THE TREE
OF LIFE

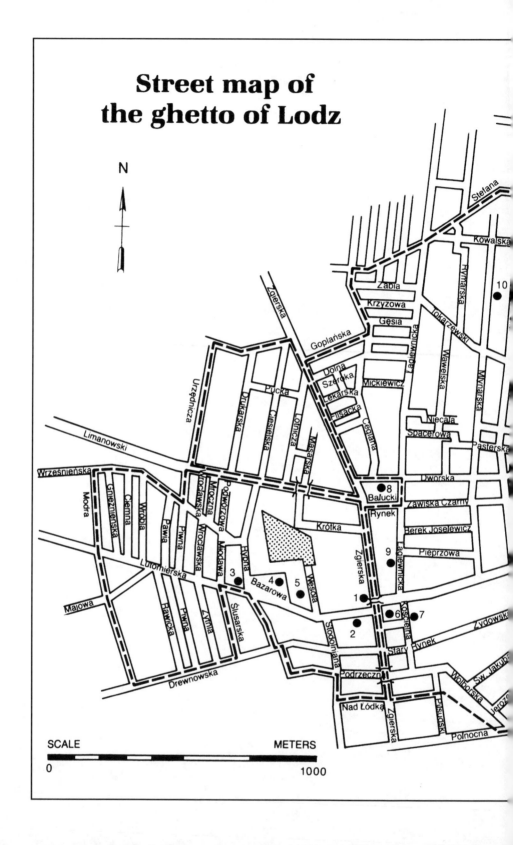

Street map of
the ghetto of Lodz

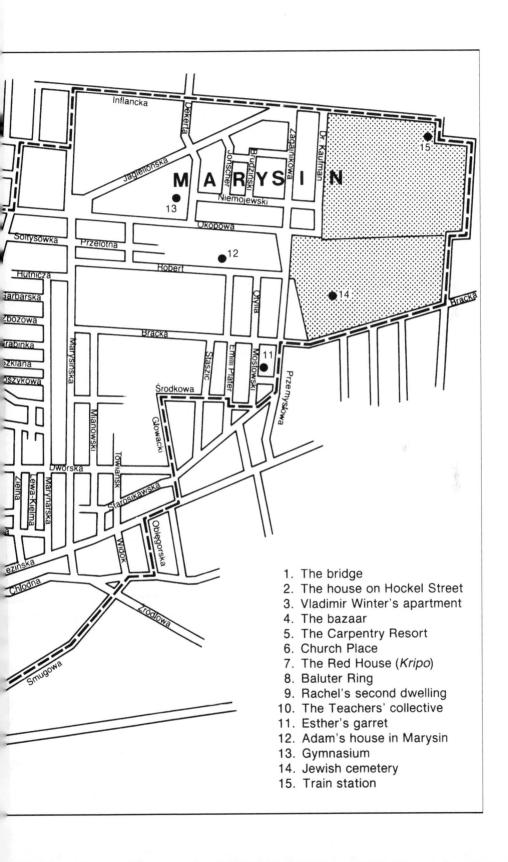

1. The bridge
2. The house on Hockel Street
3. Vladimir Winter's apartment
4. The bazaar
5. The Carpentry Resort
6. Church Place
7. The Red House (*Kripo*)
8. Baluter Ring
9. Rachel's second dwelling
10. The Teachers' collective
11. Esther's garret
12. Adam's house in Marysin
13. Gymnasium
14. Jewish cemetery
15. Train station

**NATIONAL
ENDOWMENT
FOR THE ARTS**

This publication has been made possible
with financial support from
the National Endowment for the Arts.

Terrace Books, a division of the University of Wisconsin Press, takes its name
from the Memorial Union Terrace, located at the University of Wisconsin–
Madison. Since its inception in 1907, the Wisconsin Union has provided a
venue for students, faculty, staff, and alumni to debate art, music, politics, and
the issues of the day. It is a place where theater, music, drama, dance, outdoor
activities, and major speakers are made available to the campus and the community. To learn more about the Union, visit www.union.wisc.edu.

THE TREE OF LIFE

(A Trilogy of Life in the Lodz Ghetto)

Book 3: The Cattle Cars Are Waiting, 1942–1944

Chava Rosenfarb

translated from the Yiddish by the author
in collaboration with Goldie Morgentaler

The University of Wisconsin Press
Terrace Books

The University of Wisconsin Press
1930 Monroe Street
Madison, Wisconsin 53711

www.wisc.edu/wisconsinpress/
3 Henrietta Street
London WC2E 8LU, England

5   4   3   2   1

Printed in the United States of America

Library of Congress Cataloging-in-Publication Data

Rosenfarb, Chawa, 1923–
[Boym fun lebn. English]
The tree of life: a trilogy of life in the Lodz Ghetto / Chava Rosenfarb; translated from the
Yiddish by the author in collaboration with Goldie Morgentaler.
p. cm.—(Library of world fiction)
Reprint. Originally published: Melbourne, Australia: Scribe, c1985.
Contents: Bk. 1. On the brink of the precipice.
ISBN 0-299-20454-5 (pbk.: alk. paper)
1. Holocaust, Jewish (1939–1945)—Fiction. I. Title. II. Series.
PJ5129.R597B613   2004
839'.134—dc22   2004053592

ISBN 0-299-20924-5 (volume 2)
ISBN 0-299-22124-5 (volume 3)

In memory of my parents
Sima and Abraham Rosenfarb

Acknowledgements

I wish to express my thanks to all those who contributed in helping this book see the light of day: To Bono Wiener who stood by me unwaveringly; to Dr. Adele Reinhartz and Dr. Ellen Burt for their assistance in the preparation of the first draft (Dr. Burt, Book I; Dr. Reinhartz, Books II & III); to my sister and brother-in-law, Henia and Norbert Reinhartz for their ceaseless encouragement and support; to my son and daughter-in-law, Dr. Abraham Morgentaler and Susan Edbril, for their love and consideration. But most of all I wish to thank my daughter, Goldie Morgentaler, for her selfless hard work, for the dedication and devotion she offered me throughout many months, as she assisted me in giving this book its final shape.

Ch. R.

"Love thy brother as thyself."

Rabbi Hillel

"Die Erstellung des Ghettos ist selbstverständlich nur eine Übergangsmassnahme. Zu welchen Zeitpunkten und mit welchen Mitteln das Ghetto und damit die Stadt Lodz von Juden gesäubert wird, behalte ich mir vor. Endziel muss jedenfalls sein, dass wir diese Pestbeule restlos ausbrennen.

Der Regierungspräsident
gez. Uebelhor.
Lodz, am 10 Dezember 1939"

("It is self-evident that the establishment of the Ghetto is only a transitory measure. I reserve my judgment on the point in time and the means by which the Ghetto, and with it the city of Lodz, should be cleared of Jews. In any case, the final goal should be to relentlessly burn out this pestilent boil.")

BOOK III

The Years 1942–1944

Chapter One

THE DEPORTATION had been going on for two weeks and the streets gradually became used to the sight of crowds loaded with packs and sacks, day in and day out streaming in the direction of the prison. They were seen but no longer noticed during those bright days when the sun, rather than caressing with its warmth, was lashing with frosty whips. But today was Sunday. A day of rest for the Germans as well as for the ghetto. The streets were sparkling white and empty. In the jail, those who were to leave with the transport on the following day were waiting, those who had already succumbed to heart attacks or fatal disease, included. They too were honoured by being counted. Dead, they still had to contribute to rounding out the number: a thousand a day.

A crowd had gathered along the fence of the jail. Inside stood those who were departing; outside, those who were remaining. With their fingers knotted through the wire nets, people were taking leave of one another. Words and tears flowed back and forth. Today's transport was fortunate. The deportees had time to absorb the features and the last words of those remaining on the other side of the fence. They had time to realize how strongly they had been attached to that place from which they were already so thoroughly severed. But the frost froze their sorrow after a while. It bit their hands, their noses and toes, making them hurry back into the prison hall to warm up, thus freeing a place for others who emerged from inside. Likewise those on the other side of the fence, who had come to say good-bye, became stiff with cold, leaving their places for others, while they set out at a gallop towards their own roofs.

The rest of the ghetto inhabitants spent the day in their houses, either under the covers of their beds, or sewing knapsacks. The evil decree had already touched all the relations of those who had previously been punished by deportation, and now it was the turn of those who had arrived from the provincial towns and those taking allowance. The set number of ten thousand had already been reached, but the "wedding invitations" did not stop arriving.

Bunim was lying in bed, dressed; on his raised knees was the bookkeeping register whose hard covers served as his table. He was working. Across from him Blimele lay in bed playing with her doll, Lily. Only Miriam was up and about. Wearing her winter coat, a shawl wrapped around her head, she was preparing lunch. The shutters of the window were open; the sun shining into the room seemed to follow the creases in the white tablecloth with its rays. Miriam had retained her habit of preparing each meal as if it were a festive ceremony, and as usual the thought entered Bunim's mind that the table was a sacred place, and that eating was a substitute for prayer. He followed her with his eyes, as she removed the pot of soup from under the eiderdown at the foot of the bed. The pot was not heavy, yet her hands shook. For the last few days,

Bunim had noticed that her hands were shaking. He did not need to ask why. Their knapsacks had long been standing ready under the table. Every night he had whispered into her ear that they were meant to be saved from deportation . . . all four of them. Yet her hands did not stop shaking.

A few loose flour drops, like bright little fish, swam in the red soup of conserved beets. A thin slice of bread lay on each plate. Miriam wrapped Blimele in her plaid and, along with the doll, carried her into Bunim's bed beside which the table stood.

At the sight of the soup in her plate Blimele sang out: "Sunday beets, Monday beets . . ." She fed Lily with an empty spoon. "Here, take a flour drop . . ." Bunim touched her soft hair. She raised her eyes to him. "How long will you keep on stroking me, *Tateshe*? A mother shouldn't be stroked so much."

"You are my child," he replied.

"But I am Lily's mother."

"You will always be my child, even when you grow up to be a real mother . . . or a grandmother." He watched her, weighing something in his mind. At length he added, "You know, Blimele, you are going to have a little sister, or a little brother."

His words went past Blimele's ears as if she had not heard them. Only after a while did her gaze jump like a hare over the border of her plate, straight at Miriam's face, then at Bunim's. "You mean a real child. A brother or a sister?"

"As real as yourself," Bunim said. "At first it will be as big as a dwarf, but then you will teach it how to walk and you will play with it."

Blimele grimaced, pressing the doll to her face, "I won't let you throw out Lily. Lily is my child and she will always be my child even when I will be a grandmother." She shook her head resolutely, "It's not good to have a sister or a brother . . . and who will be their mother and father?"

"What do you mean who? We."

Blimele let Lily fall on the chair as she dashed into Miriam's arms, sobbing, "I don't want to!" she gasped. "You are mine only!"

Miriam tried to calm her. "Silly girl that you are. Do you think that I would love you any less? Do you think that a mother divides her heart between her children like one divides a piece of bread? No, a mother's heart grows with every child she has, it doubles . . ."

Blimele stared at her, her wet face full of confusion. "You mean to say that Gabriel's mother has four hearts, because she has four children, and when Gabriel dies, she will have three? And inside you a new heart is really growing now?"

"Yes, something like that."

"So why don't you grow more hands and more legs and more heads?"

Miriam had to smile. "I don't mean the real heart. I mean . . . loving. A mother's love grows."

✦ ✦ ✦

All night a blizzard wailed through the ghetto. Like a beast trapped in a cage, a desperate wind danced into all the corners of the hut, attacking the walls as if it wanted to escape. It penetrated the burners of the cold stove, roaring inside them like a fire repeatedly swallowed by the pipes. With a dull long howl it called for help to its brother, the wind outside, which was carousing within the white tempest. The brother wind responded, pounding at the shutters, trying to tear them off their hinges. Until, at dawn, one of the shutters surrendered and like a wooden hand began to slap the bared window as if it were an unprotected face. Gales of snow swept past the rattling panes, clinking against them with hail stones which looked like peas pouring out from white sacks. A loose piece of tar paper cracked and fluttered, determined to tear off the entire groaning roof. It seemed that the hut would at any moment break away from its foundation and be carried off on the shoulders of the gale, into the whirling eye of the storm. The walls shook like sheets of paper loosely stitched together, their corners nothing but paper whistles which the demons blew.

Bunim reached for his clothes. He placed them and his glasses under the blanket to warm them. Then he slowly began to dress, winding long woollen bandages of rags around his legs before pulling on his wooden shoes. Feeling the cold inside them, he began hastily to march up and down the room.

"Why don't you put on your coat?" Miriam asked.

He picked up his coat which they had spread out over the cover of the bed. In its place he put a few open bookkeeping books, piling them over Miriam's legs. On tiptoe he approached Blimele who was asleep in her bed under a mountain of covers. He touched her toes and announced to Miriam, "Her feet are warm."

The wind carousing in the room penetrated through his coat. He put his gloved hands to his mouth and warming them with his breath, went to light the stove. The wind from the opened burners attacked his face. The firewood refused to kindle; each flame was swallowed by the spiteful wind. But somehow he managed to get the fire going. He uncovered the pot on the stove and a little shudder crept down his spine as the sour smell reached his nostrils. For the last week there had been nothing to eat but conserved beets. He put his hands and face against the kettle of water, until it began to boil. He filled two glasses with water, dropped saccharine into each and approached Miriam with them.

They both sipped the hot water. Bunim cast a sideways glance at Miriam. Her pregnancy was not showing yet, except in her eyes, in her face. She seemed changed. There was a mysterious air of renewal about her. What name was there for her magnificent self-control as she sat in the evenings preparing their knapsacks, as she composedly answered Blimele's questions? What name was there for her serving him, Bunim, as he lay in bed writing? Except that her hands trembled, even at night when they lay together and she caressed him. They were both welded together by that trembling, so that the border between their bodies, between their breaths dissolved.

Miriam caught his glance and smiled faintly. "I will stay in bed a little while longer. The potatoes haven't arrived and there will probably be nothing to do at the peeling shed. And . . ." she added in a broken whisper, "don't forget on your way out, to take along a mug of hot water for Valentino's sister. The child there is deathly sick, and they received a 'wedding invitation' for today."

As Bunim made himself ready to leave, he saw the face of little Gabriel, Blimele's friend, before him. He filled a mug with hot water and dropped a few saccharines into it. He pulled the visor of his cap down over his forehead, wrapped his scarf around his neck and tied the canteen to his belt. The wind and the snow threw open the door for him, and he struggled to close it. He ran through the powdery fog of dawn, the windows in the yard dancing before his eyes. Stumbling through the heaps of snow, he held on to the mug which was quickly cooling.

It was dark in the apartment where Valentino had once lived. A soft hoarse groan, a lulling singsong reached his ears, "Sleep, sleep, Gabriel, my child, sleep, sleep my soul . . ."

As if hypnotized by the voice, Bunim moved in its direction. The next room was somewhat brighter and he was able to distinguish a large bed. On it, four children lay asleep while at its side, kneeling on the floor, someone sat embracing the body of the child nearest to the edge of the bed.

Bunim touched the shoulder of the woman. "I've brought you a bit of hot water, neighbour." The dishevelled woman remained in her position, her head against the child's body. Only her singing stopped.

Suddenly Bunim's eyes met with Gabriel's gaze shining out from under his partly-lowered eyelids. Gabriel's nose and lips resembled little snowballs in the grayness of the room. Small dark shadows quivered under his nostrils. His rattle seemed to issue not from his chest but from that of his mother. Bunim touched the woman's shoulder again.

His touch seemed to reawaken her singsong, "I won't leave you alone, no, Gabriel, my soul . . ." Now she turned to Bunim, speaking in a different, a colder tone of voice. "What should I do, neighbour? Give me some advice . . ."

"Drink a bit of hot water," he handed her the mug.

She stood up, growing into a tall ghastly monster reeking of death. "What time is it now?" she asked, taking the mug.

"Seven."

She gasped, then took a sip. "Seven? So I still have a lot of time. Gabriel is a good child, like his late brother and sister were. God will reward him, you'll see. He won't have to drag himself out in such a blizzard." She returned the mug to Bunim and sank down to the floor, resuming her previous position. Now Bunim could leave the room, but he stood glued to his place, his eyes absorbing the sight of the gray morning dawning upon the world, the sight of a black morning expiring in a mother's arms. He heard the woman's voice, "Go on your way, dear neighbour. You can see that you're not letting the child sleep, can't you?"

He ran through the streets, fighting the wind and the snow which practically lifted him off his feet and hurled him against other people. The crowds were rushing to the bridge for the first shift at the Resorts. He held himself close to the walls and fences which protected him somewhat against the wind. His hazy glasses blocked the sight of the street before him and, as he ran, he had to remove them and blow the snow off them in order to see. What he saw were the white placards on the walls and fences; white wet rags sprinkled with black letters. He knew what they demanded. Yet a sudden impulse forced him, as he ran, to pull a piece of paper and his bitten-up pencil from his pocket. He stopped very close to a fence, supporting his raised knee against a board. He placed his canteen on his knee and on it, the piece of paper which, moist with snow, began to roll up at its borders. The stubborn pencil swayed back and forth as it wrote down the harsh phrases:

Announcement No. 355, re: deportation from Litzmanstadt-Ghetto.
   Herewith I command all the people assigned for deportation to report promptly at the given time to the place of assembly. Those who do not report willingly shall be deported by force. Even if they are not in their own homes, they will be found and dealt with. On this occasion I draw your attention to my proclamation issued on December 30, and I warn

the ghetto population for the last time not to accommodate any persons in their apartments who are not registered there. If those people who have been assigned for deportation are found staying with other families in order to avoid deportation, then not only they but also the families which sheltered them and the janitors of the given houses will be deported.

Signed, Mordecai Chaim Rumkowski
The Eldest of the Jews in Litzmanstadt-Ghetto.

A Jew seeing Bunim at the placard, jostled him. "Eh, better write down that an order has arrived at the Tailors Resort for five million sack shirts to bury dead German soldiers in. There will be a label on each of them, saying, 'Produce of Litzmanstadt-Ghetto'!" Bunim folded the sheet of paper and thrust it into his pocket along with the pencil. He set off at a run. It was late and he felt guilty about the "consumers" who had probably been waiting for him in line in front of the Gas Centre, so that they might warm up a bit of coffee or water before they hurried to work.

He no longer worked at the Vegetable Place. He was now the supervisor of a Gas Centre, and his "protection" was the commissar of the Gas Centre Head-quarters himself, a serious refined man who served as a "back" for some less fortunate "people of culture". The job was a "dry" one, and those who came in to warm up their food at the Gas Centre called themselves "consumers" as a joke. There was no possibility here of grabbing a carrot or a piece of turnip as there had been at the Vegetable Place. Bunim could, however, not have wished for a better position. He had no bosses over him, and apart from the occasional inspections by the commissar, he had no one to reckon with except his own conscience.

The "Centre" was located in a decrepit, partly-demolished house. All around the walls of the room stood wooden stands with black numbered gas burners. On the middle wall, above the burners, hung an old clock in a brown box. A round brass pendulum swung inside it, cutting up each hour into fractions of minutes. At the window stood an old desk where Bunim did his bookkeeping, registering each "consumer's" time at the burner, and taking care of the cashed-in pfennigs.

On a normal winter's day, the Gas Centre was engulfed in foggy vapour illuminated by the flames of the burners. The burners resembled flowers. True, the fragrance they released was not at all flowery, yet they emitted a delightful warmth which could melt one's frozen limbs. As soon as Bunim entered the room in the morning, before his "consumers" arrived, he would turn on all the burners, in order to warm himself and enjoy the beauty of their flames. The rest of the day he barely saw the flames. They were concealed by the pots and the backs of the "consumers", each one guarding his pot and warming himself without moving away until his food was ready. Very often entire families accompanied each pot, thus saving some firewood at home. It was fun to hold on to one's pot as it stood on the burner; there was pleasure in waiting for the food to cook. Now and then a woman would lift the cover, peer into the pot with curious eyes and savour the aroma of its content; she would taste it with a spoon and offer a taste to the children as well.

In the narrow corridor there was often a big queue of people. To keep order in the line was the most difficult part of Bunim's job. Everything turned inside him at the sight of the wrapped-up, shuddering and foot-stamping "consumers" with their pots between their red frozen fingers. At first, he had let them wait inside the warm room, but this had resulted in confusion and chaos. People took advantage of his weakness, grabbing burners out of turn, quarrelling or fighting, and more than one of them would leave without paying the few pfennigs. Bunim became exhausted just from appeasing and controlling them, while they would laugh at him behind his back. He was strange and so easy to cheat; a supervisor who could not handle his job. After days like that, he would have to stay longer to bring everything back to order, often also adding a fistful of pfennigs from his own pay to make the account balance. He felt a devastating fatigue. Yes, all these people were near to him as individuals. They were the people he described and sang about in his poems. But he felt pitifully helpless when they acquired one face, becoming an alien vengeful monster called "the mob".

During one such chaotic evening, the commissar of the Gas Centres arrived for an inspection. He disappointedly shook his head, while before Bunim's eyes black circles began to turn. The commissar, Bunim's sole "back" and "protection", said nothing, but his leaving without saying good-bye was a warning which had made Bunim's heart freeze.

He had to guard his post. Indeed, ever since he had begun leaving the "consumers" waiting outside in the cold, they had acquired more respect for him. Even if they still whispered, jeered at, or cursed him behind his back (they considered him to be half-crazy because he listened attentively to the children talking, or asked people to repeat one saying or another to him, and he was friends with the old mad Jews), to his face they flattered and praised him for being a good and fair supervisor. They bowed politely, thanking him for the slightest favour.

Like well-trained soldiers they stood at the burners, family to family, neighbour to neighbour. Though the steam from the pots smudged their contours, making them appear more distant, Bunim saw and heard them very clearly. He sat at his desk distributing numbers, counting, watching the clock, while absorbing the humming of the burners along with the scene in front of him. Under the cover of the thick bookkeeper's register lay a few loose sheets of paper and in his breast pocket was the chewed-up pencil. During these hours he made no use of them. During these hours he was like a sponge absorbing broken phrases: "The Presess laughed today . . . The Presess cried . . . The Presess is jubilant . . . The Presess is running around like a madman today . . ." or facetious sayings like, "The Tsar has a cold, so all of Russia is sneezing." Or philosophical remarks such as, "Do you know why we wear the Stars of David? Because God said to Abraham: 'And ye shall be like the stars.'" Or, "Yeah, the day I was born I cried, and every day that's followed has made me understand the reason for it." Or the sighs, "The only sin of the sheep is that the wolf is hungry."

Here, amidst the burners of the Gas Centre, the ghetto appeared as on a stage, in the projector light of the flames, in the coils of steam, playing out its life before Bunim. He would absorb as much as he could, then forget it, in order to absorb some more. Only later, when there were no lines outside, when there were only two or three burners going, two or three backs turned to him, would he secretively pull out the loose sheets of paper from under the register, and, shielding them with his arm, begin to glide his pencil over the lines. Then all he had seen and heard would come back to him. It was not an authentic recollection but a transformed one. Nevertheless, the air which his lines breathed was authentic.

Bunim reached the Gas Centre. The corridor was empty and he sighed with relief. There was no one waiting for him. He shook off the snow from his coat and dashed towards the burners, turning them on one after the other. Around him red fire-flowers burst into bloom and the room filled with a pleasant humming. It seemed as if he were not alone, as if a gay warm spirit had been waiting here to greet him. He put a canteen full of water on a flame at the side. When the burners were free he could allow himself the luxury of having a hot drink in the morning. As usual, he felt guilty about Miriam and Blimele. He had exchanged the Vegetable Place, where he could have a carrot or a turnip once in a while, for the Gas Centre, which he liked. But, after all, he had made Miriam and Blimele partners in his great task. This was the price they paid, while the pangs of guilt were his price. What he had undertaken called for sacrifice, demanded blood and the marrow of one's bones, almost one's life. He knew that it could not be otherwise.

He turned off the burners. The room became gray, dark, filled with the blizzard raging outside. Bunim approached the desk and took out a few damp sheets of paper and his pencil. Sipping the hot water, he sat down. The hot edge of the canteen burnt his lips. As if he were drinking a strong alcoholic drink, heat spread through his limbs, through his mind. He attacked the waiting sheets of paper. It was wonderful to have so many free hours ahead of oneself — a treasure he had to use thriftily. He was grateful to the blizzard and to the fact that people had nothing to cook. The conserved beets could be warmed up with a piece of paper at home; overcooked they had no taste anyway. On top of that there was the deportation . . . Yes, his work was nurtured at the expense of tragedy. And although he wished to have a steaming, crowded and noisy room again, with all burners going and with the queue outside, he enjoyed the peace and quiet; the threat they carried stimulated his pencil to hurry.

While he was absorbed in his work, the old clock on the wall gradually changed its rhythm, hurrying, swallowing or skipping over whole hours. Now and then Bunim glanced at it. The old clock had cut off a large part of the day. Where had he been? Had the past hours ever existed at all? Had he lived them? When? How? The clock must be playing tricks on him, mocking him just like his neighbours, like his "consumers" did. Perhaps it had to be fixed? It was required to show the exact time, because that clock was the true master of the Gas Centre. But of whom could one ask for the right time? Was it to be found in the measured rhythm of his written lines? Or in the speeding stampede of the blizzard outside? His hand hurried along with his impatient pencil. The confused clock crossed out time with the tips of its hands. He had already surrendered to it. Let it do as it wished. Bunim was here and yet not here — just like Time. All he wanted now was the wakeful silence within, the silence of melted, pouring lead, of untouched hot asphalt into which he had to engrave and seal the stride of his protagonists.

In this day's rhymed stanzas he had brought together Blimele and her little friend Gabriel. They conversed with their eyes, hers bright-blue, his coal-black. Like earth and sky they called out to each other, while the words uttered between them were the words which children utter and adults replace with silence. They crossed a bridge as narrow as a thread, it threatened to break underneath them at any moment. And along with them marched Bunim and Gabriel's mother, the wild monster with dishevelled hair. Bunim, too, was talking a childish soulful talk, Pentateuch talk, repeating the section *Lech-Lecho* with the bitter-sweet-lilt he had learned from Gabriel's mother. Miriam was helping them out. Miriam had dressed Blimele in warm panties and slips just taken off the pipe of the stove, so that Blimele would not catch a cold on the way, while Gabriel was dressed in little white shrouds by his witch mother — and the bridge, thin as thread yet strong as steel, swayed above Brutality, Horror and Fear.

How he, Bunim, had changed lately! The crazier he seemed to his neighbours and the "consumers", the stranger his talking, his silences, his confusedness and his sudden attacks of elation or sadness — the stronger he felt himself to be. This had begun both with the writing of his great poem and with Miriam's pregnancy. His former self-division was replaced by another duality. He was simultaneously living in two worlds: in the real ghetto, and in the one of his poem. They were the same and yet not the same. They were like two authentic chambers to which Bunim himself served as a common door, through which his characters moved from one chamber to the other. One chamber stood in the sharp light of the real day, while into the other the light penetrated through him — the poet, the door — as through a prism. The rays passing through him shimmered with solace and relief; they made the most horrible experiences bearable. Even his fear and the gnawing premonition, so clear and sharp, which did not let go of him for a moment, due to the daily march of deportees, even the shudder of horror which ran ahead and followed behind him — were transformed by the lament of his stanzas. His poem was the expression of a black solemn festivity.

He hated and clung to that festivity. His struggle was to reveal the truth, naked and raw. When he took the pencil into his hand, doggedly determined to bring out the images and to try to fit them into his stanzas, their reality was indeed revealed, but it was different from the reality of the day. And the fight between the two truths continued. With clenched teeth Bunim attacked his dressed-up lines, determined to tear off every adornment, in order to make them clearer, more honest, but all he gained was a new adornment. And at the edge of his soul, over the whirlpool of his struggle, the joy of creation was like a shameless pigeon cooing humbly, gratefully. He hated that pigeon, too, which made him walk about with his head raised.

At one moment in the middle of the day, he ran out with his canteen to the nearest public kitchen and brought back a bit of hot watery soup which he drank without a spoon. Later, he did not remember that he had gone to the kitchen, nor that he had drunk the soup. He himself had not been present, only his body.

Later still, two skinny little girls came in, without any pots. Their teeth chattered. Their lips were blue. Their eyes arrogantly demanded what their mouths shyly begged, that he allow them to warm themselves. Bunim lit all the burners for them. The fiery wreath embraced them and him. The children's lips melted into a smile, their faces opened up like buds. Holding hands they skipped from one burner to the next. They laughed. They danced. They danced into Bunim, danced through him. He looked at them, but did not see them; he heard them, but did not listen. He was writing. When he raised his head again the room was empty; the burners were turned off.

Then there entered a woman with a small pot hidden under her torn mud-coloured plaid; a burner began buzzing again. The woman bent over her pot; she too danced. Her wooden shoes clopped. She waved her arms under the plaid like wings. The flame could not warm her. She shook her head, talking incessantly to herself, to her pot, to Bunim, "Ey, Jews are no pigs, they eat everything. The beet preserves were ready for the garbage two years ago. You need a microscope to find a speck of potato in that coloured bit of water."

After her, a tall young man entered, his stiff snow-covered sidelocks dangling from under the plaid which covered his head. Another burner began to buzz. The young man opened a volume of psalms, swaying rhythmically over his pot as he whispered his words, as if he were pronouncing an incantation over his food. Bunim heard him sip his words along with the steam escaping from under the pot's cover.

Then a young handsome mother and her two little boys came in. They were decently dressed and spoke Polish. The mother removed the gloves from her children's hands and warmed them at the flame of the burner before she covered it with her pot. Her own hands on the shoulders of the two boys shone with a purple reflection.

Then Shiele, the street singer, entered. He insisted on paying for his cooking with a song, and as soon as he had provided himself with a burner, he assumed a theatrical pose, intoning in his chiming, girlish voice:

> Lady at the cauldron, I am not kidding
> Take the scoop and do some digging.
>
> Lady at the cauldron, you stole oil, you stole honey
> And bought yourself silken stockings with the money.
>
> Lady at the cauldron, you're fat like a barrel
> You'll be sent to *fecalia* at the Presess' referral.
>
> Lady at the cauldron, I don't envy your position
> The Presess will send you soon off 'for demolition'.

Then again, stretches of time passed when all the burners were cold and silent. There was no more light in the room. The sheet of paper in front of Bunim lost its lines, its whiteness. Bunim's eyes began to water and burn with fatigue. He shoved the pencil into his breast pocket, rolled up the sheets of paper covered with his handwriting, and made ready to go home. There was still some time left before Dr. Zonabend from Prague, who worked the evening shift at the Gas Centre would arrive. But Bunim was certain that there would be no "consumers" during that time, nor would the commissar drop in for an inspection on such a day. Secondly, he could not stay there any longer. Not being able to write, and with no prospect of "consumers", the game with the gas burners, turning them on and off, was a macabre and frightening temptation.

He covered his face with his large fur collar and threw himself into the arms of the snow and the wind. He marched along the walls and fences, peering through his foggy glasses. The street was teeming with people hurrying through the powdery darkness. They were coming from the Resorts, running to fetch water, rushing to have a look at what was new with their relatives or friends. Someone passed him, carrying a huge board, a treasure, over his shoulder. Two children were holding a third crying child by the hands. White skull caps of snow covered their heads. Two young people, a man and a woman, were running towards each other, pressing themselves between the passers-by, then falling into each other's arms. Empty wagons hurried past in the middle of the road, while another wagon, loaded with corpses, was slowly dragging from house to house. Along both sidewalks, rows of departing people hurried on, their gazes fixed at the invisible distance awaiting them outside the barbed-wire fence. Heavy knapsacks, clinking with the attached pots and pans, pressed down their backs. They held the hands of their children or old parents. Some of them were accompanied by relatives, neighbours or friends. Those leaving and those remaining behind barely shared a common language any longer.

Bunim too found himself attached to the rows of those whom the ghetto was delivering to the unknown today, as he marched behind their humps of baggage. Yesterday and the day before he had done the same, having encountered acquaintances on his way home. In this way, he had yesterday accompanied his neighbour Hersh Beer the Shoemaker, and his family, citizens of Baluty for many generations. So he had accompanied his cock-eyed co-worker from the Vegetable Place, who had so much enjoyed making fun of him, of Bunim. He had also accompanied his former "consumers" from the Vegetable Place and the Gas Centre. And once he had gone along to the prison gate with a friend of his youth. He had never met him in the ghetto, but suddenly noticed him in the crowd streaming to the place of assembly.

The packed street silently surrendered to the storm, as it submissively allowed itelf to be lashed by the wind which gagged the lost child's cry, erased the rumbling of wagon wheels, silenced the deportees' words and annihilated the young lovers' kiss.

Bunim was approaching the gate of his house when he noticed that the black hearse had overtaken him. Someone placed a white package on it, just as Gabriel's mother came out from the gate, carrying a knapsack, pots and pans. Her remaining children too were loaded down with little knapsacks, breadsacks and cups. "So, what did I tell you, neighbour?" Gabriel's mother called out triumphantly the moment she saw Bunim. "Gabriel is a good child . . ." The wind swallowed the sound of her voice. Bunim followed her. She asked him to hold the hand of one of the children. "I will remember you . . . for the better," she tried to conquer the wind with her voice. She seemed to be choking under the belts and cords of all the sacks that were suspended from her neck.

The hearse wagon shook slowly as it moved on through the middle of the road. The closer it got to the bridge, the thicker the crowds became. It seemed as if the whole street were taking part in little Gabriel's funeral. At the barbed-wire fence, everything stopped. The Jewish policeman on guard saluted the soldier on guard under the bridge. The gate opened and the hearse passed through it alone. A crowd of people climbed the bridge along with the five of them: Gabriel's mother, her three children, and Bunim. The stairs were uneven, covered with hard old snow. Bunim looked down from the bridge and saw the hearse sway past Zgierska Street, past the guard with the pointed gun. Gabriel's mother also looked down. A sound escaped her throat. The wind carried it off. The children clung to the hands of their wailing mother.

Bunim observed the little green soldier with the gun. He spat, but this gave him no relief. A painful stubbornness was consuming him. He felt like steel and iron. Over him all these wooden shoes were stepping. He was supporting them. He was a bridge — a gate, a bridge — a door. The little soldier down there could march into the first chamber, but had no power over the second. Bunim took a vow not to soil even one line of his poem, of his lament, by mentioning that green nothingness under the bridge. He spat again and watched the wind catch his spittle and dissolve it in the air. He repeated the last stammer of Israel Noble, one of the heroes in his poem. "I belong to no one, no one. You can take my body, but not my soul."

Chapter Two

KRAJNE SHAPSONOVITCH had received her "wedding invitation" in the last days of January, and she was long since supposed to have found herself on the other side of the ghetto. But although her children were well again, and her heart still longed after her Feivish, she was unable to tear herself away from her home on Piaskowa Street. During the daytime, when they were at home, one of her children would be on guard for police, and at night they all slept in a house with the wives of two former jugglers who lived around the corner, and who worked night shift in the Metal Resort.

When Krajne returned home in the morning, the room was warm. Adam saw to it before he left for work; more than once they even found a bit of cooked food on the stove. Then they all set out into the streets in search of provisions. There was no firewood to be stolen, nor were there any wagons of vegetables passing through the streets. The only solution was to hang around the houses of the *shishkas*, first investigate their garbage boxes, then to knock on their doors.

The children made good use of Krajne's teaching. There was no door that they were unable to penetrate. They would beg or steal, then quickly vanish. It was Krajne herself who had difficulties in sneaking into a house. She was too "visible", so she had to do it openly, with hutzpah, and she did it with great skill.

She had a talent for twisting the ladies of the house around her little finger, telling them tall tales and giving them regards from non-existent relatives. In the meantime she would shove under her plaid whatever came into her hand. Similarly she dealt with the husbands, the stern commissars and the booted directors who sometimes opened their doors to her. First she would distract them with her eyes, her bosom, and her entire generous figure. Of course, she had no illusions that she had retained the beauty of bygone days. Never mind, her reflection in the window pane, which served as her mirror, had let her know where she stood in that respect. Yet she would tease them coquettishly with whatever she possessed, all the while sighing and lamenting. She would tell them what a pious and good man her husband, may he rest in Paradise, had been, and that before closing his eyes forever, he had uttered the name of precisely this distinguished *shishka*, whose father had grown up and gone to *heder* with him. The *shishkas* had a few Achilles heels, which Krajne discovered and played upon. A *shishka's* heart would melt, firstly, if one strummed upon his family strings. Secondly, he had a weakness for pious people. Thirdly, he would prick up his ears when he heard what people of the ghetto were saying about him.

Having stated her relationship to the master of the house, Krajne would

13

come out with her story, namely, that she had just received her "wedding invitation" for tomorrow, and she had to report with her sparrows to the place of assembly, but she had nothing to take along for the road, not a crust of bread to her name. She poured out an avalanche of words, her polished tongue making the rough Baluty Yiddish sound so sad and sweet — and her stories so plausible — that the defenceless men had no time to properly digest what she was telling them. Soon she found herself talking from the very centre of the kitchen, while her sharp eyes spied around until they found what she needed. Her hand, hidden beneath the plaid, would pat the table and push something into her pocket, while her other hand was stretched out to the kind master, who had a big "Jewish heart" and would not let her leave the ghetto without a bite of food to eat.

Quite often, in a surge of humanity, the man would take counsel with his wife about what to give the good woman, so that she and her children would, heaven forbid, not die of hunger; since, after all, all Jews were brothers and had to help each other out in an hour of misfortune. Thus Krajne came home loaded with great treasures. Apart from bread, she would often bring a little bag of sugar, a piece of *baba* cake, and with the money she had been offered she could still buy something on the black market. Her problem was, however, that she could not visit the same place twice. She was supposed to have been deported. And if she changed the end of her story and did not mention the "wedding invitation", she was received in a considerably less friendly manner.

Consequently, she ran out of houses to visit. On top of that, the jugglers in whose homes she spent the nights with her children had begun to look uneasy and finally they came out with their fears: the police could discover them, their food cards could be blocked and they could be deported from the ghetto along with Krajne and her children. The only help left was Mr. Rosenberg, now registered as Adam Neiman. It was in his hands that Krajne now found herself.

Indeed, Adam was ready to do anything within his power to save Krajne and her children from deportation. He could not imagine how he could carry on without Krajne. For weeks and weeks his devotion to her had been blossoming. In his life he had loved no one apart from Sutchka, and Krajne was no exception, he said to himself a thousand times daily. But he could not deny his attachment to her. She seemed to him like a mixture of Reisel and all the other females who had once pleased him, out of which emerged a creature who had no resemblance to Reisel or to any of the others. She was different, unique. And with unique power she held him tied to her.

His devotion was mixed with humility and gratitude. Krajne had given him back his masculinity. If certain women had once warmed his bed, Krajne set it on fire. There were moments of wrestling, of her pinching and biting, of blows which she gave him; and there were the splendid moments of her surrender, when she considered it her sacred duty to let him know the account: "This time I'm doing it for the soup you gave Deborah, may the cholera take you! . . . This time I'm doing it for taking out the vegetables for me, may you roast in hell . . . Today it's for the glass of milk . . ."

In bed Krajne had a split personality. She sobbed and wailed, pouring out unheard-of curses in her helplessness, in her fear of punishment. He with whom she lay was not the prophet Elijah, but Beelzebub, Satan himself. It was he who kept her tied to himself with his unclean powers. She was trapped in a whirlpool of sin and her sole means of surviving was to surrender to him, while thinking clean thoughts of Feivish, thereby letting her soul separate from her body to fly off to unite with her husband in distant places.

Therefore she avenged herself pitilessly on Adam during the day. Their respective households were now one and the same. His laundry and hers no longer differed in colour or quality. She would set him to do the laundry. She sent him on errands. He stood in line for their food rations; he chopped wood, fetched water, scrubbed the floors. She did not spare him any curses and hurled whatever came into her hands at him. And what enraged her most was that he seemed to enjoy it, that often she would catch a smile on his thick sensuous lips. The fact that she was unable to understand his behaviour or the reason for his desiring her increased her confusion and the fear in her heart.

And in fact, not even in the daytime would Adam notice Krajne's haggard appearance. Even during the day she was permeated by the magnificence of the nights. And it was precisely during the daytime that there was this air of strength, of power and health about her which had brought him back to life.

He took pleasure in his health. Every morning and evening he did his exercises. Every day he braved the cold water, washing himself all over. Saturday he dressed up in a "white" shirt which was ashen gray and in his pre-war suit, which was creased and fitted him like a bag, and in this attire he paraded before Krajne, not moving out of the room for a minute. Weekdays, after work, he never failed to wait in front of the door for her until she arrived with her brood. There was no life for him outside the circle of Krajne's light.

Even her children became dear to him. They were Krajne's emanation. He respected them and let them, too, order him around. He, who had never before so much as glanced at a child, would now in the evenings tell the gang long stories about dogs, about forests and hunting and about animals; he described how each of his kills had died. He taught them how to make slings and shoot to hit. He taught them the secrets of judo, and sent them outside to practise by making people in the slippery street trip over their feet, while he watched through the window, roaring with laughter and applauding the youngsters for their agility. Once he even spent an entire *rumki* on them. He bought a chess set and taught them to play chess; and although Krajne would try to tear her children away from him, they clung to him all the more. They became chummy with him and took his side against Krajne. And since they considered him a member of the family, they did not mind his smell, for which he felt doubly grateful.

Krajne had expected a "wedding invitation" not only because she was the wife of a deported man and she was receiving an allowance, but also because she expected a punishment for living in sin. However, sometimes she told herself that it was Feivish who was moving heaven and earth somewhere, to deliver her children and herself from that hellish snake pit called the ghetto. And the fact that her heart would not allow her to leave filled her with such rage against herself, that she could not do otherwise than to unload it upon Adam, who was the cause of all the tragedies which had befallen the world, the ghetto and her family.

Krajne's "wedding invitation" had considerably confused Adam as well. When she began to sleep over with the jugglers' wives, he had spent the major part of the night at the chess-board, counting the hours until her return. At dawn he lit a fire in the stove and warmed up the room for her. Then he left for work, and all day as he walked harnessed to the *fecalia* wagon, he would search his mind for a means to save Krajne from the evil decree. A few times the police came at night to look for them. He protected them by assuring the police that Krajne had left with the transport a long time ago. Proudly, he displayed his *fecalist* identity card, as if to prove his own immunity and the reliability of his words.

The problem was that while his identity card and his new name, Adam Neiman, indeed protected him against deportation, they did not after all help him escape the long hand of the *Kripo*. On the same morning that Krajne slept for the last time with the juggler families, when Adam was in the middle of pulling on his "tin" pants, the stiff overalls which he hung outside to air, Herr Sutter himself paid him a visit. Herr Sutter was very glad to see him and greeted him with a generous "*Shalom aleichem*", saying in his wonderful Yiddish, "Finally we have met, Herr Rosenberg."

Adam showed him his *fecalist* identity card, where it was written black upon white that his name was Adam Neiman. Herr Sutter, just for the fun of it, knocked the card out of Adam's hand. At that very moment, the smell of Adam's melting overalls reached his nostrils, and he screwed up his potato nose, "It stinks, my friend." With his muddy boot he crushed the identity card and invited Adam to accompany him to the Red House.

✦   ✦   ✦

The first thing that Adam noticed as he entered the hall of the Red House was the chequered inlaid floor which resembled a chessboard. He saw a stairway leading from the basement and winding along the walls, up to a gallery at the top. The stairway was decorative, its wrought iron railing was worked into Gothic motifs, like a filigree trimming spirally woven upwards. Adam scanned the floors, one, two, three, as he followed the design of the railing up to the gallery where he noticed five people sitting. He traced their outlines through the openings in the railing's design; their necks seemed to be cut off by the straight line of the bannister. Above it he saw five white faces. Were these the faces of hermits meditating on God and the Crucified One? Apparently the former atmosphere of the hall had not been thoroughly ventilated; a sacred awe still lingered on between the walls of the former parsonage.

On the landings, doors were being opened and shut. Uniformed Germans moved up and down the chequered floor like figures on the chessboard of Fate. When they ascended or descended the stairs, their spurs lightly clicking, they reminded one of the angels on Jacob's ladder, of messengers on spring-like legs, of god-like bookkeepers, working in heavenly offices behind closed doors where the big black books of Destiny lay open. From the first floor came the sounds of blows and groans. A scream rang out like a cry *de profundis* of someone who was torturing his own body in order to feel closer to the Creator of the World and his Crucified Son.

Upstairs, a door opened and two pairs of hands delivered an emaciated limp body into the hands of two Jewish *Überfallkommandos* who, as if at a secret order, had run up. At the same time, another door opened and remained ajar like a gaping mouth on the verge of taking a bite. From the cellar emerged two *Überfallkommandos* accompanying a man with a bruised face and a bump on his

head. The man ran upstairs, glaring at the open door like a visitor who is
anxious not to keep his hosts waiting. The body with the injured legs passed
him as it was being dragged downstairs.

As soon as they entered the hall, Herr Sutter left Adam alone in the middle of
the chessboard floor, and from behind Adam appeared two tall figures in green
uniforms; two rooks placing the lonely king in the middle of the board in a fatal
checkmate. Through the terrifying silence tolling in his ears, Adam heard the
muffled singsong of people in pain, a wailing lament which came from the
cellar. Two other rooks approached him, this time two Jewish *Sonderkommandos*. Their stony Sphinx faces did not differ from the faces above the
green uniforms. They put him between themselves, and the three of them
began to mount the stairs. "Take off your hat!" came the order. There was
solemnity in their climbing, as if they were mounting the steps of a cathedral.
Adam's whole being surrendered to the effort; he, hat in hand, in front; the two
towers, behind. They reached the gallery where the five figures sat. Adam
became the sixth. "Not a word!" ordered the towers, placing themselves at
attention by the wall. The number of prisoners was complete for that
morning.

Adam sat on the very edge of the bench. For the first few minutes after his
arrival, his bewilderment and curiosity had stopped him from feeling anything.
But as soon as he sat down, fear grabbed him by the throat. He began to
swallow, his Adam's apple moved ceaselessly up and down under the loose skin
on his throat. His neighbours on the bench seemed to be silently transmitting
their anguish to him. It rolled from body to body like an icy snowball to which
each one of them added his share, finally offering it to Adam in its entire frosty
enormity. He shuddered as he listened to the chatter of the metal caps in his
mouth. He moved in his seat, trying to get away from the place where fear could
reach him, but there was nowhere to go. Unwittingly, now and then, he
touched the shoulder of his neighbour, giving him a light push. He noticed that
he had set the entire bench in motion. Thus all six of them swayed.

Downstairs, in the middle of the chequered floor, a uniform halted; a face
was raised to the gallery. In the same manner cardinals stood in the cathedrals
with their faces raised to the Crucified One. A name rang out between the clean
white walls; it shot like a bullet up in the air, hitting the first man on the bench.
Already the *Uberfallkommandos* were leading him downstairs; a seat was
vacant, but the remaining prisoners could not unhitch themselves from each
other. One of them allowed himself the luxury of a groan and, prodding Adam
lightly, he whispered, "Have you got anything to declare?" Adam was afraid to
move his head or to open his mouth. The whisper continued, "I've got nothing
to fear. I've a bit of jewellery hidden in town. So I'll buy my life with it."

The traffic up and down the stairs did not stop. Nor did the sound of blows
and screams, or of opening and closing doors, ejecting one body, swallowing
another. Adam was clear about the procedure: one new prisoner, one old. His
heart seemed to have jumped into his mouth. The whispering beside him
stopped. He lightly prodded his neighbour with his elbow, barely moving his
lips. "And those who have nothing?"

"No good," came the answer.

From downstairs a name was called and another neighbour on the bench rose
to his feet. The remaining four did not move away from each other. The two
Sonderkommandos took the summoned man between them. Adam's neighbour

was mumbling to the man on his other side. Adam pricked up his ears; every word his neighbour uttered might be of great importance, but he could hear nothing. His heart was pounding too loud, echoing in his mouth, in his ears, in his temples. He felt his bald head pricking him with the hair that he had lost long ago. He wanted to pass his hand over his pate to efface the weird pricking, but was afraid to move a limb.

The entire hall was like a precision clock. At equal intervals a figure on the bench would jump up like a doll on a spring. At exactly that moment, a door would open, but instead of a cuckoo bird, a body with lame legs would fall out, followed by the tick-tock of steps on the stairs.

Adam remained alone on the bench. His fear did not leave him, but it became frozen. His mind began to work: buy his life with the valuables hidden in town . . . give addresses . . . the exact places. Life was wonderful. *Fecalia* was perfume and gold. And suddenly, unexpectedly, Samuel came to his mind. If Adam began again to shudder, it was not with fear, but tension. It seemed to him that Samuel was sitting beside him, taking up the entire length of the empty bench. Adam wanted to smile at him, but his mouth was jammed with the metal tooth-caps and his tongue was dry and paralysed. Sweat began to stream from his bald head. He saw the cellar in Samuel's house on Narutowicz Street, in town; he saw the box of jewellery which he, Adam, had buried with his own hands. He could barely wait to be called.

He heard his name. For a moment he remained seated. Had they meant him? He wanted to take out his identity card, to prove that he was not Rosenberg but Neiman. But he no longer had an identity card. Herr Sutter had trampled it. He was neither Rosenberg, nor Neiman. He was no one. He was only aware of someone jumping to his feet like a doll on a spring, someone putting himself between the two *Sonderkommandos*, descending the stairs towards the open door. It was not he who stepped over the threshold of the dark room. It was not his mouth which was being gagged with a white rag. Then who was it that received the kick of a boot in the ribs, near his heart, and whose body was it that made such a noise? Something was being racked and crushed like dry leaves. Lightning blasted the darkness and a fire began to roar. Inside, deep inside, everything began to burn. From that depth someone was roaring through a million loudspeakers: "I have! . . . I have!" An alarm siren in a fiery night, a scream which no one heeded.

He did not feel himself being dragged down the stairs. He had never left that cellar which was roaring with flames in the darkness. It seemed to him that he was groaning with a hundred mouths; that he had been cut into a hundred pieces, each piece screaming to the other, complaining before the other. He, alone, was a wounded crowd which was jammed between the walls of the cellar, while the fire raging inside him devoured the darkness of the entire space.

At dawn, someone poured a pail of water over him. He came to himself and saw the face of the *Sonder* man illuminated by the sparse light from the barred snow-covered window. "Make ready for the interrogation!" the *Sonder* man ordered, throwing him a rag. Adam wanted to wipe himself with it, but his hands would not obey him. A laziness heavily pressed down his eyelids. He could not lift them. Someone kneeled down beside him and carefully wiped his face with the wet rag. With difficulty he opened his eyes, seeing nothing. A whisper penetrated his mind. His neighbour from the bench was talking to him.

"Poor soul, you're worse off than I am . . . Do you know why? Because I began to sing out everything right after the first kick. They'll probably let me out soon. Perhaps you want to send word to your family?" Adam wanted to reply, but his mouth hurt him. The man moved away from him. Other prisoners from their corners gave the man their names and addresses. He slowly repeated them, asking, "And what should I say?"

"Regards," someone answered. "That I am alive and unharmed," groaned another. "That they should take me out of here because I cannot take it any longer . . . Let them move heaven and earth," a third cried. A fourth whispered, "Let her bring it . . . let her cut open the mattress."

The vivacious man was full of indignation, "Now you've come to your senses."

From the corner came the rattle of a dying man. Near the little window two men were saying their morning prayers. The vivacious man joined them. He adjusted his cap, turned to the wall and began to sway back and forth, letting out a groan of pain with every movement. The remaining prisoners groaned along with him, shoving their bruised bodies closer to one another. They made an inventory of the strength left in their bodies, each inquiring of his own limbs whether they would survive the day of torture that awaited them.

A door opened. A man who had been lying like a stump of wood jumped to his feet at the sound of his name, and marched out from the cellar. Time was beginning to move with the opening and closing of the door. Some people called out for the interrogation were, like Adam the day before, brought back in a faint. Others crawled in alone, on all fours. Others shuffled in, doubled over, holding on to their bellies, as if they were about to lose their intestines. Those left waiting in the cellar passed the time in keeping an account of who left and who returned, of whose turn was next. Some of those who were called did not return at all. Their absence drilled into the others' minds with the question, "Free or dead?" They did not stop analysing, each his own fate and his chances of survival. The vivacious man had been called a long time ago, and had not come back. Adam respected him for his wisdom. All day, as he waited for his turn, Adam pondered the fact that some people who seemed to be little nothings had the strength not to lose their heads in the most dangerous moments.

Just as the daylight began to drift out of the cellar, the vivacious man was brought back. He had oddly disfigured limbs. The *Sonderkommandos* stretched him out on the floor and poured a pail of water on him. He opened a pair of bloodshot eyes and a mouth from which the blood oozed sideways. He seemed to smile. The prisoners surrounded him. They looked at him with contempt, with resentment and with a bitter self-pity. One of them wiped the wounded man's face with a wet rag, trying to clear the blood from his mouth. The man licked his red mouth with his tongue. It was impossible to understand what he was mumbling. Someone put his ear against his mouth and translated to the others the language of pain. "He says, that we should pity him . . . He says that he has a wife and children . . . He says that they should not forget him." Adam Rosenberg was called. The floor of the cellar was transformed into a spring board. Adam jumped up.

The room into which he was now led was darkened. The large wide windows, hung from the outside with snow-covered garlands of vines, shut out the dying light of the day. Three large desks, illuminated by three desk lamps, and joined at the corners, faced Adam like open pliers aimed at the head of a nail. Behind the middle desk sat the broad-shouldered, dwarf-like high priest of the *Kripo*, Herr Sutter. Adam bowed deeply, sighing with relief. It was better to have to deal with Sutter than with someone whose character one had yet to discover. At least Sutter did not apply physical violence.

Herr Sutter's flat frog-like face with its rounded potato-nose was buried in a pile of papers. A pair of pea-shaped eyes peered at Adam without seeming to recognize him. This stare reactivated all the pain in Adam's bruised body, and his courage faded. As his legs began to give way, another German entered the room. He had a jovial human face. Smiling at Adam like an old friend, he sat down at a desk by the side and with a gesture of his hand invited Adam to approach. The polite man was wearing civilian clothes and he addressed Adam in a resonant Yiddish with only the hint of a German accent.

"Good evening, good year, Herr Rosenberg!" he said warmly. "We had difficulties in finding you. What kind of idea was it to change your name? All your life you worked to make the Rosenberg name famous, and suddenly you throw it away. That is not at all noble or honourable . . . forgive the remark. I have always been eager to make your acquaintance. There was not an industrialist in Litzmanstadt, then still called Lodz, who did not speak your name with awe. So today at last I have the opportunity to introduce myself to you, Herr Rosenberg. Do you know who I am? You don't? Of course, how could you know? Celebrities are known to everybody, while they themselves know no one." The polite man forgot however to introduce himself as he changed the theme of his monologue. "And how do you find life in the ghetto? All right? American currency or, as it is called in the ghetto, the 'noodles', the 'hard' and the 'soft', help a bit in adjusting to the situation? And between you and me, how much have you got left, my friend?"

"Nothing!" Adam burst out in German. "I am a *fecalist!*"

"You are a *fec* . . ." the friendly man laughed. "You're proud of it. Quite right. A noble profession . . . a *fec* . . . *fecalist!*" The German tried to control his laughter. "*Ja wohl* . . . and it is also an important social function, apart from the extra rations. You have the opportunity to save, or perhaps even to buy a few additional 'noodles'. How much is a glass of milk on the black market nowadays? Why do you stare at me like that, Mr. Rosenberg? Don't you know what I am talking about? Don't you know what 'noodles' are? You do know what 'hard' and 'soft' are? No? Are you sticking to the pre-war terminology as far as currency is concerned? You don't mix too much in the affairs of the ghetto, I can see. And how is Madam, your wife, and the children?"

Adam was completely confused. "I have no wife or children . . . Herr . . ."

"Deceased? I'm sorry to hear that. Not from starvation, I'm sure."

Adam made a great effort to mobilize the bit of courage he had left. "I have jewellery! Hidden in town . . . in a cellar . . . I'm ready to show you . . . I have . . ."

The polite man blinked at Sutter, while both Germans leaned forward. "I am very glad to hear that," the German said now in a business-like tone. "Of what value more or less? Of course, you cannot recall right away. Don't worry about that little problem, it can very easily be resolved. We know that you are an honest man and would not tell any lies which could be easily discovered." He moved closer to the desk with his chair and became very serious. "We trust you completely, as you can see. We treat you with respect. You frequent such distinguished circles, the cream of Jewry. You will do us a favour, and we are capable of doing you a favour too, as they say in the ghetto, 'One hand washes the other'. Very true. As far as your money is concerned, it lies hidden, of no use to anyone, not even to you; even if you had it in the ghetto, its worth would be equal to mud. *Rumkis* are the gold of the ghetto, the best currency. While for us it could help solve some difficult war problems. Do you understand? You are an intelligent man, after all. We have a fine proposition to make you. You will survive the war under our protection, and you won't lack any *rumkis*. But as we said, let's proceed systematically. First comes your contribution. We shall make a little excursion into town, Herr Rosenberg. What a nice Germanic name you have!" Both Germans stood up, saluting each other with "Heil Hitler!" Adam bowed. Two *Sonderkommandos* led him down into the cellar.

Adam felt nauseous from the smell that greeted him downstairs, from the sight of the emaciated bodies and the protruding eyes filled with the madness of fear. Those who were able to do so, pushed themselves closer to Adam, bombarding him with questions, curious, jealous, hopeful. "They're taking me into town," Adam cut them short, and buried his face in his arms. He refused to say another word. He had something more important to do. He absolutely had to calm the clamour roaring in his head.

He had a lot of time to do that. An entire restless ferverish night. Only now did he see clearly what was going on in that cellar. The air was hot and raw like an open wound. The sound of the dying man's rattle was no more. His corner was empty and even more frightening than before. Thoughts tangled in Adam's mind. He wanted to purge himself of them. He had come here to learn the truth and arrive at conclusions. Here, in this cellar, one could experience death while still alive. The torture which he had gone through meant living while dying — piecemeal, disgustingly. But he would not give in. He would expel death from his life. As long as it was given to him to live, he would keep order and restore the proper sequence. Life and death must not be simultaneous. He would protect his life against the hideousness of pain, even free himself from the kind that Reisel could inflict. He had nothing more to learn. Here, in this cellar, he had finally become mature and wise. Even his attachment to Krajne was false, twisted. He had to laugh at that madness of his. What a heartache her receiving the "wedding invitation" had given him! How senseless that was!

The following morning, he was called and was led out into the street where a black limousine was waiting for him. He sat pressed between two uniformed Germans as between two stone columns; both of them wore the insignia of the Death's Head. The limousine circled the church, passing through the gate at the bridge. Then there was the stretch of Zgierska Street with the barbed wires on both sides, until Freedom Place appeared before them. Without the statue of Kosciuszko the Place looked unfamiliar. As the limousine slid ahead, Adam had a distant recollection of his own motorcar, of his chauffeur Marian. For an instant he had the illusion that he was on his way to his factory. It did not last long. They were passing through an unfamiliar city. Adam recognized the streets only by the direction in which he was travelling. The streets themselves seemed wider. Their walls were covered with swastika banners, and they were almost empty. Fear attacked him. He wanted to be back in the ghetto as soon as possible.

On Narutowicz Street where Samuel's house was supposed to be standing Adam became completely flustered. It took him a while before he could recognize the familiar gate. A maid in a black dress and white apron greeted the visitors with "Heil Hitler!" From the salon where Adam had once danced during the New Year's ball, a blond lady appeared, a "Heil Hitler!" greeting on her lips as well. The SS men exchanged a few polite whispered words with her, while Adam was unable to take his eyes off her dressing-gown which seemed somehow familiar to him.

The way to the cellar was clear. As Adam descended, a dreadful feeling swept over him. Here he had lain for long weeks with his Sutchka. Here he had become thoroughly transformed from a free man into a trapped animal.

He was given a shovel. "*Arbeiten, los!*" came the order.

He was left alone in the cellar. For a moment he stood motionless, in order to quiet the turmoil in his mind. With an effort he gathered his thoughts, straining his memory. He began counting the footsteps. The tunnel which he had tried to build should have been somewhere near the wall, and ten feet to the left . . . He put his foot on the shovel and let out a scream. The pain in his back seemed to cut him in half. The ground was hard. He clenched his teeth. Tears of helplessness blurred his eyes. But the final effort had to be made. He threw off his jacket, took off his sweat-soaked shirt and again aimed the shovel at the stubborn ground. Groaning, he wrestled with it, occasionally stopping to catch his breath and wait for the pain in his back to subside.

During one such moment he noticed Wojciech, Samuel's former servant, through the little window of the cellar. Wojciech pretended to be chopping wood, but was actually peering into the cellar. Adam turned his back on him. Panic overcame him. Had Wojciech perhaps stolen Samuel's hidden treasure? Adam no longer worried about his pain. He buried it, covering it with the heaps of soil which he freed from the ground's armour. An SS man came down to inform him that an hour had passed, and that he had only another fifteen minutes left.

Adam threw away the shovel and stretched out on the ground. Once the top layer was removed, the soil became more submissive. He dug with his hands, with his nails, throwing out fistfuls of earth like a mole. His hands reached down deeper and deeper. He no longer saw them or felt them. They had become the rakes of his despair. But he was not achieving much with them. He grabbed the shovel again, and then again fell down on all fours. The SS man appeared to announce that another half hour had passed; he warned and he raged, then gave Adam another five minutes. Adam sobbed, stammered, digging with both hands, with his entire body — until his nails finally scratched against a hard object: Samuel's box of jewellery. He lay there with his nails on the treasure, his dirty creased face over the hole, letting his tears drip into it. "I have it! I have it!" His body shook spasmodically.

The SS men found him stretched out on the ground. They grabbed him by the collar and lifted him up in the air. He handed them the box, glaring at them through his tears with humility and triumph.

On the way back, he felt like a child after a long crying session, a child who had successfully tricked someone. His gaze danced over the unfamiliar streets. Somewhere in one of them, in a wall at his factory, he had buried a full cigar box with valuables, and in the wall of his white little "palace", another one. The empty alien streets did not know about it, nor would they ever know. Herr Sutter and his colleagues did not know about, nor would they ever know. Only Samuel . . . he alone knew. But Samuel was an idiot and Samuel had a radio hidden in his cellar. Samuel could be forestalled. There had been a judgement handed down against Samuel, not by the Germans — but by him, Adam Rosenberg.

In the Red House the two guards let go of him, ordering him to report to Room No. 4. He ran up the stairs as if they were those of his own house. Herr Sutter himself was waiting for him at his desk. He did not mention the box of jewels, but immediately made the proposition: "You will be a regular confidant of the *Kripo*." Herr Sutter spoke very seriously. "You will have all the privileges, a letter of protection, an identity card. But first we have to see what you can achieve. We want names, addresses and the certainty that you will not make us search in vain. Report here every morning. Now you can go home. Have a good Sabbath."

It was late Saturday afternoon, and only the deportees with their packs and sacks were passing through the streets. Adam hurried to Krajne. The moment he was free, he forgot his thoughts in the cellar of the *Kripo*. He was again drawn towards her. He wanted to recount his trials to her, to arouse her compassion. As he hurried to see her, he saw himself in bed and Krajne nursing him. He clearly heard her yelling, he felt her hot angry gaze, while at the same time feeling the touch of her hands which spoke an altogether different language. It felt wonderful to be running to her. It made him feel festive, exultant. He promised himself to reward her for everything. He would not let her and her brood starve. He would dress her up, buy her new shoes. He would get a new dwelling in Marysin. They would not lack coal or firewood. He would take in a servant to do the dirty work, so that Krajne need only cook and sleep with him at night. Tomorrow he would intercede with Sutter to free her from deportation.

✦ ✦ ✦

The threshold of the hut in Paiskowa Street was covered with snow. Inside, the rooms had been ransacked; the furniture and the rags overturned, the stove ice cold. Adam ran outside. He paced the street for hours. It grew dark. Curfew was approaching. It seemed to him that he was waiting for Krajne's arrival, that soon she would appear on the corner with her brood. He could not believe that she was really gone. Everything seemed hollow without her. The struggle and the stubborn clinging to life lost all sense. No, he was not feeling the same kind of sorrow as at his loss of Sutchka, or Yadwiga. It was an entirely different feeling. It had something to do with a kind of religiosity which living with Krajne evoked in him. Krajne's disappearance undermined the foundations of life itself. The world could not exist without Krajne.

Late at night, he entered the house to prepare himself to leave, to report to the prison and to look for Krajne and her children, who were his family. But his knapsack was gone. Gone also was the chunk of bread he had still had when Sutter had come for him. Krajne was such a type. He did not begrudge her. On the contrary, it made him miss her more, with all her charms. It even eased the burden on his heart. He went to bed with his clothes on. Tomorrow he would rise, wash himself with cold water and leave for the place of assembly.

The next day, a Jewish informer working for the *Kripo* came to fetch him for his first day of work. Adam did not hear a word of what his companion said. He could not understand why he was going in the direction of the Red House, when his heart was galloping towards the ghetto prison. But as soon as he passed over the threshold of the *Kripo* House and saw the chequered floor and the gallery bench holding the day's prisoners, his mind began working in the opposite direction. His eyes, his ears, all his senses remembered the dread of death which annihilated everything else. Krajne's departure stopped bothering him. He saw the hand of Fate in it. Attachment was destructive. Krajne's disappearance was the omen which indicated that his road was cleared for a new beginning.

Herr Sutter had no instructions for Adam. Instead, the Jewish informer introduced Adam to his colleagues. They taught Adam about a completely new aspect of the ghetto. He listened intently. It was important that he know thoroughly his field of work. However, he needed no practical or tactical advice. Never mind. He was quite a good strategist, a systematic thinker. He decided to divide his work into two systems. One would consist of recalling the names of the Jewish capitalists of Lodz whom he had known before the war, and finding out whether they were in the ghetto. Another list would consist of the names of those whose concealed treasures he might discover through research. He also decided on a third, personal little list of those with whom he had private accounts to settle.

Thus Adam became a *Kripo* informer and a fine polite gentleman. A good listener, he took a keen interest in the lives of the people with whom he became acquainted, and who gladly opened their hearts to him. After a while, he was in possession not only of lists, but of a private filing cabinet with the names of hundreds of ghetto citizens whom he would, like an efficient spy, follow, and afterwards decide their fate. It was a breathtaking game. He became so involved in it, that if he were woken up in the middle of the night and asked about a name in his files, he could sing out that person's entire biography along with financial information about that person's past, as well as the man's current state of affairs and top it all off with his present exact address.

As soon as he received his first pay and his letter of protection, Adam renovated his rooms on Piaskova Street and installed a good stove. He had not given up the plan of moving to Marysin, but for the time being he needed this corner which was still warm with the breath of home. For a while he could not make up his mind whether to put a sign out in front of his door, or not. Advertising himself as a man of the *Kripo* had its negative side. It might scare people away from him and also endanger his future after the war. However, the positive side outweighed the negative. He would avoid the unpleasantness of night searches and accidental visits by the Jewish police. After all, Piaskova Street was a blind alley where only the penniless riff-raff of the lowest order lived. He did not intend to work on them, or to befriend them. Thus a sign appeared on his door which read, "Adam Rosenberg, *Vertraunngsmann der Kripo*". It amused him to watch his neighbours dash past his door as if Beelzebub himself lived behind it.

Adam would leave for the Red House early in the morning, after his exercise session and a substantial breakfast which included a few cups of real coffee. He liked the walk in the crisp air through the still silent streets; he enjoyed the daily tension he felt on entering the Red House, dangerous and sinister to the entire ghetto, open and familiar to him. He absorbed the awesome atmosphere, the frightful solemnity of the rhythm of time which had a completely different beat than anywhere else in the ghetto. If he sometimes also felt a kind of nervousness upon entering the building, it was not mixed with fear, but rather with something similar to the arousal he had felt in Spain during a bull fight. The muffled roar of pain escaping from under the closed doors of the cellar resembled the roar of wounded bulls, although he was well aware that here a massacre rather than a fight was taking place. Sometimes, attacked by an irrational urge, he would rush down to the cellar, to watch, listen and absorb the 'scream of blood' and become intoxicated by it. He felt no repugnance or disgust, but the excitement experienced by a man watching a woman undress slowly. Since he felt such pleasure during the few minutes he spent downstairs, he was also grateful to the half-slaughtered men. He spoke kind words to them, curiously inspecting their wounds. He secretly offered them cachets to soothe their pain, as if he too were one of them and had sneaked in to help them. He rolled his eyes upwards, consoling them, "God is merciful."

He was already on friendly terms with Herr Schmidt, the polite German who had interrogated him, as well as with Herr Sutter and the tall uniformed SS men. The only one whose sight he could not bear was the *Sturmtrupper* who took care of the huge spy dog. The Germans of the *Kripo* were in general an educated lot. They engaged Adam in conversations which had nothing to do with his work. They discussed 'philosophy' or 'religion', or Jews in general. There was one quite good chess player among them whom Adam liked to outplay almost to the end, when he let him win, or, in an attack of self-love, at least stalemated him.

As far as Jewish problems and statistics were concerned, the Germans were much better informed than Adam, not to mention the fact that they spoke Yiddish better than he. They would correct Adam's linguistic mistakes while he laughed along with them. As for their opinion of the Jews themselves, he not only agreed with them, but provided them with clever arguments of his own. Herr Sutter had even remarked once, "You talk as if you were not a Jew."

Adam replied, "Of course I am not a Jew. I never was. What does it mean to be a Jew, after all? They're not a nation. They don't even have a language of their own, or a country. A religion? I am not religious, neither is the majority of them. A Jew does not even have a definition, Herr Sutter. Therefore I think that a Jew can only be he who wants to be one. I don't want to."

Sutter rubbed his potato nose and disagreed with him, "Eh, get off it. Jews are a breed. All Jews have the same kind of blood. Could you pump out the Jewish blood from your veins? Blood determines character, idiot. Cheap blood, a cheap character, an intriguer, a liar, a swindler, a thief, clever like hell and yet a blockhead."

Adam pretended to think deeply. He knew how far he could go in his sincerity with them. "Possible, Herr Sutter. But it is a fact that I don't want to be a Jew."

This provoked a smile on Sutter's frog face. "Go down into the cellar and ask them whether they want to be Jews. If it were a question of wanting or not wanting, there would be no Jews nowadays. But since it's a question of blood, they have to rot. Eh, why do you make a long face? I don't mean you. You are helping us, aren't you? That's why I pity you. But what choice do you have? Can you crawl out of your own skin?"

Apart from the intellectual conversations and the schnapps shared with the Germans, Adam had a chance to meet with his colleagues, the Jewish confidence men who worked for the *Kripo*. There were witty and gay fellows among them, who thought about nothing but living out their days. And there were also wise and serious men who considered themselves to be good Jews, even religious. They boasted about their good deeds. For every Jew they denounced, they helped two others. They worried about and felt responsible for the ghetto. Adam gladly spent his time both with the gay and carefree and the serious and responsible. But he felt better with the serious ones. They had respect for his education, for the role he had played before the war, for his command both of the Polish and German languages, which proved that he was a man of the world. In order to please them, Adam, without effort, copied their Jewish patriotism and mentioned God's name at every occasion. They often invited him into their comfortable homes, receiving him with respect and good food. Among them he also found a few pitiful chess players with whom he would earnestly sit at the chessboard. The others respectfully *kibbitzed*, yawning, as they thoroughly realized what a good head Adam carried on his shoulders.

Playing chess became one of Adam's most important activities. After he had settled down in his new profession, he had a lot of spare time which he did not want to waste just on women and crime novels. He wanted to preserve the sharpness of his mind. He scanned the ghetto in search of good partners and for a few *rumkis* he often succeeded in getting himself a beggar with a sharp mind. Mostly, he played with them in their dark cold lairs, in order to conceal who he was. At his present level of life experience — although he was still overly meticulous about his personal cleanliness — he had developed a tolerance for dirt and muck. A clean corner of a table was all that he needed.

All in all, Adam's work at the *Kripo* stimulated his intellect. He philosophized about life, about human nature and about himself. It appeared to him that the metamorphosis of his character which had begun with the outbreak of the war, had now reached its culmination. He was now a different man, more mature, more complete.

During the late hours of the night the wail of sirens resounded over the sleeping ghetto. An air raid alarm, a frequent event of late. Adam lay in his bed, waiting to hear the roar of the airplanes. Though it did not materialise, he was unable to go back to sleep. A sequence of senseless images, both vivid and dreamlike, tangled in his mind. He rose tired in the morning, yet roused himself, jumped out from his bed and approached the window. On the window-sill stood a jar of water; the two little fish inside were basking in the sun's rays. Adam had received the fish yesterday from Schultz, the *Volksdeutsche*, whose job as stool pigeon and spy *cum* janitor was to wash the blood stains off the stairs and the chequered floor of the Red House. Schultz had once told Adam about the fish he was breeding. This had aroused Adam's longing for the tropical aquarium he had had in his office before the war. He succeeded in talking Schultz into selling him the two little fish for no less than thirty *Reichsmark*.

Adam sprinkled the water in the jar with a few bread crumbs and lit the stove. He filled the washtub with water and began to exercise. Then, without a moment's hesitation, he immersed himself in the cold water of the tub. The water penetrated his hot skin, waking each cell. When he stepped out of the tub, he was as fresh as usual, except for his tired burning eyes. He put on some new underwear which he had bought from a *Jude* from Luxemburg. His laundry had again taken on a pre-war colour; like his colleagues, he gave it to the

Ghetto Laundry, where it was treated with the same care as the laundry of the German soldiers. He hurried on his new suit which he had bought from a *Jude*, a doctor from Czechoslovakia, and he sat down to his breakfast. His appetite was not as good as normal, but he was rather content. He had to watch his capricious belly which had again begun to bulge, in spite of his exercises. He got up, put on his fur-lined coat, which he had bought from a *Jude* from Hamburg, and before leaving the room, he glanced again at the fish in the jar, worried that they had eaten too much and made themselves sick. He wanted them to be healthy and live long.

Outside, he was greeted by a bright winter morning. It was still early, but the days were already long and the sun was high above the horizon. The streets were covered with fresh untouched snow. Adam looked at it through his dark sunglasses, the sole object he inherited from his wife Yadwiga. Lately, he rarely parted with them in any weather. They not only protected his eyes but seemed to shield his entire face like a mask.

It was pleasant to be the first to disturb the smoothness of the snow with the steps of his rubber boots, which he had bought from a *Jude* from Berlin. His eyes no longer burned. Like curious squirrels they darted about the street which, through the glasses, looked greenish-bright and enchanting. He could see the entire length of Hockel Street up to the bridge, which looked like the aqua-coloured jaw of a fantastic crocodile. He fixed his gaze on it. It was healthy for the eyes to look into the distance. Suddenly, he noticed a black shadow resembling a huge bird on the top of the bridge. He had to remove the glasses in order to see it more clearly. The shadow looked like one spread wing which dived into the air and vanished. Was it possible that his eye-sight was weakening, causing him to see black blotches? His pleasure was spoilt. He began to worry about his eyes and his health in general.

The street was filling with people. Wrapped-up ghettoniks with their clinking canteens were pouring out from the gates, stumbling through the fresh snow. Adam hurried past the gate of the house where he had once lived. Here he sometimes noticed Samuel, or his daughters, or Reisel; they never recognized him in his glasses and foreign dress. Near the bridge, a Jewish policeman was ordering the people to move across quickly without stopping to look down. Adam, however, did look down and saw the "bird" lying under the bridge: the body of a young woman, her coat spread out, a thin dress moved up to reveal a pair of slim legs. Her two arms were stretched over the snow as if they were trying to embrace the earth. A gendarme stood nearby, the muzzle of his gun facing the bridge. People began to run, Adam along with them. Satisfied, he thrust his hands into his pockets. There was nothing wrong with his eyes. On the other side of the bridge, he bumped into a *Sonderkommando* whom he knew. "What happened, comrade?" he inquired.

The policeman shrugged his shoulders, "A Czech girl."

"Flew down?"

"Yeah, the sixth case. The *Judes* have fallen in love with the bridge."

Adam patted the *Sonder* man on the shoulder. "They should be forbidden to do that," he remarked half-jokingly, half in earnest. "Suicide is a private affair, not a public performance."

At the Red House, Herr Sutter and Herr Schmidt were busy. The sounds of a loud discussion in German could be heard coming from room No. 4. Downstairs, on the chequered floor, the *Sturmtrupper* was promenading with his dog. The traffic on the stairs was normal. Adam entered the kitchen, approached the window and stared into the garden. He was moody and sentimental today. The beauty of nature overwhelmed him. He longed for the mountains, for his skis, for freedom. He philosophized a bit, coming to the conclusion that after all he was a prisoner, that his life was already on the decline in terms of years, and that each splendid day which passed unrelished, would never return.

Overcome by self-pity, he poured himself a cup of coffee and inhaled its aroma. He recalled that during the alarm at night, he had been disappointed that he had heard no roar of airplanes. Yes, he wished that the war would come to an end soon, but not until the time was right for him. In his half-wakefulness after the alarm, he had had a vision. The airplanes were throwing gas bombs and all Jews and Germans, in fact, all the people in the world were annihilated. He alone survived to roam the world. He wanted to begin enjoying life, but out of a forest there appeared a hungry skinny wolf. Adam had no gun and Sutchka was dead. The wolf zipped open its belly and someone resembling Mietek stepped out of it. He fell upon Adam's neck while Adam struggled to make up his mind whether the young man wanted to embrace or strangle him. Unexpectedly, his mind, which for so long had been free from thoughts of his son, again became burdened with him for no apparent reason at all. Adam was still unable to understand himself.

A Jewish *Kripo* man came in and helped himself to a cup of coffee. He turned to Adam, "They're fighting upstairs over a sack of gold watches. The *Kripo* wants it for themselves, and Biebow wants it for himself. We'll probably have to wait here until lunch. Have you heard that the trains have stopped running?"

Adam shrugged his shoulders. "I don't travel by train."

"The evacuation will probably halt . . . temporarily."

"Maybe the war is coming to an end? They're getting a beating."

"Eh, what are you talking about? It's the typhus. They're more afraid of that than of the lickings at the front."

"Is there really an epidemic?"

"Did you just drop from the moon? Don't you know what's going on?" Adam, struck by fear, stopped sipping the coffee. He decided to take still more care of his personal hygiene. The Jewish *Kripo* man continued, "For the time being, the jail is so crowded that you can't throw a pin inside it. If today's contingent is added, it will become dangerously crowded. I'm telling you, we should count our blessings. Every time I go into the jail, my heart bursts. Yesterday I took two of my cousins out of there. Today again I have my wife's nephews on my head. Our dear relatives will not be satisfied until we put our lives and livelihoods on the line for them. Aren't we only human after all? We want to catch our breath. But they won't let us; family, acquaintances, trailing after us. You're fortunate. You're all alone and that's that." Adam did not listen to the man's confession. He was thinking about the typhus epidemic and how to protect himself against it.

Late in the afternoon Herr Sutter let them know that he would have no time that day. Adam left the Red House. The sun was already hidden behind the roof of the church. Through his glasses the snow seemed gray-green and the damp cold air even more so. Adam was tired. He felt like going home, like going to bed, and he feared that wish. Perhaps this was the beginning of typhus? He resolved to master himself. Rather than cross the bridge, he decided to remain in the larger side of the ghetto. The fresh air was the best prevention against sickness.

The people were still in the Resorts and the streets were empty. Only old people and children passed by. Here and there groups of people were walking towards the prison. Adam passed the empty Vegetable Place and reached Baluter Ring where there was a lively commotion. He looked inside through the fence. Wagons filled with materials passed in and out through the gate, while armies of porters loaded and unloaded them. Germans, wearing only their military shirts, were giving commands. Officials with briefcases and nimble secretaries came and went. At the office doors stood black limousines with red swastika pennants on their windows. Adam walked on, past a few roaring factories, then he turned the corner. From the slanted snow-laden roofs there fell a powdery drizzle. The further away he walked from Baluter Ring, the smaller, the more shrunken were the houses. Often huge masses of snow slid off them and landed on the passers-by. Adam observed three figures walking in front of him. Loaded down with gigantic sacks, two old people were clinging to a tall son who stooped under their weight.

The sight of the lanky hunched-over young man, who was letting his old parents carry such loads, while he himself carried an empty bread sack, again brought the thought of Mietek to Adam's mind. When they had run into each other at the Tailor Resort, Mietek had looked just as skinny and hunched. With that image he had vanished from Adam's mind, in order to reappear on such a strange day as this. Adam thought of turning back, but instead he accelerated his steps. As he passed the threesome, he cast a glance at the young man and sensed rather than recognised Mietek.

Adam stopped, as if nailed to the ground. Of Mietek's face, which was covered with shawls and a torn plaid, only the nose and eyes were visible. His glance reminded Adam of the little Mietek who had waved good-bye to his vacationing parents. The faces of the two old people seemed to beam with the pride of parents who were leading their son to the marriage canopy. The three barely noticed Adam. When he stood in their way, they avoided him by crossing the street. Adam followed them with his eyes. Then, suddenly, he tore off his dark glasses and set out at a gallop after the three vanishing figures.

"Mietek!" he cried out, panting. "Mietek!" The three did not stop. He was catching up to them. A mass of snow slid down from a roof and struck the visor of his cap, and his nose, stinging his lips. "Mietek!" His howl seemed to explode the heart in his chest; like a shrapnel it seemed to burst his mind and crush his skull.

A few people stopped to observe the scene. Both old people turned their heads to Adam. The old woman smiled with toothless gums. "Were you calling someone, my friend?"

"We are on our way to our children in Eretz Israel," the old man informed him.

Adam grabbed hold of Mietek's bread sack. "Don't go, Mietek, I'll save you!"

"Leave him alone," the old woman begged Adam. "He volunteered to take the trip with us."

Mietek jerked his shoulder with force. The cord of his bread sack broke. Adam was left holding it. The three backs moved ahead. Adam watched Mietek lead the old people out of sight around the corner. The cord of the bread sack was wound around Adam's finger. There was a finality in that broken cord. It was like becoming aware of a leg at the moment of amputation. That feeling surpassed the point of endurance; it dulled his exploded mind, freezing every nerve in his body with ice-cold chloroform. There was no pain, nor was there relief. Adam threw the bread sack into the gutter. Shrunken, he walked slowly back.

His room was warm. He had covered the fire in the stove with ashes in the morning, so that the fish in the jar would not catch cold. He approached the window. The grayness of the dying day and the reflection of the electric bulb were mirrored in the glass and in the water of the jar. The vivacious little fish sailed gracefully through the light and the grayness. Their scales shone like tiny mother-of-pearl buttons; the small mouths kissed the water, seeming sensuously to seek something essential which they had lost. The little eyes, like minute beads, blinked dully. The water surface above them was smooth and calm. Adam dipped two fingers in the jar and began to stir the water. He watched the fish quiver with fright in the stormy water, seeking an escape in the glass. His fingers chased after them, affectionately tickling their bellies. The water became turbid. The storm and the fear inside the jar were soundless. Adam stirred faster, as if he wanted to extricate a scream from the dumb fish-mouths.

He heard a light buzzing, barely audible, like the sound of a tiny motor. It was not coming from inside the jar, but from somewhere above it, from the window. He removed his fingers from the water and observed the window-pane. It was clear with no frost on it. The sound was coming from its corner. Adam stared with surprise at the first fly. An announcement of spring. Colourful images budded in his mind. The smell of perfumes blossomed in his nostrils. He was overcome by compassion for the tiny fly born in winter, and with his hand he began to chase after it on the pane, until the squirming speck of life was trapped in his clenched fist. The two fingers of his other hand slid inside the fist and snatched the little nothing of a body. He lifted it up against the light and began to pluck off one glassy delicate wing after another, until of the nothing of a body nothing remained — but silence.

He wiped his hands together and turned back to the fish. Animated, he snatched the jar and opened the door with a broad sweep of his arm. He swung the jar across the street, expecting to hear the smashing of crushed glass. But the jar had landed near a wall where the snow was soft and fresh. Two arched little streaks, like two commas, gave a sudden jump into the air, tracing their quiver in the snow. Then the white softness swallowed them — and everything was silent.

Chapter Three

THE HOUSES DUG OUT from under their dirty snow covers. The trees in Marysin shook off their icicles and stood in naked expectation. The melting streets became muddy. Young frivolous breezes jumped at the faces of the passers-by, tearing the hats off their heads, and inflating their coattails. The breezes filled the arches of the gates and chased each other's tails on the street corners.

The silent streams of evacuees were still flowing in the direction of the prison. All the "criminals", all the wives and children of those who had been previously evacuated, as well as those newer arrivals from the provincial towns had already been deported. It was the turn of the *Judes*, the immigrants from Vienna, Berlin, Hamburg and Dusseldorf who had not managed to die or commit suicide during their short sojourn in the ghetto. It was also the turn of those unqualified or unable to work. Ten, twenty thousand had already departed. The numbers were approaching thirty-five thousand, and there was no end to it.

Now that the air was milder, the daily streams of deportees seemed to flow in a livelier manner, as if supported by the gay breezes. Images of quiet villages bathed in the green of summer, where they would work, replacing the Poles who were in Germany, were reflected in the wanderers' eyes. They would plow the fields, harvest the grain, dig out the potatoes, not from narrow tiny *dzialkas* but from spacious fields. They would eat soup from large pots, drink sorrel borscht and chew black farmer's bread. Their children would drink milk straight from the cow. And so, in peace and serenity, they would wait with their families for the storm to pass. They marched hopefully, while those who remained in the ghetto were aflutter with fear, until they too received a "wedding invitation", until all the "protections" came to naught, until they could no longer survive with their food cards blocked, and they too joined the stream of wanderers.

One day in March, the postman knocked at the door of Chaim the Hosiery-Maker and handed his wife Rivka the "wedding invitation". Rivka was alone with her sick daughters. Sarah, the only healthy one, was at work in the Corset Resort, while Chaim was at the Straw Resort, braiding straw shoes for the German soldiers on the Russian front. Rivka hid herself in a corner of the kitchen, with the "wedding invitation", so that the sick girls would not see her from their beds. Her lips trembled. She stared at the "invitation" absent-mindedly, turning it on all sides, as if looking for something more written on it. Finally, she hid it under the oilcloth on the counter. She began to stir the red beet soup on the stove. It seemed to her that she was stirring her own torn heart.

The Almighty had been merciful to her. He had not sent down all the tragedies upon her head in one blow, because He had not wanted to destroy her. First He had taken the two sons who had not come back from the front. Then He had made sick the two youngest girls who were in the hospital. Then He had made sick the older ones. And so, gradually, piecemeal, she was able to bear the pain, and she knew that she would survive this last tragedy as well.

It was Chaim that she worried about. She could see how it "ate" at him; she could hear how derisively and arrogantly he conversed with the Almighty. There was so much aggression in his prayers that she could not bear to listen to him. Sometimes she would try to calm him, whispering, "Are you like Job that you should talk to God in such a way? We still have something to hope for and therefore we are more fortunate than Job. You'll see . . . The war will come to an end, the children will get well and the boys will come back . . . After all, we have a merciful Father in heaven, Chaim."

He would shake his head, as if to say, "Stupid pitiful woman, because of your torment you don't even know what you are talking about." And she realised that her words did not console him but merely made him silent. Yes, Chaim had been keeping silent a lot lately. When he did talk to her, he would not look her in the eye. Her heart melted with compassion for him.

She stood at the stove, stirring the pot, and prayed with trembling lips, "Great Father in Heaven, have pity, don't break him down and don't mind his arrogant words. You know, don't You, that a person in pain can say foolish things. Give him strength. Give him a breath of hope. He is so exhausted . . . dear God . . . We've brought up such children, such golden roses, such bright souls. Chaim's heart goes out to them, dear God, Sweet Father. You have created man in your wisdom, so You must understand that a man in distress can be stronger than his own self. But when? When he has a will to struggle on. Dear God, don't deprive him of that will. Let him rather struggle with You, than lose the will . . . Therefore I beg of You . . . Don't be angry at him . . ." Her tears dripped into the pot and were cooked along with the red beet soup.

When Chaim and Sarah came home from the Resort, the table was set and the sick girls were washed. Balcie, the eldest came to the table.

"What's new outside Father?" she asked, lazily stirring her soup.

"It's getting warmer," he replied, his eyes on his plate.

Sarah fed her sick sisters. There was no need to loosen *her* tongue. She gladly related the news from the street, from the Resort. Only to their questions about Esther who now worked with her in the Corset Resort, did she have nothing to reply. "Esther is Esther. It's hard to get a word out of her."

Chaim asked Rivka in a whisper, "What's new at the hospital?"

"Thank heaven, may it only not get worse," she replied loudly and cheerfully. "Their cough doesn't sound so hollow . . . they're breathing easier, much easier." It was only when she was washing the dishes and Chaim came into the kitchen that she showed him the "wedding invitation". She saw him suck both lips into his mouth, until only a thin crack remained in his beard. He stood before her not uttering a word. Her hands shook as she wiped the dishes. She whispered, "Have God in your heart, Chaim. Remember, if you, heaven forbid, don't have Him any more, we are lost."

"And if He does not have us any more, what will happen to Him?" he burst out. He vigorously rubbed his beard with both hands. "We don't leave!" he hissed through his teeth, and left the apartment.

She was glad that he had gone. He would have burst, trying to pretend before his daughters. She could bear it better. She was a woman; she could cry a bit in a corner. It was good that Chaim was not crying. He was her support, her rock. "Great Creator of the World," she whispered to the towel, wiping both the dishes and her eyes, "see for Yourself, can't You be proud of my Chaim, may he be protected from an evil eye? Isn't he a powerful man, a rock? But dear God, he needs You. Without You he will roll down into the pit of purgatory, like a heavy stone. Support him, dear God, have consideration, be merciful . . ."

Chaim came back late in the evening. In the room where the sick girls slept it was dark. Their heavy grating breathing gave the impression that there was no air in the apartment. In the kitchen where a small bulb was lit, Rivka and Sarah were warming their hands by the dying fire in the stove. They too were breathing heavily, in rhythm with the girls' snoring. Sarah had already been informed about the "wedding invitation". Chaim joined them at the stove, putting his hands against the tiles.

"I went in to see the Toffee Man," he told them. "He is surprised that he and his children have not received an 'invitation' yet. The Toffee Man said to me, 'God has mapped out the road and its trials for each one of us, and I am awaiting mine. You'll ask what I am doing in the meantime? You know, it has been said somewhere: Prepare yourself for the Other World as if you had to die tomorrow, prepare yourself for this world as if you had to live forever.' So I asked him: 'What do you mean by that?' So he answered me: 'We ought not to report to the transport willingly, because outside of the ghetto a storm is raging and God is not there. Because He is here with us, keeping our hands clean from sin.' Be that as it may, he said the same as I: not to deliver ourselves, but to leave the apartment and separate, one staying in one place, one in another . . ."

A sob escaped Rivka's throat. "Sweet Father . . . only not to separate . . ."

"What else can we do? Who will let in a family of six . . . three of them sick?" Chaim put the tip of his beard into his mouth and vigorously chewed on it.

They froze into silence. The last sparks of fire went out in the stove. There was only the sound of the heavy breathing on the other side of the wall. Chaim's face was contorted. His furrowed forehead seemed to reflect the storm raging in his heart. Rivka did not take her eyes off him. She wanted to sink down at his feet and implore him to recognize that it was bad enough that the two sick children were in the hospital, that the rest of them must not separate, because if they did, they would all be lost.

Sarah looked up at her parents questioningly. "Perhaps we could move in with Esther?"

Esther had found a new place for herself, a garret room, a kind of shed, which suited her requirements very well. Perhaps she was attracted to garrets, or perhaps she hit upon them by chance. This one was located in the building where she had once hidden when Valentino was in danger and she was searching for Rumkowski. The only piece of furniture in the shed was a bed. A box served her as a table, and a nail on the wall was her wardrobe. The walls were slanted and the window was above the roof. The window was a treasure. It had a fine view. Through it she could see a large expanse of sky, the fields of Marysin, the distant barbed-wire fence and behind it, the red chimney of a brick kiln and a frozen pond which looked from the distance like a cracked mirror. From the left side, the wire fence was cut off by the fence of the cemetery above which the roofs of a sunken city peered out: the cupolas of the rich people's monuments. On bright days she could also see a field fringed by a forest, but it was distant and dream-like.

The day she moved in, Esther was enthusiastic. What she needed was to free herself of all the impediments which threatened to trap her. She no longer needed anyone. Her experiences had strengthened her instinct for self-preservation. Every tie with another human being, even the slightest contact brought torment and might mean her own destruction. All she wanted was to have her food, her sleep and her rest which she now hoped to get, thanks to her fine little window. She recalled the poet Burstin's window, and Winter's window. Perhaps it was thanks to these windows that she had become so attached to their owners. Now she herself was the rich owner of a window with a "free" view.

The very first night, however, the little room lost all its attraction for her. As soon as she put out the light and approached the window, a strange feeling took hold of her. Outside was an endless expanse of darkness above a white snowy desert. She saw herself, barefoot, naked, wandering in the desert amidst gales; saw herself falling face down onto the sparkling ground which pricked her like nails. She heard herself calling for help. No one heard her, no one came to lift her up, to hold her. The fire in her little "cannon" oven had gone out, the wind took possession of the room. All night she lay shivering in her bed. She had no clue as to the cause of her anguish.

Her distaste for the room, her corner of escape, grew from day to day. She hurried zealously to work every morning, and after work she did anything to postpone her return home. She mocked herself. She, the revolutionary, the fearless flag-planter, the marcher in illegal demonstrations — was a coward, uncertain even of what she feared. She tried to conquer her weakness, to tear up the cobwebs of dark thoughts in which she had become entangled. She tried to make her shed cozier, more home-like. But as soon as she had finished, the eeriness of the surroundings still chased her out.

So it happened that instead of enjoying her life alone, she became envious of everyone who had family, relatives and friends, forgetting that she too had a family and friends. The lively streets seemed alien to her. She had no one to worry about, to be afraid of losing, to hurry home to. Standing in line in front of the bakeries and food co-operatives became her favourite pastime. Squeezed in among the waiting people, lost in the whirl of their conversations and noise, she felt more secure. Sometimes she listened to someone's confession and allowed herself to be invited into someone's home. Yet it did not enter her mind to visit her comrades or Uncle Chaim and his family. Only among strangers did she feel at ease. Then came the period of conserved beets and the days of great hunger, and all fears and wants left Esther, except for one: the need for soup, and for a crust of bread. There was no yesterday, no today or tomorrow. There was only the given moment, and it was a stomach waiting to be filled. At night she slept deeply, and if her hunger woke her, she dreamed about food while lying awake.

She was sitting in the hall of the Resort, bent over a pack of corsets, waiting for the lunch hour. Beside her sat Freida "the goat", the hall entertainer. Freida lived in a room above that of a rich "white guard", a flour porter, so her room was always warm. The girls from the Resort would come to "bathe" there, that is, to wash from head to toe, hair included. Esther had lately visited her only rarely, although Freida insisted, just like Uncle Chaim's Sarah: "Why don't you come up?" Esther hated these questions.

The weary girls worked slowly, as if the sewing machines were heavy iron cradles whose sound rocked them to sleep. The ringing of the lunch bell made them jump to their feet. The soup, as usual, was watery yet refreshing. The girls sat around the work tables, or on the piles of corsets on the floor, close to each other. Their spoons and canteens clinked cheerfully. Now it was time for Freida "the goat" to entertain them with songs or pranks. Esther scratched out her canteen and licked her spoon. Through the slivers of her eyes a green light shone warmly. Beside her sat Sarah, swallowing the last spoonfuls of the girls' food with her eyes. Her own canteen of soup stood beside her machine, untouched. She was saving it to take home to her sick sisters. Esther buried her face in her canteen. She was trying to ignore Sarah's presence. But Sarah would not move away from her, as if she wanted to tell her something. Esther did not want to listen. She engaged herself in a humorous dialogue with Freida.

Then she heard Sarah's whisper in her ear: "Esther . . . I want to ask you . . ." Esther looked her cousin in the face and read the news in it before Sarah even opened her mouth. They fell into each other's arms. Sarah's eyes were both demanding and begging, "Perhaps we could hide with you?"

Esther pressed her to her bosom. "Of course. The janitor never comes up to the garret."

✦ ✦ ✦

The dwelling on Hockel Street looked as if there had been a pogrom. Packs of bedding, clothing, pots and pans were strewn over the floor. On the bare bedding sat the three sick girls, watching the commotion with burning eyes. Rivka was moving about, packing. Things fell from her hands. Her body shook as if she had fever. The sick girls whispered advice to her, pointing out what she had missed or misplaced. She replied in a soft voice; a voice which remained like a nest, protective and warm.

Chaim and the Toffee Man, whom the girls called "The Jewish Dot", carried down the knapsacks and the bedding, then came up to fetch the sick girls. The oldest, Balcie, insisted on going down the stairs by herself. The others were carried down on chairs. Two other members of the society "Love thy Brother like Thyself" came to help. The girls were placed in a hand cart. The most difficult thing was to cross the bridge. The sick girls were dragged over it, hitting their feet against the stairs. A few times policemen stopped the strange procession, inquiring about its destination. "To report to the transport," Chaim replied, and the road was cleared.

The move to the hiding place was done quietly, carefully. The hour was auspicious. Esther's neighbours were busy with their evening meal and no one noticed the arrival of the new inhabitants. The Toffee Man and the other helpers shook Chaim's hand, "May it be in a lucky hour."

The three sick girls lay in Esther's bed which took up almost the entire shed, reaching to the "cannon" stove. Rivka stood over Esther's table-box preparing supper. The air was sultry; smoke escaped from the stove and from the lit candle on the box. The smell of fried oil hovered in the air. They ate in silence, except for Rivka who kept on whispering, "Let's just stay together . . . only together . . ." Before she finished eating, she fell asleep with the plate in her lap.

Chaim stepped out of the shed on his tiptoes and collapsed on the mattress in a corner of the garret. Esther and Sarah took Rivka by the arms and led her to another mattress close to Chaim's. They themselves slumped down on a red pile of bedding in another corner of the garret. They fell asleep in each other's arms. Esther saw herself in her dream: a little girl with a blue ribbon in her hair, collecting blossoms from the cherry tree . . .

As soon as Esther opened her eyes in the morning, Aunt Rivka offered her a mug of hot coffee. Sarah crawled out from under the low ceiling where they had slept, and stood up. She placed a tiny mirror on a box near the shed and combed her thinned-out tresses. Uncle Chaim was saying his morning prayers in the corner. Esther saw her sick cousins through the open door of the shed. She approached them, "If you look out through the window on a bright day, you can see a forest in the distance," she told them.

Balcie smiled, "I saw the sun rising over the cemetery, and I saw a flock of birds flying by."

"Look!" Esther whispered. "The ice over the water by the brick kiln has cracked!" She ruffled the sick girls' hair. "Here you will have something to see all day. And when it gets warmer, we'll open the window and you'll have fresh air."

From that day on, Esther too began to bring home her soup from the Resort. The first three days it was for the sick girls. Then, when the date for the family to join the transport had passed and Sarah and Chaim stopped going to work — since officially they were not in the ghetto any longer — Esther's soup, greatly diluted, became the basis for the entire meal. Aunt Rivka did not thank Esther as she had done when Esther had helped the family with soups. Nor did Esther now feel set apart as in her childhood. Finally she was an equal among equals. It was a good comfortable feeling to have a family. All day long at the Resort she would worry about the garret, the food rations and the firewood. After work, she would hurry with Sarah to the hospital to visit her sick cousins, then she would stand in the lines in front of the co-operatives, surprised that she felt so good, so cheerful, her heart so intimate with all the people, with the entire ghetto. Together with Sarah she cleaned and prepared the garret for their first Sabbath together. They had become used to doing things soundlessly, to walking around in the rag slippers which Esther had made at the Resort, and to talking in a whisper, in order not to attract the attention of the neighbours.

Friday night the building sank into silence. Doors would rarely open and every noise seemed muffled. In the garret the floor was scrubbed and covered with rags of sack cloth. In honour of the Sabbath, an additional box was moved into the shed. Rivka covered the boxes with a tablecloth and put her Sabbath candlesticks on it. She blessed the candles. The flames of the candles flickered; her hands trembled. The sick girls, their braids wound in crowns around their heads, their cheeks aflame, watched their mother's trembling wrinkled hands.

At the foot of the bed sat Sarah and Esther. They too looked at Rivka's hands, searching for her face through the fingers which covered it. When she finally removed her hands from her face, it seemed clearer, smoother, her eyes less red and misty. A warmth radiated from her shrunken figure and permeated the entire shed. And then there was the warm shimmer of the candlelight, embracing everything with a mysterious halo. The air glowed as if a spray of tiny diamonds were descending from the ceiling, or rising towards it. A rectangular carpet of light was spread out on the floor. The tiny windows reflected the candlelights along with the snow and the night. The garret seemed like a fantastic temple with tiny stained-glass windows.

Chaim returned from the place of prayer. When he appeared in the frame of the shed's door, it seemed not to be he but rather a portrait of him. Light and shadow played on his face and on the "new" gaberdine which he had acquired during the "good" early weeks of the war; they played on his beard and on his blue and red hands. His blank eye was fixed on distant worlds, while the other, filled with the peace of the Sabbath, gazed at the family as he greeted it with "Good Sabbath". Rivka served the Sabbath meal: Esther's soup from the Resort mixed with radish leaves. Then she served the "fish" and the "meat" which consisted of cutlets of the radishes themselves, mixed with a spoonful of flour and fried in a drop of oil. Then a *baba* made of coffee grinds spread with a bit of marmalade was removed from the window sill with great ceremony. The whole meal was consumed in silence, until it came to the *baba* and the coffee.

Chaim gave Rivka his cup to refill with the coffee-tea, as he called it. There was no more trace of his previous irritability. He spoke up, "People say that in our darling ghetto everything we eat tastes like . . . Radishes taste like fish, beets like herring, turnips like apple sauce. I'm telling you, Rivka, that today I really felt the taste of meat in the cutlets." He smiled into his beard and said to his daughters, "Your father has become a real glutton." He drummed against the tablecloth with his fingers. "So, what else do I see there on the window?"

"Nothing, only the bread." Sarah replied.

Rivka glanced at Chaim and then at the window, where a chunk of bread lay wrapped in a towel, and she ordered, "Give Father a slice of bread in honour of the Sabbath."

Chaim protested. "Heaven forbid. I'd rather have another mug of coffee-tea."

The bread wandered from hand to hand until it reached Rivka. They watched her cut off a thin slice and place it before Chaim. For a moment she hesitated, then she cut six more slices, thin as paper, distributing them among the girls. "This is in order that your conscience should not bother you," she said to Chaim, adding softly, humorously, "A poor man is fortunate. He is not afraid that he will become poor. Eat up and let's hear some Sabbath songs."

They slowly chewed on their slices of bread, washing them down with gulps of coffee-tea. From some lower floor the sound of a Sabbath song reached their ears. Chaim picked it up; Rivka and the girls accompanied him softly.

Because of a mistake, the family's food and bread cards were not annulled, and three weeks after the date of their supposed departure, they were still receiving their rations. After three weeks, the mistake was rectified. The day this happened, Rivka was unable to control her tears and Chaim again began to say his prayers with confusion and bitterness. The sick girls trembled like frightened birds whose nest was in danger. They muttered incomprehensibly, their cheeks burning. Balcie, the oldest, wept shamelessly on Sarah's lap. Esther stayed close to Rivka. "You'll use my food ration and my bread, Auntie."

Rivka nodded. "Yes, Esther darling, God is merciful."

The next day Esther sneaked out from the Resort and ran to Baluter Ring to see Rumkowski. At the gate of the Ring there stood a cluster of people, desperately sobbing, imploring the Jewish policemen on guard, to let them in to see the Presess. They were waving papers, documents, which were supposed to prove how important it was that they be let through. The policemen paid no attention to them. They swung their clubs and pushed the crowd away from the gate. Those who were too insistent received blows from the policemen, who treated them like nagging dogs. Esther too nagged at a policeman: "I am the Presess' ward," she implored him. "I am . . . I am . . ." The blows descended over the backs and heads of the people. The crowd dispersed through the mud in front of the gate in order, after a while, to regroup and again cling to the policemen. Guarding the gate of Baluter Ring was no longer one of the policemen's most pleasant duties. The two policemen lost their patience and began to deal out kicks and blows in earnest. The mud puddles, stirred by the running feet, were splashing over peoples' faces.

A man wiped both the mud and the sweat from his face, wailing, "Woe, slaves are ruling over us!" He spat in the direction of the policemen.

Another Jew raised his hands to the sky, "Deliver us, God, from both bondages, from the goyish hands and from the Jewish heads!"

Unnoticed by the policemen and the crowd, a young German appeared at the gate. He halted, scrutinizing the scene as he combed his blond crop of hair. Then he thrust the comb into his pocket and stood with spread feet and folded arms, observing the sky. Suddenly he roared, "*Los, aber schnell!*" He reached for the holster on his hip and the mud began to splash under the feet of the escaping people. The Jewish policemen at the gate stiffened, gratefully saluting their protector.

Esther rushed across the bridge to see Mr. Shafran. She could barely catch her breath; sweat and mud streamed down her face. The building in which Shafran now lived was familiar to her. More than once had she climbed these stairs, carefree and humming, on her way to Winter's apartment. Now, however, she had the impression that she was climbing them for the first time. Michal Levine's mother let her in, and they stared at each other, unable to utter a word. Not only did the old woman bear traces of her bygone beauty on her face, but with her white head and glowing complexion she still looked beautiful. She was neatly dressed, the white hand-knitted shawl with which she never parted covered her shoulders. But her eyes were red and tears shone on her cheeks. With great effort she finally told Esther, "They are at the prison . . ."

Esther let out a groan, "Leaving with the transport?"

"No . . . They went along . . . to accompany . . . her . . ."

Esther ran to the prison. It was dusk. The air was mild. The reflection of the vanishing sun painted the sky in pastel streaks, a warm pink, violet and aqua. The people in the transport along with their children, their packs and sacks, stood in the mud behind the prison fence. To both sides of the fence clung the departing and the remaining. Hundreds of pairs of hands were entangled in the wire mesh. Talk, shouts, sobs travelled back and forth. Eyes looked at faces criss-crossed by wires. The striped colours of the sky reflected in the tearful eyes of those outside, while in the eyes of those inside, who stood with their backs to the horizon, it was already night.

Esther paced along the fence, scanning the crowd. She moved closer, in order to recognize a familiar profile or hear a familiar voice. The hands clinging to the wire like pale spiders in a spider web flashed by her. It seemed impossible that Uncle Chaim and his family might one day be standing on the other side of the fence, while she took leave of them from this side. She concentrated on finding Shafran. Her life was in his hands, and she had to claim it from him.

From the other side of the fence a radiant little girl looked up at her. The child seemed suspended in the air. She was wearing a white knitted hat over ringlets which covered her delicate forehead. She smiled and waved at Esther, her tiny mouth full of incomprehensible chatter. Esther smiled back, waved back. A longing drummed at her heart. She moved closer and saw the child's mother, who held it on her arms. The young dark-haired woman dressed in a black suit, was also smiling, but her smile seemed artificial.

"Mina!" A man beside Esther called out, poking a pair of fingers through the wire, and waved at the child.

"Mina!" Two other men called out, doing the same.

The little girl repeated three names, distorting their pronunciation.

Esther recognised Dr. Levine, the painter Guttman and Mr. Shafran. She clung to the latter's arm. His hand touched hers, pressing her fingers; yet he did not take his eyes off the fence. She made an effort to pull him away from the others. She muttered, "You must help me, you must!" He cast such a pain-soaked glance at her, that she felt like throwing herself into his arms and letting loose the sobs which were choking her. She coughed, trying with all her strength to master her voice. "They've cancelled my Uncle's ration cards . . . They have . . . Please, come with me to Rumkowski!" She pulled at him. "I won't survive if they take them away from me . . ."

He pulled back to the gate. She blocked his way, but he brushed her aside. "The transport is leaving within two hours," he said.

Her voice became commanding. "I want you to come with me. You must save me!"

They measured each other with their eyes. "I don't want to leave this place, do you understand?" he spoke sternly, then he freed himself from her hand and turned his back to her. However, before she had time to recover, he disengaged himself from the crowd and called out to her, "Come, I'll still have time to come back." They ran through the muddy ghetto in search of the Presess. The offices were closed. The Presess was not at his home. They knocked at the doors of distinguished *shishkas*, asking after him. Shafran became increasingly impatient. He was far from his usual soft-spoken self. He was angry and he growled, "I am beginning to be afraid of meeting you. Why do you come to look for me only when something bad happens to you?" He reminded her that exactly a year before, on the eve of Purim, he had also run with her through the streets. She barely heard what he was saying. She was feverish in her despair, in her hope. She was unable to fathom the measure of time called a year. It meant nothing. The eve of Purim then and the eve of Purim today were the same point in time, the same knot in the noose at one's throat.

After two hours of running, they gave up the search for the Presess. "It's enough for today," she said, leaving Shafran without another word.

She went to visit Freida "the goat". They "bathed" and washed their hair together. Esther did everything in her power to become intoxicated by Freida's gaiety, to rid herself of her fatigue and through laughter and lively chatter regain her composure. She borrowed Freida's prettiest blouse and a clean skirt. She combed her hair and bit her lips in order to make them look red.

Freida laughed, "With whom's the rendezvous?"

"With the most handsome prince in the ghetto!"

In the street she tried not to run, but to save her strength. She kept on arranging her half-wet short hair which now looked dark-red. She reached Herr Schatten's apartment through the backyards. He was not at home. She waited for him in the arch of the gate; around her all was dark and quiet. A draught swept through the gate. She leaned against the wall, listening to her teeth chatter. Her knees began to give way, but she was afraid to sit down on the step. She did not want Schatten to see her shrunken or bent. She bit her lips and rubbed her hands, trying to keep herself warm. She had no idea how much time passed. Time was a night, a dark archway, a rough cold wall and a gale. The only thing that she was aware of through her vigil was the will to go on, the wish that her hair be in order and her mouth be warm and red. As if it were coming from some deep cave she heard the rumbling of her empty stomach. She tried to tighten her stomach muscles; she rubbed them with her fists. Yet the sound of her insides went on filling the darkness, rumbling through the gate. At the same time she felt no hunger. She felt as if she had satiated herself with cold rocks, rough and heavy ones, which were pulling her downwards, forcing her to collapse on the ground. But her will was awake. She did not surrender.

Someone was whistling in the backyard; a light melodious tune accompanied by rhythmical bootsteps. A black silhouette cut itself into the darkness of the gate, approaching, growing, filling the entire world with its form. Esther stepped forward to meet it. "Herr Schatten!" she called out and the whistling stopped. She came close to him. "Don't you recognize me?"

With his hands, Herr Schatten searched for her figure in the dark. "I can't see a thing, Madam," he called out gaily. "Please, come inside and we shall meet face to face." His hand around her arm was a clasp, the claws of a carnivorous animal. Not letting go of her, he unlocked the door with his other hand, pulled her inside and turned on the light.

The sight of the room leaped at Esther with such sharpness, that each piece of furniture seemed about to prick out her eyes. "Now do you recognize me?" she smiled crookedly. "Exactly a year ago . . . Purim . . ."

He crossed one leg over the other, scratching his bushy crop of hair. "A redhead?" He tried to remember, amusedly furrowing his brow. He caught himself. "Of course! The redhead! Woe, what a monkey you've turned into!"

Esther swallowed, "My uncle . . . I have . . . have . . ."

She was unable to talk and Herr Schatten helped her out, "Your uncle . . . Last time it was also some uncle . . ." He adjusted his jacket and with a broad knightly gesture opened the door for her. He bowed, knocking the heels of his boots together.

The electric bulb swayed before her eyes. The rocking furniture seemed to attack her, to push her; the ceiling pressed against her head while the floor became slanted, rising up and throwing her out of the room.

✦   ✦   ✦

The eve of Purim was one day and the day of Purim was another. The eve of Purim had led the heart to the precipice of despair; it could not go any further. On the day of Purim the precipice had not been crossed, yet it brought a sigh of relief. The inhabitants of the garret rose that morning as if washed and cleansed of all their sorrows. Because as soon as they opened their eyes, they felt the breath of mercy filling the sun-bathed air. Hope, like the thin dust trembling in the rays of light, penetrated the garret and pushed away the walls of fear. The world was basking in freshness. Delicate streams of golden sunshine poured down from the clear cloudless sky. A mild warmth, wrapped in the airy breezes as in transparent shawls, embraced everything alive, making people feel comfortable, light and in harmony with the outdoors. Only a person who had vegetated through a long winter behind barbed-wire fences would be capable of grasping the promise of that first day of spring.

The family's breakfast consisted of a mug of hot coffee. Their lunch was the same. Only the sick girls had a slice of Esther's bread with a bit of her marmalade. In the evening, however, Esther came home from the Resort with her soup, while Chaim brought home a soup contributed by the Toffee Man's society "Love thy Neighbour as Thyself". Esther had had a good day. From the morning on she had felt sure that something pleasant would happen. In her good mood, it was easy for her to pretend that she was fainting at work. The girl workers, in their Purim mood, also felt quite carefree. They enjoyed Esther's performance. Leaving their places, they raised the alarm and assisted Esther in her act of fainting.

The manager himself who was probably also finding the usual routine unbearable, entered the hall and stated that Esther was fainting because of hunger. He promised that at lunch time he would order the *wydzielaczka* to give Esther a substantial canteen of soup.

Esther, "revived" but very weak, stood in line in the yard, supported by her friends who delighted in the warm air and were amusedly chanting in a choir:

"Dear *wydzielaczka*, I am not kidding,
Take the scoop and start the digging . . ."

The *wydzielaczka*, in her white apron and white scarf, equally infected with the gay Purim spirit, supported the tune, singing back:

"If there were a chance, I swear by God
I'd fill with potatoes all of your pots."

The girls laughed. So did the supervisors and the manager. The manager himself took the canteen from Esther and brought her back a double, thick soup. He ordered her to sit down immediately and eat it all up, so that he could personally observe how the soup would put her back on her feet. She had to obey. She sat down on a doorstep, dug up a slice of potato from the canteen, but then she dropped it. The smiling manager and the friends who surrounded her made eating appear like such an extraordinary delight, that she could barely keep herself from emptying the spoonful into her mouth. She was dying to take at least one sip, to munch on at least one piece of potato, but she knew that if she started to eat, she would not be able to stop. "I cannot swallow," she shook her head, pitifully staring at the manager.

"Her stomach has shrunk," the manager pronounced his diagnosis. He bent down to her, asking compassionately, "Do you want to rest up and take half a day off?"

At home, in the garret, Aunt Rivka talked all day to her sick daughters, telling them about Queen Esther and the saintly man Mordecai and about Haman's defeat. The sick girls reminded her of the time they had disguised themselves on Purim, and gone from house to house with the chant: "A good

Purim to all. Wherever I go I fall. Haman the Villain rots in the earth, while Mordecai the *Tsaddik* rides on his horse." To entertain her sisters Sarah dressed up in a white apron and a white scarf, acting the part of the Angel of Justice. Then it occurred to her that in that dress she could easily sneak into the hospital and visit her two sick little sisters. Which she did. She even received a soup there, and thus she too did not come home empty-handed.

It was a day full of miracles. Aunt Rivka was beaming. "You see, children," she said, "The Almighty is sending down manna from the heavens."

Chaim was also full of energy. And it was to him that the greatest miracle happened. He was walking in Marysin, not knowing why, and in a big mud puddle behind a shed he found two unguarded boards of wood. He sold them on the black market for the price of two turnips.

Their Purim feast consisted of a delicious soup and a few slices of turnip. During the meal, Chaim talked as if he had swallowed a "talking potion".

"Purim," he said, "derives from the word Pur, which means fate. When Haman was sure that the fate of the Jews was one hundred percent decided, and that all the Jews, big and small, would be killed . . . he gaily went out into the streets with his pack of scoundrels. There he saw Mordecai the Righteous running after three children who had come out from the *heder*. Mordecai stopped each of them, and asked, 'Tell me what chapter of the Torah you studied today?' So the first boy replied, '*Al tira*,' which means, 'Don't fear an unexpected fear'. The second boy said, '*Utzu Eytza*', which means, 'They may convene a thousand councils, to no avail. Whatever they decide will have no bearing, for God is with us'. And the third boy answered, '*V'ad zikna*', 'Until old age I am the same. I shall bear the responsibility, I shall act and I shall save . . .' So Mordecai was overcome by a great joy, and when Haman approached him, and asked what he was so happy about, Mordecai replied, 'They brought me good news. You, Haman, may stand on your head, so you'll sink easier into the ground.'"

After these words, Rivka's heart began to flutter like a bird, with praise and gratitude. Her Chaim was a changed man. Tremendous miracles had happened to him on this day of Purim. Chaim's good mood was not artificial. He could never fool her in that respect. She nodded piously, as if to encourage him to go on talking. It had been so long since he had said a decent word to her.

Chaim, as if sensing her wish, talked on. "Haman said, 'I shall not raise my hand against anyone, until I raise it against these children.'" Courageously, Chaim looked his children straight in the eyes. "So, don't we all know how far his hand could reach? And another thought entered my mind today as I walked home with the two turnips. God's name is not even once mentioned in the whole of the Book of Esther, and yet it is a sacred book, and before reading it we say three blessings. Why then is God's name not mentioned in this book? The sages give all kinds of explanations, but I have found my own. Because what is the meaning of a sacred book, eh, Rivka? A sacred book means an eternal book. It refers to all time. It implies Haman's times as well as ours. And the fact that God's name is not mentioned in it, I explain like this: He, the Almighty, does not really want to wage wars for our sake, but wants us to wage wars for His sake. If that were not so, what would He need Esther or Mordecai, or the little *heder* boys for? Couldn't He destroy Haman in one blink of an eye, without their help? That's exactly it. As long as we were still in our diapers, an infantile people, the Creator wrought miracles and split seas for us, or He fed us manna. But since we have grown up and entered the world, He demands action from us. He has led us by the hand long enough. We ought to become the Mordecais and the Esthers ourselves and He, like a good father, helps us only with a spark of hope, giving us strength by His mere presence. Do you understand? And here we constantly come up with reproaches against Him, asking 'Why don't you save us?' And was I myself any better? But it is a fact that if a man takes only one step on his own, he immediately feels God's eye watching him. For instance, had I not gone to Marysin, but had stayed at home, quarrelling with the Almighty, I would not have found the two planks of wood and we would not have had the turnips. Of course, if you want, you can say that God was not present during my walk to Marysin. But was He not there, if I felt Him in all my limbs, felt Him a hundred percent better than during all my prayers . . .?"

Rivka blinked. She was no longer sure whether a new deviation had not entered into Chaim's relationship with the Almighty. Yet Chaim was a serene man today, and this was the surest sign that God had again taken him under His wing. Downstairs, on the first floor, a child was playing with its Purim rattle. Its sound was unpleasantly grating on the ears. Chaim and his family began to read the Book of Esther. After he had finished, Chaim remembered something, "Oh, yes, apart from the soup, the Toffee Man gave me a Purim gift." He reached into his pocket.

Chaim never managed to distribute the candies which the Toffee Man had given him. The garret was suddenly filled with a stampede of boots, with screaming mouths and swinging clubs. The bed broke, the box-table tumbled; plates fell to the floor. A turnip got tangled under the feet like a hard ball. The sick girls were carried downstairs. "Mama!", their cat-like mewing was heard.

Rivka flew down the stairs. She completely lost the power of speech. She wanted to say something to the tall *Uberfallkommando* who placed the sick girls on a cart, but she could not. Chaim, pressing his prayer shawl to his chest, ran up and down the stairs, from one policeman to the next. The knapsacks came rolling down past him. Esther and Sarah supported fainting Balcie under the arms and scrambled down the stairs with her. In the street stood a group of people surrounded by Jewish policemen. The carts loaded with the sick began to move. Rivka ran after them, then she turned back, and threw her arms around a policeman's neck. She wailed, "Have pity, dearest, I have two children in the hospital . . ."

Commissar Steinberg emerged from one of the adjacent houses. That day he had been a disturbed man. The last days before Purim he had had trouble rounding up the required thousand heads per day for the transport. The deportees became more stubborn with every hour and hid themselves ingeniously. And this day, the day of Purim, when the ghetto had sighed with relief, out of the required thousand only three hundred Jews had reported for deportation before sundown. The situation was growing serious, and around seven o'clock Steinberg's patience burst. He ordered the mobilization of the entire *Uberfallkommando* and explained his strategy to them. The raid had to start in the evening, in greatest secrecy, and it had to be carried out as quickly as possible. Steinberg decided to lend a hand himself, to encourage his boys and assure himself of a proper result.

As soon as Chaim saw Steinberg, he dashed out towards him, his fist aimed at Steinberg's fleshy face. But Steinberg caught him deftly by the wrist. With his single seeing eye Chaim stared deeply into Steinberg's eyes, and suddenly he began to shake, to shrink. A stream of tears poured down his face, dripping onto Steinberg's hand which had grabbed hold of Chaim's beard. "Only for this, for walking about with this in the ghetto," Steinberg pulled him by the beard as if he were about to tear it off his face, "I should have knocked your teeth out. March!" he shoved Chaim towards the group of prisoners.

Chaim pressed the prayer shawl to his chest as he began to move ahead. Rivka stopped running from one policeman to the other and joined her husband. He hung on to her arm with the weight of his shrunken body. "Rivka dear", he moaned, "I saw God's face, Rivka, my crown."

"Hush . . . Hush . . ." She pulled him along with her.

"He is Asmadeus . . . The Satan . . ." he mumbled.

"Hush . . . don't say a word . . . God is merciful, Chaim dear," she sniffled through her nose, pressed down by the weight of Chaim's body. She continuously turned her head back, "My children . . ."

Behind them came Esther and Sarah with the sick Balcie between them. They were surrounded by other families, parents with children on their arms, children by their sides. Huddled together, pressing one against the other, they shuffled through the blue of the mild Purim evening. A youngster who had listened to Chaim's lamentations, began to scream hysterically, "Haman is a Jew! Haman is a Jew!" He tried to tear himself out of his parents' arms, throwing his head around like a trapped colt.

The last sparks of the dying day were reflected in the mud puddles in the street. Rivka tripped on a stone and almost fell. Esther caught her and took hold of her arm. Now all of them walked together in one row. In front of them, on the cart, rode the two sick sisters; behind them walked the policemen swinging their clubs. They did not have far to go. The prison house was already in sight. Chaim did not stop talking to Rivka. She did not stop trying to calm him, "Hush . . . Hush . . . You are not on the same plane as Job, Chaim . . ." Her voice was gradually coming back to her. "God has not punished you with the worst . . ."

Esther was indifferent to Rivka's talk and to Chaim's strange lamentations. She felt dull, satiated in a way, at peace with the surroundings, with the world. She now had a mother and a father. When they arrived at the fence of the prison, she noticed the people clinging to the wires, their hands like spiders of light in a dark spiderweb. When had she last seen that sight? Yesterday? Last year? She had seen it when the noose around the neck of hope had still been loose.

They entered the prison yard. Now it was the people outside who seemed trapped behind the fence. A cool wind rose from the humid muddy ground. The police disappeared and the prisoners could move about freely. Rivka pulled Chaim in the direction of the carts, "Come, let's keep close to the children."

One group of prisoners and then another entered through the gate. At the back of the yard a crowd was being gathered around the huge open trucks whose platforms were walled with wooden planks. The coloured ribbons of the policemen's caps and armbands blinked in the dark. Finally the policemen linked their arms into a chain and began to heard together the remainder of the crowd in the yard, pushing them towards the trucks. A few Germans appeared to watch the loading. The new groups of people with their packs and sacks pressed against those in front of them. In the crammed throng the policemen moved about, distributing pieces of bread with sausage. Some people stuffed their mouths with the food as they moved on towards the trucks. Others saved it for a "black hour".

The loading itself proceeded in silence. Rivka still turned her head towards the ghetto, whispering, "My children . . ." while she, along with the two sick girls, and with Sarah, Chaim and Esther, approached the truck.

Esther bit into her slice of bread. She swallowed her piece of sausage. A policeman helped the sick girls as well as Chaim and Rivka climb onto the truck. Stuffing her mouth with the remainder of the bread, Esther let go of Rivka's arm. She wanted to have her hands free, so that she could climb onto the truck. She strained her eyes in the dark to see where to place her foot. As she looked down, she noticed something white on the ground. A child's little cap? She stared at it as she searched with her foot for the step of the little ladder. Someone gave her a jolt and she fell to the ground. She lay under the truck with the child's cap in her hand. Climbing feet moved past her as if they were trying to walk over her. Her mouth was still full of food. In her mind's eye she saw the smiling child — of yesterday? Of some time before? Of tomorrow? On all fours she crawled under the truck and came out on its other side. She cut through the crowd which surged on towards the trucks. Somehow she passed the cordon of policemen; she began to run, falling into the arms of one of them.

"Where are you going?" he shouted.

Her mouth was still full; the crust of bread blocked her throat. She threw her head about, trying to tear herself away from the arms which held her. The little white cap fell from her hand. "There . . ." she stammered, pointing towards the ghetto. Suddenly a light went on in her head. She thrust her hand into her pocket and drew out a green card. She raised in to the policeman's eyes. "This . . . my identity card . . . I work in the Corset Resort . . . I'm the Presess' ward . . ." She spat the words out fast, relieved that the bite of food had at last slid down her throat.

"What are you doing here?" The policeman eyed her from head to toe. Then he grabbed her by the hand and ran with her to the gate. "Let her out," he quickly said to the guard. "She's the Old Man's ward."

She ran and ran, an eternity, without turning her head back even once. On all fours she scrambled up the stairs to her garret and prostrated herself on the messy bedding under the low ceiling. It was already night, but downstairs a child was still playing with a hoarse Purim rattle.

Chapter Four

SAMUEL'S ACQUAINTANCE with Moshe Eibushitz had begun the year before, in the Spring. They had met one evening in the backyard on Hockel Street when both were taking some air in the Garden, by the cherry tree. Once they discovered that their daughters were friends, they struck up a conversation about the girls, which led them to a conversation about the old times. It came out that they were the same age and had both participated in the war against the Bolsheviks.

"It's possible then that we have already met . . ." Moshe said with a smile. Samuel offered him a cigarette. At the sight of the cigarette, Moshe's lips began to tremble. The cigarette shook in his mouth. When he finally lit it, he inhaled deeply, his eyes closed, and he remained that way for a long time, isolated from the world in his pleasure. Then, calmed, he opened his eyes, moved closer towards Samuel and told him gratefully, confidentially, "You know, every fall I gather some dry leaves in Marysin. I leave them to dry in the sun, then I crush them up and smoke them rolled in a piece of paper. Only once did I ever exchange a slice of bread for a cigarette. Smoking is a passion, but one should not let oneself become a slave to it."

"Does that mean that your will power is stronger than your passion?" Samuel asked.

"No, not so much my will power, as my unwillingness to feel guilty. To sell your bread for a cigarette is a sin."

Samuel made a mental note to bring Moshe a pack of cigarettes at their next encounter. Indeed, they began to meet in the yard quite often, to discuss the news, politics, Zionism and Bundism. These discussions were not very heated, as if each of them were somewhat detached from the platform he was defending. Sometimes, particularly when they discussed life after the war, they had the impression that they actually followed the same school of thought, although they were not clear which it was.

Then came a time when they failed to communicate as smoothly as before. Moshe was nervous. His usually calm face was clouded, his voice loud, jarring, seething with anger. "Every time I divide the bread," he complained, "I become a nervous wreck. I shudder as if I had a seizure of malaria; my tongue seems to jump out of my mouth. My wife and children stand around, watching me dissect the loaf. I add a bread crumb here, remove a bread crumb there. I am fair, I am just. Can you understand such justice? Do I deserve an equal portion with the children, I ask you? But then, how do I get the devilish strength to give them a piece from my own share, when my body seems to jump out from its skin at the mere smell of bread? But my wife, you see, doesn't find it so hard to do. She cheats us all . . ."

After that meeting Samuel began to avoid Moshe. Then the Eibushitzs moved out of the yard and the friendship between the two men seemed to be over. Months passed. Until one winter day, Samuel noticed Moshe in the street, and from the way Moshe walked, Samuel guessed that he was suffering from the popular disease of the ghetto: decalcification of the bones, as it was labelled. Samuel stopped him. Moshe's face, blue with cold, with watering eyes and sunken cheeks, lit up with a smile from ear to ear.

"Mr. Zuckerman!" he exclaimed. "God, I have not seen you for ages!" They held each other's hands for a long while, letting each other know with their eyes how glad they were to have met and how surprised each of them was by the other's joyful reaction. "Congratulate me, Mr. Zuckerman," Moshe pressed Samuel's hand. "Mother Luck has smiled on me at last! I got a position in a co-operative!"

"Really?" Samuel cried out. "In that case I don't have to worry about you. Those who work in the co-operatives manage quite well." Samuel felt relieved. Only now did all the barriers between them disappear.

Moshe winked at him meaningfully. "I know what you have in mind. But to all my troubles I refuse to add that of my own conscience. I don't want to become rich in the ghetto. All I want is to survive."

Their real friendship sprang from that encounter, even though it was almost too late in both their lives for a new friendship. Life itself was against it. Yet it was perhaps precisely that fact that gave it strength and support. Samuel never invited Moshe to his home. It was he who would visit Moshe, and their meetings depended on him, although he always had the feeling that he needed Moshe more than Moshe needed him. He was always surprised by the enthusiastic smile with which Moshe would greet him. Which of the two was the prince, which the pauper?

Moshe's apartment, its kitchen walls covered with shelves full of books, was permeated by an air which reminded Samuel of the serenity of his own study before the war. Only the problem was that the more he absorbed this atmosphere, the more difficult did he find it to stay between those walls. It seemed to him that he did not say the right things, that he smiled falsely, that the Eibushitzs felt embarrassed with him and that he had actually come uninvited. Moshe, on the other hand, also wished that they could be alone. So he invited Samuel into the little bedroom. There they were alone. Samuel would offer Moshe the pack of cigarettes which he rarely failed to bring him. They would smoke, chat, discuss politics, or confess. Sometimes they would just sit together in silence.

Once Moshe said, "Strange how the concepts of honesty change. Do you recall what I told you in regard to taking advantage of my new job? Well, you think I don't steal? Whenever I can, I smuggle out a bit of oil or a few carrots. And my conscience keeps silent. It does not even occur to me that I am harming the consumers. Perhaps if I smuggled out sackfuls of food, I would feel like a thief. If so, is it a question of amount? Is a small thief not a thief? And to be truthful, the reason I don't steal more, is not because I am honest, but because I am afraid of being caught, of losing my job."

Samuel watched the lit cigarette in Moshe's delicate hand which was covered with a blue branch of swollen veins, fully aware that every time Moshe talked about himself, it called forth an echo of his own voice within him. This time he allowed the echo to materialise into words which he had never uttered to anyone. "Now think about my situation, Moshe. I am part of the system. I belong to the clique, to the ghettocracy, and the Presess is my friend. I say friend. Of course I don't talk with him the way I talk with you. But in a certain way . . . I owe him a lot. My colleagues, the *shishkas*, also eat from his hand at the same time as they spit at it. The truth is that I respect the Old Man. When he comes to the resort and praises my achievements, I have the feeling that my own father is patting me on the shoulder. And I am also convinced that thanks to him we shall survive, because I too believe that work can sustain us, that in fact we are not working for the Germans, but for our own selves. What would I have done without the Resorts, without the chance to build, to be useful?"

"Useful to the Germans?" Moshe puckered his eyebrows.

"Do you hold it against me?"

"Who am I to sit in judgment on you?"

"My problem is that I feel low."

"I know . . . your conscience is your problem."

"I was a member of the first Jewish council under the Germans and almost paid with my head for it. It was clear to me that I could not free myself of that function even if I wanted to. And that was also a form of collaboration, wasn't it? Nowadays, the thought comes back to me: what feat is it to be innocent and free from sin, when one does nothing? Perhaps it is one's duty, as the Old Man says, to take the responsibility upon oneself and participate in the German game, in order to save as many people as possible. But on the other hand, there is another thought bothering me. Don't we know perfectly well that the German game is precisely to make the victim participate in the task of his hangman?"

Another time Samuel and Moshe touched upon even more intimate issues.

"I am a sickeningly sentimental man," Moshe said with a smile. "For instance . . . after twenty years of marriage I am, so to speak, still in love with my wife. And if you want to know, many people take me for a henpecked husband. They make fun of my meekness as a family man. But that's what I am. Without the family I am nothing. In it and through it I see the world, I see other people. To me this is the highest ideal; it leads me towards other ideals. It's not manly? A real man ought to be somewhat detached from his family, they say, a part of him should always remain on the outside. I don't give a damn about it. I've put everything I have on this one card."

Again Moshe's words echoed in Samuel's mind, and he told Moshe about his life with Matilda, about the veil of estrangement that always hung between them, about his cravings for other women, for all women, for the Eternal One. He told him what he had only recently allowed himself in the ghetto, with Sabinka. Again he betrayed his guilt feelings. "Isn't it strange that we begin to hate those whom we harm?"

Moshe also liked to let his thought wander to the past, to tell Samuel about his youth in his *shtetl*, about his barber shop and his customers. But here Samuel could not reciprocate with frankness. It seemed to him that he had nothing of importance to recall, and in fact, he remembered amazingly little of his past. All that had remained with him was the taste of constructing, of producing. But then he would have to tell Moshe about his factory and his wealth, and this, Samuel feared, would have smacked of conceit. Should he then, instead of talking about himself, have told Moshe about his forefathers' contributions to the history of the Jewry of Lodz? But what sense did it make for him to wrap himself in the glory of his parents, if his own children could not wrap themselves in his? The book which he had once planned to write did not enter his mind at all. In general, he found it easier to present himself to Moshe in a bad light than in a good.

His conversations with Moshe did not seem to have any bearing on Samuel's day-to-day life. After all, his visits were provoked by a sudden impulse and were rare. Afterwards he would immediately forget about them. In the Resorts he behaved as usual. He liked to repeat Rumkowski's sayings, to order the workers around and offer them either praise or slaps. He caroused with his colleagues and visited Sabinka. At home he walked around like a stranger, sometimes exploding with rage, at other times whistling gaily. Both his revulsion and his pity for Matilda grew. But he felt the pity most when he was away from her, when he found himself in Sabinka's arms after an evening of total forgetfulness. When he was in the house, he rarely spoke to Matilda; he avoided looking at her and did not even resort to his old repertory of feigned politeness.

Yet he became aware of a certain change in his behaviour, a change partially rooted in his conversations with Moshe. He felt this clearly on the day he had rushed to the Presess on behalf of Mietek Rosenberg, when he had spoken to the Old Man in a way he had never dared before. He also had moments during that long winter, when the echo of Moshe's voice unexpectedly echoed in his mind as he clearly heard him saying, "Zuckerman, you are like the fog . . . You have no backbone. They all talk through you as through a parrot's mouth: your father, Mazur, Rumkowski. You have no sense of self, no character. What is your supposed passion for building? Nothing but a means of escaping from yourself, a means of losing yourself and dissolving into your work, of becoming one with the things you create. Your name is Hollowness, Samuel Zuckerman."

There were days when he would wake up in the morning with the sound of that voice in his ears. The truths which it revealed irritated him. He had no means of dealing with his torn inner core, no means of making it whole. At the same time, he knew that if he continued with that kind of existence, it would eventually destroy him. He needed to be proud of himself, to be a man, to be brave and at peace with his conscience. Yet he postponed his straightening up until later, until tomorrow. To do it now was impossible. And so he continued to kick his workers around, to run to Sabinka, and to doggedly avoid his home; he continued to serve the Presess.

Lately, he had begun to shut himself up in his room, from time to time taking out the packs of notes which he had prepared for his book. He intended to start writing it. However, the notes remained on his table untouched. The only place where he still felt somewhat pleased with himself was in the cellar where he listened to the radio broadcasts.

✦   ✦   ✦

The time for spring cleaning arrived. All the windows of the Zuckerman house stood open. Reisel had washed them the day before. They were so perfectly clear that their panes seemed to have become mirrors through which the light of the day was beaming. Between the open balcony doors stood chairs laden with bedding, with mattresses and clothing. Inside the house all the doors also stood wide open. The draught coming from the windows passed through them, filling every corner with wind and with the sound of Reisel's voice. Reisel was dressed in her cleaning costume which consisted of her pre-war cloche gown, which dated from "King Sobieski's times". The scarf she wore covered all of her straw-like yellow hair, reaching down to her eyebrows. Laden with brushes, brooms, pails and rags she resembled a Turkish Ottoman in the midst of the battlefield.

Today Matilda replaced her at the stove and did the cooking. Matilda's face and neck shone with perspiration. She was in a hurry and everything fell out of her hands. She burnt her fingers on the boiling pots, she cut herself with the knife, she almost broke a few plates and she mixed up the recipe of one holiday dish with that of another. Nevertheless, she was in good spirits. She enjoyed cooking, particularly today, when all the opened doors and windows let in a wonderful breeze which carried the message of renewal.

She wore a sleeveless open-necked dress of a flowery design. Her flabby arms and full breasts felt the caressing air with every cell. A few times she left her work to wash her perspiring face and take a look at herself in the mirror. She reproached herself; she should have taken more care of her figure and not given in to her craving for sweets. She hoped that now, in springtime, when she did not feel so cold in her soul, she would be better able to discipline herself.

In her mind she heard a piano playing Beethoven's "Für Elise". The deep warm melody seemed permeated by her own longing for Samuel. Never had she loved him so powerfully as recently. It seemed to her that up to now her feelings for him had been incomplete, sickly and destructive, and had had little to do with real loving. What she now felt was generous, healing. The change had come about precisely during these last fateful days in the ghetto, with the evacuations, and also with the concerts in the House of Culture, and with this wonderful spring. She hummed the tune of the Lied, paraphrasing the words to suit her mood: "And on the day when I am gone . . ." Hope was not always a positive feeling, she thought. It led to rebellion, to frustrations and bitterness. As long as she had been hoping for Samuel's love, she had been impatient, restless. Precisely her resignation, her acceptance of their alienation as final had put to sleep her pain and helped her link herself to life again.

As she busied herself with the pots, she thought about Samuel. She was surprised that no one had noticed how much he had changed. He had completely lost his playfulness, his boyish charm. His way of walking, his looks betrayed an indecisiveness and a lack of self-assurance. His eyes had become darker; his gaze was evasive, as if he were trying to hide its expression of despair. His hair had turned gray and his forehead was crossed by a few deep furrows. His nose seemed longer, more pointed, while his mouth had lost its shape with his lips drooping loosely. His back was bent, the shoulders were collapsing around his chest, and when he walked bare-chested into the kitchen, she could easily count his ribs, as if he were a *klepsidra*. Yet, in her eyes, he seemed more masculine, more attractive than ever.

He had become a heavy smoker, and the house was full of unfinished cigarette butts strewn over the floors, the tables and plates. The smell of nicotine lingered stubbornly in all the corners of the house, as if the walls themselves were permeated with it. At first Reisel tried to react, but Matilda cut her short, herself removing the traces of nicotine as well as she could.

She liked Samuel's room and its smell. It made her feel that she was trespassing on the privacy of a stranger. It seemed unbelievable that she had had two daughters by the stranger, that he had ever touched her. It had been two completely different people who had once stood under the marriage canopy, who had built a home together and slept close to one another. She remembered it all as one remembers a book one has read a long time ago. And just as one does not miss such a book, she did not miss those bygone times. If she was filled with longing, it was immobile, not facing the past or the future. It expressed itself in her curiosity about the stranger with whom she could achieve intimacy only through his room. She liked to rummage about in it when Samuel was not at home. It became her obsession to open his drawers, to search his pockets. The former Matilda, the one of the "old book", would not have done such things. It would have been against her pride and dignity. But the present Matilda barely remembered what pride and dignity meant, just as she barely remembered many other virtues which had been the basis of her former behaviour. And when she asked herself what she actually expected to discover in Samuel's room, she could not find any answer.

It was not only in Samuel's room that she rummaged about, but also in the room of her children. The children had also become strangers. That kind of love also belonged to another woman, to a mother who had known the language of caresses, who had had a big warm heart upon which devotion had fed like sheep on a sunny meadow. Now she felt barren, her feelings for her daughters resembled those she had for Samuel — they were filled with the longing and curiosity that one feels for strangers.

This morning her curiosity had come to the fore. As she was watching her daughters help Reisel carry the mattresses out onto the balcony, she noticed a folded sheet of paper on the springs of Bella's bed. She fell upon it, but before she had managed to unfold it, Bella leaped towards her and grabbed the sheet of paper from her hand. Smiling confusedly, crookedly, she ordered, "Give it to me!" and came close to the girl.

"I don't want to! It's mine!" Bella pushed her away. Matilda surrendered, but promised herself to inspect her children's room immediately after they left the house. For the time being, in order to calm herself, she went into Samuel's room.

Lately, Samuel did not put away the materials for his book which he had spread out on his table. Matilda was familiar with every scrap of paper on it; she also knew that there had been no new pages added to the pile. Yet she sat down on Samuel's chair and attacked the papers as if she had never seen them before. The papers were yellow and creased. To her they were not the notes for a projected book, the History of the Jews of Lodz. To her they were The Long Forgotten Book. The dust between its pages was the dust of time that had covered every path leading back to the past. This was the dry barren meadow where no sheep were feeding. Matilda fingered the pages while listening to the piano echoing in her mind: "And on that day when I am gone . . ." The breeze wafting into the room helped her flip the pages and caressed her cheeks consolingly. "It is Spring," it whispered in her ear. "Fresh, luscious green grass sprouts in the meadows which were dead during the winter . . ." She heard her daughters shut the door behind them, and she rushed back into their room. She rummaged through it, smiling dully. Having found nothing of interest, she gave up the game and went into the kitchen to resume her cooking.

Bella was sitting on a pack of bedding on the balcony, biting her nails. The skin around the nails was irritated and red, and it hurt her. The spring day also hurt her. It underlined the winter reigning in her heart. The only feeling still

alive within her was her hatred of her parents; a feeling which had so
overpowered her lately, that she was barely able to keep it in check. The piece of
paper which she had refused to show Matilda in the morning was worthless.
She had wrestled with her mother over it because of the opportunity it had
afforded her to relieve her rage. The folded sheet of paper now lay in Bella's lap.
She remembered every letter on it, every mark. Mietek had written the note six
weeks ago, before leaving with the transport:

> "I am joining the deportees voluntarily. I want you to know about that.
> When the war is over, don't look for me. I am breaking away from
> everything and from you, too. You have destroyed me and showed
> yourself to be a coward. Everyone is a traitor. But it is only you who
> count. You have loved me (whatever that means). You were the only one,
> and it seemed important that we do it together. I have tried to do it alone,
> but you have turned me into a coward too. Actually you were right: there
> is no need to make the effort nowadays. Perhaps the Germans will do me
> the favour. I don't look ahead to anything. I expect nothing. I am also a bit
> curious about what's going on on the other side. Mother Luck is smiling
> on me. As you can see, I was born in a silken shirt. All my whims will be
> answered sooner or later."

Bella lay down on a pile of pillows heaped on two joining chairs. Her face
framed between the bars of the balcony's railing, she looked down into the
yard. The cherry tree resembled a bridal bouquet. Its boughs, heavy with leaves
and clusters of flowers, were barely moving. Once in a while a flower petal
circled in the air like a butterfly before it fell to the ground. Slowly Bella began
to tear up the letter, filling her palm with its shreds. She aimed at the tree, but
her thrust was too weak. The shreds of paper twirled in the air and vanished
under the balcony. The cherry tree filled her eyes with its knot of blossoms.
She whispered to it, "You are beautiful . . ." — Something sobbed within her,
"I want to die . . ."

In the yard behind the latrines two little girls were playing. One of them was
rocking her doll's carriage so vigorously, that the blue ribbon in her hair was
waving in the air in time to her movements. The other girl was filling little pots
with soil and putting them on the broken chair which served her as a stove.
Along the walls in the backyard were rows of straw mattresses put out to air.
There was a lively traffic around the water pump. Streams of water drummed
against the tin bottoms of the pails. Sheyne Pessele was scrubbing chairs with a
hard brush. Other women were scrubbing their kitchen utensils. Between the
black beds of soil, small boys chased one another, playing rag-ball. Men, women
and children with shopping bags and canteens in their hands were coming
home from the Resorts. They were calling in the direction of the open
windows. Some people stopped before the entrance to chat with their
neighbours. The first workers appeared on the *dzialkas*, building borders
around their plots, or sowing. A man, in traditional gaberdine, tails flying, his
traditional cap high over his forehead, watered the thirsty soil. A woman
squatted over a heap of soil, looking like a gigantic hen warming her eggs. She
was loosening the ground before her with a toy shovel. Two girls dressed in
men's pants were digging under a window, singing.

From behind the roof of the latrines a white pigeon flew out like a rocket of
light, circling the yard as it descended. The setting sun fringed its wings with
purple. Then the sun's reflection on its wings disappeared, and as it approached

the cherry tree, its whiteness merged with the whiteness of the boughs. The pigeon settled on the tallest branch, swaying like a huge white bud.

"*Mameshe! Mameshe!*" one of the two little girls called out. A pregnant woman, her pale hands folded over her belly, appeared in front of the latrine man's hut. The little girl pointed to the pigeon on the tree. "What's its name?"

"It's a pigeon," the woman answered.

Her little daughter was excited, "It's very nice. Where does this pigeon bird live, *Mameshe?*"

"On the other side of the ghetto," the women explained.

The other little girl laughed, "On the other side their live some people who look like people, but their heads are made of cabbage. My daddy calls them cabbage-heads."

Someone came running through the gate, raising a feverish commotion in the backyard. The pregnant woman grabbed her girl by the hand and rushed into the hut with her. The other little girl disappeared into an entranceway, along with many other neighbours. The yard was empty. The mailman with the "wedding invitations" had entered the yard. Straight after him, came Junia. He called after her, apparently wanting some information. She ran ahead, leaving him behind. She was dressed in a police uniform with a beret on her head.

Suddenly Bella heard Junia's voice behind her. "I have to tell you something. Wait for me here."

Bella heard the sound of the water tap and Junia's singing voice. She was humming the hit song which Herr Schatten, the Presess' confidante, had composed. "The silvery moon has deceived me,/the sun has mocked me with its light./Only the shadow keeps its promise/and visits me night after night . . ." This sad romantic melody coming from Junia's mouth sounded like the gayest song in the world.

Bella heard Reisel's voice. "Get up and help me take in the mattresses!" Bella stood up slowly, awkwardly grabbing a mattress by the corners. Reisel shook her head. "Your mother is right. Your hands are made of clay."

Junia approached them dressed in her slip, drying herself with a towel. "What are you complaining about, Rosalia darling?"

At the sight of the half-dressed girl, Reisel let go of the mattress and grabbed herself by the head. "Naked on the balcony? Someone might see you, you shameless brat!"

All three of them somehow arranged the mattresses on the beds. "And now, Rosalia darling, be so good as to leave us alone, because I have something very important to discuss with Miss Bella." Junia said.

Reisel straightened her headgear and putting her hands on her hips, exclaimed, "Not on your life! The table is set and I saw your father come in!"

They sat at the table. Bella kept her face buried in her plate. Samuel also looked silently into his plate. Only Junia and Matilda were in a cheerful frame of mind. However, what they said to each other did not connect somehow; their phrases passed one another, as if each of them were talking to somebody else. In addition to their awkward conversation, Reisel was carrying on her own monologue. She talked to all of them and to none of them, adding to the impression that this was a group of deaf people taking their meal. Matilda noticed that Samuel's plate was still full; he was turning it round and round, barely raising the spoon to his mouth. Her gaze met with his. She could not bear her reflection in his eyes. Her voice acquired an unnatural pitch. "A good soup," she muttered. "My own invention . . ."

At last Junia decided to come out with the news which she wanted to announce to her family. She pushed away her plate and raised her hands in the air. "Harken, harken, all those present at this table! I, Junia Zuckerman, openly declare here, that from today on I shall no longer be a member of Herr Rumkowski's police force; that from today on, I shall practise the glorious profession of an educator of the nation's new generation!"

Reisel raised her hand to her ear, shaking her head. "What is this girl blabbing about?"

Junia prodded Samuel with her elbow, "Did you hear what I said, Papa? They are about to open a school for gifted children . . . a new system of teaching. I met a teacher whom I know. He's organising the whole thing. He wants to take me on as a teacher."

It was not Samuel or Matilda who reacted to her words, but Reisel. "The blazes!" she cried out. "You're as capable of being a teacher as I am of being a dancer. All of a sudden, such *meshugas*! What's wrong with being with the police? The extra soups, the extra rations don't suit you?" Junia embraced Samuel, giving him a loud peck on the cheek. "Go ahead, kiss her, hug her, Mr. Zuckerman," Reisel carried on. "In your place I would have taught her a lesson for not being able to sit still on her behind. It's all your fault, Mr. Zuckerman, and yours too, Madam. But how do they say? Before marriage one has ten ideas about bringing up children, but after the marriage, one has ten children, and not one idea."

"What will you teach?" Samuel finally asked Junia.

"I'll teach what I know. Sports, Gymnastics. *Mens sana in corpore sano!* That means, Rosalia darling, a healthy mind in a healthy body."

Reisel shook her head, growling angrily. "Sure, sure. Fresh, healthy and *meshuga*."

Junia spoke about the program for the projected school which would be under the supervision of a teachers' collective. The children would study languages, science, dancing and painting. Her enthusiasm irritated Bella. She left the table, went to her room and threw herself on the bed. Studying, teaching, what meaning was there to it? Nearby on the desk stood her books. She had spent so many years amidst sheets of paper. She had meant them to be a boat which would keep her afloat during the storm. It had been a paper boat. She herself was lying drowned at the bottom of the sea. She covered her face with her hands. "I want to die . . ." she muttered into her palms, as if they were a pair of ears against her lips. She heard the door open. Someone entered the room. Footsteps approached her bed. She kept her face covered and the steps moved away. The door was shut.

Samuel paced in the corridor puffing on a cigarette. From the kitchen Junia's and Matilda's lively chatter reached his ears. Now and then he heard Matilda's short warm laugh. It grated on his ears. He could not bear her when she was sulking, nor when she was cheerful. She, with her haughtily raised head! The self-righteous, the morally indignant who thought that she held justice in her pocket! It had all been her own fault. It was she who had chased him out of the house. Because of her he was unable to begin work on his book. She had forced him to run to Sabinka. She had caused him to drink. She, with her eternal reproaches and resentments; she, in her flabbiness, in her ugliness. He turned back towards Bella's room. The children were his, just as much as they were hers. He had to win back Bella at any cost; he loved her, and she had become so alienated from him. He again entered Bella's room and approached her bed.

Her contorted ugly face was soaked with tears. At the sight of her, his bitterness swelled into anger. He was overcome by a sudden wish to free himself of her. He wanted to erase the sight of her face. "Stop wailing, for heaven's sake!" he exclaimed. "Stupid miserable creature that you are, what are you crying for? Have you got it too good?" He rushed out onto the balcony, eagerly sucking on his cigarette. He inhaled deeply, not the fresh air, but his rage. The white head of the cherry tree blinked at him from the yard. The sight of its beauty and the mild breath of the wind worked him up even more. He came back into the room. Bella had managed to wipe her face. Like a reddish-blue twisted mask it looked up at him with cold unfamiliar eyes. His heart shrunk. His sweet delicate daughter who had once awakened such wonderful feelings of tenderness within him — where had she vanished? He wanted to say a few hopeful comforting words, but her face expressed so much contempt that he lost his courage. "You still don't know where we are living, Bella, do you?"

Her lips twisted bitterly, "Do *you*? If we are living in hell, then you are one of its demons."

The floor began to sway beneath him. His overflowing heart gave a jump, while his fury flowed down into his arms. He slapped her loudly on the face and saw the impression his five fingers left on her red-blue cheek. He could not bear the sight of it. He wanted to erase the mark, to take it back, to annul it. So he slapped her again.

She did not move. "It doesn't hurt," she mumbled.

He shouted, "If I am a demon, I'll treat you like one. And don't you dare cry in front of me!"

"Who asked you to come in here? This is my room."

She should not have answered him. Her words drove him wild. As he saw her lying before him with her heavy defenceless body, he felt himself capable of tearing her into pieces. He wished her dead; he wished to rid himself of the memory of her. He threw the butt of his cigarette through the balcony door and lit another, pacing the room with quick, thunderous steps. It was the hour of the radio broadcast, but he could not interrupt his pacing. He would lose the most precious hour of his day, the moments to which he had looked forward since he had opened his eyes that morning. And all because of her . . . of Matilda . . . of Bella . . . His urge to throw himself at her would not leave him. He wanted to hit her harder and harder, until he had relieved himself of that corroding boil which throbbed in his guts. But he saw her lift her hands and cover her face. Her soft, delicate hands; they seemed to be, not of flesh and blood, but were like two transparent shells of a heart. He saw them wandering over piano keys. They charmed music out of the abyss of the present moment. He was compelled to pick them up, to cuddle them, as if they were two wounded birds fallen out of their nest. No, what he wished was that they should nurse him and cure the wound festering inside him.

"What do you want of me?" he asked apologetically. "Am I really such a monster? We ought to count our blessings. People are being sent out of the ghetto . . . by the thousands. No one knows whereto. You have a secure home . . . a bed. Is it not bad enough as it is? And we don't know yet what the end will be . . . Why do you carry on this childish war with me?" He sat down beside her, but she was too stiff and too cold for him to try and touch her. "Do you remember how it used to be between us?" He looked at her imploringly. "Don't deprive me of my courage. I don't have it easy, believe me." At last he dared to take both her hands into his. But her hands which looked so soft and delicate were hard, strong, glued to her face. He tore them away by force.

She stared at him with a glance which froze everything inside him. "What did you bring me into this world for?" she hissed, biting her nails frenziedly. "It's all your fault . . . all . . . all . . ." she howled. "I hate you! I don't want to be a Jew! I don't want to be, at all!"

Samuel dashed out of the room and ran down into the yard. Junia came out to meet him. They vanished behind the wall into the cellar. He bolted the door behind him, took out a flashlight from behind a beam and approached the heap of sawdust. "It's too late . . ." Junia whispered. He sensed reproach in her voice. He did not dig up the radio receiver, but let himself sink heavily onto the heap, leaning his head against his knees. Junia sat down beside him. Her fresh warm voice reached him in the darkness. She said, "It seemed to me that as a police woman I would have a chance to prevent the children from growing up to be thieves. But the truth is, Papa, that children who steal a potato when they are starving, are no thieves. I too . . . I used to steal . . . and did not really consider myself a thief. And as soon as you put on a uniform, you immediately feel righteous and just, even though you yourself act like a beast. I would even hit them. Yes, your daughter, the noble Zionist. Now, in the dark, I can tell you this. So I had to cut myself free. To be one of them and still keep one's hands clean, is impossible." Each word that Junia uttered was like a drop of oil on the fire raging within Samuel. He felt like strangling both her and her words. What did they all want of him? Why were they out to poison every moment of his life? Even here, in the cellar, there was no longer any peace for him. He was ready to leave, but she caught him by the hand. "Let's stay for a few more minutes. It's quiet here, good to talk . . . Here, in the cellar, we are both different people, aren't we? Have you noticed that I never laugh here? It is not that I am sad . . . Why don't you say something? What are you thinking about?"

He jumped to his feet, "Come, let's get out of here!"

She followed him to the door, pulling at his sleeve, "Papa, what happened?"

He shook her hand off, "Nothing happened, leave me alone, all of you!" As soon as they were outside, he left her behind and ran out into the street. He knew that Junia was following him, he could hear the sound of her steps. He stopped, turned his head back and his gaze was trapped in the depths of her eyes. "Why are you running after me?" he growled.

"I know where you are going," she said calmly.

"Are you sure?"

"Yes, for a long time now."

"Then tell me, so that I may know too!"

Her black eyes pierced through him in the dark. It seemed to him that he was staring at himself with those eyes. He wanted to say something — in order to keep together the wholeness of his life which was about to fall apart. But she had already turned away from him. The street and the darkness swallowed her. He stood screwed to the place where he had stopped. It did not make any sense to take a step in any direction. What was it that Junia knew? About Sabinka? Was that all? All and more than all. She would never forgive him, because he would never forgive himself. And if so . . . if so . . . then why not go to Sabinka? He set out in the direction of the bridge. He could barely wait to reach Sabinka's house — and yet he was unable to accelerate his steps. He had time, loads of time. The whole night. This night and all the other nights . . .

When he got to Marysin, he turned back home. In front of the gate stood the little Toffee Man with the box of candies suspended from his neck. "Buy a remedy for the heart, Mr. Zuckerman," he proposed. Absentmindedly, Samuel reached into his pockets for a pfennig. "Put it in your mouth straight away," the little man advised, handing him a candy.

Samuel paced in front of the house sucking on the candy. He saw a few people loaded with packs and sacks heading towards the bridge. The thought of Adam Rosenberg entered his mind. He had not seen him for a long time. Adam no longer came around to get money out of him. What happened to him? Samuel became curious. It seemed important to know the answer to that question. It was essential that he know it. If Adam had left with a transport, or if he were lying sick somewhere, dying, was that an indication that he, Samuel, had emerged the winner in the struggle between them? What kind of struggle was it? Why did they hate one another? Perhaps because they resembled each other so much. They were actually two brothers cut from the same mould. Samuel saw Adam's repulsive flabby face in his mind and a shudder crept down his spine. How was that possible? They were so different in their natures. Except for this one thing: the disgust which he felt towards himself resembled the disgust he felt for Adam. Adam felt no disgust for himself — and that was precisely the difference between them. If that were so, then all was not lost yet. A spark of light, however meagre, still kept the darkness from closing over his head. In a surge of energy he roused himself and headed back towards the bridge. He was in a hurry to see, not Sabinka, but Moshe Eibushitz.

The kitchen of the Eibushitz apartment was full of young people. Books passed from hand to hand. Whispered words rustled along with the sound of flipping pages. Moshe jumped to his feet from a chair at the stove, staring bewildered at Samuel. On the stove stood two bowls of soup and a plate with a few slices of turnip. At one bowl sat Blumka Eibushitz, eating. Samuel retreated towards the door. "I'll come another time . . ."

Moshe blocked his way, "Why? I've finished eating. Rachel is in the other room with her group, but let's go down . . ."

"I'll wait for you outside," Samuel said quickly, and left. He waited for Moshe by the gate, inhaling deeply. Matilda had said that today had been a beautiful day. He had not noticed it at all. He recalled that the very first days in the ghetto he had been extremely sensitive to the weather. He had enjoyed looking at the cherry tree, at the beauty of Marysin. More recently, however, entire days would pass without his relishing their sunshine, their light.

Moshe joined him and they walked over to the neighbouring backyard, where they could sit down at the water pump. Moshe was limping. He seemed thinner and more stooped than when Samuel had seen him last. As soon as they reached the water pump, Moshe immediately sat down. The dead cigarette rolled from thick brown paper, which stuck to his lips, shook lightly as he spoke. "As you see me here, Zuckerman, I have not slept for the last three nights. The number of evacuated has reached forty thousand. My strength is leaving me and fear has more power over a weak body . . . Tell me, what's hiding behind all this?"

Samuel shrugged his shoulders. "I know the same as you."

"Don't you ask the Old Man? Doesn't your party demand to be told where the people are being sent to?"

"And what about your party?"

"We sent out a comrade two months ago to find out. She vanished as in deep water."

"And what if we knew?" Samuel offered Moshe a few cigarettes, and then touched his shoulder, "If you receive a 'wedding invitation', let me know right away."

The dry cigarette on Moshe's lips shook gratefully, "I have a friend in you."

"I have a friend in you, too."

It became very dark. Curfew was approaching. They had only spent ten minutes together. Yet Samuel left Moshe like a person who had confessed and had had his sins forgiven.

✦ ✦ ✦

In the Carpentry Resort work seemed to be running normally. The machines roared, the saws gave out their groaning sounds which mixed with the sound of falling wood. Only the hammers and the planes seemed to have lost their rhythm. Samuel liked to keep the door to his office open when everything was running smoothly. With his ear in contact with the remotest hall, he would work well. New ideas would like fresh raw boards arrange themselves in his mind, before he put them down on paper. On such days he was not afraid of German inspections or of Rumkowski's visits. He would not become excited when the Germans praised him; he would not despair if the Presses did not praise him or was not friendly enough. He was satisfied with the results of his work and that sufficed him. Lately, however, he had been keeping the door of his office shut. The irregular rhythm of the tools in his workers' hands irritated him. Sometimes he panicked and ran from floor to floor, yelling and threatening. The fearful workers received his attacks meekly, and this reaction prompted him to set his fists in motion.

But more than yell and deal out blows he could not do. Could he throw them all out? So he rushed to the Kitchen Department and there made scandals, demanding that the workers receive better soups. He saw to it that the sanitation in the Resort improved and that the children and the physically weak should not be charged with heavy duties. And so the situation remained. There was no point in wrestling with the sluggishness that had taken hold of the Resort.

During the early hours of the afternoon the air of lassitude hovered most heavily over the Resort. The day seemed endless. The soup that the workers had had for lunch had served only to intensify their craving for food and to increase the fatigue brought on by the warm spring day. The windows in the halls stood open. A fog of dust vibrated in front of them. Dirty sweat ran down the faces lowered over the machines; each worker was a pillar of grayness in the thick, sultry air. Once in a while someone fainted. Probably one of those who had been denied his soup as a punishment for some misdemeanour.

The only clear objects in the halls were the boards of wood. They were like slabs of light, warm in colour and cool to the touch. The workers' fingers held on to them. Their nostrils eagerly inhaled the forest aroma which clung to them. The younger workers played with the wood like children. As they stroked it, they gave themselves over to dreams of freedom which in their minds took on the image of tables laden with food. Their empty stomachs were transformed into bottomless sacks fringed with sharp teeth. The sacks absorbed the abundance of food, never filling, while the amount of food on the tables did not diminish. The dreams were about chewing, about swallowing; each tooth was a fork, a spoon, a knife. Until the dreams were pierced by the shout of a supervisor and the workers grabbed their tools, pretending to work.

Samuel, who usually arrived at the Resort in the morning, determined to conquer the general apathy, would, during these hours, himself surrender to it. The day was stagnant — a jungle of motionless minutes, seconds, from which it was impossible to disentangle oneself. A voice within him called for help, desperately seeking the end of the maze, the hand of clarity which would lead him out. Yet at the same time he was aware of the futility of his scream. Instead of the bright hand, he saw a dark one, dragging him deeper and deeper into the airless timeless density.

Before him on the table were spread the blueprints of ammunition boxes. The order was for sixty thousand. The boxes did not require any particular style or good craftsmanship. They had to be geometrically simple, like egg cartons. They did not need Samuel's ideas and improvements, they needed no pleasant colour schemes. They were to serve only for ammunition, The simple-lined severity of the drawings cut into the jungle-like maze of Samuel's thoughts. He had to set down his instructions for the *Meisters*, give them the measurements, decide the quality of the wood to be used; he had to calculate the size of the daily production and how to divide the work among the halls. His eyes burned, his eyelids were heavy. His cigarette was burning out on the ashtray, its smoke joining the dusty haze in the room.

A policeman entered, saluting; "Mrs. Rumkowski is here to see you, Herr Commissar."

Samuel was alone in the room with Clara. She wore a black summer suit and a black hat with a large brim; half of her face was covered by a thin veil. Through its delicate mesh her eyes gazed at him, both demanding and imploring. She sat down opposite him, put her black lacquered purse on the desk and removed her black gloves. "Forgive me for disturbing you," she said.

In his drowsiness her appearance seemed unreal. He pushed away the ashtray with the smoking cigarette, as if to free himself of the fog and to see her more clearly. She looked like a middle-aged, dressed-up matron. Her thin lips were cut by deep little furrows spreading in all directions like rays of despair. Her cheeks, white as flour, looked like flabby kneaded dough. Only the gaze piercing through her veil was strong, both in its demand and its supplication. He made an effort to give her a friendly smile. "It's a pleasure, Clara . . . Hm . . . Mrs. Rumkowski."

"I won't keep you long." He detected the reproachful undertone of a neglected friend in her voice. "He . . . He doesn't know that I am here. I cannot get a thing out of him. He refuses to talk to me about these matters. But I carry his name, Mr. Zuckerman. I must know . . . I share the responsibility with him. The only place where there is any information is the Evacuation Commission. I spoke to him and convinced him that you should join the commission."

Samuel jumped to his feet, completely awake. "Are you out of your mind?"

"You must . . . We must do something. Forty-nine thousand Jews have left the ghetto. Whereto? You talked me into marrying him . . . You must share the responsibility. I cannot take it any longer." Her eyes burned through him.

Samuel was beside himself, but with all his strength he tried to control himself. "Leave me out of it, Clara. I talked you into nothing."

"You must help me, Mr. Zuckerman!" She stretched out both hands over the designs of the ammunition boxes.

"What do you mean, help? What kind of help is that?"

"You must get inside . . . find out . . . influence them. I don't know myself . . . Being there you could reach him, too. He is afraid of you."

"Of me?"

"He cannot bear to hear your name mentioned. He says that you are his enemy. That you have betrayed him."

"I?" It was as if a hammer had struck him on the head. He began to pace the office. He could no longer bear to listen to her. "I don't understand a thing. Leave me alone!" he shouted in helpless rage.

She jumped to her feet, grabbing her purse and gloves. She stood facing him across the table, a worn exhausted matron with a pair of begging eyes peering straight into his. "You're deserting me. I'm drowning."

"I am drowning along with you."

She approached the door, adding, "I won't let the matter rest."

"I'll never do it! Never!" he called after her. He was alone in the room. Sweat streamed down his face. He felt so stifled that he could not catch his breath. He approached the window. Clara was hastily crossing the yard. A murky apparition in a nightmare. She vanished, leaving behind the smell of her penetrating biting perfume.

It was raining when he left the Resort. A refreshing playful spray. The streets were full of workers on their way home. Canteens were clinking, wooden shoes clopping against the wet pavement. The hunched backs, drooping shoulders, the heads bent towards the ground made it seem as if the refreshing drizzle were a whip. Men, women and children passed him, all looking alike. The same look was in all their eyes, a look alert as a listening ear, sniffing like a nose; a look of rabbits sensing the trap and seeking an escape. Samuel's steps grew heavy. For some time he again felt that his boots weighed tons. He felt each single drop of rain as if it were Clara's sharp penetrating perfume dripping over his skull. As usual at that time of the day, there was a commotion in the yard. Neighbours greeted him. All their faces seemed the same. He could barely distinguish between them, confusing their names. They all had the same hollow clay-coloured cheeks, the same pointed noses and protruding cheek-bones, the same deep, dark eye sockets; and then there was that frantic humid gaze.

He ate his supper in silence, as usual. Lately he had acquired the habit of turning his plate around and around, a kind of nervous game. Matilda spoke with a voice which seemed unable to find its proper register, sounding now thin, now thick, now loud, now low. Junia was excitedly talking about her new job. Nor did Reisel shut her mouth for a moment. Only Bella sat at the table in silence, like Samuel. Soon he left them all and went to his room. It was not long before Junia followed him there. In spite of the last scene between them, in the street, her attitude towards him had not changed in the least; it was as if she had forgotten all about it.

"Comrade Widawski gave me a message for you. You must absolutely come to the meeting." She hung on to his arm. "You will go, won't you, Papa?" She smiled, mischievously winking at him. Yet he knew that deep in her laughing eyes there lurked a warning, a threat: her judgment of him.

He shook off her hand. "I'll go." He was tired, but Junia said that it was time to leave, and that they could go together — she to the meeting of her youth group, he to the meeting of the party board.

The rain had become heavier. Junia wore no coat. The rain washed over her bare arms, her face and her short black hair. "Wonderful!" she purred with delight. "A spring rain is the nicest thing in the world. You feel like a plant with the rain watering you to make you grow. I would like to run barefoot in such a rain. Perhaps I'll do it as soon as I reach Marysin. I'll get all my gang outside." She looked him in the eye. "Are you listening?"

"I'm listening." He could not bear her glance.

"To you it must sound stupid, what I'm saying . . ." she laughed. "You don't even feel the rain, do you? I know. You don't feel . . . life. And I can practically touch it with my hands, so to speak. That's why I think that we should forget about the history of Zionism today. Because to run barefoot in the spring rain is the best form of Zionism." She pulled him by the arm. "Why are you so heavy? Come, run with me. Can you still run?" He freed himself of her arm. He could not help himself, her friendly words were stifling him. Streams of water washed down her lively face. "You look like Atlas carrying the whole world on his shoulders. An old Atlas, almost crushed under the burden. Papa . . . It is a sin to be young and act like an old man. A sin even against the party. With joy it seems easier . . ."

Samuel smiled crookedly. "Joy? It's been a long time since I've heard that word."

"Because your ears are blocked!" Thunder rolled across the sky. She shook him by the arm. "Thunder! Has it unblocked your ears? Will you run with me?"

"Run if you want to."

She waved at him and ran off. He followed her with his eyes. Her thin tight dress danced before his eyes through the rain. She was moving her glistening arms; her bare legs seemed to soar through the air. His heart began to pound in rhythm to her gallop. He had no wish to run after her, yet he felt himself moving alongside her, there, in the distance, beside the arms of light which could perhaps lead him out of the entanglement of the jungle. From behind, however, he felt the arms of darkness holding him back — the arms of the Lady in Black. Her perfume came pouring down from the sky, stinging his nostrils.

The members of the Zionist Co-ordinating Committee received Samuel with a murmur of satisfaction. The proceedings had already begun. The youthful Comrade Widawski was presiding. He was the main provider of clandestine news for the party, keeping in close contact with all the radio listeners in the ghetto. Samuel searched him out whenever he was having trouble with his receiver. More than once had he felt like a *heder* boy in the presence of young Widawski. Widawski clearly knew what he wanted and what he was doing.

The possibility or rather the impossibility of organizing a resistance against the Germans was being discussed. The deportations had reached the number of fifty thousand. Contact between the Zionist Party and the Presess had been broken off. The Presess did everything in his power to keep the core of the Zionist organization intact, yet he would not allow any Zionist leader to approach him. He never uttered a word about the fate of the deported, and the party had not managed to find any contact with the outside world. Nor did the Jews who were connected with the *Kripo* or the Gestapo give any hints, or perhaps they too were ignorant about the issue. It was the fourth month of the "action". The only solution seemed to be to find a personal contact with the Presess, to demand that he once and for all come out into the open with what he knew.

All eyes turned towards Samuel as Widawski addressed him. "You are the only one whom Rumkowski considers a personal friend. You have to put that personal contact at the service of the community." The comrades nodded approvingly, although Widawski quickly corrected himself, "I am perhaps not expressing myself properly, Zuckerman. I mean you ought to take advantage of your friendship with the Presess in order to get through to him. But once you face him, you stop being a private intercessor and become our spokesman." Widawski scratched his head with his pencil, smiling faintly. "Let's not kid ourselves, comrades, our situation is quite unusual. Take, for instance, the communists or the Bundists . . . Between them and the Presess there is a clear demarcation. But not between ourselves and him. He considers himself one of ours, and yet we have to resort to these means in order to reach him."

Mr. Zibert, the Presess' court advisor whom the Presess had also refused to see lately, considered it necessary to make a speech in defence of the Old Man.

"What do you want him to do?" he concluded. "Should he play at democracy now? Convene a parliament and confer with his ministers? Don't we realize that if the road of resistance is closed to us, there is no other road to choose but . . . the one that he has chosen?" Zibert's speeches had in the past been listened to with little attention, for he could with the same verve defend two contradictory points of view. Lately, however, he spoke little during the meetings, and when he did, he was given full attention, as if the Presess himself were talking through his mouth. Because, in spite of the fact that they believed him when he said that the Presess refused to see him, there was no doubt that he was the only one who knew what was cooking in the kettles at Baluter Ring.

Zibert's speech provoked a discussion about the role of the Presess. It was dark and the rain washing the window panes seemed pitch black. Again Samuel had the feeling of being lost in a jungle. A storm was tearing at the very roots of life. Thunder, like the echoes of quarrelling voices, cut through the entanglement, leaving behind a still deeper darkness, a still greater chaos.

All night long he restlessly tossed and turned in his bed. He was on vacation in the Tatras. The air was cool and fresh; the sun illuminated the snow-covered mountain peaks. He was skiing over a white field, soft and yet smooth as a table. With a playful swing of his body, he aimed at the oncoming hills. He soared over them weightlessly, delighted with the lightness of his feet. Then he realized that he was not just moving ahead, but escaping. His feet felt increasingly heavy. His mind became heavy. He turned back and saw a female figure on skis. She was wearing a black ski-costume and a black hat. He immediately recognized her and accelerated his speed. A high mountain approached him. The black figure was skiing down from its top, straight towards him. "I caught up with you through the back," she said. "You must help me . . . an avalanche has buried . . ."

He wanted to ask her what the avalanche had buried, yet he only bowed to her, "Forgive me . . . My daughters are waiting for me at home." He left her, hurrying back through the field. The field was as empty as a white desert. He was unable to find his way back. He hurried on with more speed. He fell. His skis cracked and broke. Helplessly he looked around, and noticed a little skier, wearing the uniform of the mountain police, approaching him. "He will lead me out of the entanglement," Samuel said to himself.

The little skier had a boyish face and looked funny on his gigantic skis. He said to Samuel, "You must help us . . . An avalanche has buried . . ."

Samuel became furious. "You're a hothead! Can't you see that my skis are broken? That I am lost? My house is supposed to be somewhere around here and it is gone."

Moshe Eibushitz appeared before him. He was sitting on a huge icy water pump, puffing on a cigarette. "The worst thing for me is to divide the loaf of bread, Mr. Zuckerman. My gums begin to hurt because of the craving . . ." he said.

The little skier would not let Samuel listen to Moshe's words. "Hurry, you must help us," he urged him on.

Moshe took off his wooden shoes and offered them to Samuel. "You are my support," he said. "Here, take my skis."

Samuel's whole being exploded into a scream, "Where is my house!"

"On the other side of the avalanche," answered the little skier, who resembled Widawski.

That dream in many variations repeated itself over and over throughout the entire night. In the morning Reisel came in to wake him. "The blazes!" she shouted, "Mr. Zuckerman, get up quickly! You have an invitation from the *Kripo!*"

✦ ✦ ✦

The rains lasted a few days. The clouds, like gray heavy bladders full of water, exploded over the Ghetto. Then a morning arrived when the rain bags were empty. They shrank, rolled themselves up and swam away like a squadron that had accomplished its mission. The skies became blue, free, beaming with the radiance of dazzling April days, so overpowering everything with their brightness, that one could not do otherwise than gaze at the world around through squinting eyes, which barely gave protection against the glare.

It was during one of these days that a new generation of ants was born in the lush gardens of the *Kripo*. The young blades of grass were whispering the first sounds which the newborn ants were supposed to hear: "*Ki tov* . . . It is good . . ." To the inhabitants of the anthill this garden represented the universe in its immeasurable infinity. The more daring, the more curious ant-individuals could reach only to the brick wall which blocked their way. Their Queen, who had wings and used them to soar with her lover up into the air on their honeymoon, was the only one who had the opportunity to see the entire fence of the garden. But she was so much in love, that all she ever looked at was the black body of her inseminator. And after all, the ants had more important things to do than measure the expanse of the garden. What they were interested in was the cabbage leaf under whose canopy they lived. Here their ancestors had once found a huge button fallen from a monk's cassock, which they had turned into the corner-stone of their communal abode.

But this new generation of ants, like any other, had its number of daring rebels who liked to follow their own paths and search for an answer to the questions which perplexed them. They refused to obey their mentors and set out to climb the neighbouring brick wall, conquering one brick after another, until they found themselves at the edge of some kind of precipice. Confusedly they turned about it in circles, until they hit against something shining invitingly in the sun. It was slippery to creep over the shiny surface, but also pleasant and interesting. The young ants reached a sharp edge in the smoothness of that plateau, which was of course a window pane. It was now covered with cracks which looked like paths. One after the other the ants squeezed themselves through the cracks, then crawled down the other side in single file. Here it was dark, hot and spooky. Frightened, the ants began to look for a way out, but the more frantically they searched, the lower they descended and the darker and more terrifying the place became. Finally, they reached the ground.

This was not, however, the same soft ground as outside; it was hard and dry. And suddenly something blocked their way. A density. The ants, blinded, confused, became entangled in strange threads. Climbing from one onto the other, they got lost inside them, then emerged again, until they left the forest of human hair behind and began to promenade along a wet-warm yellowish hill, cut across by rows of furrows. At the end of the furrows, a bulging blue pipe was pulsating like some trembling root: a swollen vein on a human forehead. The ants proceeded to descend along two slanted elevations which moved up and down, emitting a wind: a human nose. From there they crossed the hollowness of two cheeks reaching a soft tasty foam covering a human mouth. For a while they swarmed over it, sucking in the unfamiliar drink. Then they heard a rattle and again became frightened.

Through a yellowish roundness covered with a prickling needle-like forest — a human four-day old beard — the ants descended into a valley which was a human neck, reaching a rocking surface covered with soft curling hair-weeds: a man's chest. A long and fascinating march over skin and cloth finally brought the ants to a point where they could have gone in one of two directions: along two spread out human legs. They chose instead to descend straight from the belly into the depth between the two legs — and suddenly they lost the ground under their ant-feet, finding themselves in water which was sticky and red — in a deep sea of human blood oozing through the cloth between the thighs. Ants were not created with the ability to swim in human blood. For a moment they quivered. Finally they drowned. All that they had seen on their long and daring road drowned along with them.

Samuel Zuckerman was lucky. He had cheated Herr Sutter. He had given him an address on Narutowicz Street, had let himself be led there by three *Sturmtruppers*, had taken them down to his former cellar — and finally had come up empty-handed. For such a thing he deserved to be finished off on the spot. But he had friends who interceded on his behalf, in particular the *Kripo* man, Adam Rosenberg, who used his influence with Herr Sutter and Herr Schmidt to win the life of his former friend.

"Do whatever you please with him," Adam pleaded with Herr Sutter, "but don't kill him. Because Zuckerman has never even known a decent toothache in all his life. And in my opinion there exists a kind of life which is worse than death . . ." Adam's voice sounded candid and convincing. It was for that reason that he had kept silent about the radio. He wanted Samuel to live a life which was worse than death, and he wanted to bear witness to it.

Herr Sutter allowed Adam to convince him with his arguments. After all, he agreed with him. Sutter himself, as a rule, derived more pleasure from playing games with his victims, than from finishing them off on the spot, which was like swallowing a delightful bite of food without chewing and savouring its taste.

In addition to Adam, Herr Rumkowski as well as the *Ghettoverwaltung* and Herr Biebow himself had intervened on Samuel's behalf. True, Herr Sutter and Herr Biebow were deadly enemies, unable to agree on how to distribute their loot. Samuel, however, had headed one of the most important branches of production in the ghetto and it was not so easy to replace him. Nor had Herr Biebow and Herr Rumkowski been the best of friends recently. The old Jew had begun to get on Herr Biebow's nerves. At this moment, however, it was good policy to do the Old Man a personal favour. During these days of evacuations, it was in the interest both of the *Ghettoverwaltung* and the *Kripo* that the "actions" proceed in an orderly manner, so that the income-value of the ghetto should not suffer. Thus Herr Rumkowski successfully interceded with Herr Biebow, and Herr Biebow — with the *Kripo*. Such a Jew as Zuckerman had the worth of a whole set of silverware, plus a few units of the best English material. With these gifts Herr Biebow greased his intervention. A few other Jewish *Kripo* men with "Jewish hearts", moved by the pleas of Samuel's daughters, also donated a few substantial gifts.

Softened by such strong pressure coming from all directions, and with the good of the Fatherland firmly in mind, Herr Sutter and his staff deigned to preserve Samuel's life, and finish him off only as a man, by maiming his sex-organ.

The day that Samuel had left for the *Kripo*, Matilda and her daughters had moved about as if drunk. Reisel, who had never before lost her head, wandered from one room to the other, not knowing what she was doing. "May he only not become a cripple," she prayed. "May he only be able to stay on as a commissar," she sniffled.

The first few hours they had waited for Samuel on the balcony. In the afternoon they all went down into the street. Matilda was pacing in front of the bridge, Junia went to see the leaders of the party, Reisel rushed to Church Place to keep an eye on the Red House from the distance, while Bella wandered aimlessly through the streets, hoping that on her return home she would find Samuel there.

The following day a policeman brought a note saying that they should send in clean underwear for the prisoner. He ordered them to bring a similar parcel of underwear to the *Kripo* every morning. The sisters took a parcel to the *Kripo* the following day. They were handed another parcel and ordered to go away.

"Unwrap it, perhaps there is a note inside," Bella said.

Junia who had been pressing the parcel to her chest noticed that her fingers became pink and sticky. She stopped. Her chin was shaking. "We won't see him any more," she stammered.

It was Bella who summoned her courage, "I am sure that we will see him."

Once home, Junia threw the parcel on the kitchen table. Reisel stretched out her veined arms, and unwrapped the parcel as if it were a ration from the butcher shop; she peeled off the papers and they saw a pile of red rags. The red of Samuel's blood reflected in Matilda's and in her daughters' eyes, washing away all veils of estrangement between them. They dashed towards the door. As if with one ear all three of them understood Samuel's call for help, which seemed to reach them from all the streets and backyards. Their minds were sharp and fast. Matilda ran to the Presess, Bella and Junia found the addresses of the two *Kripo* men, Vigoda and Glanz.

Mr. Vigoda was a bulky jovial fellow who saw the suggestion of a joke in everything he heard. He liked to laugh. He received Bella sitting in a velvet-covered armchair, a pair of fur slippers on his feet, a cigar in his mouth. "What are you wailing for, stupid cow, eh?" He blinked at her with his mischievous little eyes. "Your Papa won't lose a hair from his head, rely on me. How do you know that what you saw on his underwear was blood? Maybe he spilled some borscht on it. That didn't enter your mind, did it? Your Papa is an idiot, you understand . . . playing tricks on Sutter . . . taking him to an empty cellar. But on the other hand, I have great respect for your Papa. He is a true heir of Schmuel Ichaskel Zuckerman himself, eh? Great ancestry, important ancestry! Ha-ha, so why are you wailing, stupid cow? Am I not a Jew or what? Do you think I have a heart of stone? I get sick when I hear of Jewish tragedies. Ha-ha, believe me, honestly. Of course I will try to save your Papa. What do you think I am in the *Kripo* for? Of course, it will cost you something . . . It will cost you nothing. I will pay from my own pocket, greasing money . . . Then I will discuss it with your Papa."

On the surface Junia had less luck with her *Kripo* man, Herr Glanz. Herr Glanz had no sense of humour at all. He took his function as a stool pigeon with deadly seriousness. He behaved as if he had the whole of the ghetto in his pocket, and it often seemed to him that he had the same say as every German with whom he collaborated. "Eh, Jews, Jews," he shook his head with dismay. "They'd rather die, but keep on worshipping the Golden Calf."

"My father has no money," Junia looked him straight in the eye with feigned respect.

Herr Glanz shook his head with authority. "Then why did he lead us into town? Whom is he making a fool of?"

"Save my father, Mr. Glanz!" Junia came closer to him, imploring him with artificial submissiveness. "You are the most important man in the ghetto . . . You and Leibel Welner. They say that you can even wind Sutter around your finger. Father will repay you, you'll see. The war will not last forever." In response to her false humility she saw a twinkle of delight in his eyes and understood that she had struck the proper tone.

Herr Glanz remained serious. "You are a fine girl," he remarked. "But I do nothing for nothing."

"Heaven forbid, Mr. Glanz. I don't ask that from you. I swear to you that as soon as Father . . ."

He took her measure with a pair of squinting eager eyes. "I don't take any cheques. A father deserves to be paid for in cash."

She pretended not to understand the proposition. "Good . . . good," she smiled crookedly. "Tell me how much you want."

"Not how much, but what I want, you should ask," he replied, moving towards her with outstretched arms.

A flame lit up in Junia's eyes. Her small strong hand flew up straight against Herr Glanz's unprepared face. She kicked him in the shin. "My father would rather die, you dog!" She spat at the very tip of his nose, and ran out. Despite

this, Herr Glanz dropped a word about Samuel to his friend, the mighty Leibel
Welner. Herr Glanz and Leibel Welner had calculated that it was worthwhile
to use their influence.

It was Matilda who had had the greatest success with her interventions. The
Presess, when he heard the story about Samuel, forgot all that he had against
him. He left his work, in order to save the most devoted and most important of
his commissars.

At night, mother and daughters slept in one bed, huddled up against each
other. They lay awake for long hours, thinking, missing Samuel, and awaiting
the morning with trepidation. In their sleep they saw red basins of water and
their hearts dissolved in Samuel's suffering.

After two weeks Samuel was released. Rumkowski provided an ambulance
to take him to the hospital. Samuel's ribs were broken and the wound in his sex
organ was infected. In the hospital Samuel's body was walled into a cast, and a
few days before Passover he was sent home. In the yard there was a pre-holiday
hullabaloo. People koshered their kitchen utensils, scrubbed tables and chairs,
pails and basins. The sanitary wagon could not get through the narrow paths
between the beds of soil and Samuel was carried in on a stretcher. The
neighbours stared at him. He waved his hand at them and at the cherry tree
which was shedding its blossoms. When they got upstairs, he asked to be
carried out onto the balcony.

Matilda could not take her eyes off Samuel's face and his gray head. Again she
had a different Samuel before her, who was neither the stranger from
Narutowicz Street, nor from the ghetto. Even the expression of his eyes was
changed. His eyebrows were oddly pointed and his shapeless mouth, sometimes
twisted into a grimace which was meant to be a smile, revealed the dark hole left
by two knocked out front teeth. Matilda's face was soaked in tears. She was
mourning the other Samuel, the stranger who had been brutally handsome,
whom she had loved all her life — her husband. The person lying on the
stretcher bed, on the balcony, was not her man, was not a man at all.

"Don't cry, Madziu," he begged her in an unfamiliar voice, hoarse,
unpleasant, whistling through the hole between his teeth.

She could not stop crying. And so, tearfully, she served him, not letting
Reisel or the children help her. It was strange that Samuel had never been so
much hers as he was now. She let that perception penetrate deep inside her. It
gave her strange pleasure to possess him so completely and to be alone with him
for days and days. Once in a while she wished she could become acquainted
with the newcomer. it would have been a great consolation, she thought. But
she could not find a common language with him.

The same happened with the daughters. They would sit at his bedside,
talking to him with pretended liveliness, as if they wanted their noise to cover
up the emptiness which divided them, too, from the man who had come back. It
seemed as if he were a visitor who had been placed in Samuel's bed, until the
father whom they missed could return. They watched Matilda feed him with a
little spoon, the food running out through the corners of his mouth while he
helplessly stuck out his tongue to catch it, and their hearts shrank.

The second day of Passover, the Presess himself came to visit the sick man.
He came up, dishevelled, breathing heavily. He rushed into Samuel's room,
straight towards the bed.

"For how long do you intend to laze around like this?" he grumbled, shaking

Samuel's loose hand. "The Resort is waiting for you. I am waiting for you. Zuckerman, don't forget, you're my right hand!" Matilda offered him a chair, but he shoved it away. "I've no time to sit!" He gave a short laugh and bent over the sick man. "You should know that I saved your life. Those sons of bitches, they would have finished you off. You'll still have to tell me the whole truth about how and what . . ." He waved his fingers in Samuel's face, "Don't worry, one bright day I shall rid myself of them too, those bastards, stool pigeons!" His face became milder, his voice hoarser, "Are you receiving the extra food? Do you need anything?"

"Nothing, Herr Presess," Samuel answered quietly.

Rumkowski grabbed the chair which he had previously shoved away and sat down close to the bed. "The whole world is against me, do you hear?" he said confidentially. "Every Jew thinks that he knows how to deal with the Germans better than I. My so-called friends think that I am not acting clever enough with Biebow. One says I ought to flatter him more, another says I have to grease his palm more, a third says that I flatter him too much, that I grease his palm too much. And so they knock me in the head and poison my life. I am too big in their eyes; they'd gladly make me lower by a head, and would replace me, do you know with whom? With Leibel Welner! Yeah, no more no less than that underworldnik, that Gestapo servant! He and his clique have the Jewish good in mind and not I, can you understand such reasoning? Any wonder that Biebow and the *Ghettoverwaltung* listen to him? Everything runs smoothly with him, while I am like a bone stuck in their throats. Because I am like a shepherd protecting his sheep. I'm at the end of my tether, Zuckerman, honestly. So much work, so much blood and sweat I've put into the ghetto, and here they tear the ground away from under my feet. The people, the idiotic mob, what do they know? What do they understand? 'Give us Welner!' they scream. 'Welner is good, he helps us, he does things for us!' He, the *Kripo* man, the Gestapo man, the stool pigeon, he helps! How do you like that?" Rumkowski passed his fingers over his dishevelled mop of hair and adjusted his glasses. For a while he chewed on his lips, weighing something in his head. At last he spoke again. "A crazy idea has entered my wife's head. She's giving me hell. But on the other hand, I think that this time she is right. Do you know what she wants? She wants me to put you into the Evacuation Commission. Because, after all, I have no one to rely on there. Now . . . I mean, in your condition, there can't be any talk of it. Yet, let's say nominally, if only in order that she stops bothering me . . . Because before you're even able to stand on your feet, the 'actions' will have stopped."

Samuel had listened to the major part of the Presess' monologue with his eyes shut. Now he suddenly opened them wide, fixing his gaze on the Old Man. He turned to him, rolling over his entire cast-encased body. A white foam appeared on his lips. "Don't you dare, Herr Presess!"

Rumkowski wrinkled his forehead and wiped his suddenly flushed face with both hands. "And if you were well, and I ordered you to join the Commission?"

"Don't you dare, Herr Presess!"

Rumkowski shook his head, embittered. "I see . . . This means that it is true what they tell me about you. And I, idiot that I am, did not believe them. You're washing your hands, aren't you?"

"I've washed them already," Samuel whispered forcefully.

"And what do you think I should do . . . if the Germans demand from me . . .?"

"I don't know. I've barely finished with my own accounts."

"The ghetto does not enter your accounts at all, does it?"

"What has happened to the people who were sent out of the ghetto?"

Rumkowski jumped to his feet as if burnt. "That's what you want to know?" He managed just in time to catch his glasses which had slid down to the tip of his nose. "You want to know and to keep clean hands, don't you? It doesn't suit you otherwise, great lord that you are, but to leave the dirt for me, eh? . . . eh? If that's the case, then you will join the Commission, on your sick bed! They will come here. That's how I want it to be. Yes, that's what I want! You've suffered a few blows, and you shake in your pants? For your information, my whole life is in the Germans' hands, day and night. And no one will run to risk his head for me, as I did for you. That's the thanks for your life that you're giving me, for having kept you all this time in the best position? You're shaking me off! You! You!" He dashed to the door, then turned his head to the sick man. "One thing you better keep in mind, Zuckerman. It's only I who cannot be replaced!" He halted in the open door, and remained there thoughtful for a while. Then, somewhat calmed, he asked, "Is that your last word, Zuckerman?"

"Don't you dare, Herr Presess!"

The same evening Samuel said to Matilda, "You will have to find work in a Resort, and Reisel too. As soon as I am able to stand on my feet, I'll do the same." He added with a faint smile, "If we stick together, we will survive."

A few days later, he revealed his secret about the radio to Matilda and Bella. "Every evening we will go down to listen to the newscast together," he said, "and we shall . . ."

Junia interrupted him. Coldly and brutally, she informed him that the radio was gone. That the day Samuel had left for the *Kripo*, she had taken it to her comrades, because she thought that someone had informed on Samuel, and that now — the radio belonged to the party. Samuel did not move. He slowly lowered his eyelids. His pale fingers gripped the edge of his blanket. For a while he lay motionless, as if asleep.

Then he said without opening his eyes, "It's better like that . . . It's safer . . ." He said nothing more. There was quiet in the room. The air was sultry, permeated with unpleasant smells from the sick bed, with the breath of the strange gray-haired visitor in the gypsum armour. The limbs of the three women in the room also seemed paralysed, as if they too wore casts. None of them seemed capable of uttering a word which might alleviate the heaviness of the air in the room.

Now and then friends arrived to visit Samuel. Miss Diamand had found out about him, and a few times she had climbed over the bridge to see him. She asked to be left alone with the sick man. She would sit there for hours. Samuel would withdraw into a deep sleep. He would also fall asleep during the visits of neighbours, of the managers and *Meisters* and of his comrades of the party who would bring him gifts of food.

One morning Samuel said to Bella, "Go over to Mr. Eibushitz . . . Tell him to come and see me . . . and tell him also to bring his shaving tools along."

Chapter Five

(David's notebook)

The evacuation is over! Sixty thousand have left. The Party has been decimated. Among those who left: 'Mucha', our actor. He was a good comrade. How much work he had put in into organising our evenings, our entertainments! I catch myself. I say "he was". How brutal. Whatever is removed from our eyes might as well be dead, especially here, where one is so busy with oneself and with the concrete surroundings. The best proof: the deportation of my friend Marek. Our triangle, the "Flying Brigade", is broken. I sometimes pass the house where he lived. At first I continually had the impression that if I entered his apartment, I would see him, his mother, his aunt Sonia and his father; that I would find a lot of young people there, swarming around Marek. But I got over it. The chapter called Marek is over. Saying good-bye to him was painful, the faked humour unbearable. I was disgusted by my "optimistic" last words to him. We have known each other from childhood, competed in our studies, played together, discussed problems and "saved the world" together. In the ghetto we helped one another exist, if only through the fact that the other was there. How much of myself has he taken with him? How much of himself has he left with me? As I said, days and weeks go by when he does not enter my mind. We no longer share the same fate. We are dead to each other, having nothing but memories which one forgets and one recalls.

We should be depressed, but we in the ghetto are overjoyed. The deportations are over. There is a new story now: we have to be stamped. My family went to see the commission of German doctors, to get stamped too. Our ages are between ten and sixty, as required. The doctors sit at a table, examining the patients from a mile away. What will come out of it no one knows and no one cares at the moment. Mother is right. She says, "Don't worry today about tomorrow's troubles. There are, thank heaven, enough of today's troubles to worry about." I obey her. I am in a good mood. I think that I am in love. And on top of that I won thirty *rumkis* today!

I am beginning to believe that miracles can happen in the ghetto. We were supposed to live on only our Resort soups tomorrow, and here I have become rich in a matter of a few hours. All evening long I played with the *rumkis*. Mother thought that they were fake, but I checked at the co-operative. They are first class! Tomorrow we go shopping on the black market. Mother talks to me "through a silken hanky". I am not such a *schlemiel* after all.

But let me tell the story in some order. I have begun to play chess again. At first I played with the neighbours, or during lunch at the Resort. But lately strangers have begun to seek me out, and so it was with today's game. I was cutting up some parsley leaves with Abraham, when an elegant gentleman entered our "residence". His pate shone like a watermelon; he wore dark glasses. "Does the chess player live here?" he inquired.

I replied with pride and dignity that he did indeed. I took off Mother's apron and freed a corner of the table for the chessboard. The gentleman opened his briefcase and drew out his own chess set. Many players like to walk around with their pieces and board as if this were an asset in helping to win the game. I don't mind. Let it be his set, so long as there is a game to be played. The gentleman removed his glasses and I recognized the rich Mr. Rosenberg who had used to live in our yard. I did not strike up a conversation with him; my interest in him was limited to his quality as a player. He asked me how much I wanted for a game. I immediately realized who I was dealing with.

"If you lose," he decided, "you pay ten pfennig. If you win you get ten *rumkis*."

I blinked at Abraham who said to him, "You must be some player if you bet like that," and he excitedly rubbed his hands.

The visitor made an opening with the bishop. My strategy of playing the first game with a stranger, particularly when I play the black, is to stay on the defensive and thus find out my adversary's potential. I don't even mind losing the first game. It's a psychological manoeuvre. The winner becomes sure of himself and begins to underestimate me. He concentrates on the attack and during the second game he sets his mind only on proving how quickly he can mate me. Then I "innocently" begin to defend myself, imperceptibly preparing my offensive. The score is one-one. My opponent gets angry with himself for having lost to such a *schlemiel*. The third game becomes more interesting. Ambitions flare up. But my opponent still does not respect me. Then, when he loses for the second time is the war really on. The only problem is that I myself often underestimate my opponent, forgetting that he too is capable of psychological manoeuvres.

Modesty aside, there are not many players of my calibre in the ghetto. This time, however, I met one. I did indeed intend to lose the first game, but he demolished me in twenty moves which was a bit too fast. With a triumphant laugh he took the ten pfennigs from me; and I set out at full steam to win the second game. I won the advantage of a knight, but my opponent worked out a clever strategy to improve his defensive line and the game was a draw. The remaining three games I won one after the other and Herr Rosenberg counted thirty crisp *rumkis* onto my palm. His face was beet-red. I asked him haughtily, "Perhaps you would like to play with my brother?"

Rosenberg packed up his chess set and put on his dark glasses, "I will be back to play with you again!" he said, and he ran out.

In honour of my victory we cooked a soup with two spoonfuls of flour. But as I am writing this I am so hungry that I could eat up an ox along with its hoofs. My stomach is rumbling. Let it be tomorrow already, so that I can make my *rumkis* edible!

✦   ✦   ✦

The houses, now that they are dug out from the mud and snow, seem shrunken, dirty and black with foulness. Without their coats and scarves, the people also look withered. It is frightening to look at the thin legs of the children, at the yellow faces of the adults. Streets and yards full of skeletons moving in full sunlight. Against the background of the flowering ghetto earth, which becomes more garden-like with every spring, the picture of dry human bones seems macabre, in particular in Marysin which is now being called *Tsarskoye Siello*.

My rebirth is fantastic! I, the bundle of bones, have inwardly become like a beet-leaf, juicy, warm, amorous. How did this happen? I don't know, and don't want to know. My lucky star winks at me, "Not a word more!" as at someone who has stolen a treasure. To hell with wisdom and logic! I have a beautiful new bluff which supports me. Yes, I am a flute player in the orchestra of the sinking Titanic. The waters reach up to the neck, no help is arriving from anywhere — and I stare into the empty sky, playing a God into it, a God who cares, who would not let me drown. My Titanic is sinking even more tragically than the other, because it is not God, but Brother Man who has started the storm. Therefore my flute must play more powerfully, more beautifully, more intoxicatingly — and more deceitfully.

Philosophising gives me a pain in the head. Let me go back to my innocence, to spring and to love. Her name is Inka. She is like a beet-twig: petite, cute. She has a swaying walk; it seems as if the slightest breeze could blow her away. Her lips are like the beads of a *kalinka*. She laughs with the sound of cascading waters. She is naive like a child and pious like the Pope. I am her God, and this explains why I don't believe in God myself. God himself does not believe in any other gods, but in himself.

Inka's mother is a potato-peeler at the same place as my mother. Inka is Rachel's classmate. She works in a co-operative. I know no other details about her. We never discuss the ghetto, nor food or politics. Nor do we talk about literature or the sciences, not even about love. We don't talk at all. We twitter like birds. Senselessness full of the highest sense. She is thin, her breasts are round and full, her face is round and pink, her hands are soft and white. She dresses nicely, in gay dresses full of colour, peasant-like. She wears a triangular scarf on her head, tied in a knot under her chin. She smells of fields and bluebottles. I never grow tired of kissing her.

I met Inka one day when Mother sent me to return a turnip she had borrowed from her mother. They live in a tiny room and part of their household is in the corridor. Where her father is, I don't know and don't ask. When I came up the stairs, I saw Inka sitting on the landing with her feet in a basin of water. She was soaping them, sitting hunched over like a squirrel. She raised her head to me and I saw her tasty *kalinka* mouth. I felt like putting my hands into the basin and soaping her tiny toes.

Since the weather has become so pleasant, we spend a lot of time together. She brings along a huge black umbrella and a blanket and we go to Marysin. We lie down in the grass. The umbrella protects us from the sun and from people's eyes. Once I said to her, "I think I love you, Inka," but I don't recall what she replied. I don't remember what she says to me or what I say to her. We cling to each other and chatter, humming between kisses, between caresses. Our touch is not hot. It is cool, refreshing and light, altogether different from that of a certain woman I know. We never notice where the time has gone. Suddenly we find ourselves in the dark and we walk back, the rolled-up blanket over my shoulder, the open umbrella over hers. People follow us with their eyes, laughing. We laugh back at them.

Spring of 1942 — what a spring! As long as the world has existed, there has probably never been such a May. It seems as if one could touch freedom with one's fingers. I feel it inside me. The barbed wires seem pitifully weak, as if the sun were about to melt them. I feel gratitude and joy. How good it is that the Germans have no power over the sun, and consequently not over me. Never before in my life have I known what spring is. Only now do I know. It does not let me surrender to the moods at home, in the street, or the ghetto. I have my weapon: Inka and Marysin!

Mother is again irritable and angry; it's impossible to say a word to her. Perhaps she knows something. I don't want to ask her. She is pale and thin and goes to bed as soon as she comes home from work. The household is entirely my responsibility, although Abraham helps me as much as he can. He has matured. He works in a Metal Resort, has become a professional metal-turner. The dust of the turnery is not good for the lungs, but it is important that he work in a Resort, particularly now, after the stamping episode, in case a new evacuation takes place.

We are both trying to ease the gloom at home. Yesterday Abraham came back with a few jokes from the Resort. The wife of a *shishka* says to a beggar, "Why do you always come to my door?" The beggar replies, "Doctors orders. He said that if I hit upon food that didn't harm me, I should stick to it." The other joke is about a doctor who says to his patient, "You are suffering from a new disease, which will enrich medical science." So the patient replies, "What's the matter with you, doctor? I am so poor that I need a money collection myself." The third joke I don't remember. I am a poor teller of jokes. Abraham, however, does so well acting out a joke, that one could collapse laughing.

But, as I said, I escape from home and the yard whenever I can. I used to enjoy the cherry tree, but nowadays it is unpleasant to sit under it. One third of the neighbours are gone. There are many new faces. And the people are jittery, quarrelsome. You could go deaf from the noise. People fight in the line at the water pump, or they fight over the abandoned *dzialkas*, the heirlooms of the deported. We now have a fellow, a former underworldnik by the name of Moshe Grabiaz, who has taken over the command of the backyard. He was a policeman for a while in the ghetto, and therefore he thinks that everyone has to be subordinate to him. Shalom knows him from before the war. He says that before the war Moshe would not step out of his house without a gun, and that his additional occupation was strike breaking. In the yard he applies his fists at the least provocation, avenging himself on the neighbours for whatever mishap occurs to him. He has a little girl of four who follows him like a little dog. His wife is sick, bedridden.

The same jitteriness can be observed in the streets. The relaxed atmosphere of the days after the evacuations belongs to the past. The air is precious, mild, and the people are wild. There are quarrels and fights in front of the co-operatives, the Vegetable Place, the public kitchens. Any wonder that I escape?

In spite of my egoism, however, I fulfilled my comradely duties a few times. It has come out that my friend Isaac has not got decalcification of the bones, but rather tuberculosis of the bones. I went to visit him at the hospital. He did not need me to cheer him up. He is cheerful because he is not at home. He said to me, "Now I am like a prince, taken care of, pampered, and no one is demanding a part of my bread ration."

We could open a branch of our organization at the hospital, so many of our people are there. Among them, our actress Gittele and her fiancé Manik. They have red round cheeks and don't look sick. It's a pleasure to look at them. But their eyes shine feverishly. I move from bed to bed, telling them bits of news or jokes that enter my mind. When I look at them, my heart sings like a bird. I am still well. I can walk about. I have Marysin and Inka!

✦ ✦ ✦

The announcement of the new food ration has come out. Deplorable. Two and a half kilograms of potatoes, twenty deca flour (fifteen deca less than for the previous ten days), ten deca *roggenflocken*, no vegetables, no preserves, nothing. I put myself in line for yeast today. A store opened where they give out only yeast. They say that it is a remedy for swollen legs. The main thing: yeast is edible.

It is quiet on the battle fronts. I have lost my curiosity for news, or perhaps I deaden it on purpose. I want to free myself of everything that contributes to my destruction. I must protect my good mood. The war must in any case be over this year. Perhaps I am "building castles in the air", but I want to live and therefore I must hope. If I don't listen to the news, I can also bluff my neighbours and my friends better. My imagination performs well without hindrances, so that I myself become excited.

I dream about Father almost every night. I see him as he looked before the war. "What's new?" he asks me. I tell him the good news which I have made up. He shakes his head, refusing to believe me. Yesterday he reproached me, "You've eaten up my sugar and my bread." My conscience began to bother me in my sleep, so I tried to change the subject. I said to him, "Look how nice it is outside, Father." I had the impression that we were in our country house. But Father said to me, "How can I go outside if you are wearing my pants and jacket . . . and you took my shaving tools?"

✦ ✦ ✦

Half of the people in the ghetto suffer from some kind of stomach trouble. Abraham and I cannot complain about that. What we wish for ourselves is precisely to lose our appetite. This, I think, is happening to Mother, which is not such a good sign. Often she gives us her food. It sustains us and cuts our hearts like with a knife. Eh, what am I writing? Let me not allow black thoughts to attack me.

✦ ✦ ✦

An historic cursed day in my life. We called the doctor for Mother. For a few days she has been in bed with stomach pains. Our former neighbour, Dr. Levine, examined her. He told her to drink a lot. "A medicine which we can afford . . ." he joked. I was surprised that he was less preoccupied with her stomach than with her back. He gave her a note for an X-ray. As he was about to leave, he noticed Father's photo on the wall. He remarked that Father looked familiar to him, and asked where he was. Mother told him. It came out that his father had been arrested on the same day as mine. His father was a leader of the *Poale-Zion*. Mother asked him whether he knew what had happened to these people. He said that he did not know, and left.

I caught up with him on the stairs. He is not such a healthy specimen himself. He is limping, is thin and has a yellowish face. He wears a navy blue doctor's cap and a navy blue coat which makes him look spooky, a figure bringing with him the foreboding of bad tidings. As soon as he saw me, he accelerated his steps. I blocked his way. He put his hand on my shoulder. "It's possible your mother is having some trouble with one of her lungs," he said, "but at her age this is not so dangerous. See that she eats well." He aimed at a smile. "Easy to say, isn't it?"

He lightly shoved me aside. I followed him, asking, "Do you know anything about them?"

"Nothing," he said. It was obvious that he was lying. Suddenly he shook my arm vigorously, "They behaved bravely. The Germans played dirty with them before they finished them off."

My body stiffened, my head roared; everything began to spin around me. "When?" I asked.

"Long ago . . . at the beginning of nineteen-forty. I figured out the date . . . the twenty-seventh of January." The date of my birth. I wanted to run off, but Levine grabbed me by the sleeve. "I know that this was not a good moment to tell you. But when is there a good moment for such news? They were brave, so we must at least be brave in accepting the truth about their fate. We owe it to them and . . . I owe it to you."

✦   ✦   ✦

I did not tell Mother or Abraham. I carry it alone within me. The lame doctor, in his navy blue coat with the black bag in his hand, comes in to see Mother. Every time he looks at me with his serious eyes, I fear that he is again about to reveal some more distressing news to me. I am grateful to him for what he has told me already. He made a man out of me, more than a man, an old man. He has extinguished my spring, and my hope. He has deprived me of my birthday. It has already been two years since my life-giver began to disintegrate into dust, while I was seeking support in thought of him. Now I am embracing the clear pure truth, I am embracing the unfathomable. I am not even crying. I go to work, take care of Mother, of the household, and my craving for food is wilder than ever before. Why did we hang Father's picture on the wall?

✦   ✦   ✦

I cannot believe that Father is dead. I cannot accept the fact. I asked Levine how he found out. He told me that one of his patients had been in prison with our fathers, for walking on Piotrkowska without a Star of David. He bought himself out for ten thousand marks, a privilege of the non-political prisoners. Levine gave me the man's address and I went to visit him. He is already half-gone, but his mind, as is the case with most of the dying people in the ghetto, is sharp. He had known Father before the war. He saw the group of political prisoners walk about the prison yard — and he saw a great deal more. I listened to the details up to the last word, but I have no strength to repeat them here. I saw myself in Father's skin. It was I who was shot at the wall. I am a walking corpse.

Yet Father lives on in my dreams. Sometimes I see ourselves during that day in the country, when I was around thirteen years old, and beat him at chess for the first time. I feel his proud gaze. He was delighted with my first victory over him. Now I "celebrate" my last victory over him: I am alive. Another time I dream of things which never happened: Father lashing me with a long whip. It hurts, but I am happy, because this proves to me that he is alive. I sometimes dream that I am a German soldier on guard at the prison or at the ghetto fence.

✦ ✦ ✦

Once more crowds of people from the provincial towns arrive daily. Their children and old people were finished off in the forests, they tell us. They look like escapees from a madhouse. Luckily, hunger does not allow us to think too much; perhaps there is a God who sees to that.

I would like to invent a God for myself. After all, I am not a bad bluffer; I sometimes manage to believe in the lies I invent. Why couldn't I bluff myself into believing in a God? More and more I am envious of the religious people. I cannot forgive my parents for having brought me up without a religion, harming me for the rest of my life. They gave me socialism, the belief in man. What can I achieve with that kind of ideological garbage nowadays? I want a God! I want an omnipotent saviour! Let Him be a lie, but let me have the ability to cling to Him as if He were true. Let me have the patience for waiting for Him, for expecting Him. That is the only thing which might support me in this abyss.

I no longer attend party meetings. I don't study or read. All that is trash. In the evenings, my chores over, I go down and peer through the window of the Toffee Man's cellar. Sometimes I go inside to visit him and sit near the stove where he prepares his candies. I force myself to find sense in what he tells me. He tells me that there is a secret meaning in the fact that the two of us, who once met in a church and had to look death in the eyes together, are neighbours in the ghetto. He tells me what he told me then, that we are related. I listen to his strange, silly, unfounded words and to the buzzing of the *yeshiva* boys at the table; boys my age, swaying over the open volumes of the *Gemera*. How can I become one of them? I would like to, with all my being, yet I know that I will never achieve that. In what they are doing I find not sense but tragi-comic nonsense.

I told the Toffee Man that the Germans killed Father. He cried. His tears did me some good while his words irritated me. "Don't say that he is gone," he shook his head, weeping. "His soul dwells both within you and within the heavens. He protects you . . ."

"He is dust and foulness," I retorted.

The Toffee Man kept on mumbling, "His soul . . . His soul . . ."

He cries a lot and repeats the word "soul". What is soul? Let someone come and explain the word "soul" to me. Another bluff. I told the Toffee Man that in my dreams I see Father in flesh and blood, and he immediately gave me an explanation for it, "His soul dresses up like that for you, so that you can grasp it. We on earth are capable to grasping only that which has a physical form."

"Then perhaps we too are souls dressed-up, so that God can grasp us," I joke bitterly. "Perhaps we are your God's dream . . . his nightmare?"

"Heaven forbid! We are as real as the world. Don't we feel hunger or pain?"

"What for? Couldn't we have remained souls in your God's heavens, feeling nothing but happiness?"

"The answer to that, you see, is clear as day." He shakes his thin beard. "We have a mission to fulfil on earth. Because we are here to cleanse the world. The world is God's kindness, and man ought to be its emanation. You think that God has no worries on His head, don't you? But it is He who has the real wars to wage . . . with the *Sitra Achra*, with the Dark Worlds which are out to destroy the creation of God's kindness. And the *Sitra Achra* does not fight a fair and honest fight. It creeps about inside us, God's messengers, into our very humanity. Because it wants to corrode us from within. Therefore every man's heart is a battlefield. Therefore the pain and suffering which man suffers and causes others to suffer. And the competition between Good and Evil is not of equal strength. It is easy to be evil, and hard to be good. To make light you need a wick and oil, to make dark one blow from your mouth is enough. So what I am trying to tell you is, that we Jews are the victims of the war between Good and Evil, more than any other nation. If in each of our souls the same war goes on as in the souls of other people, we are still, all of us together, a common, particular battlefield where the war between the Good and the Evil of the world takes place. Therefore we suffer doubly, ten-fold, a hundred-fold. But therefore we are also the diamonds in God's crown. The soul of the soul of the Universe!"

I listen to him in order to forget myself a bit. A sad entertainment. I want to find, if not logic, then at least a symbol in his words. "Tell me," I ask, "Your God, does He too believe in something?"

"There you go again! I just told you, didn't I? Of course He believes. He believes in Goodness and Justice, and for that He wages His wars."

"That means," I go on, "that God Himself also worships a God whose name is Goodness and Justice and for whose sake He suffers. He too suffers doesn't He?"

"Of course He suffers."

"Then who does not suffer?"

"Evil doesn't suffer. He who does not have a heart or soul doesn't suffer. The Devil doesn't suffer."

"Then I am ready to renounce my heart and soul. I will join the Devil's party. Enough suffering!"

"What are you saying such silly things for?" the Toffee Man weeps. "What does the Devil know of living, tell me? He is foulness. He is corroded by hate, envy, greed. He surfeits himself and drinks, and robs, and desecrates, and is never satiated. Of the kind of ravaging hunger that the Devil suffers we don't even have a clue."

"That means that he, the Devil, is suffering too."

"Of course he's suffering. But his suffering is different."

"Then who does not suffer, I ask you?"

"Oy," the little man sighs, "Death does not suffer . . . Death alone."

"But you said that there is no such thing as death."

"There is, there is. He who withdraws from the battlefield is dead . . . Eh, we are both saying silly things, bitter silly things. May the Almighty forgive us."

I run out from his cellar, racing through the streets as if I were being chased. What is happening to me? What is there to hold on to?

✦ ✦ ✦

And on the other hand — yes, there is a God. A brutal, indifferent one. His name is Life. He is not kindness or justice, yet He is powerful and magnificent.

We bow to Him and worship Him. All of us. He lashes us like a stepfather, while we thank Him and cling to Him. He is all that we have. I go down on my knees before Him, I pray to Him. I don't want Him to leave me. He is my holy belonging. He is the beginning and the end. I don't want to ask my God about anything. He won't answer my questions anyway. He is a capricious God. To Him the Jews are not the cream of the crop, but the refuse on the bottom. Why? Are there any reasons for it, or aren't there? And what if there are? The fact is important. The fact is God. The fact is sun and moom, day and night, wind and air, and everything that I can embrace with my senses. The rest is not worth a broken pfennig. Everything that is alive knows that. Therefore — egoism and hatred. Hatred because of jealousy, of competition, of the desire to become God's, Life's favoured child. Egoism means clinging frantically to life. Egoism is the only kind of Love that exists.

And yet how good, how merciful is my brutal God. Not even two weeks have past since I learnt about Father, and I have already gotten used to the thought. There are days when he does not even enter my mind. I only feel the hollowness within me, but it does not hurt so much any more. I don't find it hard to laugh and joke with Abraham. I don't mind Father's picture on the wall. I can look at it calmly. His death has no longer happened to me two weeks ago. It fits now into its place in time: more than two years ago. Now we have to save Mother. I cook good tasty soups for her. Their aroma fills the room. But when she pushes away the full plate, I am glad, inwardly, in my stomach, and I pray that she will not touch food for at least another few days. That is a noble son!

May the devil take it, I don't want to be a Jew!

Chapter Six

IN THE *WISSENSCHAFTLICHE ABTEILUNG* where Rachel was now working there was quite a lax atmosphere; discipline was a matter of each worker's conscience. The showcases had to be ready for a certain date which the *Rabiner*, the manager, would announce months before.

The *Rabiner* liked visitors to come in to see the exhibits, or to look over the collection of old books or ritual objects, or works of art. Visiting writers and painters were allowed to sit down at the tables for a chat with the workers, or to enter the *Rabiner's* office — the door stood always open — and discuss highly spiritual matters with him. Here Rachel would meet the painters Winter and Guttman, and others whom she had not known. Here the dark-haired sickly Comrade Sender, who was a cultural institution all to himself, would pop in. Once in a while the poet Burstin would show up and sing for the workers parts of symphonies which he knew by heart. Quite often one could hear the voice of a poet reciting his poems, or the voice of someone relating folk stories, freshly concocted jokes, sayings or songs — treasures of the ghetto folklore which the *Rabiner* collected in thick pads with black covers. One day Guttman brought along a woman called Itka who had escaped from the insane asylum on the day it had been evacuated. Itka wore a red summer dress with red beads around her neck. Sitting stiffly in a chair, her enormous eyes staring into the distance, she improvised long incomprehensible poems, expressive, sombre and beautiful. The workers in the neighbouring room let their work drop from their hands as they listened, mesmerized by her lilting voice.

Rachel's problem was that these intellectual feasts were not capable of quieting the rumbling in her empty stomach, and she acquired the ugly habit of taking advantage of the *Rabiner's* kindness and rushing home for half an hour every day.

Being alone at home might have been a pleasure, because she still needed solitude as a plant needs water. However, the time spent at home made her rather restless. The doors of the food cupboards were not locked, and if hers was empty, there was always something to be found in her mother's. Then began the struggle with herself and with her hands, which were attracted to the cupboard like a magnet. She was angry at Blumka for still having a piece of bread or a bit of marmalade. She would be angry at herself, at the thought that in the beginning of her life in the ghetto, she still had had the power to offer David a few spoonfuls of her own sugar, and that she had become such a weakling now.

Until one day she got a brilliant idea which saved her. On the window sill stood Moshe's box of dried leaves which he used as tobacco. She took a piece of

79

paper and awkwardly rolled a cigarette for herself, as she had seen her father do. The thick paper surrounding the "tobacco" lit up. She inhaled. Her breath burned in her throat. The room began to spin around her. She sat down on a chair, forcing herself to inhale the smoke again and again, until she could do it no more, and she choked. She leaned her head against the table top, and it too began to circle around her, along with the room, fast and dizzily, then slower — until it stopped — at the point of victory. She did not feel hungry any more and she stared at the food cupboards courageously, cold-bloodedly. From that day on running home became not a pleasure but a need, like a daily injection. The pangs of hunger were not supposed to destroy her life. She still had so much to accomplish.

Apart from her work at the *Wissenschaftliche Abteilung*, she gave a few private lessons, the most important of which were with the Holy Shoemaker, an instructor in the prison camp for Polish youths outside the ghetto. He was one of the greatest philanthropists of the ghetto, the greatest patron of painters and writers and he kosherly deserved his fine nickname.

The shoemaker was a young man in his thirties, dark-haired, with a fine pale face and a faint smile always playing on his lips. He had an innocent child-like gaze which peered at the world with astonishment. He was slim, tall, his gait was light yet somewhat unsure. His name was popular in the ghetto and legends about his kindness circulated in the yards and along the foodlines. It seemed as if he lived in the ghetto without being subject to its laws. Evidently, he did his job at the prison camp so successfully that he could live like a free man, without tensions or fears. His little house in Marysin, nestling in a small orchard, looked like a picture postcard. The rooms inside were nicely furnished and the shoemaker's two little daughters had a room to themselves and a nanny.

Although the Holy Shoemaker had never savoured the "'ristocratic" life before the war, he quite easily adjusted to the life of the ghettocracy. His politeness and finesse were princely, and if it were not for his limping Polish and his ignorance of the manners of the well-bred, he could surely have passed for someone born in a silken undershirt. Moreover, he liked people and led an active social life. Many of the Resort commissars as well as the crafty Mr. Zibert were counted among his frequent visitors. Here they would come without any 'one-hand-washes-the-other' calculations, but rather because of the honour of being befriended by such a 'rare' Jew. There was also good food to be enjoyed here and, in general, the shoemaker and his wife were pleasant warm-hearted people.

Outside, in the green well-kept orchard, there were always a few painters standing in front of their easels. Hidden behind their canvases, they would now and then pop out their heads to look at the house, or at the shoemaker's little girls whom they painted for the reward of a basketful of vegetables, or half a loaf of bread.

Along the outside wall of the house there usually stood a group of supplicants, waiting for the master to have a free minute and lend an ear to their pleas, then take out his pocketbook, or order his cook to prepare a parcel of food. Wintertime, the supplicants would gather in the spacious warm kitchen. Amongst them were intellectuals as well as simple needy folk. The shoemaker treated them all with equal generosity and respect.

The shoemaker wanted to learn Polish as well as "'ristocratic" manners and his friend, the *Rabiner*, had assured him that a more expert teacher than Rachel he would not easily find in the ghetto. True, Rachel herself did not feel particularly sure of herself as far as "salon manners" were concerned, but she made an honest effort to share whatever she knew with her student; and what she did not know she would invent, helped by her rich imagination. She taught him how to talk to the ladies at the table and in the street. She taught him phrases of courtesy, and how to touch upon "intelligent" topics in "intelligent" company. She also taught him how to smoke expertly, since smoking seemed to be a necessity for a man of good manners; and it also seemed unfair to have loads of cigarettes in one's possession and not be able to profit from them oneself, while a ghetto full of men were dying for a puff. The Holy Shoemaker hated smoking just as Rachel did. He became red-faced, and always ended up coughing, choking, spitting and letting out clouds of smoke, as if his throat were a chimney. But he was disciplined and doggedly followed Rachel's directions as to how to hold the cigarette gracefully between his fingers, and how to tap off the ashes elegantly. Rachel had the opportunity of smoking with him and also received two cigarettes to take home for her father.

She felt much better when she was teaching the shoemaker the Polish alphabet which he had to write out every day in a new copybook because he could never find the old. He calligraphed shapeless, undulated and collapsing letters, but he was persistent and would have made great progress had he had his lessons regularly. The trouble was that he rarely had the time, and Rachel would spend the major part of her hour in the loft, where he would send her until he could free himself of his many obligations. The loft, neatly whitewashed, was full of boxes in which the shoemaker kept his supply of food and vegetables, as well as a net-sack full of tempting gold onions. Every time Rachel left the loft without having stolen an onion she considered it a victory. She was proud that she did not have to be ashamed to look her handsome student in the face.

Apart from the Holy Shoemaker, Rachel gave private lessons to the veterinarian who inspected the meat, which was quite often rotting, when it arrived in the ghetto. The veterinarian, a heavy-bodied man upon whom the ghetto diet did not seem to have any effect, wanted to learn Yiddish. With his rich moustache he reminded Rachel of a healthy country squire. He spoke a heavy Cracow Polish in a bass voice, and with his posture, his doctor's cap and high boots, he intimidated his teacher, whom he received in his basement office. He was waging a holy rage against Fate which had, all of a sudden, forced him, on top of all his troubles, to study a language which he despised and which he had to know in order to communicate with his uneducated subordinates who could not speak even a broken Polish. He wanted to speak and to understand Yiddish immediately; but, alas, he was muddle-headed and the words which came out of his mouth were unrecognizable. He was always angry at Rachel and tried to teach her how to teach him. She could feel his unpleasant breath against her cheeks and would sigh with relief when the hour was over and she had her sixty-five pfennigs in her pocket.

Rachel also gave another kind of private lesson, which in fact was not a lesson at all. This was an hour spent with the *Rabiner* himself. Her acquaintance with him had been reinforced through her father who worked at the co-operative next to the *Rabiner's* house, located down on Marysinska Street where the second degree *shishkas* lived, and where one could already breathe the fine air of Marysin. The *Rabiner* had a garden with a bower, a pretty wife and two pretty, hungry daughters. They had come from Danzig, and German was spoken at home. Only the *Rabiner*, a Polish Jew, spoke a fine Yiddish. At home he wore his black German-style frock-like jacket with a black vest. His pale face and his neat pointy goatee made a distinct contrast against the darkness of his dress. Rachel never tired of looking into his twinkling eyes as she listened to his clear yet mysterious voice. He was spell-binding, mesmerizing, a man of flesh and blood, and yet — a riddle; he seemed ageless, belonging to both past and future centuries. He was preparing a verbal translation of the psalms into Yiddish, and Rachel's function was to help with the grammar. Her reward was not money, or food, but the study of the psalms.

Usually when she left the *Rabiner's* house, Moshe would be waiting for her outside with a treat, a carrot or a few radishes. Lately, he never failed to bring her a flower from the garden behind the co-operative.

Rachel had had a dream; one of those nightmares capable of determining the mood of one's waking hours. She was convinced that dreams revealed some concealed truth, and she wanted to face that truth, but even the thinnest path back towards it had faded from her memory. All that remained was a heaviness in her heart which she was unable to shake off.

She was on her way home from her lessons. It was dusk. The air was mild, summery. Her blouse was unbuttoned at the neck; her hair, wet with perspiration, was dishevelled, sticking to her forehead. Her bare feet in the cloth slippers could feel the heat of the pavement. She was in a hurry. The hours after work had to be used carefully. She still had her work at the library and with her study group. She also had to visit Miss Diamand and attend the lectures at the "university". There were books to be read, notes to be taken, essays to be written.

She had intended to think of her projects on her way, but unfinished thoughts along with the strange mood of last night's dream were carrying her off into distant worlds. Suddenly, bells began to ring in her head, bringing her back to reality. On the sidewalk across the street she saw David trudging along with slow steps, as he carried a heavy board on his stooped shoulder. She dreaded the encounter. When she did not see him, she found it easier to wait for his return, convinced that their estrangement was not forever, that one day it would vanish and they would recognize each other again. Her accidental meetings with him always made her hope waver. Yet she crossed the street and approached him. He shook his shoulder awkwardly, and the board slid off it.

"They're taking apart the furniture of the deported," he said, avoiding her eyes, "I got 'protection' and received this board." He smiled coldly, a brutal unfamiliar smile, which did not illuminate his face, but rather related a gloomy message to her. She could not bear to look at him, yet all her being cried out to embrace him — to call back the boy who had left, whom she loved. He wiped his forehead with his sleeve and said nothing more. Nor could she bring out another word. At length he put the board back on his shoulder. "I must run on," he said, stretching out his hand to her.

"Everything is over between us, isn't it?" she muttered.

He stared at her as if he had not understood her question. A hot spark lit up in his eyes, like a call for help, like a scream of pain. He marched off, stooped under the load he was carrying. She ran through the street. In her mind she balanced his gaze against his silence. How was she supposed to explain them?

Had he wanted her to know that he was suffering alone but that she could not help him?

Despite the encounter, the rest of her evening was a success. She disciplined herself. Only at night, on her bed, did she give rein to her grief.

After the night came a new day and a new mood. Her heart was free of all clamps, her mind open, ready to absorb all kinds of new stimuli, to assimilate all that each moment had to offer. She was ready to rush about again, to run away from herself, towards herself. She had the feeling that she would not have enough time, that she would not arrive at whatever goal she had set for herself.

That summer her parents and Shlamek spent a lot of time on the *dzialka*. There was always something to do there. Tired, but cheerful, they would come home with bags full of leaves for cooking. Rachel envied them. She also liked the *dzialka*, the soothing contact with the soil. But she could not bring herself to spend more than a few minutes there, always promising herself to stay longer the next time, to chat a bit with Moshe, to give some attention to Blumka. But the next time she would again have no patience. And the same would happen during her visits with her friends. She would pop in to see one or another of them, stay for a few minutes, then run off.

The days became increasingly hot and sultry. The nights were not much better. In the morning the crowds dragged themselves to the Resorts, streams of sweat washing down their creased faces. In the Resorts inspections took place day after day. *Gauleiter Greiser* himself partook in them. Was it really so hot outside? Did one really feel so faint from exhaustion? During the inspections the heaviness of limbs vanished, as if they were infused with new energy, as if the thick air had suddenly become light and refreshing. The people worked feverishly. Afterwards, the good news circulated through the hot streets and houses: the Germans were satisfied with the ghetto. Now the people could allow themselves the luxury of sitting on the doorsteps of the houses after work, complaining about the heat. They could allow themselves a rest from the tension and permit their alertness to slacken. Lazily, dreamily, they shared their optimism: "The Germans will come to a black end any day now, and we will live to see it with our own eyes." The clank of a streetcar running somewhere through the ghetto streets laden with food and merchandise was music to the ears; it strummed the chords of hope: "The world cannot do without us. We are useful!"

In the evenings, on the same streetcars arrived hundreds of people from the provinces. They trudged through the streets and stopped to talk with those resting in the doorways, telling them, "In the *schtetl* of Turek children were thrown like rubber dolls onto the trucks . . . In Lask only a few hundred were picked out, the rest were led off into the forest . . . In Varta the first to be hanged were the Rabbi and his son, the rest of the people followed after . . ." The resting ghettoniks blinked their eyes, wiped the sweat off their foreheads, and as soon as the strangers had walked off, they talked about a new invention: making pancakes from the leaves of radishes.

Placards appeared on the street walls. Five hundred men and two hundred women were needed for work in Germany. This was not important news. Such small "actions" were a daily business. Herr Schatten was in charge of rounding up the required number of people and he did his job meticulously. First of all he had at his disposal the volunteers who were fed up with the ghetto and the heat;

the rest were caught in the streets, or taken at nights from their beds. Today's order differed from the previous ones only in the fact that this time the transport had to leave within twenty-four hours. It was better for the ghetto. This way its normal working rhythm was not disturbed.

Rachel was asleep on her bed arranged out of chairs, near the open window. Her pillow was wet with tears. She often cried in her sleep which was actually a state deeper, heavier than normal sleep. She was having a nightmare, seeing herself within a void, without vision. Suddenly, something began to pound dully, to pulsate through the emptiness of which she was dreaming. Every throb lifted her higher, causing her to surface from the depths. She heard screams, someone calling. Sweat streamed down her face, saliva dribbled from her half-open mouth. Then a scream hurled her into the air. She jumped down from the chairs, opening her eyes wide. Was she still dreaming? A pair of fists was pounding against the door.

"Eibushitz! Eibushitz!" someone roared. In the half-darkness, Rachel hit against Blumka coming out of the bedroom. They could both barely manage to unlock and open the door. A pair of hands pushed them apart; someone stepped in between them. Someone else's hand lit a flashlight, while the voice continued goading, "Moshe Eibushitz, for the transport!" Beams from the flashlight jumped up and down the walls. Shlamek leaped down from his bed. Blumka was mumbling incomprehensibly.

Rachel quickly mastered herself, announcing, "It's a mistake. He works in a co-operative. I'll show you his identity card."

"That's correct," came the answer. "He works in a co-operative; he's on our list." The flashlight was already in the little bedroom, so was the voice, "Eibushitz, get up! To the transport!" Two pairs of hands shook Moshe out of his sleep. The bed squeaked loudly and eerily. Moshe was already standing at the bedside in his nightshirt, shaking on his spindly legs. The flashlight shone into his face, "Get dressed!" came the order. "Cover the windows and turn on the light!"

Blumka struggled to hang up the window cover. Moshe turned on the light. His eyes squinting, he gathered his clothes and turned to Rachel, "Roll me a cigarette." He had barely managed to hustle on his pants, when the two policemen pinned him by the arms. "Go to Zuckerman!" Moshe managed to call out as he waved to his family and the door was slammed shut behind him.

It took Blumka and the children a second to dress. Then they stopped short in the middle of the kitchen: "What do we do now?" They began to wander about the kitchen and the little bedroom. Dishevelled, shrunken, they shuddered with cold throughout the hot sultry night, not removing their eyes from the clock.

As soon as the first morning lights brightened the sky and the first people appeared on the bridge, Rachel rushed to the Zuckermans. Reisel, half-asleep, received her with a growl. She asked her to wait, but Rachel followed her and burst into the sick man's room. She dashed towards the bed and faced the body in the gypsum armour. "They took Father last night!" she sputtered. "He told me to run to you, Mr. Zuckerman! He is counting on you . . . He . . ."

Samuel sucked in his cheeks. A heavy sigh escaped his lips. He opened his mouth a few times, but seemed unable to utter a word. At length he gave up struggling with his voice and dumbly wagged his head.

Rachel ran through the streets. It seemed unbelievable that Moshe should not be among those hurrying to work. It was unbelievable that she would not see him today, or tomorrow . . . or perhaps ever again. It did not entirely penetrate her mind and so she felt no panic. Hopeful and sure of herself, she hurried to see the Holy Shoemaker. He met her at the door, a thin smile upon his thin lips. He was on his way to work and he did not stop. She ran out after him into the street, talking to his back. "They might send him away today . . ."

He let her follow him and talk to his back. When she had nothing more to say and was waiting for his reply, he turned to her and shook her hand politely, "It will be arranged, Miss Rachel." She stared at him. It was as if her soul had moved into his clear eyes. Had she heard him properly? There was no time to ask him again. He was already far away although she still felt his presence beside her. She should have run after him and embraced him for his kindness. She was in love with him, head over heels, for making happen what she had known would happen.

Moshe came home that night. He seemed intoxicated, flustered. He embraced Blumka and wept with his head buried in her hair. Daughter and son watched the pair shyly, because of their father's tears. When his weeping turned into a prolonged lament, they wanted to avert their eyes, to block their ears, but were unable to do so, knowing that the sight of their sobbing father in the arms of their mother would remain with them for the rest of their days.

Yet the experience with Moshe was forgotten within a few days, carried away by the pulse of time in the ghetto. Even Moshe himself seemed to have forgotten that fateful night. Only the present counted, the hot sweaty Now which one had to conquer. The evacuations, some big, some small, took place almost daily. People were sought out in their homes and caught in the streets. But this had become the problem of others. Moshe was not on the lists any more. He was under the protection of the Holy Shoemaker. He had a "back".

He should have regained his strength. He was a fortunate ghettonik, working in a co-operative, able to enjoy a bite of stolen food, a bit of sugar, a lick of marmalade. But depite the bottles of *Vigantol*, the medicine for decalcified bones, which Rachel got for him through her other student, the veterinarian, he was unable to walk properly. Yet he did not neglect his visits with Samuel. Since he found it difficult to cross the bridge by himself, Rachel or Shlamek assisted him. Samuel's cast had been removed at last and he was allowed to walk about his room. A thin, tall, gray-haired man with drooping shoulders, his coal-black eyes seemed to stare at his surroundings with astonishment. Later, he would go down with Moshe into the yard; they both felt best when they were together outside of their homes. Yet, although they felt closer to each other than ever before, their conversations were shorter. They would sit together in silence for long stretches of time.

As for political information, Moshe was now the one to deliver it. He would make it short. What was there after all to tell Samuel? That the Germans had taken Sebastapol? That practically all of Egypt was in their hands? The best thing was to return to the silence as soon as possible, to feel the healing power of the cherry tree and to delight in the soothing awareness of friendship. Now and then Moshe would break their long silence. Once he remarked, "Outwardly I am calm . . . inwardly however, I feel cold. A strange feeling . . . I sometimes wake up at night to hear my teeth chatter." Or he would say, as if to himself, "In the past, even in the ghetto, making love was like celebrating. Nowadays . . . nothing."

Samuel would smile. "In the past, it seemed to me that a man carried all of his masculinity between his legs. Now, that I am no longer physically a man . . . I am actually beginning to feel like one." His voice was still hollow, whistling through the holes left by his knocked-out teeth.

Only once did he speak at length about his sojourn at the Red House. He saw Moshe's face turn red and blue, and the cigarette at his lips begin to tremble. Yet Samuel felt compelled to give his account to at least one pair of ears. His experience had to be sealed in the memory of at least one other human being — his friend. Moshe had to follow him where he had been. The beads of sweat on Moshe's forehead bore witness to the fact that Moshe was indeed with him in the cellar of the Red House.

Samuel spoke about pain. "Do you know, when physical pain crosses over the border of endurance, it ceases to be physical. Through it I saw my entire life . . . But I saw everything as if in a crooked mirror. They say that suffering enobles you. For its duration, pain only transforms you into a mass of raw flesh. You have two wishes: to stop feeling, to perish once and for all, and that those whom you love should hear your scream, and bear witness. With every burning nerve inside me I called the children . . . Bella in particular. But then, when it's over, the mirror bends in the opposite direction. Those whom you love become remote. They have never been where you called them with the voice of your blood; and they will never know. Pain severs you from those who don't share it with you. And it awakens a fear within you of its return. You fall madly in love with life. At the same time, you are aware that you must arrive at some conclusions after the experience, that you must straighten up the mirror; that your life ought never to be the same again. I think that everyone arrives at his own conclusions, depending on the baggage he carries within him. All the knots untie by themselves. I never had such clarity in my mind, Moshe . . ."

Another time Moshe repaid Samuel by evaluating his own life. He was not ashamed to talk about his love for his wife whose hands were bitten by soaps and suds, his love for the woman for whom he felt not a trace of physical desire. He spoke of his pride in his children. He had sown something of himself within their hearts. He spoke of his admiration for Rachel, of his respect for Shlamek. His son was close to him, a physical copy of himself. His actions and way of thinking were familiar to him. While the daughter was an adorable mystery. Moshe was not afraid that he would hurt Samuel by extolling his harmonious family life. He knew that his friend was free from envy; that just as Samuel's pain was his to share, so was his happiness Samuel's to share.

One evening Moshe met Samuel with the news, "The Carpentry Resort is on fire! You must hide, Zuckerman! They say it's an act of sabotage!"

Samuel shrugged his shoulders, smiling indifferently, wisely. He took Moshe by the arm and led him out into the street, towards the Carpentry Resort. The building was cordoned off. They stopped at a street corner, and watched the flames from a distance, "It's good to watch it burn," he said. "A pity that I cannot pride myself on that accomplishment."

✦   ✦   ✦

A hungry *Jude* who had often noticed Rachel waiting for her father in front of the co-operative, began to nag at Moshe, saying that he ought to buy a fur jacket for his daughter. Moshe badly wanted to buy the fur jacket, but the *Jude* was asking a whole bottle of oil for it, and to bargain with a German Jew was impossible. The *Jude* did not stop begging Moshe to come to his lodgings and see the treasure, which Moshe finally did. And as soon as he saw it, his heart began to pound at the thought of how perfectly it would fit his daughter. However, a bottle of oil was a price that he could not even allow himself to dream of.

Yet, one bright day, Rachel did become the owner of the exquisite fur jacket. It happened at the end of June. It was Saturday. All the young people who had come to borrow books from the library had left and Rachel was busy preparing her lecture for her study group. The kitchen was now full of her parents' visitors, while she was in their bedroom, near the window, sitting on the floor with a chair serving as her table. Then Moshe, dressed in a white shirt, his sleeves rolled up, came in. His face glowed peacefully, even the cigarette in the corner of his mouth seemed cheerful. "Important visitors have come to see you," he announced solemnly to Rachel.

Comrade Bracha Koplowitch, whose posture and head of curly blonde hair made her resemble a lioness, entered the little room. She was followed by Simon, the president of the youth organization, dressed in his Sabbath best, the collar of his white shirt laid out in the fashion introduced by the poet Slowacki. Behind them the smiling leader of the *Skif* slid into the room. Without much ceremony they sat down on the beds. Comrade Bracha immediately came out with what she had to say. "It's about the library . . ."

"Do you want a report?" Rachel brushed away the wisps of hair from her forehead and was thoughtful for a moment. To give an account of the achievements of the library was a pleasant proposition.

But before she could begin, Simon spoke up with reproach in his voice, "During the entire time of the library's existence you've never considered it necessary . . ."

Rachel blushed, her ears began to burn. "I was waiting for the leadership to become more interested . . ." she stammered.

"And the cash?" Simon threw the question. "What have you been doing with the money?"

"I buy new books, there is a bookseller who sells bargains."

Comrade Bracha announced composedly, "The leadership has decided to remove the library to other quarters." After that had been said, the visitors shook hands with Rachel and left.

All week after work, comrades arrived with sacks to carry away the books. Shalom removed the shelves. "That's how it is, my lady," he teased Rachel. "A library in the ghetto also has to move from one place to another."

Rachel hoped that she would be assigned to the library committee, but she was not even nominated. The kitchen was left with bare walls. Rachel felt empty too. Moshe and Blumka tried to console her, saying that it was all for the best; the family would live with less fear.

Rachel was unable to free herself of her resentment. "I know why they removed the books. Perhaps they do suspect me of some kind of embezzlement, but that's not the main reason. The main reason is that I considered the library to be my personal achievement, my work, and I did not go to ask them what to do or what not to do. A democratic party board can be as despotic as any dictatorship . . . and I hate them . . . I hate the regimentation, the so-called party discipline. Wait and see," she fumed, "if I don't free myself of it altogether one fine day."

The following day Moshe stole a bottle of oil at the co-operative and arrived home with the extraordinary gift for his daughter. Excited, he wiped off the sweat dripping from the tip of his nose and said enthusiastically, "You never had a fur jacket, Rachel. You'll enjoy it after the war. Come here, touch it . . . soft as butter. Try it on."

Rachel had the same feeling that often overwhelmed her during her work with the *Rabiner*, or with the Holy Shoemaker, or with the veterinarian: a strong sense of the grotesque. Something both funny and sad. It was hot in the room. She was barefoot, wearing only her slip. The soft gray fur jacket was a piece of beauty, a mild cuddly kitten. She put it on over her slip. The silken lining delicately caressed her skin.

"It fits like a glove!" Blumka was enraptured.

Moshe quickly rolled himself a cigarette. "I knew it would fit her!" He beamed, waiting for a smile to appear on Rachel's face. She smiled at him.

Shlamek stroked Rachel's back. "What kind of fur is it, Father?"

Moshe scratched his pate, "He told me but I forgot. He was once a great businessman in Frankfurt, that *Jude*, and the fur jacket belonged to his only daughter. She and his wife volunteered for the evacuation during the winter 'action'".

Blumka was afraid that with all the hands touching it, the jacket would become stained. She told Rachel to take it off. She would see if she could find a bit of naphthalene somewhere, then pack the jacket well and hide it for after the war. She was afraid of trouble in the event of a house search, if the fur were discovered; all the furs in the ghetto were long ago supposed to have been delivered to the *Verwertungsstelle*. Finally Blumka had a brilliant idea — to transform the fur into a pillow, cover it with a pillow case and let Rachel sleep on it. At night Rachel rested her head on the soft new pillow. She thought of the girl who had worn the fur. That night, too, she cried in her sleep.

Chapter Seven

JULY. THE GHETTO found itself in the centre of a blaze which had nothing more to devour. The ground was dry, cracked, sapped of all its juices; no longer black, but brown and dusty as sand. The trees in Marysin were withered and the worms and flies swarmed all about them. Their leaves, shrivelled like dry strips of paper, hung from the wasted boughs. The last unripe fruits with scorched skins, like the faces of old people, seemed to peer at the ground with longing. And the people were like the soil. Their faces scorched like pieces of clay, shrivelled and yellow, they looked like bundles of bones, which could barely move. They too were sapped of all their juices. Above their heads hung the sky, its blue seemingly evaporated, a deep void upon which a nebulous rotting sun lay scrambling in its own fire.

That July the food rations were more meagre than ever. There were no vegetables or potatoes. The size of the bread portions was reduced and the soups consisted of mere water. That July the children stopped playing in the streets and the yards. Old age took hold of them. The youthful men and women, those dogged evening strollers, lay on their beds after their day's work at the Resorts, or looked out the windows. Only now and then a young man or woman passed through the streets, cheeks aflame, eyes burning, blossoming in the inner heat which was devouring their bodies; these were the tubercular, or those who had "water on the lungs" — on their way to the ambulatorium for an injection of calcium. Occasionally, other brave bony young people could also be seen venturing into the streets: those who still had the courage to go to a meeting, to a study group or even to a concert. And then there was another kind of passer-by who still had a more or less human appearance, a normal face, but eyes filled with madness — the groups of Jews arriving daily from the provincial towns; the Jews who were the source of all the horror tales. It was they who would not allow one to forget the impossible rumour that was circulating through the yards — about the deportation of all the old people and the children from the ghetto.

In the bazaar, which had once swarmed with black marketeers, there stood a solitary gallows. The black corpse of a young man who had tried to escape from the ghetto dangled from it in the sunlight. It had been the third hanging that week. A fourth was being prepared for the following day — of a Czech Jew who had accidentally wandered off onto the forbidden sidewalk near the Red House. When he ran into him, Herr Schmidt had knocked him to the ground. The man had scrambled to his feet and responded with a smack to Herr Schmidt's chubby face.

The teachers' collective to which Miss Diamond belonged had fallen apart.

When they lost their work at the schools and the *gymnasium*, the teachers, like Miss Diamand, found themselves without the ground under their feet and with nothing to give meaning to their days. Of course they tried to settle down somehow, finding work at the offices or Resorts, however life devastated them quickly and thoroughly, men and women alike. Every week the hearse arrived for someone else. Miss Luba, the young Latin teacher, had been resting in her plot of land at the cemetery since the previous spring. Professor Lustikman, who had taught physics and chemistry, and who had walked about hungry and irritable, was no longer hungry or irritable, and had for several weeks himself been given over to the processes of physical and chemical disintegration. After him, followed Frau Braude, the teacher of German, the lady with the goitre who had had an aversion to men. And the same week she was joined by the teacher of arts and crafts, Mrs. Brauner. The "Karmelka", Mrs. Feiner, and Professor Hager and his wife still carried on, and so did Miss Diamand — to everyone's surprise.

She knew that according to all calculations, her turn to join her colleagues in the cemetery was long overdue, and she was herself amazed at the unfairness of Fate. Others, much younger than herself, were already gone. She read the same astonishment in the eyes of her neighbours, as if they were asking, "What is she still doing here?" She agreed with them, often good humouredly asking the question herself. During the summer, she had acquired a new knack for jokes. The entire world and human fate in particular seemed to her like a tragic farce, a mock-play. She would have taken nothing seriously, had it not been for the children of the club, the orphans left behind by her colleagues. When she looked at the children, she did not feel like laughing. She felt like raging against the invisible Mocking Clown. It was that rage which chased her out of bed every morning, which kept her on her legs, obliterating all desire for rest, or peace. Her energy was against the laws of nature and, consequently, a kind of mockery as well.

She had been feeling very well lately. The need for food did not bother her and she suffered little from the heat. She was again wearing her mauve dress which resembled a Greek tunic and she had become accustomed to her wooden shoes, not finding them too heavy. Her head was practically bald. The bit of hair left refused to lie flat against her skull, but stood away from it, its fuzzy texture turning it into a white aureola around her forehead. The mind behind that forehead worked clearly and well.

With her tiny steps, she trotted up and down the stairs, from room to room, over the yard and the dying garden, assembling the children. Nearby, at the Lingerie Resort, a school had been organized for them. There, the remaining teachers taught after their day of work at the Resorts. This was a joyful school, where the teachers themselves became students. The experienced professors, worn out as they were, revived the long dormant children within themselves. Here the children were taught to play the recorder, and the best musicians came to give concerts for them; they were also taught how to paint. In this way the teachers and their students learned to smile at things of beauty. True, the world was coming to an end, the earth was expiring, the ghetto was in agony. But here, under the watchful eyes of the teachers, the spirit of youth budded anew. The teachers became the soil, the roots and the sap for the Tree of Life which had to find its way towards tomorrow.

Miss Diamand had a new friend: Mrs. Hager. That summer the Hagers had given up their privacy and had begun to come into personal contact with their surroundings; as if their love for each other had now reached such fullness that they had to spread it around. Old Mrs. Hager volunteered for work. She had been estranged from children and was afraid of them. Children had always seemed to belong to a different race. They had seemed both fragile and wild and she had preferred to keep herself distant from them. Now she became the supervisor of the orphans' bedroom. She helped them to dress and wash; and as a result of that physical intimacy she began to change. She herself now often forgot to wash, to comb, or to make herself beautiful. She ceased to paint her dried lips or cover her creased cheeks with powder. And she became talkative, a chatterbox, like a little girl. Her old age acquired a child-like charm.

Miss Diamand did not carry on any lofty conversations with her. They would discuss thick combs and how to obtain them in order to prevent the children from getting lice. Together they made an inventory of the laundry and mended the torn pieces, an activity which Mrs. Hager performed deftly, and Miss Diamand clumsily. "Oh, Hagerowa," Miss Diamand would blink her half-blind eyes. "You are a magician!" and she would ask her friend to thread the needle for her.

Professor Hager became a gay old man that summer. Overnight he turned into a grandfather. He had a new audience to entertain with the tales of his former experiments in cross-pollinating flowers, of the marvels of living things. He also taught the children geography. Now he had not only his career as a botany teacher at the *gymnasium* behind him, but also his career as a director of the Garden and Plantation Department. From this period stemmed the story which he liked to recount. It was about the goats which one fine day had been brought into the ghetto. On account of these goats, a serious row had broken out between the Presess and the Plantation Department. The Department was of the opinion that the goats should be distributed among the population, first to the sick or to those who had large families. Each goat would provide a litre and a half of milk daily, and a family borrowing such a goat for two weeks could, given the price of milk on the black market, put itself back on its feet. The Presess however had decided differently: the goats were to be at his disposal; they would be kept in a barn and their milk would contribute to the improvement of the financial situation of the community at large. When the goats finally did arrive, they were sick, thin and worn out, real *klepsidras*, and each week ten or fifteen of them died. After a few weeks there were no goats left. All that was left was the Presess' aversion to the Plantation Department and its chief, Professor Hager, who was transferred to the Straw Resort, then to the Rug Resort where tapestries were woven out of the dirty blood-stained laundry which came into the ghetto. At present he was occupied at the Saddle Resort — while his evenings were devoted to the School for Gifted Children.

He would teach the children about countries and continents, their people, their animals and vegetation. No, the world was not called ghetto, he explained to his tiny listeners. The world was even bigger and more beautiful than Marysin. It was spread out beyond the barbed-wire fence, over fields, and forests, rivers and seas, islands and oceans. What were the rivers, the seas and the oceans like? How could there be forests where one might get lost, and where could there be such roads that one could walk and walk, ride and ride and yet not encounter any fences? And were there indeed animals which were not horses, or dogs or cats? Were there countries where the people were not called Jews, or Germans or Poles? And was there really a land where one could eat as much as one's heart desired? And was there a place where time was not cut up by evacuations and "actions"? All these questions the grandfatherly Professor Hager would try to answer to the best of his knowledge.

Some of the children, the older ones, had already heard these stories and remembered them as a dream. Now these stories seemed even more invented, more fantastic than before. But most of all, the children liked to hear "Grandfather" Hager promise them that perhaps in a month, or two, or three, the barbed-wire fence would be taken apart and they would all climb onto a cart and set out upon a road which runs on and on and is never blocked. The little hearts fluttered with excitement, saliva dripped from their open mouths. And when "Grandfather" Hager intertwined his stories with tales from history or about scientific achievements, the children found themselves on a magic carpet carrying them off between sky and earth, between time and space into a breathtaking infinity.

Often the lessons took place outdoors. The children sat on blankets on the ground, while the professor occupied an old armchair. He liked to have the children's heads at knee level, so that he could see each of their faces.

Miss Diamand also sat among the children. She too listened attentively to the stories. They seemed like a dream to her as well, and since she was convinced that the dream would never again become reality for her, she was even more moved by what she heard than the children. Her bird-like face turned towards the story-teller, she would squint her watery eyes while her hands, folded in her lap on top of the mauve dress, wound around each other, resembling the roots of a tree. It was as if she were absorbing a revitalizing elixir.

Although she was busy with the little ones, she did not fail to notice that her former "tormentors", the *gymnasium* graduates, had stopped visiting her, that they had at last forgotten her. She, however, was unable to forget them. Instead of being satisfied, she was worried. It was clear that they had taken an essential part of her with them, and to be cut off from them meant to be cut off from herself. Her students had been like plants growing out from her. She had to know what had happened to them, just like a root had to know what happened to the boughs which it had nurtured.

The ghetto was small, yet it was like a sea in which people and names drowned and were lost. Miss Diamand was barely able to recall her students' faces, let alone their names. However, one day she set out to "the other end of the world", the other, smaller part of the ghetto, in search of the "university", having provided herself with the exact address. Despite this, it still took her quite a while to discover the barn which was located deep inside one of the backyards. At first she thought that there was no one there. She walked further in, wiped her glasses and looked around. At length she noticed a table, a blackboard and a young man standing in front of it. He was guiding a piece of chalk over the blackboard, filling it with mathematical calculations. She came closer, and inquired, "Is this the . . . the university?"

The young man turned to her, bowing with both mockery and scorn, "Yes, this is the . . . the . . . And with whom do I have the honour?"

She came very close to him in order to see him better. He might be one of her former students, perhaps from before the war? One moment he seemed like a child to her, the next like a middle-aged man. It was pleasant to look at a hand with a piece of chalk between its fingers. "I am Dora Diamand. I taught at the *gymnasium*," she introduced herself.

The young man bowed even lower, "I'm very pleased to meet a colleague. My name is Reinstadt, Doctor of Physics and Chemistry. What can I do for you?"

Her lips trembled. "Where are the children?"

"What do you mean by 'children'?" he laughed in a squeaking voice. "You're probably thinking of the students, the scientists and the humanists. They're gone. They've betrayed mathematics, physics, chemistry, philosophy. They're studying applied medicine, specializing in diseases of the lungs, in dysentery and typhoid." He moved a chair towards her and seated himself on the table, playing with the chalk. "I've heard about you, Miss Diamand," he added. "They often mentioned you." She asked him for a drink of water and he brought it to her. The expression on his face was still haughty, disdainful. But she could not be fooled. She had a sad child before her. She sipped the water along with the tormented gaze of his wise eyes. "Everything has fallen apart." He spread out his hands towards the empty barn. "Three weeks already. Do you think it is because of the heat? Why weren't they afraid of the cold?"

"Perhaps you have a register with their addresses?" she asked.

He laughed, "You think that we had nothing better to do? Everything was improvised. Whoever wanted came in to listen."

"They will come back," she consoled him.

He threw the chalk into the air and caught it. "Out of the question!" he called out. "And that's how it ought to be. I come here myself because it's cool here. Let's not kid ourselves, Miss Diamand. It makes no sense. The young people understand that. Sometimes students grasp things better and quicker than their teachers. They made clear the madness of it to me. We are all about to kick the bucket . . . A brain full of knowledge and a brain without knowledge both rot just the same."

She could not bear to listen to him. "Please," she begged him. "You must not talk like that. You have a rich long life ahead of you. And as long as one lives there is a difference . . ."

"Is there? Of course. Long live science and progress! Long live the German people and their great mathematicians, their brilliant scientists! With what refinement and precision they have improved on the laws of the jungle! In the jungle one animal is still capable of hiding from the other. But no one can escape the Germans. They possess perfect technological traps, psychologically calculated down to the last detail." He threw the chalk into the air, smiling crookedly. "How do the people say? Science is a candle in man's hand. One uses it to illuminate the world, another uses it to burn it down."

She wanted to tell him something, but realized that there was no need. She was not worried about him. He was angry and bitter, sad and tormented, but he had been standing in front of a blackboard with a piece of chalk in his hand. She did not believe that he had come there because it was cool. If her heart winced with pain, it was on account of her students who were not there. She stood up, watched him play with the chalk, then said with a barely noticeable smile, "Don't drop the chalk."

She trotted through the half-empty street. The setting sun licked at the sidewalks with burning tongues and dried the tears on the old woman's face. Miss Diamand felt guilty towards her students, as if she had deserted them, and not they her. She was already close to the bridge when she recalled an address: the yard on Hockel Street.

Matilda Zuckerman was mixing dry grains of *Ersatz*-coffee and sugar in a little cup. Without interrupting her eating, she received Miss Diamand. "We keep on waiting for the new food ration," she said, the little spoon at her mouth. "In the meantime we stuff the stomach with what we can." The dry grains of *Ersatz*-coffee were cracking between her teeth. "You look quite well, Miss Diamand," she smiled, licking at the grains of sugar which had jumped out onto her lips. "Very kind of you to have come. Do you know that the bread rations have been reduced?" She pointed to the cup in her hand. "Coffee mixed with a bit of sugar fills you somewhat. But is there anything capable of replacing a piece of bread?" Miss Diamand asked her how Samuel was. Still chewing, she shook her head. "There is nothing to feed him that could put him back on his feet, and with this heat on top of it . . . But he goes to the Resort."

"And where is Bella?"

"On the balcony of course. She lives there."

Matilda was no longer fat. Her light sleeveless dress with its large décolleté revealed her loose flabby skin which looked like a yellowish drapery over a short skeleton. She led the teacher towards the girls' room. Some grains of coffee got stuck in her throat, she coughed, then said in a whisper, "She sits on the balcony from the time she comes home from work, till the time she goes to sleep." She bit her lips. "Everything has fallen apart, Miss Diamand . . . and I don't know how to put it together . . ." She raised the cup as if she were trying to hide her face behind it.

Bella was sitting on the balcony, her head leaning against the wall, her eyes shut. Her ugly face was twisted, the nose pointed, the corners of her mouth drooping, as if she were asleep. Miss Diamand touched her lightly on the shoulder and Bella's heavy eyelids slowly opened to reveal a dull gaze. "Miss Diamand?" she raised her eyebrows. "I haven't seen you for a long time." Her voice sounded raw and dry.

Miss Diamand bent down to her. "I have come to see how you are, child."

"Who sent for you, mother or father?"

"No one, Bella. Go and get me a chair. I want to sit with you for a while."

The girl stood up and stared at Miss Diamand with open enmity. "I have forgotten everything you taught me, and my good manners, too," she said with sarcasm, bringing out a chair from her room. Miss Diamand sat down, brushing away the fuzz of hair from her forehead. Bella towered over her. "Why are you so curious about me?" she asked.

Miss Diamand tried with all her strength to force a smile onto her wrinkled mouth. "I miss our conversations. Do you remember how you used to come running to see me?"

"I never went running to see you." Bella leaned against the balcony railing, and wound her hands around it. "Do you remember, Miss Diamand, that at the beginning of the ghetto you used to say that no one would be able to disguise himself here, that naked like Adam we would appear before one another? That's what is happening! You're seeing me naked now. Everything else that you taught me is a bluff . . . hollow pretty chatter! High philosophies! Art, beauty, love! Love? Who was the fool who invented that crazy word? And the word Life? What nonsense you used to chatter about life! The extraordinary interpretations you gave us! Poor Miss Diamand. The truth is that there is nothing to it — but a stomach with intestines. Food goes in one end, and out the other. Two openings and the movement between them is called life. Physiology is the only science which is not a hoax." She cast a sideways glance at the old woman, noticing that the latter had lowered her head and that her shoulders were slumped over her lap. "What did you come here for? What do you want of me?" she fumed.

The trembling gray head shook. "Child, it is not so . . ."

Bella sank down to the balcony floor, "Oh, no!" she called out. "You won't get me there again! You have wrapped my head in cobwebs and soft cottons long enough, my dear good Miss Professorka. You were the one who helped me make my bed of soft pillows and feathery eiderdowns. Do you think it doesn't hurt to be suddenly thrown out into the cold? But you have no reason to bewail me. You may even congratulate me. I am fine. Do you see that tree downstairs? It is my neighbour. We don't cheat one another. We don't talk hollow talk. We don't understand each other and that's that. It stands there, I sit here. It is alone. I am alone. Dead things, live things, everything is alone, apart, and if everything is like that, then one stops feeling . . . and that's how it ought to be."

"Your mother . . ." Miss Diamand whispered slowly, carefully. "She needs you . . ."

"Please, don't tell me about her!" Bella waved her hand violently. "Do you know what she needs me for? To unload her anger and bitterness. She needs a scapegoat, a victim. I thought that the time Father was at the *Kripo* had revived the mother within her, idiot that I was. How could it, if she never was a mother. The whole idealized concept of motherhood, Miss Diamand . . . it, too, is nothing but hollow bluff. All that exists is greed . . . a will to possess and to feed on others. Oh, poor Miss Diamand, when will you open your eyes and see things as they are?"

"Don't call me poor." Miss Diamand regained the normal sound of her voice. "It is you who have become poor. What you are saying is not true . . . not . . . not completely. It is only one face of the truth. What is crying out from you is the best proof that there is something more to life than just the mechanism, as you call it . . . the physiology. Why don't you ask your father . . . He must know more than the two of us."

Bella's face changed. Her forehead furrowed as if she were in pain. She spoke with a voice which also seemed changed, broken, "Because he is the most distant . . . That's why." She jumped to her feet. "Leave me alone, Miss Diamand!" she cried.

"Are you throwing me out?"

"Yes, I don't want to see you!"

Exhausted, lost, Miss Diamand trudged back over the bridge. She recalled that in the past when she had crossed the bridge, she had used to think of her friend, Wanda. Now she smiled at herself, Bella's smile. That childish ceremony on the bridge seemed silly to her. Her hazy gaze jumped towards the barbed wire. The wires were crossing out something, turning it to naught. She was like the stem and the roots of a tree. The wires were dull saws which had cut off the branches that were about to sprout from her. Where had all the juices that she had fed the shoots vanished? Her beloved student Bella was a dead bough. Was there any sense in searching for the others?

If it were so, then it meant that all was over; it meant that it was futile to devote oneself to the little ones. Miss Diamand felt that she was entering a dark tunnel: indifference. She lifted up her head and looked at her surroundings with new eyes. Everything was the same, and yet no longer the same.

The red brick church fell into the orbit of her gaze. What had happened to the church? It seemed to have lost its foundations, seemed to be asleep upon white clouds of eiderdown. The front door of the church was wide open and the white clouds swam in and out through it, raising a snow-like dust. She approached the church-yard; inside it stood a few horse carts. As she began to walk through the soft cloud of feathers, she noticed the blue statue of the weeping Virgin Mary, with her hands folded in prayer, sway forward from her niche in the wall. Some men hammered away at Mary's feet, until she fell down into their raised arms. Four of the men carried her away on their shoulders like on a coffin.

Hammers began to pound in Miss Diamand's head. What she was seeing was no hallucination. Flabbergasted, she walked further into the church. An unearthly coolness enveloped her. Her steps sank into the clouds of eiderdown. It was half-dark around her; only a pale light penetrated through the stained glass windows. Wherever the sun's rays touched the fuzz on the ground, they transformed it into a rainbow-coloured cloud. Swarms of women with white scarves on their heads were sweeping the clouds of down into the corners, piling them into heaps. Others were cutting open pillowcases of various sizes and releasing the "snow" into the air. They were exchanging shouts with one another, waving their hands as they stepped down through the fuzzy mountains. It seemed to Miss Diamand that they were about to soar into the air on invisible wings. One such "angel" covered with the "snow" appeared before Miss Diamand, "Who are you looking for, Grandma?" she asked.

The old woman blinked, "What happened here?"

"What do you mean what happened? Nothing happened. A new transport of Jewish bedding has arrived."

"From where?"

"It's better that we don't know."

"Here, into the church?"

The "angel" shook her head compassionately. The heat outside had probably gotten to the old woman's brains. "Where else should it have arrived, Grandma? This is the Feather-and-Down Resort. Here we cut open the pillows and eiderdown covers, we select them, clean them . . . prepare the bedding for the *Yekes*. Come on, I'll show you out." She led Miss Diamand through a mountain of down, past the carts outside, up to the gate. "Go in good health, Grandma!" she called out after her.

Miss Diamand tottered about in the heat of the street for a long time. Before her eyes was the image of the church full of feathers, full of bedding. Her student Bella had also been talking of bedding, of soft pillows, of fluffy covers. Bluff — Bella had said. The soft pillows in the church upon which she had noticed, although she did not want to admit it to herself, reddish-brown bloodstains, were not bluff. She entered her own backyard and saw the children. It was time to start the classes. She could not help herself. At the sight of the excited flock of bony youngsters, her indifference vanished. She had to start again, to believe again. The children, too, were not bluff.

The following day Miss Diamand did the last thing that she could do for her beloved student Bella. From under the pillow of her bed she drew out a fat deluxe volume, bound in leather, with gilt borders: the complete edition of Slowacki's poems; a book she and Wanda had once given themselves as a gift. Her greatest treasure. She took it to Bella. She met her on the balcony in the same position, half-awake, half-asleep, as the day before. Bella did not seem to be surprised or moved by the teacher's gesture. Indifferent, she listened to the old woman's mumbling, coolly observing the trembling hands which were handing her the book: "A gift for you, Bella . . ."

Bella shrugged her shoulders. "What do I need it for?" She pushed away the teacher, along with the book.

Miss Diamand, supporting her hip with one hand, bent down and placed the precious volume on the floor of the balcony. "Do with it whatever you wish."

✦ ✦ ✦

Miss Diamand slept very little at night. Three or four hours of sleep before dawn were enough for her. However, these were not like the sleepless nights of the year before; nights filled with a dream-like wish to become one with their darkness. Her present nights were wakeful, filled with a consciousness devoid of even a trace of dreaminess. She was fully aware of what was happening to her. All the roads that she had passed had been wrapped in a haze of half-dream, half-reality. She had been looking at everything through veils, from a distance, through a softening light. It was clear that she had wanted to wrap these veils around her students as well. Bella had been right when she spoke about soft pillows: the longing for beauty, the eternal search for goodness, for nobility, the wish to stride upon paths running not upon the real earth, but at least a head above it. She was at fault. And yet she knew that otherwise she could not have gone on, that otherwise she could not have been a teacher.

Now that the veils, torn and crumpled, had fallen off, and she was left with the severity of Bella's "naked truth", she knew that the abyss stood open, waiting for her. But just at the point of her imminent encounter with it, she lost the will to sink into it. (She had used to wrap death too in veils of beauty.) Suddenly she fell in love with existence, in the full awareness of its crudeness. It was good to be, to absorb the ugly splendour of life. Clinging to it like a spider whose web had been torn, she knew very well that soon she would spin new threads and weave them into veils, in order not to let her soul perish.

And she knew that the children in her backyard would be the ones who would sooner or later help her revive these old habits. They would help her to create a new music for herself, an inner atmosphere, which would offer her what she called a "style of being". Should she defend herself against it? Or should she tend to it? Neither was important. What was important was this present sleepless night which she was facing with her own senses. No one else felt the indifference of the resplendent sky, of the earthly fragrances, in the same manner as she did. The world, the way she perceived it, belonged to no one but her. And that was a powerful feeling. It gave her strength to accept the ghetto, such as she saw it. She heard the ghetto breathe in its sleep, heavily, filling the silence with its torment. How full of sound and motion a silence could be, she mused. Very often the silence was pierced by the razor-sharp wailing of a siren. An air-raid alarm. Sometimes it was followed by a distant roar of airplanes, at other times by a calm which tolled in her ears.

Miss Diamand thought about the birds of steel high up in the air. Her heart moved into the heart of the lonely pilot who roamed through the night sky. "What is he thinking about?" she asked hereelf. "What does he feel inside that armour of steel, as he soars above cities, over houses, over millions of beds where men, women and children are now asleep? What does he feel as he holds their fate in his hands? Does he not feel lonely up in that navy blue void? Does he not long for the corner on this earth to which his life is attached? Does he have a wife, a mistress, a mother, a child? What is the power which will make him press a button and allow him to drop the fiery rockets, the bombs, upon the roofs of other people's homes?" She did not wonder whether he was a German, a Russian, or an Englishman. He was one of her students, her son. She had taught him to read. He probably knew at least one poem by heart, at least one love song or lullaby which his mother had sung to him. Perhaps he no longer believed that from deep heights the eye of God was watching him. Yet there certainly was an eye within that pilot's soul, through which he was seeing himself. He had probably been nurtured by a civilization rooted in the commandment "Thou shall not kill", otherwise he would not be able to manipulate the mechanism of his steel bird. Then what was it that made him press the button — that student, that child who had once played in the lap of motherly kindness, who had once smiled a childish smile of innocence?

In Europe, in Asia and America, there were many teachers, many preachers and lofty sermonizers like herself, Miss Diamand thought. And these were her students, their students, who rose to the skies in these birds of steel, sowing death. Then what was she to offer the flock of children in her yard, in the ghetto? What was there to offer the new generation of German children and the children of other peoples? How could one make them grow with hands that would never be compelled to press the button and unleash the tools of destruction? How could they grow up and remain innocent? What was the seed one should sow in their hearts? Literature was not enough, poetry was not enough, music was not enough, religion was not enough. What then?

As she lay in her bed, struggling with such thoughts, the silence of the night was pierced by a sound which shook her more than the air raid sirens. Lately the children had been sleeping badly; possibly the heat or hunger, or bad dreams disturbed them. They tossed and turned on their beds which she could hear squeaking through the open window. The children often screamed in their sleep — a scream of frightened birds, an unfinished scream, which remained suspended upon needles of fear. Often a very small child would cry out with a cry that seemed to come from a deep forest. Or she heard sighs, or the word "Mama . . ." which brought a sail-boat sailing through the night to Miss Diamand's mind; a lost sail-boat, seeking the arms of a port to embrace it with tenderness and give it shelter.

Miss Diamand was afraid of the screams and cries of the sleeping children. She would climb down from her bed and in her bare feet totter down to their bedroom. She would walk from one bed to the other, unable to guess from whose mouth the sounds had come. Once back in her own bed, she herself would feel compelled to release a scream of helplessness. She would shake with cold in the heat of the night. An incomprehensible nagging anxiety was eating away at her heart; a fright, never before experienced. It made her feel estranged from her own self. It cancelled out her reason and turned in circles through morbid labyrinths of premonition.

During the last days of July, Clara, the Presess' wife, often visited Miss Diamand. She would arrive very early in the morning, practically at dawn, so that the neighbours would not notice her. Dressed up in a summer hat and white gloves, she smelled of soap and perfume. Her high-heeled shoes looked new; they shone and squeaked unpleasantly. She arrived loaded with packages: with bread, sausage, cheese and marmalade for the children. She did not stay long. She and Miss Diamand no longer had a common language. They would exchange practical remarks regarding the children's well-being.

One morning Clara suddenly said, "An order for a thousand cribs has arrived at the Carpentry Resort, and an order for seven hundred children's shoes at the Shoe Resort. That could mean that those who were sent out of the ghetto are being well cared for."

"And perhaps these things are meant for German or Polish children?" Miss Diamand said, thinking of the bedding that she had seen in the Church. What would the Jewish children cover themselves with in the new beds? Then she added, "A woman in our backyard works at the Old Clothes Resort. They are sorting blood-stained clothing which arrives by wagonloads into the ghetto."

Clara looked aside, to avoid Miss Diamand's open gaze. "It is not certain that these are the clothes of the Jews of Lodz . . . Perhaps they belonged to the people from the provinces . . ."

Miss Diamand asked strange questions. Whenever Clara came, Miss Diamand led her back to the same topic. The kind and dreamy Miss Diamand had become a brutal tormentor. It was clear to both of them that she was overcome by a revulsion for Clara. She feared Clara's visits, her smell and the squeaking of her new shoes. Miss Diamand wanted to lock her door or leave the house for the whole day. But she did not do it. There was no escape from the questions or from Clara's answers. Clara was a messenger who, loaded with gifts, arrived to deliver ugly tidings. Miss Diamand's nights became increasingly brighter. They dawned with foreboding. They grayed with the lights of judgment.

One day Clara arrived with a box of toys for the children: dolls, trumpets, animals made of rags, little dogs, bears, kittens. They had been brought into the ghetto from somewhere, to be cleaned and fixed — and Clara had taken a box of them for Miss Diamand's children. When Miss Diamand saw the display of toys, and her dry hands began to pat them, to hold them close to her nose, to her eyes, Clara turned to the window and stared out into the yard. The old woman glared at the rag dolls and animals so long, that her eyes became blurred. She smelled, she saw the gruesome tale which the toys were telling her. She asked Clara to take everything back. Her children, even the smallest, did not play anymore, she said.

The elegant Clara wept. "The Presess of the Warsaw Ghetto has committed suicide," she said in a sombre whisper. "He was asked to deliver seventy-thousand Jews to them . . . Now the Germans are doing the job by themselves." She wiped her face with her white glove. "It won't come to that here. We are useful . . ."

From that day on their roles reversed; Clara let herself go, torturing the old woman with the "most confidential" information which she could apparently not digest on her own. Every day she had a new story to tell about killings, sharing with her former teacher the poison which was eating at her. She no longer cried. Her eyes were filled with madness. She also told her dreams to Miss Diamand. "I dreamt that I was a piece of coal; the entire ghetto was a heap of coals. I was at its very top and I was black and heavy, pushing the coals beneath me into the fire . . ." She finished as usual, "Nothing will happen to us . . . We are useful. And I've heard that Germany has been bombarded . . . Hamburg . . . Bremen . . . levelled to the ground."

Miss Diamand tried to chase the image of Clara out of her memory. She occupied herself with the school, immersed herself in petty daily chores and sat in on Professor Hager's lessons in the yard. She spent a lot of time with the little ones, chatting with them and listening to their stories. She was full of energy and cheer, joking with her colleagues and the children. Indeed, she had acquired a sense of humour.

Chapter Eight

BLESSED RAINS POURED down from the skies, reviving the exhausted soil. They also did some good to the people. The children sprouted like young blades of grass. Barefoot, half-naked, they filled the air with their laughter and shouts of delight; young girls put out pots and basins in which to catch rainwater to wash their hair. During these days the price of yeast came down on the black market and it was easier to get it at the yeast co-operatives. Apart from that, a new ration of potatoes came out and there was something to put into the pot. And when people's stomachs are more or less satisfied, their imaginations begin to flourish, their hopes start to fly in all directions. That August they flew off in the direction of the distant Caucasus which would soon become the chopping block upon which the head of the German hydra would be chopped off. Or they flew to the Western Fronts, urging the soldiers to hurry and bring salvation. It seemed as if the rains and the new ration of potatoes were a message from the world: "Keep it up, brothers. It will not be long before we come to save you!" A conference was taking place in Moscow where Churchill sojourned for ten days and where the participants divided the post-war world among themselves.

Who, on days like these, thought to pay attention to Herr Sutter's words, "If the twelfth hour tolls for us Germans, you Jews will not survive the eleventh!" People laughed. Nineteen forty-two was the year of liberation. The stones in the streets were talking about it. Even the people swollen with hunger, dried out with dysentery, burning with tubercular fever, even those on their death-beds were confident that they had enough strength to save themselves. Intoxicated by the spirit of renewal, people abandoned themselves to their dreams of life after the war. Now they would know, they mused, how to enjoy it, and how to change the world.

Shalom shared the good tidings with his mother, delighted by the awareness that he was practically putting a new heart into her withered body.

"If fate wills it," Sheyne Pessele looked at her bony son of whom "there was nothing left", as she put it, "and we reach the blessed hour, I will take a whole loaf of bread, a round one, well-baked, such as only Uncle Henech was capable of baking. I'll put a knife into your hand and say, 'Eat as much as your heart desires!'"

Shalom teased her, "You are worse than Boncie Schweig, Mother. He at least wanted a white roll with butter."

"You're stupid." She wagged her head. "Why do I say that? Because the worst thing for me is to fight with you over a piece of bread. If you only took care not to eat up the whole ration in one day! You're shrugging your shoulders. Of course, how can you understand a mother's heart?"

"After the war," said Shalom, "we shall eat such food in the middle of the week, that we never dreamed about even on the Sabbath. We'll eat baked, fried, stewed dishes . . . and pastries of all sorts, and chocolates. We will drink strong tea with lemon, with half a glass of sugar in it." In order to make her laugh, he reminded her, "Do you remember the perfumed tea that I brought home from Sutter?" However, his words caused Itche Mayer's shadow to pass through both their minds; grief linked the gazes of mother and son. Itche Mayer had not lived to see that wonderful hour. Shalom was anxious to bring back the hopeful mood. "We might perhaps get some chickens or ducks of our own. Perhaps a cow? Fresh milk, eggs, butter . . ."

Sheyne Pessele shook her head. "Look at the greedy eyes that fellow has got! You think that you could devour wagon-loads of food, don't you? Believe me, you won't be such a glutton. How much do you think a person can eat? The rich never have food on their minds, believe me, because they have enough to eat."

"May I live to see the moment when I will not have food on my mind."

"About that, you see, you are right . . . I mean about the chickens, ducks, a cow . . ." she smiled shyly, wistfully. "Do you think I would mind buying myself a little orchard somewhere, with good trees: pears, apples, cherries, plums, a few raspberry bushes . . . some strawberries. I wouldn't mind having a plot of land, not a pitiful *dzialka*, but a real patch of field . . . with cabbages and cucumbers, with potatoes and onions; nice, fresh, straight from the soil. My, what a different kind of life that would be! Because, to tell the truth, I never did get used to the city. In the city people are more dead than alive. In the city I became old and cold. If you live between stones and bricks instead of trees and fields, you yourself become like a stone, and you become evil too. The world is crazy, I'm telling you. People shut themselves up in cages, through their own free will. I mean, even when we were free. How can you be free in a city? One person steps on the other's corns, one stares inside the other's pot, one eats up the other with his envy. Man was not created for that, believe me. Man was created to live in the country. His character is better there, and he is freer. According to my stupid reasoning, towns are the beginning of all the evil in this world. Who makes wars? The country men? No. The city men. Where is there theft and robbery? Where does one chase after luxury and cheap pleasures? Where does one slave away one's life in factories? Only in the city. I won't say that country life is paradise. Of course you have to labour. But that kind of labour is healthy . . . And, Shalom, a plot of land makes men more honest, you hear?"

Shalom did not agree with her, "Well, I always envied you. You spent your childhood in an orchard, while I grew up rotting away in a cellar. But there is such a thing as progress. You can learn about it from history. First, man was a wanderer, then he settled down, creating settlements, then villages, then towns, big towns, huge cities. Civilization demands that, and civilization never goes backwards, always forwards. One fine day, a few hundred years from now, the whole world will be one huge city."

"I'm glad I won't live to see that." Sheyne Pessele tossed back her gray head. "Who needs 'cibilization', I'm asking you? We need it like a hole in the head. What has man become thanks to it? Has he stopped being a fool? What has it given him? A soft pillow under his behind? A train instead of a horse and buggy? An automobile? Is man so sick that he cannot use his own feet? Machines should work for him? And what does he have two hands for? And if the machine does work for him, and if he does have a soft pillow under his behind, and if he rides in a train and has a water closet, is he really better off? Is he happier for that? He is only lazier and has more time to worry and to cook up schemes of how to do in his neighbour, how to swindle and rob, how to improve his firearms and to kill."

"Mother, you don't understand," Shalom interrupted her. "All that is on account of the capitalistic order. In a socialistic world, civilization would be at the service of man. I wish it upon myself to have all these great comforts. I wish it upon myself to be able to fly in an airplane and see other countries . . . see how people live . . ."

"Eh, let me be," she would not be swayed. "Big thing! Other countries, other shmountries! In one place it's a bit warmer, in the other a bit colder; here flows a river, there stands a mountain. What's so important? You should know, Shalom, that if you know one person well, you know all of humanity; and if you know one plot of land well, you know the whole world. You can see for youself that the more people travel, the more they hate one another. Do you know why? Because men really were created to live with one another, but when? When there is a plot of land and a little fence between one and the other. A little fence protects people from each other, and the plot of land unites them and teaches them to help each other when needed. That's what it is. People were not created to live in herds like cattle. You can do a lot for the other person only from a little distance. Then you like the other person better too. I mean your socialism. Everyone puts into it whatever he wants. If they would let me give advice to the world, I would introduce my kind of socialism: for every man a piece of land with a fence, and a little gate to go in and out."

Shalom was taken aback by her words. He had thought his mother to be a convinced socialist and Bundist. "Socialism seeks to remove all fences and borders, Mother, and here you come, ready to put up new ones? That's the kind of socialist that you have become? What you are preaching is egoism, not socialism. We want the love of humanity to rise up after this war, do you understand?"

She did not take his reproaches to heart. "Love of humanity, shmove of humanity! One could choke on such words nowadays. We have already seen the kind of love which you are preaching. One person may smother the other with love until he chokes. Man, you should know, can do a lot of good and he can be a wild beast, and because of both things there has to be a little fence between one man and the other."

"What are you harping on that fence business for, Mother? Here you have a fence around the ghetto! Do you enjoy it?"

"That is a barbed-wire trap, not a fence. It has no gate. The gate is important."

They both smiled. Shalom shook his head, "With every passing day you become a greater philosopher, Mother. Your thoughts are so deep that it's impossible to get to them." She replied with an affectionate look. They had never been as close to one another as now.

✦   ✦   ✦

Sheyne Pessele had swollen legs. The swelling started in her toes, and climbed her feet and legs up to her thighs. But she remained active. She called her legs, "my pumpkins", and discussed them as if they were two separate creatures. She cursed them angrily and when they bothered her too much, she scolded them. For the time being she was still the master of her body, not they. And she would order them around like a good general trying to muster his *schlemiel* aides-de-camp.

Her legs daily carried her to work at the Old Clothes Resort, over the bridge, and back. They carried her to the food lines, and to visit her married sons and the grandchildren. They carried her up and down the stairs to her neighbours and to the orphans in the yard for whom she was caring and who called her Grandma Sheyne Pessele. The adults had also begun to call her by that name, swarming around her just like the children. She would give them all kinds of medical advice, along with remedies of her own invention. She practised her methods on them, helping them throw off a bad mood, or overcome an attack of anxiety or depression.

The 'King' of the backyard, the former underworldnik Moshe Grabiaz, had the greatest respect for Sheyne Pessele. As soon as he saw her in the yard, he would call out to the crowd, "Move away, everybody! Let a person pass!" After which he would take her under his personal protection, report on the condition of his sick wife to her and ask her for advice.

His little daughter Masha, who followed him around like a shadow, parroting the adults with her chatter and mannerisms, would wrap herself in the loose folds of Sheyne Pessele's skirt and looking up at her with a pair of sharp eyes, would beg, "Give me a tickle, Grandma Sheyne Pessele."

Sheyne Pessele was called upon to straighten out the quarrels at the water pump or on the *dzialkas*. She mixed in everywhere, except in the quarrels between husbands and wives. "No one ought to put herself between husband and wife," she would say, wiping her mouth. She was seen most often at the cherry tree. Although the tree was now officially the property of the Community Board, she could not be indifferent to it. Even the community guardian who watched the tree considered her to be the tree's "mother". He complained to her, "You see, Grandma Sheyne Pessele, there is no cherry harvest this year. The cherries are falling before they ripen. The rains have come too late." Her heart ached at the sight of the tree. It was dying. Swarms of worms were eating away at it.

In the mornings, on her way to work, Sheyne Pessele had a companion. Reisel, the Zuckerman's former cook. To be truthful, the two women could not bear the sight of each other. Reisel's "'ristocratic" past was alluded to in every word she uttered, and "In my house, one conducted oneself . . ." was her stock introductory phrase. Sheyne Pessele could not stomach it. Reisel, on the other hand, could not bear the important role that this simple-minded carpenter woman was playing in the yard, nor the respect that people had for her, and she, Reisel, was of the opinion that the neighbours would be much wiser to take her, a "woman of the world", into their confidence. But she and Sheyne Pessele worked together at the Old Clothes Resort, and it was easier to walk if one could lean on someone else's arm. Reisel, too, was barely capable of walking on her feet lately. So they marched arm in arm. One woman's legs thin as sticks, the other's thick as pumpkins.

The Old Clothes Resort was located in a yard from which all the inhabitants had been recently evacuated. No renovations were needed to install that kind of a Resort. One had only to empty the rooms of furniture, put in tables where there were none, place some benches around them, and the Resort was ready. Mostly elderly women worked there. The work was not difficult and no qualifications were needed. What woman was ever ignorant about the quality of a piece of material? Or of how to pick out the woollens from the cheaper stuff? All they had to do was to sort the clothes according to their quality and their condition. Some clothes were blood-stained and dirty; others were brand-new. The air in the rooms was permeated by a strange smell and it took a long time to get used to it.

There was no strict discipline at the Resort. German commissions never came to visit, nor did the Presess or his people. The women did their job without hurry, yet they worked well, with precision. There was no need to watch them, because they themselves wanted to have their hands busy, so that the time would pass quickly. Moreover, if they sat idly, their thoughts were liable to play tricks on them. More than once, while looking at a garment, they would see the person who had worn it. Each garment had a personality of its own; it revealed its age, its own characteristics and especially with the children's clothing — its charm. It was better to crumple the clothes and pile them into heaps, so they would look less human. And yet, in spite of everything, the women knew that the bodies missing from the garments had belonged to the Jews from the provinces, not, heaven forbid, from Lodz, not, heaven forbid, from last winter's evacuation. Even so, it was quite spooky to work there.

The best method of making time pass was, of course, to set the tongue in motion. The women did not shut their mouths for a moment, grinding away the hours with their chatter like coffee-grinders, from morning until lunch. During the second part of the day, an additional preoccupation was added: the preparation of clothing for themselves, to take home. They helped each other wrap the garments around their bodies. The search at the exit was usually superficial. The manager, the only man in the Resort, a fragile sickly little fellow, looked "through his fingers".

Sometimes it happened that, as they busily were looking for clothes to take home, the women would find in a pocket a letter with a familiar signature, or a photograph of a familiar face. It was in this manner that Sheyne Pessele discovered Valentino's pullover. She recognized it immediately, for he had always worn it, and it had a peculiar faded mauve colour. There was simply no other pullover of that kind in the whole world. Another time, in a breast pocket, she found a button with the picture of the Bundist leader Beinish Michalevitch, the kind of button which her husband and sons used to wear. And one day a worker found the photo of Blind Henech in the pocket of a woman's jacket. Sheyne Pessele grabbed the picture and quickly hid it in her brassière along with the two baby shirts which she had prepared to smuggle out for her grandchildren. At home, she hid the photo in a cupboard, telling no one. She knew something which her children were not to know, which the ghetto was not to know.

At the Resort, Sheyne Pessele was no bigshot; her mind was not on her work, but on Itche Mayer, her husband. Nowhere else did she see him as vividly as she did here. He said important yet strange things to her. She saw him raise his clenched fist. "Sheyne Pessele," he would say. "Why do you keep the truth from the children? Why don't you alarm the ghetto? What risk is there still to take? We are doomed, Sheyne Pessele. The Resorts won't help. Rumkowski won't help. All the Jews will go sooner or later. So, if that is the case, we must fight, my wife . . ."

She quarrelled with him. He had always been a hothead. How could he say that her sons would go? So what if they were skinny? They had a healthy foundation. They would survive. "You are no Solomon, Itche Mayer," she told him. "Take a look at the people. Some fighters they are! The ghetto is barely breathing. The greatest fight they are capable of is to climb a few stairs. And on the other hand, Itche Mayer, why don't you realize that if we throw ourselves at the Germans, we are lost good and proper. What do you want us to do, cut up the barbed wires? Escape? Whereto?"

Itche Mayer raised his fist at her, "Arms, Sheyne Pessele! The ghetto must provide itself with arms!"

She asked him, "Are you out of your mind, or just *meshuga*? How would you get arms into the ghetto? Through the sky? Don't you remember that all the houses surrounding the ghetto are gone, that no one can get out from here alive? Not enough gallows have been put up in the bazaar? And if we did manage to get out, would not the Poles deliver us into the Germans' hands, without blinking an eye?"

"But Sheyne Pessele," Itche Mayer argued with her, "If there really is no way out, and if we must all perish, the Jews of Lodz should fall while standing upright . . . We, the Jewish proletarians of Lodz, have beautiful traditions. Only we should not feel degraded, Sheyne Pessele, . . . not on our knees . . ."

"Traditions-shmaditions," she copied him, her heart aching. "Who is on his knees, tell me? Our legs are swollen, true enough, but we stand upright. And we want to live, not to perish. Yes, my husband, we have to be patient and to struggle on, so that at least some might be saved . . . perhaps our children . . . our grandchildren . . . perhaps even I, myself? Itche Mayer, forgive me, but I want to live too, I want to survive. We did not sacrifice you, but you are a sacrifice. And those who left with the evacuation, are also a sacrifice. Then let it be at least for something." Thus she debated with him in her mind, unaware of what her hands were doing in the meantime.

When she returned home, she washed the blood off the baby clothes which she had smuggled out and distributed them among the orphans, or offered them to her grandchildren. She felt as if she had returned from the Other World. She forgot about Itche Mayer and the Resort. She was too busy.

At night, on her bed, she would quarrel with her two "pumpkins" and pat her belly where the swelling had climbed. That too she kept secret. In her sleep, Itche Mayer would return to continue their discussion. She would tell him only the good news, the tidings from the battle fronts, giving him the mixed-up names of localities which she invented in her sleep. She gnashed her teeth and clenched her fists like Itche Mayer. "You know that I am stubborn, don't you, Itche Mayer?" she asked him. He knew it, but he was stubborn too, and they would not give in to one another.

During the day, when she talked with Shalom, she had the feeling that Itche Mayer was talking through her mouth, "Why don't we pull ourselves together and do something?"

"What do you want to do?" Shalom failed to understand.

"Fight!"

The word "fight" on the loose lips of his swollen mother sounded both funny and wild. Shalom laughed, "My, my! You've become quite a hotshot, I can see. It wasn't for nothing that Father used to say that you should have been a general."

In his heart of hearts Shalom thought that lately his mother had begun to talk in an odd way. He did not know whether he should worry that she was going out of her mind, or whether indeed she knew the secret story about the letter which had reached the party from the *Rav* of Grabow. Shalom himself sometimes doubted whether his thoughts were normal, in particular during the heat wave, when the streets were empty. Was he not sometimes under the impression that those who had been sent away had come back, that they were walking along the heated sidewalks? Only the long-awaited rains had washed away that illusion, chasing off the ghosts. The news arriving from the fronts was good. "We will be liberated in 1942!" was the party's prophetic slogan. "Endure and Survive!" was the other slogan. But it became hot again and the good news petered out. The potato ration had been eaten up and there were no more potatoes coming in. Instead of succumbing to despair, the ghetto seemed to have gone insane, as if the sun had struck everyone in the head.

The letter from the *Rav* of Grabow had been brought by one of the newcomers from the provinces. Israel had read it at a joint meeting of the Party and youth boards and Shalom knew it by heart:

> "My dear ones, to our sorrow, we know everything now. Today a witness arrived back from the hellish place. It is in the village of Chelmno, near Dombia. Everyone has been buried in the forest called Lubov. The gipsies from Lodz were also brought there. They were all destroyed by gas poisoning or by firearms. One's heart turns to stone, the eyes dry out. Do not think that a madman is writing this to you. This is the hard, cruel truth. Tear off your clothes, Man, wallow in the dust, run through the streets wailing, or laugh like a madman. Yet perhaps the Almighty will still see to it that a remainder will be saved. Help us, God our Creator! Write whether all this is known to your community."

Shalom recalled the scene, when the letter had been read. They were all sitting in the sultry bedroom, like wax figures. Israel himself remained stooped, shrunken, his forehead wrinkled. He was biting his underlip, his gaze turned inward. The *Rav* of Grabow was out of his mind. "Don't think that a madman is writing this to you," he had said in the letter. No madman believed his own madness. There was not a word of truth in the letter. Shalom was surprised that the comrades refused to understand that. Comrade Bracha Koplowicz sat doubled up, motionless, continuously repeating the name of her eight-year-old daughter. Who would dare to do something to her child? The safest of all were the children. Nothing else but that the most reasonable people had gone out of their minds. At length, Israel declared that the letter must be given to the Presess, so that he could not pretend ignorance. The Zionists also had a copy of the letter and they too delivered it to the Presess. The Presess let them know that he had been aware of the facts mentioned in the letter for a long time.

The ghetto was full of lunatics. In the Resorts people stood at their machines, bewildered, the tools falling from their hands. "Children up to ten years of age . . ." the rumours buzzed in their heads. Then came another rumour: "Also the old people . . ." Who was considered an old person? Those over sixty? And how about those who were exactly sixty, like Sheyne Pessele, for instance?

In the evenings Shalom sat with his mother. She had become talkative lately. As soon as they were together, she began to ventilate her weird thoughts, her "philosophies". He joked with her, contradicted her and waited for her to say some more. He felt her tenderness for him through her words, her care, her fears. He was attached to her. He was the most devoted of her sons. He was her baby. He was deeply convinced that wherever she went, he would follow. He would protect her. He was a man and he would defend the only real kind of devotion that exists in this world.

The mad confusion lasted a few days. Shalom was right. It had been the result of the blown-up imagination of sick minds. What nonsense they were capable of inventing! Another day, and then another passed. The ghetto had digested the nightmare. There had never been a *Rav* of Grabow in this world and all the "ducks hatched in people's minds" about the ghetto itself had also been "sucked out of their fingers". People went back to discussing the food rations again. Potatoes were supposed to arrive after all, perhaps not in August, but surely during the first days in September. Wagonloads of food were waiting to be transported into the ghetto, and each passing night brought one closer to the moment when potatoes would inundate the co-operatives.

Shalom hated the youth meetings, yet he could not bring himself to miss them. Simon, the youth leader, would force the news items and the reports from the clandestine radio station SWIT through his lips. The Germans had begun to thoroughly annihilate European Jewry, starting with the Polish Jews. Simon was a tall fellow who worked at the Metal Resort and his sinewy hands seemed powerful. He was obstinate and stingy with words. His speeches were to the point, dry, every word came out hard, undisputable. Shalom, however, had his doubts as to their truthfulness. Who knew, perhaps the radio station SWIT was German? Perhaps they wanted to break the spirit of the Jews in that manner? It was Shalom who would finally start the singing. They sang their favourite songs, sentimental songs, fighting songs. On the way home, Simon pounded at his chest with his fist, "They will never take me alive!"

"Nor me!" the others followed suit. It sounded like hollow boasting, a children's game. These were words that never demanded any backing.

Israel remained more distant than ever, also more serious and silent. Once in a while he had supper with Sheyne Pessele and Shalom, but he seemed to listen to them only with one ear. Shalom could not forgive him his behaviour, and he was no longer ashamed of his resentment. Israel did indeed have important problems to solve, but how could he so abandon his nearest ones? It seemed to Shalom that it was more difficult to bear the responsibility for one mother than for an entire ghetto. Once, when Israel had left, Shalom ran after him, bombarding him with questions.

"So, between you and me, what's cooking, Israel?" He tried with all his strength to keep his reproaches at bay.

"There is not one single piece of firearm in the ghetto. All efforts to get some have failed," Israel replied.

"Is the 'duck' about the evacuation of all those over sixty really nothing but a 'duck'?"

Israel ignored the question. "Apart from that there is the problem of collective responsibility. One reckless step and we'll vanish without a trace. And moreover, the atmosphere in the ghetto does not favour drastic action . . . Everyone has a mother, a father or a child. This paralyses us."

"The whole thing could be nothing but a lie . . ." Shalom tried to strike a hopeful tone.

"Czerniakow of Warsaw did not commit suicide because of a lie." Israel was cruel.

"But Lodz is not Warsaw. Lodz is a working camp. Mother works in a Resort. She is useful."

"We will have to re-register her and change her age to fifty. She looks good."

"Yeah. The swelling makes her look good. Israel, if it happens . . . what should we do?"

"Hide out."

"That's all that the board has decided?"

"We settle whomever we can in the Resorts, even the children under ten. We change their birth certificates." He gave Shalom a pat on the shoulder, "Chin up . . ."

At night, before he fell asleep, Shalom would concoct clever plans of how to free the inhabitants of the ghetto. To kill the few guards at the barbed wires seemed easy. After all, there were no more than ten to fifteen of them. Shalom saw himself and his comrades along with the mass of the Jews running through all the streets of the ghetto — towards freedom. He held his mother by the hand, pulling her along and not letting go of her even for a moment. She was raising her clenched fist just like everyone else. And in front of them ran Simon, the tall stubborn leader of the youth movement. "They'll never take me alive!" he pounded his chest. Simon resembled Israel. He was Israel, while Israel was Itche Mayer and Itche Mayer was he, Shalom. They were all leading the ghetto towards freedom.

✦ ✦ ✦

Unexpectedly, it happened that Shalom forgot about all his worries and fears. Suddenly he came to himself. He had enough to eat — such an unheard-of miracle that all the pessimistic thoughts left him. It served him as still another proof that all would end well.

It all began with the new commissar who had taken over the Resort after Zuckerman. Physically the new commissar was awe-inspiring. His name was Gurny and at the beginning of the ghetto he had worked for the *Kripo*. Apparently he had not been overly pleased with his activities there, and as soon as the opportunity of getting a new position presented itself, he used his "protection", which was of the best kind possible, to get what he wanted. He was a handsome fellow, tall, blond, and healthy; he looked like a boxer. He had a pair of sharp shrewd eyes. But most awesome was his walk. He stepped with the entire heels of his boots as if he were crushing worms with every step. And he also supported the Presess' view that "If you don't treat them with sticks, they'll listen to you like to a wall of bricks." He did not actually carry a stick with him, but his rule was to slap, like Zuckerman had done, and he liked to deal out kicks to the left and right. The kicks he applied freely and frequently, while the slaps he left for more serious occasions. The workers joked that Gurny was building a boot-factory on everyone's behind. Gurny could also deal out blows with a board, or with a pair of pliers, or with whatever came into his hands. He was not discriminating.

The workers both feared and liked him. He never went any further than the blows. He never sent anyone to the *Kripo* where he still felt at home, nor did he punish a worker by putting him on the lists for deportation. He never called in the police and never let anyone be arrested. The workers were grateful to him for his humanity and they praised him to the skies. They exchanged notes about his intelligence, extolling his perfect German and repeating the fact that his father, who had been a jeweller before the war, had been very proud of his son, the genius.

Since the strange rumours had started to circulate and it was impossible to concentrate on one's work, Shalom's days had begun to drag like lead. Finally, he decided to occupy his mind with something. He secretly began to make combs, powder cases, cigarette cases and pocketbooks out of wood, and he even carved elegant clog-like shoes for women. He smuggled them out from the Resort and, as a joke, began to peddle them among the daughters of the ghettocracy, and among the office girls. The items that he produced were attractive. He had carved them with the girls in mind, imagining himself to be their lover and his feelings seemed to be reflected in his work. In time, other workers became interested in Shalom's activities and began to do the same. They helped each other, keeping an eye out for the supervisors. It was pleasant to carry something out from the Resort which counteracted the production of boxes for ammunition, while at the same time bringing in some money.

Only on the top floor of the Resort was furniture still being manufactured. The products of "The Affair Department", as the workers called it, went to Herr Biebow and his friends, and only the most privileged workers were assigned to work there. Shalom was not one of them. He had bad luck with Gurny who had nicknamed him "Comrade from the Movement".

It was a hot afternoon. Shalom sat at his workplace carving a little powder box. Things were not going well. His hands were perspiring and the piece of wood kept slipping out from his fingers. Black circles spun before his eyes, as if he were about to faint. He had to shut his eyes and wait for it to pass, but then he could not open them again. The little box fell from his hand. He heard a noise. With all his strength he tore his eyes open and saw Gurny standing before him.

Gurny was hot too. His shirt was unbuttoned, his face red, his eyes blurred. Sweat was streaming down his cheeks. He weighed Shalom's little box in his palm. "You are a good carver, Comrade from the Movement," he said quietly, wiping the sweat from his face. But then he jumped up and rushed through the hall, throwing the wood about as he searched the hall. "Sabotage!" he roared, setting in motion both his boots and his hands, as he attacked the workers. Here and there he dug out hidden "little things". Shalom was indifferent. The hall and Gurny were turning in front of his eyes. He calmly waited for his share of kicks, but Gurny did not come back to him.

The following day, a notice appeared on the door of the hall, informing the workers of their punishment: the daily soups would be cancelled for two weeks. The workers held a meeting. A protest strike was suggested. Gurny could do anything but deprive them of soup, because without soup they were lost. But, the majority of the strikers was against the strike which would only enrage Gurny more. It was proposed that a delegation be sent to Gurny with a plea for indulgence. Shalom and his brother Mottle were indignant. They were not beggars. This aggravated the other workers. "It's all your fault!" they threw themselves at Shalom. "We are all suffering because of you!" Shalom shook his head, embittered. These were his working comrades! More than half of them were greenhorns, newcomers to the trade. Of the former workers some were dead and some had left with the evacuations. Those who remained were *schlemiels*, *klepsidras*, afraid of their own shadows.

The meeting resolved to send a delegation of one person, and to Shalom's astonishment the choice fell on him. "Not on your life!" He shook his head, seeing black circles before his eyes; he could barely stand on his feet. "I won't ask him for anything," he declared. "I can only make it worse and then you'll reproach me again."

The workers insisted, "If someone else goes, he'll get a licking. You he spares. Didn't you notice that he did not even touch you?"

That had indeed been strange. Shalom realized that with all his enmity, Gurny had actually never beaten him up. Consequently, Shalom gave in and went to see the commissar. He entered Gurny's office and began his plea with a trace of fear in his heart, "I've come as a delegate from my hall, about the punishment."

Gurny jumped. He locked the door as if he had trapped a bird in a cage. But to Shalom's amazement, Gurny's face was neither severe nor angry. His forehead was red and perspiring. He seemed exhausted and shorter than usual. His voice also had a different ring. It was deeper, heavier than ever. "We were lucky with the fire," he said. "But the *Yekes* are keeping an eye on us. Anyway they suspect us of sabotage and I am responsible for everything. And what will happen if they put up the entire Resort for evacuation?"

Gurny now had a human face and Shalom, standing in front of him, on the verge of fainting, felt inwardly more comfortable. "At what did you catch me redhanded, Mr. Gurny?" He spoke as if Gurny were not the great commissar but a neighbour from the yard. "A tiny bit of wood refuse, that's all that goes into making such powder boxes. You call that stealing and sabotage?"

"Of course it is sabotage. Is ours a Resort of powder boxes? And what would have happened if a commission had suddenly come in?" Gurny asked.

Shalom pretended not to hear the question. "Why don't you punish those who take out wagonloads of wood?" he went on. "What do you think we buy with the money earned for all these toys? Potatoes? No. A bit of coffee refuse to stuff our stomachs with. And how many true carpenters are still alive in the ghetto? Soon you'll have no one to fiddle with, Mr. Gurny, I'm warning you. And where will you yourself be without us?"

Shalom knew that he was overdoing it, but to his surprise, Gurny was not angry. Instead, he justified himself. "Believe me, I'm not such a dog as you all think. Don't I want the same as all of you? Do you think that I am practising politics for the Germans in the Resort. That I am anxious to produce boxes for German bombs? I want to survive the war just like you, and therefore . . ." He bent over to Shalom, "I'd like to meet with your brother." A light went on in Shalom's head. His head began to spin even faster, but at the same time he was gay and he grinned as Gurny went on in a whisper, "I know what you will say about me after the war. But it won't be true. You must understand my situation. I am not a party man, but don't think that my stand is so different from yours. My brother who lives in Paris is an important Bundist. And have you ever seen me deliver anyone to the *Kripo* or the police?"

Shalom straightened up, feeling a head taller than the tall Gurny. What power the Bund had! How good it was to belong to it! How strong and proud this made him feel! And because of his enthusiasm, of his tension and excitement, his legs began to give under him, as if he were about to swoon. Afraid that soon he would not be able to bring out another word, he spat out quickly, "Cancel the punishment, Mr. Gurny."

Gurny shook his head, "I must show that I am the boss. But I am ready for a compromise: one week without soup!"

Gurny's head along with the entire room swam in front of Shalom's eyes, but he was still able to talk, "Remember, Mr. Gurny, the war is coming to an end."

"I'll go even further with you, Comrade from the Movement," Gurny said congenially. "I'll give you only four days."

"Not even one!" Shalom was no longer able to see the commissar's face.

The commissar's words sounded as if they were issuing from distant chambers. "Very well! I'm doing it for the movement . . . And tell your brother that I want to talk to him."

Shalom tried to find his way to the door. He wanted to leave the room proudly, with his head up. Finally he found the doorknob. He still had the strength to turn his face to the commissar and say, "Please, Mr. Gurny. You don't need all those little things that you confiscated. Give them back to us."

Shalom was unable to notice the changed expression on Gurny's face. Gurny's voice sounded now as it had always sounded. "I'll give it back to you, so that you'll see black before your eyes! Out of here, you soul of a dog! If someone shows you one finger, you want to grab the whole hand, don't you?" Then he whispered in Shalom's ear, "Do you want to work at the Affair Department?"

Shalom's voice came out hoarse, with a stutter, "My brother . . . Mottle . . . take him too . . ."

Gurny fumed again, "Such a monster! Show him one finger, and he wants the whole hand! All right! Your brother, too!"

Shalom dragged himself to his place in the hall, and fainted.

It took some time before Shalom got to work at the "Affair Department". First Gurny assigned him and Mottle to fill an urgent order for filing cabinets.

"I can barely stand on my feet," Shalom said, as he begged Gurny to release him from the job.

"As far as I am concerned, you can stand on your head. You'll work nights too," Gurny commanded.

Shalom managed to get Mottle taken off the job. "He doesn't need much more," he warned Gurny. "We might have to carry him out in just such a cabinet, and you will have one craftsman less."

The time arrived for Shalom when there were no longer any days or nights, or even hours. All that existed was a heap of wood which had to be made to stand up and turn into filing cabinets. Everything else — the Resort, the ghetto, Sheyne Pessele, the party, the comrades — vanished from his mind. Not only did his mind stop working, so also did his stomach. All he was aware of was a pair of hands sawing, planing, scraping, varnishing. The hands were strong and gave support to the body. Shalom's head no longer spun. He did not faint. Every evening Gurny sent in good soups for the four workmen who were barely aware that they were eating. One night, however, all their senses were alerted. Presess Rumkowski, who probably had a vested interest in the filing cabinets, came to have a look at the work. He walked around the half-finished cabinets, nodded his dishevelled head approvingly, and said, "You're good boys." He seemed worried, distraught.

One of the workmen prodded Shalom with his elbow, "Now is the right moment to ask him for an extra ration."

Shalom refused to listen. "Can't you see that he's angry? Perhaps something is about to happen?"

A third worker sneered, "Maybe he has a stomach ache from overeating?"

Shalom's suspicion did not diminish. "He does not look so well. Look how his back is bent. Something is wrong, I'm telling you. I don't like his face either. Look at his crumpled hair. How long ago was it that he walked around like a dandy? And why, do you suppose, has he come here? Maybe he can't sleep. He must know something."

"You're an idiot," the first worker said. "Let's not miss a golden opportunity."

The Presess was jotting something down in a little notebook. The workers went on disputing in a whisper, which of them should approach the Old Man. The choice as usual fell on Shalom. So he tried to rid himself of his sudden attack of anxiety, and approached the Presess. "Herr Presess," he bowed, his heart hammering. "May I have a word with you, please?" The Presess did not raise his head. Shalom's teeth were chattering, but he took hold of himself. "We work day and night, Herr Presess," he mumbled. "We are the best craftsmen . . . and our feet are swollen."

The Presess shut his notebook and thrust it into his pocket. "I shall reward you," he said and left the hall.

The four overjoyed workers began to muse about the amount of sugar, meat or bread the Presess would prescribe for them. "He won't make a fool of himself," a worker remarked, "by offering us one extra ration. He'll probably give us a permanent one, once every two weeks, or once every three. He saw how we look. He knows that he can't do without us."

The two firemen who guarded the Resort at night appeared in the hall. "You're getting extra rations, aren't you?" one of them inquired.

"Don't hide it, we heard every word," said the other. "You should ask us what such a word from the Presess means."

It was clear that they had come to do business. "I will give you four hundred *rumkis* for a ration, sight unseen," one fireman proposed.

A workman replied part in earnest, part jokingly, "I want a thousand!"

"I will give you five hundred!" said the other fireman.

The eyes of the four workers grew big with astonishment. They became goggled like little balls, bouncing from one fireman to the other. Shalom mastered himself. He asked the firemen to leave, so that the workmen could take council. "Let's not be stupid," he said to them. "Did you hear the price they're ready to pay, blind? They are firemen. They're already getting extra rations and know their worth. And if it is worth so much for them, then it has its worth for us. Let's wait and see."

The filing cabinets were ready on time, but Shalom was unable to get up from his bed the following day. Mottle came home from the Resort to tell him that Gurny was satisfied with the job. "Has the order for extra rations arrived yet?" Shalom inquired.

There was no order for an extra ration. But when Shalom arrived at the Resort a few days later, the workers greeted him with good news, practically carrying him into Gurny's office on their shoulders. Gurny handed Shalom a note, saying with a smile, "Here is an order for one extra double soup."

The real salvation came from Gurny himself, and from the "Affair Department" where Shalom was at last put to work. Gurny became very chummy with Shalom, often giving him his own extra soups, all the while suggesting that Shalom's brother Israel should know about his good deeds. The soup was for both Shalom and Mottle, and on account of it frictions arose between the brothers. Mottle was of the opinion that the soups should not be divided equally, but that he deserved exactly two thirds, since he had a child. And did not Shalom love his nephew? Yet Shalom found it difficult to give in to Mottle. He wanted to put Sheyne Pessele back on her feet. True, she had been re-registered as fifty years old, but she had to look much younger in order for the *Yekes* to believe it. And he himself was also barely walking on his feet. Secondly, Gurny was his friend, and a sympathizer of his party, not of Mottle's, and if it were not for him, Mottle would have had nothing. Eventually, however, Shalom gave in to Mottle. He thought that anyway it would never be given to him to have enough to eat in the ghetto.

But very soon he was proven wrong.

A set of furniture for a whole apartment had been finished at the "Affairs Department", and when the time to deliver it arrived, Gurny came running to Shalom, and pulled him by the sleeve, "I'm taking you along into town!"

The furniture was loaded on a truck and covered with a huge canvas. Gurny and three of his workers took off their Stars of David and hid under the cover. There were a few holes in it, through which they looked out at the city. "You're in town . . . You're in town!" Shalom repeated to himself. But he did not really grasp the fact. The streets and people moved past him like a film strip. They left him indifferent. He was surprised that he was not surprised. The apartment was Herr Biebow's private residence. As he entered the rooms, Shalom's impression of watching a movie persisted. Even the food which he savoured in the kitchen, the sip of schnapps, the bread and cheese, the bowl full of potatoes seemed unreal. What was real was the little parcel which he brought home: half a loaf of bread and a piece of bacon. Only at home, sitting across from Sheyne Pessele, was he capable of digesting the experience. Sheyne Pessele sold the bread and the bacon. The price of bread was sky high on the black market and for the bacon there was no price at all. They would be able to live for two weeks like human beings, Sheyne Pessele and Shalom thought.

And just as misfortune does not come alone, so good luck also comes in company. A few days later, Gurny sent Shalom and Mottle to do a job at the *Sonderkommando*, insisting of course that their brother Israel know what he was doing for them. Shalom and Mottle took along not their canteens, but the largest pots in Sheyne Pessele's possession. The *Sonderkommando*, the most distinguished unit of the Jewish police force, was well fed. Shalom and Mottle waited with their pots until the policemen had their fill. The food distribution took place in a cellar, and after their pots were filled, the two brothers would sit down on the floor, place their pots between their legs and stuff themselves. The *Sonder* men watched the two short brothers, amazed at the capacity of their stomachs. Only at the last spoonfuls did Shalom begin to groan and puff. But he could not stop eating. After he and Mottle had scraped dry their pots, the *Sonder* men would amuse themselves by asking, "Do you want some more, boys?" Two full pots were again placed between the brothers' legs. The *Sonder* men would hover over them, inciting them, betting on them, guffawing, as the two brothers panted and wheezed, but kept on eating.

After such a lunch Shalom was unable to stand up. His head was bathed in perspiration. His stomach was about to burst; the soup inside him was searching for an exit. He gnashed his teeth, swallowing whatever came back into his mouth. Food was health, was life, one was not supposed to disgorge it. He trudged home with another potful of soup. Sheyne Pessele beamed. The soup could easily be divided into eight or nine good portions. Shalom threw himself on the bed. "We are getting rich!" he moaned.

Shalom and Mottle worked at the *Sonderkommando* in accord with the slogan "T.I.E.", Take it Easy. Yet one fine day their job was finished. Shalom walked home for the last time with his pot of soup and a piece of sausage. The sausage was such a treasure that Sheyne Pessele and he could live on it for at least four weeks. He smiled to himself, impatient to see his mother's face. But then, he had a brilliant idea. He would visit his friends at the Tuberculosis Hospital and distribute the soup among them; a man was after all not meant to live only for himself. He began to walk more energetically, passing some notices announcing that the Presess would address the ghetto population in the backyard of the Fire Brigade. "He's crazy," Shalom laughed. "All he does is deliver speeches!" He could not forgive the Old Man the "extra ration" that he had given him for his night work.

He was not allowed to enter the hospital. The policeman on guard at the gate informed him, "Not today . . . that's the order . . ."

At home Shalom said to Sheyne Pessele, "I have a brilliant idea, Mother! Let's have a ball tonight! Let's call the whole family over for dinner. I'll find Israel too and drag him home by the ears." Sheyne Pessele immediately began to busy herself with preparations for the event. She cooked a *baba* from coffee dregs and made a few matzos of pure flour for her grandchildren.

Two hours later, the whole family was gathered at the table, the two grandchildren sitting on Sheyne Pessele's lap. Shalom had indeed pulled Israel home "by his ears". They sipped the soup and ate the *baba* spread with marmalade. The two grandchildren received bits of sausage to munch on. The grown-ups stared at the babies' tiny fat lips, their mouths watering. Although they were in their working clothes, and tired after a day's work, they all felt festive during the unexpected family feast. Even Israel seemed moved by their gathering. His small gray eyes revealed what he could never bring to his lips. He remarked, "Tomorrow it will be three years since the war began."

Shalom pounded against the table with his fist, "If after three years we can still sit, all of us together, at the table, then the Germans may stand on their heads, and it won't help them much."

Sheyne Pessele nestled her head between the heads of her grandchildren. She was thinking of Itche Mayer as she sniffled and swallowed her tears. "Next week, if Fate wills it," she turned to her daughters-in-law, "You must come again. At least once a week I want to see us all together. Do you hear me, Israel? Do you hear me, Mottle? And you, Yossi?" She warned her daughters-in-law, "You must obey me, or I'll take my sons back." They all laughed.

Chapter Nine

THE PRESESS WAS UNABLE to fall asleep. The window stood open and the stubborn song of a cricket penetrated the room; its thin sharp chirp grated on his mind, awakening bad thoughts. He struggled with it. He was not Titus and the cricket was not Titus's mosquito. He did not even get up to shut the window. It would not have helped anyway. One's mind could not be shut like a window. The mind did not listen to orders. Yes, he was thinking. He was not afraid of thinking. His conscience was clear.

Basically he still respected himself for his perseverance and courage. He was moulded from the clay of which heroes are made. Never in the history of the Jews or perhaps of mankind had there been such a hero as himself. Now he understood how insignificant was the generally accepted notion of heroism, the so-called "courageous act" of defiant resistance. Such heroism meant to walk a straight line, to make a cut like a knife. For that, no patience was needed, no sustained effort or even wisdom. It was quite a simple deed to put one's own life, sometimes along with that of others, on the line. Was dying in such a manner really such a great accomplishment? His kind of heroism was of a much higher quality. It was of the most thankless, the most isolating kind. He, the hero, was misunderstood even by those for whom he sacrificed himself, hated by those for whom he was ready to lay down his head; it was a heroism for which history would spit at him. For this, only the strength of someone like himself was sufficient.

Ever since Rumkowski had learned what had happened to the Jews from last winter's evacuation, many things had become clear to him. First, it was clear that his plans both immediate and distant, which had once seemed so sober, were nothing but fantasies, hollow chimeras. He was an old man who had deluded himself, believing that he was realistic and practical. In fact he was still a child and a dreamer. Then when — he asked himself reproachfully — when does a man stop being naive? When does he stop cheating himself and become mature? Was it only under the shadow of his own death? In the past, he had been so busy living that he had had no time even for the thoughts of death. Now it was not important whether he thought about it or not. It was there, and in its shadow, he was now fully aware that to him the present was still not a matter of death — but of life.

He now knew clearly what the Germans wanted and what they needed him for. He knew that he would never sit with Hitler at the same table, discussing the establishment of a Jewish state. Hitler must not win the war. Hitler was the Angel of Death for the Jewish people and for Mordecai Chaim himself. And it was against Hitler that he was waging his great struggle. Yes, a Jewish state would be established some day, but he would not be the Moses leading his people to its border. His people would not want him. His people would judge him and shake him off. Perhaps the Jews themselves would put the noose around his neck the first day after the war, after he had saved as many of them as he could. In that lay his bravery. To know all these things and to give himself up as a sacrifice; to let himself wallow in dirt, in blood, let himself be trampled on by both the Germans and the Jews, let himself be spat on — and yet do what he was given to do. The sixty thousand Jews had not been sent out of the ghetto to their deaths by him, he was not their hangman. Yet he took the guilt upon himself. He wanted to save a remainder . . . in order that the people should not perish without a trace.

And he still hoped to achieve his aim, to outsmart the Germans. Had he not built Resorts which accomplished wonders? Had he not done everything to ensure that the Germans would not be able to manage without the Jews and their deft hands? Had he not accomplished that feat, in spite of the efforts of all those of his own kind who had put stones under his feet, in spite of the intriguers and the parties which had tried to take the rudder out of his hands? They carried tales about him, they made him repugnant in Biebow's eyes. Only when it came to doing the dirty work, did they hide in corners, leaving him alone in the foreground.

If he still wanted to hold on to the rudder, to have power, it was no longer because of his personal ambitions, or his personal gain. What could he now hope for, if his highest goals had come to naught? The ladder which he had wanted to climb was broken. Even his private plans had burst like a soap bubble. He had married, hoping for a bit of happiness at home. He had wanted a corner of his own, perhaps a son. But it had not worked out. Was it because of the ghetto, because of the Germans, or because of himself? It was too late for everything.

There was some truth to the saying that love was blind and marriage was an eye-doctor. Home had become hell for Mordecai Chaim. Clara, with her constant questions and her ceaseless nagging, was the real stubborn fly which pricked at his mind. She considered him a criminal, a murderer. And he would never have a child with her. Never. All the injections were of no avail. Perhaps Fate had decreed that all his powers should remain within him, to make him strong enough to withstand the super-human trials which awaited him. He would leave no offspring. All that would remain after him was his disgraced name. So be it. He took that in his stride too — as long as his people might live on. He, Mordecai Chaim, was a Jew. His Jewishness was all that was left to him. If Judaism continued to exist, he was sure somehow to find his place in its history. He would not perhaps be praised or sung about, he would in the best case be forgotten, yet in some way he would partake in the procession of future Jewish generations.

He lay on his bed, winding one lip into the other as if kneading his thoughts with his flabby mouth. In the bed across from him lay Clara. He knew that she too was not asleep; he heard her tossing around. Unnoticeably, she had gotten into his blood stream, in spite of her destructive attitude towards him. He could have escaped her. He could have left her. But he would not do it. A magnetic power held him to her. And although her talk was so bitter, he was rarely angry at her. Sometimes it seemed to him that he needed her bitter words. Now and then he tried to open his heart to her. Never before had it been in his nature to confess to anyone. He had had no friends and he had never been very close to his brother. Now he felt like confessing — to Clara.

He tried to explain to her how he felt. "I am like a tightrope walker. I have to navigate. The Germans have chosen me to help them do their thing . . . while I am doing ours. Through serving the Germans, I serve my people. I want to postpone . . . to ease . . . to help them survive. That's my struggle, Clara, why don't you realize that? The Germans order me to keep the ghetto calm, to say to the people, 'You are safe, the actions won't be repeated.' The Germans need that in order to disguise their aims, to facilitate the execution of their evil plans. And the Jews need it too, in order not to break down . . . so that their nerves don't burst . . . so that their strength does not run out when they really need it. You're asking me to alarm the ghetto about the slaughters, to take council with the political parties. What will that give me? If the parties take one irresponsible step, all is lost. Why don't you understand that?"

She refused to understand. She demanded impossible things from him, and since it had become clear that an "action" against the children and old people was imminent, crazy ideas entered her head. "Let's do what Czerniakow did," she nagged him.

He scolded her, "Suicide does not solve any problems. And where is my responsibility? What would you say about a father committing suicide and leaving a houseful of orphans? And if I take poison, won't someone else be put in my place? Would he be any better? Sure, suicide is the easiest way out. But on the other hand . . . I have no suicidal blood in my veins."

"No, just homicidal . . ." she cut in.

On the dresser lay the prettiest gift he had ever received in the ghetto. It was an album given to him on *Rosh Hashana*. It was bound in wood and leather and in it, the good wishes of fourteen thousand five hundred and eighty-seven school children were inscribed. Every child had signed its name and each page of the album started with a prayer or a verse, written by a child. The verses were written in Yiddish, Hebrew, or Polish, while the front page bore the Hebrew inscription, *Ata nasi doeg lanu*. One of the poems he had even learned by heart, not word for word, but its meaning. "You have laid down your life for us," the poem said. "We are the goal of your strivings . . . You are severe in your appearance, but soft at heart . . . You bleed for every hurt child. From the clearest source, from the hearts of children, thousands of blessings flow upon your magnificent head." Why did he remember the album now? How would he be able to fall asleep? He cast a glance at the window, at the distant dark sky. "You are all alone . . . alone . . ." the cricket was singing. "The loneliest of the lonely." He turned his back to the window. His bed squeaked.

"Do you want a drink of water, Chaim?" he heard Clara's voice.

He did not answer. Tonight he had no strength to strike up a conversation with her. His thoughts were making such a noise in his head, that it seemed to him that Clara could hear them anyway. They began to entwine in his mind more and more confusedly, as he felt more and more exhausted. The room was filling with swaying shadows, with eyes and ears . . . with the streets of the ghetto. Mordecai Chaim was a chip of wood on the sea of panic. Screams . . . Hatred . . . So much hatred! He was a little Jewish boy in his distant Lithuanian hometown. The long-effaced image of his mother surfaced in the dark. He surged towards it: "Mother, hide me! They want to take away the children!"

His mother's face was that of an old woman on her deathbed. "You are not my son," the dead mouth said. "I never had any children. I am barren."

"What should I do with the children of the orphanage, Mother?"

The dead old woman replied, "You are an orphan yourself, so you should know."

At dawn he was woken from his sleep. A policeman arrived to inform him that nine trucks had entered the ghetto and were headed in the direction of the hospitals. Mordecai Chaim dressed without hurry. He ate no breakfast but left for his office, in order to avoid Clara's questions. After the last German inspection of the hospitals and the demand that he supply lists of all the sick, he had realized what was in the air and had already given up on the ill. He had supplied a list of three thousand patients and kept silent, for fear that the patients might escape. Quietly, he ordered a police guard in front of each hospital. His advisors had warned him not to have such well-equipped hospitals. Others had reproached him for caring too little for the sick. Be that as it may, they would all consider him the culprit. Let them. His conscience was clear. He had thought that by sacrificing the sick he would avoid or postpone the most evil decree. He was ready to sacrifice even the old people, if only the children might be saved.

He paced up and down his office, thinking of the children. The seven, eight and nine-year-olds were in some way secure; they had been re-registered as older and were working at the Resorts. And what excellent workers they were! He had seen them at the machines in the Metal Resorts and in the Tailor Resorts. Their production had been shown to him. And yet, they too were in danger. All of them.

He gulped down one glass of cold water after another. He craved for a bit of alcohol, or some other narcotic. He had the strength to endure everything but that. He would tell Biebow so, straight to his face. He could not take the "action" of the children upon himself. Let the Germans come and do whatever they wanted.

✦ ✦ ✦

Clara ran through the streets, uncombed and carelessly dressed. The morning sun was distant and high in the sky. The streets were still empty. The ghetto was still asleep. Groups of policemen passed her. She ran after them. Suddenly she found herself on Hospital Street. In front of the hospital for the tubercular patients stood two trucks, their platforms boarded like wooden cages. Something broke deep inside her. She covered her mouth to muffle her scream. White angels were flying down from the hospital windows; the sick, in their hospital dress, were jumping from the window sills and cornices, trying to save themselves. She wanted to run back and find the old gray-haired man who had chosen her for his wife. She wanted to embrace him, to fall at his feet and thank him that all this would never happen to her . . . that her name would be on no lists, that she would not be chased and caught for any evacuations . . . that she had him to protect her life.

She did not turn back but remained glued to her spot, watching the police run after the escaping patients. She heard the howls of those who lay under the windows, with their limbs broken. At the same time she watched the crowd of young men and women, their eyes burning, their cheeks kissed by the morning sun, come out through the hospital door, wearing their white nightgowns and pyjamas, and moving drunkenly in the direction of the trucks. Some of them threw themselves at the gendarmes, or at the Jewish policemen, spitting, cursing. Others cried, walking doubled up. But most of them, stunned yet majestic-looking, confused yet proud, climbed into the trucks — like young brides and grooms climbing towards the marriage canopy. The air was chopped by piercing screams. The hospital building seemed to sway on its foundations. Something sizzled inside it as if on the verge of explosion. On the roof a girl in a white nightgown, her hair flying, ran frantically from one edge to the other. Gendarmes and Jewish policemen were carrying out the consumptives who were in the last stages of the disease; mere skeletons, scraps of humanity. One after the other they were thrown onto the trucks.

"Manik!" a sick girl embraced her lover, calling out his name as if he were miles away from her.

"Gittele!" the lover called back, hugging her, as if he had arrived from miles away to save her. Together they climbed onto the truck.

"Long live freedom!" roared a few sick boys, barely able to walk.

Now and then someone, in white pyjamas or a nightgown, broke through the cordon of Jewish police and dashed off down the empty street. "Help! Help!" cried some of the sick women, as if they were trying to wake the entire ghetto.

"Mama!" wailed a frightened little boy. The hospital door was now spitting out the very young boys and girls. Woken from their sleep, shivering, they imploringly stretched out their thin twig-like arms, to the giants in the green uniforms.

The ghetto was awake at last. All the streets began to swim with people hurrying towards the hospital. Parents and relations arrived, followed by friends, neighbours, by the entire ghetto. Hundreds of hands were stretched over the police cordon. The trucks groaned and roared; each truck like an animal in agony. The sick inside could not be seen. They had sunk down on the platforms, exhausted with fright. The babies were already being carried out. Chainwork was being applied; the babies were passed from one policeman to another, until they could be handed up into the trucks.

The sun in the bright sky shuddered like a feverish consumptive. It seemed to be spitting blood upon the white transparent clouds. The mob in front of the hospital became hysterical, the people incapable of distinguishing whether they were screaming in fear for their own lives, or for the lives of the sick. Only the mothers of the consumptives knew. Their throats were hoarse. With their whole beings they held on to a face up there which was blurred, fading into the pallor of other faces — flesh of their flesh, marrow of their marrow; each mother an open wound, from which life was pouring out — a life which hurt so unbearably.

It seemed to Clara that her hair stood up on her skull. Her body was soft and loose like a sponge, sucking in everything. She had been pressed forward by the crowd, nearer to the police cordon. Peering over their locked arms, she saw two girls huddled close to each other. Their eyes sought no one. Unnoticed, they wandered about in the confusion, until a Jewish policeman caught sight of them and chased them with a shout, "Quickly, into the truck!"

A red-haired woman dived past Clara into the knot of people in front of her, shouting to the girls, "Get back into the house! From the back!" The young woman was motioning to the girls, who suddenly came alive. In the blink of an eye they vanished back into the entrance. It was strange that no one had noticed them. The red-haired woman began to plough through the crowd. Clara followed her. They came around to the rear of the building. Here the mob was even more agitated than at the front. A young man was standing in the frame of a window on the first floor. "Jump, jump!" shouts were heard from all sides. He had nowhere to jump. The building was surrounded by police. A man from the crowd broke through the cordon, so did another, then another. The women followed. The Germans shot into the air to quell the crowd. The policemen's whistles pierced the people's ears. The white angels were still flying from the windows. Many arms grabbed them and rushed off with them, while the police chased after them.

Clara lost sight of the redhead. She roused herself to a run. She would bring him over! By force would she bring the Old Man here. Let him see with his own eyes! He had no idea what it all was . . . He had not grasped it yet! She ran through the streets, noticing white hospital gowns here and there. The rescued patients were carried quickly into the gates. She did not stop. Soon she would see him, the old criminal, the murderer, the traitor! A loaded truck passed by her, followed by another. The sick were already being driven off.

Not before Clara burst into her house, did she realize that the Presess had left early in the morning, before breakfast. The housekeeper rushed towards her, flabbergasted. "You don't feel well, Mrs. Rumkowski?" She took Clara by the arm and made her sit down on the sofa. Clara wanted to stand up. She had to run to Baluter Ring and reach Mordecai Chaim, but she was unable to move. She threw back her head over the back of the sofa. She would never get through to him. She would achieve nothing. Only for herself had she achieved something. She would not be sent off by deportation. She would live . . . perhaps survive . . .

The housekeeper came back with a little bottle of *Valerian* drops. She wiped Clara's face with a cool moist towel. A maid appeared with a glass of aromatic strong tea. Clara's breakfast was placed on a little table before her; fresh rolls with butter, a bowl of curds and a soft-boiled egg in an eggholder. She ate with relish. After breakfast she got up, dressed, arranged her hair and left to visit Miss Diamand.

Miss Diamand rushed forward to meet her. "Clara dear, it is not true that they are demanding the children, is it?"

The ground swayed under Clara's feet, "They're demanding the children . . ."

The old woman stammered, "The children must stay."

"Miss Diamand," Clara groaned, "Elderly people . . . those over sixty . . . too."

Miss Diamand left her where she stood and hurried towards the stairs. Clara slumped down on the old woman's bed. Through the open window she could see the clear sky. She saw Rumkowski's head taking shape on its whiteness. His watery gray-blue eyes were staring at her through blurred eyeglasses. "What else do you want?" she asked him in her mind. "What are you still seeking if everything is lost? What are you still striving to accomplish, you corpse with hollow ambitions?" With bitterness she gnashed her teeth, "And what kind of person have you turned me into? I was straightforward, balanced . . . I knew what I wanted and where I was going . . . You made a hysterical bitch out of me, a criminal. You criminal, you murderer of children . . . you Nazi!" Yes, she felt that this stranger, the gray old man, and herself had become one. Fate had fused them together forever. And slowly her heart began to fill with pity for both of them. There was no way out of their straits but to do what Czerniakow, the Eldest of the Jews of Warsaw, had done. It would not be enough if she did it alone, nor did she have the strength to do it alone. She was frightened. Mordecai Chaim had turned her into a coward, like himself. He had demolished all the foundations which had supported her courage.

She jumped to her feet and left the room. As she crossed the yard, she saw the assembled teachers through an open window and among them the white fuzz of Miss Diamand's head, the head of a delicate rare bird. She hated that head and feared it. She was running home to him who had become part of her, to be close to him. He was her hangman and her saviour.

They sat together at lunch, both their heads hanging over their plates. They barely touched the food. They were silent. The silence was not heavy, it carried no anger or reproach. It tolled in their ears along with their loneliness. Something had broken down within Mordecai Chaim. He was not a man, not a human being. He was surprised at Clara's devotion. Why did she not yell at him any more? Why did she not attack him with her brutal questions? Or call him morbid names? He deserved it all. Why was she clinging to him so today? Perhaps it would have been better if she had thrown herself at him, scratched his eyes out, or cursed him? Perhaps this would have given him back his strength? Perhaps in the storm exploding between them, he would have felt his own self better. Yet, if at that moment he felt grateful to anyone, it was to Clara — for her silence, for her devotion. Perhaps someone would remain in this world after all, who loved him, or would at least think of him without hatred?

When he was ready to go back to Baluter Ring, he said to her, "I must speak to the mothers . . . There is not much time left. If the Germans themselves come in and do whatever they want, everything will be finished."

She wrapped her arms around his flabby neck, "Come, let's do what Czerniakow did."

He reacted immediately. His fury returned and made him strong. "You're a stupid cow!" He tore her arms away from him. "Do you think that that would save the children? My name is Mordecai, and Mordecai wants to outsmart Haman, and my name is Chaim, which means life!"

"You must not!" she called out.

"I must! I want someone at least to get out of here alive."

"You're scared! You're afraid for your life . . . for your head!"

His head shook with fury. His dishevelled hair fell over his forehead, covering his glasses. "Did I never risk it before? Should I remind you how many times I have been close to having it cut off?" He pounded his chest. "I want at least someone to survive. I am ready to pay for it with that sacrifice . . ."

"The sacrifice of children?"

"You've never been a mother. So why do you care about the children so much?"

"And you're going to avenge yourself on the fathers because you have never been a father yourself!"

He threw himself at her, shaking her by the shoulders; hate and despair reflected in their eyes. "Quiet, you bitch! That's how you repay me for having saved you?"

"Because of you I will never become a mother!"

"Woe to you if you were one now!" A foam appeared in the corners of his mouth. His loose cheeks shook. But he could not leave her like that. Not today. Grief quickly extinguished the hatred in his eyes. He put his arms around her.

"Clara, my heart," he whispered, lowering his face to hers, in order to see her better in the dark corridor, "I love children, believe me . . . I wanted to have a son by you . . . Fate was cruel to us. I must do what is beyond my strength . . . I must talk to the mothers."

"Chaim." She was beside herself. "There are things which a human being must never take upon himself."

"I must. I'm taking it upon myself."

✦ ✦ ✦

The first thing that Rumkowski did at his office was to lock the door. He also told his secretaries to let no one know where he was. He gulped down a few glasses of cold water and sat down at his desk. On it everything was laid out in the best order, reminiscent of the good old days when he had had the people behind him and had led them like a good father. It had been a great feeling to have power over them and to be kind to them. The Germans had destroyed all that. But he would not surrender. He would still show them. He would outsmart them. Only let the gruesome days of the "action" be over. He would recover everything. The ghetto would again work like a clock.

He could not bear the sight of the desk, nor could he sit at it. He began to pace the room. He should stop digging so much inside himself, he thought. He should lock his heart and his mind with seven locks, to prevent even one thought, even one spark of emotion from passing through them. He had to become like a rock. And he had to be alone. Alone he felt stronger, more self-assured. He would send Clara off to Marysin for two weeks. He would see no one.

From outside, the commotion at Baluter Ring reached his ears. Limousines were coming and going. Rumkowski's glance fell on the filing cabinet where the lists of the children of policemen, firemen, Resort directors and commissars were kept; those children had to be saved. Yes, in these cases he had to make exceptions. He had also approached the political parties, inviting them to supply him with lists of children to be protected. The head of a woman swam into his memory, that of the Bundist activist Bracha Koplowicz. The Bundists had refused to provide him with such a list. There are no chosen children, Bracha Koplowicz, the mother of an eight-year-old daughter had declared.

He had to sit down after all, to prepare his speech to the mothers. How does one prepare such a speech? What could one say? How can mothers understand and realize the necessity? It was impossible to take notes for such an address. He would say what his heart dictated. He would speak from the depth of his whole being.

The yard of the Fire Brigade was overflowing with people. The throngs had climbed onto the roofs of the latrine and the sheds, as well as onto the fire-wagons. Those who were unable to get into the yard were crowded into the neighbouring yards and the street. The entire ghetto had assembled, standing arm to arm, body to body, glued together, yet each alone with his or her fear. They stood in deadly silence, in tense awful expectation. The ghetto held its breath as it listened to the Steps of Fate. Human speech did not belong here. Words lost their meaning before they even reached the lips. The eyes of the people stopped exchanging glances. There was nothing left to think about, but one's own flesh and blood.

So perhaps had the people stood at the foot of Mount Sinai, waiting for God.

From an elevated platform the white prophetic head of Presess Rumkowski surfaced at last. The sky had acquired a pair of hands which rose above the black mass of the throng. The sky had acquired a mouth which through thunder and lightning pronounced the verdict. "Mothers, you must give up your children!" It struck a deafening blow, impossible to absorb. Words like mountains rolled down onto the sea of heads.

The faces in front of Mordecai Chaim became blurred. They were one black mass, one body collapsing into a fit. The earth shook with convulsions. A white foam appeared on thousands of mouths, "No!"

"Mothers!" the Presess called. "Save the ghetto! If we don't give up the children, not one of us will survive. We shall be erased from the face of the earth. If life continues, you will have other children. I cannot help it, brothers! They are demanding children up to ten years of age and old people over sixty-five. I took it upon myself to execute the 'action'. If the Germans come in, there will be a blood bath. Mothers! Make this sacrifice for the people! Let everything move smoothly tomorrow . . . so that we will be saved . . ." His voice stopped serving him. Others of his entourage then tried to convince the crowd to surrender to the order peacefully.

The black convulsed body of a thousand writhing heads had no ears. A gray moss sprouted on the women's faces. The hair on their scalps stiffened into wires. Water trickled from between their legs.

In the neighbouring yard, which was also beleaguered, the cherry tree shook with the spasms of the crowd. Its dry withered boughs were stretched to the sky like arms trembling in prayer, in supplication; the hands of a dried-out mother. Pressed to the tree's trunk, embracing it, stood the Toffee Man, his sparse beard glued to the trunk like a climbing vine. Back to back with him stood Simcha Bunim Berkovitch, his glasses on the tip of his nose, his upper lip between his teeth. His pulled back cap revealed his sweaty forehead, its furrows cut through by swollen veins which seemed on the point of bursting.

"So that's that," squeaked the Toffee Man, shamelessly sobbing. "If God does not build the house, the builders toil in vain . . . If God does not guard a city, the watchman watches in vain."

In Bunim's mind the wailing of the crowd mixed with Miriam's child-bearing screams. She had given birth last night. His wife had borne him a male child. Now Bunim would become an Abraham, striking down with his knife . . . for a ram would not appear . . .

"When forests are on fire don't wail over the flowers that perish!" The voice of the speaker thundered across the back yard.

"Blimele," Bunim murmured his daughter's name.

In the other yard, the speeches went on and on, but the mass of people had begun to sway in the direction of the gate, of the street. Each street turned into a stormy flowing river, each yard into a swaying ship. The ghetto was swarming, wailing, collapsing with spasms, going out of its mind with grief. At last no one was hungry. Nowhere was there a fire lit in a stove. Like poisoned rats people raced through the yards in search of lairs, of holes, in which to hide the little Jews who had such knowing eyes. The children had been to the meeting, they had heard the speeches. They would not let go of their parents' hands for a moment.

The ghetto forgot about curfew. No one undressed or went to bed. Night arrived, but it did not touch the ghetto. Here it was daytime. A full black day of acute alertness. *Waivku Haam* ... And the people cried that night. The darkness swam in tears, the air lost its breath in horror.

The next morning the wagons of potatoes arrived, raining down the "gold of the soil" upon the mourning heads. The potato ration could be picked up only in the morning. The workers had been sent home from the Resorts and offices for an indefinite period, and the house arrest, or the *Sperre*, was supposed to begin in the afternoon.

A mild Friday evening. A fiery purple sun stood on the horizon refusing to set. From the east a distant moon appeared, fastened to the sky, motionless. Sun and moon had come to watch the children set out on their road to meet Queen Sabbath who was supposed to arrive in a pink and violet chariot. The purple sky in the west was the shawl over her head, the light of the moon was the silvery dust over her delicate eyebrows. Quietly she floated down, stepping on the earth in her light evening slippers dipped in the most precious dews. A holy silence.

The streets were empty. The bridge was closed and the gates shut. Everyone was supposed to stay at home and wait for the inspecting commission. Each family alone. A loneliness which made one's call for help, one's hope for a miracle futile. God was deaf and dumb.

The commissions of physicians and nurses, of policemen and firemen walked with their lists from house to house, from door to door. They examined the withered bodies and searched for the children and old people. Suddenly there were almost no children or old people. But the policemen who were out to protect their own children by searching for the children of others, were not fools. One Jewish head could not so easily outsmart another. Never mind, they knew how to sniff out the holes and hiding places, to pull out the frightened little mice and drag them off to the trucks.

The little mice were dressed up in their prettiest Sabbath outfits: the little girls in neatly ironed dresses, with colourful bows in their hair; the little boys in colourful shirts and jackets. Their mothers had thus dressed them up for their Sabbath road, so that the good people of distant places should be dazzled by their children's radiant beauty and not have the heart to harm them; so that they should stare in awe at these sweet delights of mothers' hearts and be kind to them.

One truck after the other rolled off. Truckloads full of charm, of colourful ribbons. Truckloads full of crying eyes, of arms stretched out towards an emptiness, truckloads full of fluttering hearts. Along with each little heart a tiny bag fluttered upon each chest. In it were the name and address of the child and a letter to the good people of distant places. For it was folly to think that there would be no one ready to offer a smile to such creatures, to stroke their heads and wipe the tears off their big frightened eyes.

Funeral corteges of mothers followed the trucks. The women seemed barely aware of what was going on.

Past them, rolled the trucks loaded with the old people. There was almost no one running after them. Almost no one who mourned them. They were doomed; guilty of being old. These were the grandmothers and grandfathers who had sat in the entranceways during summer evenings, the old men who had hidden their beards in shawls or in old stockings, those who had stubbornly followed the laws of *kashrut*. These were the grandmothers who had explained life in the ghetto according to the *Tzena Varena*, their Yiddish Bible. They had taken care of their men, of their children and grandchildren, quietly serving them all. Grandmothers and grandfathers who had lived like shadows, trying not to be in the way, not to be a burden; each of their gestures an apology for wanting to live some more, for not having had enough, for being weak or sick. They had long lives behind them, lives filled with work and sorrow, chains of days during which they had gathered experience. Now they were thrown upon the trucks like stumps of wood . . . unneeded. Silently they peered out through the cracks between the trucks' boards — at the receding streets.

The wheels rolled on and on, quickly, joining the wheels arriving from other parts in the ghetto. A long procession of wooden cages, leaving empty worlds behind them. And the day was still there. The sun had not set and Queen Sabbath was still on her way. Until "the sun and the moon became black and the stars withdrew their shine". The sun and the moon had seen enough. The people were dazed by the darkness, they did not undress nor light a light that night either. The people cried on the night of the Sabbath.

The dawn of the Sabbath day. The *Sperre* was still on. Jewish policemen were seeking out the hidden children and old people. The physicians and nurses continued to examine the others, for suddenly it was revealed that the sick and the weak were also being sought. The people attacked whatever food they had. They washed, dressed up, pinched their cheeks so that they would look healthy. With pride each displayed his worker's identity card. Some physicians could not find anything wrong with the weak disintegrating bodies. Others were more scrupulous and not one pair of swollen legs escaped their notice. The policemen and their leaders were overly zealous, they wanted to have a reserve of deportees, in case one of the "protections" was freed and they would have to find someone else to round out the number. The open windows vibrated with the screams coming from apartments where the condemned were being torn away from their dear ones. In the yards scuffles broke out with the police. Confusion. Chaos.

The ghetto was alone. Not one German appeared inside it. Jews were catching Jews . . . Jews were leading away Jews . . .

✦ ✦ ✦

At night, all the lights were on in the windows of Baluter Ring. Presess Rumkowski had shut himself up in his office. The specified number of people had not been reached yesterday or today. Things had not worked out, in spite of all his efforts. Many who had been caught escaped from the police sooner or later, hiding in all conceivable places. Nor were the physicians of any use. Some freed too many, others were too slow and meticulous. It did not help much that he had ordered the numbers to be augmented by giving up the children from the orphanage of Marysin. And what would happen tomorrow, when he had no reserves left?

His orphans were gone. He should have felt relieved. His most difficult task was over. He had sacrificed his children. His heart was cut into pieces. How would he be able to go on living? And what did he still hope to save, if he had given up the future? He could barely believe that it had been he who had ordered the orphanage to be cordoned off, so as not to let any of the children escape. It had been he who, in the afternoon, had ordered that the children be decently dressed, gathered in lines of two in a row, and led off to the station. And what was that force which had urged him to be present and witness the "defilade" through the window of his summer home? Now, along the same sandy road where he had not long ago watched their festive march, they walked, holding hands. The boys wore navy blue sailor suits, the girls white blouses and navy blue pleated skirts; coloured ribbons in their hair, white socks on their feet. They proceeded in order, well-disciplined, but so very slowly. They were not singing. They were crying.

Mordecai Chaim did not move away from the window until the last child had passed out of sight. Then he had to see Clara. He could not be alone. Clara was not at home. He wanted to take a bath in order to regain his equilibrium, but for the first time in his life he was afraid to be alone in a bathtub full of water. His supper was on the table. He did not touch it. He had gulped down a glass of schnapps and hurried over to his office. He conferred with the chiefs of police, of the fire brigade, and with everyone else who could possibly help him go through with the impossible task. He made tremendous promises. He would give in to everything they wanted, if they only . . . His head was not working well. He should not have drunken the glass of schnapps. Half of the night he spent alone in the office, then he sent messengers to fetch all the members of the Evacuation Committee. Before they could arrive, however, Herr Biebow had sent for the Presess.

The Presess was not kept long in the brightly lit office of the *Ghettoverwaltung.* Herr Biebow and his colleagues wanted to dispense with the issue at hand and go home to sleep. Business-like, they asked Rumkowski why the expected number of people had not been delivered. He assured them that tomorrow it would be. They shook their heads. They doubted this possibility. They would free him of the obligation. Tomorrow they would take over the "action" and do it their own way. The ghetto police, the firemen, the doctors and nurses were to be at their disposal.

Rumkowski came out of Biebow's office, climbed into his coach and left for home. He dashed through the house and found Clara on the sofa in the dining room. "The end is approaching!" he called out, then slumped down beside her. "The Germans are taking over tomorrow."

She sighed with relief. "Thank heavens," she mumbled, throwing her arms around his neck. "We will have clean hands, Chaim. Let the ghetto see the Germans. It will be better . . ."

Chapter Ten

BEFORE THE *SPERRE*, when the rumours of a new evil decree had first begun to circulate, Simcha Bunim Berkovitch stopped writing his long poem. He only made the following note on a page of an old bookkeeping register:

> Sometimes it seems to me that the ghetto is a mountain whose name is Futility. I am at its top, and can see clearly all the roads leading up to it and all the roads leading down from it. I see forests and deserts through which generations have strayed. Way back, behind the forest of yesterday, lies the horizon of creation. There rests the secret by which humankind has been shaped. From there the entanglement leads up to here, from the first man — up to my daughter, Blimele — and up to the creature which will any day now leave Miriam's womb.
> The Mountain upon which I stand is a volcano . . . Its crater yawns. The mountain is an altar. We are the sacrificial lambs. A sacrifice of futility? Shall we ever become the torch illuminating the darkness for those who follow, indicating to them the roads leading away from here? Will they see the light shining from our burning demise? Will the flame rising from us engrave new commandments, not upon stones, but in the hearts of men? Will the blind become seers? Will the Mountain of Futility which is devouring us ever become the Mountain of Meaning?

Immediately after Rumkowski's speech in the firemen's yard, Bunim ran into his hut and let himself sink down at Miriam's bedside. On Miriam's arm, on a long pillow, lay the newborn baby. Bunim looked at it. The wrinkled little face told him of the relationship between agony and birth. Only the thin little lips bespoke a soothing freshness. Miriam was exhausted, pale. Yet there was a radiance about her. Her eyes shone with an amazing calm.

She whispered, "We will hide the baby in a drawer, Bunim. We have to save Blimele." Bunim gave a shudder. How could she talk like that? What gave her the strength to utter those words? Perhaps she was out of her mind? "You'll have to prepare a little bottle of sweetened water," she said. "I don't have enough milk in my breasts." He kindled a fire and put on the kettle. Nearby stood the basin with the baby's first dirty diapers and the stained sheets on which Miriam had given birth. Sheyne Pessele had put them in to soak overnight and was supposed to wash them in the morning. He wanted to do it now, but Miriam begged him, "Leave everything alone and call in the child."

He called in Blimele. She rushed to the bed, her blue eyes shining over her dirty face. "What's my brother's name?" she asked.

Miriam smiled, "In a few days we will give him a name."

"He looks funny. He looks like a little grandpa." Blimele pointed her eyebrows, piercing Miriam's eyes with her gaze, "They might take him away from me."

"We will hide him well . . . and hide you too, Blimele."

"I know. With Masha. In the water tank. *Tateshe* took me up there and showed me." She went over to the doll's carriage and took out her doll Lily, nestling her in her arms. "I will not let them take you away from me, my baby," she said to Lily.

The following day the commissions began to inspect the houses. In the morning Bunim dressed Blimele in her Sabbath dress. He tried to tie a blue ribbon in her hair and managed to arrange it in a crooked bow. Blimele wrapped her doll in a little blanket and threw herself at Miriam's bed, "*Mameshe*, my tummy is ticking . . ."

Miriam calmed her, "You are a big girl. Take care of Lily."

The commission appeared in the yard, but did not search the loft where the empty old water tank stood. It also left out Bunim's hut near the latrines. Late at night Bunim returned, carrying the sleeping Blimele in his arms. They did not put on the light. The lamentations in the backyard could be heard through the windows. The night was like an open sore. Bunim and Miriam talked very little. Now and then Miriam drifted off into slumber. Bunim had the impression that the walls of the hut were falling apart. He joined in with the wailing of the night, whispering all the long-forgotten psalms that came back to his mind. He was at the very bleeding core of the wound. At dawn he woke up and dressed Blimele. Sleepily she surrendered to his touch, her head falling loosely to the side. He fed her a bit of soup and pushed a bag with a few of the Toffee Man's candies into her hand. He pushed Lily under her other arm.

"Today you'll sit the whole day upstairs in the loft," he said to her. "Remember, you must not cry, or talk to Masha . . . not a word. I will come up now and then to see how you are." He took her into his arms. Miriam watched them through the grayness of the air in the room. He felt her gaze on him as he carried the child to the door. His shoulders twitched. Outside, the yard seemed empty. Here and there shadows passed, followed by smaller ones, along the walls. Through the open windows could be heard the sound of hammers, of furniture being moved around to the accompaniment of ceaseless sobbing.

In the stairway, as he climbed the stairs, he had the strong sensation of having once climbed this way through the darkness . . . up some stairs . . . somewhere . . . He had already stepped up towards an altar with a sacrifice in his arms. The cold altar of an empty rusty tank. His head swam, his knees gave under him. The nearsighted eyes saw nothing. Only his feet had eyes, finding the steps in the dark; one step after the other.

In the attic, the pale light of the oncoming day shone through the windows. Bunim moved slowly forward, noticing quick little shadows jumping along the walls, frightened little creatures soundlessly crawling past him. Then he heard the angry whispering voice of a man coming from the shed which housed the water tank. Then there was the water tank. A large stone bed. Beside it stood the High Priest wrapped in shadows: Moshe Grabiaz, little Masha's father. His burning bloodthirsty gaze fell on Bunim, and on Blimele sleeping in his arms. He jumped towards him.

"Get out of here! This is my hideout and I'll let no one up into the attic!" He raised his fist at Bunim. "Let me save my child!"

Bunim wanted to beg him for indulgence. The children had spent the day before together and had kept quiet. But his tongue was lame, stuck between his teeth. His stiff arms felt on the verge of breaking. He could barely hold Blimele. Bent over her, he searched with his feet for the stairs. Slowly he descended, leaning with one elbow against the banister. "God does not want the sacrifice," his dazed head hammered. It seemed to him that a hand was touching him. Someone was caressing his stiff wire-like hair. A voice spoke to him, "Step lightly . . . Descend from the altar with thanks in your heart . . . God is merciful. You are not walking on your own legs . . . You are being carried down from the place of sacrifice with the sleeping child in your arms . . ." He stopped and pressed his swollen lips against Blimele's cool cheek, feeling her body against his chest. He kissed her with his whole being, and her whole being seemed to respond. She stirred in his arms. "Put your hands around my neck," he whispered.

The backyard, steeped in grayness, was in confusion. Parents and children were running in and out of all the entrances. Someone was tearing away the boards around the water pump, to check whether a little creature could be hidden inside. Someone else was smoothing out the garbage over the garbage box; beneath the heap of dirt a few two-legged rats lay concealed. Only the latrines were left alone. Yesterday all the children hidden inside them had been discovered. Samuel Zuckerman and Junia stood on the stairs leading to the cellar which had once harboured the radio receiver. They let Sheyne Pessele in with a flock of orphans. Samuel bolted the door and locked it. Other neighbours were running with their children to the gate. In its archway, in front of his cellar, stood the Toffee Man. Bunim went there with Blimele still in his arms. The Toffee Man let everyone in, opening the under-cellar where his own children were hidden.

Bunim stopped in front of the opening in the floor. An open grave filled with live little corpses. He turned back, passed the yard and entered his hut. He stepped forward to Miriam, "Moshe Grabiaz has refused . . . And the basements are overcrowded with children."

Miriam puckered her eyebrows. "Into the wardrobe!" She commanded.

He let Blimele down on the floor; she swayed sleepily. He shook her, "Blimele, wake up . . . listen . . . I'll hide you in the wardrobe. Sit quietly. Don't call out . . . even if you hear shouts. Do you hear me, Blimele?"

She blinked her eyes, then threw herself at Miriam, crying, "*Mameshe*, take me into your bed . . . hide me in your tummy . . . I'm scared."

Bunim carried the weeping child over to the wardrobe and put her down inside, behind the racks of clothes. He removed a board from the back, so that she could have enough air. He caught the last tearful flash of Blimele's frightened eyes and covered her with Miriam's coat. He knew that she would not cry. As he locked the cupboard, he saw himself in the mirror on its door. He was facing a dishevelled monster. He approached Miriam. The hot heavy air around them pulsated. He could not catch his breath. He was suffocating.

He heard Miriam say, "Sheyne Pessele's Shalom popped in a while ago. You can go and fetch the potato ration before the 'action' begins. They've opened the co-operatives for an hour." He was flustered by her words. How could he leave the hut? She insisted, "We still have another hour of peace . . . Let's at least get ourselves some food to eat." She added, "Lock us in from the outside, so that you won't have to worry."

She was right. He would lock them in and bring the potatoes. He would take out the bread ration too. He too needed to eat. He would force himself. He must be strong . . . strong . . .

As he ran with the shopping bag through the yard, he was making plans. Later on, after the danger was over, he would cook some food, to strengthen Miriam. Maybe she would be able to get out of bed for a while tomorrow? And Blimele would also enjoy a bit of good potato soup. It was an excellent idea to lock them in from the outside. Perhaps he should do it every day, as long as the *Sperre* was on? Lock them in and leave the hut. It was strange how he could feel Miriam's gaze on his back as he ran. Her hand seemed to caress his head imploringly, "Calm down, calm down . . ." Tomorrow he would perhaps find a still better hideout. The Commissar of the Gas Centres might help him; he had a favourable attitude towards writers. Or perhaps, he, Bunim, could approach Vladimir Winter who had connections with the Germans . . .

In front of the co-operative there swarmed a nervous impatient crowd. There was no queue, no order. Everyone pressed towards the door. Bunim ploughed into the crowd. Around him roared a pack of wolves, a pack of wild beasts, prodding with their elbows and scratching with their claws. Bunim removed his glasses and hid them in his pocket. Someone tore at the fur of his collar; someone else was pulling him by the coattails. He himself turned into a wild beast, as he tore at the collars, the lapels, the coattails of others. Fractions of the granted hour were falling off like petals from a withered flower, petal after petal, minute after minute. Bunim wanted to give up and run back empty-handed. There were now only five minutes left of the granted hour. Bunim was already at the frame of the co-operative's door. He could already see the employees filling the bags with potatoes. Across the way, in front of the bakery, there was a similar crowd. People were emerging with loaves of bread. The smell of freshly-baked bread reached to where he was, to where everything seemed at a standstill. There was no moving ahead. A skirmish broke out. Screams. Bunim extricated himself from the crowd and crossed over to the bakery where things seemed to be moving faster. He was amazed at the strength with which he pushed himself through the mass of bodies — straight to the door. Suddenly he found himself inside. What a miracle! A warm bright loaf of bread fell into his hands — a gift of life. His heart swelled as if he himself were a loaf of bread rising on the yeast of hope.

Away from the crowd, he felt a heavenly calm descend upon him. Another wonder: at the co-operative where the potatoes were being distributed, the crowd had shrunk. It was easy to get in. In a split second he had the whole potato ration in his bag. He flung it over his shoulder, and pressing the loaf of bread to his chest, set out for home.

The street was dead. Bunim ran over it with tangling steps. A huge truck filled with colours wailed as it passed him by. Through the gate beneath the bridge rows of empty trucks came rushing in. Bunim entered his backyard. It was black with people, all swaying, circling in a vertiginous maddening dance. Women were tearing the hair from their heads, knocking themselves against the walls; they lay prostrated on the *dzialkas*. The whole backyard was united in one howl.

Blinded, bent under the load on his back, he dashed to the hut. The lock was broken. The sack slid from his shoulder; the potatoes rolled over the floor. The loaf of bread fell from his hand. He entered the other room. Miriam's bed was empty. He opened the wardrobe and with the hands of a blind man tapped at the emptiness between Miriam's dresses. The drawer of the dresser where the baby had been hidden stood open. The shutters on the windows were torn off. Through them the morning had come in to find its reflection in the mirror of the open wardrobe door. The room was full of light. The sun, a yellow cat, lay stretched out on the creased cover of Miriam's bed. Bunim fell upon it with outstretched arms, embracing it as if it were a body. The bed was still warm and smelled of Miriam. As he lay on it, he embraced the room with dry eyes. On the floor near the door lay Lily the doll, staring at him with her glass eyes.

◆   ◆   ◆

The night after the tragedy in the yard, the women gathered at the latrine, to relieve themselves from the tension in their bowels and in their minds. These were the fortunate women who had saved their dear ones. They looked at Berkovitch's hut, shaking their heads. "That's what I call crazy," one of them said. "Why didn't he think to hide his wife right after she gave birth? And I saw him carry the little girl back into the house."

"On the contrary, he's quite sane," another replied. "It's the best way to get rid of them."

They made a reckoning of the day's harvest, "The Toffee Man's nine sparrows gone like one . . . Did you see how the father stretched himself out on the threshold so as not to let the police into the cellar, and how one of them gave him a kick in the head? The Toffee Man himself must be a goner by now."

"And Sheyne Pessele also went with the truck, for no reason at all. I can understand when a person is old and weak. But merely because of a pair of swollen legs? So they took her, while they left worse cripples behind."

"They might not have taken her — because she was more lively at sixty than others are at twenty — but she wouldn't let them get to the children in the cellar. She threw an iron bolt at a policeman, and split his head."

"Fortunately Moshe Grabiaz won't be in the yard tomorrow, so we'll have no tell-tales. Thank heaven, he ran off with his bastard . . . and he also got rid of his sick wife."

"Never mind, no one can escape from the ghetto. Sheyne Pessele's Shalom has sworn to finish him off, and you can rely on Sheyne Pessele's sons."

A woman came running towards the group to impart some information, "They already know where the people are being sent to. A *shtetl* called Ashpicin or Oswiecim. A policeman said that all the children are being kept in a camp, and they don't even lack birdmilk. Nurses and governesses from the Red Cross are taking care of them and the Germans have no more say over them . . . An international agreement."

"And the old people?"

"The old are being exchanged for prisoners-of-war. They are being taken to a sanatorium in Switzerland."

"That's what the policeman said?"

"That's what they say."

"It makes sense."

The women dispersed to announce the good news to the other neighbours.

In the morning Sheyne Pessele came back from the place of assembly. Yossi, the son who worked at Baluter Ring, had used his "protection" and saved her.

When she entered her apartment at dawn, Shalom was not there. He arrived a few hours later and they stood facing each other from a distance, as if they were afraid to embrace. They prepared some food as if nothing had happened. Shalom wanted to ask her many questions. He wanted to experience what she had experienced, but the questions refused to pass through his lips.

"A policeman came to fetch me in the middle of the night and he took me to the Resort," he told her, "to construct a gallows. They are already hanging people at the bazaar. Eighteen people. To scare the ghetto. They won't be cut down until the 'action' is over. The carpenter's trade has become quite a career, eh, mother?"

She wiped her face with both hands. As soon as they had finished eating, she ordered, "You're going to bed right away! Look at that face of yours. I have a note from the police chief himself, to protect me, but you would go with the first fire with such a face."

He was so delighted to see her safely back, that he had the impression that the danger had already passed for the two of them. Nevertheless, he obeyed her, and threw himself on the bed. His eyes were burning, his hands ached from the feverish work of the previous night. Before he fell asleep, he saw the gallows in his mind, with the eighteen suspended bodies, their feet dangling above the sand of the bazaar; at the same time he remembered that Sheyne Pessele was back and with this soothing thought he drifted off to sleep.

· Like an avalanche, the trucks of the *Rollkommando* swept down upon the ghetto, branching out into the streets and alleys. Every convoy was accompanied by men in green uniforms, their guns ready to shoot. The Jewish police cordoned off the streets, one block of houses after another, and the Germans dispersed over the yards, shooting into the air. "*Alle Juden 'runter!*"

The Jewish police attacked the apartments, broke doors, broke into all the cellars and hide-outs, herding the people out into the yards. In every yard the crowd was assembled into two long rows, one of women and children, the other of men. A soldier with a loaded revolver in his hand made the inspection, marching along the crooked line-ups, scrutinizing each person. It was no longer a question of children and old people. Mothers with children were pulled out of the line; sometimes a child was taken out of its mother's arms, while the mother was left standing. Some who looked very weak were pulled out as well as some whose noses were too pointy, or whose backs were too bent, as well as those whose legs were either too thin or too fat. It happened quickly. Those pulled out from the lines swayed drunkenly, as they trudged in the direction of the gate. If someone wished to leave with a member of his family, he was allowed to do so. If one of those taken out of line tried to turn back, a shot stopped him. That morning the ghetto was dumb. Nowhere in the world had there ever been such dumbness. Mouths were shut tight. Tears stopped flowing. Everything was awake. Everything was sharp and clear. Clear and final.

In the yard on Hockel Street the two rows of people started right at the gate and reached back to the cherry tree which seemed to be one in the line of women, as if it had volunteered for the selection. The lines were crooked and winding, climbing over the *dzialkas* and descending onto the paths between them. The line of men reached to the house where the Zuckermans lived. Everything looked peaceful after the few initial shots. At the head of the lines the selection was already going on. The rows were shrinking fast. The cherry tree remained behind with outstretched boughs, as if it wanted to follow the line but could not. At the gate stood Jewish policemen pushing those taken out from the lines into the street. In the street stood other policemen who chased the people onto the trucks.

Shalom stood with his identity card in his hand, close to the gate. Before he even managed to catch his breath, a German touched his shoulder, and the next moment he found himself in the gate. He moved ahead like a puppet, dazed, mechanically rubbing his face with both hands. When he came out into the street, he saw the *rollwagons* which looked like wooden cages and the people climbing dumbly into them. At this point he woke up and took a step to run away. A policeman grabbed him by the arm, "Up on the wagon!" Shalom pleaded with him to let him see whether his mother would come out too, so that they could be together. "Up on the wagon!" the policeman roared.

The veins in Shalom's still strong hands swelled. He was ready to attack the policeman when he noticed Sheyne Pessele. The protective note from the police chief was no longer in her hand. She ran up to Shalom; policemen began to push them up onto the wagon. Sheyne Pessele tried to tear herself out of the policeman's hands and to push Shalom away from her. "Run!" she screamed at him.

She was already on the wagon. Shalom hung on to it with one foot. Sheyne Pessele was pushing him down, while the policeman was pushing him up. Shalom let the policeman do his job and he raged at Sheyne Pessele, "Let me up, Mother, you hear me?" He scrambled up to her. The wagon was crammed with people and with silence. Mother and son stood pressing against each other, their arms and legs entangled. From the street came the sound of shots being fired at those who were trying to escape. Finally, the packed wagon was bolted shut. It swayed, and the people began to fall over one another; children slid out of their mother's arms. The silence continued. Not even the children cried — as if they, like the adults, were paralysed, overwhelmed by the unbelievable unreal reality.

Shalom held on to a board with one hand and pressed Sheyne Pessele to his chest with the other. They did not fall, but remained upright, eye to eye. Their gazes were fixed on each other's faces, until Sheyne Pessele said quietly, "Shalom, we have to save ourselves." The shaking of the rolling wagon shredded her words. "Look here, jump down and run to Yossi, he will intercede . . . and . . . Go, my darling . . . jump down, don't be afraid. We must not let ourselves . . ."

Shalom's feet were aching to jump, to escape. He could not look at Sheyne Pessele's face. But he was tied to her with a thousand cords. They both wanted the same . . . and they both knew that Yossi would no longer be able to help. And yet . . . He, Shalom, would jump down. He would run to Yossi . . . His mother was ordering him to do so. She was sending him . . . But she would fall if he let go of her. No, she herself was pushing him away, yet she did not fall. She was standing on her own two feet. She was bending down, to find an opening between the boards. She pushed away some feet and raised Shalom's foot. He looked around. The policemen were far behind. The wagon first increased its speed, then slowed down. "Mother, you jump too!" he said emphatically.

Her face lit up, "Of course I'll jump!"

"First you, Mother. I'll help you. Wait . . . soon . . . when the speed lets up some more."

"No, first you, Shalom. It's better like that. Let me see you down there, and I'll have more strength."

"Swear to me that you'll jump."

"Quick, the wagon is slowing down. I swear to you!"

He felt her lift him up. She was so strong. For a moment he was completely suspended from her shoulders. He already had both feet outside the truck. He felt her hand on his. Then he no longer felt it. He jumped down; he could no longer see Sheyne Pessele. He ran . . . He was being chased. He heard shots. He found himself in a gate. Somebody stopped him. He looked up and saw a policeman's cap. Inside the yard the "selection" was still taking place. Now Shalom noticed the wagon half-filled with people in front of the gate. He was lifted up in the air. He was throwing his fists about and dealing out blows on all sides. A group of policemen gathered around him. Soon the Germans would come out and finish him off on the spot, they warned him.

Again he was on a truck. He knew that he must not stay there. He heard Sheyne Pessele's voice over his ear, "We must not let ourselves!" The wagon filled quickly and began to move. Shalom tried many times to climb up the barrier of boards, until he succeeded and jumped down. He noticed a gate in the distance, in front of which there stood no wagon. He raced to it. An empty dead backyard. He hurried through it until he came to another. Here the "selection" had not yet taken place. The road to Yossi's house was free. Shalom edged along the walls, skirting the empty streets. The ghetto seemed to be deserted. On the bazaar stood the gallows with the bodies of eighteen people swaying in the breeze. Shalom felt how badly his hands ached.

Yossi looked strange when he was not smiling. He looked like an angry stranger, with fury in his eyes. "They've taken Mother!" Shalom sputtered out.

Yossi stared at him. "The note didn't help?" He cracked the knuckles of his fingers. "I'm going straight away!" Shalom looked about the room. Yossi's wife and child were with the protected families of those who worked at Baluter Ring and were gathered in a separate building. "You can't stay here. The 'selection' will be on soon," Yossi muttered from the door. He added, "Do you know that they've taken Mottle? I've just seen Israel. He told me. They've taken all three of them."

Shalom knew that Mottle would go. Mottle, the communist, the revolutionary, had let himself be led onto the wagon, just like he, the Bundist, the revolutionary, had. But Mottle would not jump from the wagon. Itche Mayer's children, although they were no cowards, had obligations. Mottle would not leave his wife and child. Mottle was even braver than Shalom, who had basically behaved like a fool, leaving his mother, even if only temporarily. And he heard Mottle's triumphant voice within him, above him. Mottle had won "the last and decisive struggle" over all his opponents.

Yossi stood at the door, impatient, raging, "Can't you hear what I'm telling you? You cannot stay here. The 'action' is coming!"

"Let it come."

"Are you out of your mind? With that *klepsydra* face of yours you'll be on the first fire . . . At least use a bit of lipstick. Paint your cheeks." A distant shot was heard. Yossi came back into the room and dragged Shalom over to the mirror. He opened his wife's box for cosmetics which Shalom had made for her, and hurriedly painted Shalom's lips and cheeks. "I must run to find out about Mother," he panted. "Here, take one of my identity cards." He drew out a card from his pocket, placed it in front of the mirror and dashed out of the room.

Shalom looked at himself in the mirror. He looked like a clown. Yossi had put too much paint on his face. He hurriedly wiped his cheeks, smearing the rouge all over it. No, he would never survive another "selection". He had to hide somewhere. He ran to the door. The house was silent; the yard, empty. Shouts and shooting could be heard from the neighbouring yard. Suddenly Yossi burst back in. "They won't let me through. The street has been cordoned off. Come upstairs, where are you running to?"

"I won't survive another selection. Here is your identity card. I'm going to hide in the latrines." Before Yossi could say another word, Shalom had dashed off in the direction of the latrines deep in the yard.

"*Alle Juden raus!*" came the shout. The Germans entered the yard. The shed with the latrines was filled with hiding people; it creaked. Steps were heard approaching from the other side. The next moment hands were tearing at the doors of the latrines. Locks and chains were broken. A pair of policeman's hands was already dragging Shalom by the collar.

He stood in the lineup. This time he was one of the last to climb the wagon. Right behind him the cage was closed. He was riding over the ghetto. He breathed heavily. His legs gave way under him. Yet he knew that he must not let himself. By no means. He would jump. He will only wait a bit, to catch his breath. He still had time. The wagon had just passed into the other part of the ghetto. It was still far enough from the place of assembly. He looked out through the cracks between the boards. The entire ghetto was riding on the *rollwagons*. The houses were like hollow lanterns. Soon he would jump. Sheyne Pessele had ordered him to jump. She had ordered him to save himself. He had only to wait for a favourable moment. He straightened up and inhaled deeply. He was ready. Itche Mayer's sons would never surrender. Sheyne Pessele's sons would never surrender.

The sun pricked his eyes. In front of him and behind, the *rollwagons* were rolling. The wagon ahead of his was packed, bodies were tangled up into one mass. Only one woman stood apart. The sun was tinting her hair a fiery red. A familiar-looking head . . . boyish red curls. He had seen her somewhere . . . He had loved her once. He felt that her hair was still aflame within him, burning in his heart. "Esther!" he called above the silence. Or was he only calling her inwardly? Suddenly he felt powerful. "Esther, jump! Jump!" He heard his own voice, strong, loud and thunderous. The redhead did not budge. Shalom filled his lungs with air. "Esther, escape!" He roared so that the veins in his neck swelled. The redhead did not move.

They were approaching the train station in Marysin. There . . . in the place of assembly, Sheyne Pessele was waiting. Shalom knew that Yossi could not save her. Here . . . in the neighbouring wagon, rode Esther. A clear light lit up in his mind: Itche Mayer's sons were valiant people. They would never betray those whom they loved. That was the real meaning of not surrendering. He felt relieved and tired. His blood seemed to recede from his veins and flow out from his body. He gave a deep sigh. His hands let go from the boards. He sank to the platform, looking at the red head through the cracks. "My beautiful Esther," he whispered.

As if she had heard his whisper at that moment, Esther stirred in the distance, on the wagon, and began to move. Through the crack between the boards Shalom saw her head rise, move upwards. He saw all of her above the boards of the truck. The next second she was soaring through the air; he was now riding past her. He saw her lying on the pavement. He jumped to his feet, his head above the highest board. He saw her stand up and run . . . run away from him.

Shalom's truck arrived at its destination. Jewish police and Germans surrounded it. The rails twinkled like polished silvery skates — knives. Somewhere around here Sheyne Pessele was waiting; there was only one kind of devotion in this world. Soon Shalom will fly down to her, to protect her, to be protected by her. He fell into the arms of the ultimate silence.

✦   ✦   ✦

Esther was racing through an empty backyard; she was under the impression that every shot that she heard had hit her. The clops of her wooden shoes against the cobblestones also sounded like shots. She found herself in a second yard, in a third. Everything was empty and dead. At length, she could no longer run. She knocked at one door after another. The last was opened ajar and a man's face, all covered with rouge and lipstick, stared out at her with a pair of ferocious eyes.

"Let me in," she begged. "I've jumped from the truck." The door thumped shut. She had to leave the district as soon as possible. The "action" had not yet begun here.

Sweat washed down her face in streams. All the clothes that she had hurriedly put on before the "selection", stuck to her body. She had followed her neighbours' example and put on as much clothes as she could manage, in order to look fuller. It had seemed practical too, to have some additional clothes in case she were caught. But she should not have done it. She was looking well again, as it always happened, after every tragedy. She was blossoming. She had lost her Aunt Rivka, her cousins, she had escaped from the gathering place — and she was blooming. The trouble with her was that her cursed beauty tempted the most beastly men. Two wolves had stood before her during the "selection". "That one looks too appetizing!" one of them called out, and they sent her to the truck. How she hated her body! How she hated herself for having made herself prettier still, for having painted her face like the neighbours did, for having arranged her hair to please, for having put on that pair of silk stockings which she had bought at the time of her career as a *wydzielaczka*.

Actually, she might now hurry back to her own house. There, everything was over, at least for the day. But she could not bear the thought of being all alone in her garret. First she had to see a human face, at least exchange a few words with someone — this need had overcome her as soon as they had stopped shooting after her. Somewhere in these yards her comrades, her friends and acquaintances were supposed to live. But all the yards became mixed up in her mind. She had no idea where she was. And so she raced from one brutally locked door to the other. "Death to the lonely!" the doors' silence screamed at her. "Back to the truck!" The doors seemed to chase her away. But there had been no human beings on the packed trucks either. Standing on the truck amidst the entanglement of bodies, limb against limb, skin against skin, she had felt even more severed from people than she felt now, facing the closed doors. Up there she had felt infinitely, unbearably orphaned. She did not want to perish all alone, without a witness, without a trace.

Suddenly she heard a bellow, "*Alle Juden raus!*"

A cohort of Jewish policemen came running at her. Through the gate of the yard in which she found herself came two green uniforms, their guns pointed at her. She dashed towards a stairway. A cluster of people hit against her as they surged down the stairs — a crowd of painted clowns holding each other and pressing their children to their chests. Above them, hovered the Jewish policemen in their orange striped caps, pushing and prodding those who were slow. She let the crowd flow past her. A policeman waved his club at her. "Eh, redhead, move on!"

She took a step backwards and let herself down on all fours. She found some place to hold on to the stairs, and crawled upwards between the descending feet, thick and thin, big and small. There was no sharper pain in this world than the pain of fingers being stepped on by one shoe after another. Yet she kept on scrambling upwards, navigating past the policeman's boots. Then there were no more stairs. On all fours she turned, entering a long dark corridor cut through by beams of light from the open doors, each of them framing a picture: an abandoned home still filled with the breath of those who had left it. The last open door seemed the most inviting.

A sharp sour smell penetrated her nostrils. It reminded her of something intimate and distant. A cupboard stood open. On an unmade bed lay an open valise, its cover full of round holes, like eyes — a baby's hideaway. The chairs in the room were laden with the clothes of men, women and children. A cord ran through the room from wall to wall. On it swayed torn diapers — white, shredded pennants of peace. Her foot hit against an overturned chamber pot. She shuddered and ran out.

She entered another room and crawled under a bed. Scattered shouts reached her ears from the yard. She licked her fingers with her tongue. They were stiff, blue, pressed together. She did not feel them at all. As she licked them, the smell from the other room came back to her. She drifted off into slumber and saw a tiny girl crawling on all fours. Her mother sat at a sewing machine, her feet moving up and down on a pedal, close to the floor. Up above, a little wheel was quickly turning, and a thin little needle was tapping out a good sour smell. "Under little Esther's cradle a snow-white kid lies asleep." The smell hummed. Dead white kids hung on a cord which seemed to have no beginning and no end.

When she opened her eyes the silence of the surroundings attacked her, tearing at her ears, biting her eyes. She crept out from under the bed and carefully moved over to the window. Downstairs the silence was moving. The action was over. Those who had been saved wandered about the yard. Figures of lunatics. She left the room. Through one of the open doors she saw a man on a chair, stooped over a jar with sugar which he held between his knees. The sight of his arched back brought Vladimir Winter to her mind. Winter was waiting for her in his large bright room. He would take her in and protect her; he would crush her unbearable loneliness with the tip of his hump. She had to reach him, to drag herself over the bridge. But she could not run. The weight of her clothes made her too heavy. Her feet were bruised, her hands were aching.

She dragged herself through the backyards, slowly pulling off her sweaty pullover. She tied it around her head, so that her red hair would not attract attention. Tomorrow she would shave off her hair, she decided. Perhaps she would also pull out a few teeth and turn herself into a monster. Today, however, she must remain beautiful — for Winter. She longed for the touch of his long pale fingers, for his ugly face with the hawk-like eyes, for his large white forehead burning like a piece of coal, for the waves of his compulsive chatter. She had to cross the bridge and reach him. He was her destiny, her life. She was not afraid to walk towards life.

The bridge was empty. From the depths of the street she saw two *Sonder* policemen approach. Their steps resounded with a double echo. She pulled in the belt around her waist and removed the sweater from her head, arranging her hair. She ran out from the gate where she had hidden and waited for them. "Please, take me across the bridge," she begged with sweet innocence.

The policemen stopped. The flames of her hair and the green light from her eyes beamed at them. They were two serious, exhausted men; one of them removed his cap, wiping the perspiration off its border. The sight of her was refreshing. For the first time that day he was hearing a clear calm voice, and looking at a smooth relaxed face. "Let's take her by the arms," he turned to his companion. They held her by the arms, asking her to make herself heavy, so that it would appear that they were arresting her. She made herself heavy. Her wooden shoes barely touched the stairs of the bridge. It was delightful to lean against a pair of manly arms. When they got to the other side of the bridge, they continued to hold her tight. "Where is the young lady hurrying to so bravely?" one of them inquired.

"To see my fiancé," she replied.

"He must be some man, if you're willing to risk your life to see him."

"He surely is."

It was pleasant to carry on a humorous chat after a day's work at the trucks. The fresh redheaded girl helped them to forget themselves a bit. They could not let go of her right away. They were already passing the bazaar. The eighteen bodies on the gallows swayed lightly. Esther felt so secure between the two strong arms that she dared to cast a stealthy glance at the eighteen shadows on the sand. The three of them approached Winter's house. She thanked the policemen. "Is that all we get?" one of them asked. She kissed their rough cheeks.

She entered Winter's room under the impression that no one was there. All she saw were the walls covered with paintings, and the live picture through the wide open window: the distant city with its roofs and chimneys sketched against the enormous sky of late afternoon. She took a deep breath. She had arrived at last.

A pair of hot bony hands wound around her arm. "You've come to save me," she heard a whisper. All was lost again. Winter seemed smaller and more shrunken than ever, as if the time during which they had not seen each other had diminished him. His hump was pointy like a mountain peak. His face was brown and cracked, a piece of clay. Only his forehead and the sharp nose were white. His hawk-like eyes pierced through her, fearfully, imploringly.

She smiled a dead smile at him. He began to dance around her like a dwarf, helping her to remove her coat and the many blouses. Now and then he sank on his legs but immediately straightened up. As soon as she had taken off her additional clothes, he fell back on the sofa.

"Life is merciful, Esther," he sighed. "Come, sit down beside me . . . like this . . ." He took her hand and placed it on his hot forehead, "Stroke me," he mumbled. "I've a temperature. Forty degrees. Because of fear, because I was waiting for you, because . . . I stood at the palette with the identity papers in my hand. Levine came in with his old woman and begged me to save them. Levine had taken off his medical insignia, so that he wouldn't have to participate in the action. What kind of protection could I give them? These papers are for me only . . . They're my life, do you understand?" She nodded. She would never have believed that Winter could be so ugly, a monster full of endless chatter. "With you I'm not afraid." He would not shut up. "You . . . you . . . Give me a bit of milk. I'm burning up inside . . . How beautifully you walk, Esther! Take off your shoes. No, better wear them. They will serve as weights to keep you here. Barefoot, you might perhaps fly away from me." She handed him a glass of milk. "Take one for yourself too. Go ahead," he encouraged her. "Everything I have belongs to you." Glass of milk in hand, she sat down beside him. She stared at the clean whiteness of the glass in her hands. The memory of the familiar sweet-sour smell came back to her, filling her nostrils. She brought the glass to her mouth. Her eyes overflowed. "You haven't had any milk for quite a long time, have you?" he asked.

She sipped from the glass, sobbing. "I thought that I could no longer cry," she sobbed. But then she raised her head and saw the clock on the wall. "Six o'clock!" she cried out. Her lips, still wet with milk, lit up with a child-like smile. "Peace until tomorrow morning!" The dusky sky reflected in the empty milk-white glass, in Esther's wet eyes, in her teeth, in her smiling milky lips.

Winter jumped down from the sofa. "Stay like that! Don't move!" he called out. His voice made her freeze; she did not move. He went over to the window and looked at her from there. "Colossal! Extraordinary!" He was beside himself with enthusiasm. His dishevelled mop of hair stood upright on his skull, encircling his head like a black halo. He quickly fingered through a pile of canvases, looking for a clean one. His feet gave under him and he sat down on the floor. He decided on a canvas and tried to stand up but could not manage it. "Don't move . . . don't move . . ." he muttered, grabbing his chest.

He broke into a grating cough, drew out a large stained handkerchief from his pocket and wiped his mouth. For a while he stared at the handkerchief, then threw it on a chair and somehow clambered back onto his feet. He placed the canvas on the easel and pulled the little table with paints towards him. Black and shrunken, he stood there, in front of the canvas. The light of the departing day shimmered on the tips of his hair. His hand, with its five spread out fingers like five infinite paths of longing, stretched towards the canvas. Then his ten fingers were creeping over Esther. He stroked her, looking like a sorcerer about to pronounce an incantation.

She felt that with these movements he was taking her into his possession, tying her to his eyes and through them to the canvas which smelled of milk and was like a white bedsheet. Soon she would stretch out on the sheet in her exhaustion — a lamb with red curly hair. Then she would sleep a sleep from which no one could wake her, a white eternal sleep which would not hurt. The red wool on her head would no longer burn. She would dissolve like a sunset in the white void.

The palette of fresh paint shook in Winter's hand like a fan refusing to open. He mixed the paint quickly, clumsily. Finally, he threw the palette on the table and snatched the blood-stained handkerchief from the chair, spreading it out against the light, against Esther's eyes. "Sometimes beautiful designs come out on it," he said, casting the handkerchief at Esther's feet. "Like this," he panted.

"It will give equilibrium to the composition, connect with the red of your hair and bring out the paleness of your skin. Look how wonderfully the handkerchief fell . . . by itself. Don't move!" That was all he said. The first dark stripes of the night appeared on the sky. It seemed as if Winter were pulling them towards the white of the canvas with his brush.

Esther's smile, milky red, still played on her lips. Her eyes were turned towards the sky, towards the long night. Winter was no longer as small as a worm. He was growing along with the night, from minute to minute, becoming increasingly larger, increasingly darker, taking hold of her with increasing power. She let herself go, surrendering to his hands — the hands of God. A holy trinity: God, the night and Winter. She belonged to them. They were eternity — until the next morning.

They did not exchange another word throughout the remaining hours of the evening. Esther did not notice it. A dialogue without words vibrated between them. Now, for instance, she was transmitting her life to him — beginning in the pre-memory days of her existence, up to the days when she had threaded through sad loves, thwarted passions, through loneliness and grief, through lost motherhood; days which shone with the light of Aunt Rivka's face and the white hospital shirts of the two sick cousins who had flown down to her from the hospital window, but had not reached her. She gave him her abysmal moments on the *rollwagon* and the coldness of the door shut in her face. She also gave him the days which were like the red and white fragrance of cherry blossoms, the days of blood and milk. She freed herself from all these tales, to let in the Great Peace. That was Winter's power. He had achieved all that with his magic, by sealing it all on the imperishable canvas.

It was late at night when the brush fell out of Winter's hand. The canvas covered with lines and colours shone in the dark like the raw mass of a body without a skin. He leaned against the window sill and stared at the canvas, throwing his head about and biting his lips. His sharp crooked teeth lit up with his victorious smile.

"Now I don't need you any more!" he cried. "From here I can go on by myself." He approached her, looking at her conceitedly, an undertone of vengeance coloured his voice. "Do you remember how I used to struggle, unable to reach you? Now you are mine, mine!" He combed through his upright mop of hair with his fingers, then grabbed his wrist to check his pulse. He trudged over to the bed and collapsed. When she stood up, he exclaimed in sudden panic, "Where are you going?"

"To cover the window and put on the light."

"It's not necessary. Come here," he stretched out his hands. Again she saw his spread out fingers, ten stretching paths of longing aimed at her. She felt that they were beginning to lose their power over her and she was sorry. "Esther," he mumbled, "you must stay with me. I am a great artist. No one knows that as well as you. Today we have become one. A superior wisdom has brought us together and . . . we have so much to achieve. Do you understand me? Come here, let me feel your closeness . . . your skin. You'll stay, won't you?"

"Of course I will stay," she answered calmly.

He sighed with relief. She saw him lost in the large bed. She did not mind his ugliness. His voice rasped gratingly in her ears. "I have my protective papers and you . . . your beauty. In case they come again . . . You will stay tomorrow too, won't you?"

"Of course."

"Then let's sleep. I am boiling . . . I shudder with cold. Come, cover me . . . Be good to me." She undressed close to his bed. He snatched her hand, "You won't go?"

"Whereto?" She stretched out beside him. His skin burnt her, while the night breathing into the room through the open window cooled her face. The wings of the window swayed lightly on their hinges. Down below, the ghetto was shuddering in its nightmare. But she was beyond the nightmare — in peace. It was a pity to wipe out those precious hours with sleep, but Winter, who was snoring, cuddled up against her, rocked her into sleep with the rhythm of his breath.

With the first blue of dawn she jumped to her feet. She cast one single glance at the sleeping Winter and dressed. Her heart was again clamped with hoops which would not allow her to breathe. The next moment she was rushing down the stairs, running out into the street in search of a hiding place.

✦ ✦ ✦

Golden autumn flirted with the world, using all the charms of a middleaged woman. In its eagerness to dazzle, it opened up all its arsenals of beauty, and with exaggerated care tried to outdo itself with its sweet smell, with its warm light which was reminiscent of spring and summer. Each day spread its hours over spotlessly blue skies, over an earth softened with sunshine and playful breezes, followed by a velvety night — a full overturned basket, pouring out the abundance of cool ripe fruits: the moon and the stars.

The next day of the *Sperre* also unrolled its splendour over the shuddering ghetto. Everyone was under house arrest, both those who were still together and those who had been orphaned yesterday, or the day before yesterday. They sat between the walls of their homes, not asleep, not awake, not hungry nor satiated, waiting for the hour of Fate, for the scream: "*Alle Juden raus!*" The tension rose along with the sun in the sky.

Early in the morning Mrs. Satin and her daughter Teibele knocked at the door of their neighbours, the Eibushitzs. Mrs. Satin's husband insisted that he would not go down into the yard for the "selection". He was a real *klepsydra* and he had no strength to climb down the stairs.

"If they want me," he announced, almost gaily, "let them do me the honour of coming to fetch me." Ever since the *Sperre* had begun, he had "whistled" at his wife and poked fun at her. Amused by her fear, he tried to frighten her with his laughter. "Ask her," he turned to Teibele, because he never addressed his wife directly, "ask her, the cow, why she is trembling so over her life? Tell her that the longer she lives, the longer she will be afraid of dying."

Mrs. Satin took along a bit of food and went in to the neighbours. On her own door she had hung up a lock, not that she, heaven forbid, wanted to protect her husband, but because she wanted to protect the things she had in the room. She was afraid of thieves.

Apart from the food, she also brought along her bag of cosmetics. A great expert in the matters of feminine beauty, she practised her art on Blumka Eibushitz's face, making her look at least ten years younger. She also transformed Rachel into "a real doll". She rubbed some glycerine into Rachel's hair, so that it would shine and hold well, and she dressed her up in all kinds of clothes to make her look full and healthy. She also offered advice to the men of the family, to Moshe and Shlamek. "I know, Mr. Eibushitz, that advice is like castor oil, easy to give but hard to take . . . However, if you listened to me . . . Believe me, I have your own good in mind." Mr. Eibushitz was upsetting Mrs. Satin. He refused to paint his cheeks with even a speck of rouge. He paced up and down the floor and the sound of his steps gave Mrs. Satin a headache.

Mrs. Satin and her daughter Teibele had come in all dressed up. Beneath their dresses they wore the best items of their wardrobe. Mrs. Satin was wearing a colourful flowery skirt with a gipsy blouse which went very well with the large round earrings dangling from her ears and with the multi-coloured string of beads adorning her neck. Her thick eyebrows were blackened with a pencil, her large, fleshy lips were painted a dark red and her long black hair was covered with glycerine. She looked like a sturdy gigantic queen of some exotic tribe. Her dainty daughter Teibele, dressed in her mother's high-heeled shoes, was a few centimetres taller than her normal height. She was filled and stuffed with a multitude of dresses over which she wore her mother's embroidered blouse and a broad skirt. Above her puffed-up frame hovered her little delicate face with the innocent eyes. Every now and then, Mrs. Satin cast a worried glance at Teibele, and clenched her hand over her heart. She was still not satisfied with her daughter's appearance and her headache was increasing with every second.

The women sat in the kitchen, on the beds made of chairs from which the bedding had been removed. Mrs. Satin did not stop sighing. The others looked silently either at the clock or at the window. Moshe's steps in the other room seemed to be tapping out the passing minutes.

"Today is our turn," Mrs. Satin whispered, swaying back and forth, with one hand holding her heart, with the other, her head. Even her grief and her fear seemed majestic. "Today they'll take whomever they like. Teibele," she groaned, "good heavens, your second skirt is showing from under the first . . ." She began to adjust the clothes beneath her daughter's dress. Then she turned to Blumka, "As soon as they enter the backyard, we must run down and be the first in line. Firstly, we'll avoid the blows, and secondly, they don't look so closely at the first in line. And we must stand straight, heads up high, to look healthier." She stood up, removed her hands from her heart and head and straightened up like a soldier. "How do I look, Teibele?"

"You look fine, *Mameshe.*" Teibele replied.

"Now you stand up and show me how you will look." Teibele stood up and Mrs. Satin grabbed for her heart again, "I'm going to faint! Straighten up your back, push out your breasts and don't stand crookedly on the heels. You look as if you've got two left legs. Lift up your head and don't push out your stomach. They'll think you're pregnant, woe is me. And what is that?" She felt a bulge on Teibele's hips.

"That's not me," Teibele smiled forlornly. "It's the skirts with the two pairs of woollen underpants." Mrs. Satin pulled Teibele over to her, threw the girl's skirt over her head, like a photographer hiding beneath a cover, and again began to adjust the tangled clothes on Teibele's belly.

Blumka winked at Rachel. They left mother and daughter in the kitchen and went into the adjoining room, where Moshe had been pacing. Shlamek was looking down into the yard through a tear in the blackout curtain. "What do we do?" Blumka asked, avoiding their eyes.

Moshe stopped pacing. The extinguished cigarette butt on his lips shook. "We don't go down," he said. "If Mrs. Satin wants to go down, let her. Let her lock us in from the outside."

Blumka went back into the kitchen and announced their decision to Mrs. Satin. "We want to ask you to lock us in from the outside and put the key on top of the door frame."

Mrs. Satin jumped to her feet, mortally offended. Put the key on top of the door frame? Were the Eibushitzs of the opinion that she, Mrs. Satin, might be taken away? She grabbed Teibele by the hand. "I'm going down. Let them look us over. I'm not afraid. Come Teibele, let's be the first."

Blumka followed her. "You don't want to lock us in?"

Mrs. Satin snatched the lock and the key from Blumka's hand. "Why shouldn't I want to?" The lock shook in her hand. She had lost all of her self-assurance. She stared at Blumka with pleading eyes. "Do you think that I'm doing the wrong thing, Mrs. Eibushitz?"

"I don't know who is doing the wrong thing and who the right. Everyone must decide for himself."

Mrs. Satin and her daughter left. They put the lock on the door outside. Inside, the clock was hammering louder and louder. Wheels rolled through the streets, quicker and quicker, coming closer. A shot was heard. Then another. The rat-tat of a machine gun. "*Alle Juden raus!*" The screams were near and yet still distant. The sound of boots running over stairs, of doors being smashed in was coming from somewhere. Then silence. A rustle of feet. Another shot.

Shlamek reported from the window, "They must be across the street."

Blumka chased him away from the window and ordered him to sit down. All four of them sat down in the kitchen, staring at each other, then turned their gazes away from one another. It took a long time . . . a very long time. The clock seemed not to know what it was doing with its hands. One moment they seemed to hurry, the next to stand still. The noise downstairs approached and receded. Eternities passed. The trembling cigarette butt was still stuck to Moshe's lips. His hands tied around his knees, he was winding his thumbs around one another, as if one thumb were trying to calm down the other.

"If they break down the door and take one of us?" he threw the question.

"Then we all go," said Shlamek, glancing inquiringly at Rachel.

Rachel caught his glance, and replied with a nod of her head. She was tired of waiting; tired of the tension, of sitting immobile between the clock and the window. Before her eyes stood the image of the Friday afternoon when the *Sperre* had begun. Through the window she had seen the children being led off. There was no way of connecting the pink of that dusk with the richly coloured outfits of the children filling the *rollwagons*. She had seen the women, the mothers, in their insane dance after the trucks, and those other mothers strolling about, dazed, in the yard, as if what had happened were only a dream, a nightmare. And she had seen the victorious mothers who would not let their babies be torn out of their arms, but climbed into the trucks with them. Not all the mothers had done so. And that meant that "Blood of my blood, flesh of my flesh" was a lie. How then could one find strength for the forthcoming experience?

Blumka wiped her face with both hands, in the process wiping away all the paint that Mrs. Satin had so carefully applied. "No, children," she shook her head. "In case . . ."

"In what case?" Shlamek interrupted her impatiently; lately he and Blumka were unable to talk to each other without heat. "Why do you have to dig into it so much? We have decided not to go down, haven't we? If they find us here, we won't have to decide about anything."

Moshe consulted the clock; they followed him with their eyes. It was half past nine. They heard dull screams and the pounding of wheels against the cobblestones. Another half-hour passed in silence. Rachel felt like stretching out on the chairs, but was afraid that as soon as she shut her eyes and allowed her fear to relax, the Germans would enter the yard. That was not a good way of overcoming anxiety. She needed to believe in something, to find a way of thinking that would make her strong. She let David's name toll in her mind like a bell. She was calling him. No, it was he who was calling her. It was painful to think of him now, and yet also consoling. She asked herself whether he was still in the ghetto. Throughout the past few days she had had no news from him. Every evening, after the "action", she had run to peer through the barbed-wire fence. She asked her heart about him; it answered her only with the ticking of the clock.

They heard Mrs. Satin's voice from the other side of the door. "Neighbour, they are across the street now!"

In the corridor they could hear the whispering of the neighbours as they prepared for the "action". The sound of Mrs. Satin's groans approached, then receded. Blumka took Rachel and Shlamek by the hands like little children. Moshe stood up and remained motionless in the middle of the room, his eyes glued to the clock. Rachel wanted to break free from her mother's hand. It made her feel helpless, paralysed. She felt like bursting into sobs. To cry seemed a blessing. She heard horses galloping very fast, coming closer. Then there was the gallop of one solitary horse . . . a muffled sound, as if its hooves were covered with rags, or as if the horse were riding over a sandy desert, ticking with the pulse of a lonely clock hung upon a wall of fear.

Unable to bear it any longer, she tore her hand out of Blumka's and dashed towards the food cupboard. She took out a jar red with the last bit of marmalade, and offered each of them a lick of it from the tip of a spoon, then took some herself. She scratched out the jar. As the spoon touched the glass, it let out an unpleasant squeak, causing shudders to run down her spine. She stopped, licked the sweetness of her lips and felt refreshed. The faces of the others also seemed less tense. It became cooler in the room, as if something had burst open during that last moment. They no longer avoided each other's eyes.

A few shots were heard from the neighbouring yard. A policeman was yelling somewhere nearby. Another shot. A sound of steps. Many steps. Something was cracking, rolling, thundering. The roar of a leopard. A mewing of cats. A howling of dogs. Silence. Silence. How long did it last? A second? An eternity? They did not want to turn their heads to the clock. Not yet. Soon enough they would consult it. Now they had to be all ears, to measure time by their imprisoned breaths.

The house was dead. No steps, no sound anywhere.

Moshe was the first to allow himself to glance at the clock. "Twelve!" he exclaimed.

What a beautiful hour! Soothing music! The hour when the Germans had their lunch. Now the family came alive, making order in the room, rearranging the chairs. Moshe lit the stove, Shlamek crushed the peat briquettes, Rachel prepared the dishes and Blumka threw open the food cupboard. She took out half a turnip, two potatoes and her own bread ration, and put them on a plate. Today, eating her bread did not matter. Moshe rolled a fresh cigarette, to smoke before the meal, to dull his appetite. He gave everyone a puff. The pot on the stove was making a great noise. It quacked and foamed gaily. They all stood around, watching Blumka remove the cover and add salt to the bubbling water. Their mouths were watering.

A commotion began in the corridor. The door was unlocked and Mrs. Satin appeared in the room. "Half a day is over!" she called out.

Blumka served the food. Steam rose from the plates and wound around their heads. In the middle of each plate was half a potato and a few lumps of turnip, like islands in the middle of a sea. Blumka cut the bread into four equal portions; four was a sacred number.

After the meal, Moshe took both pails to fetch some water. "Be it as it may, let there be enough water in the house," he said. Blumka wanted to go with him. The water pump in the yard was not working and he would have to carry the water through a few yards. Shlamek too volunteered to go with him. But Moshe shook his head, "No one is coming along." They liked it when he was strict, sure of himself. So they let him go by himself. But as soon as the sound of his steps died away on the stairs, the clock took possession of them again. The minutes passed. In the distant yard where the water pump was located there were probably many people in line for water. Moshe could not be expected back yet. He had only left a moment ago, and there was still a lot of time — a whole half hour before the "action" would start again. Blumka did not move away from the window.

Shlamek raged at her. "What's the matter with you? Is he a magician or what?"

"Why didn't you go along to help him?" she shouted, then bit her tongue. She was glad that he had not gone. Suddenly, she exploded into hysterical sobs. Her entire body shook; her screams seemed to pour out of her every limb. She was unable to control her spasms and when the children tried to comfort her, they made her shake all the more. Moshe entered with the two pails of water. His face shone with perspiration; the dry cigarette butt was partly unglued from his lip. Blumka calmed down, yet it was clear that they barely had the strength to face the approaching hours.

That afternoon there was no other "action" on that side of the street. The hours until six o'clock, crushed into eternities of minutes and seconds, pressed upon the brains, cutting up all of their nerves, at one moment freezing the hearts to a standstill, at another moment prodding them into a wild gallop. Then the day was over at last, sliding down from the sky along with the setting sun. What a blessing it was that the Germans needed to sleep at night, just like all humans.

Blumka cooked again. She let herself go with the food, not thinking about tomorrow or after tomorrow. The evening and the night were all that they possessed. Cheerfully, festively, they sat down at the table — all four of them together. They did not talk. They were ravenous. They ate from four plates. Four spoons chimed like four joyful bells. The four were one. After the meal they set out to look for a better hiding place.

The streets were swarming with people rushing in all directions. Acquaintances stopped one another with the exclamation, "As long as we see each other!" and continued on their way to find out about relatives, friends, or other acquaintances. They wanted to tell what they had gone through, to relieve their hearts, to ask for advice, to prepare for tomorrow or to find out some news. Perhaps a miracle had happened. Perhaps the Germans had suffered such a defeat that they would not be able to enter the ghetto the next day with their Chariots of Fate. Abandoned women, orphaned men left their homes where everything reminded them of those who were gone, and wandered among the others, letting themselves be carried away by the surge, be deafened by the clamour, in order to dull themselves and escape the loss from which there was no escape.

It was dark when the Eibushitzs reached Marysin. The soil smelled of humidity and of withered grass. Rachel left her family in front of the Holy Shoemaker's orchard, and crossed the familiar path leading to her student's house. The grass in the orchard looked black in the shadow of the trees. She expected the figure of a painter, brush in hand, to pop out from behind a tree, but the orchard was deserted; the leaves falling soundlessly to the ground were swallowed by the black grass. In the shoemaker's kitchen a gust of sultry air attacked her. The kitchen was crammed with people. She could barely wade in. She noticed the shoemaker's bushy crop of hair. His warm clear eyes were fixed on the people surrounding him, but did not seem to see them. He was talking to someone, to two people at once, to all of them. He shook his head once left, once right, turning to those behind him. She pulled at his sleeve. He focused his eyes on her, his ready answer sliding down from his lips, "I can do nothing about it. I must not . . . I have a wife and two children."

From there they went to visit the *Rabiner*. Moshe and the *Rabiner* were friends. Whenever possible Moshe did the *Rabiner* little favours, such as providing him with scarce products at the co-operative, or delivering unexpectedly announced food rations.

The *Rabiner* came out in his neat black frock coat, the lights in his eyes flashing. He offered them all his smooth soft hand and politely invited them into the bower. But when Moshe asked whether he and his family could hide somewhere in the garden or in a shed, the lights in the *Rabiner*'s eyes went out. "I am sorry . . ." he shook his head sadly. "I have a wife and two children."

On their way home, Rachel left the family and ran over to the barbed-wire fence to have a look at the other side, as she did every evening during the *Sperre*. As soon as she climbed the step where she would stop every evening, a black head of hair flashed before her eyes in the distance. Was it a trick of her memory? Of her imagination? She stared at the head for a long time before she realized that he, whom she was looking at on the other side, was the one whom she had expected to see every evening. Her heart exploded with joy.

"David!" Her shout was too powerful to pass through her throat. She jumped down from the step. He jumped down from a step on the other side of the wire fence. She waved at him. He waved back. She wanted to move forward, but there were the wires, so she climbed back onto the step. He did the same. He was swaying. His face swam before her eyes. A flood of tears burst like torrential rain from her eyes, melting everything within her. "Thank you for being safe and sound," she mumbled. Looked at through her watery eyes, David seemed like someone alone on an island, making signs to a passing ship.

"I love you!" a voice carried across the barbed-wire fence.

"I love you!" another voice echoed. Blessed barbed wires. They were letting through the image of a face, the sound of a voice. Through the empty bridge Rachel and David strode to meet each other — and yet remained on the opposite sides of the fence. Up there, on the top of the bridge, they embraced; down below, the dead church hovered over the shadow which the oncoming night was spreading between them.

✦ ✦ ✦

(David's Notebook).

I have enriched my vocabulary with a new word: *Himmelkommando*. That pretty word comes from one of the Germans; he is called Fox, they say. They also say that Fox is particularly vengeful with women. He enjoys shooting at them. Today was the fourth day of the "action". How I am capable now, the same evening, of picking up the pen and sitting down to write, I don't know. How can I be so "normal"? Do I still remember? I had moments when my open eyes saw nothing, my open ears heard nothing and my mind went completely blank.

A tragic truth has become clear to me: the world will never know what we are going through. Who will be able to tell it? Even those who survive will barely believe that what happened to them was real. Who could relate what it meant to sit on a packed *rollwagon*, in the wooden cage? Then why am I trying to? How strange that during the moments of danger I swore to myself that if I survived, I would write everything down. Therefore, instead of throwing myself on my bed, shutting my eyes and gathering strength for tomorrow, I've now sat down to fulfil that senseless mission. I have heard that these last few days the writers bury all their writings in the ground — so that there will remain a "document" for the world to read. Had I done the same with my notebooks, it would mean that I was sealing my doom. I don't want this writing book to survive me.

Our backyard is probably the most unfortunate in the entire ghetto. We have already had three "actions" and who knows how many more are to come. The first day the Jewish police, with the help of Moshe Grabiaz, cleaned the yard of the children and old people. The next day, when the Germans took over, we hid with the Pudelmachers, our comrades, who live three houses away. Comrade Pudelmacher had known Father well and for that reason he always talks to me with great respect, as if I were God-knows-who. Half an hour before the "action" began, he came over. He said that Mother looked too weak to face a "selection" and he took us to his place.

Comrade Pudelmacher had begun to build his hideout as soon as the rumours that the Germans were demanding the children began to spread. Quietly, he began stealing bricks from the demolished houses, until he had enough to build a wall along the wall between his two little rooms. Two families live in these two little rooms. Pudelmacher peeled the wallpaper off the back wall and covered the new wall with it. The entrance between the double wall is through a hole covered with wallpapered cardboard, disguised by a table moved close to the wall. We squeezed into the hideaway, which is perhaps not wider than one foot and one can only stand upright inside. Air and a bit of light enter through a hole in the wall facing the yard.

Both families were already inside, amongst them four children between the ages of six and eight who never even uttered a peep. Pudelmacher entered last, covering the hole with the cardboard. It immediately became difficult to breathe. The noise in the yard could be heard very loudly through the air hole, so that we knew when it was safe to go out. Pudelmacher stroked Mother's back, saying, "Don't thank me, please."

Upon our return to the yard, we learned about the slaughter there. Overjoyed with our good luck, we devoured everything that we had in our food cupboard and had a ball. Then, as I was eating, staring into my bowl of soup, I thought I could see Rachel's eyes swimming inside. They looked at me so lovingly that I felt hot all over. For how long has it been since I spared her even one thought! I was overcome by the fear that I would never see her again. I was sure that she had been taken away — to punish me. I went down into the street and ran from one friend to the other, asking about the Eibushitzs. No one knew what had been going on on the other side.

Last evening, I stepped up on a doorstep and looked over to the other side. I was weeping, inwardly. What sense would there be to my survival, if Rachel were gone? Her face surfaced in my memory. I saw her in her blue suit. I saw her eyes, loving and dream-like, covered by a thin haze through which a hot flame twinkles. I recalled the taste of her lips — and suddenly I saw her. It was already dusk and the church was casting a huge shadow between us. I began to jump up and down on the step, waving, calling to her. Finally, I saw the gendarme on guard looking in my direction, and I ran off, so that she would run off too. I came home and threw myself on the bed. I was saved.

This morning Mother woke me with a shout, "The *Rollkommando* is here! Get dressed quickly!"

I hurried on my things and went over to the window. The Germans were already in the yard. The police were running towards the entrances. Panic in the corridor. The people half-dressed, the children not yet hidden. The police were already upstairs, chasing down the sleepy tenants. The next moment we found ourselves in the yard. "*Los! Los!*" the Germans hurried us, waving their revolvers. We tried to run over to the Pudelmachers and were already passing into the yard of the fire brigade, when the Jewish police arrived. They were chasing a woman who was also trying to escape. I heard a shot. Something exploded in my head; it seemed to me that the bullet had hit me. The same moment I saw the woman collapse under the cherry tree. The policemen were already holding us tight.

"Do you want to be shot too?" they yelled.

Abraham was working with his fists; I did the same. "Murderers!" I screamed. Abraham and I managed to free ourselves from their hands, but they were holding Mother. We began to pull her, trying to tear her away from them (we were behind a wall and the Germans could not see us). I began to talk to the policemen's conscience: "Our blood will be on your hands!" and other phrases like that. We were pulling Mother forward, and they were pulling her back. A few firemen arrived, who grabbed Abraham and me. Soon we were standing in the line-up of men. Mother was in the line-up of women and children.

"You have a better chance with the men," the firemen said to Abraham.

Abraham was struggling with them to let him get over to Mother. The Germans were looking in our direction, and the firemen finally let him cross over to the other side. Not far from Mother and Abraham, who were the last in the line, lay the woman who had been shot, a black stream of blood oozing out of her. I knew her. Reisel, the Zuckermans' maid. I did not look at her for even as long as it takes to write this down. I did not even see Mother or Abraham. I was alone with my life. I stood straight, pushed out my chest, raised my head high — to make a good impression. For a split second my gaze fell on the window of our room and this brought a smell to my nostrils; it reminded me of our summer cottage. I saw a green field. Yes. Green. The green uniform of a German was blocking my sight. The German had a candy in his mouth which smelled of mint leaves.

"*Raus!*" The candy jumped between his teeth. The butt of his gun was delicately cutting me out of the line. I crossed the yard, feeling an icy cold spreading all over me.

Outside, I saw the *rollwagons*. From one of them Abraham, who was with Mother, was shouting at me, "Run! Run!"

A policeman dragged me to the same wagon. The wagon was packed and we began moving. Mother was too exhausted to stand and she slid down to the platform. We both forced her to stand up. "You are a socialist," Abraham preached to her. "If you want us to save ourselves, you must jump down with us."

She threw her head around in all directions. I could not bear the sight of her. What was happening in the wagon? How did it feel to stand there? Not for me to describe that. All that I saw in that hellish moment was Abraham, our hero. I blessed his energy and surrendered to his power. I obeyed everything he said.

When the wagon turned a corner, Abraham jumped down. I helped Mother. Her body was like a bag. I practically threw her down. From all sides people were jumping off the wagons. The Germans arrived. Jewish police were chasing the escaping people. I was already on the ground. We were dragging Mother along, when a policeman grabbed my collar. I found myself on another wagon. I lay on its platform shaking to the rhythm of the wheels. I said good-bye to my life. Soon I was at the place of assembly. What did Dante, the great poet, know of hell? If he were here, he would not have found the words so easily.

A dance of chalk-white faces. Sky-splitting screams, moans, sobs, the howling of children. Deathly silence and giddiness. Suddenly in the blindness that overcame me, I saw my brother's face among the hundreds of faces. He was calling me, pushing himself through with his lank body, looking for me. "I'm here!" I wanted to call, but could not. Someone brushed an arm against him and he fell. I could no longer see him. Was it him, or was I having hallucinations? He had escaped with Mother, had he not? But then he surfaced again. I leapt over the bodies and limbs; I had once before soared like that over human bodies — in a little forest, during my escape from Lodz. My strength came back to me. I called him. He called back. One moment I saw him, the next I didn't. He began to give me signs to follow him. I did not know where to, but I believed in him. He was my little God of Life. As long as I saw him, I saw hope. He reached the locked door and talked to the policeman, pointing at me. Like waves the crowd was carrying me forward and pushing me back. I gazed at the policeman's face. He had kind eyes. When I finally reached him, he opened the door ajar, whispered something to one of the policeman outside, and pushed out first Abraham, then me. The policeman outside began to run and we followed him. He entered a cellar where many people were surging towards a broken window. He pushed us out through it and we were in the street. I asked Abraham about Mother.

"Everything is under control!" my proud saviour replied.

The street was empty, cordoned off by the Germans and the Jewish police. We moved towards the yards, climbing over the roofs of sheds and latrines. Everything seemed easy. When we got to the side where the "action" was finished, we decided to rest, and entered an empty room. The beds were in disarray, the knapsacks still on the table. Abraham found some dry parsley and we shared it. He said jokingly, "A *shishka* eats his breakfast whenever he wants . . . a simple ghettonik must eat whenever he has . . ."

"You risked your life for me," I said to him.

He shrugged his shoulders proudly, as if it were a trifle not worthy of mention. He told me that he had left Mother at Simon's and run to the place of assembly. He had hung on to the policemen. A few gave him a licking and wanted to force him to join a transport. He kept on asking them if they knew Father and one of them caught himself, asking if Father were inside. So he told him that the Germans had taken him away a long time ago and that his brother was inside. "I said to him, 'Mister, the war will not last forever.' And he let me in to you." Abraham concluded.

We decided not to take any chances and to return to Mother after six o'clock. We closed the door and window and threw ourselves on the beds to take a nap. Before I dozed off I thought of Abraham's heroism. Was it real heroism or only the daring of a child who played with fire without realizing the danger? I philosophized that true heroism meant to be aware of the danger, to look it straight in the face — and yet to act. How cheap of me. I wanted to diminish the greatness of Abraham's deed, in order not to feel so grateful to him. One thing I know: I am no hero. I have moments when I am more courageous than usual and others when I am less so. That's all.

We woke up very late and figured that Mother was probably at home already. The moment we entered our room, Mother swept down on us like a bird who has found her lost babies. We laughed and we cried. Mother told us that Simon's mother had died last night. "A lucky woman," Mother added, "she died in her own bed." In the middle of the night I was awoken by Mother's sobs. I asked her what had happened and she said that she was tired of running.

Mother, my Wise Knowing Sadness, you who have given me life — tell me, explain to me: what is there within you, within me, within the confused and tormented people outside — that provokes the wolves to chase after us? What is there within their blood which makes it boil up against us? Does the platitude, the pat answer about Christ fit in here? Does it not sound stranger here than anywhere else? Sometimes it occurs to me that they torture us, not because we killed Christ, but because we have given them Christ, and because we remind them too much of him. The wolves, who are chasing after us now, have rejected Christ. Perhaps with that they have quenched the desire of all Christians. Destroying us, they kill him. Killing him, they hate themselves. Hating themselves, they kill us. Killing us, they kill themselves. Suicide expressed through murder.

Mother, how much must they hate themselves if they are capable of torturing us so? We are not better than others, not holier than others, not more Christ-like than others. Only by turning us into victims, they raise us above themselves. And seeing us raised, they hate us even more, they burn us even more, they punish themselves through us even more . . . and more . . . and more . . .

How tangled the roads are, Mother! Through which of them does hatred arrive? Has it been kneaded into the clay of which man was created? Perhaps it is present in the breath of the God whom I seek? Where do the roads lead from here, my tired, my knowing Mother, my Sadness?

Today is the sixth day of the *Sperre*. Last night I was at the wire fence again, and saw Rachel. At night we slept with our clothes on. People were saying that yesterday the quota of three thousand heads had not been reached and that we could expect to be taken from our beds at night. So we are deprived of the nights as well. This morning at dawn, Mother woke us and we went over to the Pudelmachers, where we spent the whole day. When we got back we learned that it had been quiet today in our yard. Moreover, a surprise awaited me. Rachel and her father were there. I ran over to her, eager to take her into my arms, but something held me back.

Her father asked me about the Zuckermans. I told him that I had not seen them at all during the *Sperre* and that their maid had been shot. He said that Rachel and himself had come over to hide here. The "action" had not taken place in their yard yet and they had decided to split up; Shlamek and the mother went to hide somewhere else.

While he talked, Rachel did not take her eyes off me. Gradually the barrier between us vanished. I stretched out my hands to her, pressing her fingers with mine until the familiar warmth took hold of me. I asked them to sleep over in our room and during the day to hide in one of the cellars or in the garret. Anyway there was little likelihood that there would still be another "action" in our yard. As we passed Berkovitch's hut Rachel asked me about him. I told her that the first day his wife and children had been taken, and that I had not seen him since. I also told her that Sheyne Pessele and Shalom had left with the wagon, and also that the Toffee Man had disappeared from the yard after his children were taken.

Rachel came along with me to fetch water, then we went out into the street. There was a lot to say, a lot to tell, yet we were both silent. Then I said to her, "Rachel, I love you . . . Whatever happens, remember that." Then I threw the question at her, just like that, "When will there be a time for us to live and to love each other?"

"The time is now," she said quietly.

She told me that their neighbour had locked them up in their room every day, for five days. Yesterday they were sure that the decisive moment had come and they were glad — as long as it made an end to their waiting. A short while before the neighbour had come to lock them in, Rachel's father had an attack of fear and ran out to hide by himself somewhere else. The truth is that he looks horrible and there is no doubt in my mind that he would not have passed a selection. But apparently his leaving the home removed the ground from under the feet of the others. Rachel said that her mother cannot forgive him. I feel that Rachel too, although she talks about him so compassionately, resents him. At night Israel, who goes to the houses of our comrades to see who is left, visited them. He advised them to split up. That way, at least, there was a chance that the family will not be totally wiped out.

It is good even to be sad with Rachel. We stood under the cherry tree where the woman had been shot. "The cherry tree is gone," I said, showing Rachel the withered boughs. The night sky seemed to sit on the tree like a black vulture. We sat down on two stones and held each other.

"Next year," said Rachel, "There will be cherries on the tree again. We will be liberated by then." I was about to respond with my pessimism, but she covered my mouth with her hand: a white bandage over a wound. She laughed. Her laughter never had such a tone, not light and carefree, but hot and rich. It swept me along.

To my own surprise I began telling her a story: Cherries once used to be white. But they became red with the blood of two lovers, like Romeo and Juliet. The two lovers were neighbours, but their houses were separated by a wall of barbed wire. The two of them wanted to be together but the wires would not let them. Near the fence grew a cherry tree and the lovers would meet under its branches to look at each other through the wires. They were grateful to the fence for allowing their gazes and their words to pass, and raged against it for forbidding their embrace. They tried to destroy it, but the fence was stronger than they. They tried to climb over it, but it threw them off. So they decided to conquer it by dying together. They pressed themselves to the barbed wire so tightly that the wires cut their veins and pierced their hearts. Their blood, mixed together, dripped onto the cherry tree's blossoms and since then the colour of cherries has been red.

Rachel did not like the story. She said, "That's too sad and it does not fit with the taste of cherries. I have another story: The first man and the first woman came into this world in the North, where it is bitterly cold; where strong winds blow and all is dark and empty. The first man and the first woman had to be strong and stubborn in order to survive. But strength and stubbornness were not enough. They needed warmth to overcome the elements. So the first man and the first woman snuggled up to each other and realized that this made them feel warm. They snuggled up tighter and tighter. Then they lay down on the ice together. They became one, creating fire. The fire melted the ice and revealed the earth. A tree grew out of the earth. The Tree of Life. It branched out in all directions and, like a brush, it painted a sky over the heads of the two people. The sky was like a mirror in which the fire was reflected. And so the sun came about. Then the tree began to blossom and from the flower-beakers flew out newborn bees, butterflies and birds. Then the blossoms ripened and transformed themselves into fruit, into cherries. They were red because they were the reflection of the fire on the earth and the sun in the sky. The first woman picked a cherry, bit into it, and gave it to the first man to taste. They both became red in the face and understood that it was time to bring a child into this world."

We did not laugh any more. The light-heartedness between us vanished. We held each other's hands. They were hot. "Our time is now," Rachel's words rang in my ears. I led her into Zuckerman's cellar and bolted the door. It was pitch dark inside. I found Rachel's hand and said, "Now."

The ground was soft under our feet. Sand and sawdust. We undressed. Separated from one another for a moment, we shivered and slumped to the ground. A fresh cool encounter of skin against skin. Soon the sand beneath us became warm. The cellar was full of lips, of pounding hearts and pulsating veins. We were the two lovers who embraced through a wall of barbed wire. We were Adam and Eve in the cold country of the North. We were two and one. One and many. Millions and millions of people, and animals and birds were with us. There was thunder and lightning. Brightness and darkness. Laughter and tears. We were enclosed in the shell of a blood-red cherry. Between us was the core, the seed; the essence of everything, enveloped in a mystery which we wanted to solve through hunger and thirst, through tenderness and brutality. It seemed to me that we were splitting the atom of existence, reaching to the silence of death and the beginning of life.

◆ ◆ ◆

On the first day of the *Sperre*, when the "action" was still in Jewish hands, Samuel Zuckerman decided to move to the other side of the ghetto. First he went by himself to find a hiding place. It was not an easy task. He could by no means bring himself to knock at the doors of his former friends, the *shishkas*. Of his Zionist friends, some were protected by Rumkowski and the rest were as helpless as he. The only safe place for him and his family seemed to be at Miss Sabinka's little house. It had a cellar which could be easily camouflaged. Apart from that, the house was in Marysin where the dignitaries lived, and this meant that the "actions" would not be conducted there with great strictness. He took Junia into his confidence. She had known about Sabinka and he wanted to win her over first. He looked her straight in the eye. "Junia, the past no longer has any meaning."

"Everything has a meaning as long as we live," she replied. "It is not that I mind. It is Mother. Did you ever tell her?"

"There was no time . . ."

"When will there be time?"

"Can't you see that we are on the verge . . ."

"I won't ask Mother to hide there."

"You will. We shall all hide there."

Reisel, too, was faced with a serious dilemma. She did not want to be alone during these fateful days. True, she had nothing whatever to do with the Zuckermans any more and lived in a room of the house by herself; however, the mere fact of having lived with people for so many years was binding during such times, particularly since her sisters and their children had left with the winter "action" and she was left alone in the world. On the other hand, it was better during such times to be alone and to hide out alone. Finally, she announced her decision to Samuel: "I am not moving out of this backyard. Here is my destiny." And she let them leave.

Miss Sabinka had no idea that visitors had come to live in her cellar. Samuel had a key to her door, and she left every morning for the office of the *Sonderkommando* where she worked. She felt safer there. She came home only to sleep.

The cellar was windy and ruinous. Under the stairs stood a few empty boxes and on them the family spent the first night. They sat close to each other to keep warm. At dawn they heard Sabinka get up, then they watched her leave the house, her blond braids undone. Matilda too followed her with her eyes. Neither Samuel nor Junia had to tell her where they were. She had seen Samuel take out the key from his pocket. She felt abused, humiliated, trampled — and yet indifferent. Something had burst within her and fallen away like a shell. Her soul was a piano crushed by a hammer. The music was ended forever, the white keys strewn about, the chords broken, the walls fallen apart. It did not hurt or bother her.

As soon as Sabinka was out of sight, Samuel proposed that his daughters come with him upstairs and help him find some blankets. He led them into the bedroom. There stood the bed where he had spent his hours with Sabinka. It meant nothing to him. He opened a trunk filled with blankets, dresses, furs and pieces of expensive material. From among all these things Junia pulled out a white nurse's dress with an armband of the Red Cross. "She used to work at the orphanage," Samuel explained, letting Junia try on the dress with the armband. They heard a shot and distant screams. "They're coming!" he cried out. They grabbed a few blankets and ran down into the cellar.

They sat for hours holding their breaths. The noise came close, then receded. Matilda stretched out on a blanket spread on the ground. Beside her sat the silent Bella. Samuel and Junia knelt at the little opening, looking out. Samuel felt Matilda's eyes on him. Why had they hurt each other so much? Why had it been like that between them and not otherwise? Outside, the hurricane was raging. The world was about to collapse, and here they sat all four of them, shut up as in a barrel, hitting against each other, coming closer, coming apart — naked and alone.

Now that they had come this far, did it still make sense to straighten things out? Junia was right. It did. It was important that they, inside the shaking barrel which could drown at any moment, should find some thread to hold on to together. He knew that basically Matilda was the same woman who had once so enthusiastically surrendered to his caresses, with whom he had had two children; that she was the same woman who had once had such nobility of heart and such mysterious charm. Long, long ago she had, with her music, opened up all that had been frozen within him. How much had he made her suffer? No, he had never really loved her. He had never really known what love for a woman was. Only now, in his physical non-masculinity, did he sense the meaning of it. But just as he was thinking of all this, he became aware that the road back to Matilda was closed. Every bond was like a tree which needed attention and care. A bough cut off in recklessness would never grow back. Matilda and he were embracing a bare trunk: alienation. It was already impossible to create a language between them. He wanted to be capable of offering her some tenderness in their loneliness, of saluting her in their common estrangement. If only he could bring himself to give her the kind of look that he offered his children in their silence. But he was unable to accomplish even that.

For five days of the *Sperre* they sat in the cellar. A few times the commandos came into the district but did not search Sabinka's little house. Junia grew impatient. After each action she would pace the cellar, unable to relax. Never in her life had she felt so low, so helpless. It was false, it was wrong to sit here, she thought. Everything within her rebelled, drove her outside, to spite those who had imposed that fear upon her. One must not allow that, she thought, one must do something . . . do . . . do . . .

Actually, they could have left their hideout every evening, but Samuel forbade it. He did not want either Sabinka or her neighbours to find out about their presence in the house. But their food supply was about to run out and on the night after the fifth day, Junia climbed outside. It was a long time before she returned with a few turnips which she had found in an abandoned room. She told them that she had met with her comrades and had tried to talk them into doing something together. "They laughed at me," she raged. "All they have on their minds is how to hide themselves better."

Samuel smiled. "These are the Jewish Wars, Junia. Jews fight for every inch of life."

Alone with herself, Junia had to admit that in her heart of hearts she also feared for her life, just like her comrades did. Was she not filled with gratitude every day when the "action" was over? Was she not courageous at night rather than during the day? And when she fell asleep in the dark cellar, what did she dream about? She dreamt of freedom, of taking leave of her parents through a train window. It was time to fly from the nest. She was in the Tatras, rejoicing at the feel of the free gales descending from the mountain tops. She saw the mountaineers in their costumes and listened to the sound of flutes and bagpipes. She jumped from one rock to another over lively mountain streams. The waterfalls foamed and laughed their cascading laughter. Yes, she was afraid of dying, she wanted to live. She was eighteen years old and her body and soul cried out to grow older, to grow . . .

On the sixth day of the *Sperre*, they no longer had anything to eat and sitting trapped in the same place made their hunger grow wild. Junia decided once more to venture outside. For safety, she put on Sabinka's dress with the Red Cross armband. She headed for the surrounding fields where she hoped to dig up something from the *dzialkas*. It was early in the morning. The air was fresh. It was quiet all around. The sun fringed the roofs of Marysin. A pastoral beauty. Being all alone in full daylight, in the middle of the field, made her feel strangely ill-at-ease. She went down on all fours, investigating the ground for traces of beets or radishes. She was in a hurry and at first she saw nothing. She picked up a stick and began to dig with it. Finally, she discovered some beet stems, withered and trampled. She threw them into her bag and rushed back to the house.

"Halt!" she heard a shout behind her. A green uniform was running in her direction. He was a tall broad-shouldered giant with gray eyebrows and a gray moustache. "*Wohin?*" he asked, as he came closer. His gaze was not angry, but rather friendly. Was he drunk, or was he also intoxicated with the beauty of the morning?

"I am a nurse," she said boldly.

"That I can see," he replied leisurely, telling her that he could also see that she had been loafing in the field while her colleagues were so diligently working with the children. He noticed the bag in her hand and asked, "*Was ist denn das?*"

She opened the bag and showed him its contents. He took the bag and threw it far into the field. He let her walk ahead of him. Not far from the jail stood a few empty *rollwagons*. Here too the Germans, the Jewish police and a group of doctors and nurses were assembled. The row of *rollwagons* began to move and the giant soldier helped Junia climb onto the last one. Slowly the wheels turned in the direction of the central part of the ghetto. Junia noticed someone looking up at her through the spaces between the boards. She recognized Dr. Levine. She turned her head away. She did not want to see the lame man nor to look down at the ground. She flung her head up high. The sky was milky, the sun was a warm loaf of bread. She was very frightened.

The lame doctor called to her in a hushed voice. He had probably recognized her too. She should perhaps ask him whether they had once danced together at the New Year's ball at her home. She could not remember. A weird image came to her mind: the lame doctor and herself dancing here in the empty wagon, on its shaking platform. She noticed the huge German approach Levine. He seemed to look at him with compassion. He invited him to climb onto the wagon, so that he could more comfortably chat with the "*Fräulein*". The next moment she saw Levine at her side.

"Caught?" he asked.

"No . . . Yes . . ." she mumbled. "He said that they need nurses. I'm not a nurse."

The wagons increased their speed, branching out into the streets. The clamour, the whistling and the lamentations began. Levine said to Junia, "I have been hiding all the time so that I wouldn't have to participate . . . But they took me from my bed at night." He leaned over to her, "Do whatever they ask you and at the first opportunity get lost."

The wagon stopped. Its rear wall was unlatched. The huge German helped Junia jump down, but he pushed back Levine, saying to him calmly, "You stay there." He asked Junia whether she knew what to do. She nodded. He placed her in the middle of the gate and then entered the yard. From the line-ups in the yard the condemned mothers with their babies, single women, men and children began to pass by her. The huge German appeared with two babies wrapped in long pillows. He threw them into Junia's arms. For a moment she stood with them, dumbfounded. Another German pushed her with the butt of his gun towards the wagon where Levine was. "*Das kommt here!*" He pointed at Levine and called out to him, "Lend a hand, Herr Doctor." Michal took the babies from Junia's hands. Their trembling fingers met every time Junia handed him a baby.

Though the walk from the gate to the wagon was short, it seemed to be very long and Junia was soon exhausted. Sweat began to stream down her forehead, her short black hair stuck to her face; her hands became slippery. She was pressing babies to her bosom, trying not to let them slide out of her arms, holding them tighter, feeling their bodies against hers. It became increasingly difficult to tear these tiny creatures away from herself and hand them over to Michal. It seemed to her that on her way from the gate to the wagon she was learning how to be a mother. Her arms were a cradle. Her face and neck became sensitive to the touch of the tiny hands, to the tiny fingers which slipped into her mouth, winding around her teeth, and becoming moist from her saliva. The babies seemed to suck from her with their eyes, most of which were sky-blue, some clear, others tearful. Red little mouths turned eagerly towards her white dress, seeking a breast.

Each baby became hers and every time she handed the bundle to Michal, her pain increased. She looked up at the pale lame doctor with the eyes of a cow, whose calf had been torn away from her, with the eyes of a bitch who had been robbed of her puppy. And the lame doctor was no longer able to take his eyes off her. Not only did the tremor of both their hands, but also the flutter of both their gazes tie them now to each other.

The wagon for the babies and small children was full. A soldier locked it. The huge German came out of the yard. He wiped his enormous moustache and said to Junia, "You will accompany the wagon, diligent *Fräulein*."

She was supposed to walk by the side of the wagon which moved very slowly because something was wrong with the horse. The moment the whip touched the animal, it reared up on its hind legs. Junia looked up at the wagon. It seemed empty. The little children lay or sat on the platform, Michal among them. A few of the older children cried. Some sat motionless, stunned. The tiny ones, rocked by the shaking wagon, slept in their swaddling pillows. Junia held on to the boards with one hand. People were jumping out of the wagon which followed behind, and the huge German turned in that direction. Shots and spasmodic wails could be heard coming on all sides.

Through the cracks between the wagon's boards Junia saw a strip of Michal's face and his eyes. She peered into them. "I don't understand," she said to him with her gaze. "Why do I shiver? Why do I flutter like this? Is this the end of all ends? But it is only the beginning. It is morning. How does death fit in here? How can I be so afraid of it, if everything inside me is so greedily praising life? What is Death, Doctor, tell me . . . teach me to understand . . ." It was strange to see nothing of a man but his eyes, such deep hot knowing eyes. As she walked on with his gaze upon her, she felt that she was growing; getting older and older, wiser and wiser. She had made a gigantic leap ahead in her life. Their eyes were now on the same level. She held on tighter to the wagon and brought her face closer to his.

"My name is Michal Levine," he introduced himself as if they were just now getting acquainted.

"Michal!"

"There is almost no one left to call me by that name . . . Remember: Michal." These were the only words which they exchanged along the way. As they were approaching the place of assembly, he whispered quickly to her, "As soon as we turn the corner, I will hand you the children . . . as many as I can."

They approached the Lingerie Resort where Junia had worked as a gymnastics teacher at the "School for Gifted Children". They were in the very middle of the "action" here, and in front of the factory stood a half-loaded wagon. From the basement of the factory the children appeared one after the other, followed by Professor Hager and his wife. The two old people climbed onto the wagon. Junia dashed towards them. A soldier grabbed her by the arm, but she explained to him that she had to help the children, and she showed him her Red Cross armband. He let go of her and she began calling and making signs to the old pair. There was great confusion in the middle of the crowded narrow street. Wagons arriving from different directions came to a halt. Junia noticed Miss Diamand climb onto the wagon. Two Jewish policemen had carried her to it as if she were a wooden doll.

A woman and her little girl ran past Junia. The brown-blond bun on the woman's nape was falling apart and strings of long hair cascaded to her waist. A German stopped her and tried to tear the child away from her. "You are free, beautiful lady," he said to her.

The woman wanted to climb into the wagon with her little daughter, but the capricious German would not allow it and he tried to pull the child out of her hand. Mother and daughter held tightly on to one another. Finally, the soldier succeeded in tearing the child away from the mother. He handed it to a Jewish policeman. The woman with the long hair threw herself at the soldier's feet. "Shoot me, please . . ." she called out hoarsely. The German lifted her by her thick coils of hair and put the muzzle of the revolver against her heart. A shot was heard. The woman slumped down between the wagons.

Junia hung on to a Jewish policeman who stood flustered, staring at the scene. "Do me a favour," she whispered. "I beg of you . . . There . . . on the wagon . . . the teachers. Come on, no one is looking." She pulled him by the sleeve. The dazed policeman was staring at the wagon and did not hear a word of what she was saying to him. "Professor Hager! Miss Diamand!" She called, pushing the policeman towards the wagon which was still open.

"Your grandmother?" the policeman came to himself at last.

"Yes, my grandmother. Hurry!"

Together they carried Professor Hager and his wife down from the wagon.

The old people, holding hands, hurried back to the factory building. From there another German was on his way out. He tore apart the old people's hands and forcefully led them towards another wagon. Junia did not see it. She was busy nagging the policeman to help her get Miss Diamand down. The policeman proposed, "In that case, it would be better to save the children."

Yes, save the children. But Miss Diamand had to be saved too. Junia stammered, "The old woman, too . . . I beg of you . . ."

The policeman gave in, "Tell her to move closer to the back."

Junia ran around the wagon and peered into it through a crack in the boards. She called Miss Diamand and the old woman turned her gray head in her direction. Junia slid her hand inside, waving. "Miss Diamand," she whispered hurriedly. "Move closer to the edge . . . the policeman . . . Do you see him? He'll help . . ."

The teacher began to whisper to the children in the wagon and they all clustered around the edge of the wagon. The children began to jump down, dispersing in all directions. Shots followed them. A soldier, his gun ready to shoot, placed himself by the wagon. The Jewish policeman vanished. Junia saw Miss Diamand stretch out her hands to the children who were being herded and chased back onto the wagon.

The Germans and the Jewish police re-established order. The bolted wagons began to move, including the one carrying Miss Diamand. Through the cracks between the boards, Junia saw the white fuzz of the old woman's hair rise up in the air. The mauve shawl around her neck fluttered lightly, waving . . . waving . . .

Junia raced towards the wagon which she had been accompanying. Soon it would be approaching the corner where she was to help Levine. She saw his doctor's cap. He was standing on the platform, looking for her. "Quick!" he called out as soon as he saw her. The moment they arrived at the corner, he began to hand the children to her. It was an auspicious place. Bushes were growing alongside a few houses. She hid the children between the bushes, ordering them to run off into the yards.

One little boy refused to leave the wagon, "I want my little brother!" he yelled, pointing to a baby on a swaddling pillow. Immediately the gigantic German appeared at the wagon. He put his hand on Junia's shoulder and asked what was going on. She smiled at him, unable to bring a word out of her mouth. He consulted his watch. "You are free to go home, diligent *Fräulein*," he said, "*Mahlzeit!*" Then he turned to Levine on the wagon, nodding at him. "You will of course carry on, Doctor, won't you?" Then he added, "You are a cripple anyway." He asked Levine to hand over his doctor's cap and he cast it like a discus into the bushes.

Junia entered a gate and raced ahead through the backyards, along the route of the wagons. Soon she was back in the street. She noticed that the huge German was no longer accompanying the wagon. She leaped towards it, calling to Levine who was sitting on the platform, looking out through the cracks.

"My name is Michal, will you remember?" he asked, as soon as he noticed her.

"Jump!" she cried.

He shook his head, "I've seen the births of so many children. Now I want to see how children die."

She did not hear him, beside herself with tension. "Jump, you coward! Don't give them your life . . . Michal!" At the sound of his name, he winced. The hair on his unshaven cheeks stood up. The knob on his lean neck was moving up and down. Because of their anguish they could no longer see each other. The wagon moved and Junia kept running beside it. She no longer knew what was happening to her. She sobbed; she warned Michal, "I will climb on the wagon to you, if you don't jump!"

When the wagon turned into the last street before the place of assembly, Levine jumped down. They raced into a little garden and sank down to the ground, near a fence. They were lying close together, but did not see each other. Their eyes were open, but they were blinded. They breathed heavily, sweat was pouring down their faces. Outside, on the other side of the fence, the wheels had stopped rolling. It was noon, lunch break. The world became silent. The silence brought Junia and Michal back to their senses. They still did not dare to move, but their breaths had grown calmer. They listened to the silence, staring at each other questioningly, searchingly.

At length they stood up and began to wander through the backyards of the ghetto. Each backyard was a swaying sea of sorrow, the lament of one surging into the next. Junia and Michal let themselves be carried along by the mournful waves, unaware of what they were doing. Along with a group of policemen they crossed the bridge. They walked on at a distance from each other, not exchanging a word. As they passed the gallows on the bazaar, Michal mumbled strangely, "That's me hanging here . . . I am gone with Mother . . . with the children. I am walking here with you . . ."

She did not understand what he meant, yet his words made her eyes swim. "Once I only knew how to laugh . . ." she answered him.

He led her up to his apartment. It was in a frightening disorder. The beds were broken, clothes strewn all over. Along the walls lay paintings. One of them, unfinished, seemed to be a portrait of Matilda. The table was cluttered with dishes and the remainders of vegetables. Michal went over to a cupboard and took out a quarter of a loaf of bread. He broke it in half, "Mother's bread ration." They sat at the dirty table, eating the bread, drinking cold water from the same mug.

"I want you to be my husband," Junia suddenly said, with a bite of bread in her mouth.

"I want you to be my wife," he replied, with a bite of bread in his mouth. There were still some turnips left in the apartment. They took a bag, filled it with the turnips and with all the other food remnants, and set out for Miss Sabinka's house in Marysin.

Sabinka's cellar was empty. Junia and Michal ran back across the bridge, to the yard on Hockel Street. There was no one at the Zuckermans' house. Soon the "action" started again and Michal and Junia lay down flat on the balcony. There they lay until six o'clock. Then they rushed to the place of assembly. Michal was acquainted with many policemen and firemen. None of them knew the Zuckermans' fate. In any case, the major part of the day's transport had already left. In front of the jail a huge mass of people was gathered, refusing to move away. Ploughing through the crowd, they saw Samuel and Bella. It was not easy to recognize them. They were covered with dirt and they looked wild. Samuel was barely able to talk.

"Mother . . ." he said. "I thought she was still inside."

That evening it was announced that the *Sperre* was over.

Chapter Eleven

Michal Levine
Ghetto Lodz
September, 1942

Dear Mira:

It is becoming increasingly dark and nebulous. The concepts of time and space have become blurred. We long for the past, we dream of the future. In reality we are cut off from both by the barbed wire, like a sentence by parenthesis. Time between the parenthesis is both ongoing and stagnant. Space is both infinity and one point. What is ghetto, what is the outside?

I am with a woman. Her name is Junia. We are not officially husband and wife, nor are we de facto. I have been impotent for a long time and she is still a virgin. It is enough that I know that she is my destiny.

The Angel of Death has become my companion. He introduces himself to me as an optimist, as an old acquaintance. "Don't try to fool me," I say to him. "You are the end of everything. I discovered you both with my scalpel and without it." He tells me that I am wrong, that he is continuation, the other, the infinite part of the circle of which life is only a limited fragment. He asks me to remember my "Universal I" and feel myself into it, so that I will not rage so much against him. I tell him, "I want to see Mother, Nadia and little Mina, Nadia's baby, again."

He says, "You are seeing them."

I say, "I want to touch little Mina, hold her in my arms, hear her laugh, watch her grow."

"What is so important about that?" he asks.

I tell him, "I love her."

He laughs, "Idiot . . . There is no love in life, especially not for you who have an overgrown brain and a shrunken heart. Your chatter about love is nothing but a brain child of your egoism. You philosophize about humanity because you are unable to be close to humans."

"It's a lie!" I scream.

"It is true!" he guffaws.

"How much love does one need, to call it love?"

"Too much for you. You are limited by your body, by your mind, by your attachment to your being. And love, which is freedom, expires within these limitations like a caged animal. Therefore you will know love only when you are willing to step over the threshold of my kingdom. Your infinite 'Universal I' will know it." The Angel of Death, my companion, scoffs at me. He teases me and tempts me. My nights are black with premonition.

The greenery has vanished from the yards. The gray abyss multiplies its powers. When the sun appears for a moment, the people greet it from their doorsteps, their *klepsydra* faces smiling. Here and there the little girls who escaped the *Sperre* play the pebble game *strulkes*. Who will be the winner: Life or Death? The little boys play hide-and-seek. Will they be able to hide from Fate? I am followed everywhere by hearses packed with my former patients.

Great hours for the ghetto! Blessed moments and seconds ticking out victory: we are still here! We are still living! We treasure these hours as if each of them were a precious gift. My still-alive patients are stronger than I, their doctor; they are braver than I, their healer. They are blind sages while I am a seeing idiot. They are the fortunate.

I make my house calls, conversing with Nadia in my mind. I implored her not to report voluntarily for deportation. She had one answer, "The 'wedding invitation' is my child's fate. How do you know," she asked me, "that it is better to stay in the ghetto? Perhaps the Germans want to take out the women and children and the weak, then drop a bomb on all the healthy Jews who remain?" I told her what I knew, what I thought. She refused to listen. I wanted to leave with her, but she begged me not to. "You follow your destiny," she said. "I am no match for you anyway." And Nadia who used to look at me with the eyes of a beaten dog, who had clung to me, begging for tenderness, looked as proud as a queen. I consoled myself that her maternal instinct, her female intuition would not lead her astray, and I let her follow her destiny. While I, who survived the gipsy camp, have remained here with my destiny.

I have befriended a young man. His name is David. The fate of our fathers brought us together. He lives in the yard on Hockel Street and visits the Zuckermans often. We entertain each other with our philosophies. He says to me, "I don't believe in anything. My disbelief is my belief. Out of *cogito ergo sum* I have made, 'I don't believe and therefore I am.' Yet I cannot say that I am not religious. Life is my God."

I restate his argument, forcing him to come to the proper conclusions (mine of course). "If life is sacred," I say to him, "Then it is a duty to support it and it is a crime to destroy it." And from there it is only a stone's throw to my vegetarianism, which I have never before preached to anyone, but now consider important to preach. I explained to David that we are indifferent to animal blood, as if it were not blood, but a cheaper liquid; and that killing becomes easier when you say to yourself that someone else's blood is of lesser value than your own. That is exactly what happened with the Germans. To them Jewish life is the same as an animal's life is to the hunter. Is not that the basis of every racial theory? Such people can be kind, even noble in their private lives, and at the same time act like cannibals with regard to others.

Often, after such a "propaganda" chat with David, I recall how I used to go with Mother to buy chickens in the Green Market. Then the whole ghetto, surrounded by its barbed wires, seems to me like a chicken cage. My mother herself has become a hen which the German paw has grabbed and taken out of its cage. We are all hens, roosters, little chicks. I must say, my mother was more practical than the Germans. She at least nourished her family and supported life with the flesh of the dead chicken. The Germans, however, are wasting much good eating material. That is definitely a sin. Human flesh is good, Jewish flesh must be tasty. Perhaps the day is not far off, when human limbs will be served at the table, roasted, fried, baked, boiled — tasting heavenly!

P.S. Once in a while I look over my letters to you and come to the conclusion that my thoughts continuously turn in the same circle. What did that philosopher say? "Many people think that they are thinking. In reality they are only rearranging the same thoughts." Or what did that other wise man say? "The mind is an apparatus with which we think that we think."

✦ ✦ ✦

Dear Mira:

Beaudelaire comes to mind: "It is Death, alas, which consoles and makes the beds of the poor and the naked." It is constantly raining. People are drowning in the mud. It drips from everywhere. Gales sweep through unheated homes. When I come into a room I don't remove my coat. I must rub my hands and blow at them for a long while before I can touch a patient. The people wrap themselves in rags, one on top of the other and shake with cold. I ask myself what will happen in wintertime. People's resistance is breaking down. Each body is a nest for all kinds of germs.

The general mood has improved to the point of child-like frivolity. Evidently, in order to continue living in a world without children, the adults must become children. We have given reason a vacation. It had, anyway, been the reason of fools who understood nothing. If we occasionally do think, it is a kind of mindless brainless thinking. We think with our stomachs, with our rotting lungs, with our swollen legs. And we love ourselves. We caress our own worn bodies, we pamper them and are like children preoccupied with their physiological activities. Perhaps this is because we have lost those who had pampered us and cared for us. We struggle with the memories of the *Sperre*. Just like children who want to forget a painful experience, we try to blot it out of our memory, while at the same time we do not stop talking about those fateful days.

In our conception, the *Sperre* has become the turning point in the chronological system. The history of mankind has become divided into two phases: before the *Sperre* and after the *Sperre*. One Jew can in the most natural manner say to another, "I saw him last a month before the *Sperre*," or, "I moved in a month after the *Sperre*," or, "It came to my mind on the third day of the *Sperre*." Because the *Sperre* itself, just like the creation of the world, lasted one week. And just as every day of the creation had its highlight, its own miracles, so did each day of the *Sperre* have its place in the work of destruction. There is no doubt therefore that those who survived that week are the same and yet not the same people. I look at them and see the crooked double-meaning smile on their faces. A smile which says, "Nothing can hurt me any longer," and also, "It is good that I am alive and am still able to feel pain." The gaze of the people is both the gaze of the lunatic and of the prophet. I met one of these prophetic lunatics today.

People on their way home from the Resorts clustered around the placards with Biebow's signature, which announced that there would be no more deportations, that the ghetto was to become a real working camp, that now, after the period of rest (the *Sperre*), each must again fulfil his duty and work conscientiously. Next to these placards also hung the announcement of the new food ration. A full ten deca fish were offered to us and half a kilogram of carrots per head, also ten deca parsley and a few grams of baking soda. No wonder the crowd was enthusiastic. I waded through the dripping throngs. At each step, someone else stopped me, asking for my opinion about the new ration. Each gave me a report on the state of his health, taking leave of me with a lively handshake, "We have the *Yekes* a thousand miles deep in the ground!" I passed a line-up in front of a co-operative. The whole line was shaking with the cold, yet conversing leisurely. Just as before, there were scuffles in front of the bakery. We have not become any closer to each other since the *Sperre*, or any friendlier. Just like before, we love and we hate. People quarrel or they help each other out. Yet it seems as if we were performing a comedy, performing a brawl, performing a conversation, playing the game of friendship, just like children.

Amidst the crowd in front of the bakery, I noticed the Toffee Man and I felt the desire for a candy. After all, I too am like a child. I cannot understand how the Toffee Man passed the selection. If he had previously been a nothing of a man, he is at present like the shadow of that nothing.

He grabbed me by the hand, looking at me with a pair of tearful eyes. "Have you heard the latest news, Doctor? The Messiah has already arrived! You're asking, how? Don't be a dunce head. Of course with the *Himmelkommando*! He disguised himself as a German with a gun, otherwise they would not have let him into the ghetto, would they?" I pretended to smile at his joke, took the candy and tried to leave, but he held me back. "Doctor, I want to ask you a question. I mean, the green pieces of soap that we get with the ration . . . the pieces of *Rif*. Tell me, is it really possible to make soap out of . . . I mean in general, Doctor . . . I have delivered to them nine brilliant little heads. Of course, the Almighty is merciful and the *heder* boys won't miss even a day of their studies . . ." His tears were washing down his face along with the rain. "It is good, Doctor. It can't be better. What's the difference how the Messiah arrives? We live in new times, don't we? Then how can he arrive riding a white horse? A *rollwagon*, a *panzer* auto, a bomber airplane, that's the way for a Messiah to travel nowadays. He must go along with the spirit of the times, no?"

He grabbed me by the sleeve, pulling me into the gate. To be honest, I could not make up my mind whether he is sane or insane.

"Do you remember this cellar?" he asked me. "I lived there. Do you want to know where I live now? I live in the heavens. Do you think that my remedies for the heart, the candies, are made of ghetto sugar? Of course not. My children are reciting the Torah in the heavens, and I stand down here, over the pot, mixing in God's sweetness which pours down from their lilting voices. But what am I out to tell you? I am out to tell you that God has lost the war against the Devil. You ask, how do I know? Simple. Had He not lost, I would have had my wife and children here and all this hullabaloo would not have happened." He pinned me by the lapel. "You must save a human being, Doctor. Perhaps he'll listen to you, because all my talking is to no avail. He doesn't answer me. It has been four weeks since he has uttered a word . . . The man is sick with a broken heart . . . And all in all he has lost a wife and two children. Of course that was all that he had, but, since God has led him towards life . . . Yeah, our Maker is sometimes stubborn like a mule. Whatever He wants He must have."

I let the Toffee Man lead me through the familiar yard on Hockel Street, past the *dzialka* where Mother used to sit wrapped in her white shawl, knitting. The little man hung on to my arm, which made me limp even more. He did not stop talking. "For instance, Doctor, between yourself and myself there is still some understanding. I mean . . . You bought a candy from me. A thread was tied. But this madman inside has cut all the threads. That's a sin . . ." He led me to Berkovitch's hut. The shutters were closed, the door stood open. "Go inside," he prodded me.

I entered. After my eyes got used to the darkness, I noticed a rolled up body on a bed in the other room. I called out, not knowing what I actually wanted to say. The body did not move. "It's me, Dr. Levine," I said.

At that instant Berkovitch jumped to his feet and threw himself at me with raised fists. "Get out of my house!" he roared. "You bastard, you monster! You accompanied the *rollwagons*, didn't you? You bunch of butchers! Don't you dare step over my threshold. this is sacred ground!" He threw me out and slammed the door behind me. The Toffee Man was waiting for me in the gate. In order to avoid him, I passed the firemen's yard and escaped. So, I am an escort of *rollwagons*. I have no reason to defend myself against Berkovitch. All of us who are left were escorts, Berkovitch included. He was raging against me because of his own shame at still being alive.

✦ ✦ ✦

Dear Mira:

The people of the world will sit in judgment on us. We have gone like sheep to the slaughter, they will say. Let them know that sheep writhing in the hands of the butcher, and sheep willingly stretching their necks to the knife — are all the same, nothing but sheep. Vengeance, honour — the world has its conceptions about such things. More than once have we copied them. Here, however, we have shed all such notions like an alien skin, and have emerged with our own face. We are the most clumsy avengers. Throughout the ages, when we ran away from slaughter, we also ran away from slaughtering, and perhaps for that reason we so rarely enjoyed hunting or fishing. We don't make a sport out of death. We are disgusted by the sight of blood.

Perhaps in order to become a people like others we should have learned to become bloodthirsty, or we should have gone back to the times when we were warlike, at the beginning of our existence. Would it have been worthwhile? Is it not better that even here, in the ghetto, we occupy our minds less with dreams of vengeance than with dreams of peace? Don't we feel intuitively that a thirst for vengeance can do us no good, and that honour has meaning only in life? Our physical resistance — not to defend the honour of Death, but the honour of Life — was impossible from the start. We had our dear ones and feared to jeopardize their lives. Now that we have lost our dear ones, resistance has lost all meaning. Secondly, we would not have been able to save even our own lives. Perhaps I am writing like this because I am a lame coward? I want to prolong my existence in the hope that help will arrive from somewhere, in the hope that the Germans themselves will perhaps forgive us the sin of being sheep — because we obey them with such docility — and they will grant us our lives.

I wonder whether I myself am still sane. I am exhausted and long more for peace than for life. Perhaps we are secretly grateful to the Germans who have offered us sleep after generations of exhaustion — and we don't want any fuss to be made about it? We have had enough. We want a calm painless peace and therefore we help the butcher by our behaviour, in order to speed up our own deliverance. What does the Toffee Man say? The Germans are the Messiah and we surrender to him devotedly, piously. Perhaps we are gone already? A nation of corpses. Perhaps the spirit we still carry within us is not ours but that of the Germans? Their will is ours. Their wishes are ours. They don't want us, so we don't want ourselves. We hate ourselves with their hatred, and we love them with the love of the victim for his executioner.

And yet the word "power" comes to mind. We possess an unheard-of demonic power. I can read it in the eyes of my woman, in the eyes of the people in the street. The same breed of people surrounds me as that which, in the bygone generations, refused the chance to escape death by kissing the cross. A people whose sons and daughters have risked their lives as the standard bearers of lofty ideals; a people whose members, if given the opportunity, are at present engaged in all kinds of resistance movements, although they are labelled Frenchmen, Dutchmen, Danes, Russians or Poles; a people whose sons participate actively wherever they can as soldiers of many a country's freedom army. The same people. They follow their own road. They choose their own way of living and dying. And whoever dares to reproach us with "cowardice" now, may his tongue be lamed in his mouth — before he comes here to show us his own "heroism".

My dear Mira, let me tell you this last thing. In this letter I both call you and say good-bye to you. It is both a Good Morning and a Good Night greeting. All that I was before the *Sperre* belongs to you. The Michal Levine who has survived the *Sperre* belongs to another woman — and to another reality.

Adieu,

Michal.

✦   ✦   ✦

Michal finished his last letter to his former beloved whom he had in the ghetto sometimes called Mirage. He sat by the edge of the table, half-dressed. In the stove behind him roared a fire. Around it hung his clothes, drying on a cord. He looked at the written pages for a long while. It seemed to him that he had put the seal to his own fate at that moment.

Near the window stood Guttman in front of his easel. He was holding a few brushes in his mouth, and another few between his fingers. Shiele, the street singer, was posing for him as he related the story of how he had hid during the *Sperre*. His portrait was almost finished.

Michal stealthily observed Guttman. Between the two of them something had come to a close with the *Sperre*. After Shafran and his wife had been taken away, the day the orphanage was liquidated, Guttman had vanished, but returned a week after the *Sperre* was over. He did not say what had happened to him and Michal did not ask. Actually they did not know why they were still living together. There was now no lack of apartments in the ghetto and they had only to make the effort towards a definite separation. If they were postponing it, it was probably on account of their respective guilt. Here was a single saved friendship and they were destroying it with their own hands.

Michal put the pages into the drawer where he kept his other letters to Mira. He put on his still damp clothes and took his bag. His working day was not yet over, but first he hurried to meet Junia. She came down from the bridge and fell into his arms. She talked quickly, overjoyed to see him. She put her arm around his shoulders and pressed herself against him.

"Do you still love me?" she asked mischievously.

"I still do . . . a little," he smiled.

He felt the burden of her body, yet his steps became livelier. Her playfulness seemed to ease the weight within him. When he was with her, everything lost its weight and rose into the air, fluttering and pulsating with life. She escorted him to his first housecall and he was sorry that the way was so short. He wanted her to wait for him, but she shook her head, "I have no time," she said. She told him to drop in to see Samuel who was troubled by a cough, and she ran off. He followed her with his eyes. Her soaring, half-running walk delighted him. He was climbing stairs, all the while seeing in his mind — her figure, her face, the wet dishevelled bangs, the small agile mouth, the short turned-up nose dripping with rain. Her image made his legs move more vigorously. He was patient with the sick and forgot his own pessimistic prognoses. He believed that his patients would survive, just as he and Junia would.

Junia was waiting for him at home. Shiele, the street singer, was still there, arguing with Guttman. He insisted on taking his wet portrait home with him, while Guttman refused to hear of it. The singer promised to pay with his entire capital: two German marks and half a soup.

"Understand me," he turned to Junia for assistance. "I had luck during the *Sperre*, but what if my luck runs out? I have no one. If I die, no one will know that I lived. But so, if there will be a world, they will find my picture, they will see me as I stand here, and they will know that I lived."

The painting represented Church Place in autumn: leaves falling from the chestnut trees, the gray stripes of the wire fence, a part of the bridge, a bright-gray box and standing on top, the little singer in his black gaberdine, his round cap pulled down over one ear, his pitch-black roguish eyes smiling at the crowd which surrounded him. Junia explained to him that the painting had more chance of surviving the war if it stayed with Guttman, and that anyway it had first to dry and then to be varnished. Besides all that, the painting belonged a little to Guttman as well. Shiele nodded at her words and stuck to his decision. He put the two marks on the table.

"You're lucky that it's raining outside," he turned to Guttman. "Tomorrow, if God wills it, I am coming to take my picture home."

He left and the three of them sat down to a glass of hot water with saccharine. They drank in silence. Junia's eyes darted over the walls. All around them stood Guttman's paintings: still lives, portraits of *fecalists*, of abandoned children, of old people, and also an unfinished portrait of her mother, of Matilda. Junia hated the paintings. She hated the apartment. Between its walls lived the ghosts of those who had left: of Michal's mother, of the teacher Shafran and his wife, and most of all, of Nadia and her child. Junia dreamed about an apartment which would be as new as hers and Michal's love. The problem was that there was no such domicile in the ghetto. All the empty apartments were full of the ghosts of the people who had inhabited them not long ago. So she might have made peace with the present dwelling, if she had been able to live in it alone with Michal, or if the atmosphere between the two men had not been so strained.

She caught Guttman's scrutinizing gaze. It seemed as if he were reading her thoughts. He made a grimace which was meant to be a smile, and said, "It won't be long and you'll be rid of me." She was about to contradict him, when he put his hand on her arm. "Don't deny . . ." And lowering his face to his glass, he added, "I could also have had a home . . . could have taken a wife . . . But I am not an ostrich. I fought against Dolfus in Vienna, against Franco in Spain . . .

The gun has been knocked out of my hand . . . so I fight with my brush. Of course you can't understand that. I can see pretty well how you look at me, the two of you. To you my painting is child's play, an escape . . . But you will see. Something will remain of that game. I struggle . . . Yes, I create what God Himself is incapable of . . . beauty out of a heap of garbage." Raising his face to Michal he suddenly exploded, "It is you, great altruist and restorer of life, who are the coward! A hypocrite with a saintly face! You put the doomed and the damned back on their feet, so that they can in better health walk to the gallows . . . And at night, you console yourself with her . . . the wifie."

Junia and Michal sat struck by his words. But only for a moment. Junia jumped to her feet, splashed Guttman's face with the rest of the water in her glass and leaped towards him with outstretched hands as if she wanted to strangle him. "If you slept one night with a woman and were happy," she cried out, "you would achieve more than with all your idiotic paintings! And if you are such a hero, then why don't you join those who prepare themselves for vengeance? *You* are the hypocrite, a hollow stupid maniac, that's what you are!" She clasped her fingers around his neck, shaking Guttman who went limp under her touch, as if his spine had been broken. Slowly he unclasped her fingers from his neck, stared for a moment at her palms, then pressed them to his mouth.

"I want to paint. You won't let me . . ." he was sobbing. It was the first time Michal ever saw him cry. It was also the last time.

Guttman did as he had decided. He moved to an empty house in Marysin. The last time he came to fetch his food, he shook hands with Michal; they were unable to look each other in the eyes. Michal groaned, "Why should it end like this?"

Guttman shrugged his shoulders, "Do I know why?"

The same evening Junia and Michal celebrated their privacy. Michal took out the letters which he had been writing to Mira throughout all these years, and gave them to Junia to read. While she was reading, he tended the fire in the stove, observing her dark head bent over the sheets of paper. Would her eyes be the only ones to read them? Perhaps he had actually written them for her?

When Junia had finished reading the last letter, they took a large tin box in which Guttman had kept his paints. It was a red box with the word "Tea" written in English on its four sides. This had been Junia's idea. The letters had to be preserved. No, they were not only for her eyes. They had to reach a Tomorrow, either with Michal and herself, or without them. She rolled each letter up in a sheet of wax paper. They did the same with the sketches Guttman had left behind. They also threw a few photographs of their parents and friends into the box. Then they wrapped everything in rags and closed the box. The following day they buried the box in the abandoned little garden where they had hidden after Michal had jumped from the *rollwagon*.

Chapter Twelve

THE PRESESS SAT huddled up in the corner of his coach. He wore his winter coat; his legs were covered with a warm plaid. He was on his way to the birthday party which Herr Schatten had arranged for himself. The Presess was riding alone. He had sent Clara ahead with an appropriate gift, since he was busy working and, in any case, disliked arriving along with the other guests. His tardy arrival made a better impression.

Riding through the streets, he noticed the old torn placards on the walls. They led his mind to the dark thoughts, which he so much wanted to avoid, at least during the evening hours. These were the first placards addressed to the ghetto population, not by himself, the Eldest of the Jews, but by the chief of the *Ghettoverwaltung*, Hans Biebow. Historic placards. Along with them he expected the other blows to strike him; the provisioning of the ghetto and the supervision of the Resorts was to be taken out of his hands.

Along with all his other illusions, that one had burst as well. He had deluded himself that he could outsmart Biebow, that he was stronger than this selfish German merchant, because of his, Rumkowski's connections with Berlin. That was a lie. Biebow was an Aryan and he was the master. He refused to appreciate all the years of hard labour during which Rumkowski had single-handedly established almost a state apparatus. Biebow had begun to favour Leibel Welner, the leader of the *Sonderkommando*, the stool pigeon and irresponsible fortune hunter. The reason for it was clear. Yet Rumkowski's duty was to prevent this from happening, on account of the sheep whose devoted shepherd he was.

True, he longed for peace. He was tired of the responsibilities. Lately his deceased wife Shoshana had begun to visit him frequently in his dreams, telling him, "The crown that you are wearing is a crown of thorns . . ." She was right. On the other hand, however, had he let go of everything, he would have succumbed to the great fear, the fear of six weeks ago. And then, to surrender was not in his nature. He might be exhausted in the extreme, but as long as he was alive he had to struggle, to reach out . . . for the crown, though it be made of thorns. There was no denying it. It was in his blood. So he struggled on, all alone, surrounded by a pack of flatterers, of thieves and lazybones who lived like parasites on his sweat and blood, while secretly licking the boots of their new masters. It was an old truth: friends who could be bought with gifts, could also be bought by others with gifts.

As he rode on, his wish to see Schatten and his guests vanished. What value was there in pennants which turned wherever the wind blew? He ordered the coachman to turn into Hockel Street, to the house where his former, most sincere friend, Samuel Zuckerman, lived.

169

He was received by Bella.

"Where is your father?" he asked, leaving her behind before she could answer. He entered Samuel's room and saw him bent over a table covered with papers. He strode over to him quickly, and put his hand on his shoulder, "What are you scribbling so diligently?" he inquired. Samuel turned to him his bony face, which seemed to consist only of a long pointy nose. He made a gesture with his hand as if inviting the visitor to sit down. The Presess immediately slumped down into a chair and moved closer to Samuel who quickly gathered together the pages strewn over the table. "What are you hiding?" Rumkowski grinned uncomfortably. "What's so unusual about scribbling? Whoever has a hand and a foot scribbles in the ghetto. And so, between you and me, have you be-scribbled me, too? Tell the truth. Anyway I know that all that scribbling would have no value if I were not the main character. It used to bother me . . . what people were saying about me . . . I was sensitive about history. Today I don't mind a bit. Say, do you at least remember the favours I did you along with the supposed disfavours? Do you still remember that I saved your life?" With feigned ease he freed himself of his coat. "And your wife? Where is she?" he asked. "I haven't seen her for ages."

"Gone," Samuel snapped.

Rumkowski chewed on his lips for a moment and changed the subject. "You see, as soon as I found out that something was the matter with you, I came to see you. Clara told me. She met you at the Resort, eh? Are you really working in a Metal Resort? What can you do there?"

"I am a guardian of the minors."

"And what's wrong with you?"

"The same as with many others."

Rumkowski grew lively, "You'll receive an extra ration from me and two weeks vacation at the pension at Marysin. I don't carry a grudge for too long. You know me."

Samuel smiled, "Thanks, Herr Rumkowski. I am just back from a vacation. I was sent to work in a bakery for two weeks and had a quarter of a loaf of bread daily."

"Who sent you to the bakery?"

"Leibel Welner of the *Sonderkommando*."

Rumkowski, irritated, shoved himself and his chair away. "Do you know why he sent you there? Because he wants to win you over to his side. The *Kriponik*, this stool pigeon, the hangman! Yeah, he makes nice faces to the ghetto, preparing himself for after the war, so that no one will have any idea of his dirty work. People will have many good things to tell about him; order in the provisioning of the ghetto, medicines for the sick, workers for the bakeries . . . rely on him. He knows quite well how to dig holes under my feet, winning even you over to his side. Tell me openly, on whose side are you?"

Samuel smiled, "On the side of the Allies."

"Stop joking! I have come to discuss serious matters with you. You must help me."

"I was under the impression that you came to help me."

"One hand washes the other."

"My hands are clean. And I won't help you any longer."

"Zuckerman, you have been my most devoted friend. Perhaps I have not appreciated it enough . . ."

"Don't remind me of it, Herr Presess. We carry a heavy burden of sins."

"As long as you consider yourself a partner to the load, I don't mind. Do you know what is going on in Warsaw? Warsaw is on the edge of the precipice. I want to save at least a fraction . . . Can't you see that they want to wipe us off the face of the earth?"

"So you have to lend them a hand?"

Rumkowski was beside himself, "Good heavens! If you're talking like that too, then it is the end of the world. Why don't you understand that if someone else were in my place there would not be a trace of us left?"

"You are paying too steep a price. No one is entitled to pay such a price. Who are you to judge who should be left and who should go? Are there means to measure whose life is more important? You let your 'protections' stay, sending off the others instead."

"It's a lie! I need those whom I leave. Otherwise I make no exceptions. And the 'actions' during the *Sperre* were executed by the Germans themselves. For heaven's sake, what do you think I am? A stone, a block of ice? Do you think that it was so easy for me to see my orphans go? Tell me what other choice I had. Enlighten me."

"You are the head of the people. Why didn't you say, 'Brothers, the situation is such and such, do whatever you think is right.' But you shouted, 'Mothers, give up your children!' and if . . . Yes, why didn't you do what Czerniakow did in Warsaw?"

"Listen to him!" The Presess was boiling with rage. "My blood is water to you? And what did Czerniakow achieve with his deed? Bear in mind, Zuckerman, that I am not suicidal and I won't talk a people into suicide. Would you, in my place, have done what you are preaching to me? Yeah, what would you have done in my place?"

"I don't know. That has never been my problem. My problems I have already solved somehow."

For a moment they were silent. Rumkowski panted and chewed on his lips, fidgeting in his chair. At length he bent over the table and changed the subject. "What are you writing, after all?" he asked.

"Do you remember I was planning to write the history of the Jews in Lodz? Now I am spending my evenings on it."

Rumkowski was fully aware that their conversation was over. He asked for a glass of water, forcing himself to joke, "Zibert says that drinking water does not make a man sick, nor does it make his wife a widow." He gulped down the water and took out a pencil. He wrote out a 'referral' to the vacation house for Samuel, deciding in this way to finish his visit. "I'm giving you this, because you are honest with me," he said, putting the slip of paper on the table.

He was again in his coach. He felt shamed, abused and betrayed. In his great loneliness one consolation was left to him. He longed to hold Clara in his arms. Since the *Sperre* she had become his nest, a consoling pillow.

The party at Herr Schatten's was in full swing. In the crowded room stood the host himself, dressed in a black blouse and black riding pants. His face was neatly shaven and had a fresh pinkish glow, his bushy hair was stiff and shiny. The violin with its delicate form looked odd in the hands of this fellow in the black outfit with his black boots. And it looked odd that he could, with such delicacy, charm out the languorous tango from its strings, making it vibrate between the walls of the room. Pairs were circling in a dance. Along the walls stood or sat the serious spectators.

No one in the darkened room had noticed the Presess enter, and he had to stand for quite a while at the door before all eyes turned to him. Only after a few minutes did Clara come over to him, followed by Mr. Zibert. When he had shaken the Presess' hand, Zibert turned to face the room and called out, "*Meine Herren und Damen*, the Presess Mordecai Chaim Rumkowski has arrived!" As usual, it was difficult to judge whether his tone was serious or cynical, but the Presess was grateful to his court clown.

Schatten stopped playing. An ominous whisper passed through the room, "The Presess is here!" The guests scrutinized the Presess' face from the distance. Then another wave of whispers followed, "He is in a good mood . . . He's smiling . . ."

From the side, the Presess heard Zibert's wisecrack, "When the Tsar has a cold all of Russia sneezes, when the Tsar laughs . . ."

The host came over to the Presess and bowed, soldier-like, while making the face of a spoilt child whose father had disturbed him at his favourite game. The Presess shook his hand, gave him a fatherly hug and expressed his best wishes in a miniature speech. The crowd applauded, singing "May they Live One Hundred Years" in the Presess' and Schatten's honour. The latter however had no more patience for ceremonies. He darkened the room even more, leaving only one lit candle. He began to sing: "The moon has betrayed me,/the sun has mocked me with its light./Only my shadow keeps its promise,/and visits me night after night." He sang in a warm languorous voice. His eyes, hazy, glass-like, were fixed upon distant worlds. In his black outfit he could barely be seen in the dark; his face resembled a swimming moon. His hands and the strings of the bow seemed to float in the air.

The Presess elbowed Zibert, "Is this a celebration or a funeral?"

"He likes it like this," Zibert giggled. "To make the audience feel romantic. He is a demon, and demons hate electricity . . . Look at him, Herr Presess, and you'll have an idea of how the Angel of Death looks . . . Otherwise, he is a nice fellow."

The Presess chummily prodded Zibert with his elbow, "You laugh at everyone. Do you think there is nothing to laugh at about you? You mouse-in-boots!"

"A puss-in-boots, Herr Presess. The story is about a cat in boots."

"Correct. You are as false as a cat."

"Not as far as you are concerned, Herr Presess. Honestly. Did I ever poke fun at you, or, heaven forbid, cheat you? Never. And do you know why? Because you don't trust me. You know that story don't you, about a master who asked his servant, 'How could you have cheated me? I've trusted you so.' And the servant replied, 'Precisely for that reason, my master. If you had not trusted me, I could not have cheated you.'" Zibert patted Rumkowski on the shoulder. "I am only joking, dear Presess." The Presess fixed his eyes on Clara, who was quietly chatting with the lawyer, Mr. Sirkin. No, he could not take her into his arms right now, or even stand close to her. He would have to wait until later when they were alone. Zibert immediately noticed that the Presess was thoughtful and he asked, "Are you worried about something, Herr Presess? Perhaps you need a refreshment, a piece of cake . . . a bit of compote? After all, it's a celebration."

"Baloney, I have nothing to celebrate." The Presess felt Clara's gaze on him. She was investigating his face to catch its expression, to measure his mood. She too, like all the ghettoniks, interpreted his every grimace so as to know whether she could breathe with more ease, or whether something had gone wrong again. In order to reassure her, he waved to her as he leaned over to Zibert; "And what's new in the party?"

Zibert shrugged his shoulders. "All these parties, ours included, make me plain sick. They're squabbling non-stop, making order in the world for after the war. Communists, Bundists, Zionists, all the same garbage."

"Have you given up on Zionism?"

"Who said that? I understand Zionism as it should be understood. I would eliminate all of the membership from the party, leaving two people only, you and me." He noticed that the Presess was observing a pretty young woman wading through the room, and he winked roguishly, "A tasty little chick, eh, Presess? Miss Sabinka. She works at the *Sonderkommando*."

"She was a ward of mine," the Presess muttered, adding with a confidential whisper, "Bring her over to me later. I've got an idea . . . She, you see, could become a bridge between Leibel Welner and ourselves . . . Understand?"

Zibert grinned, "Of course I do. To walk such a bridge is worthwhile. And come to think of it . . . there is after all a greater distance between a communist and a Zionist than between Leibel Welner and ourselves." He stood up, made a mocking chivalrous gesture and clicked the heels of his funny little boots together, "Said and done, Presess dear. I am going to hook myself onto the 'bridge' and pull it over to you."

✦   ✦   ✦

It was not snowing, nor was it cold, but everything was enveloped in a fog. The Presess could not bear the gray light. When he rode through the streets of the ghetto, he drew the curtain on the coach window. He preferred sitting in the dark to seeing the depressing grayness. In his office or at home he kept the lights on. Yet the grayness poured in from everywhere. He went on with his work but without energy. There was a hollowness within him which even Clara was unable to fill. Moreover, the production orders for the Resorts had ceased to arrive. The Presess hoped that this was merely a transitory stage. Yet in order to reassure himself he waited at Biebow's door, begging him for a word, a hint. Biebow was businesslike as usual. He promised that the situation would soon change. Rumkowski became unsure of himself. He had been building all his hopes on work, on Jewish usefulness to the Germans. Without that there was nothing to hold on to. The senselessness of the situation began to frighten him. He was living in a world without a future, without children, on a raft which was sinking deeper and deeper into a gray swamp.

The best thing was to make a noise, to surround himself with strong self-assured people and forget that their strength and self-assurance derived from him. He assembled the commissars and managers, allegedly in order to confer with them, but in fact to read the conviction in their faces that all was not over; that he had been wrong in his reasoning. And how bitter he felt when he noticed their gazes hanging on him, aware that they were interpreting his face as one interprets a page of the Talmud. They appeared to be more sincere and genuine in their words of devotion. They flattered him as if he were a wizard, and obeyed him as if he were a father. Their every gesture expressed their trust that he would lead them out of the ghetto and save them. As a result, he felt even more downhearted, more depressed.

His brother Joseph had come to pay him a visit and was waiting for him in the dining room. Clara kept him company until her husband arrived. Although Joseph and Clara liked each other, they found it difficult to be alone in a room. Their conversation never clicked. They sat stiffly, smiled at each other, ill-at-ease, while they discussed the weather.

The Presess appeared in the house, his lips pressed together, his silvery hair dishevelled, sticking out from under his hat like a crown of thorns. Clara and Joseph rushed forward to meet him. He averted his eyes and approached the set table, sitting down at its head. His wife and his brother took their seats on either side of him. It was easy to read from the Presess' face that any word uttered during the meal would irritate him. When the meal was over and Clara had left the room, the Presess offered his brother a look which both implored him to speak up and expressed a fear of what he would say. But what Joseph had to say had to be heard and Rumkowski inquired bravely, "Have you heard the latest newscast?"

Joseph nodded, "SWIT announced for the second time today . . . All the transports from Lodz went to Chelmno where they were finished off."

The Presess immediately felt his meal pressing against his stomach. He called in the housekeeper and ordered tea. The two brothers stirred their cups of tea, clinking their spoons. "Joseph," Mordecai Chaim groaned, "Moloch has not been satiated yet . . ." He gave a hasty sip of the hot tea. "In case . . ." he coughed, not finishing the sentence.

At night Rumkowski was unable to sleep. During the summer, when he could not sleep, he could at least look out at the sky and see a few stars or the moon. He used to be glad that he needed so little sleep, considering it a blessing that at the end of his life, when there was little time left, he needed less sleep. Nowadays it was different. Nowadays the window panes were blurred; each pane resembled the tooth of a guillotine. Mordecai Chaim's eyes restlessly jumped from one shadow to the other. His heart fluttered like a mouse in a trap, while through his mind swam images, some moving slowly, others flashing by as if only to tease him.

He saw his mother in a white long apron, all covered with flour. She was busy preparing the Sabbath meal. With a few duck feathers tied together to make a brush, she was painting the *hallot* with an egg-white, to glaze the crust. Little Mordecai Chaim came in from the street, crying. He was dressed for the Sabbath. A little boy in a navy-blue sailor suit. An orphan. He wanted to hide under his mother's apron, but she chased him away. "Leave me alone," she shouted. "Can't you see that I am getting ready for the Sabbath?" And the little orphan ran away — straight into the arms of an angry strange father who wore black boots and a green uniform. The handsome strong father lifted up the orphan and thrust him onto the *rollwagon*. The little orphan rode off somewhere for the Sabbath Day.

In another image Rumkowski saw himself among the friends of his youth. They were all climbing a mountain on the outskirts of the *shtetl*. He was leading them. He helped them to jump over the huge rocks. One of his gang was a short boy with shrewd little eyes. Every time that Mordecai Chaim turned away, the little fellow, who resembled Zibert, would prick him with a pin in the behind.

Whenever Mordecai Chaim looked at him, the boy made an innocent face and told him a funny story.

Or Mordecai Chaim would see images of female breasts. Many breasts, drooping, full like balloons suspended from a straight cord, like a string of huge beads. The breasts were warm, milk flowed from them as from fountains. He saw himself stretching out his hands to them, trying to touch them, to fondle them, to knead them. He wanted to drink from them all at once. But they slid away from his touch. He could not caress them, not even feel their warmth. The milk pouring from the nipples would not reach his mouth. So many breasts, and his hand could not hold even one. So much milk, and his eager mouth could not taste even one drop.

The window grinned with its panes like guillotine-teeth. Mordecai Chaim was hopelessly calling Shoshana, his second wife. She came to him, her body a frozen tombstone, hopping on its foundation as if on one foot. She spoke to him with the letters engraved on cold granite: "Mordecai Chaim, where are you gallivanting through the night? Why don't you come home to sleep? I am cold alone in the bed."

"Shoshana," he complained, "Why are you constantly calling me to sleep? You love me only if I am asleep."

"Right," she replied. "Because only when you are asleep are you innocent."

He asked her, "How have I sinned so much against you?" She giggled with Zibert's giggle. He felt the prick of a needle, this time in his heart. He was again a little boy, an orphan. He was the street singer of the ghetto, standing against the wall with his outstretched hand. "Love me, *Mameshe*, love me *Tateshe* . . . You must love me . . ." he sang, begging the thousands of indifferent passers-by for alms.

It was cold in the room. The oven had gone out and Mordecai Chaim felt like crawling into Clara's bed to warm himself up. He did not know whether she was asleep or not, but he knew that as soon as he climbed in next to her, she would start to cry. Ever since she had become submissive and affectionate to him, she cried a lot — and her sobs increased the confusion in his head.

In the morning, Zibert, who had lately started to follow the Presess like a shadow, was waiting for him in front of his office. That was the routine. Every morning, the clownish figure would jump forward with a greeting and giggles. His sharp little eyes would scan the Presess' face. He had come to sniff out whether the night had passed without incident. He entered the office with the Presess, relating whatever he had found out among the ghettoniks, or the *shishkas*, or the parties, or the *Sonderkommando*. He rubbed his frozen little hands.

"The Zionist groups held a secret meeting. They've decided who are the traitors of the Jewish people, or rather of Polish Jewry. Do you want the names?" Zibert threw his right hand, fingers spread apart, up in the air and with his left hand, he bent one finger after another: "First comes you, Herr Presess. Yes, you in person. Then comes Schatten . . . Then Steinberg . . . then the Chief of Police . . ."

The Presess' blood froze. He felt a stiffness in all his limbs. Yes, he had long known what his own party people thought of him. He knew that they and no one else would lead him into history — not on a white horse, but on a black hearse. His ideological brothers, those whom he had protected, would do that.

Indeed what Zibert was telling him was not news to him. Yet he felt hot around
the eyes, with humiliation. But after a few moments, he regained his
composure. He would not let himself be stoned by anyone. Perhaps all was lost
for tomorrow, for the outside world, but here there was still a goal to achieve, a
mission to accomplish: to save a trace of a people, so that there would at least be
someone left to abuse his name. That would be his victory. The Presess
straightened up regally, raising his gray head. "What else do you know?" he
asked composedly.

"Two Jewish policemen demanded to be allowed to join the meeting," Zibert
continued. "They said that they had clean hands and that they would help in
the illegal activities. All those present at the meeting took an oath, like they did
at the meetings of 1905. And now listen to the resolutions. Number one, no one
would willingly leave the ghetto. Number two, use sabotage in the Resorts. And
do you know who proposed these important resolutions? Guess. Yes, your
devoted son, Samuel Zuckerman. Fancy that. But don't get nervous, Herr
Presess. Why do you turn so pale? And if they've decided, so what? Is it the same
as if you decide? They're just talking. Why do you stand up, dear Presess?"

Rumkowski began to pace up and down the room, his dishevelled hair
stiffening like the mane of an irritated lion. "What else?" he asked.

"They've decided to interfere with your and Schatten's activities, and to
collect materials to prove the crimes of both of you." Zibert waved his finger, "If
you take it so to heart, Chief, I'm telling you, that I won't ever tell you a thing.
The ghetto needs a healthy Presess, do you understand?"

"Talk!" Rumkowski roared.

Zibert made a face, as if he were frightened. "A proposal was introduced to
create a resistance movement. Don't get scared, Presess. The proposal was
defeated. They won't create a resistance movement, because the ghetto has not
a speck of arms in its possession. It is impossible to contact any partisans and
there is no lack of anti-Semites outside, not to mention the *Volksdeutsche* who
live all around the ghetto. And with the ghettoniks themselves it is also
impossible to sit down to the table. Not only don't we have what to whistle on,
but we also don't have anyone to do the whistling. The herd of people is barely
dragging itself around. And thirdly, fourthly, fifthly: If we begin fighting, with
the nothing that we have, we will, in the blink of an eye, be erased from the face
of the earth. As you can see, they have themselves accepted your policy. But
what then?"

"But they hold me responsible for accepting it, eh?"

"You have good friends too, myself for instance."

"After the war is over, you will come to my defence, won't you? I can imagine.
You will spit in my face, in order to wash yourself clean."

"To wash myself clean? Presess, of what? You say yourself that you are
innocent. And if so, I am certainly innocent. We are both in . . . innocent.
There is nothing to wash ourselves clean of."

✦ ✦ ✦

In December, winter took the world firmly into its grip. The ghetto, white
and neat, was buried under the snow. At night the frost was biting. The Presess
who had always been sensitive to the beauty of the ghetto in winter, this year
appreciated it even more. The gray air of despair vanished. The whiteness of the
snow was revitalizing. Again Mordecai Chaim's withered body was full of

energy. Big orders had at last arrived for the Resorts and in the empty hospitals new Tailor Resorts were being organized. The ghetto was now made up mostly of young Jews, and although they were not giants, they had productive abilities, so that there were no idle food consumers. Even the group of children who had managed to survive were re-registered, acquiring adult birth dates and were working just as hard as the adults. Their resemblance to eight or ten-year-olds was an optical illusion. It seemed odd that their hair was so healthily blond, black or brown, instead of gray or white as snow. The Presess was afraid to lavish his love upon them.

The Presess tried to convince himself that he felt like a fish in water. He spread out his fins, swimming ahead, forcing himself not to look backward or forward, but to concentrate on the present day. His power had indeed been limited, but what he had hoped to achieve was still possible. That was what he tried to believe.

Half of the window in the dining room was covered with snow. The frost glimmered on the panes. The Presess was alone in the house. Clara had left for a review at the House of Culture, while the servants were visiting their relatives. The Presess had lately discovered the delights of being alone. Alone, he did not have to mask his face, to pretend. He could allow himself to feel like a horse whose saddle had been removed for a moment. He could also allow himself the luxury of being a flabby old man. To make himself look younger had become an enormous effort. Indeed, he was now sitting at his desk, wearing only his pants with drooping suspenders, shirt collar unbuttoned, his feet in a pair of warm slippers. From the painting on the wall above him, the strong virile Mordecai Chaim with his serene wise face looked down on the old Mordecai Chaim, who was leaning against the table, his head buried in his arms, snoring heavily.

But then there came a dull pounding at the front door and the Presess jumped to his feet, not knowing for a moment where he was.

A green uniform appeared in the corridor. Rumkowski took the glasses off his nose and wiped them clumsily. Before he could manage to put them back on, the visitor had already said what he had come to say and vanished. Had he been an apparition? A dream? No. Mordecai Chaim had been waiting here all evening for the green uniform and for his order. The silence and the coziness of a rare moment spent in his warm house had been there — in order to be crushed by that pounding at the door. Now he had to hurry. Herr Biebow was an impatient master. All the Germans were impatient and disliked waiting too long. One had to jump for them quickly, eagerly accepting their evil decrees, their blows — and one had to bow to them gratefully.

He hurried on his vest, buttoned his collar, tied his tie and ran over to the mirror. He had to look decent. The Eldest of the Jews was not some beggarly old man. He was a regal patriarch. Let them have respect. He quickly brushed his hair and grabbed his hat. During such a calm winter evening an invitation from Biebow spelled fate. He, Mordecai Chaim, would again become the spoon feeding the never satiated belly of the Moloch. If so, how could there be any talk of respect? No, if it was a question of respect, it was respect for oneself. That was the issue. And suddenly a thought flashed through his mind. Biebow seemed lately unable to bear the sight of him. Biebow looked with the eyes of a cannibal at the Jewish Chief. And Rumkowski heard a cold whisper within him, "This time it is not the people who are in question . . . but you . . . your bones . . . your own skin." A frost spread over his heart at that thought. His fear grew.

When Clara returned from the review, her husband was not at home. She wandered about the house, looking for a sign to explain his absence at that hour. The servants who returned were unable to tell her a thing, and those whom she had sent to Baluter Ring informed her that there was no light in the windows of the Presess' office.

Late at night the Presess appeared in the house. His clothes were in a mess. His left cheek was swollen and red. He embraced his wife with boyish enthusiasm. "Only one slap, Clara dear, only one slap in the face!" He panted, leading her over to the sofa. He sat down beside her and leaned his head against her shoulder. "His hand tickles," he whispered. "He knows that without me he would have no ghetto . . . that without me he would have to go to the Front, and that, my angel, infuriates him."

Chapter Thirteen

DURING THE THIRD NIGHT of the *Sperre*, in the darkness and silence, the door of Bunim's hut squeaked open and a shadow appeared in it. The shadow, tiny and thin, bent over Bunim. "I have come to bring you good news, dear neighbour," the shadow wailed. "The gates of Paradise are open ... the Messiah is arriving." Bunim did not move. His eyes were dry, open, staring in the direction of the doll which still lay at the door. The doll's glassy eyes shimmered in the dark with a strange shine. "Dear neighbour, answer me," the shadow's voice implored. "We must have the strength to receive the Messiah ... Here, I've brought you a remedy for the heart. Take it into your mouth and you will have the strength to meet him with song and dance." A hand was seeking Bunim's mouth. The candy rolled down to the floor. The Toffee Man went down on his knees to find it. He reached Blimele's bed and threw himself on it. The bed squeaked, jarring, cracking open the skulls of mountains. "Answer me," the little bed was wailing.

Bunim jumped to his feet. He ran over to Blimele's bed, lifted the little man up in the air and thrust him towards the door: "Get out!"

"Answer me!" the little man stretched his hands out to him. "He won't come if you don't answer me."

Bunim felt the doll's body under his feet. Lily was raising her hands to him. "Answer me!" He picked up Lily, feeling her cool oilcloth skin with his fingers. He took her to the doll carriage. A cold wind was blowing from the window. He covered Lily with her cover.

The little shadow stood at the door. Bunim left him there and went outside to close the shutters. Blimele trotted over to him, naked and barefoot, upon the cool stones. "I want to see how you shut the shutters, *Tateshe*."

He let her watch him, then he took her by the hand and entered the hut. "Come daughter, let us begin the night." The little shadow stood in the frame of the open door, not letting him close it. "I . . . I . . ." Bunim groaned hoarsely, "I cannot answer you." Arms outstretched, he sank down on the bed.

He did not leave the hut and the Toffee Man did not leave him, coming by a few times a day and wailing like a madman before him. Bunim barely noticed his coming and going. His senses were dulled. Only with a pair of inner eyes did he clearly see Miriam and his children. He was constantly going out to freedom with them. The whole family. They were strolling through a sun-lit street, they peered into houses through shiny windows, seeking a new home. Miriam smiled, "I want a warm, sunny apartment. I want the stove to work well. We are so frozen, Bunim."

The closed shutters did not let in even a speck of light. In the dark, between

179

the four invisible walls, Bunim gathered all the days of his life, those of his past and those of his future, as well as the days of his wife's and children's lives. He saw minutes and seconds as if they had body. He felt the smell of Blimele's head, he touched the roundness of Miriam's hips, he saw the wrinkled old man's head of his newborn son, his *kaddish*. He heard laughter and sobs. Yesterday and today were mixed with tomorrow. Blimele was seven years old. She was going to school for the first time. She was a high-school student. She was a bride. He saw himself walking with his daughter through bright garden paths, silently transmitting to her all the treasures of his heart. He recited his poems to her. He dedicated his works to her. And the son, his *kaddish*, sat with him over open volumes of the Bible and the *Gemara*. "I have strayed, Father," Bunim complained to his new-born son who bore the name of his grandfather, the preacher of Lynczyce. The son, the big unknown man, stroked Bunim's head, consoling him, "We shall start from the beginning . . ." They opened the Bible together. "In the beginning God created the heavens and the earth . . ."

Somewhere in the middle of the night Bunim began to sing, reciting the Pentateuch by heart, pages of the Talmud, Lamentations, the Song of Songs, Ecclesiastes. The thick darkness became full of light, full of song. It was shroud-white and there was no night or day.

Sometimes, the days gathered in the room thinned and slipped out. Bunim explained to himself that the door was not shut well enough. Then he felt his heart move within him and his teeth chatter. He would jump to his feet and look for his glasses. Unable to find them, he would try, with outstretched arms, to find the door and lock it. He tapped blindly in the dark, hitting against Blimele's bed which would begin to mew like a kitten. Blimele was raising her hands to him from her bed. "*Tateshe*, tell me a story . . ." He sat down beside her, "Once upon a time there was a story . . . not at all a happy story. Sleep my little bird, sleep my child. I have lost such a love, woe is me . . ."

During the days of the *Sperre*, the police were about to enter the hut several times. But the door stood open and they were sure that there was no one inside. "I am still here!" Bunim wanted to call them. "Take me! I am on Blimele's bed and she won't let me get up!" It seemed to him that the policemen had already taken him.

Sometimes he caught himself, in time to realize that the Toffee Man was pushing a piece of turnip between his teeth. The little man would not stop chattering, "Eat, eat. You must have strength for the real leap upward. From here, from this pit, up to the heights, is very close. Eat, eat, silly boy, pain such as ours one almost does not feel." Bunim munched on the turnip, barely seeing, barely listening.

When he felt like it, he slept with Miriam on Blimele's bed. The neighbours or his colleagues, the writers who came to console him, infuriated him. They woke him with their talk and took him away from Miriam's arms. So he let them sit there, and forgot about them.

In time, he became more awake, but he would not leave the hut. He became used to pacing the room, crooning, mumbling, talking to himself. He did not find his glasses; he no longer looked for them either. His feet learned to see in the dark. But his pacing did no good. It confused the peaceful images which he had been summoning to his memory. It made him restless. It aggravated the passion within him, driving his weak feet to an increasingly faster speed, which made it impossible for him to lie down again. Now he could only collapse with exhaustion on Blimele's bed, his shrieks of pain mingling with the squeaking of the mattress springs.

Dr. Sonabend, who replaced Bunim at the Gas Centre and who was himself a fortunate man whose wife and son were still with him, would every evening bring in Bunim's soup. Bunim began to wait for him while pacing hastily, talking and singing to himself. He knew very well that he was pacing away from light and peace, entering an emptiness which hungered for soup. Dr. Sonabend was the embodiment of kindness. He whispered softly, "Six, seven pieces of potato in your soup." Dr. Sonabend, the *Jude* from Prague, was the demon who had turned off the light. Bunim chased him away. Filled with the soup, he would continue his pacing, inwardly howling. He threw himself at the wardrobe and dug into the drawers. He crumpled Miriam's dresses, her underwear, Blimele's underwear. He implored the clothes for help, in calling back the bodies which had once filled them. They led him into an ache which could not be dulled. The little girl's slip revealed the emptiness of a world which was impossible to bear.

He began to relish the food which the neighbours and friends brought him. The Toffee Man fetched him his food ration and Bunim devoured it in one session. He lit a fire in the stove to cook the bit of flour which he had received. He opened the doors of the cupboard and saw Miriam's pots staring at him like hollow eye sockets. He touched one of them and they all burst into a clattering lamentation. He ate the food he had cooked, while standing at the stove. As he stared at the fire, he reminded himself of something, entered the other room and came back with the bookkeeping register. Inside, lay the pages covered with his handwriting, the chapters of his poem. He also brought out his bitten-up pencil, approached the stove and removed the burners. He was sobbing spasmodically as he tried to push the rolled up paper sheets through the burners onto the flames. But then he saw Miriam's hands in the tongues of fire, pushing back the gift, refusing to consume it. "Don't kill me again!" she hissed from the stove. He hurled the half-smouldered sheets on the floor and finished eating his tasty meal.

He began to fear that he was disintegrating in the hut which kept him on the other side of life. He had to get out of it and save himself. The Toffee Man found his glasses and begged him, "Come with me to pray."

"Yes, take me to the Holy Scrolls."

Bunim did not see the streets, nor did he listen to the little man by his side. He saw himself standing before the repository of the Holy Scrolls. The doors of the Holy Ark were open. He held on to them with both hands. Inside it Blimele was hiding. The cover of the Scrolls was made of Miriam's house-dress. Bunim buried his head in it and felt Miriam's parchment body with his forehead. "Where are you?" A lava of senseless hollow words erupted from his tortured heart as if from a volcanic pit.

The winter began to live with him in his hut. Through the cracks in the walls the gales whistled and here and there snow flew in through the walls. The closed shutters outside clattered. Bunim slept on Blimele's bed covered with all the bedding. The nights were warm. Through paths of sleep the bright images came back to him. He moved about within an existence resembling the spiral threads upon a vertiginously rolling spool. They swept him along, entangling him in knots. He found himself in a maze of talk, Miriam's, Blimele's, in a whirlpool of smiles, of gazes, of touches and smells. Everything together, everything apart. He would wake up without regret, without joy; open his eyes and find himself in cold and in dullness. He dressed, hurried on his black coat with the hairy collar and went to work at the Gas Centre. There he sat, unaware of what was going on around him, staring at the old weird clock which seemed to hammer nails of nothingness into timeless space. He marked down the incomprehensible minutes and hours, did his bookkeeping, and longed for his soup; a longing for a canteenful of liquid which he devoured, or which devoured him.

Late afternoon. All day long the sun would not leave the sky, standing on the frozen window panes of the Gas Centre. A lively game was going on between the frost and the sun on the outside, and the steam on the inside. Bunim sat at his desk, keeping the accounts. All day long he had felt the sun on his back. It was like a friendly hand, urging him on, encouraging him, "Today! Today!"

Then the sun vanished and the frost began to fill in the gaps on the panes. The "consumers" came in with their pots to warm up the evening meal. All the burners were humming; the flames licked the gaily bubbling pots. The covers clicked, releasing the columns of steam like the breath from opened mouths. The steam wound around the heads of those who were waiting, and climbed upwards, covering the glass of the old clock with a fog. It made the walls shine as it encroached upon the ceiling, hanging there like a cloud across the sky. Only the light of the electric bulb shone through. The bulb looked like a pale distant little sun or moon peering down onto the earth through the long lashes of its rays.

The "consumers" embraced the hot pots with their stiff fingers. Here and there someone stirred his pot, releasing a wonderful aroma into the air. A woman put a spoon to her lips with a trembling hand, tasting the soup, giving it to the members of her family to taste. Single men and women ate from their pots as they cooked, then removed them empty from the burners. Along the wall stood the queue of those waiting for a burner. Bunim no longer kept them outside. He did not mind the chaos. The people in line impatiently stamped their feet. The floor was full of mud and dark snow. The wooden shoes splashed into the puddles. From the floor the cold climbed up their legs, but the faces and hands felt warm.

The "consumers" openly made fun of Bunim, the crazy manager. They checked on him, because he often made mistakes in keeping time, or he charged too much. He mixed up their names, and if it were not for their kindly Jewish hearts, which knew that there was no reason to envy him, real chaos would have set in. A few steady "consumers" saw to it that the Gas Centre functioned more or less properly. They watched to see that the right amount was paid, so that Bunim rarely needed to add money from his own pocket. He only had to put up with the mockery, and that was not difficult.

Today he was left alone. A woman had come in from the street with the news: "There are some rumours going around again. They say that Rumkowski's face spells trouble."

The row in front of the burners became restless. People took a sip from their pots to calm themselves. A woman grabbed her pot from the burner, turning to the people with vengeful satisfaction, "So I am luckier than you. I have nothing to fear any more." She focused her eyes on a little creature wearing such long pants that they completely covered his shoes, and such an enormous hat on his head that it completely hid his face. "Tell me the truth," she asked. "How old are you, nine or ten?"

"Seventeen!" the child replied proudly.

"My Seinvel was also ten years old." She shook her head and buried her face in her pot.

The conversation became general, as if the members of one big family were assembled together. A woman from the line spoke up, "My parents were wise enough to die in 1940, so they avoided all the troubles and the evacuations. I had a fiancé and . . ."

A tall lank man with a continuously dripping nose, interrupted her, "What's the difference? today or tomorrow, every one follows his own Star of Sorrow. Rescue is behind our backs, but death is before our eyes . . ."

Two young workmen from the Metal Resort, both of them dirty and grease-covered, scolded the man for his pessimism. He did not know what he was talking about. The truth was, they said, that one could practically touch salvation with one's hands. The Germans were having a difficult winter. They had had to withdraw on the Russian front. Africa was almost liberated and in 1943, the war was sure to come to an end. The workmen had to speak louder and louder, because a skirmish had broken out at one of the burners. Two women were fighting over their turn.

Bunim raised his head from the register. Talk, shouts, tension. Has the clock stopped? He cannot hear it. Cold air is rising from the floor. Wooden shoes are splashing in the mud. The steam coming from the pots is climbing towards the ceiling. The electric bulb — a mocking eye — is peering down at the weird figures covered with rags. It looks down on the crumpled faces, the pointy noses, the deep eye sockets, the hollow cheeks covered with a hairy moss, with death weeds. The mouths are twisted into grimaces, filled with grief, with pain, with horror. So much talk; words falling upon the hum of the burners, jumping, breaking up. The humming burners take them away. They ride off somewhere. The flames lick the pots, embracing them with blue-green tongues. The pots bubble, hiss, sing. Hands lift up the covers, spoons stir the precious liquids. From the noses, from the open talking mouths water drips into the pots, making them fuller. Sacred magical broths are being cooked here. Spell-binding tales pass from one pot to the other. Between the steam-covered walls a green toad is secretly panting, its green goitre moving up and down; the green toad of anguish.

Bunim looks on but does not see. He listens but does not hear. He knows that he was moved onto a wagon with many pairs of wheels made of the gas burners, that he is being carried on the wings of the fog-covered clock — to an encounter that awaits him. All he knows is that the walls are weeping tears. It is good that walls can weep sometimes.

The "consumers" vanish. One burner after the other is turned off. The noise dies out. The mud stops squishing. Someone wishes him a kindly good-night. Another "consumer" tells Bunim to give her the best burner tomorrow and let him, heaven forbid, not forget about it. The little nine or ten-year-old boy takes his pot between his hands, asking Bunim to open the door for him. There is no one there any more, except for the tall man who stands in the corner, eating his hot soup. He is already scratching the bottom. Like a clown he turns over the pot, chiming about inside it with his spoon like a tongue in a bell. "Our star is shining bright, it's time to begin the night!" When he laughs, his voice rasps with the gravel sound of moving sand dunes.

The Gas Centre is empty. The burners stop working and Bunim Berkovitch knows that he has arrived. He stands up and faces the rows of silent burners. Above them hovers the cloud of steam; through its fog peers the electric bulb. It smiles at the weeping walls. Bunim walks away from his desk. His feet are cold. The humidity of the floor seeps through his socks. His legs are stiff. He can barely move, yet he trudges over to the burners and turns them on. A fiery wreath of flowers dancing in a circle. Bunim stands over one of the flowers, warming his hands. He glances at the walls and the frosty window.

"God!" he moves his lips. "Let me be whole again. Give me back what you have taken from me. Take me into the world . . . where Blimele is, and Miriam and my son who will never grow. Set me free from my straits, God, if you hear me, offer me the balm of your merciful accord." He feels the wetness of the walls pour out of his eyes, stream down his cheeks and drip from his lips along with his saliva, making the burner in front of him sizzle and seethe. "God," he sobs, "I have the strength. Never mind . . . You will not take me away a coward. I am not afraid. I would feed my days with a hunger for vengeance, if I knew that vengeance would bring Miriam, Blimele and my son back to me. God, my account with the world will never be straight, nor my account with you, nor with people, nor with myself. Be merciful . . . Let me come home . . ."

He wipes his cheeks with his sleeve and walks from one burner to the other, turning them off. Then he turns them on again. He does not draw out the matches from his pocket. The burners hiss like conspirators, like subterranean snakes. Their sound fills the room. The air is rich with the sharp smell of gas. Bunim no longer feels the cold in his feet. He feels light and comfortable in all his limbs. He goes back to the desk and sits down, removes the glasses from his eyes and puts them in front of him. He buries his head in his arms. He wants Blimele to run out to greet him.

A squeak. A knock. A cold sharp wind lashes over Bunim's brain: The door! He has forgotten to lock the door!

The Toffee Man stands over him. "Pfui . . . pfui . . . a man makes such a stink. Blessed be the Almighty for having sent me over in time. Come on outside quick! Into the fresh air!"

His moist little eyes glisten. Excitedly, he pulls Bunim by the sleeve with all his strength. Bunim is unable to move. The Toffee Man rushes from one burner to the other, turning off the gas. He opens the door wider and comes over to the desk with a jug of water. Bunim screams at him in his mind, "Get out of here! Out!" He presses his lips together, refusing to take a sip.

The little man goes on pulling him, chattering, "You are not yet capable of being alone, dear neighbour. To be able to be alone is a high level, given only to a chosen few." He covers Bunim with his coat and realizing that he will not be able to carry him, he throws open the window. A draught dances into the room, counting Bunim's new gray hair. The little man stands over him, whining, "We have been raised to the bottom of the abyss, do you understand? We have been raised to the deepest depths. No human being has ever seen what we have, never heard what we have. No wonder we go blind, no wonder we go deaf, no wonder we go mad. Here is a desolate *Pardes* from which only a few can emerge intact. They must see and not go blind, listen and not go deaf, drown in pain and not go mad. They, the few, must dive down to the bottom where the gold mines of Truth are buried. Like divers they must gather the pearls of *Pshat, Remez, Drash* . . . They must come up with the secret. You were meant to be a diver, dear neighbour, so do what you must . . . And now give me a good burner to warm up my little pot."

✦ ✦ ✦

Bunim did not try to commit suicide again. He felt like someone who had arrived too late to catch the train and was left alone on an empty station. He had missed the opportunity. He knew that he would stay on, that he and the Toffee Man, two madmen, had to create a kind of entity of clairvoyance.

His body moved between two points in the ghetto: between his hut and the Gas Centre. He found himself in a pit of dullness. His mind was frozen. Only his body was awake, feeling hunger and cold. He served his body with robot-like devotion. The Toffee Man bothered him less. His neighbours also forgot about him. Only at the Gas Centre did he come in touch with people. But these people were figures; talking, shouting puppets with pots in their hands. He manipulated them, assigned burners to them, took their money and had no other contact with them.

One evening a woman appeared carrying a tiny pot in her hand. The woman was petite, with a small delicate face as if carved from stone. She had a pair of eyes as quiet as two clear wells. There was a dumbness, an immobile sadness about her as she stood at her burner, wrapped in the folds of her plaid. She seemed like a statue of sorrow. She had turned her back to Bunim, her head was bent over her pot. Bunim embraced her figure with his gaze. Something called to him from her back, from her whole being. He approached her.

"You have such a little pot . . ." he said. She opened her mouth as if about to say something or to smile at him. A bubble of saliva burst on her lips. She quickly turned off the burner, took her pot and moved towards the door. He jumped ahead and turned to face her, "Where are you going?"

She did not show any surprise at his odd question. "Home," she answered, wrapping her plaid around the pot, as if she were afraid that he would take it away from her.

"What's your name?" he inquired, not knowing why.

"Mine?" It seemed as if she were having difficulty in recalling her name. "Mine?"

"My name is Berkovitch. Bunim Berkovitch," he introduced himself.

"Good night, Mr. Berkovitch."

When she appeared at the Gas Centre the next time, Bunim decided to follow her and see where she lived. He went outside with her and stopped her. "Could I perhaps visit you?"

They looked at each other, not with their eyes, but with their open mouths. The little pot shook in the woman's hand. She showed him where she lived.

Another day, she came in when he was about to close the Centre and they left together. She ran ahead of him. Her partly opened plaid flew up in the air like a pair of wings. Steam spiralled out of her pot. Bunim followed her, his black heavy winter coat unbuttoned, its tails flying like a pair of wings. The woman climbed a staircase and entered a dark room. Bunim bumped against her in the dark and the soup in her pot spilled. They both let out a frightened, "Oh!" and jumped away from each other. He searched for the woman with his

hands, found her moist warm face and fell with his lips on hers. Blinded, they
both swayed about the room, glued to each other. A bed caught them in the
dark, like a swing. The empty pot fell out of the woman's hand.

From that day on, he began to see people, to notice their faces. He began to
hear their voices and listen to them talk. Again he began to absorb . . . just as he
had a long time ago. He felt clearly that he was returning from a long journey.
But when he tried to visit the strange woman again, she turned on the light.
Along the walls stood three made beds. Pointing at them, she introduced her
lost family to him. "Here I slept with my husband. That is my daughter Sonia's
bed and that is little Gershon and little Isaac's bed. I had them all locked up and
went to fetch the briquette ration. There was nothing to light the stove with."
She offered him a glass of sweetened water. Her quiet eyes affectionately
caressed Bunim's face, his nearsighted eyes, the snarls of his gray hair. "I don't
want to attach myself to anyone any more," she whispered.

"Neither do I," he replied, stood up and left. The same night he found the
seventeen half-charred chapters of his poem on the floor where he had thrown
them. He turned on the light for the first time. He began the eighteenth
chapter.

A passionate impetus carried him away. He was not aware of the days or
nights, of the hours at the Gas Centre, of eating or sleeping. He lived only in the
pages of the bookkeeping register. His poem became his home, his world, his
longing and his fulfilment, his dreams and his reality. Blimele and Miriam were
again with him, around him. They were guiding his pencil. They were his
Blimele and his Miriam, close as his own body, yet they had both grown mighty.
He was forced to look up at them. He was barely able to embrace them with his
words. The room was too small for them, the beds too narrow. They were
expanding into the streets. They slept on the sidewalks. Their breath hovered
over the ghetto.

He was feverish. Sometimes sweat poured down his face in streams, at other
times he shivered with cold. He wanted to escape the eighteenth chapter of his
poem. He could not immerse himself once again in the whirlpool of horror
brought on by the *Sperre*. He had no strength to come back to his door and look
at the broken lock. Like a stubborn ox he paced the frozen backyard for hours,
afraid of the sheets of paper, of his pencil. And like a doomed ox, whose fate
hung on the loop around his neck, he finally let himself be dragged towards his
table. When he sat down to it, having surrendered, the all-consuming fever
came back to him, thrusting him into moments which were so sharp that they
took his breath away. He bit his lips until they bled, overpowered by humility
and guilt. It was a sin to translate such an experience into words. He had
become estranged from words. It took him hours to bring himself to polish a
grief-soaked stormy stanza and fit it into the mould of rhythms and rhymes —
of beauty? He despised himself, he cursed himself, yet he was aware that the old
dove had returned to him, cooing with the joy of creation. The word, pitiful,
hollow and rubbed out as it was, still had the magical power to revive the
remembrance of vanished worlds — and to survive them.

The eighteenth chapter was finished. Bunim was relieved. But now he found
himself within another kind of void. The sight of paper filled him with disgust;
it nauseated him. His tired head longed for the pillow, the body wished for a bed
to stretch out on and sleep. But he was unable to stay under the same roof with
the full sheets of paper and have peace of mind. Again he had a wish to roll them

all up and throw them into the fire. His urge to do so was so strong that he had to escape from it and run outside.

Wrapped in his heavy winter coat, he rushed back and forth over the empty yard, circling the frozen trunk of the cherry tree. The frost burnt his face and pricked his hands and feet. The ground glittered with diamonds of snow. It was dusk and the early winter darkness enveloped the ghetto. Bunim stepped out onto the deserted Hockel Street. All the windows were dark, covered with black-out paper or plaids. Wanton winds were carousing on the sidewalks. He was awake, as if the frosty needles had pricked open his senses. Then he was overwhelmed by a worry over the safety of his written pages which he had left on his table. He feared that the fire in the stove would jump out to grab his work and devour it, or that a gale would break open the door, which he no longer locked, and sweep away the loose sheets. Suddenly, it seemed to him that he had left a treasure in his hut, which he had to guard more than his own life. He hurried back and with tender trembling fingers gathered together the sheets of paper. On their border he signed his initials. He took the written sheets and approached the window where Blimele's doll carriage stood. He took out Lily, and made a little mattress for her out of his eighteen chapters. Then he lay down on Blimele's bed, covered himself with Blimele's blanket and with all the other bedding. He slept a calm dreamless sleep.

The following days he walked around hoping to find a pair of ears to listen to his chapters. Perhaps he would thus free himself of them, or free them from himself, he mused. He decided to take them to the poetess Sarah Samet.

At the sound of his tapping, Sarah's neighbour opened the opposite door. "No one lives there," he informed Bunim.

"The family Samet?"

The neighbour shrugged his shoulders.

The wish to read his poem to someone left Bunim for a long time. Then it returned, and he again thrust the eighteen chapters into his pocket. This time he went to see Winter. Vladimir Winter was the right man. Bunim needed his sharp critical appraisal. He wanted Winter to be cutting, to tear him apart, to shred and dissect the entity which he, Bunim, had created, to see if there was something more to it than illusion. Winter was a cold pitiless judge. Almost joyfully Bunim ran to him, his face aflame like that of a *heder* boy. His heart, which had lately begun to pound wildly at the slightest excitement, was now about to jump out of his chest.

A young dark-haired woman came running down the stairs of the house where Winter lived. She looked at Bunim with a pair of coal-black eyes, then stopped him, "Don't you recognize me? Zuckerman's daughter. We were neighbours on Hockel Street." He mumbled a greeting and tried to pass her, but she did not let him. "You're probably going to see Winter? So I'll save you a hundred stairs." She pulled him along. "He is at the *Wissenschaftliche Abteilung*. Come, I'll tell you how to get there." She continued with an undertone of mockery, "Never heard of the *Wissenschaftliche Abteilung*?" He walked at her side, delighting in her liveliness and talkativeness. "They make showcases for the Germans," she explained. "The Jewish way of life. If you want to know, I don't like the whole enterprise. It smells too much . . . I don't know of what. But don't take me seriously. I have the habit of accepting nothing in the ghetto at face value . . . I must know from where the legs grow." He was so busy trying to keep up with her, that he barely heard what she was saying. She led him to Baluter Ring and showed him where the *Abteilung* was located. She took leave of him, laughing, "Do you realize how beautifully crisp the air is? I've heard that you are a poet, so you should feel it." She hurried away across the shimmering snow. He felt the freshness of the air and inhaled deeply.

As soon as Bunim entered the *Wissenschaftliche Abteilung*, his eyes beheld the figure of the *Rabiner* in his neat black frockcoat and his pale face, a face which made him think of a satisfied cheerful Christ. The *Rabiner* came forward with outstretched hands. "Please come in," he said encouragingly. His bright eyes welcomed the visitor. He scrutinized the latter's bear-like figure, the long winter coat with the hairy fur collar and the cap surrounded by strands of gray hair. His eyes rested on the creased face with its near-sighted eyes nestled in a pair of watery bags. Bunim asked for Winter, and the *Rabiner* smiled familiarly. "You belong to his crowd, don't you? Yes, he is here. We are finishing off a showcase and I've invited him to express his opinion. You have not seen our exhibition yet, have you?"

Bunim looked at the tables covered with all kind of papers, paints, materials and he noticed some familiar faces among the workers. At the same time he became aware that the room was warm. He unbuttoned his coat and allowed the *Rabiner* to lead him into the other room to see the exhibition. Winter immediately came forward to meet him. With great pomp he introduced him to the *Rabiner*, "A poet. Our poet!"

The lights in the *Rabiner's* eyes sparkled. He took Bunim by the arm and led him around the showcases. Bunim lowered his eyes to the glass panes. He saw his birth-town Lynczyce . . . his street, the well, the synagogue . . . the girls with pots of *cholent* in their hands. However, there was something unpleasantly grotesque in the scene, or did it only seem so to him? The *Rabiner* did not remove his eyes from Bunim's face, although he did not ask what impression the exhibition made on him. Then, after Bunim had finished looking at the exhibition, he invited him into his office. Winter was already sitting there with a cup of coffee. His vulture-like face was animated, almost gay.

"So you finally looked me up," he exclaimed, "And here I have been complaining about my friends. The truth is that nowadays one needs friendship more than ever, otherwise one feels stranded in the middle of a desert. My body burns up with fever and with the longing for a human face. As you look at me now, Berkovitch, my temperature is about thirty-eight degrees. Come, let's go to my place. My oven is still warm and I have cooked a *baba*."

The *Rabiner* looked at Winter with reproach, "A visitor has just come in and you already want to take him away?"

"He is my visitor," Winter snapped.

The *Rabiner* seemed to have a plan to make Bunim stay, for he vanished from the room and returned the next moment with Rachel Eibushitz at his side. He introduced her to Bunim. She smiled faintly at him, shaking his hand.

"We have known her longer than you." Winter waved his hand at the *Rabiner*.

"And do you also know that she writes?" The *Rabiner* would not give up in his efforts to awaken the visitor's interest. "She is helping me to translate the psalms into Yiddish. Come on Rachel, let's hear a poem."

Rachel's face blushed. Her shoulders drooped and she seemed ready to run out of the room. But the *Rabiner* took her hand and forced her to sit down at his side. He filled cups of coffee for her and Bunim, and looked at Rachel with fatherly expectation.

Bunim cast a stealthy glance at the girl who was eyeing the door as she sipped her coffee, as if she were waiting for an appropriate moment to disappear. He remembered her from the times when he had lived another life. The short brown hair covering her forehead in snarled ringlets shone richly, seeming to swim towards him in warm waves. He could not see her face, since she did not take the cup away from her mouth. He saw a streak of light on her nape, a strip of white skin underlined by the border of the dark-red scarf which she wore around her shoulders, tied in a loose knot over her chest. As the *Rabiner* continued to extol his worker, Bunim felt himself blushing with the shame which he read in Rachel's face. "You are a writer, you must listen to her," the *Rabiner* insisted. "Believe me, she is talented."

Winter interrupted him, "Whether she is talented or not we shall only know in ten years time. Now she is writing with the talents of youth." The *Rabiner* was called outside by one of the workers. Rachel put down her cup hurriedly and stood up. Winter snatched hold of her by the wrist. "Tell me . . . perhaps you know . . . for what diabolic purposes is all this work? I don't like it at all . . . And it seems to me that this place is about to be liquidated. An order has arrived to immediately finish everything we started . . ."

Rachel had no time to reply before the *Rabiner* reappeared. He placed himself at Rachel's side and urged her in a paternal tone of voice, "Come on, Rachel, we are waiting."

She shook her head, "You know that I don't write seriously."

The *Rabiner* tightened his smiling lips and opened a drawer. "In that case let the truth come out," he said secretively, drawing out a thick writing book. "Your father copied it for me." Rachel sat down on the chair, staring at the *Rabiner* with big astounded eyes. He was delighted with her modesty. "What's the matter, Rachel? I want to bring you in touch with connoisseurs. Here sits a man," he pointed at Bunim, "who is himself a poet." Her gaze fell unwillingly on Bunim. Only now did she notice his swollen face, so twisted and changed that he seemed like another person.

Bunim caught her gaze. "Read," he said.

She took the writing book from the *Rabiner's* hand and flipped through the pages for a moment, her other hand playing with the knot of her scarf. It seemed as if a veil had fallen off her face, leaving it clearer, more open. Bunim suddenly felt the impulse to read the eighteen chapters of his own poem to the girl. It seemed to him that her ears would absorb his lines, not the way he wanted Winter to absorb them, but the way someone absorbs a melody which has been created especially for him. Apart from that, the girl's face attracted him with its secretive air, it teased his curiosity. Open and free as the face now seemed, it was still veiled by layer upon layer of mystery.

She wet her lips and began reading a poem about Jewish boys and girls riding through Poland's green pastures; through fields and forests full of life, full of young peasants and young animals, while the world with all its charms ran away from them. It was a rhythmical half-sung, half-spoken recitation during which Rachel swayed in her chair to the beat of the lines. The words themselves were sharp, staccato. Her listeners rocked in their chairs along with her. For a moment the room became transformed into the shaking boxcar of a freight train. As soon as Rachel finished, the unpleasant squeak of Bunim's chair broke the silence.

"Good night!" he called out in an exaggeratedly loud voice and with clumsy steps hurried out of the room. Winter ran after him.

Work at the *Wissenschaftliche Abteilung* finished half an hour earlier than in other Resorts. Usually Rachel rushed home to use the half hour for herself. But today she felt heavy, lazy. She wore the red scarf on her head and the belt of her coat was tightened around her waist to make her feel warmer. She enjoyed walking slowly on the white sidewalk, between the white houses, and listening to the voices within her. She had Berkovitch's tormented face in her mind's eye, and felt guilty for having chosen to recite that particular poem in his presence. Somehow she was unable to disentangle herself from the furrows of his face.

Suddenly, she saw him emerge from a back alley. "I was waiting for you," he muttered. Their eyes met in the sparse gas light at the corner. In that light their faces took on a yellowish green hue, as if they were covered by a mask, or freed from one. The creases of his face were invisible now, his thick lips seemed almost black. They smiled at her faintly. A deep warm darkness filled the slivers of his swollen eyes. The snow soundlessly powdered the visor of his cap.

"Forgive me for having read that poem. It made no sense," she whispered.

Tenderness and pain made his face seem beautiful. All the phases of his life seemed to be sealed in it. "Perhaps there is a sense to be found only in senselessness," he said. "Ours is a sacred madness."

They began to walk slowly, facing each other. Rachel said, "I have begun to work with clay. Do you know why?"

"In order to give three dimensions to the sacred madness."

She laughed quietly, then leaned over to him with sudden intimacy, "There are two chambers within me. I have no key to them and they open when they please. The first chamber is cluttered, bubbling with noise. Everything is in a muddle and strewn about inside it. But in blessed moments the other chamber opens. It is filled with light and with peace. So, you understand, sometimes I feel guilty for entering that chamber, thinking that perhaps it is my duty to feel torn apart."

Berkovitch replied somewhat impatiently, "You are spoiled. I am not faced with that kind of choice."

Rachel thought that she had said something which she should not have said. The man walking beside her was unarmoured. She was afraid to go on talking, yet it seemed a waste to keep silent. "You don't understand me!" she cried out. "I didn't mean to say . . . Anyway, I think . . . that art, that all of philosophy and religion, everything called humanism stands on trial here. That if the world is to go on existing, it will have to think differently, to create differently . . . to be different. And we ought to be those who begin with the new . . . I don't know how . . ."

"And I, you see," he grew heated, "I am writing my poem in the traditional old form. Four lines, the first rhyming with the third, the second rhyming with the fourth. Yes, it must rhyme. I cling to the rhythm and the rhyme . . . if not I would explode. Perhaps you are right. Perhaps it is a sin to apply the old forms as if nothing had happened. Perhaps I don't have the strength to give it a new dress."

She said hesitantly, "I wonder whether it is at all possible to write a novel about the ghetto. How can you write without the perspective of time? On the other hand, if you wait for the perspective of time, it will become impossible to recreate the specific atmosphere of this place. So, perhaps our life must be registered in the present tense. And for that we do indeed need a new form." She caught her breath and shivered. She felt a buzzing in her ears. Her thoughts were scattered. She could barely recall what she had wanted to convey to him. Yet she managed somehow to go on, "But then the question arises: how can art be chaos? How can you fit that which has no form into a form?" Her face was aflame. She put up her collar. She concluded in a drunken melodramatically loud voice, "We live on the sharp edge of the knife which is cutting history apart . . ."

He grabbed her arm and turned to her with his entire body. "Yes, there will be a new chronological system, the era before and the era after us. We are the borderline. Along with us everything is being destroyed, the new will be built with us as the foundation. I want to read you my poem. Are you cold? May I come to see you tomorrow? You see," he became more and more excited, "I have a similar problem with my work, although it is poetry. Because it is also an epic. Do you understand? I cannot allow myself to wait for perspective. I have to fix every moment on paper, as it happens. That's what we must do in such times. You are right. Later on you may remember times like these, but then the memory has already put up barriers which your subconscious forbids you to cross. And also the cut of the knife . . . the axe of Fate, its sudden blow . . . And then again: a writer ought to keep himself on the outside of his epic work. The more he keeps out of it, they say, the more successful are his results. But how can I keep myself out? Even if I could, I wouldn't want to. Therefore, you see, by writing we err in the darkness. So what? Isn't that the fate of man? Why then shouldn't works about man err in the darkness as well?"

They were standing in front of her house. She stretched out her hand to him. "Forgive me for running off," she whispered, her teeth chattering. "I don't know why I suddenly feel so cold." Yet her eyes smiled warmly at him. She gazed into his face, which seemed brighter than before. Snow was falling off the edge of his visor. "Do you know when we first met, Mr. Berkovitch?"

He stared at the snow-covered ringlets of her hair sticking out from under the red scarf on her head. Her cheeks seemed to reflect the scarf's redness. He gratefully returned the smile in her eyes with a warm smile of his own. "Of course I remember. In the yard on Hockel Street."

"No, before that. On the way to the ghetto. You were pulling a table transformed into a sleigh. You jostled me. 'You see,' my father pointed at you, 'that is a writer. Berkovitch is his name.'"

With regret Bunim let go of her fingers which had been softly, pleasantly warming his palm. The year 1943 was the year of love and hope.

Chapter Fourteen

THE FOLLOWING DAY after closing the Gas Centre, Bunim waited for Rachel in front of her house. He wanted to climb upstairs and knock at her door, but he could not bring himself to do so. He preferred to meet her at the place where they had parted the day before, to stretch out his hand to her and receive hers like a gift. He had left the eighteen chapters of his poem at home. All night he had been busy writing another poem. "The Song of Joy." Joy. He was unable to find another word for the restlessness which had befallen him after he had left the girl. He knew quite well that the word was not right. It did not reflect the true colour of his mood, but he did not mind.

Upstairs, Rachel lay in Blumka's bed. Beside her, in his bed, lay Moshe. They were both running a high temperature. Before Blumka had left for work at the Ghetto Laundry, she put Rachel's and Moshe's sugar and marmalade, along with their bread ration, by their bedsides. Blumka was impatient with the sick, and she was picking fights with Shlamek. She was sure that Rachel and Moshe just had colds, yet she could not control her fears. The frost on the window panes was growing thicker, and in the streets, rumours of imminent deportations were circulating again. She had no strength to face the long day awaiting her at the Resort. She was angry with Moshe, "Why don't you get up and go to work, at least for half a day? You could at least collect your soup there," she said.

Moshe shook his head, "I can't move."

She knew that he could not move. His glassy eyes told her that, but she could not bear to see him so helpless. "If a man wants to, he can do anything," she grumbled.

Later on in the day, Moshe turned his eyes to his daughter. She heard him say, "I don't love your mother any more . . . Everything is over between us." Rachel lay stiff, stunned. Her father's voice thundered through her head, demolishing the foundations of her life. Everything collapsed into a dizzying whirlpool. Not long before, during the *Sperre*, she had experienced the same feeling, when her father had left them to hide by himself. The image she had of Moshe had split into two. One part of him was alien, while to the other part she was attached by a million ties. Moshe went on talking as if he were intoxicated by his own fever. "How could we ever make the Germans pay for what they have done to the feelings between your mother and myself? It is becoming very difficult to love, daughter."

He became immersed in a long monologue about his love for Blumka, about how her irritability, her bitterness and screaming had gradually destroyed his feelings for her, although he knew that her temper was a result of her worry

192

about the children and himself. Then Moshe embarked on a tirade in praise of friendship, in particular his and Zuckerman's. The Germans deserved thanks, too, he said. Thanks to them this friendship had come about. Such deep mutual understanding between two men could never occur between a man and a woman. Moshe smiled, "I've forgotten to take back my razor from Zuckerman. The man is so weak that he can't even shave himself . . . Now he will bring the razor and give me a shave. Today I feel weaker than he. That is the meaning of Friendship, Rachel. One friend supports the world for the other. And . . . don't worry about what I said about Mother. I talk like that because I'm spoiled. I have it too good. How many people go through their whole lives without love or friendship?"

Rachel was no longer listening to him. She was deep in a heavy sleep. Later, much later, she heard someone talking, voices reaching her through distant doors, "Typhus . . . Typhus." Hands were touching her forehead.

There was a loudspeaker in her brain through which she began to hear weird sounds. Through it she heard her father's heavy sighs. They echoed in her mind: "We are perishing . . . vanishing . . . namelessly . . . with no purpose . . ." Then the loudspeaker was silent. Everything was over. Silence covered the sighs. Columns of smoke withdrew behind the horizon. Though all was lost, her heart was still pounding. She was alive. The loudspeaker's mouth turned as blue as the calm blue sky of Passover. Airplanes buzzed in it softly, like bees. They dropped no bombs, announced no fire, they brought peace. It made no difference. Everything was over anyway. Rachel's heart was transformed into a cannon, which shook with explosions. Her mind was an airplane thundering through the skies of Passover. She fought for every breath. Her blood sizzled. Her eyes burned like hot briquettes. Screws were being drilled into her clay-blocked ears. Typhoid was playing with her body and soul.

The Sabbath eve of the *Sperre* heaved into sight from behind some precipice. She saw heads full of coloured ribbons, little mouths talking children's talk, smiling children's smiles, imploring her, Rachel, to share her body and her life with them. So she shared them with the children whose tears began to flow from her eyes. "Mrs. Nachumov!" Rachel called, "I have become a teacher at last!" Her own burning breath hit her in the face and she imagined that her old teacher was stroking her cheeks. Her bed swayed like a swing suspended from a long cord, rocking her between the skies and the abysses, between wakefulness and dream, between life and death.

As she swayed back and forth, Simcha Bunim Berkovitch appeared. He stood at the window of the little bedroom, his hands holding on to the window's white casements as though he were holding an open book covered with an invisible writing. "I have perished," he read from the book in a whisper, as he swayed over it. "Vanished . . . namelessly . . . for no purpose . . ." She saw the puffed water bags under his eyes. Suddenly he snatched at the edge of her bed, shook it and threw it up in the air. The walls collapsed. The earth swam away beneath her, the sky swam away above her. She, Rachel, was a burnt-out, setting sun, sinking faster and faster. On her way down, she shook off Bunim's winter coat, which was black and burnt and had been smouldering on her body. She would have felt light and cool as she waved with the coat from the falling swing, were it not that the coat pulled her down like an anchor, like a sack of stones, until it tore the arms off her body. Clasping the coat, her arms fell into the bottomless night. She wanted to look down and see where her arms had fallen, but her father caught her gaze and kept it for himself. "Move over, daughter," he begged. "Move over, because I'll fall down." His face had the same expression as it had worn on that day of the *Sperre*. Desperate, anxious, she began to move towards the wall to make room for him in her bed. But then she noticed him in a swiftly passing train. "Blumka! Blumka!" he called, waving at Rachel. His voice was black, final. Suddenly she saw herself in the train, sitting at a window. At the same time she was standing on the platform of a station, abandoned, watching the train fall over a precipice. Someone was howling; a shriek in the deafening silence.

Rachel felt a soft cool hand caressing her. A voice enveloped her shuddering body like a thin cotton slip. "Rachel, the grass will soon sprout . . . The cherry tree will soon be in bloom." It was Blumka's smile. "I cooked a bit of soup for you, daughter. A few pieces of potato, a little carrot. Please, open your mouth, feel the taste. Swallow . . . Breathe the wonderful air . . ."

Rachel obeyed her. She breathed. She swallowed the good air and the fog over her eyes dissolved like a cloud revealing a bright sky. Beside her sat a shrunken little woman, whispering sweet words. Rachel barely heard them, barely understood them, yet they soothed her soul, healing it; they cooled the heat of her body with their softness. At the foot of the bed stood a thin young man, his skinny long neck stretched towards her, his hands waving like thin twigs. She realized: They were mother . . . brother.

Next to her head sat David. The day was full with his face. He was beaming. "I've brought you an apple . . . here, eat it." He pushed something round into her hand, something juicy-smooth, wonderful. Rachel stared at the minute apple as if she were seeing such a thing for the first time in her life. "Take a bite," he encouraged her. She obeyed him. Juice sprinkled over her face. She wanted him to take a bite of the apple too, but he pushed away her hand. "This is for you only." She had no idea that his face could express such happiness. She wanted to offer him a grateful smile, but she could not. He was sitting between the neighbouring bed and herself, like a wall, blocking her view. She knew that the neighbouring bed was empty. She had known it for a long while. No, she had not discovered the fact from Blumka's shrivelled face, nor from Shlamek's tormented gaze. She remembered . . .

She had been in the middle of a long conversation with her father. They had been talking to each other from the depths of their souls and they had never finished. A hollowness which would never be filled. But David was strong. When they were alone in the little room, he kissed her arms; each kiss sewing together the hollowness, each kiss a bridge which he built to help her cross the void. Her fingers found their way to his hair, to his cheeks, to his eyes and his mouth. She formed the face of her lover out of clay.

"I sneaked in to you before the quarantine began," he announced proudly. "And you know, I became superstitious. Guess what I did?" He drew out a folded sheet of paper from his pocket. "Read!" She puckered her eyebrows, straining her eyes. "I want you to live," was written on the sheet of paper. He added, "I shoved it under your pillow. Later, when you were in quarantine, they would not let me see you. The piece of paper under your pillow did the work for me. I ordered you to live and you obeyed me."

He was not always there — between the neighbouring bed and herself. She could look at the bed for hours. She did not mind. Her imagination could not fathom that finality. She saw Moshe alive, talking — as if he were in the middle of saying something as he suddenly left the room, leaving his last word suspended in the air, to wait for him to come back and pick it up. He still owed her his fatherly love. He would come to give it back to her, because it was impossible to believe that the Sacred Four was broken. The End was a familiar word, but it had no relation to this sacred number. Moshe himself was the guardian of that number; yes, in spite of the fact that he had left them alone during the *Sperre*. She waited for him to reappear with his mild tired face, the dry cigarette butt at his mouth; she waited for him, to stretch out his princely hands to her. He would enter the room wrapped in his dreaminess, in the romantic loftiness in which he kept his being dressed. He, who was capable of loving so beautifully, he, the handsome father, must not be allowed to betray them again, to desert them again. She did not cry for him.

Neither Blumka nor Shlamek mentioned Moshe's name. They knew something which she would never know. They had seen something which she would never see. She wanted to read her father's last moments from their faces. She was curious, jealous, and yet relieved that for her the truth was not validated, that she could go on waiting for him. Only at night did Rachel hear Blumka utter Moshe's name. Blumka slept in Moshe's bed. She called to him, as she hugged his pillow. Only once did Blumka call his name during the day. On the thirtieth day after his death.

The last few nights air-raid alarms followed one after the other. Bomb explosions could be heard. As soon as the sirens began to wail, Mrs. Satin would come in with her daughter Teibele. Both of them wore long white nightgowns and white bonnets. They shook with cold and fear. Every time she heard an explosion, or the close shots of the Germans, who aimed at those windows where the light shone through, Mrs. Satin covered her ears with her hands. Between one explosion and the next, she bemoaned the loss of her life's companion, her protector, who had been taken away from her during the *Sperre*. As she eulogized him, he grew into a knightly giant, an achiever, a provider, a master in the art of love. She insisted on Blumka being a partner to her mourning. Were they not like two sisters in their loss? Blumka however refused to cry with her. Mrs. Satin could not understand how Blumka could "hold herself together" so well, and how Rachel and Shlamek could go on sleeping during such an eerie night.

She prodded the sleepy Teibele with her elbow, "Don't fall asleep, woe is me! Can't you hear it thundering?"

Teibele ached for a bit of sleep and at length she left her mother and crawled into Rachel's bed. Nor could Blumka keep her eyes open, and leaving Mrs. Satin to keep watch over her fear, she too went back to sleep.

In general, Blumka was barely able to keep on her feet. The skin of her face was splotched and green, resembling an old dry apple. A gray moss sprouted on her cheeks. The hair on her head was falling out; she had deep bald bays above the temples and her entire scalp was visible to the eye. The suds and detergents had so eaten away the skin of her fingers that it peeled like paper. The wetness in which she stood all day and the dampness from the steaming basins and kettles at the Ghetto Laundry had moved into her bones, making all her joints ache. She had frequent attacks of dizziness and would faint a few times a week at her basin. She secretly gave Rachel the major part of her food ration.

Mrs. Satin, who had suspected Blumka's deeds, had taken it upon herself to save her proud neighbour from destruction, and sustained her with frequent helpings of *baba* made from coffee dregs; she refused to leave before the last bit had slid down Blumka's throat.

Rachel was in the throes of a wild post-typhoid appetite. She was capable of devouring anything that could be chewed. To Blumka, her daughter's return to life was a breathtaking sight, and it was painful for her not to be able to help her gather strength. She experienced a strange kind of regret that she herself was not edible, that she could not prostrate herself before Rachel, saying, "Take me, eat me up." It never occurred to her that by giving Rachel her own food she was doing precisely that. But the craving for food made Rachel blind and deaf. She never asked where her bread or her good soups were coming from. Her sapless, stubbornly silent brother would sit beside her, wishing a typhoid fever upon himself. Abandoned by his father, abandoned by his mother, he gave free reign to his jealousy.

✦   ✦   ✦

Rachel blossomed during that cold winter. Enraptured by the miracle of her rebirth, she found a never-ending delight in walking on her feet. Excitedly she watched her breasts fill her blouse like buds awakening to a new spring. Her hips became more rounded, broader. Her eyes sparkled with life. She was hardly able to be serious, even for a moment. She felt as spoilt as a child, playful, always ready for laughter and very much in love with herself. She could stand in front of the mirror for hours, combing her hair, setting it in different styles, or trying on blouses and dresses countless times, back and forth. It took hours for her to get ready for David's visits. When she was alone in the house, she would take out of the pillowcase the fur jacket which Moshe had given her, and parade around the room in it. Intoxicated with herself, she wanted to see her mother and brother cheerful and she tried all kinds of tricks to infect them with her gaiety. Then, when David arrived, she would shamelessly throw herself at him, press her lips to his and let him know with her body how she had missed him.

They would lock themselves in the little bedroom. This was their island of escape. They would lie on Rachel's bed, the frost-covered window panes isolating them from the world. There was a mischievous playfulness in their muffled laughter, in their efforts to outsmart the bed, so that it would not squeak too loud. The fact that Shlamek was probably peering in through a crack in the cardboard wall, or that Blumka, ears perked, was mending stockings in the kitchen, was of no importance to them. Because although Rachel and David enjoyed being alone, they had the feeling that even if the bed were standing in the very middle of the world, free for all to see and listen, they would find privacy and shelter in each other's arms. Only at night, in her dreams, did Rachel's lightheartedness vanish. She would often wake up screaming. She saw Moshe in her dreams every night — while every morning she would again blot him out of her memory.

She could barely wait to go out into the street. She felt cramped with her new energy and wished she could push away the walls. She was impatient to see people, many people. She wanted to be surrounded by noise, to listen and to talk, to achieve something great, to start something new. To live.

It was a cold day when she went outside for the first time. The gales took her into their arms, carrying her ahead. She was not yet as strong as she had imagined; she was like a toy in the hands of the wind. People wrapped in rags and plaids passed her by. Their wooden shoes splashed in the muddy snow, the water dripped from the wooden heels. Water poured from the roofs and the walls and from the icicles suspended from all the lattices and gates. She approached the *Wissenschaftliche Abteilung* and imagined the *Rabiner* coming out to greet her with open arms. She was resentful of his behaviour during the *Sperre*, when he had refused to hide her and her family in his garden, and also of his behaviour during her illness, since he had not sent her the daily soups to which she was entitled. Yet she could not help liking him and she looked forward to meeting him, to seeing his saint-like face and warming herself by the light of his eyes.

The door of the *Wissenschaftliche Abteilung* was locked and boarded up. She tried to peer through the window which was also covered with boards. She blew a little "eye" in the frozen pane and saw the empty tables, the empty shelves and turned-over benches inside. She felt very cold and the fingers in her gloves began to prick. Warming them with her breath, she entered the arch of a gate to shake out the icy mud from her shoes and noticed two old women standing there. She felt a tenderness towards them, the two saved grandmothers. She wanted to thank them for still being around.

"People were taken from their beds last night," she heard one of them say.

The other shook her head, "I've been sleeping in my clothes for the last two months."

The first one stared at her. "What's there to be afraid of? They don't want us, because we are no longer here, remember? Those between seventeen and sixty-five are on the agenda now." Then she added, "You would have thought that now, when you need a lighted candle to find an old person, they would carry us around on their hands. But the truth is that it is better not to show oneself. Wherever you go, they point their fingers at you, 'She is alive, while my children are gone.' They stare at you as if you were an apparition. 'What are you still doing here?' they ask. 'Why are you eating our bread?' they shout at you in the lines. I honestly don't know what I need my saved life for. Have I lived to enjoy my children . . . or grandchildren? Goodness gracious. I've been left all alone . . ."

A shudder crept down Rachel's spine. She went out into the street and soon found herself on the half-empty Marysinska Street, approaching the co-operative where Moshe had worked. She used to wait for him here, so that he might bring out a little bit of sugar or flour to take home, and summertime, bring along a flower for her. Behind the massive fence the most beautiful flowers of the ghetto bloomed during the summer. She entered the *Rabiner's* garden, her eyes absorbing its sad beauty. Snow-covered tearful trees and shrubs; garlands of grayness along a narrow ice-covered path into nowhere.

The *Rabiner's* wife let Rachel into the house. Her smile revealed two rows of healthy teeth, as she stretched out both hands in her husband's fashion, "Rachel! Come in, come in!" Rachel asked her for the *Rabiner*. The woman shrugged her shoulders, "He is at work." Then she caught herself, "You don't know, do you? Yes, the *Wissenschaftliche Abteilung* was closed by the authorities . . . He . . . my husband is working in the city . . . in Litzmanstadt . . . for the authorities. My daughter is his secretary." It was warm in the spotless kitchen. The *Rabiner's* wife was wearing a spotless dress with a spotless apron.

She busied herself at the sparkling stove, preparing coffee for the visitor. But Rachel was already at the door.

She ran to her former student, the Holy Shoemaker. His cook recognized her. "They're having tea in the living room," she said familiarly and went to fetch her master.

The kitchen was full of the delicious aromas of freshly-brewed tea and freshly baked pastries. A baking pan with a partly-uncovered cake tempted the eye. The Holy Shoemaker, his cheeks glowing, entered the kitchen with his light agile gait, his mouth still moist from the tea. Rachel smiled at him. It was pleasant to look at his beaming boyish face. His slim figure, the well-cut suit, his graceful movements made him resemble a Matinée idol about to approach his prima donna and sweep her into his arms. "Miss Rachel!" he cried out. "I have not seen you for ages!" He shook her hand vigorously.

"I was sick. Typhus," she told him, hoping to move him and arouse his compassion.

He shook his head compassionately. "Yes, the doctor says there is an epidemic going around. We have to take care." He became thoughtful, rubbed his forehead and finally bowed, spreading his hands apart, "I am sorry but I cannot continue with the studies, Miss Rachel. Times are bad and nothing gets into my head. You must understand me."

She understood him. "I did not come about that. The thing is that I have no work."

"Is that what it is?" He exclaimed more cheerfully. "With the greatest pleasure, Miss Rachel. I'll get you a job, *prima classa*. Rely on me. You won't have to put a finger into cold water. After such an illness you deserve it, and I think I know already what and how. For instance, let's say the Old Clothes Resort. You would go there only to fetch your soup and . . . just wait a second." With one leap he was gone. Rachel concentrated her attention on the cook who had come in with a tray strewn with unfinished scraps of cake. Hypnotized, she followed the cook's every move and watched her clean the plates and gather the pieces of cake into a paper bag. She placed the bag a hand's reach from Rachel. But then the shoemaker came back, "It's arranged!" he cried, offering her his hand. "You know, don't you, Miss Rachel that for you I would jump into the fire." He followed her to the door. "Don't thank me, please."

She turned her head to him. "Perhaps I could . . . could have a little piece of cake?" Her face splotched a heavy red which covered her ears and neck. She wanted to apologize, to explain to him what it meant to suffer from a capricious post-typhoid craving for food.

The shoemaker made a magnificently broad gesture towards the cook. "Cut a decent piece of cake for Miss Rachel!" he ordered and again disappeared.

Rachel walked through the street, taking tiny bites of cake and mashing them slowly in her mouth; she was grateful that there were Holy Shoemakers in the world. The red splotches did not fade from her face. Her joy of being alive, her eating, her health, her kissing David were all sinful. They transformed her into a beggar, they deprived her of her pride. But as soon as the piece of cake was gone, she forgot about both it and her guilt. Her head filled with great new projects. She would not have to spend her days at a Resort. She would be able to be by herself, to work for herself. She had not done anything for so many weeks. She had completely forgotten that there were books in this world. Now she was curious again, ready to absorb the black poppy seeds of wisdom strewn over white pages.

Thus her soul began to envelop itself in veils. The world was again adorned with colour and light, with a mysterious newness. She was in a state both of full awareness and forgetfulness. Through it the broken motif accompanying her individuality became fused again. This time it evoked a need in her hands to knead its symbols into forms of clay.

Rachel sat in the large workroom of the Rag Resort, scratching out the last bits of soup from her canteen. The table against which she had propped her canteen was covered with heaps of creased, tangled clothes: dresses, blouses, suits, underwear for men, women and children; some already sorted, some still in disarray. A damp foul smell permeated the room. Rachel noticed it only in the morning, as she entered the room. Now the only smell she was aware of was the smell of her canteen; a peculiar smell of tin, rust and soup. Beside her at the table, sat the other women stooped over their canteens. Most of them were middle-aged. There were a few truly old women among them, but with their scarves on their heads, with their bent backs and creased faces, all the women looked old. A grayness was hovering over the room; the colourless cracked walls and the pale dirty electric bulb shining on the mountains of old clothes on the table made the room look like a place of disintegration and old age.

The women did not stop chatting; they seemed to derive a hidden pleasure from reviving the most horrible, the most frightening moments of the past weeks, and from transmitting all the most gruesome "ducks" circulating in the ghetto. "People are being taken again ... Something is going to fall on our heads again." The women's lips shook, their eyes gleamed like those of witches. They seemed to go into a trance, as if a hidden hand had chosen them as mediums for an oracle forecasting tragedy.

Rachel's problem was that although she did not have to work, she was obliged to sit with the women all day long. The manager, a meek frightened little man who walked about like a little cock amid a flock of hens, had assigned her to a workroom. He feared inspections, although no inspections had ever taken place there. No visitors, only truckloads of clothes arrived: thousands of coats, dresses, suits, underwear. Here they were sorted, then sent on to the laundry, the Dying Resort, or the Tearing Resort. Rachel's other problem was that she was unable to read during her hours at the Resort. From the tables, the blood-stained clothes peered at her seemingly filled with bodies. They made her feel dizzy and nauseated. So, instead of sitting idle, she began to kill time by learning to recognize the materials, in order to sort them. The women included her in their circle, making her realize that the work could not be performed in silence. She gradually joined in their chatter. Soon she began to feel as old as they. She found herself sinking into pits of despair which made all her projects and plans appear meaningless.

It was not long before she rebelled. She wanted the right to come only to fetch her soup. The frightened manager at first refused to listen to her, but she threatened him with the intervention of the Holy Shoemaker, and this threat worked wonders.

Now that she did not have to physically stay with the women in the Rag Resort, she constantly had them in her mind's eye. She thought that this Resort was the most frightening corner of the ghetto. And not only of the ghetto. It was related to the horror of Greek tragedies, or rather, to a horror for which there was no name. If one could only express that atmosphere, or at least suggest it, she mused. Because the mood of that place had to be transmitted, even if in an awkward manner. She decided to sculpt, in clay, a group of women sitting around a table at the Rag Resort. But all she was able to bring out were the furrows in the women's faces. The clay could not suggest the atmosphere or reveal the women's talk, which was just as important as their facial expressions. So she abandoned the clay and took up pencil and paper. She had to make peace with the unsatisfactory usage of words. They were the only means by which she could at least stammer.

However, the main thing that happened to Rachel during those days was her awakening feminity. It was as if she had gone to bed a girl and recovered from her illness a woman. She herself would not have become aware of it, had it not been for Vladimir Winter, whom she occasionally visited. As soon as he saw her, he burst out, "You must be in love!"

She let him look at her, admire her, gladly agreeing with him. "Yes, I am in love."

A romantic haze came over his sharp eyes. Then he would preach to her about how to be a real woman, "Look up to your lover as if he were a man, but never forget that he is nothing but a child. Conduct yourself with him as if you were a child, but don't forget that you are a nest, you are peace and maturity. You are the earth and he is the sky. You are green, he is blue. You stand firm on your foundations, while he floats in the air. He is eternally searching for what you have found an eternity ago. You are the background of a painting. You are green, but in that greenness must be reflected many colours, all the colours of the palette, and more. The more nuances of shading, the more beautiful your green will be to him. Change and transform yourself continuously. Dress up in newness while remaining the same. Colourless in itself, the sky loves colour. His blue, his gray, his purple he gleans from you. Hide from him, run away from him and wait for him; entice him, call him. He will come. He is curious and restless. The Creator wants him to be so . . . for His own purposes."

That curiosity and restlessness Rachel read in Bunim's face when they met for the first time after her illness. All that Winter had told her, her body seemed to know in Bunim's presence.

He had been waiting for her at the gate every day throughout all the weeks of her illness, and when he saw her at last, he was so overwhelmed, that he could do nothing for the first few minutes but stare at her. Then he reached into his breast pocket and proclaimed, "I have a poem!" He led her back into the archway and quickly recited his Song of Joy to her. When he had finished reading, he handed her the sheet of paper. "It is yours."

She folded the page and slid it down into her pocket. "I have Joy in my pocket," she joked, gratefully. "Come!" she called out. "I'm on my way to your backyard. My friend lives there." She walked by his side, sprightly and light.

He did not take his eyes off her. His heart jumped uncomfortably in his chest. He could barely keep up with her. "Come first into my place," he begged, "at least for a moment." She agreed. He asked her to wait in front of his hut until he had fixed up the rooms a bit. She waited near the cherry tree which dripped with the melting snow, and she looked up at David's window. There was no light in it. Bunim reappeared on the threshold and called her in. He looked much younger without the black coat, dressed only in his brown checked jacket. From its breast pocket there peeked out a yellow bitten-up pencil and the top of his glasses case. The big side pockets were bulging with blank sheets of paper.

A pale electric bulb shone in the kitchen. The other room was dark. Bunim placed himself between the darkness and Rachel, not letting her go inside. "Come over here," he pointed to the table near the stove, "I'll light the stove in your honour."

"You invited me in only for a moment," she reminded him.

"Two moments," he begged her.

"I will stay for three moments," she said. "My friend is not at home."

He was delighted. Then he seemed to weigh something in his mind before saying, "I will start reading my poem to you today. Do you want me to?"

He removed the burners from the stove, preparing to start a fire, but noticed that he had nothing to kindle it with. He vanished into the dark room. Rachel cuddled up in her coat and put up the collar. It was colder in the room than in the street. There was something gnawing and sad about the cold stove, about the walls, about the dust-covered plates on the shelves, the few sooty pots, the nets of cobwebs embroidering the ashen curtains. The room seemed shut off from the world, like the rooms in the Rag Resort. She was unable to disengage herself from the grayness and had an urge to escape as soon as possible. But then Berkovitch reappeared. He had found nothing in the other room to feed the stove; but he had found a sweater of Miriam's. She let him drape the sweater around her shoulders on top of her coat. It was good to stay with him and not to run away. She made a mental note of the date on which he had started to read his poem to her. It seemed an important event, she did not exactly know why.

The following day, she began to work seriously on her short story about the Rag Resort. It was a difficult and painful task to find the proper words to render its particular atmosphere. At length she grew tired, furious at her own helplessness. She grabbed her coat and ran down into the street. She met Berkovitch waiting in the gate. They almost fell into each other's arms. "Are you running to see your friend?" he asked.

"Yes . . . No . . . I just came outside . . ."

"Then come!" he called out. "I took out my ration of briquettes today." He looked at her with expectation and when he read approval in her face, he proposed shyly, "Call me Simcha from now on."

They hurried across the bridge. In the yard on Hockel Street, David appeared before them. He hugged Rachel, kissing her on both cheeks, "I was on my way to see you!" he said as he began to pull her along.

She let herself be pulled by him, throwing a radiant smile at Bunim, "I will come in to see you tomorrow!"

David was gay. He had just fetched the new food ration. She joked, "You love me only when a new ration comes out and you've filled your stomach."

"In that case I don't love you at all, because my stomach is never full." His good mood was contagious. He told her that a German order had been issued to say a prayer in all the churches for Hitler's health, since the poor Führer was very ill. He told her that today he, David, had a real attack of optimism and that he was sure that the two of them would survive the war, and that this called for a special celebration, on the spot. He said that they absolutely had to find a place where they could be alone for a while, for instance the little bedroom of her apartment.

Finally, he could no longer restrain himself, "I have a surprise for you!" He made a tiny pause to keep her in suspense, then he came out with the news, "You're going to receive a referral to the Rest Home!" He proudly pounded his chest with his fist. "And that, my dear, I arranged all by myself! I hope you realize my heroism. Why are you staring at me like that? You don't believe that I can be an achiever too? You think that I owe it to Dr. Levine? Not in the least. He only took the necessary steps, but I moved heaven and earth!" He pressed her to his chest, looking devotedly into her eyes. "For a full week you will surfeit yourself and become as strong as a rock!"

Chapter Fifteen

(David's Notebook)

Not long ago I had a few days of optimism. That now belongs to the past. Interesting that this optimism was not due to political news but rather to something connected with myself. It seemed to me that I was not such a great egotist after all. I never loved Rachel as much as I did during those days when I looked after her. Usually when I tell her, "I love you," I mean rather that I love myself. I love her love for me. But during the time when I was afraid of losing her and was relieved that she survived, all that was different. For the first time I gave her a slice of my own bread and bought an apple for her. My running around for "protection" and my nagging Levine about a place at the Rest Home for her, put me into a mood which nothing could equal.

I visited Rachel at the Home a few times. They have regal meals over there, served at regally set tables. They have entertainment and all kinds of musical and literary evenings, so that they can forget that the ghetto ever existed. The only problem is that they won't let me in, and that Rachel must spend all seven nights of the week there. So we had to satisfy ourselves with a conversation over the fence. She has changed unrecognizably. Her face shines and she seems to have grown taller. A few times I met our neighbour Berkovitch at the fence. What business of his it was to come to see her I don't know. As soon as he sees me he disappears.

✦ ✦ ✦

Rachel is back at home. She looks very well, but her mood has deteriorated. She refuses to go up with me to their little bedroom. During our walks she keeps silent. I asked her what the matter was, and she told me that it had to do with her father; that only now, that she has come back, does she realize that he is gone. I understand her, yet it irritates me. As if she were ungrateful. She spoils my mood. It is clear that it is my duty to stay by her side, to give her support; but it is not easy. I feel like running away from her, which means that I am back in my egotistic shell. So be it. I am not an angel. I cannot look at Rachel when she has a sour face. I no longer visit her; four days have passed already and today is the fifth. She doesn't come to see me either. Has she become indifferent to me? Does she not love me any more? That question bothers me a bit. But I will not crawl to her on my knees. Anyway, I am seeing Inka again, and also Zosia, another cute girl.

✦ ✦ ✦

Rachel came by today to find out what had happened to me. She is gloomy. Some time ago that sad haze in her eyes would have tempted me to take her into my arms. Nowadays it irritates me. "I am restless . . ." she whispered to me, asking me to go down into the street with her.

The devil sitting inside me prompted me to reply, "I don't feel like it."

She stared at me as if she did not understand. She asked me to kiss her. I hate kissing on order, and gave her an ice-cold peck on the cheek. That made it worse, and she ran out. I did not follow her. I looked down through the window and saw her enter Berkovitch's hut. That cheered me up. There is no doubt that she loves me and this will help me hold out longer without her.

In general, I think that the people of the ghetto have cheered up, have recovered from the *Sperre* and the winter. Water is dripping everywhere and it is still impossible to sit outside; but the yard has become lively. Mother has found friends among the new neighbours and she too goes down in the evening to chat with them. Abraham and I have our permanent place in the gate where we meet with a gang of communists who have stepped up their propaganda ever since the news has spread that Moscow is again recognizing the Polish Communist Party. They don't talk readily about the Molotov-Hitler agreement, but if pressed, they declare that this meant salvation of the world and of the world's proletariat. Their philosophy is that the darker the night, the nearer the day. In general it is Abraham who gets into discussions with them, because to me all these squabbles seem ridiculous. Each of the disputants chants his own chant, without listening to the other. They are just as fanatical as the religious Jews, clinging to what they believe and ignoring reason or logic. Faith in the Soviet Union keeps the communists alive.

I think that we should postpone all discussions. Let us first get the war over with. I don't understand the political parties, mine included. They squabble over outdated concepts, since everything will be changed when we get out of here. After all, we are going through a cataclysm which effaces not only life, but also theories and ideologies.

Basically, I am still an optimist and I hope that all will end well (at least as far as I am concerned, because for those who are gone, all has ended; period). Perhaps I delude myself in order to be able to go on? Sometimes, I miss my conversations with the Toffee Man. He never gave me any satisfactory answers, yet he gave me something. I don't know what. Now the Toffee Man has gone mad. During the *Sperre*, he wanted to protect his children and a policeman kicked him in the head. He walks around talking and crying. Impossible to understand him.

After curfew I sometimes visit Zuckerman. He has a map of Europe, Asia and Africa, and it is doubly precious because it contains the precise positions of the war's development from its inception to the present day. At Zuckerman's I meet his daughter Bella, Rachel's classmate. She is skinny and ugly. Once I jokingly concluded in these pages, that this is probably the case with all ideals when one looks at them closely. Today I have reached the conclusion that Bella is somehow beautiful in her ugliness. (Can that be true also for ideals?) Bella has magnificent eyes; warm, sad, distant. Another riddle intrigues me: Why do I find Rachel's sadness so unpleasant, and Bella's attractive? Who can understand that?

Whenever I go to the Zuckermans, I automatically cheer up. I entertain the sick father and his daughter, playing up my hurrah-optimism. My good spirits increase when Junia, Zuckerman's younger daughter and her husband Michal Levine arrive. Junia and myself ignite clownish sparks in each other. Levine's presence does not bother me. True, whenever I see him, my heart begins to pound with fear that he might again convey some terrible news to me. But the similar fate of our fathers make us feel close to each other. We are brothers in Fate. Every now and again we have interesting conversations.

Spring is approaching. People are already measuring the ground in the yards, dividing it into *dzialkas*. There are skirmishes among the neighbours over who will get the *dzialkas* left by the deported. It does not enter my mind to fight for a *dzialka*. The shouts and squabbles disgust me. Mother reproaches me and criticizes me. She has again discovered that I am a *schlemiel*. Abraham nags me too. I cannot help it. I have not got the slightest bit of energy.

Lately I constantly dream that I am a German soldier.

✦ ✦ ✦

I was energetic for a few days. I submitted an application for a *dzialka* in Marysin. I don't have much hope. The *shishkas* grab the best plots of land as well as the gardens and fruit trees for themselves. Fifty square metres to a head is supposed to be the share of every citizen of the ghetto. But evidently some heads are bigger than others. The Presess' head for instance is gigantic. He assigned no more nor less than forty thousand square metres to himself. So, what can remain for such tiny heads as ours? I also submitted an application for a pair of shoes for mother. The wooden shoes that she wears have fallen apart, eaten up by the mud in the shack where she peels potatoes. So we shall see the results of my requests.

At night a noise in the yard woke me up. I heard a pounding at doors. People were taken out of their beds, to be deported. The ghetto must supply another thousand heads. No one wants to leave. The police had actually assembled the required number, but those who were caught ran away.

On the first of May it will be three years since the ghetto was closed. Many resorts are celebrating their birthdays. Banquets, performances and exhibitions of the production take place. The Presess loves it. He comes to the celebrations, delivers speeches, yells, "My Resorts, my workmen, my ghetto!" and is showered with praise in return. He accepts gifts, pays back with gifts; put simply, love reigns supreme.

Today, in the very heat of preparations for an exhibit in my Paper Resort, a policeman arrived and "secretly" took his brothers and a cousin home. Right away people began to whisper that a raid would take place in the streets after work. On the way home there was a panic, people were running like mad, and I with them; although it did not even enter my mind that I could be caught. They say that the required number of men had already left. They say that the deported were reciting psalms and that the policemen escorting them cried.

A miracle is happening to the cherry tree. We had given up hope for its survival last summer when it was being eaten up by worms. The grass surrounding it is already sprouting and we have a "Garden" again. Our neighbours kneel in the yard, working the soil. Bella takes her father out on the balcony every evening. He coughs. He is disintegrating, practically before our eyes. People in the yard say that he is suffering from galloping consumption. I visit him on the balcony and try to cheer him up with the good news.

Rachel often appears in our yard. Sometimes she leads the study group, to which Abraham belongs, in our apartment. Then she sleeps over with us. We spend the evening together and stroll in the yard. Sometimes Berkovitch appears on the threshold of his hut. Dishevelled, hands in his pockets, he stares at us myopically, smiling stupidly. Or he jumps back into the hut as soon as he sees us, slamming the door. An oddball. When I poke fun at him, Rachel becomes angry. I don't understand how she can communicate with such a character.

I heard an extraordinary news item today about a revolt in Warsaw. Jews and Poles are supposedly putting up an armed resistance against the Germans, not letting them carry out the deportations. People say that the Resorts in the Warsaw Ghetto are on fire and that the Germans are bombing the ghetto from the air.

✦ ✦ ✦

My application for a *dzialka* and for a pair of shoes for Mother brought no results, of course. (Luckily, summer is approaching and Mother will have good ventilation through the holes in her wooden shoes.)

I met with Simon, our youth leader. He listens to the broadcasts of SWIT every day. The news from Warsaw has been confirmed. The resistance is localized in the Ghetto. Unbelievable. Today is the first day of Passover. All my comrades are dressed in their best clothes, their mouths grinding on non-stop about the Warsaw Ghetto. We shudder with excitement, with pride, with tension and with fear. If the Germans have begun to liquidate the Warsaw Ghetto, it is a bad sign for us too. Our optimists say that this cannot happen to us; firstly, because we don't belong to the Protectorate; secondly, because we are in a working camp and German industry cannot exist without us; thirdly, because . . . and because . . .

✦ ✦ ✦

It is true! The Warsaw Ghetto is fighting! A revolt! I run to all the meetings of our organization. Everybody is talking about Warsaw, yet thinking about Lodz and about our fate.

I see Rachel every day. Twice this week I slept over at her place. We are both restless. We say we go for a walk, when in fact we run through Marysin. The trees are in bloom, the beets, the carrots and potatoes are sprouting. The grass is soft and the sun is mild. It is probably the same kind of weather in Warsaw too. Passover. Celebration of freedom. I try to imagine how it looks there . . . in the ghetto of Warsaw.

We were at Rachel's *dzialka* today and she gave me a bunch of radishes. Then we went over to the *gymnasium* which has been transformed into a Resort. It is quiet there in the evening. We found the bench under the window of Rachel's former classroom. I asked her whether she believed in heroism. She replied that she did. I asked her whether the Warsaw Jews were heroes. She stared at me, astonished, "Of course".

"Do you believe that if we were faced with liquidation, we too would defend ourselves?" I asked her.

"I doubt it," she replied.

"Then how come one Jewish community is made up of heroes and the other of cowards?" I asked.

She said she did not know how come, that perhaps it depends on the leaders of the community, on the general atmosphere, and on the conditions. In our hermetically sealed ghetto an armed resistance is impossible. She said that she was not sure whether we are cowards or not, but she was sure that the Warsaw

Jews are heroes. I told her that I did not believe in heroism. Everyone has moments of heroism and of cowardice. For instance, during the *Sperre*, I sometimes shook in my pants with fear and sometimes I was quite brave. That's how it is.

What does it actually mean to be daring, or courageous? I think a lot about it. Children often play with fire, because they don't realize the danger. There are adults who are like that, but they are called courageous. Real courage means to know of the danger, and yet dare to act. I think of the people who commit heroic deeds. Are they afraid of death? If they are, then how can they act? Because fear is paralyzing. The truth must be that they dissolve into their act to such an extent, that they forget about death. Their actions put them in a feverish state of mind which calls for so much concentration, that it excludes everything else. That happens when one has a goal more important than one's life.

I would like to be in the skin of a Warsaw Jew, to know his purpose. My comrades insist that the Warsaw Jews aren't as concerned with saving the remaining ghetto population (there are only forty thousand left), and saving them all is impossible — as about saving their dignity; the dignity of their perished parents, children, comrades and neighbours, the dignity of us all. The fighters want to erase the shame and prove that Jewish blood is not water. But is it not like water anyway? And when I hear the chant about shame, I gnash my teeth. Has it become *our* shame, not the Germans'? What I see in the revolt is both an act of courage and an act of despair. The Jews of Warsaw had the possibility of contributing actively to the struggle with the Germans, and they used that possibility. Doomed one way or another, they fight not for their lives or for an honourable death, but for the ideal of freedom.

The last youth meeting took place in Marysin, on a grassy plot of land. The setting sun was shining softly. The air was delightful. Simon reported the latest news; we discussed Warsaw. A fellow was rambling on about how we, the Jews of Lodz, behave like cowards. It burned me up. I asked all of them whether they thought that we had been moulded from a different clay than the Warsaw Jews. I explained to them that the courage that we display every day of the year, without armed resistance, is not to be discounted so lightly; that I saw heroism in our lives, and yes, in rare moments, also in mine.

✦ ✦ ✦

It is unbelievable. It has already been two weeks and the Warsaw Ghetto is still fighting on. With every passing day the fighters grow in stature in my eyes. With every passing day I admire them more. I would like to know so many things about them. How do they supply themselves with arms? How do they look, physically? Do they have swollen legs? Decalcification of the bones? Tuberculosis? I am praying for them.

✦ ✦ ✦

Today I had a game of chess with Mr. Rosenberg. Everyone says that he works for the *Kripo*. I am afraid of winning from him, and yet I cannot make myself lose and give up the few *rumkis*. When he wins, his pate begins to shine and he laughs at me, showing all the metal toothcaps in his mouth. When he loses, he looks at me so fiercely, that ants begin to crawl down my spine. However, as I said, I try to win — and that is my act of courage.

An additional food ration has come out. Four deca margarine, five deca curds, half a kilogram of carrots, ten deca "stink-fish" and three kilograms of parsley. We cook parsley soups every day and I feel a parsley garden growing in my belly.

The revolt in the Warsaw Ghetto has already lasted two-and-half weeks. As soon as I remember about it, I feel a twinge, like a hidden toothache, and I must talk to someone. Yet it is impossible to talk about it with Zuckerman whom I visit very often. As soon as I mention Warsaw, he begins to shake — I don't know whether it is out of fever or enthusiasm. The words come out jumbled from his mouth and he begins to pant.

But I find a good talking companion in Junia, who is, just like myself, fascinated with the topic. I asked her what would have happened, in her opinion, if the Warsaw Jews had had no weapons. Would they have thrown themselves on the Germans with their bare fists? Junia said yes; I doubt it. They would have brought about their destruction faster, and I don't believe that such a conscious suicide by a ghetto community is possible. We have paid for our lives too dearly. In such a case one must first of all be sure that all the roads to life are definitely barred, and that there is nothing else left to hope for. However, up to the moment of death, no one believes in its inevitability. Junia asked me what, in my opinion, we should do if it comes to a total liquidation of our ghetto. I told her honestly that I had no idea, that I could not even foresee my own behaviour. Perhaps I would become paralysed with fear, and perhaps I would throw myself at the German who was leading me to my death. Hard as I try to put myself in such a situation, I find it impossible to imagine. Should death come to claim me? Up to my last breath, I would wait for a miracle, and I would probably perish, waiting.

◆   ◆   ◆

I had a good day today. Adam Rosenberg, the fat bald pig, came again for a game of chess. I have an almost moral problem: should I be playing with such a character at all? Today I told him that if I win, I don't want to be paid in worthless *rumkis*, but that I want either sugar or bread or marmalade. To my surprise, he agreed. I won, and he owes me one kilogram of sugar and ten deca of bread. I told him that Zuckerman had "galloping consumption", and as soon as he heard that, he guffawed like the devil and delightedly smoothed out the few hairs still left on his pate. I was almost ready to tell him that I never wanted to see him again. But I bit my tongue and swallowed my rage.

After he left, Abraham joked, "There is nothing uglier than a bald man pretending that he has hair. Only in one thing are the bald lucky. They never have to comb and always look combed."

Rachel is very happy about the creation of the illegal School Department. The rescued children who are working at the Resorts will be taught in classes arranged in hidden places at the factories. Rachel was assigned to Metal Resort Number Two, as a teacher. I have finished with my teaching career. It's been months since I took a book into my hands. I could not care less about studying. The only thing that interests me is the question of when the war will come to an end. My sole aim is to sustain my body and to win first one day, then the next from the Germans.

At the Resort my mind goes completely blank. Before lunch, I count the hours until I get my soup, and after lunch — the hours until we go home. At home most of my time is taken up by cleaning, cooking and standing in the lines. Mother is of little help. She comes home from the Peeling Shed and immediately goes to bed. Abraham does lend me a hand, but home is not on his mind. He runs around. He has become active in the organization, a pillar of the Youth Movement. He still sniffles and wipes his nose on his sleeve, but he has become a *mentsch*. He wears his hair in a "porcupine" and walks arm-in-arm with the girls of his group. Yesterday he asked me in a whisper whether I too belong to a "group-of-five". I did not know what he meant and he refused to give me any explanation. I, on the other hand, am not such an idiot. Most probably the party has created a kind of fighting organization. Why have I not been assigned to a "group of five"? What are the qualifications that Abraham has and I lack? I am resentful. But, on the other hand, I am also quite pleased. I don't believe in these silly games of fighter's organizations. They have been inspired by the Warsaw Ghetto — but nothing will come of it.

Chapter Sixteen

SAMUEL WAS FEVERISH. He was lying in the room which had once belonged to his daughters, close to the balcony. From his bed he was able to see part of the cherry tree's crown and the roofs of the firemen's barn in the opposite yard. When he turned his head away from the balcony, he could see Bella at the other side of his bed. She did not move away from him.

Their attachment of years ago now seemed like a preparation for the intimacy which bound them at present. The period of their estrangement was erased. They talked very little — yet everything was clear. To Samuel, Bella's eyes were like quiet boats which, after storms of rage and bitterness, had reached a peaceful port. It seemed unjust that despite her devotion and despite his serenity, he should not get well. For he too did not feel rebellious, or furious. He felt proud. He had achieved something. He had victoriously conquered the waves which had tried to drown him. He had two beautiful daughters who would raise the flag of freedom over the land of his dreams. He himself was too exhausted, too tired.

One evening, he called Bella and asked her to gather together his notes for the book which he had intended to write; to wrap them in thick cloth and hide them well.

She stared at him in astonishment, "Why, Papa?"

He replied, "At some point in his life, every man thinks about writing a book. Only the writer actually writes one."

She did not understand. How naïve she still was. Her belief that he would get well made it more difficult for him to tell her what he had to do. She smiled wisely, devotedly, wiping the sweat from his forehead. "You will write the history of the Jews of Lodz. We will work on it together. It is time that I knew something about these things . . ." She said this both out of conviction and out of the wish to please him. "We will lock ourselves up in your room and let no one in before the book is completed."

"Yes," he agreed, but nevertheless insisted. "Wrap it well. A pity that the notes should perish. Hide them in the cellar . . . in case of an 'action' or a search."

"For the time being then . . ." she gave in. "Until you get well."

He bit his lips. How could he hurt her by awakening her to the truth? Yet he had to, for her own good. And one evening, when he felt better and stronger, he said to her, "Bella, you know my condition, don't you?"

"Yes," she replied softly. "Michal told me. Your lungs are affected."

"Badly affected."

She felt mature, experienced and maternal. "You will get well. It is warm outside and the summer is coming."

"I want you to do with the notes what you promised me. After the war, they should be kept in archives until a historian shows up . . . Perhaps you could find a piece of oilcloth to protect them from humidity."

"How many times must you tell me that, Papa?" She stroked his wet forehead.

"Then why don't you do what I ask you to?" he shouted in frustration.

She embraced him. "Hush, Papa, don't be mad at me. I'll do it. I swear to you." She bit her nails and burst into tears. He was overcome by guilt and tried to raise his hand to her head, but his arm was too heavy. Bella sat for a long while with her wet cheek glued to his sweat-soaked shirt. The blue of dusk crowded into the room. Warm shadows crept over the furniture and the walls. Through the open balcony door a lazy mild breeze entered. The leaves of the cherry tree outside rustled softly.

At length she went to wash her face. He was left alone, his senses free to absorb the lights and the shadows, the thinnest threads of silence. He was a burning thornbush within the silence, an all-devouring flame with a hissing breath. Thus, aflame, he enjoyed the peace, not only around him, but also within him. All the wars had been won, all the storms calmed, all the debts repaid, all the sins redeemed. What splendid boundless freedom! He could soar from one eternity to the other, above all the borders, all the horizons, singing with pure abandonment.

He thought a lot about life. He was feverish with life, he exploded in the silence with life.

But this very enthusiasm led him on towards cold thoughts. His reason had become a severe judge. He had freed himself of his guilt too soon. For the freedom within life was not boundless, not infinite. It ended where the freedom of another's life began. Not to hurt, not to harm — that was the border-line of life's liberty. For instance, he had to harm and hurt Bella by preparing her for the truth. But if in reality that helped Bella, then what about his harming her as well as Junia and Michal — the stranger who had become both a brother and a son to him — by eating their curds, by drinking the milk which they bought with their food rations? Were they not exchanging their bread portions for the medicines which did not help anyway? The fire in his body was devouring not only him but also his children. How could he allow this to happen and still feel that all his wars had been won?

Bella came back, refreshed. The smile which she reserved only for him was again on her face. She had brought in a dish of curds and sour cream, and she began to feed him. He swallowed a few spoonfuls, then pushed her hand away, "Go down, take a breath of fresh air for a bit," he begged her.

She shrugged her shoulders, "The air is fine here too." The air in the room really was fine. Samuel inhaled it with effort, along with Bella's smile.

The evenings were usually difficult, critical. Later on he felt better. Junia and Michal would arrive and sit by his bedside; they would talk to him, talk past him. It was good to listen to them, to know and yet not to know the content of their words, to hear the rustle of their voices as if the cherry tree's leaves were rustling above his head, to be part of that rustle — and yet apart from it. Michal would examine Samuel and never say a word. Samuel had long before stopped asking him questions.

After one of Michal's visits, as Bella was accompanying him and Junia outside, she noticed that Junia's face was twisted as if she were about to cry. Bella embraced her, "You don't have to bring anything. Father eats very little." she reassured her.

Michal took Bella's arm and, avoiding her eyes, said, "Come, I promised your father I'd take you for a walk."

They strolled through the narrow path between the blossoming beds of soil. The beet and potato leaves were swaying in the evening breeze. Michal held Bella tightly by the arm. A remote memory visited her, of how it had felt to walk leaning against a young man's shoulder. Her head was buzzing. Something hummed in her blood, making a noise through all of her body.

"Do you know, Michal," to her own surprise she became confidential, talkative. "I once loved a boy . . . He was different from you . . . But when you hold me like that . . ." She bit her lips and was glad that neither Michal nor Junia were paying any attention to her silly words. Then her mind was cut as if by the blade of a knife. She stopped, tearing her arm away from Michal's hand. "You want to tell me something about Father."

"Yes," he replied softly.

She quickly covered her ears with both hands. "I don't want to hear it!" They were standing under the blossoming cherry tree. White petals were falling down on their heads. Bella's face between her hands looked shrivelled and shrunken like the face of an old woman. Her eyes were black, deep and full of fear. It was not easy to look at her. And it was altogether impossible to look at Junia's small tearful face. Yet Michal had to force himself. He had promised Samuel. Bella jumped away from him. "I don't ever want to see you again!" she shouted hysterically and ran into the house, white petals falling from her head and shoulders.

Once in a while, Samuel's temperature would come down to normal and the strange exaltation brought on by his fever would leave him. It was then that he developed an amazingly precise sense of time. It did not run too fast, nor did it drag on too slowly. During those years when he had been absorbed in building, in creating, time had run too fast. In the ghetto he had more than once despaired at its stagnant eternities. But, now, when the fever left him, his sense of time became synchronized with the clock. He could easily guess when an hour or two had passed. It became a pastime, a game — to measure time.

Yet, in spite of that fine sense which he had developed, the face of the world surrounding him had changed. He created a theory of his own about it. He thought that keeping the body in a horizontal position influenced a person's mind. It changed one's point of view. Perhaps man was so conceited and arrogant because he walked upright, he pondered. The pressure of the air against his head is slight, therefore man feels light, he feels like a ruler. When he lies flat, however, the air pressure is upon his whole body; he becomes crushed by the weight of the entire universe. That was why people felt humble and insignificant in that position. And Samuel came to didactical conclusions from that observation. He was of the opinion that every young person, before beginning to act in life, ought to be submitted to the experience of lying in bed for about six weeks, day and night, in a horizontal position, alone in a room. That would teach modesty and sharpen sensitivity. When afterwards, he walked on two legs, the individual would remember that he was not the navel of the earth and that his view of things was not necessarily true; that there was a truth beyond man which was objective, in contrast to man's subjective and illusory truth.

Samuel thought that only now, when he was looking at the world, not from the centre, but rather from the side, from below, had he become a full person. Only now had love and tenderness, of which he had had a pale conception before, taken possession of him. Now he altogether differently, more candidly, loved his daughters, his son-in-law, and also his wife Matilda to whom he had never responded with love. How well he understood Matilda now. How beautiful she seemed to him, in her generous offering of herself. Man was so hungry for love, Samuel mused, there was so little love in this world, yet he, Samuel, the fortunate, the blessed, had in his conceit neglected that treasure, not appreciating it and not watching over it.

These thoughts led his mind towards reflections about the world in general, about the ghetto, about the Germans. The Jews believed that by destroying one single human being, a world was destroyed. A subjective world. For in reality the Germans were not destroying hundreds or thousands of worlds — not even one. The grass did not stop growing, the wind did not stop blowing, the sun did not stop shining, and life all over the globe went on as if nothing had happened. All that was happening was a murder committed by worms against worms.

Impatiently, he would await Michal. He needed to discuss these subjects with him. And as soon as Michal appeared before him, he came out with what was bothering him. "We have lived with illusions, Michal. For us every man's life was equal to an entire universe. Therefore it was impossible to fathom the destruction of hundreds, of thousands of universes. We almost made man into a god."

He looked at Michal with expectation, and Michal knew that Samuel was waiting for him, to give him back his respect for man. Michal did not disappoint him. "You know my opinion on the subject," he replied. "The universe is indifferent. In the spheres of indifference a godly spark glimmers, put there or created who knows how, who knows by whom. That spark is man. Truly a speck of dust, truly no more than a little worm, but the only creature which is not indifferent. He is the sole creature alive, as far as we know, who not only exists, but changes, shapes and colours life. And as I once told you, man, in my opinion, is the most tragic part of creation. In his arrogance, he is aware that he is basically nothing but a worm and that he shall return to the earth as one . . . thus he appreciates life. If all of mankind perished, the world as such would not vanish, according to objective truth, for which I don't give a hoot — yet it could not exist because conscious existence would not be there. Consequently, the fact that I see myself as a worm obliges me to respect the life of another worm. Hm . . . They say that one cannot force oneself to love. It depends on what kind of love. To the love which spells obligation of one man towards the other, one has to force oneself. Why? For our own sake. Have you noticed how little time the people devote to hating the Germans? Do you know why? Because we don't want to perish. Hatred corrodes the soul, destroying one's life, even if one goes on living. We cling to life-sustaining thoughts, just as fiercely as we do to our bit of soup and bread."

Samuel smiled. Michal's words were of course in the vein of his own thinking, only his thoughts became entangled from time to time. But he did not give in. "You're talking like some kind of a Christ," he remarked.

Michal smiled. "I cannot preach that we should offer the other cheek, because we are getting blows on both cheeks. And if you want to know, I hated the Germans during the *Sperre* violently; I almost destroyed myself with it. But then . . . Then I fell in love with your daughter. When I really got her under my skin, the feeling for her so overpowered me, that I simply forgot my hate. The Germans became increasingly smaller and less significant in my eyes. What seemed important to me was to protect my love. And so, all my so-called naive philosophies about mankind, about tearing down the barriers between peoples, have come back to me."

Samuel cheerfully patted Michal on the arm. Michal was indeed naive. He, Samuel, first of all wanted a home and a refuge for his own people. When that was achieved, there would be time enough to devote to further dreams.

A few times the comrades of the Zionist Party held their meetings in Samuel's room. He was surprised that they listened to him with so much attention, and even more surprised that whatever they discussed interested him still so much. Later on, however, he rarely followed the discussion for longer than a few minutes. There were times when he could by no means grasp what they were saying. The same happened with the news items which they announced. He who had once clung to a radio receiver, who had been an expert in the language of the communiqués and a wizard at explaining the news broadcasts — was now on the level of a moron. The war map of the three continents was erased from his memory. He could not forgive himself for that, because he considered these things to be of utmost importance.

Often his comrades' talk would rock him to sleep. He would emit loud grating sounds, snoring. The comrades would quietly move into the kitchen. Once, when he woke up alone in the room, he caught snatches of a conversation reaching him from the balcony. He recognized the voices. Comrade Widawski was demanding something from Michal. They were juggling with the word "cyanide". Samuel could not recall what "cyanide" meant. A funny foreign word. Michal seemed angry at first, but he gradually gave in. Widawsky said, "I know too much . . ." The wordgame was over. Widawski had won.

When the heat in his body increased, Samuel had the impression that he was a gigantic firefly tattooing his love upon the indifference of the universe.

✦ ✦ ✦

The warmer the days became, the greater became the fire in Samuel's body. Before Bella left for work at Central Bookkeeping, she would come in with a basin full of cool water and with her refreshing smile. The sight of her filled him with pride. Someone who was capable of carrying such a heavy basin and smiling at the same time — surely had the strength of a giant. She washed him with a soft cloth. He was not shy to expose his body to her. Nor was she shy to look at it. Everything was simple; as clear and as pleasant as the touch of the mild water against his hot sweaty skin.

"I love you, daughter," he mumbled.

She took leave of him, kissing him on the forehead. Alone, he would measure the hours which separated him from her. In the meantime, he let himself go. He was transformed into a boy with a light empty head, the former Samuel, the mischief, the clown. He turned somersaults on the big table in his father's house. He spread glue on the seats of his teachers' chairs at school, and the teachers became stuck. He tripped up his father and rolled with laughter when he noticed that it was Rumkowski who fell into the mud.

Around noon he felt a cool hand on his forehead. He opened his eyes and saw Bella. He was sure that she had witnessed all these games. He had been performing all these tricks for her, so that her sad eyes would light up with gaiety. Sometimes on seeing her, he would shut his eyes again, quietly and contentedly returning to his amusements. Yes, he had been born for pleasure and joy. For so many years they had been trapped within him, only to become liberated now, through his loud free laughter which was as young and as carefree as that May afternoon.

The daylight played along with him upon the walls. The opposite wall was a huge sports stadium, cut in half by a net of barbed wire. Samuel was playing tennis with himself. He was dressed in white, white pants, a white shirt, white shoes and stockings. He was hot. Sweat was streaming down his face. He smiled at himself — his partner, his opponent — on the other side of the net. Soon the game would be over. They would approach the net and shake hands above the wires. They both wanted to win, and it was not important who did, as long as the game was interesting, challenging. Somewhere nearby, Bella was probably standing with a cold drink of water. He only had to leave the sports stadium and raise his eyes. He was thirsty.

Once, when he tore his gaze away from the wall and stretched his hand out towards his daughter, he felt an unpleasant handshake, and a strange breeze from the figure at his bedside. Who was the owner of such an obnoxious face? Samuel had to smile to himself. The face reminded him of the Angel of Death. But the Angel of Death usually appeared as a *klepsidra*, a skeleton, and this one was as fat as a pig. A nightmare. It shone with a red pate and a mouthful of metal caps. "*Shalom aleichem*," the mouth said. Where was the glass of cold water?

This fat Angel looked so funny that Samuel, although thirsty, became lighthearted and gay, "Give me a glass of water," he grinned roguishly at the visitor.

The fat visitor began to turn uneasily, looking about the room. Laughter was bubbling within Samuel's head. He pointed to the bottle and the glass at his bedside, while he listened to the panting of the flabby stranger. They touched each other's fingers upon the glass. Their eyes met. Samuel swallowed gulps of cold reality.

Adam wiped his hands with a spotless handkerchief and moved over to the far side of the bed. "You see, I've come to visit you," he said. "Yeah, you are still my only friend. I've sinned a great deal against you, but believe me, I didn't do it for pleasure. I beg your forgiveness."

It occurred to Samuel that his visitor had himself become a little clown, perhaps even a better one than he himself was, because Adam had not even smiled as he declaimed his lines. "You're talking as if I were about to die," Samuel declaimed his own lines. "Idiot, what is there to forgive? You have done me no harm, not even a speck . . ." He winked mischievously. "And if I am dying, it is better to do so before I've done something which deserved death. Don't you think so?" Adam was very hot, hotter than Samuel. He too had to have a glass of water and he asked where he could find a clean glass. "This glass is clean," Samuel offered him his. "Take it, drink."

"I know it is clean," Adam groaned, "but ... Don't you have another glass?"

"What do you mean 'don't I have'? May we be protected from an evil eye, we are a big genteel family. Go into the kitchen and guzzle to your heart's delight. Why should you drink from the same glass as I, after all? Did the same mother bear us, or did we tend pigs together, or what?" He was amused at the sight of Adam dragging himself to the door.

Adam did not reappear for a long while. Samuel stared at the door, calculating how much water a person could gulp down during such a stretch of time. He began to worry about the pail of water which Bella had fetched in the morning. At length, Adam came back. He removed his jacket to reveal his spotlessly white shirt, as he sat down at a sufficient distance from the bed. But Samuel immediately said to him, "You say that you are my friend, don't you?"

"Yes, honestly."

"Then do me a favour. You emptied half a pail of water or perhaps even more . . . then be so good as to lift up your distinguished behind and fetch me a pailful of water, so that Bella won't have to do it." Adam grimaced, fanning himself with his white handkerchief. "So," Samuel insisted. "Fetch me two pails of water. Show me the generosity of your heart . . . Move! Aren't you a sportsman, after all?"

Adam stood up heavily and left the room. Samuel listened to the clinking of the pails while he inwardly roared with laughter, as if he had played a most hilarious trick on Adam. From the distance he heard the squeaking of the water pump. Its sound seemed to have moved into the room and into Samuel's chest. He wanted to inhale deeply the fresh May air, but his breath was stopped by a wall within him. He tried again, hopefully, playfully. This time he felt a prickling in his chest and in his back. Adam was panting on the stairs outside. He soon entered the room and sat down on the chair.

"A heat outside . . ." he grumbled. Then he sank into silence, in obvious preparation for what he wanted to say. Finally, he spoke up, "Listen, Zuckerman, I am ready to do a lot for you . . . Your daughter . . . She looks awful. Where does she work?"

"At Central Bookkeeping."

"Some job! What can she fill her mouth with there? With ciphers? One big round zero. And your other daughter? I heard that she got married. *Mazal tov* to you. You see, I know everything about you. I was interested. And listen, I will send you a supply of food every day, you'll see. And an extra portion of curds will also be given to you regularly. They say that curds are a remedy for your disease. And your daughter . . . Bella is her name, isn't it? You see I still remember. A fine child. She loved my Sutchka. I will get her a job in a bakery. You're surprised? I can do it easily, I've got the whole ghetto in my pocket. Yeah, even the King of the Beggars himself, little Mordecai Chaim shakes in his pants before me. So you've got an idea, eh? But you, Zuckerman, will survive the war, thanks to me. No one will save you but I. They say that you're suffering from galloping consumption, that you won't last longer than four weeks. Laugh at it . . ." He noticed that Samuel was slowly lowering his eyelids, so he interrupted his monologue and moved a bit closer to the bed. With the tip of a finger, he touched Samuel's arm, as if to wake him, and he continued speaking, but more slowly, to give his words time to penetrate the sick man's mind. "Do you know what you need most? Fresh air. Marysin, you see, could put you back on your feet. Zuckerman, I said Marysin . . ."

"I heard you, Rosenberg," Samuel replied, keeping his eyes shut.

"I'll get a house for you in Marysin, or I will offer you my own. A house just like in the country . . . with a nice garden. Do you hear me? As for me, I will move in here. I don't mind doing you this favour. We can do it even tomorrow. And about transportation you don't have to worry either. So, how do you like my plan?"

"Some plan."

"So what do you say?"

"I say that I am quite all right here."

"You're an idiot. A man must not surrender. One must try everything. You are a father of two daughters and the war is about to end. Secondly, as a friend . . . I mean, one hand washes the other. I am ready to pay you."

"Why do you want my house?"

Adam did not expect such a direct question. He coughed and went on wiping his face with his handkerchief. He hurriedly moved his chair closer to the bed, and even more hurriedly moved it back.

"Listen, it's a secret . . ." he began with effort. "But you I can trust. It's not a question of the house. It's a question of the shed in the corridor. The thing is this: I am going to get a puppy. A German has promised it to me. Tomorrow or after tomorrow. I can't keep it at home, the walls of my house are too thin. After all, I am a Jew of the ghetto and am not allowed to keep a dog. This is a solid stone house. As long as Sutchka was here, nothing happened to her. Understand? The new dog will be tiny . . . I'll let it get used to the shed and will hide it there if something happens. I would have waited with the exchange of the houses, I swear I would. But it is urgent. I am a lonely man, Zuckerman . . ."

He waited for a word of compassion. Samuel was silent; he kept his eyes shut. Adam was becoming impatient and edgy. Here he was talking from the depth of his soul, while the man before him lay like a mummy. "Do you know," he said incensed. "If I wanted to, I could get Sutter to evict you from here in no time."

Samuel blinked his eyes. Suddenly the truth cut into his consciousness like a blade, dazzling him so brutally that he jerked in his bed. "You are . . . you have . . .!" he wanted to bellow, but he did not have enough breath. His tongue remained suspended in the middle of his open mouth. Adam smirked slyly, watching Samuel struggle with his breath, throw his head about and move his open mouth. "Nazi!" Samuel's mouth hissed out at last.

"If only I could be a Nazi!" Adam cried. He had had enough of playing the comedy, enough of watching the disgusting cadaverous face of the sick man. He stood up and began to pace the room. "And if you want to know," he now spoke freely, "I saved you from Sutter's hands, I, who suffered so much from you. You consider yourself a better man than I, don't you? You are a noble ethical human being, aren't you? Then have a good look at your daughter, and you'll see how ethical you are. You think that it took me long to figure out that you feed on her like a parasite, on your own flesh and blood? Well, aren't you a greater criminal than I? Don't you know that nothing can help you? Why don't you put an end to yourself, my great hero, tell me? You don't feel like it, do you? You'd rather steal a morsel of life from your own flesh and blood with every bite of food that you take. But you consider me a devil for wanting the same as you, although I don't do it at the expense of my child's life."

Samuel did not hear him. He only felt the presence of a mighty awesome Adam within him and around him. All his battles were still far from being won, and of all of them there was still the most important left to fight — with Adam. Samuel stared at the wall. The last lights of the day were playing upon it. He found himself at the sports stadium again. "Endure! Endure!" he commanded his hands, his feet, his heart. A net of barbed wire divided the space. On one side stood Samuel, on the other, Adam. They were playing passionately, with their whole beings. All the pulses in Samuel's body were pounding, sweat flowed in streams down his face, tears poured from his eyes — helpless tennis balls. He wept.

A cool hand touched his forehead. He opened his eyes and saw Bella. Her lips were moving. She was saying something, he did not know what. He puckered his eyebrows and strained his ears. "Do you understand?" she asked. "The whole ghetto is buzzing. Even the Presess said in his speech . . ."

"Who was here?" he asked.

She shrugged her shoulders, "No one . . ." She stroked his face. "And do you know what else? He said that we ought to prepare ourselves."

"Yes, we ought to prepare ourselves," he repeated absentmindedly.

"People are beside themselves with joy on account of the good news. It makes one's head turn. They say that they will begin taking apart the wire fence in a matter of days. The Allies and the International Red Cross demand it."

His eyes began to glow with such light that she had to divert her gaze from them. "Endure!" he pressed out from between his teeth.

Her eyes were swimming. She bit her nails. It cost her an effort to continue speaking, "Downstairs people are saying that the ghetto would have been opened a long time ago, but Rumkowski didn't want it . . . because of security. Anti-Semites, Poles or Germans, might attack us . . . This way we are safe."

"Give me a glass of milk," he said.

She rubbed her face, enlivened, "A carrot with sugar, perhaps? Perhaps a bit of soup?" Avoiding his glance, she turned away.

"All right, a carrot! All right, a bit of soup!" he called after her.

She halted at the door, "Do you know, Papa, politics are beginning to interest me." She left but was back in the blink of an eye. "Someone was here, Papa! The pails are full of water."

"Who was here?" he asked, and then remembered, "Adam Rosenberg. He wants to get us out of the house."

She fed him, and it seemed to him that he saw saliva foaming at the corners of her hungry mouth. He ate, although he was not hungry. He had to accept the sacrifice, for her sake. For her sake he had to get well; more than for her sake: for the sake of a higher justice which must not allow that of the two of them, Adam should be the one to live to the day of peace. He said to Bella, "We won't fight with him over the house. We must concentrate our enegy on essential matters." She nodded gratefully, "Nor shall we run away," he added. "Let's see what that *Kriponik* is capable of."

"The *Kriponik*?" she stared at him astounded.

He was on the point of bursting out with the truth which had just been revealed to him, but he bit his lips. "Yes," he said with feigned indifference. "He has made friends of a few *Kripo* scoundrels, so he acts important."

It was not yet completely dark outside, when Bella undressed and went to bed. She wanted the night to be as long as possible. She loved her sleep, it was her greatest treasure. She stared at the slice of sky in the balcony door, inhaling deeply the fragrant breeze that wound through the room. She was exhausted. Each passing day was a long path through magical circles, moving slowly round and round the dying wick of a candle. She knew that she was a spellbound moth, driven to become one with the wick, to become food for its flame. It was important that the flame grow stronger, that complete darkness should not swallow her, so that she might dare to inhale the May air, to taste the sweetness of summer evenings which were surely waiting somewhere for her. It seemed strange that her father's illness should awaken all these cravings within her. She discovered an unsatiated desire within her, to relish, to flourish, to ripen. Here, coming in touch with her father's intimate wounds, with his raw helpless body, she realized how wonderful everything physical, everything sensual was. And if she had again begun to miss her piano, it was due to her longing to express, through music, her enthusiasm for all earthly beauty. Every night she would shut her eyes with a prayer that she might get up in the morning and something would happen. She had great plans for herself, for herself alone. Samuel would get well and she would set out into the world — on her own flight.

Samuel kept his face turned towards Bella, yet he barely saw her. He heard her regular breath, and its rhythm carried him back to the days when she was a tiny girl and he would stand over her crib. He had always thought her fragile; his heart had always been full of tenderness and of the fear that something might happen to her. Yes, and he had always known that her ugliness was a mask. That in reality she was a fragrant flower blossoming in his garden, that the man who discovered her beauty would be fortunate and blessed. The face of her mother, of Matilda, swam out from the depths of his memory. Bella was a copy of her. That was why he had never been happy. It had not been given to him to discover the beauty of Bella's mother. He was capable of taking only the child into his heart. He called Matilda in his mind.

Then he thought of Junia, his other daughter. He had never worried about her. At six months of age she had sped on all fours along the corridor of the house on Novomieyska. From the start she had set out to conquer the world with her free expansive arrogance. At the same time, she was just as stubborn as her forefathers, and she strongly resembled her father, in her looks, in her love of mischief; perhaps also in her strength? Perhaps he was, after all, not the weakling he had thought himself to be, perhaps he had lived with that misconception because it had been convenient. Wasn't he aware of his inner strength right now, during his illness? Yes, that strength now told him something unpleasant, which he had to recognize. Adam Rosenberg was right. An enemy was sometimes more capable of appraising a person, than a friend. He, Samuel, was guilty. Bella was withering . . . Junia was as thin as a stick. Perhaps Michal's hot metallic eyes were burning with condemnation? Perhaps these blossoming days of May were also a reproach? Fear of death? The will to live? Was he not stronger than both?

The next day, they waited in vain for Adam and the visitors from the *Kripo*. Nor did anyone show up in the days that followed. Samuel and Bella were triumphant. The days became increasingly hot and the ghetto's enthusiasm grew. The air was full of promise. Freedom seemed close enough to touch. Samuel and Bella told themselves that Adam had become frightened by the good news and had given up his evil intentions.

✦ ✦ ✦

To mark their third anniversaries, many of the Resorts organized celebrations, and Central Bookkeeping, although it did not participate in such lighthearted events itself, arranged a lottery, with tickets to the performances of the various Resorts as prizes. Bella won such a ticket to the review at the Millinery Resort. Although it did not enter her mind to use the ticket, she was glad to have won it. Mother Luck was smiling on her. She waited for David on the balcony, in order to offer the ticket to him. He deserved it on account of his frequent visits, for diluting the heavy atmosphere in the house with a bit of cheerfulness.

When she saw him sitting under the cherry tree, she ran, barefoot, down to him. She liked to walk around barefoot. It gave her the feeling of having an additional sense, of allowing the world to enter her through still another path. It was delightful. Yet, just as she reached him, her knees gave under her and she almost fell upon David. Something began to roar in her head. There was darkness spreading before her eyes. She held the ticket tightly between her fingers and sank down heavily beside David, as she waited for the darkness, turning in circles before her eyes, to disappear. She was calm and patient. It was not the first time that this had happened to her. And indeed, light soon began to dawn before her eyes and she raised her head to David.

"I have a ticket for you, for the review at the Millinery Resort." He was chewing a blade of grass and did not even glance at her. She became sad, disappointed that her good luck meant so little. She stretched out her hand with the ticket, "Here, take it . . . If you don't want to go, perhaps your brother will."

His fingers slowly began to crawl over the damp grass. He covered her hand with his and a pleasant warmth climbed up her body, colouring her cheeks. He took the ticket and thanked her, she could not understand why. It was she who owed him thanks. And she wondered how sensitive and grateful a hand could be, just like a heart. She felt like sitting for a while beside this stranger who was so familiar, to inhale the merciful kindness of the earth, of the grass. But to sit like that was a sin. Upstairs, there stood a bed whose occupant meant every-thing to her. Thanks to the body in that bed, there was day and night, there was May and the light of the sky. With her eyes fixed on the balcony, she stood up and said goodnight to the young man.

He did not reply or follow her with his eyes. But then he heard a thud and a muffled scream. He jumped to his feet and ran to the entrance of the Zuckermans' house. Bella was lying near the stairs with her head on the stones. Women came running from all directions. Soon the entrance was full of people and of noise. A few men carried Bella upstairs and put her in the bed opposite Samuel.

"It's nothing," David said as he bent over the sick man. "She fell down the stairs."

Samuel wrinkled his forehead, twisting the blanket with his hands. "Call . . ." he mumbled.

David ran to fetch Michal. When they came back, the house was full of neighbours. Women scoured the rooms, investigated the kitchen, opened cupboards and drawers, as if the house had no owners. In the room where Samuel lay, the women who were experts at revivification were busy working on Bella, sprinkling cold water in her face, rubbing her hands and smacking her cheeks. She was given oddly smelling flacons to sniff and someone was blowing into her mouth.

Michal sent them all away, leaving one woman in the kitchen. He ordered her to cook a bit of soup. And indeed, as soon as the spoon with the hot liquid touched Bella's lips, she opened her eyes. When she had devoured all of the soup, she stood up as if she had just had a good rest, and approached the sick man. "Did you see the silly thing that happened to me, Papa?" she asked, dressing up her face with her special smile. She smoothed out his wrinkled forehead with her hand and arranged his pillow.

They spent a pleasant evening by Samuel's bedside: Michal, Junia and Bella. Samuel seemed to have forgotten the incident with Bella. He was in good spirits. His temperature had dropped and this seemed to revive the others as well. They discussed the situation on the battlefields and the fact that the war was indeed coming to an end. Junia, half in earnest, half jokingly, described how the Jewish homeland, which would have to be created right after they left the ghetto, might look. She and Michal kissed Samuel at leave-taking. It was an ordinary, yet festive evening.

Bella was in bed, ready to receive the night, when Samuel's voice reached her ear, "It won't take much longer, daughter." His voice sounded hopeful. She answered him trustingly, "I think so too," and she shut her eyes.

A hot day. This year's May had character. From early morning the sun took hold of Samuel's room, filling every corner with dazzling light. Samuel greeted it as one greets a favourite relative who has come to pay a visit. He was in a clowning mood when Bella washed him.

In the bright light of the day his wounds and bed-sores looked sharp and shiny. The pus stuck out clearly from the red raw flesh. As usual, Bella's every finger ached at the touch of his skin. The smell from his rotting body was unbearable, biting, as it filled her nostrils and seemed to penetrate her brain. Her head spun as she powdered and blotted out the fissures in his skin. Meanwhile she chatted cheerfully. Samuel was burning up with fever, but that seemed to make no difference to his wonderful mood.

"Now," he said, "After you have so elegantly powdered me, daughter, I want another thing from you." He cast a glance at the open balcony door in which the sheet of sky shone so brightly that it looked transparent. Its sight made him shudder. "I feel so splendid today," he went on, "that I can allow myself to be arrogant. Bella, do you know what I feel like doing? I feel like going out on the balcony . . . Such a caprice . . ."

Bella became excited. Her head began to swim. Samuel's wish was a wonderful sign. "Do you feel so well, Papa?"

"Excellent, daughter! I know that I burden you . . . but . . . arrange a few chairs so that I can lie down, as you used to do. Perhaps you could call up someone to help you?"

She shook her head energetically, "I don't need any help."

"Good, we'll do it together," he said. "It is not far . . . from the bed to the balcony. Four steps at the most."

"Yes, four steps at the most," she agreed, "Do you want to move right away?"

"Right away."

They looked at each other solemnly. Bella inhaled deeply and approached the closet, because first he wanted to dress. She found his clothes which he had not worn for a long time. Her hands shook and sweat covered her forehead. She felt faint. An extraordinary thing was taking place at this moment. As if intoxicated, she approached Samuel. Father and daughter were so absorbed in what they were doing, that in spite of their closeness, they did not see each other. Finally Samuel was dressed. His pale unshaven face seemed attached to the loose suit. The suit itself seemed without a body, collapsing in the hollow of the bed. "Give me a bit of water," he begged her. She raised him on his pillow and gave him a drink. She too gulped down a glass of water eagerly. They looked at each other proudly, searchingly.

She arranged a place for him on the balcony. It was still early in the morning. A huge shadow covered one side of the yard, making the other side look all the brighter. Standing in the centre of that brightness the cherry tree bathed in gold. The air was hot.

Samuel wanted to take the few steps outside by himself, but it immediately became clear that this was impossible. He was even unable to drag his feet down from the bed. Bella had to hold his knees and move his limp legs towards the floor. He flung his arms around her neck, and in this way she got him to sit up; then she lifted him to his feet. As she dragged him towards the balcony, he moved his legs and it seemed to him that he was walking by himself. Both of them panted heavily, loudly, glued to one another, entangled with their bodies, their limbs, their hearts aflutter — both of them united by one intent — to reach the chairs on the balcony.

They fell into the open eye of the sun. Another few minutes and Samuel was resting on the chairs. The unpleasant smell of his body, of his feet, reached Bella's nostrils; washing him daily did not make the smell vanish. She covered Samuel with a blanket. He kept his eyes shut. She thought that he was tired and wanted to sleep, but he said to her, "Move me up . . . I want to sit. I know that I am exhausting you . . ."

She helped him sit up. "What do you mean you are exhausting me?" she panted. "You made it out all by yourself."

He opened his eyes wide. "Really?" he smiled faintly. "Oh, I will thank you in bulk for everything . . . Now only give me another bit of water and you can go to work. I'll wait here for you until your lunch hour." She gave him the drink and he inhaled as much air as could reach the painful barrier in his lungs. "Bella, look, I am dressed, sitting up, feeling like a normal human being," he said. "But you know, before you leave, do me one more favour. Give me the shaving tools . . . not mine, but Eibushitz's. Do you remember that he left them here and never took them back? Fine professional tools." She stared at him in wide-eyed astonishment. She did not know whether she should cry with joy, or hug and kiss him. He caught the expression on her face and forced himself to widen the smile on his lips. "Come on, girl, move. Do what your father commands. Why are you staring at me like that? You're afraid that I won't be able to do it myself? Silly child, I have been shaving . . . guess how many years . . . After all, I don't have to do it with perfect precision at this moment, do I?"

She muttered, "I'll help you."

"Out of the question! Am I a man, or not? Secondly, there is no hurry. I'll do it a little later. It's great to be out here. Let's have breakfast together."

"Are you hungry?"

"Like a wolf."

As soon as she left, Samuel shut his eyes. The tumult in the yard reached his ears. People were already rushing with pails to the water pump, or with clinking pots to the coffee centres. Canteens and spoons chimed like bells. Windows were opened, pillows and eiderdowns dusted with carpet-beaters.

His sitting position on the chair-bed made the bedsores burn like fire. Samuel was barely able to keep his head upright, it constantly fell either to one side, or to the other. Everything was clear and sharp and yet foggy. The light breeze playing with his hair brought goose pimples to his skin, each hair on his head pricked like a needle. The noise in the yard reached his ears in one roaring sound, with the rustling of the cherry tree as a part of it. The same was true for the buzzing of the irksome flies which attacked and swarmed around him.

Although each part of his body was a separate source of pain, there was a wholeness within him. There was a corner within him which the pain could not reach; where he felt calm, light, sunny. He had experienced this same feeling after receiving his "treatment" at the *Kripo*. That had been the beginning of his great recovery — through pain. Yes, suffering could work in two directions. It was capable of destroying and of restoring. It depended upon whom it hit. Him it had restored as one restores a castle from its ruins. He was a magnificent airy castle now, doors and windows wide open to all directions of the world. Pride and dignity dwelt within the castle. And in its Holy of Holies, the candle of tenderness, of care, of non-indifference, as Michal called it, was lit.

Bella sat beside him, pushing spoonfuls of curds into his mouth. He kept his eyes open, trying to make his glance forceful. The curds were cool. He held them on his tongue for a while. With clear eyes he swallowed the sight of his daughter. "Thank you," he said when the dish was empty.

She stared at him. Today he had kept on apologizing and thanking her. "Didn't you say that you would thank me in bulk?" she remarked.

"Don't forget the razor," he reminded her.

When she appeared with the shaving tools, she was dressed in a white summer dress, her long brown tresses braided in a tight crown around her head. The light from her big eyes seemed to wash her entire face. A pure light. She smelled of innocence, of freshness and renewal. She brought out a chair.

"Here, I've laid them out for you," she said. "Here is the mirror, a bottle of water, a dish . . . a glass. And remember, be careful, don't strain yourself. If you find it difficult, wait for me."

He asked her to kiss him. He had never asked her before. Usually, she kissed him whenever she felt like it. She pressed her lips against his hot forehead.

The next moment there came a thud, as if the door had been shut forever. With all his strength he wanted to break it open and call back the figure which had vanished from his sight. Something crept over his forehead, then it tickled his cheek. A fly. It was not important to shoo it off. Above him, the clouds swam by. One of them had the shape of Adam Rosenberg's face. Then it dissolved. It was meaningless, insignificant, just like the fly. A playful thought entered Samuel's head. He said to the cloud, to Adam, "You yourself suggested what path I should choose in order to conquer you."

He opened his eyes wide and sighed. This time his lungs allowed him to sigh deeply. There were no locked doors. There was only an open May day which was slowly receding, becoming incomprehensible, in order to make way for another kind of day and another kind of clarity. He, Samuel, was a restored palace into which a new life had moved. Soon, very soon, he would be celebrating the housewarming. Visitors would arrive: comrades, friends, so many of them. Matilda would play the piano while he would sit near the fireplace, watching her. Then he would offer her the gift for which she had waited so long. He would take her into his arms, press her to his body and they would join the other guests in a dance; join all their guests, Adam Rosenberg included. Adam would have to be invited — out of gratitude . . . of humanity . . . of pity. He would have to be invited on account of the tiny eternal light burning in the Holy of Holies, burning also within poor Adam, probably weeping and gnawing at his heart in its longing for redemption.

Samuel stopped feeling the pain in his body. He gathered all his strength, concentrating it on the hand which he stretched out towards the chair. He followed the hand with his gaze and had to smile. Naive Bella had brought no soap . . . no towel. Perhaps she had known that all that he needed was the razor knife with the black handle.

Between Samuel's hand and the razor stood the glass of water. His fingers unwittingly turned it over. The fingers became wet and cold. The glass rolled along the seat of the chair and fell. Something cracked, reverberating inside his skull. He was surprised that a breaking glass could make such a noise. His arm stiffened like that of a thief paralysed with fear. It seemed to him that Bella might arrive at any moment and disturb him. His fingers quickly snatched the handle of the razor. The handle, warm from the sun, felt like Moshe Eibushitz's warm handshake. That was good. Friendship was a blessing; it gave support. Samuel felt healthy again, cured of the galloping consumption. Without great effort he opened the knife. All the light of the sky was reflected in the blade.

He was fully aware of what he was doing. He took out his left hand from under the cover, turning it palm up — not like someone begging for alms, but like someone who had sown his fields and was waiting for the rain. On the wrist of his left hand the twig of blue veins under the skin was clearly outlined. Samuel brought his right hand with the sparkling blade to it. With it he sawed once and once again over the blue branch of veins.

A stream burst out from under the skin of his wrist. Samuel sighed, letting the razor fall from his hand. Both his arms fell to his side. His head shook for a moment, then remained resting on his shoulder. The stream flowed out from him, oozing, making room for freedom. He felt good. The open face of his beautiful ¡laughter Bella smiled at him. The perfume of her white dress penetrated deep inside him. How powerfully he loved life! What he had just done was proof of it. He wanted to worship it in this manner, through the only means possible. One needed superhuman, god-like power to do that.

He kept his eyes open. The blood which did not stop oozing from his wrist, dripped onto the balcony floor, making a pleasant sound. Samuel's heart so overflowed with tenderness, that his eyes became blurred. The open balcony door began to lose its outlines, as did the sky with its light. It grew darker and darker around him. A wind blew through his head. He was riding into a tunnel which did not let fear or joy pass. All his luggage fell off, leaving him only with his own haste. Bella was supposed to arrive . . . He had to hurry even more, so that she would not catch up to him. Hurry? An illusion. Bella was with him.

Samuel stopped hurrying. His pupils circled the horizons of the eye-whites for the last time, setting like two black suns under his half-lowered eyelids. Not far from the balcony the cherry tree was rustling. Tiny red balls had appeared on it: dots of fruit. Newborn cherries.

Chapter Seventeen

IT TOOK QUITE A WHILE before Adam Rosenberg realized that the German who had promised him a puppy was making a fool of him. The twenty-four year old fellow who adorned his uniform with a black armband with a *Totenkopf* on it, walked about the ghetto with a police dog and headed the raids and searches. At first, Adam was afraid of him, not so much on account of his uniform or his acts of cruelty, as on account of his looks, his height and his youth, all of which reminded him of Mietek.

Adam was at first also frightened by the SS man's dog whose name was Churchill. Then the dog began to remind him of Sutchka, and in spite of himself, Adam would now and then give the dog a few affectionate pats; until a friendship was established, which led to the rapprochement between Adam and the dog's master. This in turn had inspired the order, that Adam should take care of the dog, should wash and brush and walk it when its master had to leave for the city. Along with this function Adam was given a nickname by the *Kripo* men. They called him *Hundsmann*. Adam accepted the nickname cheerfully, even with a certain pride. Serving a dog seemed to him less humiliating than to serve a human, since in his view the dog was superior to man. Dogs possessed more humanness than human beings; they were devoted, sought no profits and were not exploitive or sadistic. Now that he had so thoroughly learned about man, both German and Jew, Adam doubted the accuracy of his opinion less than ever before.

Thus his powerful longing for Sutchka had suddenly come back to him. He felt frightfully lonesome. More than once his sorrow grabbed him by the throat, stifling him. Tears often filled his eyes as he abandoned himself to self-pity. The problem was that he was becoming bored. His work at the *Kripo*, along with his activities as *Hundsmann*, filled only a few hours of his day. That gave him ample time to brood, and even those nights which he spent with a woman did not save him from the gloom of loneliness. Female devotion bought with bits of sugar, flour or bread, evoked his craving for what he could not buy. Even his semi-permanent woman, whom he had fattened up with food to suit his physical appetites, was unable to satisfy that need. He missed the warmth of a Sutchka.

He lost interest in the things which had once absorbed him. He collected foreign currencies, "soft" and "hard", and the jewellery which was still in the hands of the most prominent *shishkas*. He had once enjoyed the game of impoverishing others while enriching himself. Now, however, although he had already tasted starvation, valuables began to lose their attraction for him. They meant nothing more than security against hunger. Nowadays he considered a day without anxiety his greatest treasure. To worry about the future seemed silly. His most remote worry was about the next day. And with such a conception of time, the possession of valuables meant very little. Of course he was sure that he would witness the end of the war. He even had, like every other practical *Kripo* man, an outfit consisting of female clothes and a female wig, with which he planned to disguise himself, should the ground begin to burn under his feet; he also knew that his road led towards Switzerland. But that was a planning prompted by reason. His imagination was incapable of visualizing such a moment. His solid conclusion was that man lived in the present, not in the past or in the future. And that was why sadness engulfed him. The present, the given moment was hollow — a wasted treasure.

He urgently needed a friend, a dog. And here that dog, Sutter, refused to give in to Adam's pleas. In a leisurely way, Sutter explained to him that a dog could not be kept trapped in the ghetto like a Jew. A dog would not respect any barbed-wire fences and might become a carrier of germs. Adam shook his head in despair. Sutter had no idea of the nature of dogs.

He was left with the option of secretly working on the young fellow from the SS. The latter should have understood him. And indeed he did. He said, "*Ja wohl*," and Adam could barely believe his own ears. He was ready to prostrate himself with gratitude before the SS man. The SS man smirked mischievously and said, "Tomorrow morning."

Tomorrow morning seemed distant. Adam thought it would never come. But come it did. Holding his breath, he ran out to greet the German, his eyes blurred with anticipation. The fellow put his hand chummily on Adam's shoulder and said, "You didn't tell me what kind of dog you want, *Hundsmann*."

What an idiot he had been! How could the young fellow guess that he wanted a dark young Doberman. Dobermans were intelligent and devoted. Adam would give anything to have a young Doberman. In the meantime, he sought a home for the dog and left for the Zuckermans' house to have a look at the shed in the corridor.

At first, every time that Adam ran out to meet him, the SS man would say, "Tomorrow morning." Then he began to say, "Next week." Adam asked him whether he should pay him in advance and the SS man said, "*Ja wohl*." Adam gave him a golden ring as an advance on the account. The fellow slid the ring into his breast pocket which was embroidered with a black eagle. Only then was the deal really made. Adam had every right to expect the young Doberman.

The German did not change his chant during the days that followed. "*Morgen, nechste Woche . . .*" he would say. Until the truth struck Adam like lightning, at the same time underlining the validity of his philosophical thoughts. Tomorrow or the day after did not exist. "*Morgen*" meant never. Today meant everything. He would never have a young brown Doberman to fill the emptiness in his life. As a result, the emptiness became more devastating. He had lost his hope. Adam mourned for the dog he would never have.

The house in Marysin in which he lived had one great fault. In front of it passed the funeral cortèges on their way to the cemetery. And one day Adam watched Samuel Zuckerman's funeral, recognizing the dead man's daughters as they followed the hearse. The funeral itself did not impress Adam more than any other. On the contrary. He felt somewhat relieved, like someone who finishes an account book, knowing that he will never have to open it again.

Nevertheless, thoughts of Samuel began to nag at him and the more he thought about him, the more he was filled with the dread of his own death.

He reproached himself, "Your life is all that you possess. Don't waste it. Look, such a beautiful time of the year. Your house is bathed in green. On the trees the apples are flashing like girls' cheeks, the cherries are like lips, the prunes like eyes, and the grass is as soft as the most velvety skin. Your house is clean and comfortable. You have a good bed, a fine mattress. You have shelves full of goodies. Remember: This is paradise. There is no other." He wanted so much to enjoy himself. Life was so precious. But instead of relishing it, he lay on the fragrant grass, abandoning himself to thoughts of death, brought on by the buried Zuckerman. Yes, his garden, although surrounded by a fence, was nothing but an extension of the cemetery. And whenever Adam became aware of this fact, he had the impression that his heart was about to stop, that he would not be able to get up, but must remain lying there forever.

The earth began to frighten him. The flowers and the juicy grass were a mask over its face. In reality the earth meant death, his own as well. How silly then was his wish to have a dog! It was nothing but a wish to forget himself, to ignore what Samuel's shadow whispered in his ear.

He avoided sitting in the grass and moved over to the threshold of his house. Later, he gave that up as well, and spent long hours napping in his sultry room. Although sleep resembled the state which he feared, at least he was not tormented by worry about his health during those hours when he slept. Later on, sleep also ceased to be of any help. He had nightmares.

All that was left for him was to escape into the street. True, he hated the crowds, and when he passed the queues in front of the co-operatives, he always recalled a trace of his Latin education: *Odi profanum vulgus.* Yet he felt safer in the crowd. Thus he arrived at another philosophical conclusion: being alone was reminiscent of death. Death was final loneliness. That was the reason why men sought companionship. Love, friendship, political, national or racial affiliations, all these were simply coverups for the desire to silence the scream of loneliness and death.

As he wandered through the streets, it occurred to Adam that although he had been happiest with Sutchka, he had experienced another particularly powerful feeling of wellbeing for a short while, at the beginning of the ghetto, when he had sat at the table with Yadwiga and Mietek, and even more strongly — when he had lived with Krajne the Gold Digger. That meant that relationships with people, even if one hated them, gave one something which the most devoted dog was incapable of giving. Adam inferred, that if it were impossible to escape death, he had, as long as he was alive, to try and escape the dread of it. And man was the only creature that could help him in that respect.

Dressed in a clean shirt, flowered tie, a straw hat and dark glasses, he strolled through the streets in the evening air, observing the passers-by. A woman stopped him, "Mr. Rosenberg, may I have a word with you?" He measured her with his eyes. She was of the same indefinite age of all ghetto women and could as easily have been thirty as well as fifty years old. She had hollow *klepsydra* cheeks, a sharp nose and blue lips. Her forehead had deep bald spots extending above her temples, like that of a man beginning to lose his hair. Her eyes were also like those of all the ghetto women, dark, large, restless and sharp, full of fear. On her skeletal body there limply hung a cotton dress, obviously made of a tablecloth. "My husband is being kept in the *Kripo*, Mr. Rosenberg!" she ran after him when he accelerated his steps. "Perhaps you can help me?"

With dignity he shook his head, saying, "I will do whatever I can. God will help you." Still running after him, the woman told him her name, and when she noticed him jot something down on a piece of paper, she began chanting a litany of thanks and blessings behind his back.

The little incident put him in a cheerful frame of mind, which surprised him, since such an encounter would have enraged him only a few days ago. Lately his name had become known in the ghetto. People ran after him in the streets, imploring him to intercede on behalf of their relatives or friends. He was unable to rid himself of them. He could not bear their lamentations, their pleading eyes. But today he felt differently. He was not sure whether he would go down into the cellar of the *Kripo* to check on the man whose name he had marked down; but at the moment he had good intentions. His own name rang in his ears with the lilt of the woman's voice. It was pleasant.

Passing a fence where a few daisies were growing, he picked the prettiest and tucked it into his lapel. He removed his sunglasses and cleaned them with his clean handkerchief. The sun was already setting and he could easily do without the sunglasses, but wearing them had become too strong a habit. The moment he stepped outside, his eyes and his entire face felt the need to hide behind the dark glasses. On the thresholds of the houses women were sitting and chatting. Now and then he nodded a greeting to them. It was the first time he had done such a thing, consciously and soberly putting his recent resolutions into action.

Adam had an ache in his chest. He spent a whole day massaging the region of his heart and applying compresses to it, certain that his end had come. The next day, his stomach began to hurt and again he thought that everything was over. The same happened on the following days. On each day of the next two weeks, he felt that he was one step away from the grave, and he again saw Samuel Zuckerman's funeral cortège in his mind. Samuel had mesmerized him. In his nightmares, Adam saw the black glassy eyes with which Samuel had looked up at him from the pillow. Samuel's gaze was neither kind nor hostile, yet it was commanding.

As a result, despite his great pain, Adam forced himself to go to the place which he feared most — the cemetery. He told himself that in order to be conquered, an obsession had to be faced rather than avoided. And his obsession was, he told himself, to see Samuel's grave.

He did not have far to go. He had barely finished explaining to himself what it was that he was doing, when he saw the cemetery's brick fence and iron gate. From behind the empty hearses standing outside after their day's work, two packs of beggars emerged, headed straight for him. They looked like corpses which had escaped from their coffins. The beggars clicked their tongs and cracked their knuckles as they begged for alms. They pulled at him, jostled him, crying, "Charity saves from death! Charity saves from death!" He did not understand their chant. It seemed to him that they were accompanying him to his own funeral, moving ahead to show him his own grave. They had accompanied him far inside the cemetery before they gradually dispersed, heaping curses on his head.

He became aware of the silence which hung over the place. The tombstones cast long shadows. The trees and the grass swayed. Tall weeds grew over the graves and their black wrought-iron enclosures. Weeping willows stretched their long hair-like boughs to the ground as the last rays of light furtively shimmered on the leaves. The darkness of the night unrolled like a carpet under Adam's feet. It seemed to him that behind every tree, every tombstone, there lurked a shadowy figure which might pop out at any moment and cover his mouth with a cold hand. That would be his real end; his heart would stop forever. But to his own amazement, he discovered at that moment that the pain in his heart was completely gone.

He walked over to the new part of the cemetery. Here there was no park, no trees, no grass. Hundreds of clay-like brick-red heaps were scattered densely over a raw field. Here and there someone stood in front of a heap. Sobs reached Adam's ears. He walked on hypnotized, past the heaps, lost in the labyrinth of paths. Here had the dead ghetto come to rest. Momentarily, Adam felt like someone looking for an apartment.

It made no sense to try to find Samuel's grave. Every grave was Samuel's and each conveyed the same message to Adam, "Even if you chance to escape the deportations, you will come to rest here, too, even if you are still healthy and working for the *Kripo!*" That was what Samuel was telling him and he agreed with him. For he had read somewhere that people who had no clear images or dreams about the future were approaching their own deaths; and he had stopped thinking or dreaming about the future. If he died now, the result would be that he had not beaten Samuel after all, that the score was zero against zero — a draw. The difference between the two of them would be only that Samuel had had two daughters who had accompanied him to this place.

Mietek entered his mind. He imagined that Mietek were with him now and fantasized how they might live and eat together. He saw Mietek picking fruit from the trees, devouring jars of sugar. Then he thought of Sutchka and he asked himself which of the two he would prefer to have with him. Life with Sutchka would be simple: pure unconditional devotion, without any obligations. With Mietek life would be much more complicated. Even if they led the idyllic existence his imagination had concocted, there would be mixed feelings, complexities, misunderstandings and obligations. And yet he had no doubt that he would have chosen Mietek, that only Mietek could have filled the emptiness and subdued his anxieties.

He accelerated his steps so as to get out of the cemetery as soon as possible. After he had passed the exit, he felt light. What weird thoughts he had just had! Of course he had conquered Samuel. He was still alive. He had conquered him with as many victories as the number of days by which he would survive him. Now, however, his sense of victory was not tinged with a sense of vengeance. He was positively inclined towards the loser. He sentimentally recalled their ill-fated friendship and regretted the way it had ended, just as he regretted the end of his relationship with his wife and his son.

His walk to the cemetery contributed to the pleasure of his walk through the streets the following day. He was on his way to seek entertainment at the review performance of the Straw Resort, which was located on the premises of the former Gipsies Camp. He felt as if he were on his way to a pre-war opera. He felt this especially when he saw the crowds gathering at the entrance. The review was a great success. The chaos in front of the box-office was similar to that which took place in front of the butcheries when a meat ration came out. People pushed one another, quarrelled, wrestled with the policemen, and fought over the tickets. The only difference was that in spite of the congestion, the faces were cheerful, a playful childish twinkle in the eyes.

Adam had no problem getting a ticket. Earlier, on his way home from work, he had visited the director of the Straw Resort and expressed a wish to see the performance. The director, bowing politely, called in a blond girl and ordered, "A ticket in the first row for Herr Rosenberg."

The blond girl led Adam into a cubicle where he could choose his ticket. The girl had long braids. Her figure was perfectly shaped, its forms both mature and youthful. She viewed him with a gaze which was both innocently submissive and vulgarly feline.

"Sit down for a moment, Mr. Rosenberg," she invited him. Her voice was warm, hoarse and vamp-like. "You are the famous Herr Rosenberg, aren't you?" she inquired, offering him a cigarette. He noticed her long red fingernails. "You don't smoke?" she smiled, revealing two rows of pearl-like teeth to which she gracefully raised the cigarette. She resembled Yadwiga in her younger years, but was in every respect more perfect and enticing. Above the low neckline of the girl's white blouse, he saw the indication of a full rich bosom, an asset on which Yadwiga could never pride herself. "And you refuse to sit down too?" the girl carried on with her coquettish monologue, encouraged by Adam's eager gaze which shamelessly passed over her. "Do you realize how everyone honours you?" She charmingly tightened her mouth, blowing out a thin column of smoke. "Without delay you receive a ticket in the centre of the first row, practically next to the Presess himself." She shook her blond head. "I am keeping you . . . hm . . . wasting your time . . ."

He bowed chivalrously. "A little chat with such a ravishing young lady I do not consider a waste of time."

That remark encouraged her. "You took one ticket, Mr. Rosenberg . . . That means that you are going alone. If . . . If you want to, we could go together. My name is Sabinka."

He bowed again, took her hand and lifted it to his mouth. "I shall be delighted, Sabinka." He planted a kiss on the tip of her slim fingers. Before he left, he managed to catch a glimpse of her suddenly changed face and the confusion in her eyes. With that she pleased him even more.

So this evening he was going to the theatre with a lady; a fact which of course enhanced his strange yet pleasant impression of going to a real theatre, with a real lady. Now he waited for her at the side of the cluster of contending people. The excitement and light-heartedness of the dressed-up crowd infected him. He already saw himself sitting inside, arm-in-arm with the coquettish girl. The lights would go out, he would take her hand in his as the curtain rose. He adjusted the daisy in his lapel. Basically he was a romantic, he thought, not at all indifferent to beauty, or to the enchantment of such a mild summer evening.

A coach stopped at the front door of the Resort. "The Presess!" a whisper passed along the box-office queue. The coachman scrambled down from his seat and opened the door of the coach. First, a white silken scarf appeared, then a stiff hat, then the Presess himself, dressed in a light summer coat. He leaned on a walking stick as he strode with quick, somewhat shaky steps, his shoulders stooped. From all sides people bowed, calling, "Herr Presess! Herr Presess!"

Hands stretched out to touch him, to stop him. A more daring hand pushed an envelope into the Presess' pocket. The policemen tried to protect the Presess as much as they could, but they, like the mob, were taking everything lightly. After all, they had come to enjoy themselves.

"Where is his wife?" someone pulled a policeman by the sleeve.

"She's suffering from gallstones," someone else replied.

Someone called, "Herr Presess, why such a small ration of turnips this time?"

Another, in a more revolutionary mood, exclaimed, "Why don't you stop the additional rations for the *shishkas?*"

Another was even more rebellious, "We demand bread!"

A woman blessed the Presess, "May an evil eye never rest upon your head, Presess dear."

The Presess navigated with his stick, waving it in all directions. At length he disappeared through the entrance. Adam smiled. The Old Man looked years older than he had imagined. It was the first time he had seen him since the establishment of the ghetto.

Then Rumkowski's rival, Leibel Welner arrived, surrounded by his entourage of *Sonderkommando* officers. He roguishly raised his hands as he greeted the crowd which responded with good-humoured exclamations, "Leibel! Leibel!" Welner chummily patted those standing close to him on the shoulders. A woman pulled him by the tail of his jacket, telling him something to which he pretended to listen. "What did he say? What did he say?" people called to her from all sides.

"May he be blessed with a long life," some shook their heads with satisfaction. "Since he began to have a say in the ghetto, life has become easier."

"And what about his quarrel with the Presess?" a woman inquired aloud.

"They were reconciled at the review performance of the Tailor Resort, but at the review performance of the Paper Resort they became enemies again," someone informed her.

"To be honest, they are both riding on our backs", another concluded.

The conversation continued until Welner vanished into the entrance and a few *shishkas* and their wives appeared. The smell of soap and cheap perfumes reached the nostrils of the public which listened to the *shishkas'* loud chatter in Polish. Someone commented, "Do you see the ghettocracy? Dressed like royalty, they go every night to another performance, and after that, they really live it up! Believe me, before the war they never had such a taste of paradise."

"Right!" someone added. "Not only is the war already over for them, it never even began."

The *shishkas* ignored the questions thrown at them by the crowd, and passed through it with their heads haughtily raised. Someone commented, "Those who love money, hate humanity."

Adam listened to the people with satisfaction, enjoying the performance before the performance. At that moment he felt no distaste or hatred for the mob, he rather liked it; the crowd reminded him of a parade of circus clowns.

Sabinka approached. She wore a broad bell-like skirt and a black blouse with a low neckline. Her braids were pinned in a crown around her head which made her look older and still more attractive. As soon as Adam noticed her, his playful disposition vanished. He became serious and tense. Sabinka too looked serious. She shook his hand and he read a kind of confusion bordering on fear in her face. They plowed into the dense cluster of people, pushing ahead without exchanging a word. She pressed against him and he could feel the outlines of her body. They entered the hall and took their seats. Without a word, they stealthily observed each other, now and then uncertainly exchanging smiles.

Soon the lights went out. The public became quiet, and with bated breath watched the curtain rise over the stage, which was constructed of raw boards. The sole stage decoration was a drawing of stairs which were meant to symbolize the ghetto bridge. A cardboard panel shook backstage, a door opened and a group of young people leapt out, dressed in traditional frocks and skullcaps. They performed a Hassidic dance. The band in front of the stage played a Hassidic tune. The crowd joined in, humming and clapping. As soon as they finished, the hall erupted with ovations, "*Bis! Bis!*"

The performers, the majority of whom were young girls dressed up as *yeshiva* boys, repeated their dance, although it was obvious that they were barely able to stand on their feet. As they danced, the flustered crowd noticed the Presess' head rise and move in the direction of the bandleader. A whisper passed through the rows, "He gave him a note . . ."

"He gave him an order for an extra ration."

"All the dancers will go to the Rest Home for a week."

The dancers' legs began to tangle as they turned their eyes first to the head of the Presess, then to that of the bandleader. The crowd forgave them their mistakes and again applauded energetically.

Then a skit was performed which poked fun at the Kitchen Department, by recreating a scene in front of a public kitchen during the distribution of soup. The crowd in the hall roared with laughter, stamped their feet and clapped their hands after every humorous line. The next skit dealt with a romance between a *fecalist* and a girl who worked at the Dairy Resort which was transforming the spoilt milk products into edible food. This was followed by a satire on the managers of the most important Resorts, and a series of "portraits" of *shishkas*. The public was left to guess whom each portrait represented. For the finale, a choir sang Yiddish folksongs. The public hummed and sang along, so carried away, that it forgot to applaud at the end.

Adam was fully aware of the quality of the "art" that he was being offered. Yet he too was swept along by the general enthusiasm. He laughed when everyone else did and applauded when they did. He even became sentimental when he heard the songs which he could not understand. Evidently the girl at his side was making his heart soft and susceptible.

As soon as the lights were turned on, the chaos and the hullabaloo began again. Adam took Sabinka's arm and pushed himself through the crowd with her in tow. Suddenly, he found himself face to face with the Presess. He heard a man behind him say, "People, do you know what the Old Man prescribed for the actors? Candies!" Adam felt the Presess' eyes fix on him. It was clear that the Presess was searching his mind for a name that would match the familiar face before him. Finally, he pointed his eyebrows, wrinkled his forehead and cleared a way to Adam with his stick.

"What's your name?" he asked.

"Adam Rosenberg, Herr Rumkowski. We knew each other well before the war." Adam replied.

The Presess retreated a step, "You're still alive?"

"Alive and kicking, Herr Presess!" Adam laughed freely. He bowed with great ceremony and introduced Sabinka, "Meet Miss Sabinka, Herr Presess."

The Old Man's eyes fell on the girl. Stunned, he began to cough, pounding his stick against the floor, "You! You!" he roared hoarsely, between one cough and another.

"Do you know each other?" Adam was amused. "What a small world!" He politely shook his head at the Presess and, guiding Sabinka by the waist, moved on towards the exit.

Adam walked with Sabinka in the direction of his house. He was impatient because of the double hunger that had attacked him. A philosophical conclusion had ripened in his head: when a person exposes himself to people, things begin to happen. He congratulated himself on his own wisdom, as his eyes devoured slices of Sabinka's neck and the regal crown of her braids. She was talking to him. Yes, she preferred the straight road, she said. She disliked pretending. She was not the innocent girl that perhaps she seemed to be. He assured her that he loved innocent girls who were not innocent.

She said, "I picked you, because . . ."

He replied with a little giggle, "It is I who picked you, little fool."

They had a gay leisurely evening meal and then Adam took the opportunity to satisfy his other appetites. Later on, just when he expected her to leave, she surprised him by saying, "I will stay with you overnight, so that we can have it more cheerful." Bells began to toll in his head. He saw a beautiful, devoted, human Sutchka before him. She told him about both her day and her nighttime experiences in the ghetto. For a year and a half she had worked at the *Sonderkommando*, she said, as she concluded the ghetto chapter of her biography, but she had been thrown out of there for stealing strychnine, *Vigantol*, glucose and Coramine for the Zionists. The only one of her entire collection of commissars and policemen whom she had loved was a Zionist by the name of Samuel Zuckerman. He had been her last lover. But just as she was about to tell Adam more details, he cut her short. He ordered her to dress, go home and never show herself to him again.

The next day he waited for her in front of the Straw Resort, to apologize. The day before, he had forgotten for a moment that all that counted was the present, and that Sabinka too had never existed before, as far as he was concerned; that both Rumkowski and Samuel belonged to the meaningless past, and the fact that he had inherited Sabinka from them meant that he had emerged victorious in his struggle with them.

However, as soon as Sabinka saw him, she ran away. He had no intention of following her. He went to the review performance of the policemen, which he enjoyed tremendously, for it was conducted in Polish. But his return home was sadder than it had been the day before. His house seemed more desolate than ever and he decided to bring back Sabinka at any price. This resolution held for him the pleasant anticipation of a game, because he knew that here, between the wire fences of the ghetto, there was no power which could take her away from him, not as long as he wanted her. He felt like a boy who had trapped a butterfly in his net.

Every day he waited for her in front of the Resort. He would jump out from behind a corner, from behind a wall, right in front of her startled face, taking pleasure in the sight of her frightened eyes. When she dashed off, he did not follow her. He found out where she lived and one evening he surprised her by knocking at her door. She refused to open it, and peering in through the window, he could see her sitting huddled in a corner. To frighten Sabinka became a favourite pastime for him. But it also increased his desire to have her for himself, frightened, trembling, yet devoted. So after a while he had had enough of the game, and one evening he grabbed her, before she managed to enter her little house.

"I'll scream!" she warned as she wrestled with him.

He laughed, "Do you want to sleep over in the Red House?"

That worked like a spell. She burst into sobs, "What do you want of me? What have I done to you?"

He told her that all he wanted was that she should go home with him, that he would never frighten her again. He would be good to her. She obediently accompanied him, looking at him submissively, yet not without suspicion.

In bed it was impossible to touch her. Her body and all her limbs were ice-cold and the awareness that she wanted to flee as soon as possible deprived him of the pleasure of being with her. He could not forgive himself for having destroyed the sweetness of her willing submission, by treating her as the scapegoat of his silly re-awakened frustrations. Again he ordered her to dress and leave. She vanished into the night. He wanted to run after her and bring her back, but he was surprised at his own behaviour, and he stayed in bed to analyze himself. He wanted Sabinka to be attached to him by a devotion mixed with a drop of fear. And he wanted her willingly to accept such a state of affairs. But he came to the conclusion that this could only happen if she were sincerely in love with him. How then should he behave to make this possible? He pondered over the necessary tactics.

Adam began to enjoy the summer more than ever. He relished the taste of every bite of bread, the delicate fragrance of butter, the flavour and sweetness of fruits. In particular he enjoyed washing with cold water on summer mornings. He installed a faucet in the wall outside, attached a pipe to it and took his showers on the grass of his garden. Every pore in his skin took delight in the cleanliness of the underwear which he changed every day.

Sabinka disappeared from his life for good. This time it was impossible to trace her. Adam continued to play the detective game, devoting all his free hours to his search. He spent a lot of time walking vigorously, cheerfully, He interrogated many people, then checked on their information. He enjoyed the game so much, that he prayed for his search to last as long as possible. His only problem was that his masculine impatience did not agree with that wish. Thus he arrived at another philosophical conclusion; namely, that if a man resisted temptation, it was due to the temptation's weakness rather than to his own will power. This was of course not entirely applicable to Sabinka. He saw no reason for renouncing her, so that his will power was not exposed to a test at all.

Chapter Eighteen

SUMMER BROUGHT CONTINUOUS heatwaves. The *shishkas* abandoned their winter houses, moving into their summer residences in Marysin, or *Tsarskoye Sielo*, as it was called. Those *shishkas* who had no summer residences, because they did not want to worry about two households, spent two or three weeks in one of the rest homes where the guests would complain of overeating. In the evenings the residents of the homes visited each other, moving from one garden to the other. They grouped themselves according with their place in the hierarchy of the ghetto, and according to their sources of income. Rumkowski's people visited Rumkowski's people, Welner's chums visited Welner's chums, while the stool pigeons of the *Kripo* gathered with members of their own clique. In fraternal harmony they discussed politics and wished for a quick successful end to the war. The better the radio bulletins were, the closer the end of the war was drawing, the more reason there was to arrange all kinds of parties and celebrations. The participants nervously, restlessly enjoyed themselves, while repeating Herr Schatten's favourite saying, "*Après moi, le déluge!*" Herr Schatten himself had become a great drunkard and everyone was glad that he never showed up at these exciting garden parties.

Late in the evening a gramophone played discreetly. People would rise from their deck chairs, leaving the uneaten food for the servants, or for their relatives or acquaintances from before the war, and they would gather in the grassy clearing. The men paraded about in their white shirts, the women in their custom-made dresses, sewn by the best seamstresses at the Resorts. The air was romantic. Crickets sang in the grass. Frogs croaked. The couples nostalgically danced in the moonlight. Not far away was the barbed-wire fence and a German guard marching with a gun slung over his shoulder.

Presess Rumkowski set out for a stroll along the sandy road of Marysin. His devoted companion, Herr Zibert, was with him. The Presess was now sleeping no more than three or four hours a night and tonight his head was in such turmoil that he did not even try to go to bed. The previous night his rival Leibel Welner had been arrested and led away from the ghetto. The Presess had been cheered by that news and was so excited, that he tripped over his own feet and needed the support of both his stick and Zibert's shoulder. "Eh, Zibert," he sighed with fatigue and delight. "All signs indicate that I will come out the winner. And what did you say is the name of that island?"

"Lampedusa, Herr Presess."

"Is it really as important as you think?"

"It's the beginning of the end, Herr Presess."

The Presess was happy. Lately, in spite of the danger, he was unable to keep himself from visiting the Resorts, to announce to all the news that the war was coming to an end. The workers applauded him gratefully, as if he himself had been winning the battles on the fronts.

"You see, Zibert," the Presess said, leaning on his companion. "Now they begin to realize . . . Yes, I will have saved a flock of Jews from the trap. No one else has achieved that, you can see for yourself. Warsaw has been blotted out, Warthegau blotted out. In all of Poland my ghetto is the only one that exists. Oy, Zibert, when will I live to see the hour . . ." The Presess' dishevelled silvery hair rose lightly with the evening breeze. His satisfaction was a double one, because he was also tired of the burdens and worries that he had borne all these years. He craved a rest, to be, at least for a short time, free of responsibility for anyone or anything; after a while, he would return to lead his liberated people. "Another time I would have worried," he said to Zibert, "about the reason the Germans are sending in so few vegetables, but not today. What's important is that they are about to open three ammunition factories in the ghetto."

Zibert's little eyes lit up roguishly in the dark, "Will you give the crowd ammunition to eat, Herr Presess?"

"You don't know my Jews yet, Zibert. My Jews can do with a trifle. Just give them hope. Of that they need a lot." The distant sound of a gramophone reached their ears and they stopped. "What's that?" the Presess asked.

"They are drowning the worm that eats them. It must be at Sondermann Reisman's house party."

The Presess adjusted his glasses and stamped his stick on the ground, "I'll show them!"

Zibert took him by the arm appeasingly, "Listen to my advice, Presess, and do nothing of the sort. How does the saying go? 'Man is superior to the cattle by his talk. A wise man is superior to the fool by his silence.' Why should you create enemies for yourself? My system is to hit the enemy from behind, and not to show my own face but someone else's. That's what I've learned from the Germans' psychological methods. It is difficult to hate an enemy who does not show his face." The Presess realized that Zibert was right. He must not provoke an open war, particularly now, that their chief had been made lower by a head. Rather he had to win them over to his side, to get around them from behind, diplomatically. Zibert kept both hands in his pockets, letting the Presess lean against him with the entire weight of his body, like a devoted son leading his blind father. At this moment he also led him with his wisdom, "Listen to me, dear Presess. If I were you, I would quietly appear at the celebration and let myself be received by the crowd . . ."

The Presess shook his head categorically, "I will never step over that threshold!" For a while they walked on in silence, then the Presess, already composed, asked, "What did you say was the name of that other island?"

"Panteleria."

"Let it be Panteleria, as long as it is good for the Jews. But I am afraid that the ghetto politicians will prepare some crazy surprises. Who knows what these hotheads can do at the last moment."

A few days later, Herr Biebow ordered all those who were living in Marysin to move back into the ghetto, and a great traffic of handcarts began. Curious ghettoniks watched the move, smiling maliciously. The Presess himself expressed his satisfaction.

The Presess gave a great banquet in honour of the third anniversary of the Work Department. The crowd was unusually excited. Zibert wandered among the guests and whenever someone approached him for some news, he would first cover his mouth with a finger and say, "A fly would never get into a shut mouth." Then he would confide with great secrecy, "The Old Man says that Jews have been wiped out from the rest of Poland and that of all the ghettos only ours remains. He says that all the Eldest of the Jews have been made shorter by a head, and that only his head has been left intact." When he was asked about Leibel Welner, Zibert shrugged his shoulders, "In Warsaw it began the same way . . ." He pointed to the table, shaking his little head. "*Après moi, le déluge!*" Then he giggled and roguishly warned his interlocutors, "Remember, brothers, don't go to sleep, because you may wake up too late!" They stared at him as if he had gone out of his mind.

When the time came for the speeches, the Presess, his face aglow after his bath, sat down at the head of the table. His wife Clara sat down beside him. Her hair was badly arranged and her face seemed to be covered with chalk. She sat stiffly, motionless, like a wax figure. Beside her sat Countess Helena, the Presess' sister-in-law, regal and elegant. She wore a feathered hat, her impressive head adding an unmistakable lustre to the head table. It was she, and not Clara, who played the role of First Lady. On her other side sat her husband Joseph, the Presess' brother. Thin, straight, he held his aristocratic head high and stared at Clara.

About ten speeches had already been delivered, all in praise of Presess Rumkowski. "When can we call a man great? We can call him great from the moment when he begins to understand the small!" Herr Biederman of the Approvisation Department concluded his speech pathetically. Herr Schatten, dressed in a semi-military black uniform, looked sober today, and he delivered a soberly severe speech in German. He spoke about the behaviour of the ghetto populace. The Jews were attracting too much attention from the Germans; they failed to remove their caps on greeting the passing representatives of the authorities, and they were lazy at work, always looking for an opportunity to potter around and to steal. "That Jew who was recently hanged for stealing leather brought shame upon the entire ghetto and upon Presess Rumkowski as well!" Herr Schatten promised that he would do everything in his power to help the Presess transform the ghetto into a working camp without lazybones or swindlers.

When it was Presess Rumkowski's turn to reply to the speeches, he stood up and like a good psychologist announced, "My dear guests, I will not deliver my speech now, because these tables want to speak before I do. So I will keep my speech in my belly until you have all filled yours."

The crowd bellowed with laughter, then applauded energetically. Immediately, the chairs began to squeak as they were pushed closer to the tables. The Presess gave a sign to begin eating, and the next moment, the guests forgot both him and the rest of the world. The tables, set with all kinds of tasty foods, were so absorbing that they left no room for conversation. It was not that the guests, heaven forbid, arrived here starved. But even a *shishka* appreciated a tasty morsel of food as well as the business of eating in general. At length the visitors discreetly pushed away their plates of food, for which they could no longer find any room in their stomachs, and raised their heads to see where they found themselves. Suddenly everyone was heavy and drowsy.

The Presess stood up and raised his arms. "My dear guests," he began slowly, "A while ago you were too hungry, now I can see that you are too full to hear me out." The guests burst into a stormy laughter and tried to shake off their sleepiness. They hoped that the Presess would not deliver a long speech. "I will therefore not keep you long," the Presess guessed the general wish. "I only wish to announce, that I offer my best wishes to the Work Department, and I am giving every officer of the department an extra ration of half a kilogram of meat and half a kilogram of sausage." Bravos and cheers interrupted his words. He waited for the noise to subside before going on. "My friends, all of you who are assembled here. Each of you has in his own way helped me to keep the ghetto going. I know quite well that in helping me, each of you has also helped himself, but I have disregarded a great many of your trespasses, in consideration of the responsibility resting upon your shoulders, I mean the responsibility of not letting yourself be caught in *flagranti!*" The Presess laughed at his joke and the crowd laughed along dutifully, then applauded again. "But jokes aside, I am appealing to you and to your social conscience. In this present historic moment, let us all remember the duties with which Fate has entrusted us. Let us remember our people, brethren!" He raised his eyebrows dramatically. "It will not be much longer, my friends. The glorious hour is approaching. You all probably feel it as well as I. Let us brace ourselves. Let us be strong, and may we very soon leave this valley of tears. *Am Israel Chai!*"

The Presess received a standing ovation. The guests were again fully awake and talkative. They commented on the Presess' speech. If he could talk like that and be in such good spirits, then it must really be close to the twelfth hour.

A policeman appeared and whispered something in the Presess' ear. The Presess called over the Chief of Police who buttoned his jacket, adjusted his cuffs, put an expression of importance on his face and marched out of the garden along with the Presess. Immediately the crowd surrounded Zibert. "What's going on?" They pulled nervously at his coattails.

Zibert waved his hand, "Nothing special. A murder, that's all."

The guests first sighed with relief, then shrugged their shoulders in amazement. A murder in the ghetto? The women began to whisper among themselves, intrigued. The evening was now full of excitement and sensation. The guests considered it their duty to wait for the Presess' return, like children awaiting their father. Besides, they also had to wait for Zibert who had run out to catch up with the Presess.

It was Zibert who came back first and it was from him that the crowd learned about the sensational event. "Do you understand?" he began, his eyes fixed on the ladies in the crowd. "A girl of about fifteen, with a pair of shapely little legs and a head covered with gorgeous locks. And she was walking home from the bakery, the happiest girl in the world. Yes, imagine, my friends, the body of a fifteen-year-old, fresh, tasty, walking along Miodowa Street with a fresh tasty loaf of bread in her arms." Zibert's voice sounded mockingly romantic as he continued in a singsong. "And the air is as intoxicating as wine, the sky is as blue as . . . the girl's eyes. What passions such an enticing sight could awaken in one's heart! So . . . he was following her, hypnotized. Who? A twenty-year-old good-for-nothing, in three-quarter-length pants and a dirty shirt with holes at the elbows. Imagine, ladies, a pair of eyes black as night, burning and licking the princess and the bread as she tripped along Miodowa Street. His nostrils were full of the smell of bread, of the smell of her body . . . And so he followed the smell to the house and up the stairs. He was barefoot, so she did not hear or see him. She entered her room, leaving the door open, because, you understand, my friends, she was also intoxicated. She took a knife out of the drawer. She lived alone, you see; all of her relatives were taken during the *Sperre*, while she hid in a garret, because she thought that fifteen was too young to leave . . . So she was left with her life and with her loaf of bread. She sat down on her bed and due to her impatience did not even turn on the light. However, in the apartment across the corridor the lights were on and the door was open too. The light coming from there illuminated the girl like a projector. The fellow, our ragged hero, stood at the side of the door, gazing on her as she sat with the loaf of bread in her lap, ready to cut a slice for herself. He saw the saliva dripping from her hungry mouth, and the saliva began to drip from his as well. And then, my friends, he threw himself upon her, his hands on her round hips, on the round loaf. The girl lost her voice . . . but she hung on to the bread . . . to her life . . . to her loaf. So they wrestled over the bread. Until he grabbed the knife from her hand. He cut into the fresh loaf, into her fresh body. He then snatched the loaf with both hands, and in the room, beside the bed, devoured it entire. From the opposite apartment a woman peered inside the room, surprised at the scene. She was so surprised that she began to scream and so the police were called, and that is the end of the story."

The guests listened to Zibert's tale open-mouthed. Little shudders crept down their spines. The women wiped their eyes. The men lit cigarettes.

✦ ✦ ✦

Clara was eating breakfast alone. A new commission was supposed to visit the ghetto to find the appropriate buildings for the ammunition factories, and the Presess had left early to look over some buildings by himself, in order to form an idea of which buildings to suggest. Clara ate without great appetite. She had not been feeling well lately. The doctor had been unable to find anything wrong with her and had finally concluded that all her complaints had a "nervous basis". This, however, did not make her feel better. But she would not give in to her symptoms, and insisted on continuing with her activities. She was taking care of the children who had been saved during the *Sperre* and were now working at the Resorts. Today she had a bag full of candies to hand out to the children at the Tailor Resort.

This particular Tailor Resort consisted only of child-workers. They were registered as adults and were producing like adults. They worked at the sewing machines and did all the necessary handwork. Clara walked from one child to the next with her gift of four candies per child. She saw the corners of their mouths water, the tips of their tongues pass over their lips. They thanked her, quickly pocketed the candies and picked up their work. Clara respected these little adults.

She knew about the illegal schools which had been organized for them in the cellars and garrets of the factories. During certain hours, they would disappear in groups according to their real ages and attend classes. She would have gladly helped out with these activities. But she was not officially allowed to know about the classes and had to content herself with the information provided by Zibert, who helped out in the illegal School Department. And so she learned that the children had created a mutual aid society with a communal bank which gave out loans to those of them who were family providers. She learned about the committee whose members visited their sick comrades and helped out with home duties when necessary. She also found out that, just like the grown-ups, they were divided into political factions and carried on heated discussions among themselves. But in contrast to the adults, Zibert told her, the children made no plans for after the war, nor did they "make order in the world". For they barely had an idea about the world. Politics was a game to them. They were hungry for games.

Before Clara had managed to empty the bag, she noticed that the children suddenly became unusually noisy; their eyes made joyful somersaults in all directions. Then a youngster blurted out, "Mussolini has fallen!"

She hurried to bring the news to the Presess. The Presess received her in his office with an unpleasant growl, "Let us first be finished with the commission," he said. "The Germans want the Church for an ammunition factory and the Feather Resort will have to move." He sent Clara off and called in Zibert. He inquired about the radio communiqués, about which he had already heard from his brother. Zibert told him that the Germans themselves had declared that they had given up Orel on the Eastern Front and Catania in Sicily. Where was Orel? Where was Sicily? The Presess had not seen a map for a long time, but today he had to know the location of these places and especially how far away they were from the ghetto. He felt increasingly like an exhausted messenger who had to deliver a treasure and yet could barely keep on his feet. Zibert promised to bring him a map.

These days the Presess was feeling particularly united with the people. He reacted like a seismograph to the moods, to the fevers of the ghetto, which was like a hysterical woman, capable of moving in the blink of an eye from tears to laughter; the ghetto could, from the heights of enthusiasm and exultation, plunge into the deepest pits of fear and despair.

At first, the people excitedly congratulated each other on the good news. They shook hands in the streets and ran gaily to the Resorts. Until the question arose: "What will happen to us?" Rumours were buzzing from Resort to Resort, from street to street. Nerves were taut. Patience hung by a hair. Everything was turning in a dizzying whirl. Ripe summer beamed at the world with its warm light; but the sunshine irritated the people even more. Its light was confusing. The nights were agonizing. Memories of the *Sperre* returned, stifling the bodies with horror. The ghetto was like a narrow cage, swarming with creatures who were awaiting their sentence.

Until one night the tension burst. There was a knocking at many doors. Many people were taken from their beds. That night too the Presess slept with his clothes on. Lately, every demand to provide a certain number of people for deportation cut into his heart like a razor blade. Now that the war was so near the end, each life seemed more precious, the German demands more arrogant, his own remorse greater than ever before. The Presess wandered about his dining room, surrounded by the walls covered with portraits of himself. Clara was awake with him. Her sick twisted face irritated him. He could not bear the sight of her.

Finally, he sent her back to bed and began to pace the room more freely. In order to avoid the sight of the clock, he put out the light and opened the window. The garden emitted the sweet aroma of ripe fruits. The smell irritated the Presess. From distant streets came the sound of talking, of wailing. He could hear hurried steps ... people running ... The thin sound of whistles cut through the air. The Presess dipped both hands into his mop of hair, combing it over and over. Then he put his hands on the window sill, as if he were about to deliver a speech. The trees stood like a crowd of listeners. "I am Mordecai Chaim Rumkowski," he sighed as if introducing himself to the trees. Above hung the clownish face of the cock-eyed moon, with a slice of cloud over it, like the crooked visor of a cap. A policeman's whistle shrieked in the distance. It drilled into his heart. He was unable to bear the tension any longer. He had no strength. His old tired feet were about to give out under him. He raised his creased face to the moon, "God, what do you want of me?" The roguish, mocking eyes of the moon blinked at him. In his loneliness, the Presess tried to call back his strength, his stubbornness. "Persevere! You have put up with it for so long, hold on for a little while longer!" He clenched his fists.

He had never been a thinker and hated digging into himself. He was still certain of one thing: he was here to accomplish a mission. It was not for him to question or rebel against fate. He heard the call of destiny within him and he followed it blindly. It was the only commander to whom he submitted — just like Moses. Then what sense did it make to ask one's heart: What do you feel? To ask one's tired body: What do you want? Mordecai Chaim used them like tools. They had to help him follow his will. And if they fulfilled their duties, the moment of redemption could not fail to arrive. He, Mordecai Chaim Rumkowski, would leave a trace behind him. He would not perish like the nameless hundreds and thousands. He would be like a star beaming its light upon the sky of eternity. This was still important to him.

In order to accomplish his mission on behalf of his people, he had to be wise and use his body, his tired servant, with understanding, the Presess concluded. He had lately neglected his health, and it showed. He would go to sleep now. He would achieve nothing by thinking of the thousand people who had to be rounded up tonight. He still had seventy thousand working Jews at his disposal. He had ordered the sick, the hopeless, the tubercular, the *klepsydras* to be taken, and to make up the balance: the men and women who lived alone, without families, in order not to lower the morale and to avoid lamentations and tears. He felt an affinity with those who were leaving. That was their destiny — to be a sacrifice for the sake of those who remained, just as it was his destiny to save those who remained. His neck too was exposed to the German knife. Now that all the Jewish leaders of the ghettos were gone, his turn was at hand.

Still, he could not go to bed. He was not in a frame of mind conducive to caring for his health. He remembered that he had a little bottle of schnapps in a drawer and he took a sip from it. The warmth spread over him. He looked around the room which was washed by the pale metallic moonlight. From the portraits, his own face looked down at him. "I am Mordecai Chaim Rumkowski, the guardian of the people," each face introduced itself proudly.

The moon was grinning in the window. "It's a lie!" it squinted roguishly. "The real Mordecai Chaim Rumkowski is paying with other lives the price for his own senile existence!" Mordecai Chaim removed his glasses and wiped his hazy drunken eyes with a trembling hand. He would go to bed to spite the moon which wanted to destroy him, to spite all the forces that were out to erase him from the face of the earth. He would sleep a calm healthy sleep.

He heard a noise in the garden. Someone was snapping twigs and whispering. He realized that the policeman on guard at the gate was squabbling with an intruder. Rumkowski leaned out through the window and immediately noticed the policeman's cap. He also saw the figure of a woman.

"Herr Presess," the policeman saluted. "She says that she is your ward. She fought with me. The transport is leaving within two hours."

The woman leaped towards the wall and raised her head. Her red hair glittered in the moonlight. "I am your ward, Herr Presess! My name is Esther!" she called out. "You must not send me away, Herr Presess!"

He recognized her; he still remembered her red head when so many other heads had vanished from his memory. Was it indeed he who was sending her away? That was impossible. That was folly. He winced with grief. "Are you on the list?" he leaned out to her, like a judge leaning over his bench to see a defendant.

"Yes, because I am alone. I escaped during the raid. They are waiting for me outside the fence. I am young and healthy, Herr Presess. I am a good worker!"

He looked down at her. She was young and healthy. Her figure was slim and graceful, her head on fire. In the light of the moon she possessed an unearthly beauty; a beauty which increased the pain in his body and soul. Once, in the past, she had sat in his office, also demanding something from him. In the past he had sent for her, and she had not come. Had he punished her then? Should he punish her now? His legs began to shake. He felt dizzy. "Get out of here!" he groaned. "Get out! To the transport!"

Her face looked like a block of hard cold marble. "Why me?" he heard her stammer. "I am the last of an entire family!"

"That's exactly why!" he heard his own voice say. "So that there will be no one to mourn you."

"I am the last . . . the last . . ."

"Take her away!" The Presess ordered the policeman.

The policeman, also moved by the woman's beauty and the scene in front of the window, stepped towards Esther. But she jumped aside, spitting in the Presess' direction. "Murderer!" she cried.

The policeman pulled her to the gate. Outside, two other policeman took hold of her. From the way that they were leading her off, the Presess judged that they would release her and let her escape. She was too beautiful. The fellows could not allow her to leave with the transport. Mordecai Chaim felt a lump in his throat as he imagined what the Germans did to such beauties . . . what they did in general.

He decided to avoid facing the deportees at any cost. It was not good for him. He had felt the same way during the *Sperre*, watching the children of his orphanage depart. He would severely punish any policeman who allowed anyone to enter this garden. "Murderer!" the girl had called him, spitting in his face. He did not feel offended. He knew he was a murderer, although he had not committed any murder. His hands were soaked in blood, although he had not spilled any. He had taken death for a partner in order to save lives. It was a difficult, unbearable task. But that was how it had to be.

Esther's face refused to vanish from his mind. It haunted him, tortured him. Her body had been created for hands to caress. Her green eyes, the fire of her hair had been created to be adored. Even now, in his old age, Mordecai Chaim was still quite capable of appreciating a woman's qualities. Esther was the embodiment of femininity, of life itself. He was grateful to the policemen who would release her. She was his ward, his child. He was filled with fatherly pride. It had been he who had raised that flower in his garden. Suddenly, he became frightened. And what if the policemen had led her off to the transport, after all? "Let them!" the moon blinked at him. "She called you a murderer. If you let her live, she will become your prosecutor, your Angel of Death." Rumkowski leaned out of the window and called the policeman on guard. "The girl, the one who was here, run after them and tell them to free her right away!" To assure himself that his command would be followed, he wrote a note.

He sighed deeply with relief. He felt as if he had just saved an entire transport from deportation. He stepped out into the garden. The soil smelled sweetly. The trees were rustling. The moon now seemed distant; it had lost the resemblance to a human face. Rumkowski noticed another moon, a closer one: Clara's face in the bedroom window. Her mouth looked like that of a corpse. A cold wave surged down his limbs at the sight of her figure clad in the white nightgown. She stretched out her hand to him, the white waxen hand of death.

"You did well, Mordecai Chaim," he heard her say. Then she added, "But do you realize that someone else will have to go instead of her?"

In order to escape Clara he went out into the street. There he met the policeman who was returning from the place of assembly. "She ran away, Herr Presess!" The policeman saluted.

Rumkowski felt like smiling, but instead, he puckered his eyebrows and commanded severely, "Fetch the policemen who led her off. Go! That's an order!"

In the morning a murmur passed through the ghetto: a thousand people had been taken during the night. The ghetto felt like a body from which leeches had sucked blood and relieved the tension. The people put themselves back on their feet. The war was about to end and it was summer. One fine day they would get up in the morning and it would all be over. In the meantime, they had to survive the day. They had to concentrate on the given moment and not think of anything else, so that the liberation would be a surprise. They pretended not to await it and went about their daily business, so as not to scare it off. Yet it was difficult to carry on with that kind of game. The longing for freedom was so strong that they had to betray it. And again the ghetto inhabitants allowed themselves to be thrown from laughter to tears, from tears to laughter.

Presess Rumkowski's moods were no different. His body shrank from day to day and he could not move about without his walking stick. Thus he rushed from one Resort to the other, trembling over the ghetto, as if it were a house of cards. He no longer delivered hopeful speeches. He was reproachful, admonishing the people and waving his stick, "Remember, you lazybones, you crooks, that you may bring a calamity down on our heads with your behaviour. You must work and not play at politics! Work is our passport to life. Don't forget that, you loafers! The ghetto must tick like a clock!"

The workers of the Corset Resort had assembled to listen to the Presess' speech. He was standing on top of a box with a sea of dishevelled faded female hair in front of him. But then he noticed one colourful splotch in the sea of colourlessness: a fiery red. He did not recognize the face from the distance, yet he was sure he knew whose it was. After his speech, he cleared a way to the woman, with his stick.

"You!" he called out. "Your name is Esther . . ."

"Yes, Herr Presess," she replied loudly, in a cold rusty voice, while he wished that her voice were as warm as the colour of her hair.

"What are you doing here?" he asked angrily, because she was not about to thank him . . . because she was not beautiful at all. That memorable night had transformed her into a beauty. In reality her face was yellow, freckled, smeared with dirt and sweat. Her green eyes seemed extinguished, her cheeks hollow. She was as thin as a stick. Only the snarls of her hair seemed to blossom, burning his eyes with their spiteful devouring fire.

"I work here," she replied.

He did not know what to say to that and he asked more composedly, "You're one of my orphans, aren't you?" That was a silly question. Did he not know who she was?

"All the Jews are your orphans," she shot back, and the extinguished eyes of the women around her lit up playfully. He could not make up his mind whether to be satisfied with her answer or not; whether to smile and give her an extra ration, or to chastise her.

On his way back, sitting in his coach he thought about her. He was sure that he could never win her over and that she would never forgive him, although thanks to him, she was still alive. He stopped at another Resort and scrambled down from the coach, tired, his body limp. He leaned heavily against his stick, his friend, his support; unlike other friends it did not torment him.

In the evening he sent for Zibert, without whom he could no longer manage. "Tell me," he turned his creased face to him. "Why do they all hate me so?"

Zibert blinked his small eyes mischievously, "Laugh it off, Presess. It is not you they hate. Through you they hate the Germans. You are the mask upon the Nazis' face. Don't hold it against me for telling you. Now that the game is almost over, it would be worthwhile for you to step aside a bit, so that the ugly German face can become more visible. Then they will love you more and hate them more."

Chapter Nineteen

EVERY DAY ESTHER vowed that she would move into another place. So many apartments now stoood empty. But every evening she came home exhausted and had no energy to put her plans into action. She was also aware that escaping the garret where she was constantly reminded of Aunt Rivka and her family would not help her escape the fear to which she had surrendered. She would lie in her bed, the cover pulled up over her chin, and tremble. She heard the sound of policemen's boots coming closer and closer. Over and over again she imagined that they had come to fetch her . . . until sleep overcame her.

All the lights within her soul were extinguished, except for one thin flickering flame; the flame of being, of existing. Weak and forlorn though she was, she was still capable of turning herself into a lioness in order to protect that little flame. How much strength had she possessed to wrestle with the policemen who had caught her! It was as if she were not one worn-out woman, but an army of ogresses.

She was not sick, had no swollen legs, no decalcification of the bones, no weak heart. The problem was only that within her something was withering. It hardly ever crossed her mind that she had once been a communist, a social activist. She was estranged from her comrades, from her co-workers at the Resort, from people in general. Her loneliness did not bother her, yet walking home from work sometimes took her hours. She dragged herself through the streets, turning into side-streets, or placing herself in a queue which she saw on her way.

One day as she was roaming the streets, she met Vladimir Winter in his flowing cape, with the painter's cardboard sheets under his arm. He still moved quite vigorously on his feet. He jumped towards her and snatched her hands between his long cold fingers. His hot gaze pierced through her as if seeking a spark of life in the extinguished green of her eyes. "Why don't you come to see me?" he whispered nervously. "I am not mad at you for having run away from me during the *Sperre*, I assure you. You look so pale . . ."

"Will you give me a piece of bread?" she asked.

"Oho!" he hooted enthusiastically. "I'll give you bread with sausage! Don't you remember anything?"

"How often?" she asked.

"What do you mean, how often? Whenever you come. I'll share with you. You can be present at the literary meetings if you want to. It has become a fine circle of artists. We meet every Saturday night. There are new talents . . . Great works are being read and discussed. You could sing for us . . ." She left him in the middle of the sentence and walked away.

It was the first of September. The fourth anniversary of the war. Esther sat in the Resort bent over her work, repeating in her mind: four years . . . four years. She could not grasp how four years could seem so long. She tried to remember what had happened during those four years, but was unable to. On her way home she heard people remind each other of today's date, so she again strained her memory. At Baluter Ring the wind was sweeping the sand, ruffling the huge swastika flags hanging above the barracks. There, behind the fence, in the windows of the *Ghettoverwaltung* the lights were already lit. Before the gate stood a German guard with a gun. She recalled that she had found herself a few times before that gate. Once she had even succeeded in seeing Rumkowski; she did not recall on what occasion. Further on she saw a queue in front of a co-operative and she went over to inquire what it was for.

"Fly catchers! Two to a head!" Someone informed her. "All summer when the flies were swarming, they would not give them out, but now that winter is approaching they provide you with fly catchers."

When she arrived at her street a woman neighbour, also on her way home from work, got hold of her. The woman considered it her duty to give Esther an account of all the news she had heard throughout the day.

"And do you know that fifty consumptives have been taken from the hospital again?" As she talked, her canteen and spoon clanked. "And do you know what happened to the people taken during the *Sperre*? Have you heard of a place called Chelmno? I heard of it for the first time today, and may I never hear of it again. They say that all the Jews from Lodz were finished off there. And they say that in the vicinity of Cracow there is another place . . . may our eyes never see it. And as you see me here, I would spit in the face of all who spread that kind of story. It is clear as day that the *Yekes* are letting out such rumours on purpose, so that we keep quiet and shake with fear as if we had malaria. I myself know from a reliable source that all those who left with the *Sperre* are safe in German camps and have enough of everything. The children and the old people are in Switzerland, under the supervision of the Red Cross, and may we all be liberated as truly as I've heard of people who are receiving postcards from there. As you see me here, I hope and believe that I will soon receive such a card myself, with news of my children, written by a nurse in Switzerland, because my children can't write yet . . ."

Scattered clouds raced through the sky and the evening cold rose from the ground. Esther put up the collar of her coat as if to protect herself not only against the cold but also against the woman's talk. She turned to go home, but could not summon the strength to climb up to her garret. She took leave of the neighbour and continued her stroll. She tightened the belt of her coat, pulled the canteen handle up her arm and put her hands into her pockets.

She felt a hand slide under her arm, press it tightly and pull her forward. Before she could manage to turn her head, she heard a voice whisper in her ear, "Come quick, don't look around!" She remained facing forward, but caught a glimpse of a face through the corner of her eye. The voice whispered, "Let's turn left into a gate." Once inside the gate, she turned her head and scrutinized the stranger. She wanted to ask him where he was taking her, but they were moving too quickly. Her heart pounded. The stranger's nervousness made her whole body shake. He was dragging her along, practically carrying her off with him, his fingers tightly pressed around her arm. At length, she could no longer take it. She lagged behind, her feet stumbling. The voice nagged at her, "Hurry . . . do me a favour and hurry . . . they're following me."

She raised her eyebrows. A memory stirred in her mind. Her eyes lit up with the recollection of familiar features. A snowy first of May . . . "Hersh . . . Hersh . . ." a name beat against her trembling heart. She no longer minded hurrying on; she abandoned herself to the strength of the man's hand and allowed herself to be dragged through the backyards. But now she did not take her eyes off him. She saw his wrinkled forehead shining with sweat, his lips pressed together, his gaze restless. She had not absorbed the sight of a face in such a manner for a long time. Who could the man be? At the moment that was not important. What was important was that she had a purpose — his purpose.

Finally, he relaxed his steps and looked back less often. Their walking arm-in-arm became pleasant. It was delightful to lean one's head against a man's shoulder. Her memory flipped through images of the past, until it halted for a moment in the vanished eternity, to recall a little bottle of perfume someone had offered her in her room on Hockel Street . . . a pair of adoring eyes following her every time that she passed the yard. These were not the same eyes, not the same face. The stranger had for no reason at all brought the recollection back from oblivion.

They stopped at a street corner. "Thank you," he said. "A stool pigeon of the Gestapo has been following me for the last two hours." He was about to leave her, when he cast another glance at her. Suddenly he caught himself, "It's you!" he exclaimed. "Chaim the Hosiery-Maker's niece, aren't you? Your name is . . ."

"Esther," she helped him out. "And you are Itche Mayer the Carpenter's son!" she now remembered him without difficulty.

"Yes, I'm Israel." He shook her hand energetically, "Thank you very much."

She felt all the bones in her fingers soften under his handshake and wished it could last forever. Another image came to her mind. She was standing in front of the locked gate on Hockel Street; it was before the ghetto had been established, after her Uncle Chaim and all the inhabitants of the street had been led away. Israel had been standing there too, and she had been unable to let go of him, just like now.

"Where are you going?" she asked. "Maybe I should still walk on with you for a bit . . . It would be safer."

He looked around in the street and waved his hand, "It's getting late. I'm sleeping over on the other side of the bridge."

"On the other side of the bridge! You can't cross the bridge now. Look!" she pointed to the empty bridge in the distance.

"That's not good," he rubbed his forehead.

She gathered her courage and this time she took hold of his arm and pulled him along, at first slowly, then with increasing haste. "Why is the Gestapo looking for you?" she asked, trying to distract him.

He let her drag him along. Suddenly he asked, "Perhaps you know of an empty flat . . . where I could sleep over? In case the stool pigeon is still keeping an eye on me. I can't endanger my comrades."

"Yes, I do know of an empty flat, in my house." She stared at his tired face, at the wrinkles around his mouth. He was not much taller than herself, yet he seemed tall and powerful; he seemed to fill the entire street. A sudden wish entered her head: to hold him in her arms like a child.

When they arrived at her shed, he asked, "You live here, don't you?" He seemed to be reading her secret thoughts. "Alone?"

"Alone," she replied.

She admired the brightness of his bluish, almost childlike eyes. She invited him to sit down in the only chair she owned and sat down across from him on the bed. They avoided looking at each other and did not even try to converse. In their uneasiness, they began to smile, not at each other, but rather past each other, a silly shy smile. Finally, he put an end to it. "Are you inviting me to sleep over here?"

"I invite you to have supper with me."

He jumped to his feet, "Out of the question!"

She jumped to her feet as well, "I have potato peelings . . . a lot of them. I beg you . . ."

He impatiently began to pace the floor of the shed. She rushed to the "cannon" stove and looked inside it. Then she had an idea. "If you want to," she proposed, "You can light the fire in the stove in the meantime, so that it'll be ready faster." She pointed to the bits of wood and the few peat balls on the floor. He silently approached the stove and finally took off his blazer. She cut the potato peels into a pot. She felt weak in her limbs; something was waking within her and she barely had the strength for it.

"Do you keep your window covered during the day too?" Israel asked as he lit the stove. "It looks as if you had no window."

"Who needs a window?" She shot a sideways glance at him. "Also, I'm too lazy to remove the blackout cover and then put it back on." He cleaned his hands and approached the windows to remove the cover. She ran over to him. "Don't do it. The light will shine through."

"You're easily frightened," he said, taking his blazer and turning to the door. "Goodnight and thanks again."

She blocked his way and stared at him imploringly. "The food will soon be ready." She hung on to his arm. "I swear to you that I am not frightened. Come, help me move the table to the bed. Take the chair," she ordered, and he took the chair. She asked him to sit down. The pot on the stove was boiling. They sat at the table and listened to it, the empty table top separating them, silent expectation hanging like a cloud between them.

Soon the soup of potato peels and parsley leaves stood in bowls before them. They ate hurriedly. It became unbearable to sit opposite each other. Israel's face turned stony. Esther knew that he was only sitting with her out of gratitude or politeness, that he was at this moment wondering about how to leave without hurting her too much. She was grateful to him for his consideration. She quickly removed the bowls from the table, put out the light and pulled the cover down from the window, opening it wide. The wind swayed the casements and blew in her face. The pond behind the brick kiln on the other side of the barbed-wire fence was silvery pale. In the distance the outlines of the cemetery tombstones cut into the horrizon. Further on, a dark forest marked the sky like a thick black line of a pencil.

Israel stood beside her. "You have a nice view," he said. "What frightens you here?"

"How do you know that something frightens me?" she asked.

"I know."

"There," she pointed. "In the brick kiln there is something going on every night, or perhaps . . . perhaps it is in the cemetery. I hear screams, sobs. Sometimes I hear it from very close, almost from under the window." It was pleasant to pull out the threads of fear which had lain knotted within her for so long. "Sometimes, at night," she went on, "I cannot take it. I jump out of bed and want to run somewhere . . . Then I hear bootsteps on the stairs and I feel trapped. I've spent more than one night sitting fully dressed on the bed. And when I fall asleep I hear whistles. The police are after me, I think. You should understand that . . . You must know . . ."

"Tonight no one will come," he said in a voice as clear as his eyes.

"Tonight I am not afraid," she assured him.

In his honour, she decided to make pancakes out of coffee dregs. She asked him to cover the window and put on the light. This time when they faced each other across the table, the distance between them seemed smaller. Something had been dissolved and untied. They ate the hot pancakes and sipped the hot coffee. It seemed to Esther that Israel was smiling into his cup. Keeping her eyes buried in her cup, she said, "You're laughing at me."

"I am laughing to you," he said. "I am glad that we met."

He wanted to sleep on the floor of the attic. She told him that she had had another bed and more mattresses when Uncle Chaim's family had lived with her, and that she had burnt everything but her own bed. And she invited him into her bed.

The window was open. The wind played with its wings, rocking them on their squeaking hinges. The narrow bed was uncomfortable. Their unfamiliar limbs tried to move away from each other as far as possible, but the bed would not allow it. They wanted to sleep, but sleep would not come. There was a noise between them. They wanted to exchange a few words, but did not know what to say. They smiled in the dark, until they were no longer capable of holding back, and burst into laughter. Their laughter made their bodies move, bringing together Esther's head with Israel's shoulder, her waist and his arms, her cheeks with his, her mouth and his.

At some point during the night, she told him about Hersh, about Valentino. At some other point he told her about Faigie, his wife, and his daughter Masha. He also told her that his brother Yossi with his wife and child had been caught in the street during a raid last February, and that he, Israel, was, like Esther, all alone in the ghetto. Inside them something simultaneously wept and was jubilant.

"Don't leave me alone," Esther whispered.

"I won't leave you alone," he promised.

"It's all over anyway."

"It's not over yet. But I won't leave you alone."

"We will perish."

"We will live."

After that night, they did not seek words to clarify their situation or their feelings. Things were as they were. Israel did not always sleep over with Esther. He often disappeared for nights in a row and his disappearance brought back Esther's moods of the past, when she had lived with Hersh. Just like Hersh, Israel was guarding a secret which she had guessed. And she also guessed that Israel was an opponent. Yet it was precisely this opponent who revived her interest in her own party. Her acquaintance with him began to straighten everything out within her, not only mentally but also physically. The yellowness in her face vanished. Her eyes acquired a lively sparkle. She needed a mirror again and she found it amongst her things. She again began to make herself pretty every day after work. And she kept her window open, so that she could look out for Israel.

Israel's belongings consisted of a knapsack containing a few articles of clothing and his food cards. Esther began to wash his shirts and mend his socks. She took out the food rations for two and now when she queued up, it was not in order to be with people, but for a purpose. She no longer had ample time. She was important. She had a family.

Israel proposed that they move out of the shed and find a better room for themselves. She shrugged her shoulders, "It's not worthwhile." She looked into Israel's eyes, enjoying the sight of her own reflection. In his eyes she could see herself grow and blossom. And she noticed that he was surprised at the change in her. She explained, "I am like a flower which is incapable of living without water . . . I could die without love . . . I mean really die. When love vanishes from my heart everything disintegrates within me, everything withers . . ."

When Israel slept at home, they left for work together, Esther for her Resort, he for his. They exchanged half-words, broken sentences, and Esther did not mind, that quite often Israel did not hear a word she was saying as he walked, his brow wrinkled, steeped in distant thoughts. Yet her hand was cradled securely in his and the conversation of their fingers was vital.

She worked diligently at the Resort. Her hands were quick, her feet strong, her head light. Her thoughts, carried by the rhythm of the machines, tormented her with nagging silly wishes impossible to fulfil; sinful wishes which had never in the ghetto, never in her life been as powerful as now. She wanted to have a child. She had savoured so many tastes of life, she wanted still to savour only that one; she had to. Often, sitting at the machine, she would fantasize how it would be to have the two things together: freedom and a child. It was a simple wish, yet arrogant, as if she wanted too much. Tears lit up her smiling face as she bent over the sewing machine. She would not be able to bear such happiness. It would be beyond her. Her heart would burst with joy. Along with her fantasies, she was overcome by a wild craving for food.

More than once when she was thus steeped in thought, would she hear the buzzing of voices around her. Words, whispers reached her ear. Her friends were again spreading news about lists. Who would have to leave this time? Of course those who lived alone, with no family ties, with no one to mourn them or shed a tear for them. Esther accelerated the speed of her machine. She wanted its humming to blot out what she heard. It was all a lie, a figment of someone's imagination.

The pile of pink corsets grew on the box beside her. Every time she shook a finished corset to rid it of the loose threads, she raged at the thought of the women who tied themselves up in such garments. She did not think with words, yet her heart was full of curses. She would look around the hall and see pink corsets for thousands of fat German bodies. They laced themselves up with cords of hatred, Esther thought, with the curses which, through the bony fingers of those who shaped these garments, penetrated every stitch, every pore of the material. She felt that every stitch she made was full of poison, and she visualized the poison pouring into the pores of female skin. She saw that skin come in touch with the skin of German officers, generals. She saw the poison contaminate their male bodies, destroying their seed. It seemed strange that the Germans were afraid only of sabotage and not of that other Jewish weapon: the curse permeating the uniforms, the dresses, the coats and shoes which the ghetto produced. She was sure that wherever the products of Jewish hands reached, they accomplished a secret mission — to destroy the users, to haunt them to their graves. She wanted the curse to take effect right away. She had no patience. People were again talking about lists . . . and she still wanted to savour the taste of being a mother.

When she experienced these moments of powerful hatred, she would begin to sing and the girls at the machines would pick up the tune. Their voices were defiant, stubborn. The machines hummed along with them. Esther was not particular about her songs. Revolutionary songs and love songs, lullabies and humorous folk-songs followed one another. But all of these well-known songs sounded different here, filled with new content, new meaning. Thus the singalong would go on for an hour or two, until suddenly the thought of lists would again begin to peck at the women's hearts. The songs which had sounded so powerful and free, now died away. A screaming silence would inundate the hall. The machines stopped for a while, as one girl stealthily observed the other. None of them needed corsets. On the contrary, their protruding bones needed a lot of flesh to round them out. Which of the girls would be missing tomorrow? Whose machine would be silenced tomorrow? And after tomorrow, the corsets produced by those missing hands would be laced around living bodies.

It was difficult to bear such a moment for too long, and just as the overflow of joy could lead to tears, so could the overflow of despair lead to laughter. Freida, "the goat" could not bear the mood of gloom and doom, and, with her jokes and tricks, she steered the hall out of its heavy mood, as one steers a boat out of a whirlpool. The bells of Fate were tolling for someone, perhaps even for herself, but at that moment the sound of laughter deafened them.

Fate. Although Esther had become a communist again, she had created an uncommunistic theory for herself. She believed that the fateful incident was the main shaper of human life and that this was a force against which there was no use fighting. What, after all, had each important event in her life been, if not an accident? Had it not been an accident that Israel had taken her by the arm in the street? And how that fact had influenced her life! Or, for instance, the physical beauty with which she had been endowed by Fate. Would she ever have had anything to do with Schatten, or even with Winter, if not for her beauty? And how often had she cursed that beauty precisely because it had put her life in danger.

On her way home from the Resort, she often met the neighbour who kept her informed about all the rumours. "I have a nephew at the Metal Resort who heard from a reliable source that an inquiry from Berlin asked Biebow how many wagons would be needed to transport all the Jews of Lodz, with the machines and everything else, to a town not far from Lublin. So Biebow has apparently replied that at least six thousand wagons would be needed for that purpose. So my nephew, who is not stupid, says that six thousand would not be enough and that the whole thing does not make sense. Because where will the Germans get six thousand wagons nowadays, if they need all they have for their army? And why to Lublin, of all places, which is closer to the Russian front than Lodz? Be that as it may, it's a strange story, and either it is a sign for the better, or heaven forbid, for the worse."

Esther listened to the woman's talk, evoking Israel's features in her mind, evoking his face which she was leaning to read by heart. This helped her tell the woman that she should not worry. She climbed up to their room and waited for him, praying that he would spend the night with her.

The next day at the Resort resembled the day before it. Again the sudden changes of mood to the accompaniment of the machines. Again a song awakened by the will to persevere and the thirst for vengeance. Again restlessness, nagging fear, sudden silence, and then — laughter.

The machines were humming, while the hands ran ahead, shoving the pink material under the needles. The machine's wheels were turning . . . unscrewing memories . . . the reflection of an image . . . Once, so long ago, at the very beginning, a mother sat, turning a little wheel, her feet stepping back and forth under the sewing machine. A tiny girl crawled on the floor, then looked up. Up high, there was the mother's face shining like a sun with the promise of happiness. And now that mother was again sitting at a machine, and the tiny girl, not yet born, was looking up from the floor, crawling somewhere nearby . . . somewhere far away; the unborn little girl's face: a sun, a promise of happiness. The entire floor of the hall, if not the entire earth, was full of expectation.

As soon as she arrived home, Esther took a basin full of greenish-red beet leaves and went down to the water pump to wash them. There was a commotion all around her. Other neighbours were also washing their vegetables. The sky was gray. From far away there came the sound of something roaring. The neighbours raised their heads. A formation of airplanes sawed the air. They came down so low that one could see the swastikas on their wings.

"They're heading East," a neighbour remarked.

As soon as the airplanes had swept over, Esther cupped her hands and took a drink of water from the pump. She sipped it and watched the water run through her fingers. She made herself a sign. If she could manage to take three more sips before the water ran out through her fingers, Israel would come to spend the night with her. She succeeded, and quickly wiped her face and her hair with her wet hands; like a satisfied young hen she shook off the drops and grabbed the basin with the swollen leaves. Upstairs, she busied herself cleaning the room, cooking, making herself pretty.

She was in the middle of combing her hair when she heard a sound. Israel's steps were coming up the stairs. She had known that he would come. She turned to him as he entered. Afraid that he might read too much joy in her face, she immediately turned it away. As she was absorbed in setting the table, Israel took her in his arms; his dirty unshaven face smelled of sweat. She wished to stay in his arms forever, but she pushed him away.

He took the empty pails and vanished. She heard the pails clinking on the stairs like bells. She hurried to the mirror to finish combing her hair and stared into the reflection of her smiling eyes. She wanted to look beautiful, to be beautiful. She wanted Israel to tell her that she was beautiful. He had never told her that. Her beauty seemed to be of no importance to him. She had thought that she would like that, but instead, doubt gnawed at her heart. Perhaps he did not like her? Perhaps she was not beautiful enough for him? Perhaps she should find out in which dress he liked her best?

Israel returned with the pails full of water and removed his wind-breaker and shirt. She filled a basin with water for him and watched him wash. His shiny wet skin told her of his strength, although his shoulders were slumped, his spine and the shoulder blades bony, protruding. He was not tall, but in her eyes he seemed like a giant, almost as tall as Valentino. Yes, when she looked at Israel's hairy chest, that bulky fellow with the curly black mop of hair, with the burning gipsy eyes that had charmed her, came to her mind. The two men were so different and yet so much alike. The closer Esther felt to Israel, the closer she felt to Valentino, the closer she felt to all the men in her life. It seemed to her that all that she had felt for them had been poured over into a new form, in her attachment to Israel, like precious wine in a new container.

At the table, they looked at each other for a moment before they lowered their eyes to their bowls. Esther sipped slowly, asking herself whether Israel's face were not more serious today than usual. She was still orienting herself to his moods with difficulty. After all, he had not once smiled at her since he had entered the room. Actually he had not yet uttered a word. She realized that he was not eating, but was looking at her, his eyes clear and yet solemn. She saw the two deep furrows in his cheeks, reaching down from his nose towards the corners of his mouth; his forehead was creased by two parallel lines. His wet hair, which was beginning to dry, fell in strands shot through with heavy lines of gray.

"Why don't you eat? What are you waiting for?" she asked. "Do you see how thick the soup is? The spoon can stand upright in it." What a difficult talker he was! She had no idea how to strike up a conversation with him. Why was he not eating? Didn't he like her cooking? Was he not hungry? Why did he not take his serious eyes off her? She sipped in his gaze along with the spoonfuls of soup. She took a beet leaf on her spoon. "Beet leaves are good," she said invitingly.

The two sharp lines linked above his eyebrows. He pressed his jaws together and stretched out his hand, covering hers. "Lists are being compiled," he said.

She asked indifferently, "Of whom? Those who are single?" She had no reason to fear. This time she was not meant. She was not single. She had a family, a home, established in a time when homes were being destroyed, and because of that, all the more sacred. And she also had someone to mourn her. He, the man with the creased face, the stingy talker who sat opposite her, would ache after her. She did not need him to tell her that. She knew it.

At that moment, a strange inexplicable smile appeared on his face. "I think that we should get married," he said.

She laughed brokenly, "We?" The room began to sway before her eyes. She understood. They were in danger.

He sat down beside her on the bed. "What do you say?"

She nodded. He was right. They had to announce to the world that they were lonely no more. This had to be fixed in the ghetto books, where names were being crossed out. She freed herself from his embrace and stood up to clean the table. Her hands shook, her fingers tangled in the tablecloth. A bowl slipped out of her hand. She heard Israel's voice following the sound of broken glass, "*Mazal-tov!*" Her head was swimming. Israel stood beside her and wrapped her in his arms. He raised her chin with his hand. The bright green of her eyes shone at him.

"*Mazal-tov*, my bride." For a moment he put his forehead to hers. Then he proposed, "Come, let's go for a walk."

"A walk?" She was surprised. They had never gone for a walk before.

"Yes, let's . . . In honour . . ."

"You're not leaving today?"

"Later on. Now we're going for a walk."

Slowly, solemnly they went out into the dark street. Israel held his arm around Esther's shoulder; her head leaned against it. The air was cool. The smell of rotting leaves rose from the ground in Marysin. The beds of soil were dug up, raw. Esther and Israel strolled between them, their heads lowered. Little by little Israel's tongue began to loosen. "I don't know who you were . . . up to now. You don't know much about me, but at this moment in my life you are the dearest thing I have." He noticed her head sinking even more. "Are you crying?" he asked.

"Probably with joy . . ." she whispered.

After a few minutes he spoke up again, "I've been thinking . . . how superficially people once took each other, even husband and wife. A contact of surfaces. I said that I don't know you? It's silly, really, Esther. I was being chased like a dog . . . Had they caught me that night, you would have shared my fate. You opened not only your door for me . . . I have a home." He bit his lips, which were spread in a smile. "That I should talk like this . . . about my feelings for a woman . . . Who could have imagined that?"

"Then stop" she said, her heart swelling with unbearable gratitude.

He did not stop. "Interesting," he smiled. "What I just told you is not the only thing. There is also the shine of your eyes, the colour of your hair . . . your body. You are the most beautiful . . ." She put her hand on his mouth. It was too much. Her joy hurt her. Moments of happiness were sometimes impossible to bear and one should not prolong them. On their way back, Israel added, "One important thing about me you must know. I am a Bundist." She did not react to his remark, although she was about to tell him something too. She had to tell him about her own political affiliations. She owed it to him. Yet her mouth refused to open.

The Presess did not perform any marriage ceremonies during the two weeks when the lists were being compiled. When the last five hundred people had left the ghetto, the Presess again began to unite pairs in wedlock. Esther and Israel became husband and wife according to the laws of the ghetto. Israel broke open a door in the same building where they lived, and they moved down two floors. The new apartment consisted of one large room. Israel fixed the windows and installed a new stove. "You won't shake with cold again," he said to Esther, as he worked at the pipes which he fixed to run along the ceiling to spread more warmth.

She held the ladder on which he stood, which gave her the feeling that she was assisting him. "Do you think that we shall stay here over the winter?" she asked.

"Probably . . ."

She did not believe it. All the signs indicated that the war was about to end, that Israel and she would survive. She also saw a good omen in the fact that the "action" had passed and they had not been touched.

It was pleasant to arrange the room. She did it at dawn or during the few minutes after work. She did not have much time. Israel could not stand in the queues, and she had to cook and mend their clothes which were falling apart. Then she had to rush to her meetings. She was again enthusiastically immersed in her party work, although she had been accepted by her comrades with great reserve. They remembered her weaknesses and her capricious character, and there could be no talk of assigning her to a closed group whose task it was to prepare the ground for a reception of the Red Army and to begin a resistance movement against the Germans. But she was allowed to take care of the party's rescued children, the "Pioneers", and she was grateful for that. It was strange. Her adherence to the party made her feel closer to Israel. On the way to her meetings she was able to guess what he was experiencing. And that was good. Because her real home was not the new room — but he. She dwelt within him, and she was curious about the quarters into which her heart had moved. She always got home before he did, and she would go to bed to wait for him. Often she fell asleep before he arrived, but she always sensed when he was at her side and cuddled up to him.

"Today you will cook a big *baba*," he said to her one morning as they sat down to their breakfast of coffee and minute slices of bread.

"Are you expecting visitors?" she asked.

"We are going to have a meeting here."

The bread she was eating stuck in her throat. Then she caught herself and began to eat hurriedly, so that he should not notice her nervousness. "I will prepare everything and leave. I'm not a Bundist . . . I . . .," she stammered.

He looked at her, grateful, satisfied. "Where will you go?"

"To my friends."

"You will have to sleep over there."

"No. I'll come back at night, through the backyards."

He told her about Rumkowski's encounter with the parties of the Left. She had no idea that such a meeting had taken place. The Presess had delivered a sugar-sweet speech at the conference. Israel quoted him: "'Sure I've made mistakes, but I am only human. You as people with experience in social work should have pointed out these things to me!'" Israel smiled, "The Old Man sent extra food rations to our people and they sent them back to him. He is prostrating himself and he has become very chummy with me. He used to call me a hooligan and a derelict and he made sure that I didn't get a decent job. Now he pats me on the shoulder whenever he sees me. One day, not long ago, I asked him what his plans were for after the war, and he told me that he would submit himself to a trial, and after he would rehabilitate himself, he would leave for Eretz Israel to live out his last years in peace. He wants nothing else . . . no honours."

Until late at night Esther sat in a gate across the street, waiting for Israel's comrades to leave. Israel came down with the last of his visitors, probably to wait for her. She ran over to him and fell into his arms.

"I would like my comrades to meet you," he pressed her to himself as they lay in bed. "But you see, I feel a bit uneasy. They know Faigie, and to them it means that I have left a wife and child in Warsaw, and am living here with another woman. And it is possible that Faigie and the child are still alive. Sometimes it seems to me that I should not have tied myself to you, to anyone. A dilemma. It is no little thing. I came here to be alone, to devote myself completely to the party work. So I sometimes feel like a traitor. I've never experienced such . . . such inner storms. And here I have to be a whole person, concentrating only on one thing. It makes no sense to hide these things from you. I must be . . . I ought to be . . . I demand this from myself and others demand this from me. The comrades trust me. The young look up to me. I give orders, and that obliges me . . ." He was silent for a long while, then added, "To the two of us, to you and me, everything is clear, natural, and I would say, sacred. And yet . . . Do you understand?"

She tore herself away from the pillow. Her head was buzzing. She was barely

capable of absorbing all that he had told her. "No, I don't understand!" She
burst out, barely able to put her confused thoughts into words. "Now you are
asking yourself whether you have the right? Is it not a bit too late? What have I
done to you that you should lift me up to such . . . such happiness, and then
throw me back into the darkness? Would it not have been better if you had left
me alone, if I had not tasted this kind of life? Did you want to play games with
me, with my life, to tease me?"

He tried to calm her and would not let her escape from his arms as she
wrestled with him. "Keep quiet, silly woman. So what if I ask myself these
questions, so what if I answer them. So what if others sit in judgment on me. I
could not leave you anyway, Esther. It's a lost cause. You are my weakness and
my strength."

She was amazed that he could, with such a few words, calm the turmoil
within her. What he had said to her was magnificent, each word her victory,
each word a knot which tied her to him more tightly.

The autumnal rains began their monotonous reign over the ghetto.
Everything fell into nets of grayness. The outlines of the houses, the faces of the
people became vague, unclear. The foggy streets seemed both short and
infinite. Esther barely noticed the fog. She had a purpose, not like in the past,
when the streets had been clear and her purpose foggy.

One such day, as she walked through the haze, she noticed Israel on the
opposite sidewalk. She ran over to him, falling against him with her whole
body, pressing her face to his cheek. "You . . . Here?" she laughed, about to
move on with him.

His face was cold, his gaze alien. He grabbed her by the arm with hard fingers.
"Yes, me, here!" he hissed. "And I was looking for you. You're a Red aren't
you?" He did not wait for her answer, but squeezed her arm more tightly.
"Comrade Stalin's methods, eh? They have assigned you for the mission, didn't
they? To sleep with me and trick me, to extricate the secrets of the social
traitors, the Bundists, eh?"

"Israel," she groaned.

He shook her with all his strength, looking into her face with cold hateful
eyes, pierced by sparks of pain. "The hell! Why didn't you tell me?" He let go of
her arm. She remained as if suspended in the air. The downpour inundating the
street was dividing her from Israel with a needle-like curtain. Now they both
kept their hands in their pockets and walked with their backs bent, at a distance
from each other; she in her helplessness, he in his rage. His forehead was red,
each crease shining like an arrow. As they climbed the stairs he added, "I can no
longer live with you."

The walls of the room were gray. Sad shadows lay across the floor. Israel took
out his knapsack from under the bed and filled it with his belongings. Esther
blocked his way to the door, "Israel, you must not . . . You promised me . . ."
She threw her arms around his neck and hung on to him. "I swear to you . . . If
you want me to, I will give it all up . . . If you want me to . . . Please, I beg of
you."

He pushed her away from him, "I don't trust you."

"Trust me, I will do whatever you want. I will help you. I will . . . become a
Bundist."

He grinned bitterly, "That's how one becomes a Bundist, you think? I thank
you for sacrificing your principles . . ."

"I don't mean that. Israel . . . Don't leave me."

He offered her a bilious glance, "I had the impression that I was dealing with an honest person."

"I love you."

"Why didn't you come out with the truth, if you love me?" He was standing at the door, his hand on the knob. Esther, shrunken, stood beside him, her head bent. He could have left now. Yet he did not move. "What a riddle you are!" he said in a calmer tone of voice. "I don't know what kind of fortune brought me together with you. There is no time for love in the ghetto, anyway; not for me. I am here to do work. I am responsible and I have a conscience." He looked at her sadly. "If you had at least told me . . ."

He opened the door and she came closer to him. "You are my husband," she whispered, "I will follow you everywhere, unless they send me off, unless I die . . ."

He erupted, "I am a free man with a free will and I respect free people. You will not keep me tied to your apron strings!" He saw her slump down, her shoulders beginning to shake. "I am disgusted with you!" he raged. "I thought that you were a whole person, not a rag."

"I am a whole person only with you," she sobbed, her legs giving under her. The room whirled before her eyes, until everything stopped and she found herself in darkness. The floor swayed and she fell to Israel's feet, her wet coat spread out over her. Through the deafness in her ears she clearly heard the echo of his voice.

"I will discuss it with my comrades, let them decide . . ." she heard him say. In her darkness she suddenly felt like smiling. So that was how a whole and free man talked. How whole and free was he, if he could not decide about his own life? Then she heard him say, this time imploringly, "Don't stand in my way. Don't make it harder for me than it is. You ought to understand me, if . . . if you ever served an ideal."

She really felt like smiling, like a mother smiles at a child who is absorbed in a game. With her mouth close to his shoes she said loud and clear, "I shall wait for you."

That night he did not come home, but the following day he was back. Esther received him as if nothing had happened between them. She did not ask about anything and he said nothing. A few days later he tried to strike up a political discussion with her. Esther smoothed out his furrowed forehead and did not react to his invitation. He insisted, "So, what do you have to say?" When she laughed, refusing to pick up the challenge, he added earnestly, "I would prefer us to ventilate all these things openly, like free people."

She offered him a motherly look. "The only difference between you and me," she said "is that you are a man and I am a woman. And as far as political discussions are concerned, let's postpone them until we are really free."

The same night he told her that the Presess had again called together the representatives of all the leftist parties and appealed to them to accept co-responsibility and to offer him advice — and that they had sent him to seek counsel from those, from whom he had sought it up to now. Later still, he caressed Esther, whispering, "My beautiful Esther, there is no power that could separate us, neither the ghetto, nor the liberation."

She shuddered, "Only one thing could . . ."

He shut her mouth with his.

Chapter Twenty

THE FIRST QUARREL between Junia and Michal Levine took place over a bag of carrots. She had come running to the ambulatorium, to show him the full bag. He asked where it had come from and she said, "From Marysin. Rumkowski's people were digging up his fields, so I pretended that I was one of them; I filled the bag and ran away." She looked at him, expecting him to praise her.

He shook his head. "Which means that you stole it."

"Look at him!" she drew up her nose, offended. "To take from Rumkowski's fields means stealing to you?" She knew that he viewed her "left" tricks with disapproval, but in the case at hand she felt innocent.

"I don't want to have anything to do with it," he said cuttingly.

She began to boil with anger. "I know, my darling saint. Your only aim in life is to be a corpse with clean hands." For three days in a row the atmosphere between them was strained.

Their second, more serious quarrel involved a more basic issue. Junia again visited Michal in his office. He was in the middle of preparing a lecture for his colleagues about the mortality rate in the ghetto, to be delivered the same evening. She placed herself behind his back.

"Hurry up, my dearest, sweetest Michal." She restlessly chatted on, pulling him by the collar. She was impatient. She hated to wait. Realizing that she was not achieving much, she began dancing around him, straightening his hair, tickling him behind the ears, and in general seeing to it that he would not be capable of putting down another word. He took off his white coat, gathered his papers and left with her.

He leaned against her arm. Lately he had begun limping more than usual. It was not so much Junia's behaviour that had not allowed him to concentrate on his lecture. It was rather that morning's order to send a number of patients home from the hospital within forty-eight hours. There had not been many patients in the hospitals lately. Those who were accepted usually had no one to take care of them at home. He wondered about the reason for the order, and, immersed in his thoughts, did not realize that Junia was not leading him in the direction of their house, but away from the bridge. When he suddenly became aware of it, he asked, "Where are you leading me, gipsy girl?"

She offered him a playfully sly glance, "Somewhere," she said, and showed him the tip of her tongue.

She was full of charm. She made him feel lighter, more hopeful. He kissed her on the cheek. Yet he must not give in to her; he still had so much to do

258

before he could enjoy being with her. Not only was he not finished with his house calls, but in spite of everything, he had to complete his notes for the lecture and attend the meeting with his colleagues.

Apart from that, he had taken an additional task on himself. His friend Shafran, who had been deported, had left his psychological study unfinished, and he, Michal had decided to bring it to a conclusion. It was not an easy job. He was ignorant of the subject. He had to become acquainted with the methods and the technique of recording the observations. He had no idea whether what he was doing had any scientific value. He would sit poring over works of psychology until late at night, coming in contact with psychoanalysis for the first time. He began studying the modern philosophers who seemed to have influenced the field of psychology. His problem was that it was extremely difficult to explain psychological phenomena in the ghetto according to all these theories. Man existed here in conditions which no scientific imagination could have fathomed. Moreover, he himself was mostly interested in man as victim and man as persecutor, as seen from the vantage point of the ghetto. Here, the soul of the victim was under a microscope, yet on the basis of the victim's nature one could hypothesize about the nature of the persecutor. These were his reasons for asking the questions which Shafran had formulated: How did man behave as a male, a female, or a child; as a worker, a *shishka*, a judge, a policeman or a *fecalist*.

He let Junia lead him on for a little while longer, then he stopped. "I must go . . . It's almost evening."

She held on to him, "You must come with me. It's more important than anything in the world. You'll talk about first aid. You can shake it out of your sleeve. My friends are waiting for you. They will ask questions and you'll answer."

He stared at her, confused, "What kind of madness is this?"

"Madness? Michal, my gold, this you call madness? I thought you would be enthusiastic. These are truly important activities. The command of the hour! Why are you making such a sour face, sweetest?"

"You know very well what every hour means to me."

"We want you to come to us two or three times a week."

"What is that, an order?" His face became overcast. She had never seen him so offended. "Perhaps you think that because I am lame and I lean on you, you have the right to lead me by the nose?"

He should not have said that, for it was not true. But he was restless, worried and dissatisfied with himself. She let go of his arm. First an expression of astonishment appeared on her small face. Then a flame lit up in her eyes. "And because you are lame," she was incensed, "do you think that you have the right to wheedle out of your most important obligations?"

"And who are you to tell me what my most important obligations are?" he shot back.

"Do you think that it is enough for you to bury your head in that Sisyphean work of healing the doomed, and to hide between the pages of your silly scribblings . . . your rotting books? Your handicap is no excuse. Not for me! And you know quite well that we are doing the only thing which makes any sense, you coward!" With that she left him in the middle of the street and ran off.

They were not on speaking terms for a long time. Junia, who found it difficult to be in a silent room, and was usually the first to make up, this time resisted, not reacting when Michal spoke to her. He, on his part, was too depressed to find the energy to explain to her what had actually annoyed him. He needed her to ease the burden on his heart. One hundred and thirty-nine patients had been taken away from the hospital. One hundred and thirty-nine files full of case-histories had been thrown into the garbage. He looked at Junia, who, without her mischievous gaze, without her smile, resembled a lost, confused rabbit, and he reproached himself for the silence between them. How could they allow themselves to play such childish games nowadays?

Finally she made up with him. She did it awkwardly. No longer able to bear the silence, late one evening she leaned over Shafran's papers which lay on the table. "The Psyche of the Ghetto Jew," she read the title aloud, her voice coloured by an undertone of irony. "Do you know what it is, the psyche of the ghetto Jew?"

"I am studying it," he replied.

"Then what for instance do you know about the psyche of the ghetto Jew who is preparing himself to fight?"

He answered demurely, "As far as I have come to understand the ghetto Jew and the conditions here, I don't foresee that he will put up any resistance."

She jumped to her feet, "That's what you think! And I am telling you just the opposite. If you want to know . . . Take for instance Bella. She is also a ghetto Jew, isn't she? And she is the most passive creature in the world on top of it. Do you know that she lives exclusively and absolutely with one thought, namely that of revenge?" Michal was careful not to allow another quarrel to flare up between them, not because he was ready to give in to her, but because he could not do without her smile, without her cheerfulness. So he accepted the issue of Bella. That was a topic which united them. It was not long before Junia sat down in his lap and braided her arms around his neck. She was still serious, but there was a smiling twinkle already lurking in the depths of her black pupils. "It is strange, isn't it," she said thoughtfully. "I am completely different from Bella . . . and yet both of us want the same thing."

"For different reasons," he remarked.

"And what do you mean by that?"

"You love life, and she has begun to hate it."

She bent her head sideways, looking at him suspiciously. "And even if that were true, don't you think that she is justified? I am proud of her anyway. She has a better character than I. If she undertakes to do something, she does it thoroughly. You should see how involved she has become, how she studies Zionism and Hebrew. And she will know the language, not like me, who knows nothing but a few Hebrew songs. And do you know what else? She has begun to study the Bible."

Michal smiled, "Does one need to study the Bible in order to take revenge?"

"But it can't hurt, can it?"

"Nor can it help."

"Then why do you think she has taken up Bible studies?"

"I think that Father's death was a terrible blow to her. And I think, the fact that she studies . . . is a sign for the better."

Junia visited her sister every day. Bella now lived all alone in the big house.

She had locked the balcony door and the room in which Samuel had spent his last days. She also kept the doors of the other rooms closed and had moved into the kitchen. She refused to listen to Junia's offer that she live with her and Michal.

Bella's movements had lost their languorous slowness and her eyes were no longer covered with a wistful haze. Sometimes it seemed to Junia that Bella had lost something essential which had formerly been characteristic of her. She seemed cold, unfamiliar. Even her voice had become harder, as if she had dried up not only physically, but also in her soul. Her face was greenish, her eyes puffed, her cheekbones protruding. With her long pointy nose she looked like an ugly bird of prey hovering in silence, but ready to attack at any moment. Junia despised herself for seeing her sister in such a light, and the more alien and frightening Bella appeared to her, the more often she went to see her.

They would go together to the meetings of the Zionist Youth group. Bella was active. She had taken up a position of responsibility and she volunteered for the most difficult assignments. Soon she became, like Junia, a member of the board. They clashed often. Bella was against any activities in the field of culture, being of the opinion that, firstly, there was no time for it, and secondly, such activities weakened organizational discipline. She was against singing and dancing the *hora*, even for the very young members. In her opinion, even the children had to behave like adults. Junia, on the other hand, could not do without an occasional hour of song and dance. She thought that in spite of all the serious preparations, they must not forget that they were young. She was amazed at how Bella, who had previously had no interest in politics and had shunned any organized activity, fitted so easily into political work. Junia could not hide her enthusiasm.

"Bella, it is wonderful to do Zionist work with you." She did not stop chatting on the way home from their meetings, as if she were trying with words to fill the abyss between herself and Bella. She was helpless against what was happening to them. Often she tried to convince herself that there was no barrier, only a misunderstanding, and she made an effort to strike up a heart-to-heart conversation. But she never succeeded. Her admiration and respect for Bella grew in direct proportion to their alienation.

Although Junia had never aspired to becoming a first-class cook, she always tried her best when preparing the Friday-night meals. Friday, when there were no meetings, she could allow herself more time to try out the recipes of the holiday dishes: the "fish", the "chicken soup" or the "*tzimmes*", made out of beet leaves, parsley and radishes. As usual, Michal was still not home from his house calls, and when Junia finished with the housework, she still had time to run over to Bella and for the thousandth time insist that she should, just once, join them in the Sabbath meal, if only to see what a good cook her sister had become.

This time Bella again refused to come along, and Junia ran home confused, with the uneasiness in her heart which always followed her encounters with Bella. She could not stay alone in the apartment and wait for Michal, so she went upstairs to Winter's place, in order to kill some time there.

It was cold in Winter's room. The window was open. Winter stood in his work coat, with a shawl around his neck and his beret pulled down over his ears, hovering at the easel. She rushed to shut the window, but he pushed her away with his elbow. "Do me a favour and don't disturb me," he said. "Can't you see that I'm painting the city from the distance."

She shrugged her shoulders. "I don't see why you can't paint the city with your window shut."

"Because I need to feel the density of the air," he said, addressing the canvas. "The nuances of gray . . . its interplay with the rain which can't be seen, but which is there. I don't want to have a barrier of glass between my object and myself. Is that clear now, you total ignoramus?"

She wrinkled her nose, "For that you find it worthwhile to risk your health?"

"I'm not risking yours," he snapped, adding, "If you want to stay here, you must be quiet, and peel some potatoes, so that I will at least have some use out of you. You can prepare the *baba*. I am expecting about twenty people tomorrow night." Junia grimaced, but she obeyed him. To prepare a *baba* was a tedious job and she did not intend to do it in silence. She did not stop talking, and as soon as she had finished, Winter began to nag her, "Go home. I can't concentrate when you are here." She pretended not to hear and stretched out on the sofa. Winter was working quickly, manipulating the brushes stuck between the fingers of his left hand. Junia followed his movements with her eyes, commenting on every bit of paint which he put on the canvas. Winter was beside himself, "I've never met a human being so little related to art as you. No sense for it whatsoever. You're just the opposite of your sister."

Junia winced, the sofa squeaked. "How come you know my sister so well? And do you know too that she would block her ears if she had to hear your sermons on art and literature?"

"She would, would she? And yet she has a sense of intimacy with art, of which you don't have even a hair."

"I do so!"

"Not a speck!"

"Then why don't you begin your artistic soirées until I arrive?"

"I don't wait for you but for Michal."

"You're a scoundrel!"

"You yourself come because of Michal. Never mind, I've seen you yawning more than once."

"I have my tastes. And if they don't agree with yours, it's not my fault."

"Of course they don't agree. You are not receptive. You have no sense for things which are fine or profound. If anything appeals to you, it is the vulgar, the strident, the superficial. You haven't got the slightest idea of what elation of the soul means."

Pretending to be offended, Junia sat up, "If you say one more word, I'll leave!"

"Please, do me the favour. You are too great a contrast to my work, and I cannot manage with both at the same time."

"Scoundrel!"

He winked at her. His large mouth spread into a smile. "You are the antipode of art, because you are the embodiment of life. Superficial, vulgar, strident and delightful."

She jumped down from the sofa and dashed towards him, shaking her black dishevelled hair in his face. "Phraseologist! Declamator! Bluffer! I don't give a broken penny for a word of yours, and certainly not for a smear of your brush!"

The pot with the *baba* in it began to bubble loudly on the stove and she jumped to remove it from the flame. Then she stretched out on the sofa again, pulled up her knees, and turned her eyes to the dreary evening sky which looked like a background for the easel and for Winter's humped figure. She was quiet. In reality she did not want to disturb Winter. She liked his room because it was different from all the other rooms she had ever seen. It had a particular air, a particular atmosphere of which she was aware, although she often joked about it. Perhaps Winter was right, she thought. She did not understand art properly, nor did she understand him. But she did feel related to him in some way. There was a freshness about him, as if he were in the process of constant renewal. She was never bored with him, just as she was never bored with Michal, although for different reasons.

At length she saw Winter put away his brushes. He checked his pulse, wiped his forehead and took off the beret. He turned around, calling out, "You're still here!" He sat down beside her. "Tell me the truth," he shook her arm. "What does Michal think about my condition?"

"He thinks nothing."

"And he calls himself a friend?"

"Do you think that you are the navel of the world? That we have nothing more important to discuss but you? Anyway, everyone knows that you have halted your disease, because you are a sorcerer, stronger than ten healthy people."

"Who knows that?" he asked, childlike disbelief in his eyes.

"Everyone. Michal . . . myself."

"My, my, how gorgeous your lies sound!" he exclaimed. "But if that is the case, then get off the sofa, shut the window and cover it." As soon as she stood up, he took her place on the sofa and unbuttoned his work frock.

"The painting here, of the naked woman with the red hair," he heard Junia ask, "why did you turn it to the wall?"

"Because it's no good. My greatest fiasco," he replied. "Do you know her? Esther? She will be here tomorrow. A strange thing about her. She is like a candle, sometimes lit, sometimes extinguished. One day I meet her and she looks like a shadow, another day she looks radiant. And this time . . . There was something particular about her. It doesn't show yet, but I have a good eye for the . . . the milkiness of the face, the black shadows under the eyes, the veins in her cheeks and hands, and the main thing: the melancholy sweetness of her gaze."

"Your ex-mistress, isn't she?" Junia winked at him playfully.

"You're banal. There's no word to describe . . . I would like to paint her now . . . in her pregnancy. That would be my swan song."

Junia covered the window and began to wander about the room, stopping before the portraits of Esther. "Here she looks as if she were pregnant," she pointed to the painting of Esther on the sofa with a glass of milk in her hand.

Winter hooted. "A good observation, my ignoramus! Perhaps at the moment I painted her, I impregnated her soul . . . quite possible!"

Junia was no longer listening to him. She heard steps outside, and shouting "Michal!", she dashed out of the room. She fell upon Michal, throwing her arms around his neck, almost toppling him over. The next moment they sat at the table, their faces buried in their plates. The first spoonfuls Junia devoured in silence, but then she moved close to Michal, caressing him, kissing him, telling him about her day. Finally, she described her conversation with Winter and finished with a stammer, "Michal, if you could talk Bella into coming tomorrow to Winter's evening. She would enjoy it, I'm sure."

"I've just left her," Michal said. Junia tensed. She felt a discomfort around her heart as she noticed Michal's face become serious, overcast. "I wanted to see how she was There is something about Bella that we have not known. Imagine, she sat in the kitchen dressed in a white blouse, the table covered with a white tablecloth . . . two lit candles. Around the table sat a man, a woman and a few children. And guess who sat at the head of the table? The Toffee Man. When Bella saw me, she smiled at me strangely, as if she did not recognize me. Then she stood up and came slowly over to me. 'Good Sabbath, Michal', she said in Yiddish."

Junia jumped to her feet and grabbed her coat, pulling Michal by the sleeve. "Come, we must go to her! She is sick!"

He did not move. "We can't help her. She is struggling for her life. Zionism is evidently not enough."

Junia was beside herself, "Forget your psychology, Michal, come on, help her!"

He stood up, facing her, "What do you want me to do? Give her an injection?"

"Then I am going by myself!" Junia rushed to the door.

He called her back angrily. "Take off your coat!" he ordered. "You must not disturb her peace." He began to pull the coat from her. At first she would not let him and she struggled with him, but finally she gave in and burst into sobs. He pressed her to his chest and for a moment they stood embracing each other. "I promise you," he whispered, "that I will take care of her as much as I can."

They sat down to finish their Sabbath meal. "Why is it," she smiled confusedly into her plate, "that I used to feel so sure of myself . . . so grown-up and that ever since I have been with you, I feel like a child, so stupid?"

"It's fine to be childish and stupid sometimes, my gipsy girl," he replied. "You have put too much salt into the chicken soup, which means that you are in love."

✦   ✦   ✦

On the Sabbath Michal usually had the greatest number of house calls. The strength which kept the ghettoniks on their feet during the week reached its point of exhaustion on the Sabbath, allowing all kinds of aches and pains to take over their bodies. Dressed in his navy-blue raincoat, the Red Cross band around his arm, his bag in one hand, his list of patients in the other, he made his rounds. The people in the street usually recognized him and greeted him. Some considered it their duty to stop him and report on their own state of health as well as on that of their families and neighbours. Others accompanied him part of the way, giving him all their symptoms and asking for on-the-spot diagnoses. Still others would, out of gratitude, tell him all the reliable "ducks hatched in people's minds", or share with him the most precise radio information which they had heard from someone who had heard it from someone else . . .

He was patient with them and took them very seriously. Sometimes this saved him a visit. He did not miss an opportunity to give each of them an injection of courage. He too told them bits of news, but only good bits, which he adorned and added colour to, whenever necessary. He was aware that his news reports and cheerful words had weight: "the doctor himself said it" and that this was actually the most effective remedy at his disposal.

With the women he was particularly mellow. When he looked at the younger ones, it hurt him physically that they were so bony, so devoid of feminine beauty. His life with Junia made him feel closer to them. They were complicated, loaded with frustrated longings and moods, and yet they were down-to-earth and cunningly practical. He would stroke their cheeks and hands, while he caressed their ears with the promise that the war could not last much longer. As for the elderly women, the feelings he had had for his own mother helped him give attention to them. He acted the role of a strong wise son who knew everything and had a cure for every complaint. He stroked their gray heads and spoke the words which he knew would have soothed his own mother's heavy heart.

There were also women who were like witches. Crying with forced tears, they pulled him by the coattails, always demanding something from him: a bottle of *Vigantol*, of glucose, of strychnine, a few drops for the heart, or a few sleeping pills. "You, dear Doctor, can get it for nothing. And the prices on the black market are sky high . . ." Others waited for him in the dark arches of the gates, a little bottle of oil, or a little bag of sugar in their hands, offering it to him with thanks. "Doctor, I swear to you, you must take it. A doctor who does not take anything is not worth anything . . ." They irritated him. He did not need their oil or sugar and he hated them for tempting him to take the gifts. Still others ran after him in the street, spat at him, cursed and abused him bitterly — for not having saved someone dear to them.

There were days when he felt not at all stronger than his patients. He was, just like they, grateful for what he still possessed, and he prayed to be able to save Junia and his home. During such days, he allowed his patients' sighs to penetrate him, and that was not good for either patient or doctor, because then he was less tolerant, less confident. During such days, he walked faster through the streets, pretending not to see those who greeted him, his thoughts escaping into abstract worlds which had no relation to the present.

During such days, he was not only unable to sit down to Shafran's work, but he could not even think about it. It seemed meaningless, futile to dig into those papers. Did he really understand what Shafran had been aiming at with his observations, with the notes he had left behind? Shafran had recorded the behaviour of the Ghetto Jew, his reaction to tragedies, the impact of starvation upon his psyche, the effect of his being trapped between barbed wire. On the surface that was the clear intention. However, the choice of facts and their illumination, even if objective on the surface, depended on Shafran's personality, on his intellect. Michal saw the same phenomena differently, yet he also thought that he was seeing them objectively. Perhaps Shafran had been trained to see the problems from a proper point of view while he, Michal, had not.

Even in formulating the questions themselves there was a difference. By finding out more about the victim and the executioner, Michal wanted to formulate a comment on man in general. Even before the war, he had entertained himself with a theory that man was a transitory creature in the process of evolution and at the same time a turning point in that process. Man was the great news that had happened to the animal. Michal had thought that the more time elapsed in the process of evolution, the more room the human spirit would take up; the better, the more precisely the human brain would work, the less of an animal and the more human man would become. But ever since he had heard about Chelmno, where the sealed trucks of the deportees had been filled with gas, in 1941; ever since he had learned what had been done to the deported during the *Sperre*, to his mother, to Nadia and the child, to Shafran and his wife, to the children of the ghetto; ever since he had been in the gipsy camp; ever since he had come down with typhoid fever — he had begun to think that the animal was more instinctively ethical than man, that the animal was only a killer out of necessity. Consequently, man seemed morally inferior to the animal, because he used his reason and intelligence to perfect the sport called murder, in order to satisfy his aggressive corrosive hatred. Was that evolution? Or was it the end point in the development of life?

And Shafran, what had he wanted to find out? What was the great question that he had put to himself in his work? Would he also have come to the conclusion that the human spirit, of all things, was the axe in the hand of the *Golem*, with which he would destroy everything, himself included? Would he also conclude that if one put the positive achievements of the human mind — in technology, in medicine or in the arts — on one scale, and the German murders on the other, the other would weigh down the former into the deepest abysses of despair? Would he then conclude that the killer and his victim were not only German and Jew, but man and man? Cain and Abel? And at what conclusions would Shafran have arrived after observing his friend, Michal Levine, for instance, who preferred to be destroyed rather than destroy?

This particular Sabbath day was a day of broken reflections. Michal's mind was like a blackboard on which thoughts appeared and were erased. He hurried through the streets with a full list of patients in his and. He had also promised Junia to bring Bella along to the gathering at Winter's.

Under the bridge stood the German guard, his head covered with a wet green cap, the collar of his uniform, up. Near the collar was slung the gun, its muzzle facing upwards like a dark eye. Hands in pockets, the guard briskly paced back and forth, to keep warm. As Michal came down from the bridge their eyes met. If hatred were an expression of masculinity, then both Michal and the gendarme were neither men nor heroes at that moment. Their linked gazes were rather the greetings of two wet dogs, shivering in the autumnal cold, hungry for a bit of warmth at the hearth of home. And yet Michal was convinced that had he approached the gendarme and asked him, "Do you hate me, *Herr Offizier*? the answer would have been, "*Ja, Ich hasse dich kreziger Jude, mach das du fortkommst!*"

Michal had a consoling thought. Hatred was madness, hysteria. The human mind was too splendid a mechanism to be despised because one of its elements worked poorly. It had to be cured. The only question was how? Michal was sure of one thing: Nation would only stop raising its sword against nation when there were no nations. But that still did not mean that hatred would vanish from man's heart. The Germans, for instance, were only the most unhampered, the most limitless channel through which hatred poured out to inundate the world. But where was the source of the channel itself?

The door of Bella's apartment stood open. The kitchen was neatly cleaned; on the table lay the same tablecloth as the day before, during the Sabbath-eve meal. The other rooms were also clean and empty. Michal left, and as he passed through the gate he remembered that the insane, eternally weeping Toffee Man, whom he had seen yesterday at Bella's table, had once lived in the cellar with his nine children. As Michal descended the few steps to the cellar, he heard a singsong coming from inside.

Someone grabbed his arm, "Where are you going?"

He shook off the hand, "I'm a friend."

"What friend?" The hand did not let go. Michal gave his name and the voice became friendlier. "Good evening, Doctor! Forgive me a thousand times, but the Rabbi told me to let no one in. Do you want me to call someone out for you? With the greatest pleasure." The voice sounding partly female, partly male, spoke with a *Gemara* lilt.

"I want to ask your Rabbi if he knows where Zuckerman's daughter is."

Only then did the hand let go of Michal's arm as the young voice sang out with enthusiasm, "Zuckerman's daughter! Small thing! The holy woman! Of course, she is inside. She cooks and cleans for the Rabbi and the *yeshiva* students. The Rabbi says that she is the incarnation of Mother Rachel herself. She does the greatest deeds for the broken and the poor. Yes, ask anyone in the yard. And do you know that she is being taught Yiddish and also the Pentateuch with *Rashi's* commentaries, too. May I live so long as this is true. The Rabbi says that she has a *gaon's* head. You would not believe that a female could have such brains, that's what the Rabbi says. And didn't I hear her explain a piece of *Rashi* with my own ears? It sounds a bit crooked in her broken language, but the explanations are straighter than straight, and my, the good deeds that she does!"

"Call her out," Michal broke into the stream of enthusiastic words.

The young man laughed, "What do you mean call her out? Do you think that because you are a doctor . . ."

Michal lost his patience. He threw open the door and an unusual sight appeared before his eyes. Around the walls of the cellar stood a few tables, a lit candle on each. In the light of the candles shone pale young faces bent over the open pages of huge volumes. As soon as Michal entered, the singsong stopped and the faces turned in his direction. At one of the tables a sparse long beard began to shake. Beside it, Michal noticed Bella. He barely recognized her in her black dress and black scarf. She whispered something to the Toffee Man and went over to Michal.

"Are you looking for me?" she asked. "Has something happened?" He took her tightly by the arm and led her out into the corridor.

"Disrupted the studies, oy, disrupted the studies!" the young man on guard called after them squeakily as they entered the gate.

In the darkness, Michal drew his flashlight out of his pocket and turned it on Bella's face. In its light she looked like a woman long past her youth, her ugly face expressing the weariness of life. When he reassured her that nothing had happened, her face cleared somewhat and her eyes lit up warmly.

"I've come to take you along to Winter's," he said. "It's going to be interesting . . . Please, do it for Junia."

She did not move. "I don't want to, Michal."

"Come, you will find . . ."

"I have already found everything. Goodnight. Give my regards to Junia." He would not let go of her. He noticed her smiling. "I know what you think," she said. "You think that I am crazy."

"You are not, Bella."

"Do you understand me?"

"I think I do."

Silently she searched his face. "Then explain it to Junia. Tell her that all my life I was wandering in the dark. That's why I was always so frightened . . . always egotistically busy with myself. I was lost in the emptiness, do you understand, Michal? But here . . . a light has gone on inside me. Father lit it. And now not even a speck of dust seems lonely to me. Nothing gets lost . . . nothing dies . . . Father is still my father and I am still his child. Everything is united and the wholeness means peace . . . You feel that everything around you, just like yourself, is aiming towards a centre. You feel related to it all. Every man is close to you . . . and, Michal, one feels so . . . so eternal. So many generations behind you. So many generations ahead of you. Do you know, death exists only for those who fall out from the wholeness, for those who deny the sacred web or want to destroy it . . . for the Germans, the godless . . . not for Father, or for me."

"Why do you avoid us? Why do you shun Junia?" he interrupted her.

"I must do so for the time being. My steps are still shaky, the slightest blow . . . Do you understand? In reality I love you both more than ever. Tell her that. You see, I am building my world anew and my hands tremble. I am learning to live and I am like a dancer on her toes for the first time . . . a beginner." She moved closer to him, stroking his rough cheek. "I knew that you would understand me. I felt it the first time that I met you, at the New Year's ball at our home . . . remember? Something in your eyes told me then that you would understand me today." He heard her quiet rustling laughter. "I'm glad that you put out the flashlight so that I could tell you these things. Such people as you and me, Michal, should fall in love with each other. But we are attracted precisely to unreligious types . . . I to Mietek . . . you to Junia. And it is for the best. Goodnight." She shook his hand. He could not keep from lighting the flashlight again. He looked at their clasped hands, noticing that the skin around her nails, which she had used to bite, was pink and healed.

It was raining heavily. The empty streets surrendered to the night and the muddy waters. Michal put up his collar and limped on through the backyards. His head was full of Bella's talk. He was not sure whether he pitied or envied her, whether he despised or admired her. He did not know whether she was normal or insane, just as he could not decide about the Toffee Man. The border between normalcy and madness had become difficult to find. Suddenly he felt a spasm of fear clamping around his heart. And he himself, with his thoughts and searching, with his attacks of feeling absent and present at the same time, with his weakness for the colour white, which brought back the clear image of his mother wrapped in her white shawl — was he normal?

He hurried. He wanted to see Junia, to touch her, to hold on to her.

The sound of a woman's voice came from behind Winter's door. Someone was reciting a poem in a melodiously vibrant voice. Michal removed his wet coat and waited. He did not want to disturb. The voice flowed on and on without becoming heavier or lighter. He tried to catch the words but all he could hear was the rhythmic flow of syllables, pouring out with the waves of the voice. His curiosity grew. He slowly entered the room. It was partly lit. The doors of the "cannon" oven stood open, reflections of playful tongues of fire danced over the faces of those present, over the walls hung with paintings. The person from whose mouth the voice was coming sat on the floor close to the oven. Michal was unable to divert his gaze from that mouth. There was something awesome, breathtaking, in the sight of a moving mouth, without a face or a body. The fire in the oven quietly crackled as it accompanied the strange voice.

He scanned the faces of the listeners. A pair of arms was stretching out towards him. Junia was sitting on the floor, wrapped in his mother's white crocheted shawl. Her thick black hair covered her face, allowing only her glowing eyes to shine through. Carefully, he waded between the legs spread out on the floor, until he reached Junia and sat down beside her. Her warm hands took his face between her fingers. They glided over to his forehead and slid down along his wet hair. A rounded, full moment of peace. Junia asked in a whisper about Bella, and he lowered his mouth to her ear. "She sends regards. She asked me to tell you that she loves you more than ever."

Then the reciting voice took hold of him completely. From where he sat, the mouth was not visible; instead, his eyes embraced a female back; a figure framed by the light from the oven, as if cut out by a scissor made from the tongues of flame.

Winter, his eyes shut, was lying on the sofa with one hand under his cheek, while the other rested at his side, partly folded, like an ear, listening. A crooked exalted smile played on his mouth. Leaning against the sofa sat Berkovitch, his gray mop of hair upright, each strand an exclamation point, his puffed face red with the reflection of the flames from the stove. From beneath his glasses there peered a pair of blinking dots. Their gaze was like a pair of rays reaching to the other end of the room where Rachel Eibushitz sat. The girl kept her face turned towards the oven. Berkovitch seemed to take in Rachel's face along with the voice which flowed on, loud, heavy and warm. His lips moved, as if he were mumbling along with the incomprehensible phrases. Near Berkovitch sat a few people whom Michal did not know and among them the redhead, Esther. Her face looked transparent, her hair a sharp contrast to her palour. Her veined hands rested loosely braided over her belly. Michal immediately noticed that she was pregnant. A hazy dream-like recollection: he had once delivered her child. A dead child. Or perhaps he had merely seen himself at such a scene one night, in his sleep?

Near Esther sat the violinist Mendelssohn. Michal and he rarely met nowadays, since they had even less to say to each other than before. Mendelssohn had become apathetic. He busied himself with caring for his body, with getting cigarettes and worshipping his hands. Only when he needed something that Winter could not provide for him, did he seek out Michal. Mendelssohn's face expressed no feeling, no sensitivity to the voice hovering over the room.

The declaiming voice began to fluctuate. It became increasingly fast, stormy, tragic. Michal could understand every word and sentence separately, yet he understood nothing. What a weird long poem it was! It seemed to wind around the roofs of houses, to sing around the church with its red turrets and the dead clock, to describe the sick crows, each crow a house in the ghetto. The spread wings of the crows were the roofs over empty nests. The poem sang about a bed used for firewood. The words of the poem filled the bed with the bodies of a man and a woman. Then it spoke of the fire which devoured the bed; the voice seemed to jump along with the bed into the blaze, roaring from inside with a wild awesome roar and abandoning itself to a hysterical frenzy, unbearable to listen to.

Then the stream of words stopped, but their echo lingered on in the air like the smoke after a fire. Winter opened his eyes, his hand began to flutter in the air. "Magnificent! Unbelievable!" he exclaimed.

No one responded. The two dozen people, sitting one against the other, seemed like one paralysed body. Then the voice resumed its outpouring of words. At first it was shaky, but soon it climbed to its measured height, setting its images afloat over the silence on rhythmically swaying waves. The voice talked about the strings of rain which resembled the woven beards of praying grandfathers; it sang about autumn and dried-out water pumps squeaking and groaning, wishing for the winter to freeze their sorrow. The voice sang about a sky without birds and a town without children. Soon it grew heavier, until it began to squirm again in hysterical spasms. Sighs and murmurs could be heard in the room, a kind of anti-lilt which the listeners started in order to protect themselves against the frenzied voice.

One of the listeners could no longer bear it and turned on the light. The recitation stopped. The people began to stretch their limbs and wipe their eyes. Michal stood up and ploughed through the crowded room towards the man who had turned on the light, and grabbed his arm. Guttman had a thick beard and looked like an old man. But he seemed lively, cheerful.

"Look at her," he pointed to the woman who had been reciting, "I'm painting her."

The woman had a head of dishevelled blond hair, a milk-white face with red chubby cheeks and doll-like, round eyes. They were wide open, full of sky blue, they seemed to look and see nothing. One deep furrow cut her forehead into halves, reaching down between her pointed eyebrows. Her mouth, colourless and puffed, was spread in a dull smile. She stroked the floor with both hands as she rhythmically rocked herself back and forth.

"Who is she?" Michal asked.

"Itka, a sort of poetess ... You heard her improvise. I am the one who brought her," Guttman said, not without pride. "At the beginning she is always better, more in equilibrium. But as soon as she gets tired, she falls into such a tone ... impossible to listen." He leaned over and whispered in Michal's ear, "She escaped from the madhouse during the raid. My ... that weird beauty ... the music ... the treasure of images ..." They were discussing Itka, while their gazes spoke about themselves. They looked at each other with the same curiosity as they had an eternity ago, when they had first met.

✦   ✦   ✦

Junia became busier and busier with her party work and barely had any time left over to spend with Michal. He would wait for her while trying to work on Shafran's manuscript. It still did not progress smoothly. Often he abandoned the work and went upstairs to visit Winter. But Winter lately had no time for him either. He was painting feverishly; finishing everything off, as if he were preparing for an exhibit. He was absorbed in his work and the presence of people in his room irritated him. And when Winter was not pleased to see someone, he did not mince words but let that someone know exactly how he felt. He could not even bear Michal's silence.

"It bothers me," he told Michal in his hooting voice, "when Junia putters around here. But she is so remote from what I am doing that she cannot affect me. But you ... You are like the autumn rain. You get into my bones, even with your silence. So I don't want you here. Come Saturday night. I reserve Saturday nights for my guests."

Michal did not hold it against him. He would even have been glad that Winter was so energetic, so positive and self-assured, had it not been for the fact that he, the doctor, needed the companionship of his patient.

One day after such a reception from Winter, Michal set out to visit Guttman, who lived near a muddy garbage dump in Marysin. His house was dilapidated, its only decent room serving Guttman as a studio. On the outside, the house was earth-black, the shutters broken, the beams rotting, but inside, the room looked almost like a museum. The walls were whitewashed and covered with Guttman's paintings. The paintings were related to each other by the play of rainbow colours. Guttman used pure blues and yellows, sharp reds and greens, without any mixture. Although the paintings depicted life in the ghetto and with precision brought out scenes which were not at all gay, their atmosphere was, thanks to the colours, rather bright, optimistic, reminiscent of multi-coloured peasant tapestries.

Here, in his studio, Guttman also seemed more cheerful. He received Michal with the heartiness of old times and with the same talkativeness. "Do you understand, Michal," he pointed at the walls with pride, "Chagall was right in saying that colour is a state of the soul. The new tone . . . Do you see? That's how I feel nowadays. I'm working non-stop. Guess what I am doing? You'll laugh. I am preparing an exhibit for after the war. As soon as I hear that we are free, I'll load everything onto a wagon and travel from town to town, from country to country . . . and let the world see." He offered Michal a piece of bread and a jug of coffee. "Eat with a quiet conscience," he encouraged him. "I have a patron. Ever heard of the Holy Shoemaker? I am painting his wife and little daughters. Half a loaf of bread weekly, until the end of the war. And do you think that he protects only me? Take Berkovitch, for example. Berkovitch is writing a great work, doing with the pen what I am doing with the brush. Do you understand, Michal, there is a relationship between the pen or the brush and the gun. The relationship is in the difference between them." Michal nodded. Here was another friend who no longer needed him, whom he needed. "If I begin imagining," Guttman continued, "how the sirens will start to sing and the churches to toll with the good news, I almost burst with tension. It seems to me that when the hour arrives I will faint or have a heart attack. How will it be possible to take such news? And do you know what's going on in the Resorts, how Rumkowski and the *shishkas* are trying to please the crowd? Do we need a better sign? Michal! We have to be ready for the great hour, inwardly ready. A new world will rise from the ruins. We need a clear outlook . . . a clear vision." He stopped in front of Michal. "Did you hear about the order to submit all musical instruments to the *Yekes* before the first of January? They don't want us to play at their funeral."

Michal left Guttman's bright hut and fell again into the arms of autumnal grayness. He walked through the dark wet streets, thinking of Mendelssohn. He would gladly have visited him too. Mendelssohn would perhaps need his companionship today. He thought about Mendelssohn's violin as if it were the musician's sick wife who was about to be taken away. But to see Mendelssohn he needed Junia at his side and he hurried home to wait for her.

Like a murderer who stealthily throws the noose over the head of his victim, winter sneaked into the ghetto, strangling it with its cold. With six kilograms of heating material per month and the diminished food rations, there was nothing left with which to resist the frost — but hope. The people put on their threadbare winter clothes which they had worn the year before, two years before, or three years before; they wrapped their legs in rags, and chopped up the last pieces of furniture for firewood. All they had to warm their hearts with was — good news.

But there were also days when the good news lost its power to warm. One such day was when two green uniforms appeared at Baluter Ring, entered Rumkowski's office and invited the Presess to step outside. They put him into a black limousine and led him away. That day and the following night the ghetto waited anxiously. Only in the morning, when they heard that the Old Man was back, did the people sigh with relief.

Then a merrier day came. An order was issued to send delegations of workers, instructors and managers to a meeting at the House of Culture. The chief of the *Ghettoverwaltung*, Herr Hans Biebow himself, came to address the assembly and he talked for an hour and then another hour. It was a severe speech. He reprimanded his listeners for the conditions in the ghetto, for the badly paved streets and the chaos in the offices and departments. He spoke about raising the productivity of the Resorts and about saving on raw materials. He spoke on and on — while the ghetto rejoiced. For the first time in history, the distinguished Herr Biebow had turned for help directly to those who up to now had only deserved to be commanded. His criticism and reproaches had almost elevated the hordes of slaves to the level of equals.

It was burning cold. Michal limped through the streets. Lately he had begun to visit his hopelessly ill patients, those dying of starvation, those with corroded lungs, with intestines exhausted by dysentery, those who had fallen victim to unknown diseases. Rarely were any of his patients unconscious. On the contrary. Most of them were aware of where they stood in the struggle for life. Michal felt an affinity with them.

He saw little of Junia, and they almost willingly destroyed the little time that they had together before going to sleep, as if they wanted to make bearable the good fortune of being together. They quarrelled mostly over Junia's reproaches that Michal devoted too little time to her comrades, that he was negligent about the first-aid lessons which he had finally undertaken to give, and most of all that he had not a speck of enthusiasm for the cause to which Junia devoted every spare minute. They both feared their increasingly frequent quarrels, and yet provoked them. Deep within, they knew that their fighting would not break them, that they were like two kites which hit against each other, but could not fly too far apart, because the same hand held both strings.

On the Sabbath night before the deadline for surrendering musical instruments, Mendelssohn appeared at Winter's door with the violin in his hand. He had brought it, not with the intention of playing, but because he could not part with the instrument. Wherever he went, he took it along.

The beautiful instrument lay on the table. Its mouth, open and dark, covered with the rows of strings, was dumb. Out of that dumbness it seemed to talk. Winter's guests were unable to take their eyes off it. Mendelssohn cried shamelessly, "Why are they such sadists? What would they lose if they left me my violin?"

Guttman consoled him, "They don't want us to play at their funeral."

Berkovitch gave his advice. "Throw it into the fire rather than give it up to them."

"Burn it, yes, burn it here, before our eyes," the others picked up the idea.

They made a big enough fire in the "cannon" oven to embrace the entire violin. "At the waters of Babylon, there we sat . . ." Berkovitch mumbled.

Mendelssohn wiped his eyes, lifted the violin from the table, and pressed it to his chest as if it were the body of a lover. His face changed gradually, until it became again the face of a proud virtuoso. "I won't break or burn a violin," he said in a controlled voice. "Let the violin survive me. Let someone's hands hold it . . . Let someone's ear lean against it. From the violin's insides, that ear will surely hear my voice. I am inside it . . ." He placed the violin on his shoulder, leaned his chin against it and picked up the bow. He wanted to give his last concert, but could by no means find a work suitable to his mood. He began to play a composition of his own, then he began to improvise. But his hands trembled and he had to stop. Finally, he wrinkled his forehead, smiled crookedly and placed the instrument in its case. "The poet Rilke said," he turned to the gathering, "that when music speaks, it speaks to God, not to us. We stand in its way, so it passes through us. It is we who are the violins."

Chapter Twenty-one

THE YEAR 1944 HAD BEGUN. During the day the ghetto, frozen, snow-covered, harassed by blizzards, looked like a ghost town. There was no smoke coming from the chimneys. The yards were empty; the frozen waterpumps with long icy beards looked like exotic glass figures. Through the white empty streets there occasionally passed a shaking *fecalia* wagon covered with brown icicles, pulled by human horses; or a truck with raw materials, headed for the Resorts, or a cart with food for the co-operatives; a tiny cart surrounded by an army of policeman with clubs in their hands. Above the ghost town hovered its faithful guardian: the Church of the Holiest Virgin Mary. The church's tower with the snow on its back looked like a priest dressed in white, its face, the dead clock, expressing stagnation; the hands still pointed to ten minutes before ten — the long hour of loneliness.

Yet there were in that town beyond time, some places where time did count. For instance, in the Resorts, and in the stomachs of those who worked there. In his last speech the *Amtsleiter*, Herr Biebow, had strictly forbidden people to leave the work places and appear in the streets beween seven in the morning and five-thirty in the afternoon. When that hour arrived, the empty streets revived for a while. They looked like the branches of a frozen tree along which crept swarms of black ants. People rushed to the food co-operatives, or to warm up their pots at the Gas Centre, or to arrange the burial for a loved one, or to drop in on a relative, or to hear the latest radio news.

Soon the ghetto was desolate again. For a while the people moved about inside the houses. Neighbours assembled to seek advice: how to protect themselves against the "epidemic of dying" which had lately attacked the ghetto with full force. Or they heatedly discussed whether it could be true that the *Yekes* had withdrawn from Lvov. Then they went home and straight to bed, covering themselves with whatever there was, and letting the rest of the rooms be taken over by the frost and the wind. Soon sleep came, erasing also that illusion of time. The ghetto was suspended in a void.

It was before noon. The Presess sat in his well-heated office at Baluter Ring. Around him, on the walls, hung charts and artistically executed diagrams of the production of the various Resorts. There were also amongst them framed poetry-and-prose reports about the achievements of some departments, institutions or executive bodies, while on a special table lay the albums filled with words of praise for the Presess, intertwined with blessings, odes and colourful illustrations.

The interview hours were over and the Presess was tired. He had received too many women today. Their coquettish manners which had once made him move his chair closer, now made him push his chair away. Today, however, he was aggravated by two women who were, on the contrary, without a speck of coquettishness or flattery, they had been the "Comrades from the Movement", the communist, Comrade Julia, and the Bundist "Lioness", Bracha Koplowitch. Two women of steel. The Presess had an ice-cold dread of such females.

He had called them in with the positive intention of conferring with them. He wanted to collaborate with them and their parties on a secret project: to prepare the ghetto for the hour of liberation, so as to retain order and avoid chaos and unnecessary bloodshed. But the two women had told him bluntly that his first step should be to open the stashes of the buried food supplies which were being kept for a "black hour", and to distribute them amongst the populace. He patiently explained to them that, given the situation of the moment, with the winter and the difficulties of transportation, new supplies of food would not soon reach the ghetto and therefore he had to be thrifty and plan the food distribution well.

The two women shook their heads, puffing themselves up like proud turkeys. They declared that at this very moment, people were starving, the mortality rate was great and that his plans led only to the rotting of thousands of kilograms of food. He almost jumped to his feet with rage. What did they know about planning? Did they carry a speck of responsibility on their shoulders? Yet he had not lost his relaxed tone of voice. He invited them, along with the representatives of other parties, to a secret meeting. Then he inquired how they were and whether they had enough heating material at home.

As soon as they left, he gave free rein to his fury. He hated the women, hated all women, his own included. He sent for Zibert who entered, hopping comically in his shiny boots and rubbing his ears with his little red hands. He jumped over to the oven, rubbed his back against its tiles and smiled clownishly. "May all Jewish children have such warm rooms as this one, Presess, may you be well and healthy." The Presess had to bite his lips so as not to smile, in spite of his nervousness. Zibert looked ridiculous in his boots, with his figure bent sideways, as he stood like a little teddy bear at the oven. The shrewd Zibert did not fail to see the expression on the Presess' face and reacted immediately. "I don't mind a bit that you laugh at me, Presess. So what if I look like Puss-in-Boots. As long as I am warm and comfortable, the devil may take the rest. It is not given to everyone to be tall, just as it is not given to everyone to be smart. What a man lacks in one thing, he compensates for in another. Not so, Presess?" Finally he moved away from the stove and approached Rumkowski's desk. Immediately he had a ghetto joke to tell, apropos the heat in the room: "A commissar was asked in his office, 'Tell me, why is it so hot here?' So the commissar replied, 'What do you expect? After all it's here that I bake my bread.'" Zibert giggled, stretching his warm little hand out to the Presess. "*Shalom aleichem!*" He lifted Rumkowski's hand from the table and shook it with the tips of his fingers. "I'm at your disposal, Herr Presess".

The Presess, calmed down considerably by Zibert's presence, began to complain good-humouredly, "I had a women's day today, Zibert."

No sooner had he said that, than Clara, dressed in black as usual, entered the office. Zibert bowed roguishly, "My respects, Mrs. Presessova."

She did not give him even a glance, but spoke directly to the Presess, "Chaim, I must talk to you!" Zibert scratched his head and made for the door, although he noticed that the Old Man's eyes were calling him back. Left alone with Clara, the Presess grimaced. He had positively had enough of women for the day.

"Chaim I want to defend a case at the Court of Appeals," she immediately came to the point.

The Presess' face grew even more twisted. Lately Clara had begun to get on his nerves, bothering him with all kinds of court cases. She wanted to practice her profession. Basically he had nothing against it. It would give her something to do and she would perhaps leave him alone, but he feared her female head. Her way of reasoning was often in sharp contrast to his, and she was capable of "cooking up a soup" that would blacken his face. As soon as it came to the so-called issues of justice, she might forget who it was that had the say.

Furthermore, the case in question, a story about a young fellow who had produced false bread cards, touched the Presess personally. It was unheard of for a fellow, through a swindle, to become a distributor of bread and thus be in rivalry with the Presess himself. "Can you make excuses for him?" he asked after she had presented the case to him. "Someone like that should have been deported, but all he got is eight months."

She said reproachfully, "Eight months of jail in the ghetto cannot be compared to the same elsewhere. And then . . . he is still a minor."

The Presess knew that she would not leave him alone, and he wanted to be rid of her. After all, he had no reason to fear her. He had given the lad eight months and even if the court stood on its head, nothing could alter his sentence. He smoothed his forehead and stretched out both hands to her. "What should I do with you, Clara dear? You insist on defending him? Defend him." He kissed her forehead. "But then you will have to repay me with a delicate little favour. Tell the ladies, the wives of our friends, to stop painting their faces — no rouge or powder, and not to wear hats; a new decree, which actually does not touch you. You don't use these tricks anyway, nor do you need them." He pushed her towards the door.

Thus the "female" part of the Presess' day was over. The light of dusk was already vanishing from the dirty snow outside, in Baluter Ring, as a prison van slid into the gate, halting in front of the Presess' office. Two Gestapo men disembarked and entered the Presess' warm room. They politely invited the Eldest of the Jews to board the van.

The next twenty-four hours were exclusively "male".

The following evening, when the Presess returned into the ghetto, there was a blizzard raging. The prison van appeared in Baluter Ring after office hours and no light could be seen in the windows of the barracks of the *Ghettoverwaltung* or the other departments. The Gestapo men accompanying the Presess were too lazy to help him disembark. A white gale of snow dashed past the open door of the van, tearing at the Old Man's white hair. His hat flew off his head, danced in the air and rolled into the whirl of wind and snow. The Presess put his leg on the step clumsily, holding on to his glasses with one hand. Something pushed him and he fell into the snow.

He stood up slowly. He saw the lines of the wire fence around Baluter Ring through his wet glasses. Behind the wires he saw black shadows, one beside the other. He dragged himself over to the wall and leaned against it. His mouth was too tight to let more than a strangled sob escape. There, on the outside, stood the people; in the snow and the wind they had waited for him. He, Mordecai Chaim, had just lived through twenty-four hours of horror for their sake. Were they waiting out of love and care for him? Or had they come to see him, the great man, fall into the snow? Be it as it may, they were now hurrying home, and from house to house the joyful message was probably circulating: "The Old Man has come back!" No, the Old Man was not such a fool. He knew that all they had on their minds was themselves.

He could barely remember when he had ever cried in his life. At this moment he welcomed his tears. They relieved his tension after the long hours of abuse. He now allowed himself the luxury of self-pity, of bemoaning the fate of a lonely unloved shepherd of a people, of weeping over his humiliation, over the fact that instead of the warmth that he might have expected from the people, he had to content himself now with the warmth of the dying fire in his office. All that he wanted from them was a bit of affection, a speck of recognition for the sacrifices he had made for their sake. Had he not done everything to deserve that bit of love? He had put his own head on the line. There were leaders of other nations who had risked much less for their people, yet they were popular with the masses. Why not he? Why had not even one friendly exclamation, not even one word of encouragement reached his ears?

His tearful eyes darted over the walls of his office decorated with framed odes, with words of praise. All that was cold, calculated flattery. He knew it and yet he collected it all and held it dear, soothing his heart with lies. And he would go on expecting the lies and the flattery. He would remain the same as he was before these fateful twenty-four hours. And they, his Jews, would also remain the same. "There is something about you, Mordecai Chaim," he said to himself, "that does not allow people to love you, while it is your fate to need the love of people more than anything else . . ." That was the truth about him. The past twenty-four hours seemed insignificant in comparison to the moment when he had seen the black shadows on the other side of Baluter Ring. He would have been capable of singing out victoriously, had he heard at least one voice, at least one expression of devotion. Mordecai Chaim slowly combed through his dishevelled hair with his hands, as if he were caressing his head.

At length he wiped his face and straightened up. He clenched his fists. He would force them to love him, force them to be grateful to him. He would save a remainder of the people, in exchange for a remainder of love. And as if in reply to his resolution, the door opened slowly, and the Presess' coachman carefully poked his head in.

"Herr Presess!" he called out, "You have come back, thank heavens! A stone rolled off my heart. Here, Presess, someone handed me your hat." Rumkowski practically fell into the arms of the hefty broad-shouldered coachman and let himself be guided to the coach.

At home, Clara's open arms waited for him. Her face was puffed and her eyes tearful. Strangely enough, her worry was distasteful to him. "They didn't hurt you?" she patted him, searching his eyes.

"Not at all," he groaned, freeing himself from her embrace, "We had a conference."

"You look exhausted, Chaim," she whispered. But then she remembered that he did not like to be told such things. "You look frozen," she corrected herself, helping him to remove his coat.

She led him into the dining room, brought him tea and pastry and sat down beside him, expecting him to tell her what had happened. What had happened? Nothing. The games which had been played with him were a gruesome dream which he refused to remember, which he never would remember. Now he was back in his kingdom, awakened from the nightmare. He quickly sent Clara away and sent for Zibert. He wanted to hear the latest political news.

The ghetto rose in the morning to the news that the Presess had come back from the city, sobbing. The same day a "duck" began to circulate that the Chief of the *Ghettoverwaltung*, Herr Biebow, had not appeared that day at Baluter Ring, but had been arrested for swindling, and that the ghetto would probably be the scapegoat. Yet the ghetto went to sleep in good spirits, since during the late hours of the evening another "duck" had begun to circulate from street to street, from house to house, from bed to bed: The *Yekes* were indeed pulling out from Lvov.

The following day a German commission appeared in the ghetto and visited all the Resorts. It was followed by a new "duck", namely that the commission included the commander of a camp near Lublin. He had come to investigate the possibility of transporting the Jews of that camp to the ghetto in Lodz. There was another "duck" which claimed the opposite: The commission was looking for ways of transporting the Jews of the Lodz Ghetto to a camp near Lublin. Little by little it became clear that the visit of the commission was related to the Presess' trip into town, and with his sobbing on his return. The people waited impatiently for the evening when the news from the secret radio listeners would begin to spread. There was no doubt that the front was coming closer.

The ghetto was feverish and this time the fever attacked not only the workers of the Resorts, but also the managers, the policemen and the high officials. The ghetto had acquired new prophets: the few radio listeners who from hidden nooks explained the messages of the laconic oracles coming from the sacred radio receivers. The names of these listeners who throughout all these years had secretly guarded the thread of waves connecting them to the world, became known to everyone overnight. They were blessed and praised by all, the stool pigeons of the *Kripo* included. It did not even enter the latter's minds to tell on the few heroes which the ghetto still possessed.

Presess Rumkowski himself had completely lost his equilibrium. If up to now his moods had been changeable, it now became completely impossible to know what to expect from him. When one might expect praise, he reprimanded, waving his stick; when one shook with fear in his presence, he would smile good-humouredly and give out an extra food ration. But in both, his good and bad moods, he was impatient. He seemed to be in a constant hurry, racing towards his goal with his last bit of strength. Barely capable of remaining for an hour or two in his office, he would rush to the Resorts and departments. Here he was silent, there he delivered speeches; here he patted the people on the shoulder, there he slapped their faces. He commanded, "Work, work and more work!" then ran off, preoccupied and excited.

On one such day, his secretary appeared in the Presess' office, announcing, "Herr Rosenberg of the *Kripo* wishes to speak to you, Herr Presess. Should I let him in before his turn?"

The Presess, busy with paper work, exclaimed without raising his head, "Out of the question! There must be justice here!"

Adam Rosenberg walked into the office an hour and a half later. He was wearing his complete winter outfit. The fur coat had been bought from a Czech

Jude, the fur hat from a Berlin *Jude*, and the dark glasses were inherited from Yadwiga. He looked doubly well, doubly fat and his face was beet-red from sitting in the heated waiting room for so long. Without waiting for an invitation, he sat down in the empty chair at the desk and slowly removed his fur hat to reveal a shiny pate. He wiped away the drops of sweat from his upper lip and grinned, "Good morning, Herr Presess." With his hand he checked whether the few hairs left on his head were properly spread over his pate, then he stretched out the same hand to the Presess.

His hand remained suspended in the air. The old man on the opposite side of the desk glared at him with a pair of stupefied cold eyes. "You?" he panted. "Who let you in here?"

Adam swallowed the "you" with its accompanying tone of voice and replied, still grinning, "I asked for an interview and patiently waited my turn." With a broad gesture he unbuttoned his fur coat and drew out a clean batiste handkerchief. After blowing his nose loudly, he resumed, "I'll get to the point immediately, Herr Presess. I have come both on business and for private reasons." He inhaled deeply, playing with his fingers as he talked. "You know Herr Presess, that through all these years I've asked you for nothing, in spite of our close acquaintance before the war. Now too I have not come to ask for anything. I am a proud man. I have my dignity and I don't need anyone's favours. Therefore I can talk to you like an equal." Adam was fully aware that the Old Man's patience was hanging by a hair. With feigned nonchalance he threw one foot over the other, while the speed with which he began to wind his fingers betrayed the fact that he was beginning to lose his self-assurance. "I am an advisor to the *Kripo* and I have no doubt that you are aware of this fact . . . Indeed, I have come to see you on that account, namely, I want a good position from you."

Rumkowski raised his eyebrows and opened his mouth, uncertain whether Rosenberg was acting out some clownish role of his own, or whether he had been sent by Sutter. But he caught sight of Rosenberg's nervous hands and a little flame lit up in his eyes. "That's what it is!" he called out.

"That's what it is. I told you, Herr Presess, I have not come to beg, but to propose a business deal."

"And what kind of business is it, for example?"

"Do you understand, Herr Presess, the war is about to end. And as soon as this happens, Herr Presess, the two of us, you and I, will be in the same boat. So, for the job that you will give me now . . . I have substantial capital secured in Switzerland. I will make you my partner. We can vanish into a nice little country and live out our years in peace."

The Presess began to enjoy himself. "You are worried about saving your skin."

"The same as you, Herr Presess."

"How many Jewish souls do you have on your conscience; you stinking stool pigeon, tell the truth."

"Never as many as you, Herr Presess."

Rumkowski guffawed, "And I, you see, don't want to escape anywhere!"

The more self-assured the Presess became, the more unsure Adam began to feel. "Do you really think, Herr Presess," his voice began to vibrate, "that you are a great hero? So I am telling you that you're acting foolishly. It might happen that too many Jews will save themselves, and don't you worry, they will recognize you after the war and catch you. You have delivered hundreds . . . thousands . . . And those who will remain . . . even if one of them remains . . ."

"I am praying to God that more than one should remain. And why do you need a job from me? Don't you enjoy your work at the *Kripo*? You no longer like watching your brothers being tortured and killed?"

"Herr Presess . . . I in your place . . . would not mention that. Secondly, they are not my brothers."

"Really? Aren't you a Jew?"

Adam wanted to tell him that a Jew was only he who wanted to be one, but he bit his tongue and lowered his head. "Not all Jews are brothers, Herr Presess."

"That's certainly so," the Presess snapped with pleasure. "I, for instance, don't consider myself your brother."

Adam's shoulders drooped. His voice began to ring desperately, "I can't work at the *Kripo* any longer . . ." he muttered. "I . . . I know too much. Do you understand? If you gave me a job, I would change my name and appearance. I'll dye my hair . . ." With an awkward gesture he circled his hand over his pate, "I want to pay for it. I've saved a few gold pieces. The ghetto's treasury is empty. I know everything, Herr Presess. We are in the same boat. One way or another, the noose is tightening around our necks. Let's run off together." Adam dared to raise his head and look at the Presess with a gaze of indescribable sorrow. "I am a lonely man, Herr Presess. I have no one in this world. And bear in mind, if you refuse me . . . Sutter's still my best friend. You have been taken into town twice, three times, haven't you? You got away by the skin of your teeth, but you've missed only by a hair . . ."

The Presess jumped to his feet, pointing his finger towards the door. "Out of here!" he bellowed, shaking so violently that his loose eyeglasses jumped to the tip of his nose and he barely managed to catch them. "And remember, if you say one more word, I will call Sutter myself and tell him what you came to see me about!" Adam, bent under the torrent of the Presess' curses, and slipped out of the office.

When Zibert appeared that day, the Presess immediately told him about his encounter with Rosenberg. Still shaken, he asked, "How can you explain such an anti-Semite, such a monster?"

Zibert rocked himself on the heels of his boots. "Let's not kid ourselves, Presess." He tied his lips into a little chuckle. "There is an anti-Semite hidden in each one of us; within one—more, within another—less. A question of degree, nothing else. How many of us would not jump out of our own skin if given a chance? Do you think that only the stool pigeons of the *Kripo* want it? What about our policemen? And our Steinbergs? And even just a simple nobody, a ghetto Jew, and even myself, the great Zionist, for instance? But why should we go so far? What about the Creator of this world, our Daddy in heaven, isn't he a little anti-Semitic? Believe me, more than once have I imagined Him as a Hitlerite with a swastika on his arm."

The Presess blinked. Zibert was not "in his soup" today, and it was preferable not to indulge in a serious conversation with him. "Spare me your wisecracks," the Presess ordered. "Better tell me what's new on the fronts."

Chapter Twenty-two

(David's Notebook)

I've been thinking a lot about my sister Halina, about Warsaw. Halina probably had a baby. What happened to them? I think a lot about my two deported friends, Marek and Isaac. Also another figure comes lately to pay me visits in my mind: Socrates, who accepted without protest the beaker of poison from those who stood so much lower than he. How should one understand Socrates' death?

I suffer terribly from hunger, I'm incapable of thinking of anything else. A madness. I knew and yet did not know that the craving for food is the strongest of all passions. I am becoming an animal. I care about nothing when I need a bite of food, not even about the news. But as soon as I have eaten a bit, I become a smart alec, a philosopher, a saviour of the world, a world politician. I talk about freedom, heroism, love.

For as long as I could, I postponed my contribution of five deca bread for the sick comrades. Today, an hour ago, I took out our bread ration. I cut off and weighed a slice of it on our scale (the highest technological achievement. It consists of strings, two preserve cans, and small stones serving for weights). I immediately took the treasure to Simon, our distinguished leader, and at the same time swallowed a litany of reproaches from him, because I don't attend the meetings and am not socially active. I came home with a fresh collection of information straight from the radio box, and with a burden of obligations towards the movement: to become one of the Nursing Group serving sick, lonely comrades, to lead a children's group, and so on and on. When my stomach is more or less satisfied, my mind becomes so energetic that I can take the most fantastic obligations upon myself. Fulfilling them is of course another story.

✦ ✦ ✦

I am diligently preparing myself for my lectures to the children. I read them a fine book about the Spartacus uprising. Children admire heroes. I am not indifferent to the subject myself. The question of what is a hero interests me. Apropos, during my last conversation with Simon I had a moment of tension. I expected him to ask me to join the resistance movement, but he mentioned nothing of the sort. Yet I know for certain that both mother and Abraham have become involved in clandestine activities. I am curious about the kind of psychological formula our leaders used to eliminate me, setting me apart from my family. My relations with Abraham have grown shaky because of this. He looks down at me. Perhaps I should have asked Simon straight-out and heard what he had to say. And what would I have replied, if he had asked me straight-out: Do you want to join?

I don't know whether I want to join. I am actually quite glad that they have excluded me. I had better not analyze the reason — I mean the deeper reason. The superficial reason is that I don't believe in my strength, in our strength. I don't see what we could achieve by going out into open battle; we, the barely-walking skeletons, rotting with tuberculosis, hungry, swollen. What could we accomplish by throwing ourselves at our armed guards? Acts of meaningless courage which end in death only play into the hands of the Germans. Honour-shmonour is not worth a farthing. I don't want us to be buried in the ground, while the world erects monuments in our honour, lays wreaths and sings the praises of our heroism. No thank you. I still remember a conversation which I once had with Zuckerman. He said to me that the Germans have not abused our honour, but rather their own and the world's; that for us Jews the fight for survival is our sole means of defending our honour, and that willing death is dishonourable. He was right.

As I said before, all these "philosophies" pop into my head when my belly is more or less full. Then I throw optimistic phrases left and right. I am an artist not only in bluffing others, but also myself.

✦   ✦   ✦

We are hungry. It is unbearable. It has never been so bad before. A kilogram of potatoes costs one hundred and fifty *rumkis* on the black market. A bit of oil costs a thousand. Calcium or a little bottle of *Vigantol* is impossible to come by, not to mention glucose. The mortality rate grows from day to day. There are no medicines. We cook at the Gas Centre and wear our coats at home. We sleep in our clothes. The comrades used to bring peat balls or rags for the fire to our meetings; now we sit in the cold rooms, huddled up, body to body, keeping each other warm.

In spite of everything, those people, who are still on their feet, have become agile. If one says that miracles happen in the ghetto one ought to believe it. The party work has become activated. The cultural life of the ghetto is flourishing again. The scarecrows, the *klepsidras*, smile from ear to ear, greeting each other with the exclamation, "May they go to hell!"

I rarely meet Rachel in private. During meetings we sit close to each other, but it is to keep warm rather than for any other reason. Sometimes, during a discussion, I purposely defend a view that is contrary to hers, in order to irritate her. She is so positive and knows a hundred percent what she wants. It shocks me. Apart from that, she is hanging around with that crazy Berkovitch. What she sees in that gray-haired nut only God knows.

✦   ✦   ✦

Perhaps there is a bit of truth in the saying, "God shall not abandon you". Last week I earned a fortune — not, heaven forbid, at the Resort, but from playing chess. The *Kriponik* Adam Rosenberg visited me day after day, and either he has lost his head, or the quality of my game has improved. I easily won every game. The problem is only that he no longer pays me with food but with *rumkis*, and on the black market the prices are sky high. But let's not complain. To be truthful, I am afraid of winning so often from that bore. The whole business of having a *Kriponik* in our home makes me uneasy. Garbage. The main thing: I've bought twenty-five and a half potatoes.

✦ ✦ ✦

As soon as I have a free moment, I crawl into bed with my Spinoza. I bought the book in the street for ten pfennig, accidentally, although there are no accidents in the ghetto. The Toffee Man says that everything that happens to a Jew in the ghetto has a high and deep meaning. So the fact that Spinoza has fallen into my hands precisely now must also have some significance.

It is hard to get into the work: long entangled German sentences with connected words as well as minute print. The book itself — unbound, torn, covered with mud — is falling apart. Interesting: I bought the book with the Toffee Man in mind. Spinoza is a pantheist, it occurred to me. He thinks that God is everywhere. If so, I thought humorously, perhaps Spinoza will convince me that the Toffee Man is right and that God is indeed present in the ghetto. For the time being I am having nothing but trouble with the book. I have had no preparation for such "heavy artillery" and I have to read the same passages over and over again, and still leave them undigested. In spite of everything, however, the book absorbs me.

Today I was in bed with my Spinoza when Rachel entered. She was frozen, her nose and cheeks red. Seeing me in bed she ran towards me, crying, "Are you sick?" I could not bear her questioning worried eyes. I assured her that I was healthy as a fish and had nothing else to say to her. She remarked, "There is snow on your walls." I confirmed that yes, there was snow on our walls. She went over to the window and touched the blackout blanket. "Stiff as a sheet of ice," she said.

"Stiffer than that," I replied.

I asked myself whether I torment her because I love her or because I hate her. Anyway, I put my Spinoza away and called her over to sit down beside me. I put my arms around her, pressing my cheek against hers. She immediately said, "Do you know what I think? I think that it is not the wire fence that stands between us, but something else."

"What?" I asked, not curiously but rather automatically.

"Something else."

I laughed and said that between us stood her clothes and I suggested to her to get undressed and creep into my bed, since Mother and Abraham were at a meeting and would not come home soon. She removed her coat and shoes and crawled in under the covers. She was like a slab of ice; her dress and stockings were unpleasant next to my warm body. I wanted to help her unbutton the dress, but she began to cry. That froze me completely. Soon she got up from the bed and put on her coat and shoes. I asked her whether she knew anything about the resistance movement. She said no, and dashed out of the room.

As soon as she left, I felt warm around my eyes. I picked up Spinoza but it did not help. My eyes ran over the print while what I saw was Rachel's gaze. Why can I not bear it? What is there about her that I have come to hate? Is it because when she is beside me I become more aware of the barbed wires, of my craving for food, of my own weakness? Or is there, as she says, still another reason?

✦ ✦ ✦

A darling of a "duck" is quacking all over the ghetto. A committee to save the remainder of European Jewry has been formed in America. We shall receive parcels of clothes and food. And we are being reassured that the distribution of all these goodies will be in the hands, not of Rumkowski or the *Sonderkommando*, or of the Germans, but of the International Red Cross. I, the remainder of the remainder of European Jewry, think that this would be quite nice if it were true. The people are overjoyed, as if their bellies had already been filled by the contents of the Red Cross parcels. In the meantime a completely different "duck" is circulating: the Germans are again demanding a thousand heads. I have heard that many have been taken from their beds at night. Who is meant this time is not clear. Apart from that, German commissions arrive every day to visit the Resorts. There have never been so many of them.

+ + +

The Germans are demanding fifteen hundred of the intelligentsia and semi-intelligentsia. (What is the definition of semi-intelligentsia? There is a saying that half a wise man is a whole idiot.) They are afraid that the intellectuals and half-intellectuals might rouse the crowds, inciting them to acts of resistance. Which means that the transport will without doubt, be "scrapped".

A team of doctors has begun to work. There is talk about a deportation of ten thousand people to take place soon. I put one and one together: first the intelligentsia, then the entire ghetto.

+ + +

I am on the list! I've received a note to report to the doctors' commission. We have moved in to Rachel's apartment. If only I had gone into hiding, they would have taken Mother and Abraham as hostages. People are saying that at the Tailor Resort coats and suits are being sewn for the men of the transport. That is supposed to mean that they will be sent to work, not be "scrapped". There is a "duck" going around that the men will work in factories where instruments of precision are being produced. I am curious as to how they have classified me — as an intellectual, or as half an intellectual? Devil take them. I will not leave. I will not let them catch me.

+ + +

Our food cards have been cancelled. We cannot pick up any food. Mother brings bread and vegetables from the party headquarters. The rest comes from Rachel's family. We live together. I have heard that others assigned for deportation have also gone into hiding. Only five hundred and thirty people have reported to the jail. Fools. No one should report voluntarily. There are rumours curculating that the *Ghettoverwaltung* wants to sell the ghetto to another business company for thirty-five million marks. The company wants to pay only thirty million. We, the merchandise, ought to be proud of our high value.

In the meantime I am trapped here and do not exchange a word with anyone. I sit in Rachel's corner, in the little room, between the bed and the window. I am alone in the apartment now. Rachel and her family are at work and Mother and Abraham, who do not go to work because I could be traced through them, run around all day in search of "protection" to free me. I have moments when I go out of my mind with fear.

+ + +

The days are terribly long, but I don't write much here. I read Spinoza a bit and the rest of the time I do nothing but count the hours until Rachel's arrival. We don't talk much, but I feel best when she sits down beside me on the floor. She has taught me how to smoke. It gives me no pleasure, but it does kill the appetite. Mother and Abraham are constantly running around. I sleep under the bed, in case the police come to raid the house at night.

✦   ✦   ✦

An order has been issued that on Sunday no one can leave his house. There will be a search all over the ghetto for those who are hiding. Today is Friday. I want to believe that there is a God who will protect me. I feel low, miserable. How good life would be if the world were led by a fatherly spirit, by a kind, caring hand. I am crying like a baby.

✦   ✦   ✦

Today, Sunday morning, I was caught. I am in the prison. I took this pad along. A light bulb is burning in the hall. It is night now. All of us prisoners are lying on the floor. The hall is well heated. We have also received a tasty soup and a slice of bread with sausage. Everyone is calm, but no one is asleep. I am also calm. I will wait another hour and try to escape. I am writing here in order to keep my nerves at bay and to kill time.

I stood all morning at the fence of the prison. Rachel stood on the other side. I am unable to write about her now. I shall try to escape through the latrine.

✦   ✦   ✦

Hurrah! I am free! Free! Not thanks to my heroic deeds, heaven forbid. But let me tell it in some order. I hid in the latrine, and around midnight dashed to the fence. But that fence was not made for such a hero as myself to climb. A policeman pulled me down, gave me a going over and paraded me back to the hall. Two hours later I repeated the bit with the latrine. The policemen immediately got hold of me on the fence, and once more gave me a treatment with their fists.

"Idiotic bastard," they said, "you've nothing better to do than to climb a straight wall?"

This time the policeman at the door was ordered not to let me out. The policemen do their jobs devotedly. For participating in today's action they and the firemen and chimney-sweeps receive one kilogram of bread, ten deca of sausage, ten·deca of fat, ten deca of marmalade, twenty deca of white sugar and the rest I don't remember. The watchman at the door boasted about it himself.

I had to leave my definite escape for the moment when the group would be led outside. But at dawn a policeman appeared in the hall and called my name. I waded through the bodies. Only now, on my way to "freedom", did I see the faces of those on the floor. I was not ashamed of leaving them. I was proud of being freed, of having "protection". The policeman who let me out gave me a friendly pat on the shoulder. I fell into Mother's arms. Abraham kissed me, then Mrs. Eibushitz, then Shlamek. I ran ahead with Rachel. It was seven in the morning. People were on their way to work. The clop-clop of the shoes and the clinking of the canteens were music to my ears. We immediately left for work. All day long I barely knew what was going on around me. I did not find it difficult to act according to the slogan "T.I.E." (take it easy). In general, if what we are doing in the Resort in the "field" of sabotage is ever discovered, I don't envy us. We waste as much material as we can. Machines break down every day and no order has yet left our hall on time.

After work I went to the bazaar. I took off Father's sweater and sold it for three kilograms of potato peels. We celebrated my homecoming and our last meal with the Eibushitzs. We did not shut our mouths for a moment.

✦ ✦ ✦

Everything is back to normal, including the craving for food and the cold. Mother is very weak after the experience of my arrest. Two days ago as I was shaving in front of the mirror, I was flabbergasted by my resemblance to Father. It is weird. Not that I mind resembling him, I just don't want to think of him. Firstly, it hurts to remember him, secondly, he was my ideal of a man and thinking about him makes me realize how worthless I am. I feel obliged to try and be worthy of him, to follow in his footsteps, etcetera. My dilemma is both that I want to follow in his footsteps and I don't want to. I want, as a man, to discover my own truths. At the same time I want to be sure that he would approve of them.

I feel Father's presence within me and around me, even when I don't look in the mirror and don't think of him. Probably the interplay of imagination and reason in the mind of a hungry person is different from that in the mind of a satisfied person. Sometimes silly thoughts come into my head. I think, for instance, that a person can be destroyed physically only, that only matter can disintegrate, that there is such a thing as the eternal breath of life, a mysterious non-matter. (The Toffee Man would be delighted to hear that from me. Michal Levine perhaps too.) And so say I, the rationalist, deluding myself with such crazy mystical medieval tales — that my father's life's breath, for instance, is within me. And not only my father's but the life's breaths of all the Jews who have left are with us in the streets, the yards, the houses. They move through us day and night. They advise and lead us, they reproach and console, they warn and demand. More than anything else they demand. We cannot bear their demands and try to drown them out with our chatter, to exorcise them like *dybbuks*. They obsess us, refusing to acknowledge our weakness, refusing to vanish.

I am writing stupid things. Never mind. Paper is patient. So let me continue with my illogicalities. It sometimes seems to me that the air around us is full, and not only with the souls of those who left the ghetto. Because if the soul is immortal, then the air must be crowded with the souls of all the generations that had once lived. How crammed the air must be! Perhaps that is why the souls of the living are also crammed and muddled, full of chaos? Each of us must be carrying the souls of his ancestors within him. Our present wishes, cravings, passions, must be gleaned from some remote beginning, passing through us, aiming where? To the souls of our children. We probably carry within ourselves the souls of those who will be born some day, or of those who will never be born.

✦ ✦ ✦

In my opinion, the ghetto is too preoccupied with culture. The fact that the Germans tolerate this is a bad sign. They want us to relax our watchfulness. We must make the poets and the artists shut up. We should boycott the House of Culture. We should stop singing, dreaming, making plans for after the war. We must be on guard.

How strange that in spite of the cold, the hunger, the epidemics, art is blossoming, negating the Latin proverb: *Inter arma silent musae*. There is not a backyard where the people do not gather, I mean mostly the young, to discuss, sing, or read together. And I, am I not infested by it myself? My Spinoza is absorbing me more and more. I have become sentimental about the book's dirty torn pages. Just to think that between page fifty-four and fifty-five my life was hanging by a hair! There is no trace in the book of that fateful interruption. Where is there a trace of it? Is there a place where a night of danger in a person's life registers? Eh, something must be wrong with me. My rationalistic legs are beginning to shake . . . precisely now when one ought to be smart, practical and alert. I must pull myself together. I will throw away Spinoza.

✦ ✦ ✦

I almost quarrelled with Rachel today. She is hanging around with that scribbler Berkovitch and I often see them together. She holds his arm while he wears a broad smile. We stop and greet one another, then I run off in one direction, while Rachel walks off with him in the other, as if nothing had ever happened between her and me. This infuriates me. What does she have to chatter so much about with that no-goodnik? Also, he is perhaps fifteen years older than she and as gray as an old man.

✦ ✦ ✦

This evening I went strolling, hands in pockets, in the fifteen degree cold. It was dark, but the white sidewalk, the white walls made the darkness seem brighter. Suddenly I saw the two of them, Rachel and Berkovitch that is, a few steps away from me. They were standing under the gaslight, steam rising from their mouths. In the dark their faces looked like red beets; the visor of his cap was turned sideways. He was holding a sheet of paper in his hand, letting the light of the lantern fall on it, while he read something to her. She embraced the lantern, her gaze buried in his face. Objectively speaking, this was quite a strange-looking scene and some passers-by smiled at them. But, my heart began to pound at the sight. I came closer, very close, and pulled her by the sleeve.

"*Servus*, Rachel!" I cried out.

They both stared at me as if I had woken them from sleep. But soon Rachel's eyes lit up pleasantly and she shook my hand. "What are you doing here?" she asked.

"I am out for a stroll," I said, staring straight into her eyes, and ignoring her companion. "Come with me," I commanded.

She turned her head to her companion and so did I. He glared at her with such slippery eyes that I felt like giving him a smack between his teeth. He smiled like a moron and handed her the sheet of paper, "Take it, read it by yourself," he said. He shook her hand, and then mine. I pulled her away so fast that she begged me to stop, because she had no strength to run. Nor did I have any strength, but I was propelled by my nerves.

She wore a dark-blue thick scarf on her head; it looked in the dark as if she had blue hair. She was beautiful, delicate, fragile, in the evening light of snow and gas lanterns. This made me explode, "Why do you go around with him?" She did not answer and I became even more furious. "I can't understand what you see in him. I see the two of you together almost every day."

"You see me every day?" She looked at me astounded.

"Almost."

"And I have not seen you for nine days," she said, looking like a wounded Madonna.

"Why do you look at me so reproachfully?" I asked, "Why do you go around with strange men?"

"I don't go around with strange men. He knows that I love you."

"Yet he goes around with you, and he knows that you are doing it to spite me."

"It is not to spite you."

"Why then?"

"I don't know why."

We were silent for a long time. We were very cold and entered a gateway. It was only a few minutes before curfew. I pressed her to myself to keep us warm. In the dark I saw her eyes run over and my heart filled with tenderness for her. I held her tighter. "Rachel, you're mine ... Why don't you understand that?"

"Explain it to me," she whispered.

I did not know how to explain. I only said, "You're right."

She said, "And if I am right, will that make you love me more?"

I could not fall asleep at night, thinking of my meeting with her. A few important things became clear to me. First, that I could lose her forever; second, that I love her; third, that I have the need to free myself from her. In one word, a very clear chaos. Due to that intense thinking I got hungry. I ate up half of tomorrow's bread ration, and now, two o'clock in the morning, I am putting all this down on paper.

✦   ✦   ✦

I visited Rachel today and told her of the three confusing truths which I discovered last night. She said that they did not surprise her and that she had known it all for a long time. She also added that Berkovitch had proposed to her, suggested that she move in with him, and that she had refused because she loves me.

After that exchange, everything between us became simple and clear. Yet I was surprised and overwhelmed by what followed. I squeezed her hands between mine, saying, "Rachel, I want to become a man." When I said it, I was so moved that I felt a lump in my throat. "I must go away from you ... to be alone. Your love is good and beautiful. But I am not ready for it. It binds my wings. I must be free. I don't know why, but I feel that it must be so. I feel, I am sure that I will come back to you." Here I had to wait for my inner tension to subside. I kept silent for a long while, holding my head close to hers. Then I gathered all my strength to add, "Perhaps my feelings of today are not dependable. I must not promise you anything, nor must you promise me anything."

After I left her, I felt relieved, yet not lighthearted. A chapter of my life is over.

✦   ✦   ✦

Mother died two nights ago.

Chapter Twenty-three

THE YARD OF the Metal Resort was cluttered with broken parts of machinery, rusty kettles and metal refuse covered with snow. The walls of the building shook; the window panes trembled. The pounding of hammers could be heard from near and far, followed by a sharp metallic sound as it joined the general cacophony of squeaking, grating, swishing noises.

Rachel had to climb many stairs. The door to the halls stood open and she could see the black monsters, the machines, through the gray dusty air. Beside them, stood the human machines with black faces and hands, and eyes whose whites flashed like tiny electric bulbs. Some small human machines dressed in dirty overalls turned their black faces to her, exposing bright rows of teeth as they smiled. They were her students from the illegal school which was harboured in the garret.

In the garret the floor shook under her feet, swaying with the roar of the building. Over the roof, the winds wailed as they crumbled the snow and threw it against the frozen panes of the tiny windows. In spite of the noise, it seemed to Rachel that complete silence reigned here. She entered the little shed which served as a teachers' room and took out the books which she needed. Then she began to straighten up the rows of benches in the classroom, moving the blackboard closer to them. She liked to sit close to her students and would often perch on the top of a bench, facing the class. She placed her bench in the middle row, opposite the student Freiman, a charming fourteen-year-old who lived alone; he had jumped from the wagon during the *Sperre*. He had very big black eyes and when he listened to Rachel, he kept his mouth open, so that the mouth too seemed to be listening. Indeed, there were a few youngsters whose absence Rachel would have deeply regretted. There were, however, others who did Rachel a favour by not attending. They did not allow her to concentrate; either their appearance gave her the feeling that what she was doing made no sense, or their arrogant bitter remarks confused her.

She put her canteen in a corner so that her students could not see it. She felt a little ashamed of receiving a soup for teaching them. She paced the floor. The frost bit her fingertips. Not long before, the principal had still received a bit of heating material, and he would light the little furnace in the garret. But those times were gone.

As she wrapped herself tighter in her coat and put up the collar, she heard the sound of many steps, some light and rhythmical, others heavy and tired. The garret filled with sixty black little devils. Sixty black faces shone bright eyes at her and she felt warmer. At that moment she was certain that the profession she had chosen as a little girl was the most beautiful in the world. She sat down on the bench, removed her gloves, placed the open book on her lap and embraced the class with her eyes. Her favourite students were there. Their faces, smeared with dirt and machine grease, were open; the dirty black hands lay relaxed in their laps.

"We shall study a story by I.L. Peretz today, called 'Miracles at Sea'," she announced, raising the book. "In the Kingdom of Holland," she began to read, "In a half-sunken hut near the seashore, there lived a humble Jewish fisherman by the name of Satia . . ."

The garret was transformed into a sea. Satia and his wife were drying the nets, their children were rolling in the sand or looking for ambers. Satia, the only Jew in a village of gentiles, knew little of Judaism. The sea did not allow him to leave the village. His father, his grandfather and great-grandfather had all perished at sea. Such power did the sea possess. It was man's most dangerous enemy, often treacherous. And yet the fishermen loved it; they were attracted to it and could not tear themselves away from it . . . For they wanted to live and to die on it.

The sixty boys swayed in the powerful stormy sea. They could not tear themselves away from it . . . They wanted to live and die on it, too. As if through a fog Rachel caught sight of the principal counting the children, then entering the "teachers' room". She went on with the story:

". . . Tonight is the eve of *Yom Kippur* when Satia followed a Jewish custom. He would catch a large fish and leave for town to be present at the synagogue, to listen to the cantor and the choir sing, and to eat the fish after the fast . . . So Satia is now leaving to catch the fish. In the morning the sea is barely swaying; it barely breathes, one can barely hear it whisper. Lazily, as if still dreaming, it stretches and shrinks. Yet the chain of Satia's boat growls a warning, 'Beware, beware!' And his neighbours, the fishermen, tell him 'Beware!' A barefoot old man points out a black dot in the sky and says, 'That will grow into a cloud . . . You have a wife and children, Satia'. But Satia replies, 'And a great God in the Heavens.' And now he is on the sea and the sea sways and rocks stronger and more wildly. The sun has swum into the sky, but its lustre seems moist. A weeping sun. And Satia pulls out empty nets."

A piece of loose tar-paper flapped angrily against the roof of the attic; the gales seemed determined to tear it off. The class swayed sadly, with awe, and Rachel swayed with them.

Then the storm breaks out. The sea rages; the waves climb higher and higher . . . Here is a fish! Satia must catch it. But the fish only teases him, with its dazzle. Within Satia a voice cries out to turn back, but the fish tempts him on. The gales lash at him with an obscene rage, smiting him as they whip up the sea even more. The sea roars and thunders as a thousand basses play inside it; mighty kettle drums are hidden in its waves. "Home! Home!" Satia's heart is pounding. He begins to row quickly. The boat jumps like a nut over the waves. But he is dazzled again, and again something tempts him to turn back and move further out to sea. He sees his wife's body in the waves. She is calling him, "Satia, help!" He struggles with the waves. But suddenly he remembers, "*Yom Kippur* today!" And he lets the oars fall from his hands. "Do with me, God, whatever you wish!" he calls out to the sky, "I don't row on *Yom Kippur*."

Rachel read a few more lines, but she heard a noise coming from the benches. Freiman was pounding his fist against the top of his bench. He stood up and turned his dirty face to Rachel. His eyes were sharp, full of anger, "That story is for the dogs!" he snorted.

The wind pounded fistfuls of snow against the frozen attic windows. It roared in the pipes of the cold furnace. Rachel inhaled deeply, pulling the coat more tightly about her. She moved her hand over her hair to fix it, and suddenly it seemed to her that she was Miss Diamand, her old teacher, and that Freiman was herself. "Sit down, Freiman", she said calmly. "Let us first finish the story." Her eyes returned to the book. Satia is humming a tune which he suddenly remembers, a tune which the choir used to sing on *Yom Kippur* every year. Satia wants to die singing.

The entire class was now in an uproar. The noise increased. Freiman jumped to his feet again, burning her with his gaze. "If I were Satia," he exploded, "I wouldn't be such an idiot! If I were Satia, I would go on rowing until I had no strength left, and I would not want to die singing! If I were Satia I would not let anyone do with me as he pleased, not even God!"

A forest of black fingers rose in the air. This was her moment, the moment when she, Rachel, had to prove what kind of a teacher she was. And she was so inexperienced! She prepared herself, embracing the class with a gaze which was both hers and Miss Diamand's. With encouraging nervous nods she tried to help the youngsters express what they had to say.

The discussion was at its height, when the principal broke in to announce that the lesson was over. He invited Rachel in to the "teachers' room" and admonished her severely.

"Next time, Miss Eibushitz, you must not wear your coat during a lesson. It is not pedagogical and makes a bad impression on the students. We must create the atmosphere of an institution of learning, not that of a streetcar."

She wanted to ask him why sitting in a coat in a cold room created the atmosphere of a streetcar, but he, with his books under his arm, was ready to take over the class. As soon as he went out, a bell began to ring discreetly and a commotion began in the garret. The principal opened a side door and let the boys out through it. Rachel ran over to a little window, climbed on top of a bench and saw a German automobile in the street.

She went down to the factory office to wait for the inspection to be over. Soon she heard the news. The commission had come in connection with the six wagons of machinery from the concentration camp of Poniatov which had been liquidated. The Germans had come to decide whether to place the machines in the existing Metal Resorts or to build new factories for them. The office girls speculated on what had happened to the people who had worked these machines at the Poniatov camp.

As soon as the commission departed, Rachel fetched her soup and ate it up in front of the kitchen window in the yard. When she raised her eyes, she saw Bunim standing beside her, his nose red with cold, his face blue, his eyes squinting; steam rose from his smiling mouth. "I stepped out from the Gas Centre for a minute," he said. "Come with me. It is warm there."

She took hold of his arm and leaned over to him, "Impossible."

They could not talk. The wind was blowing in their faces, taking their breath away; it tried to tear them apart while it tangled the tails of their coats. Their eyelids were stiff with frost, their lashes hard, frozen; their gazes could distinguish only a small stretch of sidewalk. Now and then Rachel managed to steal a glance at Bunim. His puffed red lips looked like an open wound. He thrust her hand into his pocket and whispered into her ear, "I have a new chapter!" The wind cut short his words. She was unable to reply. She hid her face in the collar of her coat and allowed herself to be led by him. He led her into the Gas Centre, offered her a mug of hot water and refused to let her go before she had agreed to come to see him that evening.

✦   ✦   ✦

Bunim's hut came into view in the evening darkness, adorned in its wintery splendour. The roof, covered with a thick layer of snow, shimmered. Long icicles dangled from it like the fringes of an exquisite curtain. Icicles were also suspended from the protruding beams and the closed shutters; these were thinner, more delicate and resembled unlit candles.

Inside the hut, the walls shone with parallel streaks of frozen snow which had entered through the cracks between the boards. The torn, white-gray curtains were like a frozen cobweb, stiffly clinging to the window-panes. It was half dark in the kitchen. A candle in a corner cast a pale light. From this corner Bunim emerged and slowly walked towards Rachel. She unwrapped the scarf on her head, but had no courage to unbutton her coat. In the lit corner, on a chair, stood a tin basin.

"Doing your laundry?" she asked, avoiding his shining eyes.

"I'm soaking a shirt . . . I brought home a kettle of hot water from the Gas Centre," he mumbled and moved in the direction of the other room. "Come in here . . ."

At the beginning of their acquaintance he had never let her enter the other room. Lately however he would receive her only there, getting her out of the kitchen as soon as he could. He did not want her to see how awkward he was in his housekeeping chores. It was dark in the other room, where Bunim never turned on the electric light. Rachel moved forward, with both hands outstretched, until she touched Blimele's bed and sat down on it.

He brought in the candle from the kitchen. "I don't know whether I should read to you tonight," he said. "Tomorrow will perhaps be more appropriate. My shirt will be dry and . . . I will clean up the room a bit." A few moments later, the new chapter of his poem was in her lap. He took apart a chair and fed it to the fire, covering it with peat dust and sand. "That way" he said, "the fire will burn throughout the entire chapter."

A cold oven was a sad sight, but the sight of a warm oven in a sad room was almost unbearable. The fire with its pleasant hissing and crackling seemed to reveal even more sharply the homelessness of that half-dark home. Rachel had the impression that the walls were chasing her out. The beds, the wardrobe, the mirror, the doll's carriage at the window, where a dirty empty flower vase stood behind the stiff torn curtain, haunted her. Between the two windows a tiny red velvet pillow in the form of a heart hung on the wall. A few pins and needles were stuck on it; a thin black thread dangled from one of the needles.

Bunim took out a woman's coat from the wardrobe and threw it over Rachel's shoulders. Suddenly she felt hot, unable to breathe. She wanted to throw off the coat and escape. But she remained sitting on Blimele's bed and allowed Bunim to cover her feet with Blimele's blanket. He sat down beside her. His stiff hair looked like a gray crown of twisted thorns pointing in all directions. From between his swollen eyelids and his puffed cheeks his gray eyes blinked at her, called to her. His cracked lips burnt on his blue face like a painful wound. "*Ahava* . . ." Had she heard him whisper the Hebrew word for love, or had she imagined it? She picked up the manuscript and handed it to him.

He began to read quickly, swallowing the words. He read with the lilt of a *Torah* student, as he swayed to the rhythm of the stanzas. The chapter was about winter and about the young man called Israel Noble who had been caught escaping from the ghetto and was hanged on the bazaar. The poem described his calm proud walk to the scaffold and the footprints that the young man left behind him in the snow. The poem rang out with the freedom of a neck inside a noose, as it repeated Israel Noble's words like an echo: "I belong to no one, no one. Only my body is yours but not my soul . . ."

Bunim was rocking over Rachel's lap, holding on to it as if it were a table. He read about the cherry tree from whose branches tenderness like white doves flew down upon the tortured body of the ghetto. He read about nights as deep as a sigh, as loud as a cry, as entangled as nightmares. He clenched his fists, letting them rest on Rachel's knees. His voice broke. The chapter was finished. They had no idea how it happened that a kiss sealed their mouths, like a dot after the last word of the last line. It seemed to her that his mouth was the velvet pillow which hung on the frozen wall. She left her lips on the wounded mouth, cradling Bunim's gray head and stroking his unshaven swollen cheeks. Soon she was surrounded by his arms completely, and she let him absorb the soothing sweetness of their embrace.

But the next moment she tore herself away and stood up. He helped her wrap herself in her coat and tied the scarf under her chin. He insisted on taking her home. They walked the streets like two blind people. He held her hand in his pocket as they led each other on. "Will you come tomorrow?" he asked.

When she was alone at home, Rachel often felt like wearing the fur jacket which her father had given her, so that she could be warm. But she did not have the courage to do it, fearing the thoughts that would attack her as soon as she was embraced by the warm fur. She was sure that she would think about the girl to whom the fur had belonged, a girl perhaps as old as herself — who had never grown older.

However, the night before, she had sat on Blimele's bed, wrapped in Miriam's coat, her legs covered with Blimele's blanket. And this morning, a few minutes before she left for work, she dared to remove the fur from the pillowcase and put it on. She felt warm. The fur caressed her neck. She did not fear the thoughts which came to her. She thought of the very things she had been afraid of thinking, and yet she enjoyed parading about the room in the fur. She smiled at herself in the mirror, sorry to have to take off the fur and hide it again. She put on her threadbare gymnasium coat, wrapped the scarf around her head and neck and took her canteen; she threaded her belt through its handle, put her spoon into her pocket and left the room.

No sooner was she outside than she fell into Bunim's arms. "I was waiting for you," he blinked. "I've sneaked out of the Gas Centre. No consumers. And I have a new poem!" He pulled her back to the stairway, climbed up a step, and took out a sheet of bookkeeping paper from his pocket. "'*Ahava*' . . . that's the title." He read quickly, as usual. She stood a step below him as he swayed over her head. His voice galloped with the rhythm; splitting, crushing the sounds of words, of syllables, while he wiped his wet nose and his wet wrinkled forehead with his hand. Then he folded the sheet of paper and handed it to her. He cleaned his glasses and led her out into the street. He put her hand into his pocket, inquiring, "Where is your first lesson?"

"At the Tailor Resort," she replied.

They walked on in silence. Vapour issued from their mouths and nostrils. Rachel protected her face from the cold by hiding it behind Bunim's shoulder. They stopped at the Tailor Resort. "Will you come tonight?" he asked.

She went that night. Bunim fed his last chair and two doors of the water bench to the fire and it was warm in the room. He invited her to sit down on Blimele's bed and she obeyed him. He was wearing his washed shirt, his checked jacket and a crooked tie. He was shaved and his gray hair was combed. He looked young and festive. His expression of joy, so often mixed with a grimace of pain, was subdued, softer. His squinting eyes smiled wistfully. "Take off your coat," he proposed. "You won't be cold." He unbuttoned her coat and untied her scarf. Knots of wavy brown hair fell over her forehead and cheeks. For the first time he switched on the electric light in the room.

She hung on to him with her gaze as if she were afraid to look around. His lips were moving. He mumbled some quiet, incomprehensible words. He took her by the hand as if to encourage her. In the corner stood the wardrobe with the mirror. In it was reflected the opposite wall with the windows, the stiff gray curtains and the tiny heart-shaped pillow. At one of the windows stood the carriage with Lily, Blimele's doll, in it. A bluish carriage with a fold-up hood. It was easier to look at the reflection of these things than at the things themselves.

But Bunim pulled her hand, forcing her to stand up. He turned to face the room with her. He led her towards the carriage and took out Lily, handed her the doll and let her hold it for a while. Before putting it back, he showed Rachel the finished chapters of his poem which served Lily as a mattress. He covered the doll with the little blanket and led Rachel back to Blimele's bed. There they had used to sit in the dark by the light of a candle. Now he wanted her to see the bed, to touch it with her hands.

He led her over to the large bed where he had slept with Miriam. "I made the bed for the first time today," he whispered. "In your honour." He led her to the table and watched Rachel put her hands on it. Here Miriam, Blimele and he had taken their meals. A white tablecloth covered the table. "In your honour," he said. "And do you see, I swept the floor." He left her and disappeared into the kitchen. Soon he was back with a plate in his hands. He stepped slowly, so as not to spill a drop, placed the plate on the white empty table and ran back to fetch the spoons. Carefully, they carried the table over to the large bed and sat down. He handed her a spoon, "You must not refuse," he whispered. She ate his ration of soup with him from the same plate. Their heads were close, their eyes, their lips opposite each other. The steam rising from their mouths mixed in the air between them. "You . . ." Rachel heard him whisper, "Call me Simcha."

"Simcha."

The plate was empty. Bunim began to pour out impassioned words. He talked about Miriam and Blimele and his little son without a name. He was so full with all that he had to tell her, that he had to stand up. Hands in pockets, he began to pace the room. Finally his talk changed into a hum. He was humming *Hasidic* tunes; lofty, exuberant, exalted tunes. Suddenly he leapt towards Rachel, grabbed her into his arms and lifted her up high above his head.

His legs gave under him and they both fell to the floor. They sat there silently, their mouths twisted into bashful grins. They stared at each other for a long while. Rachel's gaze jumped towards the wall, above the floor; she felt a draught, and noticed an opening the size of a nut. "Why don't you block it with something?" she asked. "It would not blow so much."

The smile was still on his lips. "When I was alone, a little mouse used to come in through that hole. Sometimes a poem would also come to me through the hole. If you promise that you will keep coming to see me, I will block it with something.

"From where will your poems come to you then?"

"From you . . . *Ahava*."

She jumped to her feet, "I must run."

He took her home.

✦ ✦ ✦

Bunim waited for Rachel every morning, often with a new poem in his hand. He also waited for her after work. In the evenings he would accompany her to her meetings and then wait for her again. Finally, he would come up to her home and wait for her there. He became familiar with Blumka and Shlamek and sometimes had supper with them. Rachel grew so used to his presence, that she was no longer surprised at meeting him wherever she went. It came to seem natural that whenever she emerged from anywhere, he should step forward from behind a wall, or from some dark nook. When she did not immediately notice him, she automatically searched for his black winter coat with the fur collar and for his face with the heavy glasses. She expected him to put her hand into his pocket and with his shoulder to protect her face from the cold. He accompanied her also to her meetings with David.

On taking leave of her, he would beg, "Drop in at my place for a minute, later on."

With David everything was as before, on the surface. But they both knew where they stood, and whenever she saw him, she remembered what he had said to her not long before. David was no longer with her. He was searching for the Holy Grail. He had left her to participate in knightly battles. He had gone to find the man within him. While she, who was so close to him, was waiting for him somewhere else, distant and lonely. They exchanged simple clear words, yet Rachel was amazed that they could still hear each other across the distance. No, this was not a time for running away, she thought. This was a time for keeping together, for clinging to what one possessed. It sufficed that one had to deal with the external hand threatening separation. To separate of one's own will was a sin. Rachel knew this and she read in David's face that he knew it as well; but they knew it only with their reason. The strange powers working within each of them, independent of reason, were pushing them onto the unsafe roads which they had chosen for themselves. In their estrangement, they would touch. Their bodies would sometimes become drawn to each other and they would remain in an embrace reminiscent of the past, though no longer the same.

More than once did she leave David, intoxicated by his present-absent kisses, full of a gnawing sweet longing, yet also sad and humiliated — to fall into the cold air of the yard and Bunim's arms. He would be waiting for her in the gateway, in order to see her once more, or to lead her to his hut, to look at her, to read to her. At such moments his moods resembled hers. He too felt humiliated, ashamed of himself, full of longing. His talk would lapse. He would stammer. Between one word and the next, his love begged for hers. It caused

her to hang on to him with her whole being, seeking protection from him —
and from herself.

When she came to see Bunim after her meetings with David, the intensity of
Bunim's feelings seemed to grow. Dazzled by her physical beauty, starved for
her vitality, he would hold her tighter and longer in his arms than ever. He
wanted to know nothing of her previous experience and he asked no questions.
Being with her at such moments was all that he wished for, as if his joy could not
reach any higher.

During such an evening, he would busy himself around her more than usual.
He would feed pieces of furniture to the oven, would offer her spoonfuls of his
sugar ration and force her to taste his ration of marmalade. His face radiant, he
would entertain her, and it seemed as if spring had entered his life, making him
look younger and stronger. He would caress the knots of Rachel's dishevelled
brown hair, repeating, "*Ahava . . . Ahava*," and forcing her to sit down on
Blimele's bed.

"Read a new chapter of the poem to me," she asked one day.

Flushed, he sat down beside her. "There is no new chapter."

"Aren't you writing?"

"You know very well that I am."

"I mean your long poem . . ."

He threw his arms around her, pressing her mouth, still warm from David's
lips, to his. She felt his presence everywhere, around her, within her. He was
between her teeth, in her eyes, filling her nostrils. She was lying on Blimele's
bed across from Miriam and Bunim's bed, opposite the wardrobe, the table and
the carriage. The sight of her naked body filled the room. Suddenly he jumped
away from her, "Are you crying?"

Weeping, she slowly put on her clothes and wrapped herself in her coat. For
the first time he did not accompany her out. Outside, everything was dripping
with ice. She absorbed the cold air with her hot face. At the bridge, Bunim came
abreast of her with an open umbrella.

"Take it, you might catch cold."

The following day he was waiting for her again.

Rachel gave up her work with clay and began to write short stories and
poems which she also gave up after a while. She was dissatisfied with the results.
They were too far from what she was striving to bring out and only emphasized
both her helplessness and the entanglements of her soul. Up to now she had
thought of herself as living on two levels, in two worlds, an inner and an outer.
In the outer world she might arrive at some clarity, at an awareness of what she
wanted and where she was heading. It was the inner world, however, snarled
and complicated, in which she was unable to find her way. All she knew was her
confusion and the moods it created. All she knew were the accompanying
motifs, the colourations of these moods, and only through them could she
define herself — to herself.

But now she discovered a third level of life within her. It was a painfully
murky pit into which she used to descend only in her dreams. Now she was
immersed in it during her wakeful hours as well, like a blind person. She asked
herself whether her father, by vanishing from her life, or whether her parting
with David had caused her to slide down into that pit. She felt attuned to fate
like a fly entangled in an autumn cobweb, like a blind dancer whom someone

was teaching the choreography of a dance she could neither control nor grasp.

She would see her father within these dark chambers. He would walk with her to the co-operative to fetch the food rations. He would call her "Daughter", telling her about his life as he gestured with his princely hands in an eternal greeting, an eternal farewell. Inside these dark chambers, she could see the cherry tree covered with blossoms and with snow at the same time. There it was both summer and winter. She would joyfully roll with David over white pastures, over cool sheets of peace, while above their heads there was lightning and thunder, blades of knives and the howl of dogs. She saw herself in the *Sperre* of eternity, rushing to hide with her family, with David, with Bunim, or by herself. Someone was racing after her — an eternal race. Between David and herself there were forests of barbed-wire fences. The Hebrew teacher, the "Karmelka", had written on a blackboard before she was led off during a raid, "Mimamakim . . . De profundis . . ." Rachel heard herself call for help within that black chamber. Something was about to happen to her.

For some reason she felt so very guilty — she who had been wrapping herself in Miriam's plaids, who had been lying naked on Blimele's bed, who was enjoying her fur jacket . . . she who ate bread and sipped soup from her canteen, who was able to laugh and to cry, who had a pair of living warm arms which were ready to braid themselves around a lover's neck. There, inside these dark chambers, she hated David for holding her trapped. It was by him whom she loved that she would be destroyed, not by the Germans. There, she hated Bunim. It was by him who loved her that she would be devoured, not by the Germans.

She would decide not to see either David or Bunim, so that she could cement her inner strength anew. But the day when she did not see David was a day without a spark of light. And Bunim? He stood behind a wall, waiting for her with a poem written during the night. Bunim held her hand in his pocket and led her to work through the slippery streets. He forced her to eat his soup with him and he washed his shirt every day, so that he could wear it when she came to see him. He turned on the light in the other room, kindled a fire and fed it the doors of the wardrobe.

In Bunim's room the walls were weeping, reproaching, chasing her out; and yet they were embracing her. She sat with Bunim on Blimele's bed. Across the room, leaning against the wall, stood the mirror of the partly-burnt wardrobe. Rachel saw Bunim and herself in it. She knew that today, like yesterday, she would cry and he would jump to his feet, irritated, confused, asking, "Why are you crying?" She would not know what to answer. One thing she was clear about: the angrier he got with her for her tears, the more ready she was to stay with him. His anger, his shouts released something within her.

"Why don't you go?" He would wait for her to dress. "Why do you come to see me? Why don't you leave me alone and stop torturing me? Never mind, I don't need your pity. I can bear it alone."

She would stretch her hands out to him, humbly waiting for him to come nearer. When he took her into his arms again, she heard a voice within her, whisper, "That powerful man, with his swollen face, with his sick heart, wants to devour me in order to stand on his feet. I want him to devour me." And she would smooth out his furrowed brow with her lips, whispering. "Forgive me."

Then, in love with herself, seeing herself so splendidly reflected in his eyes, she would allow him to serve her; because she cherished the image of herself which he gave her. She deserved to be waited upon. She was the Rachel of his poems, whom he called *Ahava*. She was adored. Her soul and body were one and they were full of light. As she ate Bunim's food with him, his soups, his sugar and his bread, it was she who felt generous, proud that she was capable of offering herself to him in her kindness.

He surrendered to her every whim. She surrendered to him. Sometimes when they stared humbly at each other, Bunim would whisper "We are perishing, *Ahava*." There was no fear in their eyes. What he said also meant, "We are imperishable".

◆   ◆   ◆

Long rainy days. The snow was melting; the ice was beginning to crack. Yet, although it was the beginning of spring, the air was permeated by a wet biting cold. The ghetto was swimming in water and mud. Dissolving heaps of snow floated through the streets and yards. The roofs were constantly cracking, slabs of ice were falling from them. The bridge stood sunken in mud, a turned-over gondola in the Venice of a forsaken world. The church was a red ship which had forgotten to which port it was bound. The ghetto sploshed in the mud, buzzing like an inundated behive. In the hearts of the ghettoniks, spring had already arrived, and as they rushed in their rotting wooden shoes to food queues or to their meetings, their eyes shone like a thousand suns. They were unable to stay home. They had to be outside, to move, to talk.

Rachel and Bunim spent a lot of time outdoors. It was cold in her apartment and the floor of his hut was flooded. They moved through the streets until, soaked to the marrow of their bones with rain and cold, they would enter a gateway, sit down on a step and call it home for a while. They would eat together or Bunim would read, until she exclaimed, "I must run!"

"Running again," he would usually say, and she was never sure whether it was with reproach or only with regret.

One evening she met him with the news, "The Zionist Widawski has committed suicide. He took cyanide. Someone from the *Kripo* told on him."

That evening Bunim talked a lot. He spoke quickly, a foam appearing in the corners of his mouth. For the first time he did not look at Rachel and seemed to have forgotten that she was there. He was talking about Widawski whom he had once met — a young man who, afraid of betraying his comrades during interrogation, had taken cyanide. The young man was a real man. Suicide was no weakness. Only those who were themselves cowards denounced such acts as cowardice. Even a person who took his own life out of a fear of life was also crying out his scorn against God, by becoming the master of his own fate. Then how much more respect did that man deserve, who took his own life out of a reverence for life?

Chapter Twenty-four

THE SUICIDE of the Zionist Widawski shook the ghetto. Nor was Bunim able to think about anything else. The shadow of the young man moved into Bunim's hut and at night would place itself at the head of his bed, asking stubbornly, inquisitively, "And you? And you?"

Bunim lay on his bed, his arms under his head, his eyes turned to the closed shutters. The shadow of Widawski brought with it Miriam and Blimele, Bunim's parents and sisters, the poetess Sarah Samet and the poet Burstin who had known entire symphonies by heart and had left with the "action" of the single people. Widawski's shadow brought along the neighbours from the yard, the characters of Bunim's poem. Bunim flipped through all these faces as through the pages of a book. He whispered their names and heard them ask, "Why have you abandoned us?" They wailed, they demanded, they cursed, "You were supposed to carry us within you. Don't let us vanish namelessly. Take your pencil into your hand again."

With the help of Widawski's shadow, Bunim lit the candle at his bedside. He took an empty bookkeeping sheet and a pencil and stared into the darkness. Slowly he began to sway, trying to recapture the rhythms of his long poem and move his mind back into it. But then he saw Rachel's face in the warm flame of the candle; her beaming eyes called him. Bunim was still swaying, but the rhythm was new, young, pulsating with vitality. He covered the white sheet of paper with fragrant dancing words. Widawski's shadow was still at his bedside, but the more Bunim felt his presence, the more eagerly he gave himself to the new rhythm, the more intoxicated he became in his exhilaration.

When he finished and the pencil fell from his hand, he sighed, relieved of the ten stanzas of a flamboyant love poem. But then he picked up the page, crumpled it in his fist and lit it with the candle's flame, allowing the fire to lick the tip of his fingers. He extinguished the candle and covered his head with the eiderdown. The shadow of Widawski brought the characters of his poem to him again. Bunim shut his eyes tightly, "Let me live!" he called to them in his heart.

Blimele touched the tips of his toes with cold fingers, "*Tateshe*, take me in your arms . . . Come across with me . . ." she begged him.

Bunim went with Rachel to the writers' meetings at Vladimir Winter's. He was asked about his great poem. He was asked to read a chapter aloud. Rachel too was tormenting him with questions. "Have you stopped?"

"Yes, I've stopped," he told her.

"Why, Simcha?"

"I can't write!"

"Why?"

One day he exclaimed, "You know very well why!" She left him and walked away. He caught up with her and grabbed her arm, "I cannot go on without you." He took her hand and squeezed it so forcefully that she got cramps in her fingers. He panted heavily, exhausted; the fur collar on his chest moved up and down. She knew that his legs were becoming increasingly swollen. The doctor had told him that something was wrong with his heart, that he must rest often. She went home with him and forced him to lie down.

He began to stay in bed. The Toffee Man became his frequent visitor again; he also brought Bunim's food rations. When Rachel wanted to help with Bunim's housekeeping, he scolded her, "If you have come to do charitable work, you can leave right away!" But when she was on the point of leaving, he would apologize, then call her over, "Sit beside me . . . Just sit beside me."

The hut acquired its former sad appearance. Now, with the partly-destroyed wardrobe, with the table without chairs, with the wet walls around it, it seemed as if despair itself had moved in. The moment she entered, Rachel wanted to run out again. She would sit a bit with Bunim and when she could no longer bear it, she would stand up and, averting her eyes from him, mutter, "I must run."

He would grab her hand, "Why are you running away from me?"

"I am not running away from you . . ." In order to convince him, she would sit down again, taking his unshaven puffed face between her hands. "What's new with the poem?" she would ask.

That irritated him. He raged. Finally he would say, "Go, go if you want to!" and would show her the door.

✦   ✦   ✦

The first smells of spring. Blue streaks of sky, pastel stripes of gold which the breeze, like a magician, pulled out from its hat of clouds where the sun was hiding. The soaking muddy earth of Marysin, swollen, waiting to be fertilized. Budding trees. Leaves of a delicate sea-green. The ground was already being measured in order to divide it into *dzialkas*, and this time people were saying that the *shishkas* had renounced one hundred and fifty square metres *pro publico bono*. The Toffee Man talked Bunim into working the plot of soil in front of the hut.

Bunim was standing in line to fetch two kilograms of potato peels on his and the Toffee Man's food cards. The line was thick with people pushing and shoving. But there was a playfulness in their movements, an undertone of lightheartedness in their words. This was due to the delicious air, to the fact that there would soon be an end to standing in line. It was due to the two kilograms of potato peels which the people had been expecting for so long. The women saw themselves preparing pancakes, dumplings, "fish", or "meat", or "tzimmes" out of potato peels.

Bunim's ears were full of the hullabaloo. He let himself be pushed back and forth and thought about his *dzialka*. He was afraid of it, afraid of Miriam and Blimele who would come to be his partners. They had the right. The moments when he had knelt on a bed of soil with Miriam, planting beets, carrots and cabbages while Blimele stood next to her doll's carriage, watching, were moments that had poured into him like wine, filling his soul to overflowing. Those rare moments, of which he had then only superficially been aware, seemed now round and complete in their simplicity and peace. Thus he feared that Miriam and Blimele might come to claim their right in the name of those moments. And yet he wanted to have a plot of soil. It would not weaken his heart, but strengthen it, he thought. He wanted to have beets and radishes in order to prepare little feasts for Rachel. He kept his ears open to the chatter of the women in line, to catch the recipes they were exchanging. Indeed, he was standing here in line now, in order to prepare a *baba* of potato peels for Rachel's visit that evening.

Today was an important day. He was to fetch his new coat from the tailor who lived in the yard on Hockel Street. The tailor was a very sick man, and he had sewn the coat by hand after his Resort hours. That was why it had taken him two months, although Bunim had promised to reward him with an additional five deca of bread, on top of the half a loaf which he had already paid, if he hurried up.

The line was slowly moving ahead. The Toffee Man was wandering along it with the box of candies suspended from his neck, calling out in his tearful voice, "Remedies for the heart! Good, delicious remedies for the heart!"

His beard and sidelocks were wrapped in a dirty brown stocking. He had done this to please Bunim who insisted that he cover his "forbidden" beard and sidelocks and not endanger his life. Sad rivulets of water dripped down from the Toffee Man's eyes and nose. And if someone called him over to buy a candy, he became even more tearful, enthusiastically wiping his nose with his sleeve and heaping blessings and optimistic quotations on the buyer's head. The crowd knew that he was not in his right mind, and to his strange questions they would give strange answers.

At length he joined Bunim in line. He did not suspend his chatter for a moment, keeping his little eyes fixed on Bunim, as he wept, "Oy, God's light has vanished from your face, dear neighbour. I used to see it in you. I saw it then, oy then, during that winter I saw it clearly on your face . . . Your wife, the holy woman, was reviving the fire in the stove with a sheet of cardboard, cooking a soup of parsley leaves. And the little girl in the winter coat, resembling her Mother like one drop of water resembles another, was going for a walk with her doll around the table. And you, yourself, dear neighbour, lay in bed with your gloves on, a pencil between your fingers, and you were writing . . . writing. Then God's light was upon you, I could swear it . . ."

"Will you stop bothering me and shut up?" Bunim growled, pushing the Toffee Man away. "Go ahead, you can earn some money while you're waiting." The little man moved only one step away from him.

The Toffee Man haunted Bunim, speaking burning, tormenting words in his crying voice. The words remained sealed in Bunim's memory, drilling away in his mind at night. The Toffee Man had also taken to coming into the hut when Rachel was there; she sat on Blimele's bed, in her white blouse, her face fresh, her hair shamelessly dishevelled and her cheeks flushed. Or he would see her in the kitchen, warming her long white fingers over the burner of the stove.

He would quickly nod, halt at a distance from her and inquire, averting his eyes, "How are you, Daughter?" Bunim would try to chase him out. "Good, I shall come back later on," the little man would say. But instead of leaving, he would enter the other room and stop in front of the wardrobe, patting Miriam's dresses. "Burnt the doors, burnt them . . ." He would wipe his eyes and walk over to the doll's carriage, making it squeak as he rocked it. Or he would say, looking around, "The chairs have disappeared, dear neighbour, haven't they?"

Bunim had to lead him out by force. The little man would sob, "Dear neighbour, answer me. Why don't you answer me?"

"Crazy fool!" Bunim would call after him furiously.

The few minutes that the Toffee Man had stood with Bunim in line were enough to make the spring vanish from Bunim's heart. He hated the Toffee Man ferociously and feared that he would lose his self-control and tear him to pieces. What did that creature want of him? Why did everything around him seem determined to poison his life? He would not let himself be dragged down. He would fight — and Rachel would help him. She must help him, especially today . . . when he was to wear his new summer coat for the first time. He would cook a *baba* and sit down beside her. He would ask her again to come to live with him. He must convince her that this was her destiny, their destiny. "You must decide," he would say to her. "I cannot go on like this . . ." He would confess this to her as he had many times before. He knew what she would reply.

"Good, I shall decide," she would say and not show up for a few days, leaving him restless, his heart aflutter.

The air became lilac-gray, dusky. A barely visible pink sheen covered the bright blue of the church's windows and those of the houses in the street. The supply of potato peels was about to run out at the store; the people in line grew irritable, and began to shove each other in earnest.

The Toffee Man refused to move away from Bunim.

"It won't be long, dear neighbour, and we will be done with it." He peered sadly into Bunim's eyes. "I swear I know what's on your mind. You can chase me away as much as you like, but I can't allow this to happen. Your soul is soaring through the skies, isn't it? And how long is it since you wallowed in dust, crawling like a worm? Now you have come out of your cocoon, you have become a butterfly, haven't you? And that's all, dear neighbour? You can accomplish nothing else? So I'm telling you that you must not . . . Anyone else may do it, but you must not. Anyone else may let you, but I must not. You know very well that you are related to me, more than a relative, so I may give you a piece of my mind. Out of those thirty nice gas burners which you once turned on, something more than a butterfly must hatch. Sure, sure I know that you are capable of becoming both intoxicated with death and intoxicated with life, but this must not make you weak or overcome you. You must come out of *Pardes*, dear neighbour, with the fruit which carries the seeds of *pshat, drash, remez, sod* . . ."

At last they passed through the entrance of the shed. A flock of nervously squeaking women stood around the heap of soaking potato peels. One of them grabbed a fistful from the top, thrust it on the muddy scales and emptied it into Bunim's open bag. Between the cracks of the shed's dark planks, rays of bright violet entered, making the women look like the blue figures in a Chagall painting.

On the way home, the Toffee Man continued his tearful sermon. But this time Bunim was not listening to him. He was exhausted, so exhausted that he could barely walk. His mind stopped working, making him feel that there was nothing to understand, no burden to carry, no obligations to fulfil. He owed nothing to anyone. He was on his way home with a bagful of garbage. He would throw himself on his bed and that would be all.

The last streaks of light vanished from the sky. As he walked on, Bunim saw himself in captivity in Egypt, carrying bricks for the construction of an enormous pyramid. A dusk just like this one descended over the desert.

Someone removed the burden from his back and invited him to stretch out on the cool sand.Someone covered him with sand, whispering, "Rest in peace . . ." He blinked. A blue reflection still beamed from a window pane. Where could this blue have come from, if the entire sky was dark? It began slowly to weave the gray-blue striped material of his summer coat. As far as he could remember, it was his first summer coat. What a paradox! To come by a summer coat precisely here, in the ghetto! He saw himself dressed in it. It was not the night that was dawning but the day, its light as delicate and soft as Rachel's skin. A sun would rise as fresh and juicy as Rachel's lips. His heart began to beat as if dozens of drumsticks were pounding against it, awaking him. "The coat is ready! Run to the tailor's to fetch it. Hurry!"

Bunim turned to the Toffee Man, "Take the bag, divide it yourself. I'll be back soon".

When he left the tailor's with his new coat, it was already very dark. In the sky the black rags of cloud swam by. They were his old black winter coat with the disgusting fur collar swimming away from him. If only his legs were not so weak, if only his shoulders did not droop as if still pressed down by a heavy load. How could everything be as before? Was there still an obligation to fulfil . . . bricks to carry? The black coat which had seemed to swim away hung instead above his head. So it would remain. It was not finished. Only that now Bunim had two coats: one black and one blue, a winter coat and a summer coat. They would quarrel with each other and torment him. But he refused to be torn apart, although his swollen feet were lagging behind and his heart was tired. The Toffee Man would not let him drown. Bunim would wear both coats. Both would serve him and adorn him, they would not weaken him but make him stronger.

He was on his way to meet Rachel — but suddenly he turned back. He would not see her tonight. Tonight for the first time he would give her up of his own will. He would come to her through a different way, a more Bunim-like way. His feelings for her had to become a flame that instead of devouring him kept him warm. Now that he was drunk with longing and love, he must go back home. Together with the Toffee Man he would prepare a *baba* and they would both eat it in the other room, where he would not turn on the light. He would keep his ears open and his heart hungry for the Toffee Man's insane-sane words. He would swallow them along with the dish of potato peelings.

That night the Toffee Man slept in Blimele's bed. For a very long time he talked and cried in the darkness. The room was a large absorbing ear. Through it Bunim heard the first lines of a new chapter of his long poem. At the break of day he arose and took a few pages of bookkeeping paper.

✦ ✦ ✦

Bunim stood in the stairwell of Rachel's house and heard her shut the door upstairs, heard her feet hopping down the stairs, his ear registering the soft squeaking rustle of her hand against the banister. She stood before him, her coat slung over her shoulders, the thin dark-red scarf tied in a knot over her bosom, the tips of her ringlets touching it. Strands of hair trembled on her forehead. Her face was still covered by a veil of sleepiness, in her eyes the reflection of her dreams; astonishment mixed with fear. She looked at him through a haze. Then her face lit up.

"Congratulations!" she cried, gliding her hand over the coat. "Turn around. Let me see how it fits." He felt her stroke his shoulders and back. "A gay colour!" her voice reached him. Then she moved to face him. "You look great!"

He took her hand. It was good that today was a day of rest, she said, and observed him from the side, surprised to see him so changed. He reproachfully thought that she had not even asked why he had not shown up the day before, but he immediately checked himself. Why succumb to destructive thoughts? This was an important day for him, for the two of them. He was taking Rachel to the cemetery, to his parents' graves. He had a poem in his pocket, dedicated to them, a chapter in his long epic. He had made two copies of it. He would read it to Rachel and then bury one copy in his mother's grave and the other in his father's.

Now and then they stopped at the window of an empty apartment and peered inside. "Why don't you move in here?" Rachel pointed to a little house with a neglected garden in Marysin.

He mumbled, "Only if you come to live with me . . . Otherwise I prefer it there." At the cemetery, he felt her pressing tighter against him. "Live with me . . ." he whispered in her ear. She hung her head. He saw the white of her neck between her hair and the red scarf. He talked to that whiteness, "Rachel, it's hard for me to live like this. My work . . . I need peace of mind, equilibrium. With you I could achieve that, and . . . the Toffee Man says that the ghetto is a gruesome *Pardes*. Only a few can bring back the fruit . . . Those who are able to, must. I must try at least . . . We must. There is nothing more sacred than that now."

On both sides of the main path there vibrated a silence that was full of life. Between the old trees and the graves, the ground was humming with bees and flies, with bugs and butterflies. Birds were singing on the boughs. In the overgrown side paths the boughs braided nets of lights and shadow. In the large field full of raw graves without tombstones, the young grass was sprouting. Wooden markers with the names of the deceased peered out from the green. The markers looked like big butterflies sitting at the head of each grave.

Bunim walked among the graves of 1940, reading the markers. Rachel followed behind him; withdrawn, uncertain. She stared at Bunim's new coat, and observed his bear-like walk. She felt like running away. Her heart began to pound and her legs to tremble, because of the restlessness that overwhelmed her. But then Bunim turned, indicating, "Here lies my father."

He put his hand on her shoulder and drew out the few sheets of paper from his pocket. In his fast slurring voice he began to read the poem dedicated to his parents. Then he took out another sheet of paper on which he had set down a love poem, the one he had burnt and then recalled that morning. The air was warm, the sun burned Rachel's back. Bunim's face was clear, beautiful. Even the sharp deep furrows on his forehead were now barely visible. Yet she was cold. She envied the fly buzzing above her head, envied the birds in the boughs, the leaves on the trees. Bunim rolled up the two sheets of paper and buried them near the marker with his father's name. Holding on to Rachel's shoulder he set out to find his mother's grave. When he found it, he repeated the ceremony. This time he asked Rachel to sit down beside him on the grass at the grave. As they sat huddled up against each other, he said, "Now you are mine." She opened her eyes wide. He put his hand to her mouth.

She stood up, "Come, let's go."

"*Ahava* . . ." he grabbed her hand, squeezing her fingers. He pulled her forcefully down to him. She lay in his arms.

"I love David . . ." she mumbled between his kisses.

"It's a lie," he replied. "You love me. You are my *Ahava*. You must stand by me." At length he let go of her, smiling softly, "*Ahava*, I understand you. Of course you cannot help yourself. I will help you, make you ready . . ."

She tore herself away from him, "Leave me alone with your talk."

He kept on smiling. "You know that what I say is true, because if it weren't, you would have broken with me a long time ago. Why aren't you running away?"

"You don't let me!" She freed herself from his grip and from the red scarf around her neck and set out at a run, jumping over the graves and between them.

Bunim was left alone in the field. He stretched out on the grass, burying his face in the palms of his hands. Then he clenched his fists, leaning his forehead against them. "On all fours . . . on all fours I will crawl . . . and I will arrive," he whispered to himself.

The following day he cheerfully waited for Rachel. He showed her the canteen in his hand. "Guess what I have for you," he called out.

"A soup!" she tried to guess.

"No, a *tzimmes* of radishes! I've got a recipe. Come into the corner and taste it!" He took out a spoon from his pocket and handed it to her. She tasted a spoonful of the *tzimmes* while he kept his eyes on her mouth, "So?"

"Heavenly!"

He took the spoon out of her hand and began to feed her. "I have eaten already," he assured her. "This is all for you, and come, I'll show you something. My new *dzialka*. I've exchanged my old one for a plot in Marysin. And yes, do you know that the cherry tree is blossoming this year?"

✦ ✦ ✦

During the days that followed, Bunim moved back into his long epic. He worked until late at night, taking the written pages along to the Gas Centre in the morning. He waited less frequently for Rachel. All day he longed for his place by the window of his hut. There the cherry tree peered in with its festive mop of leaves and blossoms. Its revival was a miracle. In its honour Bunim opened the shutters. As soon as he entered the room, he would place a box at the table near the window and put the canteen with his soup on the table. He always found it difficult to eat alone. Now the tree kept him company. It sat with him, ate with him, talked with him.

Then he busied himself with his laundry. He hung it outside on the line which he had tied between the tree and his shutter, then he returned to the window in the hut, placed a few empty sheets of paper before him and took out his pencil. He dressed up his soul in its pre-writing mood, calling on Biblical Jeremiah for assistance. Then the pencil went racing off by itself. Never before had his pencil galloped so victoriously through the lines as it did during those days of his renewed enthusiasm. Deep, deep inside him another pair of eyes looked out at the blossoming tree and another mouth whispered, "*Ahava*, you are with me. You are Miriam. You are Blimele. You are the dove."

The young neighbours gathered around the cherry tree. Sometimes one of them would whistle warmly, while the others hummed: "The golden peacock flew over the Black Sea . . ." Some older women would tell morbid stories of what had happened last year, or the year before last. Further away from the tree, young and old alike were kneeling on the ground, digging, planting, sowing.

On a few beds of soil the delicate leaves of beets were already green, young onions were tracing their way upwards with faint thin lines. Somewhere else a woman, as playful as a little girl, stepped along a bed of soil, a bag of seeds in her hand. Slowly she let them sift through her fingers.

The hours ran on. The image of the yard framed in the window began to fade. The beds of soil sank into the darkness along with the neighbours' silhouettes. The evening was a dark sponge, absorbing, erasing everything; the night — a blackboard on which only the outlines of the cherry tree remained. And in front of Bunim remained the white sheet of paper, which the sponge could not erase.

Bunim's near-sighted eyes could no longer make out the letters, yet his pencil ran on. It seemed that the pencil had no point and left no trace behind. That made him feel freer, less restrained. He soared between the sky and the earth — every written line becoming the line of the horizon. Yet what he was actually writing was a chapter about the Toffee Man. He put him into his poem as he was — his minute figure, his flying gaberdine, his thin beard and sidelocks, and the box suspended from his thin neck. He copied his chant, "People, buy a remedy for the heart!" and described his tiny eyes — the source of his great tearful lament. He repeated his sayings — the incomprehensible and the clear, the insane and the sane — from which he, Bunim, had so often wanted to escape. The Toffee Man's day-to-day talk acquired astonishing dimensions in the poem.

Finally the pencil began to slow down. The thread unwinding from Bunim's heart was slowly running out. His hand stopped. He raised his head from the paper and looked at the tree outside with hazy eyes. A smile played on his lips. His heart was light, calm. A peaceful pride. The white dove, the joy of creation, was cooling on the borders of the written sheet of paper.

Then he stopped seeing anything; beads of sweat appeared on his forehead. He felt a pain in his back, his spine was stiff. His heart pounded with a hasty irregular rhythm. He rose from the box, letting it fall behind him and, doubled up, both arms outstretched before him, he moved towards his bed and fell on it like a log, placing both hands on his heart as if to restrain it. The heart transferred its motion to his hands and they too began to jump. Along with his hands his entire body began to pulsate. He craved a sip of cool water and looked with longing at the door, in the direction of the kitchen. But he had no strength to get up. The pail of water was too far away. He became frightened. The morning would never come, never again. He would never finish his poem . . . Never. He had only reached the outer gates . . . had only got to *remez* and not further, and already he was so exhausted, so blind . . .

Sirens began to wail. An air-raid. Bunim pricked up his ears. Airplanes were approaching. The earth was shuddering. Bombs exploded. Anti-aircraft guns ticked loudly and rhythmically. Lightning. Thunder. A shaft of light laughed demonically, illuminating the window. The walls of the hut began to hum. The devil was sitting on Bunim's heart which was pounding wildly. Bunim's mouth was open. He swallowed the air, his dry tongue protruding. But then, amidst the roar and the thunder he heard a thin faint buzzing. The cricket in the wall began to sing a tune for Bunim which was as refreshing as a drink of water: "Perhaps you will arrive. Perhaps you will . . . in spite of everything."

"Water," Bunim groaned, seeing that the cricket had acquired a human face; a little face with a beard and sidelocks wrapped in a stocking.

When he opened his eyes, the shutters of the windows were closed and the light in the room was on. The Toffee Man was bending over him, wailing. "Dear neighbour, how can a person pass out while alone in a room? And in addition, at a time when the entire backyard is jubilating in their nightclothes? I have come to announce the good news to you. All of Lodz is sitting hidden in the bunkers, only we, the ghettoniks, are celebrating in the middle of the night. The Ruskies are approaching! Do you hear the thunder?" The Toffee Man swayed over Bunim. "Some more water? Here, take some more. After all, water is not rationed." Suddenly he burst into a flood of tears. "Woe is me, how you look, dear neighbour! And your legs are swollen like pumpkins, woe is me! And look at the face that you have put on! Why don't you take care of yourself, for heaven's sake! Don't you know that in a person like yourself mind and body are tied together? You think that I don't know what you're doing? I mean . . . sharing your food. I mean, eating your soup together . . . from the same plate . . . Yeah, perhaps this feeds the soul, but not all that feeds the soul satisfies the body . . . And the jug must be whole dear neighbour, so that it can hold the wine. So, open your mouth, here, have a remedy for the heart. Take it, suck it, like that. I can see that you feel better. Caught your breath? You hear? It's thundering again; it's tearing the earth asunder. A blessing upon the Ruskies' heads. All of humanity is awaiting them like the light of day."

During the Toffee Man's monologue, Bunim's heart slowly began to calm down. In his mind he compared him to the Toffee Man of his poem. There was a difference between the two. But within Bunim, the two were one. Bunim wanted to pick up his pencil again. He sat up and faced the Toffee Man who was standing before him with the mug of water in his hand. "Thank you," he said, pushing him lightly aside. "Now I am busy. Go in good health."

They heard an explosion. The Toffee Man pricked up his ears. "Do you hear? Such an alarm! Not since the ghetto is a ghetto has there been anything like it!" He took out two toffee candies and threw them on the bed. "In case of this or that, put a toffee in your mouth, dear neighbour. It's the best remedy for you."

As soon as the Toffee Man left, Bunim went back to work, but he had no patience. He stepped outside. The yard seemed empty; until he caught sight of shadows moving along the walls; white faces, one near the other, were turned toward the slice of sky cut out by the surrounding roofs — towards the lights that were going on and off. Faces shiny like beggars' plates. With every explosion they clinked with thin muffled sounds of joy. The air-raid watchmen of the yard tried to control the crowd. One of them came over to Bunim.

"Are you out of your mind?" he scolded him, "You think that I'll let you putter around in the middle of the yard?"

Bunim took cover under the cherry tree. A few neighbours stood there, looking up at the sky. He sat down in the grass. He would soon go back into his hut and take up his writing. The Toffee Man was right — one had to take care of one's body. A petal fell from the tree, circled in the air and landed in Bunim's palm. He looked at it. Was there someone behind that flower petal? Was there someone behind that fragrant night torn apart by explosions? Was there someone behind those shadows with faces like beggars' plates? Was there someone behind him, Bunim, the poet with the swollen legs, with the wild heart and the myopic eyes? Was there someone behind that mirror, or was all that was reflected in it an illusion — on the one side, and nothingness — on the other?

He enclosed the flower petal in his fist and stood up. He entered the dark hut, lit a candle and put the little petal on the table. The white petal absorbed the warmth of the candle and curled up as if in a spasm of pleasure or pain. As Bunim watched it, he remembered Rachel. For a moment he had the impression that she had been there. But then he remembered that his eyes had not looked upon her yesterday. He became curious about the time and glanced at the clock, beginning to count the hours until morning. He looked at the written pages on the table. He had not even read what he had written in the dark. He looked at the paper but saw only Rachel's white blouse. Tomorrow he would see her. He would not read the pages now, but read them in her presence.

The next moment he was sitting at the table, his head near the candle, working. Through the white sheet of paper led the shortest route to Rachel, through the stanzas swaying with rhythms, through the rhyming words. Bunim climbed over them as over brightly lit stairs, jumped over them towards the dark-red scarf and the white neck under the waves of brown hair. But then the stairs gradually began to shake, becoming heavy and rough. The words he chose were not good; they were cold, flat and false. Now, with the lit candle beside him, he felt blinder than he had been before, in the dark.

The white dove had stopped cooing, it had flown away. The pencil still limped over the paper — a hard pointed crutch. Bunim's heart was burning with frustration, raging against the dove. It was capricious, but he would conquer it and not allow it to leave him. He would sit at the table all night long and finish the twenty-first chapter. He wanted to creep back into its lines, but they rejected him. The words screamed at him, "You have not carried us full term! We are not yours! You have cleverly construed us. We are dry. Because you have in mind not us — but her. It is she who takes you away from us. It is she who has chased away the dove." Bunim wrestled with the stanzas, quarrelled with them, "It's a lie . . . She is the dove." In a sudden flash of rage he extinguished the candle and remained in the dark with his arms spread out over the sheets of paper, his head leaning against them. The sirens wailed. The alarm was over.

He undressed and got into bed. Turning and twisting restlessly, he surrendered to his hatred of Rachel. A siren wailed in his mind, "I hate you, *Ahava.*" He must not allow her to destroy him. At the same time worry picked at his heart. Why had she not come to see him? Was she sick? Had something happened to her family? He could not forgive himself for not running before curfew to check how she was. He reproached himself for being so absorbed in his writing. "Egoist! Megalomanic scribbler!" he scolded himself.

When he fell asleep at last, Blimele appeared in his dream. Miriam was blowing with all her strength into the open burners of the stove, unable to revive the fire.

In the morning he rushed to see Rachel. He met her in the street. She was wearing a summer dress which he had never seen before. It was of a pale aqua colour, sprinkled with little flowers. The dress was tightly fitted, revealing the shape of her hips and bosom. Bunim's face and ears flushed. It was as if he were seeing Rachel for the first time, naked; a woman — a bough, her head — a flower bud.

She too became red in the face and said, "I know it is too tight . . . too short. That's why I never wore it before." She lifted her hand to her neck, not knowing whether he was staring at the Star of David on the dress, or at her bosom, and she tried to cover both with her arm. "Does it really look so bad?"

He removed her arm from her chest. "No, it suits you very well."

She became serious. "I got this dress from the Rag Resort . . . I have a few blouses from there too, but the stains can't be removed. Only this dress is like new. I have nothing to wear. And I no longer mind wearing such things. On days like these I feel like putting on something new."

They looked up at the sky which held the promise of sunshine. Rachel wound her bare arm around Bunim's. He asked, "Why didn't you come yesterday?"

She laughed. "I did come. I looked in through the window and saw you working, so I left. You have a new chapter, don't you, Simcha?"

"No, it's not ready yet . . . and don't call me Simcha any more." Their eyes met, hers astounded, his full of a sudden hostility. Her bare arms, her swaying figure, the bare feet in the sandals, the high white neck and the mouth full of sweet poison only now made him realize that she was indeed the Snake.

"We still have a lot of time," she said apologetically. "Come, let's walk over to your *dzialka.*" She let her arm slide down his and took hold of his hand. He felt her cool fingers in his. Even the nakedness of her fingers burned him.

"Come rather to my hut for a moment," he proposed.

"Sit in your hut on such a day?" But she gave in to him. On the bridge she ran ahead of him. He looked at her feet, at her pink heels. His tired heart was aflutter. He could barely lift his swollen legs.

In front of the gate on Hockel Street stood a cluster of neighbours, the Toffee Man with his candy box was among them. At the sight of Bunim he came forward sobbing, "The tailor, poor soul, is gone. Went to sleep last night and never woke up. Your new coat is alive, isn't it? And he is dead." He moved with Bunim and Rachel across the yard. "Hear the screams?" he asked. "They're coming from the tailor's place. Two neighbours are fighting over the heirloom. They found a quarter of a loaf of bread under his pillow."

As the Toffee Man went on talking, Bunim observed Rachel out of the corner of his eye. He saw her gaze wander over the windows. Then he saw her eyes fix on the cherry tree. David was standing there. Bunim saw Rachel's face light up. The next moment she was gone from his side, soaring with her white arms towards a pair of hands which took hold of her waist. Her arms locked around David's neck.

Bunim sent off the Toffee Man and burst into his hut. He did not want to approach the window, but there he stood a moment later, glaring at the pair who were embracing under the tree, their mouths close together. They were talking fast. They were laughing. Bunim was not angry or jealous, not bitter or hurt. He had only one wish: that the white snake-like arms should unwind from David's neck and the aqua flowery dress should disengage itself from him and come over to the hut. He was patient. He was sure that the meeting of the two under the tree was nothing but another step towards their parting forever. In the other's arms Rachel seemed more snake-like, more enticing and more Bunim's, than ever before.

Indeed he soon saw her take leave of David, and almost dancing, her hips lightly swaying, approach the hut. Bunim's heart began to pound with exhaustion, jumping forward to meet her. She filled the window with her flowering sea-coloured bosom. "I can't come in," she laughed, "I must run to work." When she saw the expression on his face, she added defensively, "I can see by your face that you are inspired. I will come tomorrow and the chapter will be finished, I'm sure." She waved and ran off.

"Snake!" he hissed after her.

Bunim no longer read his poem to Rachel and avoided talking to her about his work. He decided to free himself of Rachel completely. Yet his attraction to her was a passion which he was unable to master. It was a wild stream cascading downward. If only that stream could, instead of inundating his pastures, help him fertilize them, enrich his soil, how easy the most strenuous labour would become for him! He could not forgive her for not having understood that, for not having yielded. But he, Bunim, was anyway a giant. All that he had to achieve, he would achieve, in spite of her, in spite of the downward-rushing stream.

He invented a boyish pastime. He enumerated Rachel's faults to himself. She was not at all as beautiful as he saw her in his delusion, neither physically, nor in her soul. She created the illusion of having an inner richness. In reality she was much more superficial, more shallow, and at the same time spoilt and not at all as clever as she had seemed to him. He had smelled out the wickedness in her gaze, disguised under the veil of caressing sweetness. It was the snake that peered out from her eyes.

However, he was unable to think these thoughts without a certain tenderness. Her faults did not make her more distant. Nor did the blade of the knife which he had put between her and himself do his work any good. Because he worked best when he felt his love, when Rachel watched over him in peace. She was the *Shechina*, the dove. It was his passion for her that caused him to sing passionately about life, about sorrow and loss, about the thirst for vengeance, about pride, about being trampled and yet remaining free. During such moments he would knead Rachel's image into his best lines. Not in vain had she dressed up her nakedness in the flowery dress which had arrived with the wagons of blood-stained clothes. It was for his poem that she had done so. She was Miriam and Blimele. In her desecrated beauty, she wallowed in the gutters of the ghetto. The gendarmes at the fence were aiming at her. She was bullied by the Germans during the *Sperre*. She was being led through all the "actions", to all the evacuations; she climbed to all the gallows. He lamented over her, mourned her. He wrapped her in capes of manly, fatherly tenderness, in the capes of his purified verses, cuddling her in his arms as one would a desecrated Holy Scroll.

And so, gradually, he began to accept both the blade between Rachel and himself and his affinity with her beyond any barrier. And in his day-to-day life, during the hours when he was not with her, his generosity would sometimes replace his conceit, his love would replace his bitterness. He was proud of having conquered Rachel and of having retrieved his creative power. Yet he was humble and submissive, for he knew that he would not have been able to have that strength, had Rachel refused to offer him the little of herself that she did. Now he became restless for a different reason. He himself had no notion of how he would receive her; whether he would be calm and happy, or aggressive and hostile. It happened that he waited for her a few times a day, and it happened that he would leave his hut when he expected her to come. More than once would be chase her away when she visited him, calling her "Snake!" and warning her never to come back. But he would wait for her the next morning with a cup of *tzimmes*, with a piece of coffee *baba*, with toffee candy, or with a poem, and he would call her — *Ahava*.

Chapter Twenty-five

ADAM ROSENBERG'S GARDEN belonged to the few plots of ground in the ghetto that were neglected that summer. It stood steeped in dishevelled greenery, full of tall grass and weeds. Adam had more important worries that May than tending to the beds of soil. He had to worry about his life. He felt that a grave had quietly been dug under him and that one bright day he would sink into it and everything would be over.

Of course he had had similar moods many times before, but those had been hypothetical worries, the danger imagined rather than real. Now the situation was serious. The Angel of Death could now arrive on tiptoe, quietly grab him by the neck, so that no leaf was disturbed or flower deprived of a petal. It would be as if nothing had happened; with Adam or without him, everything would go on just the same.

Adam did not dare step out over his threshold. He was afraid of the cracks in the fence through which he could see the hearses on their way to the cemetery. And indeed, two of his colleagues, both *Kripo* men, had been led past his house the week before, walking to their own funerals. They went "loo-loo", as his colleagues, the other *Kripo* men, who were great cynics, used to say, instead of using the expression "a matzo ball in the head". His colleagues, the *Kripo* men, also chanted with sad voices: "Under Rumkowski you will never eat enough, under Sutter you will never be smart enough, and you will lose the war anyway." Indeed this time Adam was not alone in his fears. The ground was burning under the feet of the "Confidants of the *Kripo*". They knew too much and were too close to Sutter and his gang. Apart from that, Herr Sutter no longer needed them. The treasures of the Jews of Lodz had long been in German hands anyway. Herr Sutter did not need the help of the stool pigeons to invite any ghettonik to the Red House, if only for fun.

Now if Adam had to appear before Herr Sutter or Herr Schmidt, he would become paralysed with tension, with the fear that any minute someone would grab him from behind and lead him off. Every time he stood before Herr Sutter, he tried to read his own fate in Sutter's frog-like eyes, or in his voice.

Adam worked diligently and nervously. True, there were no longer any treasures to be discovered amongst the gray ghetto masses, but there were the *shishkas* who possessed the last remaining valuables. They had provided for themselves for after the war, when neither *rumkis* nor German marks would have any value. And Adam specialized in smelling out which *shishka* had lost his usefulness and was keeping himself afloat through inertia. With refined sensitivity he analyzed the power structure of the ghetto and acquainted himself with the entanglement of intrigues: who with whom against whom. This was not an easy task, for in spite of their frictions, the *shishkas* were a closed superior caste and rarely took a Jewish *Kripo* man into confidence. After all, none of them had delivered his own brothers to the Red House for torture; they had only surfeited themselves, abandoning their poor brothers to consumption and death; they had only served on commissions which compiled lists, deciding whom of their poor brothers to send away. Adam laughed at that "basic difference" between them and himself. There were no greater hypocrites than the *shishkas*; no one who could prove more decisively that man was the lowest form of life on earth. They convinced Adam that the best thing would be to rout out the entire human species and make the dog the King of Nature.

Thus his pleasure in removing a *shishka* would have given him the same delight as winning a game of chess, had it not been for the fact that at this very moment he was a figure in a chess game himself, a figure left alone on the chessboard, about to be mated, decapitated. It was high time for him to become a pawn, for only the pawns had a chance of survival.

Eventually, Adam realised how hysterically he had acted, running to Rumkowski to beg for a good position. He had done it during an attack of real madness, after a night when he had heard fast steps under his window. He could not get over his amazement at the fact that fear could turn a clever man into such an idiot. What did he need the good position for, if the only thing that could save him was to be lost in the mob?

He prepared himself to change his name and his appearance and every night he tried on his female dress and wig before the mirror. The mirror seemed about to burst with laughter and disgust. And he also had his doubts whether this was such a fine solution; there were no longer such fat women in the ghetto. He would have to lose a lot of weight. Yet eating was the only consolation left to him. Moreover, becoming lean threatened him with disease and new danger.

During one of those days Miss Sabinka fell into Adam's hands like a bird which had returned to its cage. Not long before, he had been looking for her, playing the game of detective. Now she stood in front of his house, waiting for him.

It was not easy to recognize Sabinka. Her golden tresses were gone and she had become thin and ugly. Her troubles had begun during the winter. One of her former patrons had evidently wanted to remove her from his conscience, and Sabinka, who was single, had received a "wedding invitation" to join the transport of single people who were deported the first week in February. She went into hiding, never sleeping twice in the same place. Her ration cards were cancelled and when the "action" was over, she did not go back to work. She was sick with fear.

Fortunately, she found a food card in one of the abandoned apartments. A few times she got through to Presess Rumkowski and implored him for help. But Herr Rumkowski remembered that he had seen her with the *Kripo* agent, Rosenberg, and he sent her back to him. She had also tried to approach some of her former admirers, but no one wanted her. The soft-hearted would push a few *rumkis* into her hand, or ask her to come to their Resorts with a pot, for their extra soup.

When she visited her educator, Herr Schatten, he spat with disgust at the sight of his ruined "masterpiece". He was busy educating a new generation of girls who had blossomed into ripeness in the last four years. Precisely at that time there had been an "action" to round up five hundred women, and Herr Schatten had suggested to Sabinka, "You are disintegrating in the ghetto, Sabinka, why don't you . . .?"

At length she followed the Presess' "advice" and went to see Mr. Rosenberg whom she feared very much. He noticed her as he stepped out of his house on his way to work, wearing his dark glasses and his straw hat. Sabinka grabbed him by the hand and shook it fervently, "How are you, Herr Rosenberg? Don't you recognize me? No one recognizes me. I am Sabinka. I just came by . . ." Anxiously, imploringly, she searched for his eyes under the dark glasses.

Adam, confused, held her hand in his for a long while. For a moment he considered taking her in, but how could he? He had to be alone. Alone it was easier to carry out his plans. He let go of her hand, mumbling, "I have no time". He pushed her away and set out in the direction of the Red House. Hearing the clop-clop of her wooden heels following him, he felt as if Sutchka were accompanying him. A pleasant feeling. He halted and waited for her to come abreast of him. "Will you stop following me like a dog?" he tried to shoo her off.

"Have pity on me, Herr Rosenberg," the girl pleaded.

He twisted his mouth with disgust, "Scabby cow!" He wanted to dig out a few pfennigs from his pocket but his hand touched on the key to his house. He handed it to her, "Go home and wait for me." Their fingers touched on the cold key. Adam marched off, wondering at what he had just done, at how he could make life so difficult for himself.

Adam lived with Sabinka. He would beat her when he was mad at her, or at himself; he kissed and caressed her when he pitied her, or himself. And it did not work. Fear stood between them. It did not let Adam concentrate on his pleasure, and the pleasure herself was bony and dry, giving Adam the impression that he held a skeleton in his arms. Sabinka submitted to his will with every bone and protruding rib; she was so eager to please him that Adam felt nothing but revulsion for her. Sometimes he would even lose the will to beat her. Yet he could not bring himself to throw her out.

Sabinka would whisper to him, "You are the best person I've ever met in my life, Mr. Rosenberg," and saying so, she would shake, her teeth chattering.

"Why are you shaking like that?" he would growl.

"I am cold, Mr. Rosenberg. I am always cold."

At dawn, when he woke up with the realization that a night had passed and no one had come for him, his heart would fill with gratitude. He would observe Sabinka. In the light of dawn she looked beautiful; her face transparent, delicate, the mouth fine, while the hair strewn over the pillow resembled the sun's first rays. He carefully touched her hair, his heart swelling with tenderness. Sabinka looked like a saint in a Christian icon, a Madonna. "You are an angel," he would whisper softly, in order not to destroy the illusion. Often his tenderness transformed itself into an urge to devour her, and his senses would awaken. He enjoyed Sabinka's frightened screams which aroused him, inciting him to further avenge himself on the angelically sweet creature and to enjoy a moment of complete forgetfulness.

Sabinka took care of the house. She cooked, shined Adam's shoes and dusted his suits. She ate the leftover food on his plate and he enjoyed watching her attack the meat bones, purring and licking her lips. This made him good-humoured, approachable. She was a two-legged Sutchka. But she had one great fault. She did not like to wash, insisting that she was too cold and that the water made her feel stiff. And Adam feared germs more than anything else in the world. He was an exaggeratedly clean person by nature.

Every morning before he left, she begged him, "Don't go away, Mr. Rosenberg."

He laughed, "Scabby idiot!"

"I am on the list, Mr. Rosenberg. They will find me. Lock me in!"

"Under one condition," he would say with a smile. "If you promise to wash properly."

He would lock her in from the outside, locking away a part of his own fear as well. Indeed, since he had begun to live with Sabinka, he feared the Red House less and he did his own work with more composure. He also became more impatient to go home at the end of the day. Every time he opened the door, he had the feeling that Sutchka was about to leap forward excitedly, to greet him. He would call Sabinka over and check whether she had kept her promise. Although she did not seem dirty, he doubted whether she had done as good a job as he might have wished.

One day, Adam became aware that spring had actually arrived. He walked home energetically, musing that man worries about the lost days of his life, while he does not worry about the days which he destroys with his own hands. How many days had he lived, unaware that he was alive, corroded by moods which did not help to change the situation anyway. He resolved to give his despair a vacation that afternoon, and to provide himself with a bit of entertainment. He decided to give Sabinka a bath. As soon as he entered the house, he saw her sitting on the edge of the bed, doubled up, shaking, her teeth clinking.

He lit the stove, put two pails of water on it and rolled up his sleeves. Then he cut off a slice of bread from his loaf. "Here!" he threw it at her with a broad gesture. "And get up. Peel some potatoes and open a can of meat. We'll have a good dinner. I must fill you out a bit. A female without a bosom is like a bed without a pillow." As he checked the water on the stove, he began, to his own amazement, to whistle the tune of one of his favourite hit songs from before the war. Whistling, he opened the door and sat down in the doorway. "Come here!" he called. She left the potatoes and the piece of bread that she had been chewing and approached him with restrained steps. "We have to start work in the garden," he said. "That will be your job." She stared at the garden dully, until he yelled, "What are you gaping at? Go, fix the meal." He heard the pails sizzle and he entered the room, locked the door and removed his shirt. He pulled out the washtub from under the bed and filled it with the pails of hot water. The room filled with steam. Beads of sweat immediately appeared on his forehead. His beet-red face shone. "Come here!" he called through the haze. "Get undressed!" He waited for Sabinka like a child waiting for an exciting game. But he soon lost his patience and leaped over to her, grabbing her arm. "Come, I will undress you." He panted as he diligently unbuttoned her dress, pulling it down over her thin body. The steam wound between them. His bare torso surrounded by a roll of fat shone moistly and shook like jelly.

Sabinka peeled off her underwear. She too was shaking. "No, Mr. Rosenberg, no!" She threw her head around. Her short blond hair stood up stiffly on her skull. Adam could see the goose pimples on it. He scrutinized her bony body, the protruding joints, the thin dangling arms, the rippled caved-in belly and the small dry breasts. Her body surrendered to his touch and he was overcome by compassion.

He placed his hands on her hips. "Crawl in," he invited her tenderly, pushing her towards the bathtub.

She dipped a foot in the water and removed it with a scream, "It's too hot! I can't, Mr. Rosenberg!" Her teeth chattered. "Add a bit of cold water!"

"Look how you are shaking, idiot, get in and you'll be warm!"

"No, Mr. Rosenberg . . . A bit of cool water . . . please!"

He lifted her over the tub and let her down into the water. Sabinka screeched, roared, lifting one leg, then the other. She tried to climb out, while he pushed her back, delighted with her screams and the spasms running down her body which shrank and stretched like rubber. He gave her a vigorous push. She slipped, prostrating herself with a splash in the tub. Then she rose again, roaring wildly, animal-like, again trying to escape. He wiped his splashed face and tickled her with the bar of soap.

"If you holler like that, I will hand you over for the transport," he threatened her, immediately cutting short her screams. She looked funny with her childlike mouth pressed together, not letting a sound escape as she struggled with the boiling water. "Stay there!" he ordered. "I am going to get the floor brush." She remained in the water, motionless, her eyes, glassy and bloodshot. She held on with both hands to the edge of the tub, breathing heavily. Adam came back. "The floor brush!" he panted. "Only this will remove the dirt . . . and this bar of good soap, too. Do you see it? I will rub its perfume into your blood, so that you will smell nicely forever." He soaped the hard brush and began to scrub her. Her skin became striped, the red lines grew. Her body seemed wrapped in a red net. He worked so diligently and with such great delight, that he did not notice Sabinka swoon onto her back, her head and the upper part of her body dangling over the rim of the tub.

He was sorry that she was clean so soon, reluctant to give up the game. But at length he came to himself and began talking to her. He noticed her limpness, the hanging head and the protruding eyes. He lifted the red mass of flesh from the water and placed it beside the tub. A puddle encircled her. She seemed to have been peeled from her own skin. Adam was overcome by an extraordinary affection for her. He took off his clothes and threw himself on top of her.

He remained on the floor beside Sabinka and almost fell asleep in the warm wet puddle. Yet he forced himself to get up. He threw a jug of cold water in Sabinka's face, but one jug was not enough. He brought more, until she moaned and began to move her head. He wiped her, picked her up and slinging her over his shoulder, carried her to the bed and lay down beside her, exhausted and happy. He had once before lain like that beside a fainting woman. Then the experience had been gruesome. This time it was magnificent.

Adam devoted a few moments to a philosophical thought: similar circum-stances could sometimes be pleasurable and sometimes not. Sutchka entered his mind. He had loved to bathe and brush Sutchka too. Yet with Sutchka he had never had the water too hot, and had never scrubbed her so violently. On the other hand, with Sutchka he had never had the particular pleasure he had experienced today. Thus Adam arrived at the conclusion which had lately become increasingly clear to him, namely, that although people stood in general on a lower moral level than dogs, he was doomed to be tied to them, and that he had to accept these ties if he wanted to continue with his life. Even having contact with people in such a weird fashion as in his relationship with Sabinka was better than total loneliness.

He cast a tender glance at Sabinka and slapped her on both cheeks. The whites of her eyes began slowly to move, until her pupils were fixed on Adam. "Ey, you!" he began to to shake her vigorously. "The potatoes are ready!"

But then he decided to cover Sabinka with the blanket. He listened to her breathing. She was asleep. He got up from the bed and made order in the room, feeling as if he himself had been washed and cleansed. He sat down to his meal and ate with great relish. He reminded himself that he had decided to fatten Sabinka, and left a few pieces of potato on his plate for her. He became very sleepy. He covered the window through which the sun was still shining, and went back to bed.

Through a fog he later saw Sabinka creep out of the bed. He heard the clinking of a spoon against a plate. Then he heard a noise from outside and Sabinka's shout, "A group for the transport!" In the blink of an eye she was beside Adam, covering her head with the blanket.

Blinking sleepily, he muttered, "What are you afraid of, idiot? I won't let anyone take you away from me."

Slowly the blanket moved, revealing Sabinka's face with two rows of bright teeth shining between her smiling lips. The sight captivated him. Those magnificent teeth made him forget about the metal caps in his own mouth. The dainty white teeth in Sabinka's mouth were his. Then he saw the teeth and the mouth move as he heard Sabinka say to him, "Marry me, Mr. Rosenberg, please".

Adam wrinkled his forehead, "What did you say?"

"Marry me, Mr. Rosenberg, only . . . as a trick. They are chasing after the lonely, the single . . ."

Adam choked with spasms of laughter. He, who had been preparing his imminent transformation into a woman, considered her marriage proposal an extraordinary joke. He could not contain himself and said, "What do you need to marry me for? We shall live like two sisters . . ." and then he confessed his plans to her. Still guffawing, he jumped off the bed and playfully, drew out the female clothes and wig from under the mattress and dressed himself in them. He waited for Sabinka's appraisal of him. After all, she was a greater expert in this field than he. He did not notice that Sabinka had begun to tremble and her teeth to chatter.

✦   ✦   ✦

Sabinka slowly regained her former appearance. But she did not stop nagging Adam with her marriage proposal. He had one way to make her shut up: to give her a few blows. In the meantime Adam himself was also changing. He slept through the nights without fear, did his exercises in the morning in order to lose weight, and cheerfully marched to work at the Red House. The date of his transformation was already fixed in his mind and he awaited it with pleasant anticipation.

Notwithstanding his plan to move out of the house, he decided in the meantime to seriously take care of the garden. He ordered Sabinka to start weeding and watering the ground. For that reason he refused to lock her in, in spite of her pleas and tears.

While she was working in the garden one day, she felt tired and fell asleep on the warm ground, under the shade of a tree. Outside, in the street, there passed the last column of people who had been caught for deportation. A woman escaped and burst into the garden through the gate. She dashed past the sleeping Sabinka, turned the corner of the house and vanished through a hole in the fence on the other side. Two policemen chased after her. They entered the garden and saw a woman lying under a tree. Had she collapsed while escaping? They did not remember her face and anyway it did not matter. They picked Sabinka up by the arms. She did not struggle with them. The horror in her eyes bore witness to the fact that they were not mistaken. They carried her all the way, and she never uttered a word. Sabinka paddled with her feet in the air and thus she sailed away from Adam's hut.

Adam came home early. The ground had been burning under his feet at the *Kripo*. Danger was suddenly hovering in the air again. Everything seemed changed and every German whom he saw betrayed a horrible secret with his glance. Adam succumbed to an acute attack of fear and never before had he so hurried home as he did today. He had to be with Sabinka. With her he had learned to master himself. She, the humble, the submissive, gave him strength. His conscience was even beginning to prick his heart, for tormenting her so. But he calmed himself immediately. If there were people who liked to torment, there were also those who liked to be tormented. And why did he think that he was tormenting her? He had saved her. She owed him her life. And if he hurt her, it was on account of his tenderness for her which he was somehow unable to express otherwise. Perhaps it was due to his love for her? It must be love that he felt for her. Perhaps he had at last learned to love a human being. He wanted to be with her forever.

Having entered the yard, he looked around. The door to the house stood open. He stopped on the threshold and let out a groan, stupefied. The covers and pillows were missing. All the cupboard doors stood open, all of the food had vanished, and pieces of Adam's underwear and clothing were gone. He jumped towards the windows, lifted the sill and removed a brick. He sighed with relief when he found the sock filled with his treasure still in the hole. He lifted the mattress of his bed and sighed with even more relief when he saw the female clothes, which he had prepared for himself, lying untouched.

He sat down on the bed, wiping the sweat from his forehead and pate. He smiled like a cheated fool. So he had allowed himself to be tricked into the sack by Sabinka, had believed in her pretended helplessness, had deluded himself with her attachment to him. He had compared her to Sutchka, imagined that he was in love with her. He could not forgive himself that he, with his hatred of humankind, could have trusted and naively believed a human creature. He had left everything open, all his possessions accessible to that cunning false stranger.

He stretched out full length on the mattress and shut his eyes. He saw Sabinka's delicate figure in his imagination and wondered that in spite of all that she had done to him, he was not as angry with her as he should have been; that, on the contrary, he was ready to forgive her. Because he feared for his life. She alone could have given him support. Then another thought entered his mind: Perhaps this was a good omen, like the time when Krajne had left. In order to save oneself it was best to be alone.

He slowly removed the female clothes and the wig from under the mattress, took a bag and gathered all the things that remained and were still of some use to him. He tucked the sock with his treasure into his breast pocket, put on the sunglasses and the Panama hat and went outside. In the garden he stopped for a moment, took off the sunglasses and threw them onto the jasmine bush by the fence. He also removed the Panama hat and with a nonchalant gesture hung it on the fence.

He went to the bazaar to buy a bit of food, then set out through the yards to look for a hiding place. On the way he remembered that he had not brought any pots or cutlery along, so he went back to his house. He was exhausted and decided to sleep. His fatigue dulled his fear somewhat and he told himself that sleeping one more night in the house would not matter. He did not even lock the door or cover the window. He cried in his sleep. He dreamt about himself: a little fat boy with whom no one wanted to play. Then he saw Samuel Zuckerman who looked up at him from his bed, and asked, "Why are you unlike all the other people, Adam?"

Adam answered him, "That is my way of being like all the other people."

Samuel grabbed him with his thin hands, shouting, "You are a Nazi!"

Then followed the hour of the ghosts. There were three men trotting side by side on the pavement. Their steps echoed louder and louder. Two marched at the side and one in the middle. On one side was Samuel, on the other, Mietek. Both wore SS uniforms with the *Totenköpfe* on their caps. Between them walked a little boy, a monster. All three of them were disguised. They pretended to march to the cemetery. It was only a game. Yet the little monster was frightened and he implored his companions to have pity on him; he implored all those who followed behind: Yadwiga, Krajne, Sabinka. They were all marching together to join the transport. "I could not help myself!" the little monster cried, begging for his life. The two at his side were leading him away and were themselves being led.

In his sleep, Adam saw the green uniforms at his side become adorned with Stars of David. From these stars ran a ray of light to the Star of David on his own chest. When he peered deep inside the Star he saw the face of his mother, the slovenly merchant of metal scraps. "Mother, don't chase me away! help me!" the little boy cried. The mother was sewn onto the clothes and refused to stretch out her arms to him.

Samuel, the tall companion at his side, said, "No human being has the right to make another suffer."

Suddenly the monster grew into a flabby man and he too was wearing a green uniform. "Why don't you understand, Zuckerman?" Adam talked to his companion like an equal. "I could not live without a candy in my mouth." And now it was Adam's turn to rage, "And you yourself, Zuckerman," he shouted, "have you inflicted suffering upon no one? And you, Mietek," he turned to his other companion, "have you inflicted suffering upon no one?" Now they all led each other away and were being led.

Then Adam saw himself writing a letter. He had written so few letters in his life. He had no one to write to. Nor did he know in his sleep to whom the letter was addressed. He was sitting in the office of his roaring factory. No, he was sitting on the mattress in this very house reading his letter: "In that manner was I attached to you. All the good that was within me I have offered to a dog . . . I am a *Hundsmann* by nature . . ." As he read the letter, he heard steps approaching. Adam found himself in the cemetery which was rustling like a wilderness. He was alone; a hunter with a gun on his shoulder. A red wall popped up from between the trees. Adam squeezed his eyes together tighter and tighter, so as not to see, not to hear. There, in the distance, was the bull's eye: the Yellow Star . . . his mother's face . . . his own face. He aimed and a shot followed. Adam was liberated from the Yellow Star . . . from his mother . . . from himself. He, the shooter and the shot, were free. Yet a dog was still howling somewhere. Where was that howl coming from? Why did he feel so related to it — he who had never felt any relatedness, he who had always been an alien? Could it be that even after the shot . . .

Adam opened his eyes. Sweat was pouring down his face. His clothes were glued to his body. The uncovered window was full of night. He got down from the bed. On his toes, as if afraid to wake someone, he approached the cupboard, removed a pot and a spoon, and went outside.

In the garden the trees, the bushes and the grass stood motionless. There was not the slightest breeze in the air. Adam inhaled the silence deeply and smoothed out the few hairs over his bald head. He left through the gate, closing it quietly, so that it would not squeak and disturb the peace of the night. Once across the street, he set out with light soundless steps towards the backyards. Although his steps were so light, his shoulders weighed him down as if he were carrying a heavy load. "I am carrying my dream on my back," he whispered to himself. Actually he had the impression that he was still wandering about within his dream. But then he heard steps on the sidewalk outside. Heavy boot steps. He shuddered and roused himself to a gallop through the yards. Someone was running after him. He could no longer distinguish between the sound of his own steps and that of those chasing him. "Halt!" he heard a shout. "Halt!" his own tired heart begged him.

Finally he was no longer able to run. No one was coming after him. No one was calling him. The air was quiet, cool, full of night. He climbed up to the room which he had chosen for a hiding place. There was a mirror in the room. Adam approached it and immediately jumped away from it. Before him, in the mirror, there stood a flabby female with a bald head. Adam could not recall when and where he had put on the female clothes, or when and where he had lost the wig.

Chapter Twenty-six

AFTER EVERY TRAGEDY Esther withered and then came back to life, becoming healthier and stronger than before. She often repeated Winter's saying which he had borrowed from Nietzsche: "What does not destroy me makes me stronger." The tragedies were the yeast on which she matured. They gave her the wisdom to distinguish between what really counted and what was only of momentary importance. Now the time had arrived when she had to learn not from her suffering but from her happiness.

It was a hot day. She was lying on her bed, her eyes fixed on her protruding belly which seemed to move in waves. It rose and fell now on one side, now on the other. The child was moving, prodding with its leg or arm against the walls of her belly — a pleasant although uncomfortable feeling. She placed both veiny hands on her belly and closed her eyes.

She remembered how she had felt during her first pregnancy. This time everything was different and the experience was even more powerful than then. And how she wanted everything to be different! That was the reason why she was seeing Dr. Levine. He himself was the best proof that it would be different this time. For could a person ever change as much as Dr. Levine had changed? He was limping now. His limping evoked trust, it made her feel related to him. Apart from that, she had chosen him, for she wanted to prove to herself and to the world that she was not superstitious, that she was an optimistic mother. She did not know how she had become so attached to Dr. Levine. The touch of his wise hands calmed her. The expression on his creased face made her feel both motherly towards him and protected and secure. She worshipped him. They seldom exchanged words and always avoided each other's eyes. Their contact was through his hands, through his ear against her belly, as he listened to the other heart that pulsated within her.

She scrambled down from the bed and poured herself a glass of milk. She felt every gulp flow down through her to the little mischief who was so impatiently moving inside her. Soon he would arrive into the bright world. His time was approaching. She had already stopped working, to wait for him. She avoided being among people. She guessed the neighbours' secret thoughts. So she protected her belly from their stare, although she herself did not mind. She laughed at the world. She was light-hearted and carefree and although she shunned people, she missed them. All day long she would sit at the window, looking down into the yard. She wanted the neighbours to notice her, to greet her. She wanted them to see how beautiful she was, despite the dark brown stains on her face. That was a sign, said the women, that she would have a boy. She was in love with herself, even with the marks on her face.

She decided to do what she was compelled to and left the room, slowly moving along the hot street, her hands folded over her belly. She pretended not to see people's sideways glances. Walking in the shadows of the houses, she crossed the bridge; she was on her way to find an apartment in the yard on Hockel Street. She hoped that Aunt Rivka's apartment was empty. She was not superstitious or capricious, but she had that one double caprice: to give birth to her child in the yard where her aunt had lived and where she had spent her childhood, and to be closer to Dr. Levine.

Aunt Rivka's apartment was completely empty, without even a trace of furniture left inside. Esther moved about it for a while as if taking possession of it, then she went down into the yard and sat down under the cherry tree. She leaned against its trunk and mused about how strange life was. From that yard both Israel and herself had left for the wide world. They had both made such large circles before coming back, in order to bring a new life into the world.

She was waiting for Israel who was supposed to join her and help her find a place. She had no worries about installing herself. Israel had a pair of "golden" hands and could do wonders to make life more comfortable. He was already at work, constructing a cradle out of a drawer and some wood.

When he arrived, she sent him up to have a look at the apartment. Then he came and sat down beside her. He unbuttoned his shirt and she could see his damp hairy chest. They were both silent. That was another circle they had made. At the beginning of their life together they had often been silent. That had been followed by a talkative period. Lately, however, they needed no talk. In her excitement, her anticipation, with her head full of dreams and plans, Esther did not notice that she rarely uttered a word. Sometimes she was curious about what Israel felt in regard to the baby. He had arrived at that moment through different experiences than she. He had already been a father. But she saw no sense in asking him. Words would only pale beside what she could read in his face. She was sure that soon a time of great talkativeness would arrive for them, when their chatter would mix with the chatter of the third — the newcomer.

Israel sat with her for only a short while. Soon he vanished through the gate. She stretched out on the grass and shut her eyes. The earth was lazy and sleepy. Not even a blade of grass stirred. The boughs of the cherry tree hung motionless. Esther played with a fistful of soil, letting it sift through her fingers. She lay on the grass, Mother Earth and Mother Esther communicating with one another, both listening to themselves, both heavy and ripe. Esther lay with her eyes shut, imagining her child's form. She was curious about the hair colour. Perhaps it would be a boy, blond like Israel, or perhaps resembling one of his brothers, the youngest, Shalom, for instance, who used to follow her about with eyes full of devotion. It was about Israel that Shalom's eyes had spoken to her, but she had not perceived it. Or perhaps she would have a little girl with black hair, who would resemble Sheyne Pessele, or reddish-yellow hair and resemble her own mother, or Aunt Rivka? How strange and how exciting! So many possibilities. So many combinations of heredity in one tiny creature!

She smiled to herself. She had lately become banal and limited in her thoughts. They all had only one topic which bore no relation to the outside world. She had a lot of time but it did not even enter her mind to read, nor did she feel like meeting her comrades or attending Winter's artistic gatherings, and she certainly had no interest in the news, in any news, neither about the ghetto nor the world. All that she felt like doing was singing. Snatches of silly old songs constantly echoed in her memory. She was idle, lazy and sleepy, waiting for that moment when she would be lying like she was now, but with a tiny mouth tied to the nipple of her breast.

After an hour's nap under the tree, she woke up hungry and thirsty. She stood up heavily, awkwardly, tapping her belly as if to check how it had taken the changed position. The belly was silent. It had been silent all afternoon. She felt somewhat lonely with the silence inside her, and yet content. The little creature was probably asleep. It felt the heat of the day. Let it rest, so that it would have more strength for the great voyage which awaited it. She dragged herself to the water pump. A neighbour set it in motion for her and she filled her cupped palms with water. She drank from them. With her dripping hands she wiped her forehead and combed her hair. She took out a tiny potato from her pocket and washed it. The potato had a thin soft skin revealing its bright body. A new potato. Esther cracked it with her teeth. She liked raw potatoes.

Slowly she went into the street. She peered into the windows, looking at her own reflection. She looked funny and yet beautiful and majestic. Then she noticed Israel in the distance, running towards her, waving his hand. Something had happened. But she would not run to meet him. She would keep on walking slowly and wait for him to reach her. What could she care about whatever happened? She was here, in the middle of the street, and her tiny companion was also here. There was no reason for her to hurry. Israel approached her. He smiled. Thank heavens.

"The invasion has begun!" He pressed her to himself, kissing her face. "I had to run home to tell you that, Little Mother! This morning at nine! The English and the Americans have crossed the La Manche . . ."

Esther laughed and shuddered, tears overflowing her eyes. "My eyes are sweating," she whispered jokingly, leaning against him.

On their way home they were caught in the rain. All afternoon a heavy cloud had been approaching, now it burst open with lightning and thunder, releasing its waters. A summer storm. Esther and Israel waited in a gateway for it to pass. It was quickly over, leaving the streets refreshed and wet. The wet windows shone gaily, tearfully, The street was full of noise, the people soared through it as if on wings. The invasion had begun! Israel left Esther and ran off to see his comrades. This time Esther was incapable of climbing up to the room and being there alone. She decided to visit the Eibushitz family. She had lately become friendly, not with Rachel, but with Blumka who reminded her of Aunt Rivka.

The following day Israel and Esther decided to move to the apartment on Hockel Street. Israel was busy all day with his party duties and had asked Esther to pack everything and leave it for him to move in the evening. She did as he asked. Although their belongings were equal to almost nothing, she worked the whole day, taking a nap every few hours. The packing seemed an enormous effort. Yet she was not resentful that Israel was not there to help her. Had she not once worked for an ideal herself? Were not Israel's activities of the utmost importance for the future of their child? They both wanted their child to grow up in a free Poland. No, these days there were no political differences between them. Like a full-fledged communist, Israel rejoiced in the victories of the Red Army. And at night when they heard the cannonades, they would both exclaim with delight, "Ours!"

Esther left to wait for Israel in the new apartment. The day was again sultry and damp. It rained and stormed a few times and only at dusk did the air begin to cool. The ghetto swam past Esther in restless waves. Expectation hovered in the air. Esther held on to her belly with both hands as if to protect it against the exhilaration, against the restlessness. She was alone in a foreign noisy world. All she wished for at that moment was silence, peace, and to have the hand of someone close touching her head. She missed Aunt Rivka badly. Suddenly, tears began to wash down her face.

The yard on Hockel Street was like a ship during a storm. People were treading amidst the beds of soil, with their heads raised to the sky. A rainbow had appeared above the ghetto. Esther looked at the windows of her new apartment. It seemed to her that it was Friday and Aunt Rivka was about to call, "Esther, come up to wash your hair!"

Berkovitch came out of the latrine man's hut. She recalled that he had had a little girl, and she felt as if a hand was pulling her backwards, so as not to show him her belly. But he was already standing in front of her, hands in his pockets, blinking myopically. "Do you see? A rainbow!" Their gazes met in mutual understanding. "Sorry, I must go back inside," he said confidentially, after a while. "I am in the middle of holding the Muses by the hair." She nodded. They were related to each other. Their souls moved about on tiptoe, trembling over something sacred that was about to come out of them. They wanted nothing but to be left in peace until the moment of deliverance. The rainbow united her with Berkovitch in an entirely different way than with all other people.

The rainbow faded and the air turned gray. The people in the yard dispersed. Esther saw Israel arrive with the cart laden with their belongings. She immediately noticed that he was disturbed. She asked him no questions, praying that he would not tell her anything, not now. She wanted to help him unpack, but was unable to. She felt very heavy and her back bothered her. She asked Israel to help her sit up on the window sill in the kitchen. She needed more air. Here, to this window sill, Uncle Chaim's hosiery machines used to be fastened. Her heart was buzzing like a machine. Israel stood beside her, both his hands on her knees.

"Esther, the cantor . . . and the other radio listeners have been arrested."

She wrapped her arms around his neck and grinned crookedly. She understood that he wanted to leave again. She let him help her down from the sill and slowly accompanied him to the door. "I am sure that they won't betray anyone," she said reassuringly.

"No, they won't," he agreed with her.

"Be careful!" she called after him.

He came back late at night. He was glad that she was awake and that he was able to talk to her. She did not stop him, although she did not want to hear anything. "The cantor," he said, "devoted himself to listening to the broadcasts through all these years in the ghetto. He spent day and night at the radio box. He had a phenomenal memory, immediately translating from English, Russian, Dutch . . . accurate to the last letter. Even the story about Widawski did not scare him." Esther shut her eyes. She needed a little sleep at least. Her back ached and she felt particularly uncomfortable.

✦ ✦ ✦

The baby arrived with the dawn. Israel barely had time to bring the doctor and make the necessary preparations. The baby arrived practically by itself, fast as lightning — and with a great cry. It was a boy. It was not blond like Israel, nor redhaired like Esther. It arrived with a mop of pitch black hair at the very tip of the head. Its eyes were not green like Esther's, nor bluish-gray like Israel's, but were orientally slanted and velvety black.

"Do you know whom he resembles?" Israel asked.

"Your brother Shalom."

Esther lay on the bed, feeling the tiny head on her bosom. She looked at the creased little face twisted with the grimace of an old man, at the thin lips which did not stop sucking, at the minute hands with the tiny fingers clenched into tiny fists — and she could not believe that this marvel had come from her, to her, for her. It was an intoxicating truth. If during her pregnancy it had seemed to her that she was not walking on the earth, it now seemed that she was celebrating in the heavens, that her bed was a cloud.

Although everything within her was crying to get outside, to the neighbours, to her comrades, to announce to the world that she had a son, she kept the news to herself, so that the jealous world would not cast an evil eye. She stayed indoors, relying on Israel for everything, and herself not taking a step away from the cradle. She had one wish: to have her breasts full of milk for the eager tiny lips. She wanted to hold her son in her arms all day long. When she offered him her breast, a voice inside her bubbled, calling out to him joyfully, "Here, take it, devour it!" She wanted to feed her whole being to him, to make him strong with her strength. She wanted to prostrate herself before him so that he should learn to walk, her body a carpet for his steps.

She received Dr. Levine with awesome admiration, blushing, mumbling shyly. More than once did she feel the urge to kiss his hand. It hurt her that Dr. Levine paid so little attention to her son and so much to her. He had not complimented her on the son even once, although the entire world knew that he was extraordinarily handsome. On the contrary, Levine seemed resentful of the little one, as if he wanted to say, "The brat is fat and full, while the mother is barely alive."

In reality, Dr. Levine did not look at Esther either. When he scolded her good-humouredly, telling her to rest at least two hours a day and take some fresh air, he seemed to stare somewhere between her son and herself. So she was a bit disappointed in him for his lack of enthusiasm. But she followed him to the door, leaving it open, so that he would not hurt himself in the dark corridor. She blessed his every step.

Visitors began to arrive, Esther could not avoid that. Everyone was eager to see the marvel, to refresh themselves with the sight of a newborn baby in the ghetto; and of all her visitors Esther liked Bella Zuckerman and Berkovitch the most. Bella had appeared in the room one morning, saying, "I heard that you gave birth to a baby. May I have a look at it, please? I've never seen a newborn baby." She looked at the baby the way Esther wished people to look at it. And out of gratitude she allowed Bella to do some of the difficult chores for her.

Berkovitch often brought along the Toffee Man who would bring "remedies for the heart" for Esther and, in his weeping voice, speak to her words she barely understood but which soothed her heart. Berkovitch brought her diapers and clothes which exactly fitted the baby. She never asked him how he had come by these things. Berkovitch would also bring carrots from his *dzialka*. He often strained them himself, sprinkled them with sugar, then insisted that Esther eat them.

Blumka Eibushitz would also come. She praised Berkovitch for bringing the carrots. Carrots were good for the eyes, both of the mother and the son. She herself was knitting a little outfit for the baby, made from the wool of Moshe's old sweater. She taught Esther how to take care of the baby and would laugh, scolding the young mother, "Why do you pick him up the moment he lets out a squeak? Let him scream a bit, it will give him healthy lungs." She would bend over the wailing baby and encourage him, "Scream, scream as hard as you can! Make the foundations of the world shake!"

In the evenings the guests would surround the cradle. Esther proudly checked the impression her son was making on them. "May he be protected from an evil eye," the Toffee Man would whine, trying to rock the crib with one finger. "What do you call him, may he live in good health?"

"We call him Shalom."

"*Shalom* to you, Shalom." He shook his long beard at the baby.

Esther did not fear the Toffee Man's tears. She was not aware of her own tears when he talked. It was the kind of weeping which both soothed and gave relief. Each time the Toffee Man asked her son's name and repeated it, it seemed to her that he wanted to remind her that when the war had broken out, she had given birth to a dead child. This time she had given birth to a live child whose name was Shalom.

Israel was becoming more preoccupied with his party work and was unable to assist even during the ceremony of bathing the baby. But Berkovitch replaced him very well. Berkovitch would come up straight after work, bringing along a pail full of hot water which he had warmed on a gas burner. As a reward Esther would allow him to take the baby into his shaking arms and let him mumble incomprehensible words to it. If he suddenly did not feel up to witnessing the whole ceremony and made a dash towards the door, she would not call him back, for his sake and her own. In reality, she preferred to be alone with her son. Then she could set free her bottled-up exhilaration.

The baby boy's skin was bright like the sun and smooth like fine leather. His legs were strong and his marvellous behind hard like two little balls. As she washed and soaped him, his skin became slippery and delightful to the touch. She soaped his few strands of black hair, softly curling the foam as she massaged his scalp. The little fellow screeched, squinted, bending and stretching his legs as if they were on springs. He splashed her all over as she groaned with his pleasure.

"Scream!" she called out to him like an experienced mother, enticing him to conquer the world, "Scream, my boy, louder! louder!"

She softly soaped his little belly. The soap squeaked as if it too were enjoying the touch of the belly and its little navel. In the meantime the little fellow forgot to scream, realizing that the water was quite agreeable and his mother's soft hands — ticklish. His mouth spread into a smile, revealing red gums which were awaiting teeth. The slanted eyes, still filled with tears, lit up mischievously, like bulbs. Now he stretched and pulled playfully, splashing his mother's sweaty face. She soaped one leg, then the other, letting her fingers slide down to the tiny heels with the ten little toes the size of peas. She played with them for a moment and then hastily soaped the alien little something between his legs, a something which would one day stiffen into masculinity. Somewhat shyly, lovingly she scrutinized it, wishing to kiss it. A wish for which he punished her with an arch of water that sprouted straight into her face, into her nostrils, her mouth and her bosom. She turned him over. Riding on her hand, he really began to splash. His wet head was raised high, his neck and back full of pink folds.

The bath was over and as soon as Esther took the baby out of the water, he began to holler again. His fun was spoiled. She placed him on a blanket on the table and wrapped him in a towel, beginning to roll and to knead him. She made faces at him, laughed and smacked her lips. After he was dried and "salted" with powder, she really let herself go with him. She buried her head in his belly, shook her red hair against his face and tickled him under the chin, talking senseless words whose sound convinced him that she was very funny, and he began to giggle and roar with laughter. She was wet with water and sweat, drunk with the light from his body.

The only trouble was with the baby's sleep. There was noise in the yard every day. The good news from the fronts, the arrest of the radio listeners, starvation and the heat made the people irritable and restless. Neighbours would quarrel, others would sing or laugh. There was constant talk.

Esther decided to no longer hide herself and the baby, but to go down with it into the very centre of the tumult, so that he might perhaps fall asleep easier. After all, they both needed the fresh air. She did indeed fear the stares and the words of the neighbours, but never mind, she now had enough strength to bear everything and not take it to heart. She wrapped herself and the baby in the plaid which Berkovitch had given her, and went down to the cherry tree. She sat down in the grass and leaned against the tree's trunk. Little Shalom was asleep in her lap, his tiny fists above his head, his legs bent and relaxed, his whole body at rest. She stared at him. She had so much to discover in him. She listened to him breathing and it seemed to her that she could see him growing as he breathed. She looked at his closed eyelids fringed with thin black lashes like brush strokes. How lightly the thin lids covered his eyes! Each lid a piece of such weightless tissue, that it seemed as if the slightest breeze could blow it away and reveal the pupils of his eyes. So she bent down over her son to protect him against the slightest breeze. Her back began to hurt, yet it seemed to her that it was comfortable to sit like that and rest with Shalom.

Around her the yard was in an uproar. She did not pay any attention to it. Just like Shalom she heard nothing, saw nothing. However, little by little an echo of the clamour stole into her heart and began to dig deep inside it. She wanted to escape it, to shut her eyes, to let her head hang down over Shalom, and sleep. After all, she was a bit tired. Little Shalom was a glutton. And he was ill-behaved, wetting many diapers; he would holler, refusing to stay put in them. But she could not sleep. She had to watch over her son.

Sometimes, when she sat like that with the sleeping baby, a din would rise into the air as if from underground. It would double its intensity and transform itself into loud wails, heavy, deafening. The sirens. She would jump to her feet with the baby in her arms and remain doubled up for a moment, not knowing what was happening to her.

When she entered her room, she began to shake. The room was full with the sound of the screaming sirens. She put the baby into the cradle but picked it up again immediately, pressing it to her bosom. The sirens would stop only to be followed by a growling sawing sound. The roar of airplanes. The ticking of machine guns. She tried to master herself. "They are ours . . . ours," she whispered to Shalom, forcing herself to sit down on the bed. She put the baby beside her, mumbling, "You must help me, Shalom." Tucking her fingers into his little fists, she pressed her lips against his cool forehead. More and more squadrons of airplanes cracked across the sky. From near and far came the sound of explosions. Again she was on her feet, pressing the baby to her bosom as she paced up and down. Where could she escape with him? She, with the child in her arms, was exposed to all the wantonness of the world. She was abandoned. She would have to discuss it with Israel. They must find a place to hide. She felt that it was approaching. Fate was coming closer. She was weak, but she must not be helpless. She had to do something . . .

The alarms did not last long, but for her they never ended. There were days when she felt the ground shaking under her feet. She told herself that it was her fatigue that made her so confused, but she knew that there was also something else to it. Fear took hold of her like madness. She counted the hours, waiting for Israel; she wandered about the room, everything falling from her hands. There was a voice screaming within her which she was unable to silence. She bit her lips, cracked her knuckles, tore up every piece of cloth or paper that came into her hands. When she could bear it no longer, she bent down over the crib, unbuttoned her dress and pushed her nipple into the little mouth. Impatiently she waited for the mouth to begin sucking. "Here, take it," she whispered. As soon as she felt the pleasant flow in her breast, felt the tiny bent fingers touching her skin, her nervousness subsided, slowly, gradually, as if the tiny giant were sucking out her weakness.

Israel came home accompanied by neighbours eager to hear the latest news. Esther would ask them to leave. "The baby is asleep," she would say with a crooked smile and shut the door behind them. She busied herself at the stove, preparing food for Israel. She did not look at him. She did not want him to tell her anything. Yet she was aware that it was better to know, that she had to know. So she sat down opposite him and inquired, "What's new?" He sipped his soup, avoiding her eyes. Just like the others, he had lately become unable to look her in the eyes. Like the others, he was distant, although he was the closest. She told herself that it was not he who was running away, but that it was she who had removed herself from her surroundings. She listened to what Israel was telling her and not a word reached her.

Finally one day, she interrupted him. "Israel," she said. "I think we must find a hiding place."

He cleared his bowl, making her wait a long time for an answer. At length he nodded, "I think so too." He rubbed his fists against the table. "That does not exclude the other plans. We must keep the youth groups organized, not allow ourselves to be deported, and in case the moment comes, have people around who are able to act . . . Why are you crying?"

"I want you to promise me . . . I want a place to hide . . ."

"There will be a place to hide." He took her by the hand, and approached the cradle with her. "What has he done today?" he inquired.

A noise rose from the yard. She shivered and ran to the window. "What's going on?" she asked.

"I told you," he said, remaining at the cradle.

"What did you tell me?"

"Biebow has gone crazy today. No one knows any details, but he gave the Old Man such a licking that he got a haemorrhage and they took him to the hospital.

He even beat up the Old Man's secretary. He broke the furniture in their office and spared no one and nothing. And there is a new order to surrender five hundred people. The people in the streets are saying that the Soviets have crossed the Vistula and are marching on Warsaw from the South." He noticed that Esther's shoulders were shaking, and he went over to her, "What has come over you, Little Mother?"

She did not answer. There was not enough time for her to relieve the load weighing on her heart. He had to leave. She took his hand and led him to the door. "Remember," she folded her arms around him. "A hideaway." As he went out into the corridor, she called after him, "Be careful!"

◆ ◆ ◆

Like lightning the news struck the ghetto: Deportation! Six thousand people had to leave before the end of the month. Three thousand per week. After a few days, more details became known. The deported would be sent to a district in the vicinity of Leipzig or Munchen. The liquidation of some Resorts or perhaps of the entire ghetto was imminent. A commission compiling the lists was already at work at Baluter Ring. These steps were supposedly being taken for the sake of the ghettoniks who had no protection in case of bombardment. The ghetto was a ship without a captain. Presess Rumkowski was still in the hospital and there was no chance of commenting on his speeches or guessing the truth from the expression of his face.

Esther waited for Israel until late at night. She ran out to meet him with the question, "What's new?" He flatly told her about everything that he knew: a few buildings near the prison had been emptied to become the place of assembly for the deportees. Tomorrow the first "wedding invitations" would be sent out.

"Who will leave?" she asked.

"No one knows as yet. I met Berkovitch in the yard. He wanders about outside all night. A strange man. He gave me an idea however. Bella Zuckerman showed him the cellar where her father had been hiding a radio receiver. My mother and a few children were caught in that cellar, it's true, but there is a shed above the cellar, in the apartment upstairs. We could figure out some arrangement, cover the entrance to the cellar with bricks, so that nothing can be seen from the outside and make the entrance from the house, or make two entrances. I must think it over. Anyway, we start work on it tomorrow night."

The following nights were full of unrest. The police were taking people from their beds, those in hiding were being sought. Whistles and screaming pierced the air. Israel and Bunim worked in the cellar every night until dawn, rarely exchanging a word. Once, however, after a night of work, Israel turned to Bunim, "I want to ask you a favour, Berkovitch." He found it difficult to express what he had to say, and tried with his eyes to find some understanding with Bunim, to make the words come more easily. "I mean . . . As far as Esther and the baby are concerned . . . I, you understand, shall not hide in the cellar . . . So I want to ask you, Mr. Berkovitch, to take care of them." Bunim mumbled something as Israel began to talk faster, more heatedly, "I am a Bundist . . . we are seeking contact with the other parties. We must not allow the people to leave. We want to have a core of activists, to organize a resistance at the moment of the liquidation of the ghetto."

Bunim muttered something again, then he burst out, "You are saving your comrades aren't you? And if, in their stead, others leave, it will be all right, won't it? And why are you inventing excuses with your talk about resistance? You know perfectly well that it will not come to that. And what meaning would it have now anyway?" Here he cut short his heated words, running his hands through his dishevelled hair. "Of course, if you don't come to hide, I shall take care of your wife and baby, but I demand from you permission to take in another family. The Eibushitzs. I have already spoken about it to Bella. Without the Eibushitzs I will not hide here, do you understand? And also, Mrs. Eibushitz could be of some help to Esther."

The following day the hideaway was already in use. Simcha Bunim Berkovitch had received a "wedding invitation". He brought his knapsack down into the cellar. It was filled with sheets of paper from a bookkeeping register and with a few vegetables from his *dzialka*; Lily, Blimele's doll, was in his hand. Before he hid in the cellar, he rushed to see Winter and his writer colleagues, to talk them into compiling a list of names and submitting it to the Evacuation Committee to protect the writers and artists against deportation. He eventually compiled the list himself. But when it was ready, he tore it up. He took a candle and matches with him into the cellar.

At night Israel came down to continue with the work. Bunim said to him, "Do you know, I am the last of the entire family of Berkovitchs. According to the theories of the Deportation Committee, it seems that wiping out an entire family is a better deed than breaking one up."

Before he had managed to finish his thoughts on the subject, the Toffee Man appeared before them. "May your hands be blessed, brethren," he wailed. "I can lend a hand too, if you have no objection." Israel was beside himself. They had obviously been doing their work too loudly, if the Toffee Man had smelled them out. He feared that the latter would spread the news amongst the neighbours, and he was not eager to admit any more people into the hiding place. The Toffee Man immediately guessed Israel's thoughts and he proudly pounded his fist against the yellow star on his gaberdine. "I too have a hiding place ready for my entire *yeshiva*. And this time the Almighty will assist us, because He will not know Himself where we are hiding. So cleverly have I and my boys disguised my undercellar." He took the hammer out of Israel's hand. "You go and get some sleep, because you must be at the Resort tomorrow."

Bunim stared at him with wide-eyed astonishment. "And you must not be at the Resort?"

The little man shook his head, "I have already finished with the Resort chapter of my life. I received a 'wedding invitation' too, and that's why I have to take care of essential issues." He looked about the cellar and scratched himself beneath his skullcap. "So, so," he groaned admiringly, "I can see you have made another exit through the hole in the ceiling, so that one could climb up to the shed upstairs. Quite clever. But don't forget to leave the ladder inside. Sometimes a great thing can become spoilt on account of a trifle."

Every evening Esther's room was filled with neighbours. She no longer chased them out. Along with them she waited for Israel, and in the meantime she listened to their talk, her body stiff with tension. The neighbours told her that the Germans were treating the people of the transports quite mercifully and were not splitting up families. They told her that the evacuees were being transported to German territory, between Frankfurt and Munich, and that a cauldron of coffee was placed in each wagon, and straw was strewn over the floor. Someone reported that a German officer or a general had supposedly declared that the evacuees would be cleaning up the rubble of the bombed-out German houses. A neighbour said that the Evacuation Committee had fourteen thousand names on its lists already, which meant that with three thousand people leaving per week, one could be safe for more than a month, that is, of course, if one was not on any of the lists.

Israel appeared in the room. The neighbours swarmed around him, but he was only able to repeat the rumours which they had already heard. They asked him for advice, to which he had one answer, "Don't join up."

As soon as the neighbours left, the silence began to set off alarms in Esther's ears. She took the baby into her arms, wrapped both herself and the little one in the plaid and followed Israel into the yard. Israel sneaked away to work at the cellar, while she wandered among the neighbours. Women gave her advice about what to do with the baby in case she should receive a "wedding invitation". They advised her to attach a string around the baby's neck and a little card with the baby's name on it. She could not understand the idea. Would she herself not tell the name of her child, if asked? Her stomach began to rumble and she could barely wait for the last neighbours to disappear from the yard, so as to be able to steal away into the cellar to Israel and sit through the night with him.

Days followed during which Esther was unable to take little Shalom into her arms. As soon as she picked him up, her hands would begin to shake and her belly to rumble.

Chapter Twenty-seven

NOT ONE NIGHT would pass without the wailing of the sirens, the sound of detonations and the ticking of air defence weapons. The people of the ghetto would try to guess how far away the sounds were. Here and there people lay prostrate on the ground, listening to its vibrations the way a doctor might listen to the palpitations of a human heart. In this manner they would try to guess how far away the front was from the ghetto and from which direction the Messiah's steps were approaching. They shared the results of their observations and quarrelled heatedly with each other over the number of kilometres. Every male became a fullfledged military expert, a strategist, reviving the memory of his military service.

With the capture of the radio listeners, the ghetto was isolated from the world. Snatches of information reached only the few. Most of the news stemmed from Baluter Ring where someone had had the opportunity to glance at an old German newspaper found in a garbage can. The majority of the ghettoniks fed on the "ducks hatched in people's minds" and on the information from the IWIT "Station" whose initials read "I Wish It Were True".

The days were sultry. The ghetto succumbed neither to the heat nor to the hunger which exceeded all previous experiences. The delivery of food stopped completely, possibly due to the difficulties of transportation and more possibly still, as a means of making the ghetto population more amenable to joining the transports. Flour and potatoes belonged to the memories of better times. Mainly the ghettoniks lived on what the soil of the ghetto could provide and on the bit of watery soup received at the Resorts. But the ghetto had a much more important problem to worry about: Fate. Day after day, under a blazing sun, transports of seven or eight hundred people left from the station in Marysin. Eight thousand Jews with "wedding invitations" went into hiding.

Michal Levine limped along the hot street, his doctor's bag in hand. He was making his few daily rounds. The sick were in hiding and he was being called only in particularly serious cases. The street was empty. There was a raid in progress. During these hours the police hunted for those who were in hiding. On the street corners and in the gates stood policemen. The coloured stripes on their caps flashed from all sides. To Michal they appeared like overgrown boys playing hide-and-seek. They did not touch Michal. On the contrary, they saluted him respectfully, "Good day, Herr Doctor."

"Dogcatchers!" Michal growled back. It was unbearable to watch the cat-and-mouse game. The policemen's chummy greeting made him their partner. His protection was at the expense of the unprotected. But he shook off the thought along with all his other thoughts. It was better not to think and to let every drop of sensitivity evaporate from one's head along with the sweat.

He heard a shriek. "Help! Help me!"

As soon as he turned, a woman fell into his arms. A policeman came running after her. The elderly woman with the wrinkled face and flying gray hair was unable to utter another word. Her open mouth turned to Michal was shaking, her loose lips were moving in and out. There was a darkness inside her mouth as if she had no tongue or teeth. Her eyes, screaming with fear, moved from Michal to the policeman and back. Unwittingly Michal embraced the woman with one arm, pulling her with him. The policeman put a hand on his shoulder.

"She goes with the transport!" he panted.

"Dogcatcher!" Michal was about to scream out, but instead he spoke with feigned respect, "Let her go, she is my aunt."

The policeman weighed that in his head, reluctantly removing his hand from Michal's shoulder. He swung his club. "If so, that's another story." He stopped, letting Michal move on with the woman on his arm. The woman, unable to bring out a word of thanks, waved at Michal and vanished through a gate.

Michal could no longer chase away his thoughts. He had saved a drop in the sea, he, the mighty Doctor, the partner of the policeman, of Rumkowski and the Germans. He had saved an old woman in whose stead perhaps a young and pretty one would leave. He slowed his steps. He was at a loss. What sense did his work still make? His house calls? What would he achieve in the best case? Put back on their feet those who would tomorrow or the day after receive a "wedding invitation"? He would make them strong enough to join the transport. Yet his physician's conscience prodded him on, "I have to do my duty to the best of my ability. The Hippocratic Oath is valid even here." That was his professional duty: to try and save the tiniest bough even when the whole forest was doomed to be consumed by the fire, a task more absurd than that of Sisyphus. His lame foot rhythmlessly clopped after the healthy one. Two feet, each with a separate goal, although moving in the same direction. He, Michal, would not win his war against his own annihilation, the lame foot seemed to chant. He was on his way to see a person who was sick and needed him, chanted the healthy foot, sure of itself.

He decided to offer himself a treat after his round of the houses, and visit Esther and her baby. Of course the baby was also an absurdity. Objectively speaking, that man and this woman were reckless and irresponsible. They had extended the reach of annihilation. And yet what a splendid expression of the will to live! Michal felt elated every time he looked at Esther. Eternal motherhood peered out at him from her eyes. Every time he mustered his courage and looked into those eyes, he felt cleansed. Today he would force himself to catch a glimpse of the little creature as well, not only to touch it with his hands and his ear, but to face it with his eyes and heart open. Let come what may. The mother and her son were the light; they gave one strength to meet the night and whatever it had in store.

The patients were alone in their apartments. Either they had no one to take care of them, or the members of their families were being kept at the Resorts on account of the raid. The air in the rooms was unbearable, stifling. Michal was used to it and did not mind. Actually he only touched the patients, talked to them and gave them home-spun advice. He had no injections or drugs for them. He rarely opened his bag, but took it along as a symbol; it enabled him to pass through the streets and it caused the patients themselves to view him with more respect and trust. He totally agreed with Voltaire that the art of practising medicine lay in entertaining the patient until nature cured him (or God destroyed him). So Michal turned into a real chatterbox during his visits. His words were the remedy. He related wonderful news from the fronts, naming towns, countries, rivers and seas. The front itself was only a cat's leap from the ghetto. He shook the jokes out "from his sleeve" and smiled falsely. His patients' complaints he dismissed with a shrug of his shoulders. Sheer delusions. Tomorrow they would rise and go to work, and after tomorrow the Russians would enter Lodz. The sick allowed themselves to be fooled easily, practically begging for the enticing lies. And if "the doctor himself said it", these were no lies.

He left their homes disgusted with himself. He was vacillating between two moods which were tearing him apart; each mood seemed to be imposed by his two feet, the crippled and the healthy. He had to find and hold on to some stable idea in this macabre vertiginous chaos. People like himself were unable to live without a clear conception of life and their place in it, just as they could not exist without a bite of bread and a sip of water. He had to find that clarity of meaning even now when his existence might come to an end any day; even during days such as this, when his feet barely carried him and the world withered in the hopeless heat. A conclusion had to be reached. There was nothing else left, but to arrive at a conclusion.

He was aware that all the gates were shutting before him too, which should actually have made him indifferent about what was to follow. Yet while abandoning himself to the search for clarity that should accompany him on the days that he had left to him, he caught himself still worrying about the future. He wanted to find a path leading that clarity across into the future, beyond his own life or death. But all that he was able to discover within himself was that he hated hatred and was ready to resist it, without knowing how. All that he was capable of discovering was the desire to live joyfully and be as free as possible.

He remained in his confusion. He was no philosopher. He did not know whether what he was thinking was naive, or clever and valid. And as the days wore on, his irritability grew. What was about to happen was no more speculation, no game of hypotheses, no dream. In the face of that reality, there was one indisputable imperative left: the human face must never become the face of the Angel of Death. Michal would think humorously, ironically: if God were an approachable democratic ruler and he asked him, Michal, "Here, as you see all my wonders, my merciful bounty, my miraculous powers, tell me, what miracle should I perform for you?" Then he, Michal, would reply: "Deprive all living creatures of the privilege of killing each other."

By the time he finished his round of house calls, the raid was over and the people had begun to rush out of the Resorts. Michal gave up the intention of seeing Esther and the child, and went home instead. Junia was not yet back from her party activities and he was glad to be alone. He did not try to continue with Shafran's work in psychology. He had given it up a while ago, burying the material in the tea-box where he had hidden his letters to Mira. For some time now he had been absorbed in a medical book about the causes of decay in old age; the book hypothesized about the prolongation of human life. Today he was not even able to look at the work. Why should he be interested in prolonging human life, if the main issue was not to shorten it.

He took a sheet of paper, thinking that perhaps his pencil might help him find his way through the labyrinth of thoughts. However, to his own surprise, he saw himself scribbling with large letters: "My Testament". He became furious with himself. He was not yet ready to write any wills. He tore up the paper. The next moment he found himself back in the street.

He was jostled and pushed from all sides. People were falling into each other's arms, "The evacuation is over!" The street swayed. Indeed, he soon noticed people released from prison. Loaded with packs and sacks they stumbled along the sidewalks, dazzled, staring at the ghetto as if they had arrived at a splendid foreign city.

"A miracle! A miracle!" All the faces were beaming. "We shall sleep in our beds again!"

Someone was running from gate to gate, crying, "People, tell those who are hiding that their food cards are valid again!"

Michal paced among the overjoyed crowds. He heard the excited exclamations, saw the radiant faces and wondered why he felt nothing but compassion and painful tenderness for those around him. He noticed Junia running towards him from the distance. He limped faster. She fell into his arms.

"It's over!" she panted, shamelessly kissing him in the mouth. Her nimble lean body clung to his heavy one. "We have gotten through it, Michal, dearest! It's over!"

He freed himself from her embrace. "Are you sure?"

She stared at him, unable to understand his indifference, his cold voice. "Haven't you heard?"

"I have."

Her little face became overcast; anger lit up in her eyes. "What more do you want, Michal? Let us catch our breaths. You are always cawing like a crow. If it were bad news you'd believe it right away."

"And you are always singing like a humming bird." He felt offended. They quarrelled.

The following day the news of the total liquidation of the ghetto became known. Fear returned with double force and only in the evening did people feel somewhat relieved. A ration of half a kilogram of new potatoes was announced, and young and old rushed to line up in front of the co-operatives. Before bedtime, the general mood had improved considerably. Rumours were circulating that the Presess was preparing a militia and defence bodies to protect the ghetto during the period of transition. Before they went to sleep, the men put their ears to the ground, to hear whether the steps of the Messiah's donkey could already be heard. They could. The front lines were now one hundred and twenty kilometres from Lodz, the people said.

In the morning the news of the total liquidation of the ghetto was confirmed. People rushed eagerly to the Resorts, trying to hold on to their usual routine by force. But soon they dispersed again. Work had stopped. Clouds of people streamed over the streets; out from the backyards, back into the backyards. By evening time, just as on the day before, their fears were exhausted. The air was cool, mild. Hearts calmed a bit. Lodz was close to the front lines and a blitz evacuation of nearly seventy thousand people was inconceivable. And in the meantime . . . how much time did an army require to cover such a trivial distance as one hundred and twenty kilometres? Before bedtime, a rumour spread that only the machines and the merchandise would be evacuated, not the people. During the night, although there was no air raid, people twisted and turned in their beds.

There was no time left for Michal to carry on with his thoughts. Days of nightmarish reality had arrived. With sharp brutal strokes they crossed out everything that was or would be, keeping one's body and mind captive to a present which contained not a trace of the present. Time spun in circles around a maddened spool. It was not only Michal who had that weird sensation of time, but every person whom he saw. It was as if the spool were twirling in front of thousands of crooked mirrors in which one person's madness reflected another's, raising it to a frightening power. There was in the blinding whirlpool only one thing which kept Michal attached to a solid point as if by an umbilical cord — Junia's hand; and during the nights — the touch of her body. Yet Michal barely saw Junia herself. She too was entangled in the twirling maze. She was talkative, confused, desperate, courageous. He did not listen to her; she did not listen to him, although they did not leave each other for a moment.

Bella rushed over to see them. "We are building a hideout in our cellar!" she announced. Neither Michal nor Junia wanted to hear about hiding. They took their knapsacks over to Bella's house and began to sleep over there, in one of the empty rooms, so that if something happened at night, they would be together.

Bella, barely alive, would drag herself along wherever Michal and Junia went. She followed them to Michal's few patients, to his short meetings with his colleagues and to Junia's meetings with her comrades. She stood with them in line in front of the co-operatives, in case there were a distribution of food. There was chaos everywhere. The spindles were twirling. A thousand eyes, a thousand mirrors reflected loneliness, with one point to hold onto: the hand of a loved one.

They went back to the building where Junia and Michal had lived to see what was happening to Winter. He received them with a broad welcoming gesture. His face, which had never smiled properly, was beaming. Standing by his easel, he worked feverishly with his brush. He inundated his visitors with a torrent of boisterous incomprehensible words.

"I have won! I, Vladimir Winter, have won! This morning they tore up my letter of protection at the *Kripo*. They politely invited me to leave with the first transport of the tailors. They're going to turn me into a tailor! Is it not a bit too late?" He roared wildly. "Let them go to hell! Look at the works they've helped me to create! Look at my walls! And now they've given me back my freedom, too. Because, Doctor, listen, I was no traitor but a slave. Now I am beginning to work for real . . . like a free spirit. Look here, I am overwhelmed by a sacred inspiration. Of course, you can't see a thing yet. Do you want to know why I am applying such dark colours? What I have in mind with that navy blue? Don't worry. It's not going to be a gloomy canvas. It is a summer night in the ghetto. Do you understand? The idyllic . . . the ideal . . . that's what I want to bring out. The navy blue will be as soft as velvet, the stars will be like diamonds, the houses like gondolas floating into infinity. And do you know what I will do as soon as it is finished? I will invite all my colleagues, the entire intellectual élite of the ghetto, to have a good look at my work. Then I will pack everything up. Oh, God, why do I still feel so cold and so hot? Doctor, don't make any mistake, I'm not running a high temperature. It is only because I'm tense. Come closer. Junia, you too. Even you will understand me today. Put yourselves at the window . . . Do you see the sky? There is only one such sky in the entire world. The sky over the ghetto." He checked his pulse and turned to Michal with a business-like voice, "Doctor, don't you think that I am perspiring because of tension and the stuffy air? Give me a glass of milk, little goat," he turned to Junia. They asked him whether he intended to join the transport, or to hide. He picked up his brush again, after he had taken one sip of milk. "I intend to do nothing, until I finish this work," he replied. "Then we shall see."

"You know what the situation is, don't you?" Michal pulled him away from the easel by the sleeve.

"Take your hands off me, Doctor!" Winter pierced him with his hot hawkish eyes. "There are no longer any bosses in my life!" he shouted, "I am a free spirit. And now forgive me, all of you, and get out of here."

They went to see what was happening to Guttman. In his hut near the garbage dumps, paintings were covering the walls in neat symmetry, as in a museum. There was a white card pinned to the wall below each painting, with its name and the date when it had been painted. Guttman was scrubbing the floor.

"My gallery will be finished just on time," was the first thing he said. He motioned with his hand, indicating that they should not step into the room, so as not to dirty the floor.

He asked Junia about the most recent news from the fronts. She did not hear his question. She and Bella were staring at the portrait of Matilda hanging on the wall opposite them. Guttman had started to paint it years ago and had probably only recently finished it. Although he had depicted all the folds and creases in Matilda's face, there was nothing of the ghetto air about it. This was the lofty Matilda, the woman who had sat at the piano in the high-ceilinged salon, playing Chopin's études. It was obvious that admiration, or perhaps love guided Guttman's brush. Thus her daughters saw their mother at that moment in all her sad beauty; they saw her as she had essentially been. Perhaps they realised that the image of Matilda which they would carry within them from now on would be that which the painter had created with his brush; for suddenly they felt unusually close to Guttman. They proposed that he come and stay with them in the house on Hockel Street.

"I too want to be with you," he said, getting up from the floor and approaching them, scrubbing brush in hand. "But I still have a few canvases to frame and hang up. Some I must still correct. Maybe in a few days . . ." Obviously moved by the expression on Junia's face, he took hold of her hand, smiling, "What's the matter, little goat?" She tore her hand out of his and ran outside.

Michal stammered, "She is disillusioned. She thought that she would . . . that we would . . ." Guttman's face changed. He turned away from Michal and Bella. They understood that he wanted them to leave.

The three of them continued to roam the streets, knocking at the doors of friends, to find out what each of them had decided to do. In front of one gate a cluster of people had gathered. A policeman disengaged himself from the crowd and accosted Michal.

"Doctor," he called out, "You have fallen down like from the sky! Come with me! Herr Schatten . . . He's kicking the bucket. For three days and three nights he hasn't stopped drinking and hollering like a hog. Delirium tremens," the policeman diagnosed.

Junia and Bella waited for Michal in front of the house. The people in the crowd were constantly changing, some left while others arrived to find out what was happening. "If that enemy of the Jews is drinking himself to death out of fear," a woman remarked, "it means that his skin is not safer than ours."

"Of course," a passer-by agreed with her. "If there is a total liquidation of the ghetto, I don't give a pfennig even for Rumkowski's head."

A man, an optimist, considered it his duty to console the crowd, "And I am telling you that things are not so bad. The neighbour of one of my relatives, for instance, has received a referral to a bakery for a whole month."

People stared at him in astonishment. Soon there was another to give support to the man's views and help him calm the crowd, "They say that the Tailor Resort has received a new order, to produce . . ."

"To produce what?" he was asked.

"Yeah, to produce tailors . . . for the transport!" called someone who refused to be reassured.

✦ ✦ ✦

Five thousand Jews were supposed to leave the ghetto daily. They were supposed to leave by Resorts, along with the machinery and materials. The tempo of the whirlpool increased. A late summer's nightmare. The dead clock on the tower of the dead church seemed to smile mockingly with its dead dials, "It's not I, not I in my deadness, who will be sent off. Only I, only I in my deadness, shall remain." People would glance at it, defend themselves against it, "That is impossible!" They each seemed to reply, "That will not happen. And if it does, then it will not be I who is led off . . . Only I, only I shall remain."

The directors, commissars and managers of the most important departments convened in the Presess' office. The Presess delivered a speech. He dabbed at the sweat on his face, coughed hoarsely and inflated his cheeks. No, it was not yet known for sure when the "action" would begin, he said, but they must expect it at any moment. Nor were any other details yet known. After the conference, the ghetto became exuberant again. A rumour was spreading that the evacuation had been postponed for twenty days. People cursed the Presess and the *shishkas* for having frightened them.

The directors of the Tailor and Metal Resorts were invited to a conference, this time not in the Presess' office but in that of Herr Biebow, where the gentlemen from the *Ghettoverwaltung* were gathered. An unfamiliar *Herr*, a representative of the *Reichsristungkommando*, delivered a fire-and-brimstone speech about the proximity of the front lines and about the general war situation which required that the Tailor and Metal Resorts should be moved to a safer locale in Germany. The Tailor Resorts had to leave the following day. The directors left the meeting with their heads raised high. The issue was clear. Biebow did not want to leave for the front and he had interceded in Berlin for the relocation of his business, so useful for the Reich, to a place more distant from the front.

Not one tailor reported for the transport the following day.

An important speech by Herr Biebow to the entire ghetto population was announced. Michal, Junia and Bella rushed to the yard of the Fire Department. The sun was spitting fire. Streams of sweat poured down the red twisted faces of the crowd. Herr Biebow's words poured down over the heads like a cool refreshing spray.

"Workers of the ghetto, my dear Jews!" The German language which had once smacked like a whip against Jewish ears, now caressed them softly. "I hope that you will take what I am about to tell you very seriously. Some of you believe that it is wiser to remain in the ghetto to the last. This, my dear friends, is wrong. Because whoever deludes himself that the ghetto is not moving towards total dissolution is making a great mistake. Bombs have been dropped already in the vicinity of Litzmanstadt. Had they fallen in the ghetto, there would not be a stone left on a stone. Therefore I am appealing to you to allow the transfer of the ghetto to proceed in an orderly manner, in peace and good will. It is sheer madness on the part of the workers of the Tailor Resorts numbers one and two to resist joining the transport, and it leaves me no choice but to apply forceful means. For four and a half years I have worked with you, always trying to contribute the best . . . And I assure you that we shall all try to do the same in the future, and by moving the ghetto to another place, to protect your lives. There is a war going on. Germany is struggling to the last . . . It is necessary to conserve all possible working power, since at the order of Herr Himmler thousands of Germans have been sent to the battlefields. They must be replaced. I am telling you this for your own good, and I hope that Resorts numbers three and four will also report like one man to the railway station. The families will leave together for the various camps which will be rebuilt and the factories installed. You surely want to live and have enough food. And that you will have. After all, I am not standing here like some silly boy," Herr Biebow's voice grew a bit harsher, "who will keep pleading with you while you refuse to show up. If you push me to apply force, there will be many dead and wounded . . ." Here he controlled himself and became soft-spoken again. "Food will be provided for each wagon. The voyage will last sixteen to eighteen hours. Take along luggage not exceeding twenty kilograms. There is enough room in the wagons. Come with your families. Take along kitchen utensils because there is a shortage of them in Germany. I assure you once more that you will be cared for. Go home, pack and sign up!"

A few decrepit tailors signed up at the place of assembly.

The following day there was another speech by Herr Biebow, at the Metal Resort. Michal, Junia and Bella rushed there as well. This time Herr Biebow's pleas were even more arduous. The crowd was delighted with his supplicating voice, soothing their hearts with the fact that the mighty master was bowing to them. But they did not sign up. Biebow drove to the other central points of the ghetto. The *Oberbürgermeister* of the city rode with him and also delivered speeches, as did the other *Herren* of the *Ghettoverwaltung*. They all begged the Jews: "Be willing . . ."

Presess Rumkowski gave some speeches of his own, calling for obedience. Perspiring, exhausted, his shrunken figure appeared before the crowds. He heaved heavy sighs and spoke hoarsely to his brothers, without a trace of his former histrionics. He no longer shouted or raised his arms prophetically. As a matter of fact, the people could barely hear him and the number of his listeners decreased with every speech; they preferred to listen to Biebow. There at least they had a bit of satisfaction.

The days passed. The speeches were to no avail. The police began to work at night, taking people from their beds.

Herr Biebow did not give up making speeches. He had a new reassuring argument. Not only the ghetto, but all of Litzmanstadt, the former Lodz, with its German and Polish population, would also be evacuated within forty-eight hours. Now and then a warning pierced the slippery smoothness of his words. But he immediately noticed the fury lighting up the eyes of his listeners and he controlled himself, adding another dose of sweetness to his pleas. Practically on his knees, he implored his sloppy, barely-living audience to do him a personal favour and allow him to take care of them for their own sake.

People went on listening to his speeches and then not appearing at the place of assembly to be deported. Instead, they haunted the streets and gathered in the backyards to interpret Biebow's sermons. They came to the general conclusion that, firstly, Biebow, the "craven *Yeke*, the idiotic pighead" was afraid that the Jews of the Lodz Ghetto would do what the Jews of Warsaw had done, since he did not have the faintest idea of how "deeply buried in the ground" the remaining Jews of Lodz were; and that, secondly, the plan which he was presenting of "transplanting" the ghetto into Germany was a hollow bluff. Because why should the *Yekes*, who where themselves buried "deep in the ground", begin now to bother about Jewish security? That, thirdly, the *Yekes* no doubt wanted to finish off the last bit of Jewry, but they were so broken and confused that their heads were simply derailed; and that, fourthly, they themselves would flee from here any day now, possibly in the same wagons which they had prepared for the ghettoniks.

The raids took place a few times a day. Those hunted were supposedly the tailors and the metal workers, but the police grabbed whoever happened to fall into their hands, and "the awl came immediately out from the sack". The raids became constant. Two thousand people had to be rounded up every day. The policemen who had begun to work near to their homes, in order to protect their families, chased after neighbours in their own streets. They swung their clubs and bellowed hoarsely, beside themselves, just like the people whom they were chasing.

Huge trucks appeared in the ghetto. Out of them jumped German soldiers and quickly surrounded the blocks of houses. Shots, screams and lamentations pierced the sky. The sound of doors being broken, locks torn apart, windows shattered accompanied the thud of boot-steps. People were rounded up and herded on foot, or on trucks, or on wagons, or on the tramcar — to the train station.

Red cattle trains arrived at the station which had a separate line from the ghetto. The sun baked the heads of those who clambered over the wooden ramps onto the cattle cars. The black herds of people were split up, filling one car, then another, then a third. The heavy knapsacks swayed, suitcases shook, pots and cutlery clinked, while from the Marysin road masses of people came streaming on, sand and dust upon their cracked lips and between their teeth.

Those who climbed the planks kept their heads turned backwards, scanning the green of Marysin, the *dzialkas*, the trees. The smell of pears, apples and cherries filled their nostrils. They felt as if they themselves were fruit filling the open snouts of the empty hungry boxcars. The doors were wide open, swallowing seventy bodies each. Then the doors were shut tight, bolted, locked. Each car had an eye which peered out at the world remaining behind: a tiny barred window. In it the sky, cut into pieces, began to sway as iron touched iron with a screech. The locomotive began to heave. The wheels began to turn slowly, rolling away with increased speed. From the barred windows, hands were thrust out, people were calling, asking, "Where are we going to?"

On the walls of the ghetto placards appeared, announcing that the smaller part of the ghetto would immediately be cut off and that all those living there had to move over the bridge into the central part; whoever was found in the cleared-up district after forty-eight hours would be shot without warning.

All night long, shadows with loads like big humps on their backs streamed over to the other side of the bridge. People moved into abandoned apartments, or with relatives or friends. The streets in the central part of the ghetto were packed with the throngs, since even those who lived in that part refused to go to sleep. Everyone was outside, in the hullabaloo. Clouds of restless shadows, hitting against each other, pushing each other back and forth, around in circles. At the same time a great silence hovered in the air and the darkness was deep. Faces shone like moons in a town of lunatics.

All night the men, under Israel's leadership, worked to finish the hideout in the cellar. In addition to Israel, the workers were: Bunim, Michal Levine, David and his brother Abraham, as well as Shlamek, Rachel's brother. The Eibushitzs had been accepted into the cellar, thanks to Bunim. However, Rachel had refused to move in without David and his brother.

The men were shirtless; their backs shone with perspiration. They worked feverishly and carefully, so as not to attract the attention of the neighbours who were moving past the yard all night. The large outside door of the cellar was already walled up with bricks. In its stead an exit was prepared through the barred window of the cellar. It was covered with a canvas and a layer of soil, which made it look like a *dzialka*. If one needed to escape, this would be the nearest way to run across to the firemen's yard. Air entered through a hole in the wall, camouflaged by the rain-pipe which descended from the roof. The second exit gave into the shed of the Zuckerman apartment. The shed and the cellar were joined by a ladder. Thanks to outlets which Samuel had prepared for his radio, there was electric current both in the cellar and in the shed, which enabled them to have light and use both a small electric stove and David's electric kettle. Food suplies were stored inside the cellar along with pails of fresh water.

Blumka Eibushitz took over as principal housekeeper, directing the women who had been busy all night making the hideout as comfortable as possible. First of all they arranged a corner for Esther and the baby, and another one for Bella who could barely stand on her feet. As soon as Esther came down into the cellar, they waited for little Shalom to become hungry and start to cry. Rachel slipped outside to check whether his wailing could be heard in the yard. It could not, but Blumka ordered Esther's corner to be separated from the rest by a heavy blanket, just in case. Blumka also hoped that the blanket would protect Shalom against the germs that the adults might contaminate him with; specifically she was thinking of Bella who had a cough which she muffled with a rag. Blumka, an expert on Koch germs, had no doubt in her mind that Bella was affected by the "real thing". The rest of the inhabitants of the cellar were assigned sleeping places, some in the shed, others in the cellar.

Their work made the women excited, nervous and, in a way, cheerful. Blumka even allowed herself to joke with Bella who had brought into the cellar a volume of Slowacki's poems, the gift from her teacher Miss Diamand. "We don't even lack culture," Blumka said, helping Bella make herself comfortable in her corner.

At dawn, when everything was more or less ready, they all sat down around

Bella's bed and rested. They listened to the silence in the yard. The hiding-place seemed like a rescue boat about to reach a shore.

Esther had not felt so calm for a long time. Israel was with her and with Shalom, and she wished for nothing more. She felt protected and safe in the presence of her man, who no longer had anywhere to run to, and whose only party was now his son. She could not understand why Israel had not yet made peace with this fact, why his face was twisted, tormented. He refused to accept the peace that had been offered them and seemed again like a boy deprived of his games. She herself had known for a long time that this would be the only way left. And she was also glad that she would have her "other" man so close, he who had had so much to do with her child's coming into the world; because Michal and Junia had also come to hide with them.

She put her son on a padded box and arranged and rearranged her corner. She placed a little mirror on a protruding brick in the wall, winking at Abraham, the second youngest inhabitant of the cellar, "That will be for you men, so that you can shave properly." She cast a glance at Shalom who was sleeping rolled up, his big toe close to his eternally-sucking mouth, and she added, "Soon my Shalom will also have to shave."

Abraham, his face smeared with dirt, glanced at himself in the mirror. He puffed out his cheeks, rubbing the place where a few hairs had begun to sprout. "I will let my beard grow, starting from today," he announced. "It will be a souvenir of the hideout for the rest of my life."

Esther felt Michal's eyes on her. He no longer avoided looking at her or at the baby. She winked at him daringly, pointing to her son, "Here is your masterpiece, Doctor . . ." she whispered.

He winked back at her, "At least there is someone who considers me an artist." Michal too had become calm as soon as he had entered the hiding-place. His bitterness and rage had remained on the other side of the wall. Medicine was again the most beautiful profession in the world.

He was able to look at Esther and the child, but not at Junia. Junia walked about as if she had a stomach ache. The dull gaze with which she looked around the cellar was that of a bird trapped in a cage. Her little face was twisted and creased with despair. It called forth such a painful longing within him for the Junia of the past, that he could hardly bear it. He did not try to console or cheer her. They had even managed to have a little squabble on the way to the cellar, as usual over a trifle. Junia had insisted on breaking into a co-operative to check whether there was any food inside to take along. He had refused to let her do it. In reality, he feared that she would change her mind in the meantime and leave him. Yes, it was he who had brought the bird into the cage. He did not feel guilty. There was no other choice.

Later on, they all discussed the issue. They had to set out and collect as much food as possible. They postponed it to the following night. When Junia volunteered for the job, Michal did not object. It had been his duty to arrive there together with her, but he did not want to keep her by force. She was a free person and the master over her own life. His heart overflowed with tenderness for her. He sat in a corner across from the box where Shalom lay asleep and thought of the children that lay dreaming in Junia's womb. What free birds they would be! He stared at sleeping Shalom and, in his mind, saw his own heir, his unborn son.

In the morning the raids began on the other side of the ghetto. Shots were heard. With the exception of Esther and the baby, they all climbed upstairs into the apartment. Shlamek and Abraham kept watch at the windows. If Germans or Jewish police appeared in the yard, there was enough time to open the door of the cupboard which concealed the entrance to the shed, to remove the cupboard's inner wall, and crawl into the hiding place.

The purpose of coming upstairs was to inhale a supply of "freedom"; for Junia was not the only one with uneasiness in her heart. The first moments of cheerfulness and peace of mind were over. They all had to adjust to the place slowly. Blumka Eibushitz, whom everyone began to call *Mameshe*, immediately became aware of the change of mood and proposed that they eat a bit of food before they went to sleep for the day. To her surprise, no one wanted to eat. All they wanted was to enjoy a bit of daylight. So they puttered about in the empty rooms for a while and then one after the other crawled into the shed and slumped down in their assigned places. Israel appointed guards which were to change every two hours, and soon silence enveloped the cellar. No one slept the entire day. They had their first meal together: a watery soup, their only meal of the day. They only had a five-day food supply. All the sugar and marmalade went to Shalom.

As soon as night fell, Michal, Junia, Bunim and Shlamek left the cellar to search for food. They rushed to all the houses which had harboured co-operatives. The doors of some were broken, and there was not a trace of food left inside. Others were locked tight and the group had no tools with which to open them nor could they make too much noise and attract attention. They were not well prepared for the expedition and Junia bit her fists in frustration.

On the way back, as they apathetically moved along the walls in the yard on Hockel Street, someone jumped toward them from one of the entrances. "Michal!" they heard a whisper. Guttman stood before them. He pulled Michal and Junia into the stairwell, and began to sputter heatedly, "We never said good-bye, so I decided to come over. I had to find a painting anyway . . . Shiele, the street singer's. He hid it under the bed. I have it here. And you know, Michal, I've left a letter in my studio . . . I wrote . . . God, I must run! I'm glad I found you. I am joining up in the morning. It's the best way to ecape. They say there are partisans in the vicinity of Lodz. The gun will again become my lover." He grabbed the street singer's portrait which had been leaning against the wall and waved his hand, "Adios!"

Junia hung on to him. "How will you escape? Tell me! Tell me!" He tore himself away from her and dashed towards the gate. "Wait!" She ran after him, "Take me with you! I beg you, take me along!" However, she stopped abruptly in the gate and let Guttman vanish. She turned back to the group which was waiting for her, took Michal by the hand and silently entered the hiding place with him.

The forty-eight hours allocated for moving into the central part of the ghetto had already passed, but another twelve hours had been generously offered. Israel decided to cross the bridge with the crowd. Michal and Junia went with him. They hoped to "organize" a substantial supply of food on the other side. Once across the bridge, they separated. Junia and Michal ran first to Guttman's hut. They did not expect to find him there, but they had his *dzialka* in mind. They had seen cabbage leaves growing on it during their last visit.

The streets in the central part of the ghetto were like crowded beehives.

Thousands and thousands of people, dazed, preoccupied, swarmed back and forth. Some were still searching for a place to install themselves, carrying pieces of furniture as if they were ready to settle down again. Others were simply unable to stay put in their homes, where everything was ready for a voyage which could begin at any moment.

The door of Guttman's hut was not locked and Michal and Junia entered the room. On a table covered with a white cloth stood a vase with late summer flowers. In front of the vase lay Guttman's letter to the world:

"This is an exhibition of paintings by I. Guttman, born in Lodz, in the year 1910. Throughout all the years of my captivity in the Ghetto of Lodz, I have tried with the help of my brush to reflect the life of the Jews trapped between barbed wires.

Whatever happens to me personally, I beseech you, whoever you are who opens the door to this house, to respect my work and not to destroy it."

Junia glanced at the opposite wall and met Matilda's wistful gaze. Her mother seemed to be sitting at the piano, playing a nocturne by Chopin. Michal flipped through the catalogue of paintings, written in Guttman's hand. Then he put it back on the table along with the letter, took Junia by the hand and left the hut. He shut the door, writing on it his and Junia's names. Then they filled their bag with what they could dig up from Guttman's *dzialka*.

When they returned to the cleared part of the ghetto, they decided to see what had happened to Winter. As they climbed the stairs, they bumped into Mendelssohn, who had come rushing down the stairs with a knapsack on his back. He shook their hands vigorously.

"My friends! My dear friends!" He beamed from ear to ear. "I thank you! Thank you for everything!" He told them his good news. Tomorrow's transport was leaving for Hamburg. He, Mendelssohn, was to return to his *Heimat, ja wohl*. He was already heading for the place of assembly in order to be on time. Punctual. He also had to secure a place for himself in the wagon. He had heard that there were crowds of people at the train station . . . The next transport was heading for Berlin and the one after that for Munich. He must leave for Hamburg.

Michal grabbed him by the shoulders and shook him furiously. "*Dummkopf! Dummkopf!*" he roared. "How can you believe such things? Don't you understand it's all lies?"

Mendelssohn shrugged his shoulders, "Please, Doctor Levine, it is a fact. Everyone knows that the first transport leaving in the morning has Hamburg as its destination. Ask Herr Biebow himself. No matter what you may think, a German tells no lies." He grabbed their hands into his once again. "*Adieu! Auf Wiedersehen!*" Michal was about to rush after him, but Junia held him back. She said nothing but stared at him with her dark eyes. She looked like an old woman.

Winter was lying on his sofa. It seemed as if he were talking to someone on the ceiling. He was running a high fever. The painting on which he had been working stood on the easel, unfinished. White splotches of canvas shone between the dark colours like letters written in an illegible handwriting. The other paintings, removed from the walls, leaned against the furniture, tied together; some were wrapped in bedsheets.

"How can I leave him like this?" Michal mumbled.

Junie responded with a groan, "Have you got a choice? Can we take him along?"

Michal checked Winter's pulse, then put a chair with a pot of water near the sofa and took Junia by the hand. "Come, I will drop in every night. I must still have an injection somewhere."

On their way back, they stopped in those backyards where there seemed still to be something left on the *dzialkas*. In the gate of their house on Hockel Street, they saw Bella sitting on a doorstep. The Toffee Man sat beside her. As soon as he noticed Michal and Junia, he jumped to his feet and grabbed Michal by the lapels.

"She does not want to understand, the girl," he whispered, sniffling, "That I have nothing to do here without my business. Who will buy remedies for the heart from me, I ask you? I hid for twenty-four hours with my *yeshiva* boys, so it still made some sense. But they all ran away. They want to be with their families. Yes, a man discusses the issue with himself. What do I have to fear after all? If my children have gone down the same road, does it suit me, their father, to be afraid, tell me?" He talked to Michal for a long time, his words becoming more and more incomprehensible. Bunim was standing a few steps away from the group. He had also just taken leave of the Toffee Man.

Little by little all those who had left the hiding place gathered at that spot. There was too much traffic in the yard for them to be able to sneak into the hideaway, and aside from that, they wanted to use the remaining few hours to find some more food. They dispersed again. When they met at the appointed hour, they were all loaded down with vegetables; Shlamek and Abraham who had succeeded in getting into a co-operative had brought along a treasure: bags of flour and rice, and even a bit of sugar.

Although they had all decided to stay awake during the night, when they were able to move about outside, and to sleep during the day, they all crept into the hiding place and collapsed on their lairs. They slept through one whole night and only the sound of shooting from the other side of the ghetto woke them in the morning. The shooting lasted only half a day. It was Saturday and the Germans did not work beyond noon.

✦   ✦   ✦

Sabbath afternoon. An awesome silence. God and the Germans were at rest. The inhabitants of the cellar lay on the floor upstairs, in the room with the balcony. The balcony door was wide open and the cherry tree was blinking upwards with the few cherries left on its crown.

Esther lay on one of the beds with Shalom beside her on a spread diaper. He was busy with his favourite game: stretching and bending his spring-like legs. Nearby sat Blumka Eibushitz, sorting through a pot of peas. On the other bed lay Bella, her head leaning against her fist, in front of her the open volume of Slowacki's poems. She was not reading. She was far from Slowacki's poetry at that moment, but she would not part with the book. It evoked the memory of Miss Diamand, and she could often hear the old woman's rasping voice within her: "My child, listen to the sound of the piano within you . . . Be faithful to your music and you will not be lost or afraid." Bella did not worry about the fate of the book itself. She had decided with Rachel that one or the other of them would take care of it and take it with her wherever she went.

The others sat on the floor. Bunim was flipping through the loose pages of the bookkeeping register, reading to himself the chapters of his unfinished epic poem. Michal Levine also held a sheet of paper on his knees. On it were written, in the barely legible handwriting of a physician, the words "My Will", and beneath them a few phrases: "I am a Jew. I love my people. But I long for the time when it will be sufficient for me to say: I am a human being." Nearby sat Rachel cradled in David's arms. Her eyes were fixed on Bunim. Gradually fatigue overcame them all. Their heads sank low. They fell asleep. Abraham, Shlamek and Junia were on guard at the windows and the balcony door.

Shalom caused an alarm with his yells. Israel, who had been fixing something in the shed, rushed in and covered the child with his body to muffle the screams. Then he grabbed the baby into his arms and rushed down to the cellar with him. "Never bring him upstairs again!" he ordered Esther. She took the baby from his arms and put it on the box. Trembling, she blocked the baby's mouth with her breast.

The inhabitants of the cellar did not talk much to one another on that Sabbath day. It seemed as if each of them were busy with his or her self, and even though they were physically close, they did not see one another. Their imaginations played with vague dreams. They felt dissolved in the silence of the strange Sabbath peace.

That night also belonged to them, along with the following day. How much more could they ask for? Except for Esther, Israel and the baby, they all slept upstairs. Israel did not trust the Jewish police and feared that during the night or on Sunday, they would come to search for those who were hiding on that side of the ghetto. He assigned regular guards for the following twenty-four hours.

Michal lay with Junia on the bed in Samuel's former room. He liked to look at Junia when she was asleep, her limbs entangled with his. He missed her smile and her gaiety. Yet she was doubly dear to him in her disillusionment and grief. He sensed her strength, not only in her firm attachment to life, but also in her painful craving for it. In her white slip, the skin of her face and arms seemed mulatto-dark, and although she was lean, there was something bronze-like and indestructible about her — a statue sculptured by the sun itself.

Michal's mind turned to the will which he had begun to write. With Junia's hand on his chest he did not feel the despair of No Exit. Just the opposite. His testament had to be a greeting, a message. In his mind he chose the words carefully, slowly. In the other room, close to the open balcony slept Berkovitch, the poet with the sick heart and the swollen legs. Michal envied Berkovitch's familiarity with words. Human language was so poor, it was of so little help here, in the hiding place. Yet he had to resort to it. He had to transmit what could be transmitted, even if imperfectly, even if unclearly. After all, the words sprang from a source which was also not perfect or clear.

They woke up to a sunny Sunday morning. It was quiet outside. They had no idea of how the day passed. It was like a dream from which they refused to awake. At twilight, Bunim stood guard at the window and it was he who saw the Toffee Man arrive, the candy box suspended from his neck; he looked just as he had during the normal days of the ghetto. From the distance the Yellow Star on his gaberdine reflected the sun's rays. Above his box his long sparse beard swayed freely, uncovered. It flew up in the air to the rhythm of the little man's steps, as if delighted with its freedom, its strands stretching in all directions. Bunim consulted Israel and they decided to let him into the hideout.

The Toffee Man, his face washed with tears, but no longer crying, appeared

346 The Tree of Life

in the apartment upstairs. They noticed a bread sack suspended from his shoulder. From it, there peered out a prayer shawl, phylacteries and a psalm book.

"Neighbours!" He raised his hands as they all surrounded him. "Since the train is not leaving today, I have decided to come and say good-bye again." He noticed Bunim open his mouth, about to say something, and he stopped him. "And it came to pass," he crooned, "that they struck us and I remained . . . I fell upon my face and I said: 'Woe, God, our Master, do You really wish to destroy the remainder of Israel?' Night after night I wept, asking that question. This night I stood up and not waiting for an answer, I said to Him, 'If it is so, Ruler of the Heavens, then whatever happens to all of Israel, may happen to Reb Israel. And may Your will, Master of the World, be done . . . And then You will see whether or not it pleases You'." He noticed David and his face lit up. He stretched out two fingers of his hands to him and shook two of David's. "Do you remember, my son, what I once told you, that in case one of us two should remain . . . You . . ."

David took the little man's entire hand between his fingers. He wanted to beg him to stay with them and he also had a strange idea — to ask him to conduct a marriage ceremony for Rachel and himself that very day. But the Toffee Man waved his hand at him as if to let him know that his words were useless.

Blumka offered the Toffee Man a bowl of soup. She expected that he would refuse it too with his raised hands. But to her surprise, he took the spoon from her hand, placed the bowl on the glass cover of his box and eagerly began to sip from it. They all watched his beard and sidelocks tremble with each spoonful that he swallowed. Bella moved very close to him. With her dark feverish eyes she stared at his creased face.

"Don't go, Rabbi. Please don't . . ." she implored him.

He pushed the empty bowl into her hand, swaying as if in prayer, "Dear Child," he said. "What do you mean that I should not go?" He adjusted the string of the box on his neck. "Do you see the toffees here, which I spent all day making? Do you know what I made them for? To sweeten the voyage, I've made them. There will be enough customers, may they be protected from an evil eye." He drew out a toffee from under the glass cover and handed it to Blumka, "That's for the woman with the red hair, for her son Shalom. Tell her to wrap the candy in a piece of cloth and give it to him to suck when he begins to holler."

The next moment he was gone.

Chapter Twenty-eight

AT DAWN, SHOUTS, laments and shrieks could be heard coming from the central part of the ghetto. Often, through the silence on their side, the inhabitants of the cellar could hear the clear words of someone begging for pity, as well as the slashing response in German language. Even at noon, when the inhabitants of the cellar expected a break in the "action", there was no change. The hunt went on from six in the morning until eight in the evening. The part of the ghetto which included Hockel Street was dead. The Germans still had enough to do on the other side. The inhabitants of the cellar followed Israel's plan of sleeping during the day and staying awake at night. But it was not easy to sleep to the accompaniment of the screams.

At night all of them, except for Esther and the child, went outside. Under protection of darkness they rushed through the backyards to the abandoned homes and to the co-operatives in search of food. They also provided themselves with pails of water, praying that the waterpumps would not squeak too loudly. Often during these night activities they noticed other "mice" leave their holes. They discovered that in the yard on Hockel Street there was a family hiding in the attic of the old water reservoir. And there was another group of neighbours in the Toffee Man's cellar.

A collective guard of the people from all the hideouts was organized in the yard. The watchmen had their observation posts in the chimneys on the roof. They had to warn the others when the Germans or the Jewish police crossed into this part of the ghetto. They also contacted those hiding in other backyards and agreed on a set of signals.

Michal Levine, a few sleeping pills in his pocket, began again to make his rounds on this side of the ghetto. But his visits to the empty rooms where the lonely sick people had been left behind came to an end very soon. On the seventh day of the "action", the watchman in the chimney signalled that a wagon on rubber wheels had entered through the gate in the ghetto fence. After a few hours the wagon rolled back, loaded with the sick.

Life in the cellar was organized down to the minutest detail. They ate only twice in twenty-four hours: at dawn before the "action", and in the evening, after the "action". They saved every drop of water, for the pumps screeched too loudly. The lookouts in the chimneys who could see what was going on on the other side reported on the progress of the "action". They reported that despite the confusion of the raids and the hunts, cabbages and turnips were being distributed somewhere. People could be seen running across the yards with full sacks. Those who were caught were chased to the trucks or wagons and the sacks were knocked out of their hands.

Rachel and David kneeled on the dug-up ground of a *dzialka* in a remote yard. They had set out along with the others for "night work". The aim of the inhabitants of the cellar was to gather enough food for a month, and since they expected that their side of the ghetto would soon be raided, they made the best use of the quiet nights that they could. The earth was cool. A fresh breeze danced lightly in the air. Rachel and David dug hurriedly and only occasionally did they hit against the root of a vegetable. But they rejoiced in the opportunity of being alone together under the open sky. When their bags were more or less full, they allowed themselves to sneak into an empty room and call it home for an hour or so.

Rachel was calm. Everything had ended. The ghetto belonged to the past. She found herself in No Man's Land, where yesterday and tomorrow were cut off from each other. The fact that one bitter chapter had come to an end gave her a sense of relief, although the arrival of the next chapter gnawed at her mind with biting question marks. She thought that the love between David and herself could not have survived much longer. The ghetto alienated people from each other. Even if they carried the same chains, their souls parted, each following its own road of torment. Of course the ghetto had also caused people to become attached and deeply involved with one another, yet both the attachment and the alienation were brought about by the abnormal conditions, and therefore they too were often abnormal and false. In some attachments there was more hatred than love, in some separations more love than hate.

Only the present fact of being together with David held any meaning for her. David was aware of it as well. They had acquired a sensitivity which allowed them to listen in to each other's thoughts. His way of reacting aloud to her thoughts was not always pleasant, yet she knew that whatever he told her was neither veiled nor disguised any more than the patch of soil on which they sat.

Their bags were almost full and their fingers were stiff, when they stopped working. They moved closer to each other and huddled in an embrace. They were exhausted, incapable of moving their limbs, yet touching was easy. With his bent stiff fingers, David stroked Rachel's hair. Much later he spoke, "Do you know," he said, "when we said good-bye to the Toffee Man, a strange idea popped into my mind. I wanted him to give us the marriage blessings."

She laughed quietly, "You're funny."

"Why? I meant it, symbolically."

"We have been married for a long time, you sillyhead, and not only symbolically."

"Do you think so?"

"Don't you?"

"No, I think that we are not married yet."

"Do we need the Toffee Man's blessings for that?"

"No. That was just a strange idea. At that moment I was in such a mood. I wanted to marry you . . . in such a manner."

"And in what mood are you now?"

"Rachel," he pressed her closer to him. "I must become a man. I must mature on my own, away from you." She tore herself away from him and sat up. He asked softly, "Why did you move away?"

"Always the same kind of talk! Still the same . . ." she raged.

"Do you find it strange? Probably I am a strange person. Perhaps I should have spoken differently. To talk about it now is perhaps silly. Sometimes, when it is quiet and we are alone, I forget myself. And yes, now I do feel differently.

Now I know that no matter how far I shall go away from you, I shall always come back." He took her into his arms, whispering, "Rachel, if you only knew how scared I am to lose you."

They walked back through the backyards. The night breeze chased the rags and papers which were strewn all over the ground. David picked up a large sheet of hard paper. "A drawing!" he whispered. He picked up another sheet, also a sketch. In the dark they were unable to make out the signature and took a few drawings along to the cellar with them.

Bunim recognized whose drawings they were even before he saw their signature. Junia called out to Michal, "Come, something has happened to Winter!"

Michal did not move. She understood. She only asked him when, and he told her, "With the last group of sick . . ." Abraham and Shlamek ran out to gather up all the drawings they could find in the street.

Another day came. The watchman in the chimney announced that the other side of the ghetto was almost empty. The inhabitants of the cellar gave up their nightly escapades. They stayed in the cellar all the time and after another day, they began to suffer stomach troubles.

The Clearing Commando appeared on this side of the ghetto. They moved into Hockel Street and before long, they were in the yard. Israel ordered everyone to take up his or her position both in the cellar and in the shed, so that both exits should be clear. Esther sat beside the peacefully sleeping Shalom, her blouse unbuttoned, ready to give him her breast in case he awoke. Blows, shouts could be heard from outside, "*Los! Los!*" The sound of hammers, of boots running over stairs, the sound of breaking glass, smashed locks, splintered wood filled the air. Suddenly it was quiet. In the silence, a sigh of relief. The hearts of those in hiding still pounded furiously, but their minds had already freed themselves from their paralysis.

The following day the Clearing Commando appeared again. Those who had hid in the Toffee Man's cellar were discovered and led out. The steps and shouts came closer. The noise surrounded the house, rolling up the stairs. Heavy boots seemed to step on the hearts of those in hiding, cracking them like nuts. The boots were already upstairs in the apartment, roaming through the rooms. Someone opened the door of the cupboard which covered the shed. German voices thundered through the thin walls. It was strange that the hunters did not hear the thunder coming from the hearts of those in hiding.

After the visit — a mighty feeling of victory. The hideaway had stood the test. The inhabitants of the cellar kissed Blumka who had categorically opposed the idea of cooking their meals on the stove in the kitchen upstairs; she had feared that the smoke from the chimney would betray them and that even the warm stove would be a risk.

More or less calm dream-like days followed. The anxiety subsided. The stomachs were cured. The minds were lulled by silence. It was as if they had all taken tranquillizing drugs. Anguish was still within them somewhere, but they were not conscious of it. They felt like ghosts with bodies so light that they were both here and some place else. Rachel lay beside the sick Bella, playing with the pages of Slowacki's poetry. Her eyes stared at the lines but she did not grasp their meaning. Bella and Rachel rarely exchanged words, yet they both felt as if they were not simply Miss Diamand's students, but her heirs. As she fingered the book, vaguely thinking about this fact, Rachel became acutely aware of Bunim's presence. He seemed to follow her everywhere with his eyes. She felt guilty towards him. Perhaps because he spoke to her with a good-humoured smile, without a trace of bitterness. He looked at her the way her father had once looked at her, when she was a little girl — with adoration, with devotion in his gaze — the way he had looked at his daughter Blimele. Yet she had the feeling that she owed him something and that she could never repay the debt.

She often thought and dreamed about her father. She saw herself walking with him through the streets of Lodz. She, a little girl with braids, her head raised high. She had to look up when she talked to him, or if she wanted to see his face when he talked to her. He would often say, "Come daughter, let's go home to Mother . . ." Then he would take her home to Blumka.

Rachel would open her eyes awakened from her dream, see Blumka, and know that she was at home. She and her mother exchanged casual words, commonplace phrases, but they could do without words as well.

Now as she played with the book, and felt Bunim's gaze on her, while she was thinking all these vague thoughts about herself, about her parents, about David and Bunim, she turned her head to Bella and remarked, "My father often read poetry to us on Saturday mornings, when we stayed in our beds longer."

"My father never held a book of poetry in his hands," Bella replied, smiling faintly. "And you see, your father and mine became friends."

"Yes, great friends."

Bella's eyes lit up. "Superficially it seems that both of them are gone and their friendship is gone, but that's false. Don't you agree? Isn't their friendship here, on this bed, at this very minute?" She was perspiring, running a high temperature, but her voice was clear. It was the voice of the former sad and dreamy Bella. "And generally . . . it is present within God . . ." she added. "Because God is the collective soul of everything alive. He holds our hearts on threads like a balloon-seller with a huge bunch of them in his hand. He ties them together and unties them, in order to enrich us with experiences . . . to make us sense Him better. Love and God are one, Rachel. When all the shells are peeled away and devotion flows freely back and forth, from heart to heart, then we are within God and only then can we perceive Him."

"And hatred, tragedy, all the evils . . . what about those?" Rachel asked.

"Those," Bella replied, "occur when hearts are locked. I sometimes think that physical illness also comes because of that."

"Rachel wondered whether Bella was talking feverishly or whether her mind was clear. The image of that Friday night when the children had been led off during the *Sperre* entered her mind. That day had made it impossible for her to ever recognize the existence of God, especially a God of Love. But she did not want to ask Bella about it again. In spite of everything, there was some truth in Bella's words, even if they were said in a fever, even if they were not supported by logic; a beautiful truth which had nothing to do with reason.

✦   ✦   ✦

(David's Notebook)

We had moments of great fright when our hearts seemed about to jump into our mouths. I had no idea that such fear could exist; it is a feeling which only people facing imminent death probably experience. I am thinking: If death means not just the moments when life expires, but also the moment prior to it, then how many times have we already died here, and how many more times shall we die? But as soon as the searches are over, the fear vanishes, and we carry on with our imitation of life.

It seems as if we have all been living together for ages; we have come to know each other so thoroughly. I am familiar with every weakness, with every grimace of my cohabitants, particularly of those whom I was previously not so fond of. I have Israel and Berkovitch in mind. Israel was a leader of our party, and when I was younger I respected him. But later on, I realized that he was the typical party official with whom you could only talk about party business and politics — in a word, a limited man. Berkovitch, on the other hand, got on my nerves because he went around with Rachel and is generally an oddball. The first days, I felt quite uncomfortable that it was thanks to his intervention and through Rachel's mediation that we were accepted into the hideout.

The difference between my present attitude towards these two men and my former one is, that now I recognize them both as members of my family, which means that I have a certain sentiment for them. This, in turn allows me to admit that the two of them arouse my respect; I even look at them now through a kind of idealising prism. I see the man of action in Israel, a man who believes in what he is doing. And I see the true artist in Berkovitch.

I think that we have all changed since we began living in the hideout; that if we, this family, this group of people, were the ones chosen to build a new life on earth, we would know what to do . . . although I can hardly see myself as the builder of a new society. How great is my own moral worth, if I am unable to mourn even for my own mother? I feel that a load has been lifted from my back and am glad that she died in her own bed. But here I am entering the path of self-criticism which leads directly to self-pity, and that I don't want.

I would like to know what happened to our youth leader Simon who used to pound his chest and boast, "They will never take me alive!" And I would like to know another thing: What is a Jew in America doing now? Is he taking a walk? Is he on vacation? Are his children gambolling on the beach? I in his place, would not be any different. What man does not see with his own eyes does not exist. When he is not involved in, or touched by an event, he rarely reacts to it.

I am going to sleep now, having written this during my watch at the window.

Last night we sat around the cherry tree. It was quiet. The ghetto is dead. It seems as if only our family populates the world — and perhaps we are the only ones left? From the other side shots are rarely heard. We are beginning to believe that we shall await freedom. However, there have been no air raid alarms or bombardments lately; it is as if the Russians were waiting for the Germans to clean up the ghetto. So our belief is sometimes shaky.

Junia, who used to be gay and vigorous, has become quite subdued. She talks seriously, not at all in her former style. It was she who spoke first when we sat down under the tree. She said, "I can sometimes see myself in our own country, see myself walking there, feeling ashamed because . . ."

We all understood what she meant with the "because". Israel supported Junia, and said, "I keep on digging into the same entanglement and cannot get out of it. The revolutionary Lodz, which bled during so many strikes and demonstrations, during the battles for freedom, joining all kinds of movements . . . We, the proud, enlightened Jews of Lodz . . ."

Berkovitch did not let him finish. He became enraged. "Shame on you two, for being ashamed of yourselves, and for abusing the community. What are you out to say? Didn't we fight as much as we could? The Germans allowed us to feel the pain of separation, the fear that it might be forever . . . but we did not truly realize what was going on. Even now, the Jews of a city . . . a community . . . Has it really penetrated our minds that all those who filled the streets and yards are gone forever? Does it enter your minds that you yourselves, too, may . . . It is impossible to fathom, in spite of everything that we know, in spite of your so-called reliable information, Israel. Our mouths only repeat the same stories. So I don't know what would have happened, if we had seen with our own eyes . . . And if it is a question of revenge, do you think that throwing ourselves at the Germans with our bare fists would quench our thirst for revenge? Are you capable of measuring out the exact amount of revenge to equal the crime? It is not only Lodz that has been effaced, not only Warsaw. And if revenge means an eye for an eye, a life for a life, who possesses such diabolic guts? And on the other hand, could it heal our wounds? Revive the dead? As you see me here, I have filled one hundred and fifty pages with handwriting. You will say that it is garbage. To me this means struggle . . . my revenge . . . my life."

Of course, I too put my two groschens' worth into the conversation. I spoke about the Germans tricking us, about the psychological game they played with us. First, they let us starve, so that we would fight with each other over whatever food there was. Later, when there was still for whom to fight, whom to protect, they imposed collective responsibility upon us. Then they bled us, drop by drop, allowing us to hope that not everyone would go . . . And on top of that, for a long time, we had no idea of what was going on. And as Berkovitch said, we did not believe and don't believe even now in the finality . . . And since we were all speaking personally, I told them that it is not my ambition to die beautifully, that I don't consider myself capable of being a hero. And I also said that every form of struggle for life is honourable, so long as it isn't to the detriment of others. And therefore I considered that the *shishkas*, who sent others away in order to protect themselves, were criminals. But perhaps they were in that respect also not completely guilty, because when it comes to choosing between me and you, the problem is difficult. But what I did accuse them of is that they feathered their nests at our expense and that they sent others to their death so lightheartedly.

Michal Levine also participated in the conversation. He said that since the Germans did not reveal their true face to us, just like God, we feared them as one fears the hand of God. Then he turned to Junia, saying that even after our liberation, when the Germans are in our hands, we will also avoid cutting their throats because we are a people which is disgusted by the sight of blood. Because during the course of our history we have unlearned our bloodthirstiness. He asked Junia what she would do after the war, if she had to choose between killing Germans or building a Jewish land? He was sure that she would choose the second. Then he said that if it had come to active resistance in the ghetto, he would have participated, not out of strength, but out of weakness. Because while fighting, he would nurture the hope that he might still save himself, and also, in the fever of the fight, free himself from the fear of death.

He said that sometimes he tries to feel himself into the thoughts and emotions of the masses of people who vere led away. Were they fully aware of what awaited them? If they were, then they probably had something more important to do during their last moments, than to throw themselves at their hangmen. They probably barely had time to spit in their faces. Because what should a mother or a father with a child in their arms do? Attack the Germans, or gather together all the love in their souls to bestow on the young, on their own flesh and blood? Michal asked what the great heroes of history, all those freedom fighters and martyrs, had done when they were led to the gallows. Did they throw themselves at their hangmen, or walk with their heads raised high, without even glancing at their torturers? When Michal said that he sometimes sees the image of his mother in his mind, and that he knows, that rather than hating the Germans, she was thinking of him, of her son, Berkovitch burst into an animal-like howl.

A shudder crept down my spine. I suddenly felt in the grip of pain and grief. I was glad that no one saw me cry. It was good to release the tears. I had been waiting for them as one waits for a rain. At last I was mourning my mother. I think that the others were also glad of the chance to cry. It did not make me feel weak. I felt fortified. However, Israel said that we should avoid such conversations in the future. I agree with him. Once is enough.

An hour later, the sirens started up again. An alarm. We remained in the yard. Formations of Russian planes appeared above the roofs. While they roared deafeningly, we allowed ourselves to scream with excitement. To my surprise, Junia went mad, dancing over the yard. She roared, trying to outdo the thunder of the airplanes. The rest of us raised our fists in the air or waved our hands. It was wonderful to let go, under the protection of those birds of steel. At dawn there was another alarm. That one we barely heard. We slept to the accompaniment of the planes and of Shalom's screams. The little fellow greets the alarms with tears. We let him scream himself out in the general noise, so that he will be quiet when he has to.

We figure that we shall be freed any day now. In the meantime I behave as if I were on vacation. The girls are also in a good mood. We have decided to fight hunger and idleness with a little lecture that each of us has to prepare every day. Apart from that, Israel discusses the political situation in the world, and Michal explains biology, bacteriology and other "ologies" related to his profession. In addition to that, Berkovitch reads us a chapter of his long poem regularly. I, and perhaps Israel too, would be happier without his readings. They get on my nerves. I must admit that some stanzas are morbidly beautiful; I did not expect to be so sensitive to poetry, especially his. However, I am of the opinion that this is not the time for Jeremiads for us. Perhaps I shall tell him that straight to his face.

I have been having long conversations with Michal. We are coming increasingly closer to one another, ideologically and philosophically. Strange, he reminds me of the Toffee Man. Probably because he also tells me that he is sure that I will survive. (May it go from his mouth straight into God's ears!) But I can't stand it when he begins talking as if he expected me to be his philosophical heir.

Nothing came of our plans about lectures and studies. We are too hungry, too tense, too tired. From all that, only Berkovitch's nightly readings are left. I gave up my decision to tell him not to read to us any more. I have become more positive about it. It has become for us a kind of prayer, conducted by our own rabbi.

✦ ✦ ✦

The Clearing Commando passed daily through the streets of the cleared part of the ghetto, stopping every time in the yard on Hockel Street. Those in hiding rarely left the cellar during the day or the night, for fear of leaving traces behind. The "lid" between the cellar and the shed was closed, so that if one group were discovered, the other would have a chance to escape. It became so stuffy in the cellar, that it was barely possible to breathe, and little Shalom whined constantly. Israel had to drill a hole and remove a brick from the wall for more air. Esther stood at that "window" with the baby in her arms. The new hole also served as an observation point. Both Bella and Shalom were given a broth of poppy seeds daily, so that they could sleep better.

The Cleaning Commandos loaded everything they found in the houses onto their wagons. They also hammered and picked, piercing walls wherever they expected to find hidden treasures. During these searches they sometimes broke into hideaways, and sent the occupants off to the other side of the bridge.

Now and then Israel would free the opening between the cellar and the shed for the night, and remove the back wall of the cupboard which covered the entrance to the shed, for ventilation. Sometimes he gave permission to one person or another to go into the apartment and stretch his stiff limbs.

Bunim carried his bread sack wherever he went. He would not take it off even when he went to sleep. Junia began to nag him to hide his poems. She and Michal had brought over the tea box, inside which they had hidden Michal's letters to Mira and Shafran's unfinished work, along with other documents. They buried it under the cherry tree, so that they might be close to their hidden archives. They added Samuel's notes for his book on the history of the Jews of Lodz, and Winter's drawings as well. Junia insisted that Bunim should also secure his unfinished epic by hiding it in the buried box.

But Bunim shook his head, "I must have the whole thing with me . . . I want to complete it. Anyway, I am unable to part with it . . . and . . ." He did not finish the sentence, although he had the impression that he had. This often happened to him lately. He talked very little, yet his head was full of talk. He was involved in a continuous dialogue with those around him. More than once they would ask him why he was so stubbornly mute. He was unable to understand what they meant. "But I am talking all the time," he protested.

That day was marked by frequent visits of the Clearing Commando. Israel gave orders to be on guard. They could hear German talk and exclamations as well as the pounding of hammers. Once in a while they heard someone call for help. The family living in the water reservoir was led off in the morning, but there were apparently others hiding in the yard. Israel ordered the majority of the group to stay upstairs in the shed, to leave more air for Shalom and Bella. Esther stayed with Shalom and Junia with Bella. Michal sat on the ladder and watched over them. Israel did not move away from the observation hole. Nearby lay Blumka, the boys Shlamek and Abraham, David, Rachel and Bunim.

Bunim could barely discern Rachel's and David's contours in the dark. Only the pale shimmer of their faces reached his shortsighted eyes. But he was aware of their presence. Now and then they would move, touching him with an arm or a leg. He also heard their whispers. A few days before, he had still bitten his lips at the sight of their closeness; his heart had contracted. It was not easy to take leave of Rachel in that manner. She lay in the arms of the alien yet close young man, and was his, Bunim's love. He wanted to love her without being jealous or desperate. But that he could only achieve at night. Then, when she looked at him in the dark, he was overwhelmed by feelings which sprang from the same source as his love for Miriam and Blimele, from the same source as his poems. "I accept it with love . . ." he was capable of saying to himself at such moments, and to accept much more than David's arms around Rachel. But during the day, when Fate rang in his ears with the sound of hammers against neighbouring walls, he felt compelled to be close to Rachel, to cling to her and whisper, "*Ahava*, save me . . . Let me protect you with my life". In the same manner he was at such moments incapable of accepting the incompleteness of his work.

Eventually, however, he acepted both: his parting from Rachel and the incompleteness of his poem. There was a finality also in incompleteness. He, Bunim, had arrived, although he was still on the road. He had achieved, although he was still in the middle of his endeavour. The dove, his creative restlessness, was now cooing a new kind of tune. His uncomfortable heart still would not allow him to catch his breath, and yet it no longer seemed trapped. Devotion was awake within him, branching out in all directions. Its rays reached not only to Rachel, but to David as well; not only to everyone in the hiding place, but to all those outside of it. He missed that rare moment when he had sat with the others under the cherry tree, when they had relieved themselves of their sorrow and felt an affinity with everything that perishes and rises again. From now on there was only silence for Bunim, a silence torn apart, yet healing with mute pain.

The sound of hammers was coming from the last entrance in the yard. Steps could be heard climbing the stairs very close by. Exclamations in German resounded from the other side of the cellar's walls. There were also German words in a Polish accent: a stool pigeon. A treasure was supposed to be hidden here somewhere. Israel with his ear against the hole heard the words clearly. They were searching for a canteen full of gold watches.

"It must be hidden in this cellar!" someone shouted.

"They're coming!" Israel called out. He knocked three times on the floor of the shed, the sign of extreme danger. They held their breaths, their bodies paralyzed, their mouths dry, their eyes blind.

Down in the cellar, Esther sat doubled up, offering her breast to Shalom. Shalom, weak, dazed by the sleeping potion, was breathing irregularly, wheezing. She searched for his mouth with the nipple, unable to get it in. The sounds were very loud now. The voices echoed clearly in the ears of those hiding in the cellar. Someone was disputing some measurements, counting aloud, hammering again. Half an hour passed — an eternity. From behind the house there came a voice. A canteen had been found with two watches in it. A few moments later all was quiet. No one moved in the hiding place. Esther fainted with her breast over Shalom, her body slumped over him. It took Michal a long time to revive her.

At night, they all had to go outside for an hour at least. This time they took Esther and the baby; only Bella remained with Junia in the cellar. Esther lay with her head leaning against Israel's knees, the snoring baby in her lap. Esther herself was barely conscious. She whispered in Israel's ear, yet all those sitting around the tree could hear her.

"I am not afraid. What do I have to fear? . . . I have lived enough anyway. It's not a question of years . . . People don't live equally, some live slower, while others live faster. I have lived fast and managed to taste everything. Look at the tree, Israel." She looked up and the others followed her gaze. "Berkovitch told me that the man who guarded the tree used to call it The Tree of Life." She suddenly began to shake and saliva dripped from her mouth. "I am going mad . . . My baby!"

Israel tried to calm her, "Catch your breath, Little Mother. The night is ours. You must gather strength for tomorrow morning."

Sirens began to screech. Abraham and Shlamek dashed to the centre of the yard and counted the airplanes. Rockets illuminated the sky. Shlamek prodded Abraham with his elbow, 'If only they threw some leaflets, or a scrap of paper . . . something".

Abraham winked at him. "Do you know what's hypnotizing me at this very moment? The cherries there, on the top of the tree."

The boys approached the tree. Shlamek and Bunim helped Abraham to climb onto the branches. Rachel brought out a cup. The cherries were over ripe and had rumpled skins. Rachel threw a cherry into each mouth, then Michal took the rest of them inside to Junia and Bella.

✦   ✦   ✦

At night, the sky looked like a hospitable table covered with a velvety dark tablecloth. In its middle stood the horn of the moon; a dish full of warm sweet honey. A sleepless strange night: hearts exhausted, limbs heavy, minds like those of lunatics, words strangely reverberating in the heads.

Michal and Junia watched over Bella. When the others came down to have a look at Shalom, Michal gathered them around him and drew a sheet of paper out of his pocket. He spoke in a hoarse heavy voice. "I want you to listen to me for a few moments. It is personal and not so personal." He drew the flashlight out of his other pocket and began to read a letter to his unborn child.

> My name is Michal Levine, son of Malka and Eli Levine. My father Eli was shot by the Germans soon after they came into Lodz. My mother left with the deportation in the year 1942. My wife Junia Zuckerman is the daughter of Matilda and Samuel Zuckerman. Matilda left with the *Sperre* of 1942. Samuel shortened his days on earth by his own hand, in the year 1943, so that his daughters could live. We are hiding here in a cellar and a shed, along with our friends — our family.
>
> We have with us my wife's sister Bella. She brought along her treasure into hiding: a volume of Slowacki's poems, a gift from her teacher, Miss Dora Diamand who left during the *Sperre* of 1942.
>
> With us is Mrs. Blumka Eibushitz and her two children Rachel and Shlamek. Their husband and father Moshe Eibushitz died of typhoid fever in the year 1943.
>
> In addition, two brothers, David and Abraham, are with us. Their father was shot at the same time as mine, and their mother died of a heart attack at the beginning of 1944. Their sister Halina was in the ghetto of Warsaw.
>
> Hiding with us also is Israel, the eldest son of Sheyne Pessele and Itche Mayer the Carpenter. Itche Mayer died of an unknown disease in the year 1941, and Sheyne Pessele left during the *Sperre* of 1942. With that deportation also left their second son, Mottle, vith his wife and child, as well as their youngest son Shalom. The middle son Yossi was caught in the street with his wife and child, and left with a transport at the beginning of February 1943.

Present with Israel is his wife Esther. Her closest relatives, Chaim the Hosiery-Maker and his wife Rivka, along with the four of their eight children who were still with them, left with the 'action' in the year 1941. The two youngest ones were deported from the hospital for the consumptives, in the year 1942.

Israel and Esther's son, Shalom, is twelve weeks old. He bears the name Shalom, after Israel's youngest brother.

Hiding with us is also Simcha Bunim Berkovitch, who lost his wife Miriam, his daughter Blimele and his not-yet-named newborn son, during the *Sperre* of the year 1942. His parents and nine sisters expired one after the other during the years 1941–2.

This letter was written during the night between the tenth and eleventh day of our hiding. If we perish, we will not leave any trace behind, nor any material possessions. We leave the buried tea box, in which this letter is hidden, along with all the other documents which are meaningful to us.

This letter is written in my own name and is addressed to my child, whom my wife Junia and I hope to bring into this world. If Fate decides otherwise, then I address it to all those who will be willing to consider themselves our heirs.

If it happens that we share the fate of those who are gone, and if there is a life after us in which our passing has some meaning; if we are remembered and there are some who try to guess our wishes and dreams, then let these words be joined with the wishes of the others who share our fate, and let my testament be counted with theirs.

If I could only make you, who live on after us, feel my trembling at this moment, by means other than words, in a different, more direct and truer manner — I would not resort to words. But I cannot help it. Awkward as words may be, in particular when written down by someone like myself, they are the only means of communicating with you. And at this moment, I rejoice in the fact that I know how to write and that you, who live after us, know how to read. With it, I bless human civilization, those achievements of the human mind which Man can use for his benefit and the benefit of others. With it, I bless the human hand which had with words and with actions made holy the word "Life", and I curse the hands which had with words and with actions sealed the word "Death".

I am a Jew. I do not follow the traditions of the Jewish religion, but I consider myself a product of that tradition. I am part of the community united by Fate which has through centuries of suffering brought us here, to this moment.

I do not believe in life after death. But I nourish a conception of a transcendental collective 'I' of humanity, an 'I' which is as eternal as humanity. I believe that I shall in some manner survive within that 'I'.

Therefore I allow myself to trust that we shall be with you, who follow. *Non omnis moriar.* We shall not perish totally and you will never be able to free yourself completely of us. Therefore you should know that with our destruction, you have also been partly destroyed. Let this awareness assist you, my child and heir.

These words will perhaps sound too arrogant to you, too pathetic and too sermonizing. No, I am not a preacher, or a chastising self-appointed prophet. I am a lame orphan whose beautiful profession became the laughing stock of hyenas. And I am crying out to you, not from the top of Mount Sinai, but from the depths of a dark cellar, the most forsaken, most lonely corner of the world. I am prayerfully calling out the old unfulfilled commandment to you: 'Thou shalt not kill!' Following it, my child, you will not cross out death from nature, but be merciful to yourself, and by your actions do not take upon yourself the responsibility for it.

When I lie at night under the cherry tree which is growing outside in the yard, when I rest during the breathing pause between one moment of danger and the next, I long for you, my unborn child, you who will come to inherit from me. I dream out your life and I follow you on your road.

Rejoice, my child, in the treasure that you possess: your spirit, which makes you God-like and raises you above the animal to a richer kind of being. Rejoice in the home which harbours your treasure: your body, which is so beautiful and perfect, each limb a masterpiece of precision, each cell — a source of wisdom unto itself. Rejoice in the beauty that you see in your mate, in your child, in your neighbour. And use them both, body and spirit, to take care of, to nurture and protect that beauty. Use them both to discover the tempting secrets of your surroundings and to profit from them. Use them both to combat the external forces which are out to destroy you, and don't avoid meeting them face to face within yourself. Love yourself wisely, generously. Give and take and be free. Break all the laws, all the barriers which you have created for yourself, in your fear. Expand your home, let is become as big as the universe.

The road to you, my child, leads though entanglements and precipices called race, religion, nation. True, here and there gardens and orchards have been planted as well as fields full of flowers and grain. However that road leads mostly through gaping deserts of alienation, through forests of distrust, through weeds of hatred. Gather only the flowers and the fruit on that road, my child. Bring them together from all corners, and call your brothers from all the ends of the world — to one place, where you will exchange your treasures, mix the fruits and celebrate life together under the canopy of the only sky.

Let a new language spring up amongst you: the language of care. Let all things transitory and unimportant fall away from you like a used skin. Remain as you are in your innermost being, and yet be joined into one with all the others — so that you should not praise yourself above your brother in your uniqueness, and that he should not praise himself above you. Let the peculiar qualities separating you from others become a source of joy, a worthwhile discovery which awakens your brother's curiosity and respect for you, and yours for him.

Life is complicated and mysterious. Life is painful and short. Life is easy and simple, joyful and rich. Don't shorten it. Shorten your brother's pain, expand his joy as much as you can, in order that he may do the same for you. Care . . . Care. Become another kind of Cain. Rise from the ground and answer God with glee, "My brother Abel is alive and I am his keeper."

Michal had barely managed to finish reading, when Shalom awoke with a scream, opening his black eyes wide. They all surrounded him and watched as Esther pushed her breast into his mouth.

✦ ✦ ✦

The following day, while they were in the middle of sipping their daily ration of hot water and saccharine, a noise reached them from the side where the door of the cellar was disguised by a brick wall. The inhabitants of the cellar listened, stiff and motionless. They heard a heavy panting. Then it was quiet, until quick steps were heard on the stairs. Someone had entered the empty apartment upstairs, and was puttering around at the cupboard which covered the door of the shed.

Quickly the inhabitants of the cellar pulled themselves together. Israel let down the flap over the hole to the cellar, and they all gathered below, in front of the exit which was covered on the outside with the sheet of canvas and the heap of soil. Israel and David stood ready to open it.

Upstairs, in the apartment, someone was moving the cupboard. Someone entered the shed and manipulated the flap over the hole. Abraham peered out through the observation hole. Suddenly he exclaimed, "They're coming!"

A howl was heard from the shed. Israel ordered Berkovitch to adjust the ladder and open the flap. The head of Adam Rosenberg appeared in the opening. Bunim quickly pulled him down into the cellar, shut the flap and peered out through the hole into the yard. Two Germans were approaching from the centre of the backyard.

Adam lay on the floor of the cellar, moaning, "Save me, people, save me!"

"Rosenberg, the stool pigeon!" Abraham recognized him.

"No . . . no . . . I haven't betrayed you," Adam whined. "They are after me!" He raised his locked hands prayerfully to Abraham.

"They've entered the last stairway!" Bunim called out.

Adam stood up with difficulty, and looked with bloodshot eyes at those gathered around him, breathing heavily. "I swear. I did not betray you. Don't throw me out. I wanted to hide in the shed. Biebow is chasing me. There are two of them. All the trains are leaving for Auschwitz . . . a concentration camp where . . . where . . ."

Junia gave him a shove with her elbow, "Shut up!"

"They're here!" Berkovitch whispered.

Boots were marching unhurriedly up the stairs; they could be heard in the apartment, in the corridor; thudding irregular steps. A voice was heard stating calmly, "There is something wrong here." The cupboard upstairs was cracking. Someone was crawling into the shed. In the silence hovering in the cellar someone's heavy breathing was heard through the flap.

Israel blinked at David, and they both pulled the cord which freed the exit from the heap of earth. A gale of fresh air attacked their faces. Israel gave a signal to the group. But before they could manage to move outside, Michal leapt to the front, running out through the opening. He called out into the cellar, "Run to the firemen's yard!"

He himself dashed out into the light of the day, heading, not towards the firemen's yard, but in the opposite direction, towards the water-pump. At the entrance to the Zuckerman house stood a German with his back to Michal. Michal ran into an entrance, watching from the side as the group hurried out from the cellar in the direction of the firemen's yard. David and Berkovitch came out last. They were dragging Bella, while Junia followed them from behind. Right after Junia, Michal saw Adam crawl out of the cellar. Instead of rushing towards the firemen's yard, he was heading in Michal's direction, running like a blind man and stumbling over his feet.

At that moment Hans Biebow emerged from the house. The German who had stood at the entrance turned around and noticed Adam. He fired a shot in his direction. Biebow made an abrupt turn about and saw the escaping group with Bella and Junia.

In the blink of an eye Michal was outside, in the yard. He let out a wild shriek as he dashed forward on his limping feet and threw himself at Biebow from behind, hanging on to his back, his hands clasped around Biebow's neck. Biebow struggled to free himself from Michal's hands which were cutting into his face with their nails. For a while he dragged Michal along the yard, until Biebow's companion discharged two shots from his revolver.

Michal fell onto a bed of soil. The letter to his unborn child, the letter which he had not managed to bury under the cherry tree, flew out of his pocket, covering the bald pate of Adam Rosenberg who was lying nearby. Michal's dead hand touched the tips of Adam's fingers.

Junia came running towards them with outstretched arms. Biebow and his companion grabbed her by the arms and dragged her into the firemen's yard, where the escapees had been rounded up by the Clearing Commando.

Bella was placed on a wagon, along with a few other sick people. The rest were marched through the streets of the empty ghetto, between the empty houses, past the empty yards. The sun lay on the sidewalks, faded, autumnal, apathetic.

At the train station, Biebow appeared again. He held a handkerchief to his cheek, covering the blood marks and the scratches left by Michal's nails. The station was full of Germans. At one side stood the group of captured Jews. The long cattle train with the red boxcars stood waiting on the rails, its doors open. The group was led to one of the cars. One after the other they were ordered to climb the plank leading up to the door. Two Germans carried over the gratefully smiling Bella by the arms. They had granted her permission to travel with her sister. They were kind to her and had even allowed her to take along the volume of Slowacki's poems.

The train stood on the station for a long time. The door of the boxcar remained open. Through it one could see the heads of the Germans in their green helmets and the butts of their guns, as if cut off from the trunks to which they belonged. More groups of people who had been caught hiding kept arriving.

In the middle of the platform, in front of the wagons, stood Mordecai Chaim Rumkowski, his wife Clara, his brother Joseph and his sister-in-law Countess Helena, surrounded by a group of green uniforms with pointed guns. The stooped Old Man with the dishevelled silvery hair, the "Eldest of the Jews", bowed before the Germans, particularly before Herr Hans Biebow. He pointed to the slim gray Jew with the knapsack on his back, to his brother Joseph, mumbling, "I humbly entreat you, Herr Biebow, to leave my brother and sister-in-law with me in the ghetto . . . with the eight hundred Jews assigned to clean up the . . ."

Biebow bowed to him in turn, with mock politeness. Without removing the handkerchief from his cheek, he said, "If you wish, Herr . . . Herr Rumkowski, you may accompany your brother on the voyage." All the eyes under the green helmets twinkled amusedly, with expectation.

The Old Man chewed on his flabby lips and shook his head lower and lower, more and more humbly. But after a while, he slowly began to draw himself up. He wiped his gray mop of hair with his hand, almost knocking his glasses off his nose. He adjusted them, took his wife Clara by the hand and along with her, and his brother Joseph and his sister-in-law Helena, approached the plank leading to the wagon.

"Enough *Lebensraum*, isn't there, *Herr Älteste der Juden?*" A green uniform asked with feigned courtesy, pushing the old man up from behind.

The Old Man entered the wagon, and toppled over onto Abraham who was sitting on the floor, leaning against David. It was not long before a whistle sounded. The green uniforms slammed the doors together. It became dark and quiet inside, a sparse shaft of light entered through the barred little window. Outside a bolt screeched as it was slid over the door.

Abraham tried to free himself from Old Rumkowski's body pressing against him. He finally succeeded. He reached out for his breadsack and drew a little cup out of it. He touched the Old Man's knee, "Here, Mr. Rumkowski, taste a cherry from our cherry tree . . . It's a remedy for the heart."

The wagon shook, screeched and slowly began to move.

Chapter Twenty-nine . . .
Thirty . . .
Thirty-one . . .
ad infinitum

AUSCHWITZ. WORDS STOP, UNDRESSED, NAKED, THEIR MEANING, THEIR SENSE SHAVEN OFF. LETTERS EXPIRE IN THE SMOKE OF THE CREMATORIUM'S CHIMNEY . . .

After The Voyage

ON MILD QUIET AFTERNOONS, the inhabitants of some of Brussels' side streets liked to spend their time "outside". They would open their windows wide, rest their elbows against soft pillows, and look out. Nor did their cats and dogs dislike this method of taking the air and could frequently be seen alongside their masters, looking down into the street.

At first, Rachel looked at these sleepy bourgeois with disdain. What pleasure could there be, she asked herself, in such monotonous staring into the street, when the only chance of seeing something of interest was to steal a glance into the depths of the neighbours' half-darkened rooms across the road? But before long, whenever she had a little time at her disposal, her head too would lean out of one such window. She realized that these promenades with her eyes could turn into great voyages of the heart and carry the mind far away; voyages that depended, of course, on the view from one's window and on the scope of one's heart and mind.

And she had a favourable view. Instead of houses, she saw a large expanse of sky, and beneath it, a field full of tracks. From the railway station nearby, the trains rushed quickly by, heading in different directions. The rails criss-crossed and multiplied, the trains followed or avoided one another, until they vanished into the hazy depths beyond the horizon. The gusts of wind arriving from far-off places breathed into her face, transforming Rachel as well into someone who was here, yet here no more.

Distant voyages. She sat at the window, gazing at the flickering lights, her ears tuned to the screeching iron, to the rhythmical song of wheels — and so she let herself be carried off. The trains before her eyes were speeding forward, biting into hours still to come. Her trains were running backwards, sweeping away the dust of hours already lived.

Besides the trains, she also had the sight of a cherry tree which grew below. It stood alone, close to the fence that divided the railway yard from the street, and seemed to be afraid of the empty space and the wanton wind dancing around it. As if a heavy sorrow weighed down its leafy boughs, it pressed them against the rough planks of the fence as if against a consoling cheek. Only two of its branches, the fullest and longest, pointed upwards, to Rachel's window — like fingers.

For most of the year, Rachel did not notice the tree. But in the spring, when it burst into bloom, it would remind her of the cherry tree she had known in the ghetto. Its large boughs, clad in their leafy sleeves, caught her eyes, preventing her from seeing anything but a white cherry-blossom holiday against the background of ghetto darkness. The leafy fingers pointed out to her where her trains should travel, and when the wind swung them, she clearly heard them whisper, "There . . . there!" Thus it was in springtime that she thought most often of the ghetto.

Today was no different, and today too, like many times before, she decided to put an end to her trips into the past. Across the street, on the other side of the fence, the cherry tree was quietly shedding its blossoms. "Let the ghetto mood fall from me like the blossoms from the tree," she prayed. "I shall put an end to my divided life, for the sake of my children. For their sake I will live to the full the days Fate has granted me."

Then a train rattled past her window. Dirty vapor ballooned out of it, winding itself around the belly of the locomotive. A wild stubborn wind kept gathering the cherry blossoms from the ground, throwing fistfuls of them into the kettle-dance of smoke and wheels. Rachel saw a black fog climbing to the sky, and in it, twirling, a white snow of flower petals. Through this fog of black and white, she saw the face of the conductor on the platform. He waved to her, as the conductors usually did when they passed her window. And this time, as often before, the train reminded her of the cattle train to Auschwitz, while the conductor brought Bunim Berkovitch to her mind. It seemed to her that it was he who greeted her from afar, inviting her to board his train; that his voice was telling her, both tenderly and angrily, that her heart, once again, would lead her — there.

And so it happened that precisely today Rachel left the window, sat down at the table, reached out for a white sheet of paper, and picked up her pencil.

She heard a scream from the other corner of the room, a baby's demanding, arrogant cry. It was as sharp as the whistle of the train at the station across the street. Rachel did not hurry to calm the crying baby. Let the mischief yell a bit, she thought. Her mother, Blumka Eibushitz, had used to say that screaming was healthy for little lungs.

The baby stopped crying for a moment, as if it were waiting for the results of its alarm. It was about to burst out again, when it heard its mother walk about the room. It hastily began to throw its hands and legs about, shaking with excitement and ready to explode with laughter. But the sound of the mother's steps was cut short, only to resume again from the distance. The little fellow felt cheated. With great furore he began his screaming all over again.

Rachel picked up the envelope the concierge had shoved under the door. To the accompaniment of her baby's cries, she sat down at the table to read Junia's letter from Israel:

Dear Rachel,
First of all I owe you and David a *mazal tov* on the birth of your son Shalom. He must already be a big fellow by now. Forgive me for not replying right away. I have become negligent about my correspondence since I am awfully busy with a million things. Don't you know me? I have no *zits-fleish*.

It is going to be ten years soon since I arrived in Israel. The most beautiful years of my life. If I have grandchildren some day, I will have stories to tell them which only a grandmother of my generation could tell; about how I witnessed the birth of their homeland (and perhaps contributed a tiny bit to it). But let my mentioning grandchildren not lead you to incorrect conclusions. I have no matrimonial plans as yet.

I have become a comrade in a kibbutz on the *Kinereth*, as you can see from my new address. This is the second part of an old dream which I am just realizing now. Are you curious how life in the kibbutz and my temperament get along? The answer is: splendidly. My restlessness and the patient quiet earth harmonize and complement one another, just like Michal and I, the two contrasts, once complemented each other. And the Sea of Galilee which I can see through the window of my tent carries both the restlessness and the peace upon its waves. It teaches me to be patient in my impatience. I must be patient first of all because I am a teacher. Indeed only a teacher of gymnastics, but I ascribe extraordinary meaning to it. Here the time to correct our disproportionate attitudes has come. In the past, we used to move heaven and earth to be able to develop our minds, our spirit, while we neglected the body, a fact which did our spirit no service either. The pursuit of perfection, of harmony, is eternal, and I am working in that direction in my tiny corner, teaching my flock to raise their legs to the sound of a *halil*.

You write that you are getting ready to leave for America as soon as David receives his medical diploma. That means that soon we shall live on opposite sides of the globe. Oh, if we could only embrace that globe with our arms, you from your side, I from mine, we might perhaps help realize the testament of my husband, Michal.

Kiss your daughter Blimele. (She must be quite a young lady by now, not so?) Kiss your Shalom, tell him that we need him . . .

Rachel sat with the letter in her hand for a long while, then she put it aside, picked up her pencil and faced the blank sheet of paper in front of her. Then she began to write:

"Samuel Zuckerman was born in Lodz. His great-grandfather, Reb Shmuel Ichaskel Zuckerman had been among the first Jews to leave the ghetto . . . and it was he who in the year 1836 . . ."

The little fellow in the crib let out such a scream that it stung Rachel's ears. She put away the pencil, rushed towards the crib and lifted the baby into her arms, crying, "Hello, Shalom!" She raised him above her head, rocking him on the palms of her hands. Then she pressed him to her bosom and approached the window with him. Across the way, a train was again passing along the field of tracks. The conductor waved. Was he greeting her? Was he saying good-bye? Rachel took Shalom's hand by the wrist and waved it in a greeting, a good-bye.

"Mama!" a voice shouted up to her from the street. Rachel saw Blimele on the opposite sidewalk. The little girl was standing, schoolbag in hand, near the fence where the two large boughs of the cherry tree peered out. "Mama," she called out. "There will soon be cherries on the cherry tree!" Then she saw David approaching from the distance and she ran to meet him. Rachel saw David pick Blimele up in his arms. She heard her laughter from the distance, "Let me go! You're hot. You're pricking me! You're tickling me!"

Rachel picked up a corner of Shalom's bib and wiped her eyes with it.

Glossary

Ab damit!	Take it off! (Ger.)
Achtung!	Attention! (Ger.)
afikomen	Piece of matzo hidden during Passover feast, for children to find.
Aguda	Political party seeking to preserve orthodoxy in Jewish life.
ahava	love (Hebr.)
Alle Juden raus!	All the Jews out! (Ger.)
Älteste der Juden	Eldest of the Jews (Ger.)
Am Israel chai!	Long live the people of Israel! (Hebr.)
angst	fear (Ger.)
apikores	heretic (Gr.)
arbeiten	to work (Ger.)
Aufmachen!	Open up! (Ger.)
Aufschnitt	cold cuts of meat (Ger.)
baba	a kind of pastry (Slav.)
bellote	a card game (Fr.)
brodyage	riff-raff (Yidd.)
beschlagnahmt	confiscated, requisitioned (Ger.)
Bund	Jewish socialist party
chalom	dream (Hebr.)
cholent	dish served on the Sabbath (Yidd.)
chutzpah (or hutzpah)	impertinence, nerve
Das ist er!	That's him! (Ger.)
Das stinkt doch!	This stinks! (Ger.)
Der hat eine Nase wie ein Horn	He has a nose like a horn. (Ger.)
Du sollst arbeiten, jüdisches Schwein!	You must work, Jewish pig! (Ger.)
dybbuk	soul of dead person residing in the body of a living one. (Hebr.)
dzialka	plot of land (Pol.)
Eifersucht ist eine Leidenschaft die mit eifer sucht was Leiden schaft.	Jealousy is a passion which with passion seeks to inflict suffering. (Ger.)
Einkunftstelle	In the ghetto: post for turning in forbidden items, in exchange for some ghetto money (rumkis). (Ger.)
eintreten	line up (Ger.)

373

Eine jüdische Hure mit einem jüdischen Hurensohn	A Jewish whore with the son of a Jewish whore. (Ger.)
Eintopfgericht	stew, all the courses in one. (Ger.)
Ersatz	substitute (Ger.)
Familienandenken	family souvenirs (Ger.)
farbrokechts	vegetables for a soup (Yidd.)
Folks-Zeitung	the people's newspaper. Name of Yiddish socialist daily in Poland. (Yidd.)
Gemahl	husband (Ger.)
Gemara	the Talmud
gemütlich	cosy (Ger.)
Gettoverwaltung	German ghetto administration (Ger.)
golem	dummy, artificial man (Hebr.)
goy, pl: goyim	non-Jew(s) (Hebr.)
grober yung	person with no manners (Yidd.)
hachshara	preparatory training farm for Zionist youth.
Haggadah	text recited on Passover night (Hebr.)
Halacha	legislative part of the Talmud (Hebr.)
halah	white bread eaten on the Sabbath (Hebr.)
har . . . nar	master . . . idiot (Yidd.)
Hasid	follower, member of Jewish religious movement (Hebr.)
Halutza	female pioneer settler in Palestine (Hebr.)
hosen-kala	groom and bride (Hebr.)
Hashana habaa birushalayim!	Next year in Jerusalem! (Hebr.)
heder	Jewish religious school (Hebr.)
Himmelkommando	commando of the heavens (ghetto expression)
Holzschuhe	clogs (Ger.)
Hutzpah (or chutzpah)	nerve, arrogance (Hebr.)
Ich liebe dich, mich reizt deine schöne Gestalt.	I love you, I am tempted by your beautiful form. (Goethe: "Erlkönig")
Ich möchte dich nur für mich haben.	I want to have you only to myself. (Ger.)
Ich werde krepieren.	I will kick the bucket. (Ger.)
infolgedessen	consequently (Ger.)
Ja, ich hasse dich, kratziger Jude, mach das du fortkommst.	Yes, I hate you, mangy Jew, get lost! (Ger.)
Jude	Jew (Ger.)
Judenrein	clean of Jews (Ger.)
Junker	Prussian aristocrat, member of reactionary militaristic political party (Ger.)
Junkerheimat	Junker homeland (Ger.)

kaddish	prayer for a dead parent (Hebr.)
kalinka	Barberry tree (Slav.)
kibbitz	watch a game, offering unasked-for advice to players (Yidd.)
kiddush	the benediction over wine (Hebr.)
Kiddush-Hashem	to be martyred for being a Jew (Hebr.)
klepsidra	announcement of death, ghetto expression re someone's face
Kohelet	Book of Ecclesiastes
Kommst du vom Reich?	Are you from Germany? (Ger.)
kosher, kashrut	Jewish dietary law (kosherness. Hebr.)
Kripo (Kriminalpolizei)	Criminal Police (Ger.)
lody	ice cream (Pol.)
Los aber schnell!	Vanish, but quickly! (Ger.)
Lechaim	To life! (Hebr.)
Lech-lecho	Go forth ("The Lord said to Abraham, 'Go forth . . .'" Genesis. Hebr.)
mameshe	endearment for mother (Yidd.)
matzo, matzos	unleavened bread eaten during Passover (Hebr.)
mazal-tov	good luck (Hebr.)
menorah	a candelabrum (Hebr.)
mentch	a person, a decent human being (Yidd.)
meshuga, meshugas	mad, madness (Hebr.)
mezuzah	small tube, containing blessing, attached to doorpost (Hebr.)
Mishna	part of the Talmud (Hebr.)
mitzva	good deed (Hebr.)
Morgen . . . nächste Woche	Tomorrow . . . next week (Ger.)
Nach oben!	Up there! (Ger.)
Napoleonkis	a kind of French pastry (Pol.)
panienka, panienki	young lady, young ladies (Pol.)
Pardes	pleasure garden, paradise, according to esoteric philosophy (Hebr.)
Passierschein	a pass, a permit (Ger.)
pintele Yid	the dot of Jewishness
Poale-Zion	Zionist workers' party
Polizei	police (Ger.)
Presess	chairman
pshat, remez, drash	three methods of interpretation (Hebr.)
Rabiner	non-orthodox rabbi
Rashi	commentator on the Bible and the Talmud
Ressort (Arbeitsressort)	name for factories in the ghetto (Ger.)
Sehnsucht nach der Heimat	longing for the homeland (Ger.)

sheigetz	non-Jewish boy, Jewish boy who misbehaves (Yidd.)
Shalom-aleichem	greeting: Peace be with you.
Sejm	Polish parliament (Pol.)
servus	students' greeting
Simchat-Torah	A holiday celebrating the completion of the year's reading of the Torah.
Shishka	privileged person in the ghetto
Sitra-achra	the forces of evil
Seuchengefahr	epidemic, danger of infection
Sonderkommando (Sonder)	special unit of the Jewish police in the ghetto
Sperre	ban, house arrest or curfew
shlimazl, shlimiel	unlucky person (Yidd.)
shnorrer	beggar (Yidd.)
shochat	ritual slaughterer (Hebr.)
shtetl	small town (Yidd.)
Siehe mal diese hübsche Dame im Pelzmantel!	Look at this pretty lady in the fur coat! (Ger.)
Sie sollen . . .	You should . . . (Ger.)
So was!	such a thing! (Ger.)
Sperrkonto	blocked bank account (Ger.)
tateshe	endearment for father (Yidd.)
Torah	the Pentateuch (Hebr.)
Totenkopf	death's-head (Ger.)
treyfa	unkosher food (Hebr.)
tzimmes	vegetable or fruit dessert (Yidd.)
Überfallkommando	raid commando (Ger.)
Übersiedlung	resettlement (Ger.)
Vertrauungsmann der Kripo	confidence man of the criminal police (Ger.)
Volksdeutsche	a German born in Poland (Ger.)
Warthegau	Polish territory incorporated into the Third Reich
wirklich	really (Ger.)
Wissenschaftliche Abteilung	Scientific Department (Ger.)
Wohngebiet	place of residence (Ger.)
Wo ist das Brot?	Where is the bread? (Ger.)
wydzielaczka	woman distributing soup in the ghetto (Pol.)
Yeke	a German, (derisive) (Yidd.)
Yid	a Jew (Yidd.)
yeshiva	institution of higher Talmudic learning (Hebr.)
Yom-Kippur	the Day of Atonement
yomtov, or yom-tov	holiday
Zukunft	the future (Ger. Yidd.)

Library of World Fiction

S. Y. Agnon
A Guest for the Night: A Novel

S. Y. Agnon
In the Heart of the Seas

S. Y. Agnon
Two Tales: Betrothed & Edo and Enam

Karin Boye
Kallocain

Martin Kessel
Mr. Brecher's Fiasco: A Novel

Chava Rosenfarb
The Tree of Life: A Trilogy of Life in the Lodz Ghetto
Book One: On the Brink of the Precipice, 1939

Chava Rosenfarb
The Tree of Life: A Trilogy of Life in the Lodz Ghetto
Book Two: From the Depths I Call You, 1940–1942

Chava Rosenfarb
The Tree of Life: A Trilogy of Life in the Lodz Ghetto
Book Three: The Cattle Cars Are Waiting, 1942–1944

Aksel Sandemose
The Werewolf

Isaac Bashevis Singer
The Manor and *The Estate*

Hans Warren
Secretly Inside: A Novel